MARVELOUS TRANSFORMATIONS

For Pauline -
With very best
wishes
Jennifer
& Christina

MARVELOUS TRANSFORMATIONS

AN ANTHOLOGY OF FAIRY TALES AND CONTEMPORARY CRITICAL PERSPECTIVES

EDITED BY CHRISTINE A. JONES & JENNIFER SCHACKER

broadview press

Library and Archives Canada Cataloguing in Publication

Marvelous transformations : an anthology of fairy tales and contemporary critical perspectives / edited by Christine A. Jones & Jennifer Schacker.

Includes bibliographical references.
ISBN 978-1-55481-043-7

1. Fairy tales. 2. Fairy tales—History and criticism. 3. Folk literature—History and criticism. I. Jones, Christine Anne, 1969- II. Schacker, Jennifer

PZ8.M44754 2012 398.2 C2012-905819-X

Broadview Press is an independent, international publishing house, incorporated in 1985.

We welcome comments and suggestions regarding any aspect of our publications—please feel free to contact us at the addresses below or at broadview@broadviewpress.com.

North America
PO Box 1243, Peterborough, Ontario, Canada K9J 7H5
2215 Kenmore Ave., Buffalo, New York, USA 14207
Tel: (705) 743-8990; Fax: (705) 743-8353
email: customerservice@broadviewpress.com

UK, Europe, Central Asia, Middle East, Africa, India, and Southeast Asia
Eurospan Group, 3 Henrietta St., London WC2E 8LU, United Kingdom
Tel: 44 (0) 1767 604972; Fax: 44 (0) 1767 601640
email: eurospan@turpin-distribution.com

Australia and New Zealand
NewSouth Books
c/o TL Distribution, 15-23 Helles Ave., Moorebank, NSW, Australia 2170
Tel: (02) 8778 9999; Fax: (02) 8778 9944
email: orders@tldistribution.com.au

www.broadviewpress.com

Copy-edited by Betsy Struthers

This book is printed on paper containing post-consumer fibre.

Book design and composition by George Kirkpatrick

PRINTED IN CANADA

For Jackson, Chloe, and Frida

CONTENTS

PREFACE

THE JOURNEY THROUGH FAIRY TALE history that we offer in this volume does not follow a straight and well-worn path. Armed with a sense of adventure and a critical eye, you are guaranteed to find some surprises—stories you have never encountered, heroes and heroines who subvert expectations, and perspectives on the best-known tales that reveal them to be very unexpected indeed. In our introduction we offer a much more detailed map to *Marvelous Transformations,* but before you embark on your readerly journey, we would like to point out a few things to help you navigate your way through this book.

First, we invite you to explore the Contents, which includes in Part I: The Tales some familiar titles but also many that are less well-known and even more that will seem obscure to most contemporary English-language readers. We are delighted to be able to offer here new translations of many classic French and Italian fairy tales, as well as some works that are appearing in English translation for the very first time. For centuries, translation has been an important part of English fairy tale history, and it is our view that translations themselves stand as creative interventions in that history, inviting close reading in the same way that other fairy-tale texts do.

As you work your way through the tales, you will find a short critical introduction to the work of each writer you encounter. These are not strictly biographical notes but instead are focused on where these texts fit in a larger history of the fairy tale as we have woven it together here. It is our hope that you will use the information in the introductory notes as well as the vision of history that emerges from this volume to engage in historically situated close reading. This is a way of reading and analyzing fairy tales that we detail and exemplify in Part I's introduction (entitled "How to Read a Fairy Tale").

In the introduction we also explain the principles of tale selection for the stories that appear in this anthology. As you will see from the Contents, there are several longer readings, including an early English chapbook and a full pantomime script, marked as "web texts." These are available at <http://sites.broadviewpress.com/marveloustrans/>.

Most fairy-tale anthologies neglect longer works, essentially because they are inconvenient to publish in a print volume that does not want to exceed a certain heft. We have availed ourselves of modern technology to avoid those omissions. Abbreviated introductions to these web texts are included in this book, and we hope they pique your curiosity so that you will explore the full texts provided online. The web offers us the opportunity to shed the constraints of the material book and to bring these interesting (and generally neglected) works back into the fray of fairy tale history.

Part II: Contemporary Critical Approaches offers original, and in that sense new, critical statements on key ideas in fairy-tale studies, from both literary scholars and folklorists working today. One of the shaping principles of *Marvelous Transformations*—and one that most sets it apart from other fairy-tale anthologies—is our commitment (as scholars, teachers, and editors) to exploring the complex relationship between literary history and folklore history, specifically the history of the field-based collection of oral storytelling. The ways in which the discipline of Folklore has impacted ideas about the fairy tale from the nineteenth century to the present day are an important part of the story we tell in this book. As you'll see, we conceive of fairy-tale studies as a truly interdisciplinary enterprise. You will find a list of suggested readings or works cited attached to each of the essays in Part II, and each of these reflects the specific critical space relevant to that scholar.

* * *

This project began as the modest idea to create a volume of essays that would help specialists and non-specialists alike teach the fairy tale. It has turned into much more. For that transformation, we owe a debt to Marjorie Mather at Broadview Press. She planted a seed by encouraging Jennifer to transform her frustrations with current fairy-tale anthologies into a vision for a new kind of volume. In our conversations together we realized that an anthology we ourselves could use in our classrooms had to be a collaborative effort: the fairy tale is too diverse a form, its history too complex, to be addressed by a singular critical vision. Together we were able to realize more than either of us could have imagined working alone. The contributions of 15 colleagues and a broader support network became crucial to that effort.

Several people have been exceptionally generous in their support of this project, from its nascent stage as a possibility through its fruition. First and foremost, we would like to thank our partners, Muriel Schmid and Greg Kelley, for their unwavering encouragement, critical insights, and patience. Donald Haase's faith in our vision and enthusiasm for every idea that seemed to come out of it, no matter how small or ambitious, buoyed our faith in ourselves. From Broadview Press, we thank editors Marjorie Mather and Tara Lowes for their support of this project, and Betsy Struthers for her careful copyediting of our long and complex manuscript. Finally, special thanks to the scholars who provided original tale translations, published here for the first time: Nancy Canepa, Gina Miele, and Allison Stedman.

In the process of collaboration on this volume and in our undergraduate and graduate teaching, we have challenged ourselves and each other—clarifying and developing our shared understanding of the genre and its unruly history. Our students have been a vital part of this process, and we want to thank our wonderful collaborators from ENGL 6621 and ENGL 3960 at the University of Guelph and the students of FRNCH 3910 and FRNCH 4620 at the University of Utah. We are especially grateful to the University of Utah's College of Humanities for awarding Christine a Great Ideas in the Humanities Grant that allowed us to visit each other's classes in spring 2012. It is to our students and to readers like them—curious, creative, and passionate about the genres of fairy tale and fantasy—that we dedicate this book.

Christine A. Jones
Jennifer Schacker

unwavering encouragement, critical insights, and patience. Donald Haase's faith in our vision and enthusiasm for every idea that seemed to come our way, no matter how small or ambitious, buoyed our faith in ourselves. From Broadview Press, we thank editors Marjorie Mather and Tara Lowes for their support of this project, and Betsy Struthers for her careful copyediting of a lengthy and complex manuscript. Finally, special thanks to the scholars who provided original tale translations, published here for the first time: Nancy Canepa, Gina Miele, and Allison Stedman.

In the process of collaboration on this volume—and in our undergraduate and graduate teaching—we have challenged ourselves and each other—clarifying and developing our shared understanding of the genre and its unruly history. Our students have been a vital part of this process, and we want to thank our wonderful collaborators from ENGL [illegible] and ENGL [illegible] at the University of Guelph and the students of ENGL [illegible] and ENGL [illegible] at the University of Utah. We are especially indebted to the University of Utah's College of Humanities for awarding Christine a "Best Idea in the Humanities" Grant that allowed us to visit each other's classes in spring [illegible]. It is to our students and to readers like them—curious, eager, and passionate about the genres of fairy tale and fantasy—that we dedicate this book.

Christine A. Jones
Jennifer Schacker

PART I

THE TALES

INTRODUCTION: HOW TO READ A FAIRY TALE

Jennifer Schacker and Christine A. Jones

FAIRY TALES SEEM TO BE everywhere in contemporary culture—featured in picture books and anthologies of classic children's stories; providing inspiration for postmodern fiction, young adult novels, animation, feature films, and popular television series; depicted in fine art and fashion, on ceramics and quilting fabric; and referenced in advertising, journalism, and political speeches. Approaching the reading of a fairy tale with an open mind and a fresh perspective can be something of a challenge, but that is just the task we would like to set for you as a reader of this volume.

As scholars trained in the fields of French Literature (Christine A. Jones) and Folklore (Jennifer Schacker), we share a passion for teaching and research centered on the genre of the fairy tale. In our own experiences with undergraduate and graduate students, and in our conversations with other academics in this field, we have observed how close study of fairy-tale texts can explode and transform perspectives on this (seemingly) familiar genre. We have also noticed the enchanting effect that scholarship can have on popular ideas about and ways of reading fairy tales. Significantly, though, there is something of a lag in the impact academic discourse has on the wider culture, which means that present scholarship awaits a future audience and past scholarship often shapes how we read *now*. In fact, some past scholarship has become so ingrained in us as North American readers that stories can appear to mean *only* what such approaches could see in them. It is our hope to challenge the trends we have inherited by introducing teachers and students to new ways of talking about fairy tales. We want to emphasize that the perspectives foregrounded in this volume are those that are currently emerging in scholarship—some fully formed, others in an embryonic state, but all representing attempts to reinvigorate the academic field of fairy-tale studies—and thus the cultural reception of fairy tales—for the twenty-first century. Ideally, the generations of students who study the fairy tale through these emergent approaches will themselves generate new critical and creative visions for the genre.

One insight we hope to impart in pairing our own critical point of view with the voices of other present-day scholars is the historical nature of criticism itself and of a project such as this one. An explicit goal of this anthology is to reveal and explore how critics, including ourselves, have tended to draw the maps of folk- and fairy-tale studies according to national traditions and recurrent motifs. We are taking a modest stab in this volume at *re*drawing those established borders, and as a result this anthology juxtaposes many tales and also many critical ideas that are rarely considered in dialogue. We have been motivated to do so by the explosion of perspectives that characterized scholarship in Folklore and literary studies of the late twentieth century.[1] These developments shaped us as scholars and teachers, but we also hope that the re-envisioning of fairy tale history we are encouraging here will result in new research by future generations of fairy-tale scholars and provide creative inspiration for future writers, filmmakers, and artists.

In the millennial era, the very idea of the "anthology" has become a bit of a conundrum for critics who seek new conceptual paradigms through which to think about and teach tale history. Even as we edit this collection of fairy and folktales, we do so with respect for the vastness of these fields and a clear sense of *any* anthology's limits. On the one hand, we regard the present volume as just one contribution to an ongoing history of tale collections, each of which has the potential to mold our shared vision of the genre, and each of which has its limits. On the other hand, we are conscious that what sets the present volume apart from other available tale anthologies is that our fundamental shaping principle is historical: we are seeking to (re) integrate related histories across national, linguistic, generic, and communicative boundaries, and we draw on contemporary scholarship to do so.

As a team, we are most interested in the points of overlap and tension between the histories of the literary fairy tale and that of folklore study. In the past 60 years,

1 Major innovations in late twentieth-century scholarship include (but certainly are not limited to) the turn in Folklore towards performance-oriented perspectives and ethnopoetics; critical reevaluations of fieldwork practice and the role of print in the history of folklore; the important work by feminists to restore women writers (particularly French seventeenth-century writers) to their rightful place in the development of literary tales; critical attention to a rich and highly exploratory tradition of late twentieth-century tales (many of which now bear the theoretical appellation "postmodern"); bold cultural rereadings of the Renaissance Italian tradition; attention to previously neglected periods and places in which the fairy tale flourished, such as the Soviet era; and scholarship on the genre's role in new media, such as graphic novels and manga.

these histories have tended to be treated as distinct in the fields of literary study and Folklore—and also in terms of anthology publication. This means that several generations of critics grew up working separately.[1] But this has not always been the case. If we look to centuries past, we see that our scholarly predecessors had a much more fluid understanding of the relationship between oral and print traditions, so there is precedent for the kind of collaboration out of which this volume emerged. That said, many of these earlier intersections of folk- and fairy-tale studies were connected to a search for universal forms and meanings across time and place—an enterprise that scholars now find problematic and certainly less compelling than questions that lead us to see the cultural *specificity* of stories. The present volume situates itself squarely within the newer cultural tradition in interdisciplinary scholarship, as we will detail in this introduction and throughout the volume.

We can trace the trajectory of these disciplinary conceits back some 300 years when readers and writers began engaging in the study of the fairy tale, developing theories about the genre and its significance. Although English-language commentators were by no means the only ones weighing in on the issue, then as now they played a significant role in the public perception of fairy tales in Europe.[2] As

---

1 Adverse effects of the disciplinary alienation of folklore and literary studies include, for example, a deeply biased vision of fairy tale history in favor of literary print matter, with orality cast as a kind of backdrop, and, analogously, a vision of performance history that does not account for the influence and variability of forms of print culture. In Folklore, relatively little work has addressed the role of print in the circulation of ideas and texts, and in literary studies notions of orality often rely on outdated models. In the study of the fairy tale, dramatic performance and media studies—forms that can fall between the cracks of these disciplines—have been largely neglected until very recently. These and many more exciting avenues open up when we ask questions that are informed by the dynamics *between* the literary and the oral, or between print and performance.

2 One small but significant example is the description of Charles Perrault's heroine as Little Red Riding Hood in the very first English translation of his story collection by Robert Samber in 1729. In Perrault's language, what she has on her head, a *chaperon*, has a fascinating and spotty etymology that involves several leaps of logic for translators. According to the *Dictionnaire de l'Académie française* (DAF) of 1694, the word *chaperon* refers to a medieval and Renaissance style of headpiece with a tufted top and a kind of fabric tail that falls down onto the shoulders. Why should Samber cast this item as horseback riding gear? As it turns out, *chaperon* is a diminutive in French for *chape*, whose first definition is a long robe worn by the clergy, that is, a cassock. The word "cassock" was used in seventeenth-century England to refer to the long cloak that horsemen wore (*OED*). Thus, a *chaperon*, or little riding cloak combined with the idea of a bonnet, becomes "riding hood" in Samber's translation. The early English name has endured through history, baffling scholars, but proving tenacious to the point that they hesitate to change it for fear the eponymous heroine's identity will be destroyed. Jack Zipes, Maria Tatar, and Christopher Betts all keep the name in their translations of the Mother Goose Tales. Stanley Appelbaum hazards a minor change, Little Red Hood, but prints the old title in parentheses next to it. Christine A. Jones favors "Little Red Tippet" to capture the idea of a fabric trailing from the bonnet to cover the shoulders, but has retained the recognizable title in her translation for this volume.

of the early eighteenth century, when English writers raced to publish continental and "oriental" tales in translation, they noted in print what role these stories could play in the transmission of their own cultural values and refined behaviors. By the late eighteenth century, Romanticism gave rise to theories about the adaptation of fairy tales for use both in the acculturation of young children and in emergent interests in national character and national identities. In the Victorian period, scholarly debates about both the fairy tale and folklore captured the imaginations of general (non-scholarly) readers, and many of the theories and approaches developed in the late nineteenth century continue to resonate today in popular writing and thinking about the fairy tale.

The introduction of field-based research, and especially the international publishing success of Jacob and Wilhelm Grimms' collection of German oral traditional tales (what have come to be known as Grimms' fairy tales), inspired generations of folklorists and amateur collectors to create national archives of tales and fairy tale books of their own. The genre the Grimms had found so prevalent in Germany—*Märchen,* or what English translators and readers referred to as "popular tales," "nursery tales," "fireside tales," or "fairy tales"—was sought in cultural contexts from Africa to Japan and beyond. While oral narrative traditions can be found in every human culture, current scholarly practice emphasizes the importance of "emic" notions of genre—studying categories of story as they are defined, understood, and used by the community in question—as opposed to "etic" or outsider notions of genre, which shaped the varied (and often doomed) attempts to replicate the Grimms' work around the world. In short, versions of stories that have come down to us as part of the "fairy tale" tradition are culturally specific: there are certainly parallels and resemblances between various narrative traditions, but what contemporary readers tend to think of as "fairy tales" do *not* comprise a universal genre. Rather, this category of stories has emerged as significant, in different ways, in a select number of specific historical and cultural contexts.

Some of the most influential and enduring tales emerged in late seventeenth-century France and nineteenth-century Germany, but both their influence and their durability are rooted in their international success: they were and are texts that have been translated widely (and repeatedly) and now stand as "canonical" in English-language print culture. The long history of translation and international reception has had the effect of making the stories appear universal, as though they were not penned by historical people but by transcendent voices of humanity. The volumes known in English as *1001 Nights* or the *Arabian Nights,* Charles Perrault's "Mother Goose tales," and Grimms' fairy tales are the primary examples of this phenomenon, especially when they are translated for children's editions.

Not surprisingly, then, even today the collections destined for the university classroom in North America center on a fairly narrow canon: tales first published in seventeenth-century France (including the "oriental" tales made popular in Europe by French writers of this period) and nineteenth-century Germany, with the Italian Renaissance writers Straparola and Basile sometimes included as inaugurators of the fairy tale's print history, and Hans Christian Andersen as their heir apparent, along with a few current reworkings of these classic tales thrown in for good measure. Anthologies tend not to position this relatively small sampling of tales (represented by the European print corpus) within the vast sea of stories generated in performance and in print by cultures across the globe, many of which have by now been influenced by the ubiquity of the European print traditions. Consequently, too, the crucial contribution that editors and scholars who reprint, translate, and annotate fairy tales make to their meaning and canonical status goes nearly unnoticed. As a result, fairy tales may be one of the most pervasive and intimately familiar forms of narrative for English-language readers, but less familiar are the theoretical and ideological assumptions we have inherited from centuries past, ideas developed and popularized by scholars that often shape the ways in which we read and interpret and use fairy tales today. Because critical approaches tend only to appear in anthologies once they have been accepted by the university community, we can also forget that the ideas of tomorrow are already emerging quietly in scholarship today.

In the past 25 years or so, the genre of the fairy tale has inspired a vibrant new body of scholarly and critical writing, including some heated debates about the fairy tale's form, function, meaning, history, and the definition of the genre itself. As we have suggested, much of this recent research has challenged older paradigms and ways of thinking about the genre. In particular, recent scholarship has shifted towards an interest in tale texts, oral and written, as situated events and artifacts, whose potential meanings emerge in their contexts of production and reception. In Folklore scholarship, performance theory in the late 1960s and early 1970s emerged from ethnographic studies of tales in social context and had a revolutionary effect on approaches to oral traditions. In literary studies, a parallel turn towards the study of the dynamics of print culture and book history had a profound effect on fairy-tale studies.

In both cases, tale "texts" are now seen in terms of layers and levels of context—for example, the social context in which a particular tale text is created or performed, the political or ideological context in which it is received, and the broader generic and discursive context in which the text circulates (including not only other texts categorized as "fairy tales," but also other forms of written and spoken language that resonate with the text under consideration). At the same time, much contemporary scholarship is highly attentive to textual detail and textual form—the particularities of the text itself. The reading process implied by these contemporary critical processes may be a bit different than the one ordinarily practiced by many readers of fairy tales. Rather than seek out tales' seemingly universal messages or morals, the reading practice we encourage requires heightened attention to detail, a focus on texts' potential ambiguities and internal contradictions, an exploration of intertextuality—that is, the relationships between tale texts and between related discursive forms—and, above all, a very inquisitive mind. Along with our colleagues and our students, we have found that this approach to reading fairy tales can yield multiple and sometimes surprising interpretations: it is demanding, it is productive, and it is fun.

As many scholars before us, we now turn to "Little Red Riding Hood"—as Alan Dundes put it "one of the most beloved and popular fairy tales ever reported" (ix)—to open our own tale of twenty-first-century criticism. We begin with the scarlet-caped heroine because she presents an exceptionally clear illustration of how we have been trained by many critical theories not to see the trees for the forest of tale history. "Little Red Riding Hood" serves then as a case study for how to build a cultural lesson around just a few salient poetic details offered by the text and explored through basic research that begins with resources as readily available as a dictionary.

We grow up with Red Riding Hood. She feels familiar, especially because her transgression or disobedience—doing something she was told not to, in this case going into the forest—is a universal experience. As readers, we tend to see her foolishness—she does not recognize her grandmother, but also does not realize she is actually a wolf in disguise—as a function of her youth and apparent simplicity (or naiveté). The tale of Red Riding Hood appears to be loaded with timeless lessons and morals: don't talk to strangers; the forest (and any other unknown terrain) is potentially dangerous; maturity is a difficult but necessary rite of passage; girls on the verge of a sexual awakening should take care and heed their mothers' advice. This is, in any case, the "Little Red Riding Hood" many of us who grow up in the West have been told to see in the story. But if, as we argue in this volume, the meaning of the story is not predetermined or singular, but shaped in the details and particularities of each and every telling, then there are innumerable identities and potentialities that can be associated with this character.

Many contemporary writers and storytellers have explored these possibilities, rethinking and reworking this well-known heroine and her seemingly well-worn adventures—and there are always many more avenues left to explore. While each modern text appears to deliberately cast new light on this tale, the habit of revising a known storyline (the tale's familiar plot elements) in order to shift the meaning is nothing new at all. In fact, even (and especially) the best known versions of "Little Red Riding Hood"—namely, those of Charles Perrault as a literary author (1697) and Jacob and Wilhelm Grimm as collectors and editors (1857)—should be seen as creative acts. In their respective cultural and political contexts, both Perrault and the Grimms were taking risks and making a statement by attaching their names to this genre (in seventeenth-century France, the *conte*, and in nineteenth-century

Germany, the *Volksmärchen*). The details and the specific ways in which they are articulated distinguish "Le Petit Chaperon Rouge" (Perrault) and "Rotkäppchen" (the Grimms) from each other, but they also form the building blocks of meaning in each of these texts. It would surprise many adults to know that the seeds of other and very novel interpretations of "Little Red Riding Hood" are contained in the very versions of the story that they learned and loved as children.

Re/reading Little Red Riding Hood

Perrault's version of Red Riding Hood, the first to be written down and published with an author's name attached to it, tells the classic tale of a girl who encounters a wolf in the forest on the way to grandmother's house and ends by being eaten by him. Interpreting the story in terms of how it speaks across time is tempting, especially since it is followed by a short rhyming text called a "moral" that came to be a standard feature of the stories we associate with children. We have found that many young adults (our own students) have learned to read fairy tales (both those that are followed by a thing entitled "Moral" and those that are not) by searching for relatively clear-cut moral lessons that would seem to sum up the stories' meanings. If we can put aside that habitual reading practice and focus closely on the details of the text itself, then the implications of "Le Petit Chaperon Rouge" and the moral of Perrault's tale emerge as both more subtle and more complex than they may appear at first glance. In fact, our reading emphasizes their ironical and playful dimensions: rather than sum up the message of each of the seemingly simple tales that they conclude, Perrault's morals complicate the meanings and implications of each text, encouraging the reader to reread, rethink, and reconsider. We can already begin to make the text strange and new for ourselves as readers by looking for distinctive features of the story and exploring why they take this particular form in this particular narrative.

Here is the moral to "Le Petit Chaperon Rouge," both in its original French and in an English translation by scholar Maria Tatar:

On voit ici que de jeunes enfants,
Surtout de jeunes filles
Belles, bien faites, et gentilles,
Font très mal d'écouter toute sorte de gens,
Et que ce n'est pas chose étrange,
S'il en est tant que le Loup mange.
Je dis le Loup, car tous les Loups
Ne sont pas de la même sorte;
Il en est d'une humeur accorte,

Sans bruit, sans fiel et sans courroux,
Qui privés, complaisants et doux,
Suivent les jeunes Demoiselles
Jusque dans les maisons, jusque dans les ruelles;
Mais hélas! qui ne sait que ces Loups doucereux,
De tous les Loups sont les plus dangereux.

From this story one learns that children,
Especially young girls,
Pretty, well-bred, and genteel,
Are wrong to listen to just anyone,
And it's not at all strange,
If a wolf ends up eating them.
I say a wolf, but not all wolves
Are exactly the same.
Some are perfectly charming,
Not loud, brutal, or angry,
But tame, pleasant, and gentle,
Following young ladies
Right into their homes, and into their chambers,
But watch out if you haven't learned that tame wolves
Are the most dangerous of all. (*Classic Fairy Tales* 12)

Even if one works only with a single English translation of this moral, there are signposts to suggest that the text is operating in complicated ways. The moral frames the tale it concludes as the story of a young girl whose walk through the woods brings her into contact with a wolf, but it also emphasizes that one can understand the text in terms of the particular dangers that face "pretty, well-bred" young ladies (rather than children in general) and in terms of the heightened danger posed by charming, quiet, polite, unassuming, complacent, sweet, and gentle "wolves"—not your run-of-the-mill wolf, and not one readily recognized *as* a wolf. If we keep these details in mind when rereading the text, then it becomes more difficult to see our heroine simply as a naïve girl: if she represents a well-bred young lady, then why doesn't she know a bit more about the world that surrounds her? Importantly, there seems to be a level of irony here: how good is a young lady's breeding if it doesn't prepare her for a walk through the woods that are at her own back door (so to speak)? What is the nature of the danger that she faces, if the most dangerous of wolves is charming, polite, and gentle—in short, a perfect gentleman? Can she learn to avoid this dangerous disguise?

If we expand our study to consider these themes in a seventeenth-century context, then some of these questions unfold further. Two elements of the scenario that stand out in the French are *humeur accorte,* associated in the moral with a specific kind of wolf, and *dans les ruelles,* one of the places into which wolves may pursue young girls. These two phrases bear discussion because they can further the line of inquiry we began when considering the English text and because they have specific resonance in the period during which Perrault wrote this tale.

Humeur accorte has several period-specific meanings: the phrase takes its primary connotation from the word *courtois,* which refers to the kind of behaviors expected of knights in the Middle Ages (200 years *before* Perrault wrote his text) and courtiers in later centuries. In the *Dictionnaire de l'Académie française* (1694), *courtois* is defined as *complaisant,* meaning given to accommodation, or the courtesy of conforming to the disposition of the person with whom you are interacting. In contemporary terms, we may think of this as a positive behavior—a kind sensitivity and thoughtfulness that we see as almost inherent character traits. But the mode of conduct suggested by *courtois* (and the temperament implied by *humeur accorte*) was once regarded as a skill, an art to be learned and cultivated, a social mask that was required and highly beneficial for courtiers who hoped to succeed under Louis XIV. Indeed, this seemingly innocent quality (from a modern perspective) or this set of courtly skills (from a seventeenth-century perspective) is associated in the moral with the wolf, our villain; *humeur accorte* is an attitude and behavior about which readers are *warned.* What, then, does the danger signaled in the moral actually look like? This is a question to which we will return in a moment; first, let's consider the spaces with which this danger is associated.

In the *Dictionnaire de l'Académie française* (1694), the word *ruelle* is defined as a small street (from the root *rue* or street). But as the *Dictionnaire* entry continues, it becomes clear that the word had additional usages, such as the one quoted above in Tatar's translation of the story's moral: "chambers." In the seventeenth century, *ruelle* refers specifically to two spaces associated with women: 1) an area of the aristocratic bedroom between the bed and the wall where one might place seating and where guests (even ones of the opposite sex) could be received, respectably; and 2) a salon, or social gathering of authors usually hosted by women and held in their homes, where ideas were discussed and texts read aloud. Salons were a famous institution during Perrault's lifetime and authors of fairy tales belonged to them. While it is not clear which meaning is being invoked in this line from the final moral of Perrault's "Le Petit Chaperon Rouge," these secondary meanings throw culturally relevant light on the phrase and on the warning that wolves may not only pursue girls when they are out in the street, but also when they are out in society, and even in their own homes. All of these spaces are figured as the "forest" in the story. Significantly, the dangers faced by the girls addressed in this moral are found in the arenas of sociability that were familiar to women of the French court—and which they therefore might not recognize to be just as dangerous as an unknown forest.

Whatever the universal elements in the fairy tale, the moral offers culturally specific details that appear to be signposts meant to help the reader interpret these broader themes through the lens of local concern, in this case, young women at court. Read in this light, the story is about something wholly *other* than the fear of the wolf in the forest or a general warning about talking to strangers. Instead, the real problems are social wolves in sheep's clothing, who do not look or act like wolves at all: they are more pernicious than clear dangers and seem to be unavoidable (hence Red Riding Hood's unfortunate end in the wolf's belly). Now the moral looks something like a lesson in court antics. Perrault suggests that in late seventeenth-century society, there was a very specific brand of danger for female courtiers: male courtiers who had mastered the art of courtesy and who took advantage of ingénues—young women whose education could not prepare them for the full range of codes and behaviors to which they would be subject when they began moving in high social circles. Madame de LaFayette wrote a novel about this very phenomenon, *La Princesse de Clèves* (1671), published about 25 years before Perrault's tale. It is now considered one of the first modern novels, and its subject is a hapless young girl raised in the country who finds herself devoured by the sexual tensions at court. Whether or not this is a time*less* concern, then, in Perrault's day the lesson was modern and timely.

Indeed, if we interpret the tale of Red Riding Hood through the insights of the moral's language, we can conclude that the heroine is not a simple peasant girl but a young society woman who cannot dodge the wolves that inhabit her world by taking another path or avoiding the forest. She must move through the forest and learn to reckon with the ubiquitousness (*ruelle*) and the duplicity (*humeur accorte*) of courtly romance. To take this a step further, we could look at the plot detail that feeds Red Riding Hood to the wolf as a suggestion that women may be asked to embrace this kind of danger—to get in bed with this particular breed of wolf—in the form of a politically expedient marriage. The moral of the story may be that, alas, there is no escaping social and sexual politics. It is almost as if Perrault is suggesting that the fate of young ladies is to be devoured by these social practices; the best a young woman can do is to understand the unavoidable dangers that surround her.

Read this way, Perrault's story is a good bit more pessimistic in terms of its social message than it sometimes appears. Readers are perhaps more familiar with versions of "Little Red Riding Hood" that end happily and redeem the heroine. In the history of fairy-tale publication, this variant on the tale emerges in the collection of Jacob and Wilhelm Grimm. The Brothers Grimm first published their tales in 1812 and 1815, but the process of editorial revision continued for several decades, culminating in what is often called the "final edition" of their *Kinder- und Hausmärchen* in 1857. It is this version of "Rotkäppchen" (Little Red Cap) that is best known and that we will discuss here.

As in Perrault's text, the Grimms' heroine seems ill-prepared for the task she is given by her mother, despite her mother's accompanying litany of commands, reminders, and injunctions. To begin, let's consider Jack Zipes's translation of an early part of the tale, when the mother's words to her daughter are quoted:

> Come, Little Red Cap, take this piece of cake and bottle of wine and bring them to your grandmother. She is sick and weak. This will strengthen her. Get an early start, before it becomes hot, and when you're in the woods, be nice and good, and don't stray from the path; otherwise you'll fall and break the glass, and your grandmother will get nothing. And when you enter her room, don't forget to say good morning, and don't go peeping into all the corners. (Zipes, *Tradition* 747)

The mother's speech stands out in the text—and is forceful—not only because it is detailed but also because it is quoted directly; as readers, we hear the mother's voice along with Little Red Cap. In the heroine's shoes, we are likely to be seduced by the tone of this voice, for who has not received the advice of a mother (or mother figure) and failed to act on it! Our tendency then is to attend to the content of the mother's speech, which seems to provide a moral compass for the text and to set the stage for the heroine's disobedience. By focusing on the content, however, we tend to overlook the form. In fact, this is only one of several notable examples of quoted speech in the Grimms' text; examples include not only the words of the mother, but also those of Little Red Cap herself, the wolf, the grandmother, and the huntsman. While many well-known fairy tales contain small amounts of quoted speech—often quite memorable, from the evil queen's "Mirror, mirror on the wall, who is fairest of them all?" ("*Spieglein, Spieglein, an der Wand / Wer ist die Schönste im ganzen Land?*" in the Grimms' "Schneewittchen," or "Snow White") to the disguised wolf's "Lift the bobbin and the latch will open" ("*Tire la chevillette, la bobinette cherra*" in Perrault's "Le Petit Chaperon Rouge")—this particular text stands out as unusual. Analysis of the varied uses of quoted speech in "Little Red Cap" offers another path into the tale's meaning and implications.

On a cursory read of the mother's language, the reader may want to assume that this woman is simply concerned for her daughter's well-being, but the mother's quoted speech is focused almost exclusively on the girl's "proper" behavior to ensure that the wine and cake reach Grandmother intact and that Little Red Cap presents herself politely once she reaches her destination. Furthermore, Little Red Cap is sent into the forest by her mother—grandmother's house is "out in the forest, half an hour from the village" (Zipes, *Tradition* 747)—wearing bright red and, we can assume from everything her mother imparts, ignorant of the dangers that lurk close by. In fact, she is not given any of the tools she will need to face the challenges that we know await her. That said, when Little Red Cap meets the wolf the moment she enters the woods, she encounters him fearlessly *because* she "did not know what a wicked sort of animal" he is: her moral education has not prepared her for this encounter, and her ignorance makes her appear courageous.

The text does not fault (nor credit) Little Red Cap for being fearless, but her fearlessness manifests itself in language use: she is curiously, excessively forthcoming in her responses to the wolf's questions, offering *more* information than he requests. For example, she explains why she is carrying cake and wine, including who baked the cake, for whom, when, and why; she gives a detailed accounting of the location of her grandmother's house, including the amount of time it takes to walk straight there and the landmarks that mark the site. Like her mother, she is a talkative character aware of detail. And this perspicacity could be just the thing she needs to survive her journey. Of course we also know that this turns out not to be the case. Why would that be? A possible answer to that question can again be found in the conversational dynamics of the story.

At this point the conversation between the title character and the wolf shifts from Little Red Cap's reason for being in the forest to a focus on her body. In this text, the nourishment for grandmother is not carried in a basket, as it is in "Le Petit Chaperon Rouge," but *under* Little Red Cap's apron, against her body. The wolf's second question to the girl is "What are you carrying under your apron?" (Zipes, *Tradition* 747). Her response—cake and wine—is true enough, on two levels, because the wolf is also interested in what lurks a little further below: the girl's own flesh and blood, another kind of cake and wine (revolting as that may sound), and the wolf's ultimate nourishment. When the wolf becomes/dresses as Little Red Cap's grandmother, it is the yummy stuff under the girl's apron that he desires. Once he has the chance to gobble up "poor Little Red Cap," the text indicates that he has "satisfied his desires" (Zipes, *Tradition* 749). Little Red Cap's immediate willingness to give liberally of her speech—to open up more than she has to—foreshadows the unwitting offering of her whole body as she walks freely into the house that has become the wolf's lair.

Interestingly, the next verbal exchange Little Red Cap has with the wolf following their initial encounter is one in which she would seem to have some real agency and the opportunity to direct the conversation—but she doesn't turn this power to her advantage. The text quotes her thoughts upon reaching grandmother's house, where she is "puzzled" to find the door open. As she enters the house it "seemed so strange inside that she thought, 'Oh, my God, how frightened I feel today, and usually I like to be at grandmother's'" (Zipes, *Tradition* 749). Her inner thoughts, with their language of anxious concern, should logically influence the rest of what she will say. Yet, the words Little Red Cap then speaks aloud are in tension with her quoted interior reflections. Since grandmother looks "strange" and Little Red Cap feels "frightened," active interrogation of "grandmother" (the wolf in disguise) would be appropriate here: she should ask, "Are you really my grandmother?" Instead, she issues a series of (infamous) exclamations starting with, "Oh, Grandmother, what big ears you have!" These declarations invite formalized response from the wolf, ones that do not impart any helpful information whatsoever. It could be that in denouncing "grandmother's" attributes, Little Red Cap hopes to dissimulate her fear. Indeed, the rapid exchange that we have all come to know demonstrates a curiously keen ability on her part to size up the things about this creature that give her pause and to voice them aloud. But that is *all* she is able to do. Rather than move from declaratives to interrogatives, and from speech to action, Little Red Cap just moves closer to her own demise, from statements about the oddness of ears to the oddness of the mouth—the last words she utters before being "gobbled up" (Zipes, *Tradition* 749). It would seem then to be Little Red Cap's lack of skill as an interlocutor—what she says or doesn't say and how she uses her words rather than her knowledge of the forest—that places her in the gravest danger and (in the terms of this analysis) renders her interpretation of the situation feeble at best.

In contrast, the quoted words of the wolf reveal and then help him to fulfill his desires. His quoted interior reflections indicate his goal of eating Little Red Cap and her grandmother, and his quoted verbal exchanges with the girl demonstrate his ability to use language skillfully and strategically in order to actualize his thoughts. He manages not only to conceal his intentions but also to achieve his goal, using his discursive skills to dissemble and then to exploit interlocutors less skilled than he. The disjuncture between what the wolf says and what he does, both in the woods and at grandmother's house, is readily apparent to readers of the text. Further, and in contradistinction to Little Red Cap, it is the wolf's ability to manipulate language that makes him so powerful.

The one character whose thoughts, words, and actions are in perfect harmony is the huntsman, who may be a well-known character to many contemporary readers and who ultimately saves Little Red Cap and her grandmother. In the Grimms' text, the huntsman is introduced after Little Red Cap is gobbled up: he happens to be passing by as the wolf, now sated, sleeps in the grandmother's bed. The huntsman thinks to himself: "The way the old woman's snoring, you'd better see if something's wrong" (Zipes, *Tradition* 749). Although his thoughts are presented as quoted speech—by now a familiar textual strategy—they include a curious use of the second person singular ("you"), as if he (or perhaps his social conscience) were addressing himself. At the same time, the use of the second person in a text can be seen as a form of addressivity; that is, the text is pulling us, as readers, into a didactic conversation, signaling that it has something pointed to say *to us*. Unlike Little Red Cap and in the spirit of how the reader is meant to react to the text, the huntsman acts on sensory clues that indicate something is amiss. He enters the house, recognizes the wolf immediately, prepares to shoot him, realizes that the beast "could have eaten the grandmother and that she could still be saved," and proceeds to save both the grandmother and granddaughter by cutting open the Wolf's belly (Zipes, *Tradition* 750). The actions that ensue from the huntsman's internal reflections are indeed exemplary. This is a character who has mastered the use and subtle understanding of the power of language.

This reading is supported by the addendum to the tale—the short narrative epilogue that follows the text. Read in terms of the emphasis we have placed on the use of language in this text, it demonstrates that both Little Red Cap and her grandmother have learned something from their experiences. It is not simply staying on the path or avoiding the woods (or not that alone) that saves them from a future wolf. In the addendum, Little Red Cap is "on her guard" when she meets the next wolf, and despite his attempts to "entice her" she "went straight ahead." But her success is also due to the fact that she uses her words and her silence appropriately, and this leads to appropriate action: she kept silent when he "wished her good day" and spoke up about the incident when she reaches her grandmother's (Zipes, *Tradition* 750). Grandmother locks her door, and when the wolf attempts to impersonate Little Red Cap to gain entry, the two women remain silent within. While the wolf plans to wait them out and then to gobble up Little Red Cap when she emerges after dark, Grandmother anticipates this plan and counters with one of her own. Her quoted directives to Little Red Cap call the girl to action, and the girl sets out a trough of water still fragrant from boiling sausages, as instructed. The wolf's subsequent drowning in the trough and Little Red Cap's safe journey back through the woods to her home are thus due to much, much more than the conventional rendering of the story's message would suggest: they are due in very large part to Little Red Cap's acquisition of skill in social discourse, her newly found understanding of the implications of speech and silence, and her ability to think on her feet and to act accordingly. Indeed, this text does not so much imply that through obedience a girl can avoid danger—since *nothing* in her mother's quoted speech would have prepared Little Red Cap for her encounter with the first wolf!—it emphasizes instead that danger (as embodied by the two wolves) is *inevitable*. The text suggests that both girls and their grandmothers need to understand and master the subtleties of social interaction and discourse to navigate their way safely through the world.

Approached in this way, "Little Red Cap" is a story about the power of language and its use in discursive strategies (above and beyond simple politeness, as emphasized by Little Red Cap's mother). As the Grimms' story shows, the acquisition of these skills is not only socially useful but also vitally important to bodily well-being. This is a text in which the heroine and, by extension, the reader must learn to become suspicious of the surface-level meanings of utterances. In this way, "Little Red Cap" may offer some very specific and pointed life lessons, but it also offers ones applicable to the process of reading itself: this particular text can be seen as operating on a meta-level, offering a critical perspective on its own interpretation and the reading of fairy tales more generally. One lesson the reader can take from a critical reading of this sort is that to take the tale at face value is to remain as passive as the young and easily victimized Little Red Cap—all declarative comments but no probing or illuminating questions. If we instead approach texts as always potentially double-voiced, coded, subtle, and strategic forms of discourse, and interrogate them accordingly as the huntsman does (and as both Little Red Cap and her grandmother learn to do), then we can gain a tremendous and liberating amount of agency.

Finally, we would like to underscore the fact that these kinds of interpretive perspectives are productively applied not only to tale texts but also to the words of writers and collectors themselves. Perrault, for example, claimed to be writing *au style du bas peuple* (in the style of common people), but placed in a social, political, and ideological context, these claims can be seen as strategic utterances, ones that draw on associations between telling stories and folk wisdom, and that downplay his tales' implications for (and references to) a courtly and adult audience. Likewise, one must take with a grain of salt the Grimms' claims to offer in print form the pure and unadulterated oral traditions of the German *Volk* (folk). Such claims resonate deeply with the Romantic Nationalist ideology that inspired their search for oral traditions (seen as pure, ancient, natural, and untouched by outside influence) set in opposition to literary traditions (which were then seen as cosmopolitan, modern, artificial, and heavily influenced by foreign literary models). The Grimms' work has an important place in the history of folklore study and the emergence of fieldwork methodologies, but it would be a mistake to take their claims simply at face value. For example, their own methods included the collection of tales from literate friends and neighbors, and the content of their collection of *Märchen* included tales that already had a "foreign" print history, as did "Little Red Cap" itself. While we don't mean to suggest that Perrault and the Grimms are wolves—that they are tricky speakers who sought to deceive in order to destroy (although that would be an interesting avenue to explore!)—still it is crucial to our argument to point out that *all texts* use the complexities of language strategically. Fairy tales, like any other print tradition, should be approached with a healthy dose of caution and a well-developed arsenal of interpretive strategies and discursive sophistication.

Our readings demonstrate that you don't necessarily need to read a postmodern version of "Little Red Riding Hood" to find new insights into the title character and her misadventures. Part of the fun of (re)reading these old texts is decoding their tone, style, form, and word choice—a process that can unlock previously overlooked levels of meaning in the texts and that can lead to marvelous transformations of their own. This is precisely the process that twenty-first-century fairy-tale scholars promote and hope to encourage in their students. There is evident pedagogical benefit to suspending our belief in time-honored interpretations and allowing the specific versions of "Little Red Riding Hood" treated above to speak to us in fresh ways, ones that honor their distinctive textual features and their respective historical contexts as well as the reader's own individuality. In the following pages we hope to arm teachers and students alike with a variety of weapons they can wield in the challenging and exciting confrontation with fairy-tale complexity.

Tangled Webs

Reading fairy tales as literature and as situated narrative performances can engender many of the same issues that we encounter reading the Bible as literature in the classroom: there are few print documents to which readers bring more presuppositions and convictions. Texts that are near and dear to us also tend to elicit an emotional response that can be difficult to surmount for further reflection. Sometimes, too, as with biblical texts, the question of authorship is unclear or difficult to discuss in conventional ways—and without that familiar anchor, interpretation stalls or goes wild. In an effort to stave off these problems and move towards a pedagogy of textual engagement, it is helpful to outline what precisely we hope to accomplish by reading stories in this way.

In the literary and folklore classroom we want to encourage beginning with the premise that individual documents in their narrative specificity are our subject of inquiry. In that case, our job is to engage primarily with specific texts, contexts, tellers, and authors—even when some of these details have been obfuscated or erased in the historical record—rather than transhistorical traditions or themes. Our first concern, in short, is the exploration and interrogation of what there is to be read, that is, what has come down to us as print matter. In the case of oral traditions, we must always be mindful of the complicated processes of "entextualization" through which oral narratives were and continue to be transformed into the specific *written* forms in which we encounter them. These processes include a number of players and can include individual tellers, listeners, transcribers, editors, and translators. One of our objectives as scholars should be to do justice to each document in its cultural and contextual specificity.

Ever since the mid-nineteenth century, scholars have been debating genre definitions and terminology, including the use of the highly contested and admittedly problematic term "fairy tale." This is an issue whose history emerges in our chronological selection of tales and the introductory notes we have provided for each group of texts in Part I of this volume; it is also an issue we theorize in Part II, because it is remains critical to contemporary scholarship on the tale in several related disciplines. We have chosen to use "fairy tale" as an umbrella term to categorize the various forms of story contained in this volume because it has powerful and enduring cultural currency among general readers today. What we want to emphasize here is that the collective histories of literary tales and entextualized oral traditions are tangled webs whose many tendrils interlock and whose pattern changes depending on the vantage point from which one looks at them. Rather than concern ourselves with teasing out all of the connections among the dots, we might set as our goal to understand how the web has been constructed by the critical discourses that brought these stories down through history.

As someone who has even a casual acquaintance with fairy tales, you have been influenced as much by fairy-tale criticism as by fairy tales themselves. What you know (or think you know) is not the fairy tale itself but a critical interpretation that has been culturally accepted as normative. These normative readings have become lenses through which we tend to view all new stories that we encounter. The organization of this anthology and the critical texts included in Part II are both meant to promote a different series of lenses—some cultural and some purely heuristic—that allow us to see otherwise. Far from exhaustive, the list of stories in this volume (as in any anthology) reflects the ideological commitments of its editors. We would like to take a moment to share with you the presuppositions that drove our choices so that you may better position this volume within your own pedagogical frame.

- **Chronology versus national tradition.** Rather than position stories within their national traditions, we present them here within a long history of tale production to avoid associating a particular period with a single linguistic tradition, and vice versa. Chronology demonstrates the flexibility of tales within a national culture, allows for examination of border-crossing, and also reveals the polyphony of contemporary influences and divergences within historical periods.

- **Stories representative of place and time rather than theme.** We have delineated periods according to the conventions of literary history, employing the terms for the most important aesthetic movements in Europe. While this vision of literary history is strongly Eurocentric, in this context it underscores and allows for critical examination of the fact that the history of this genre *has been* written and shaped by Europeans and, more recently, by North Americans. The advantage of this organizational principle is that it can help to situate texts in relation to the other arts and letters of their period, foregrounding elements of the tales' poetics and thematics—traits that are harder to see when stories are grouped transhistorically and transculturally by type or motif. To give modern readers a sense of how fairy tales have looked through various periods of print history, we have maintained most period spelling and punctuation choices, even when they look slightly odd. This is part of what it means to read texts from the past.

- **Stories from traditions that are currently being researched and debated.** Once chronology rather than theme or nation drives the choice of texts, it is easy to drown in what Salman Rushdie called the Sea of Stories—that body of somatic and poetic matter from which tales everywhere seem to be drawn. An anthology that attempted to tackle "world tales" would face a formidable challenge, and we make no claim to representation of global tale traditions. To remain afloat and create an anthology that would be useful pedagogically, we gravitated towards traditions that have generated at least a modest body of scholarship and are on the minds of specialists working on the fairy tale today. This includes many of the stories now considered "classic" fairy tales—the ones you might expect to find in a volume of this kind—but also many that are now rather obscure, both for general readers and even for scholars outside of this field. The history we have constructed here reflects both the state of fairy-tale studies today and our own conviction that exploration of the breadth and depth of fairy tale history brings fresh perspective and new life to even the most familiar of stories.

Our decision about what types of critical readings to include was influenced by three main concerns:

- Fairy-tale anthologies have tended to reproduce excerpts from the earliest critical perspectives to the end of the twentieth century. Those lists rarely include pre-twentieth-century critics of the fairy tale as a genre, of which there are several that helped shape its history.

- Classic approaches to the fairy tale, while important, do not take account of the work that has been done in the past 15 years, which has dramatically reoriented the work of many young scholars.

- Reproducing critical work that was written for a different purpose in an anthology necessarily excerpts it from its own socio-historical context.

As the contextualization of fairy tales and critical traditions is a vital concern of ours as editors, we asked scholars to generate new material written specifically for this volume, essays that reflect upon the questions that interest them most and that draw on their own areas of research. We solicited essays organized around five key terms that have both historical and current resonance in fairy-tale studies: Genre, Authorship, Reception, Ideology, and Translation. Three essays are included for each key term; within each group of three, you will find different approaches, different arguments, and sometimes disagreement. In this way we take up twenty-first-century debates and present the ideas generated by these debates in the historical and cultural contexts for which they were written. These pieces necessarily and intentionally bear the publishing date of this volume and will be remembered, we hope, as a sign of the times of fairy-tale criticism in 2012.

Although this volume is bound and its stories are presented in a linear history, readers need not receive it as a closed or predetermined (and thus overdetermined) narrative. Instead, we hope that you violate its limits and allow questions other than historical descent to determine the tales you choose to read and the order in which you do so. As you enter the tangled web laid out for you here in its fullness, please allow yourself to be caught up in it, jump around, wrestle a little with its tendrils, discover new textual strategies and new ways of reading in the process, and (most of all) enjoy the ride!

Suggested Readings

Bacchilega, Cristina. *Postmodern Fairy Tales: Gender and Narrative Strategies*. Philadelphia, PA: U of Pennsylvania P, 1999.

Bottigheimer, Ruth B. *Fairy Tales and Society: Illusion, Allusion, and Paradigm*. Philadelphia, PA: U of Pennsylvania P, 1986.

Canepa, Nancy, ed. and trans. *Giambattista Basile's The Tale of Tales, or Entertainment for Little Ones*. Detroit: Wayne State UP, 2007.

Dundes, Alan. *Little Red Riding Hood: A Casebook*. Madison, WI: U of Wisconsin P, 1989.

Haase, Donald, ed. *Fairy Tales and Feminism: New Approaches*. Detroit, MI: Wayne State UP, 2004.

Magnanini, Suzanne. *Fairy-Tale Science: Monstrous Generation in the Tales of Straparola and Basile*. Toronto: U of Toronto P, 2008.

Opie, Peter and Iona, eds. and trans. *The Classic Fairy Tales*. Oxford: Oxford UP, 1974.

Schacker, Jennifer. *National Dreams: The Remaking of Fairy Tales in Nineteenth-Century England*. Philadelphia, PA: U of Pennsylvania P, 2003.

Seifert, Lewis. *Fairy Tales, Sexuality, and Gender in France, 1690–1715: Nostalgic Utopias*. Cambridge: Cambridge UP, 1996.

Stanton, Domna and Lewis Seifert, eds. and trans. *Enchanted Eloquence: Fairy Tales by Seventeenth-Century French Women Writers*. Toronto: Centre for Reformation and Renaissance Studies & Iter Inc., 2011.

Tatar, Maria, ed. and trans. *The Classic Fairy Tales*. New York, NY: W.W. Norton, 1999.

_____. *The Hard Facts of the Grimms' Fairy Tales*. Princeton: Princeton UP, 1987.

Tucker, Holly. *Pregnant Fictions: Childbirth and the Fairy Tale in Early Modern France*. Detroit: Wayne State UP, 2003.

Zipes, Jack. *Fairy Tales and the Art of Subversion*. 2nd ed. New York, NY: Routledge, 2006.

_____, ed. and trans. *The Great Fairy Tale Tradition: From Straparola and Basile to the Brothers Grimm*. New York, NY: W.W. Norton, 2001.

_____. *Spells of Enchantment: The Wondrous Fairy Tales of Western Culture*. New York, NY: Penguin, 1992.

_____. *Breaking the Magic Spell: Radical Theories of Folk and Fairy Tales*. Austin, TX: U of Texas P, 1979.

A: EARLY WRITTEN TRADITIONS

1. Anon., Egyptian Tales (New Kingdom, Dynasty 19, c. 1298–1187 BCE; *translated by Edward F. Wente, Jr., 2003*[1])

The "Tale of Two Brothers" has fascinated and baffled English readers ever since it was translated from hieroglyphics in the nineteenth century. The convention of opening English versions of the story with "Once upon a time" reflects the fact that it is often cast as an ancient fairy tale, but that categorization continues to be debated. Some themes and plot elements do seem familiar: it echoes several tale types and motifs now associated with classic fairy tales. However, it is also brimming with details that feel distinctly foreign—featuring characters who are both royal and divine, numerous images of rebirth from Egyptian mortuary cults, and an astonishingly complex plot.

THE TALE OF THE TWO BROTHERS

ONCE UPON A TIME THERE were two brothers, so the story goes, having the same mother and the same father. Anubis was the name of the elder, and Bata was the name of the younger. Now as for Anubis, he [possessed] a house and had a wife, [and][2] his younger brother was just like a son to him, so that it was he (Anubis) who made clothes for him while he (Bata) followed after his cattle to the fields, since it

1 [Source: William Kelly Simpson, ed., *The Literature of Ancient Egypt*, 3rd ed. (New Haven, CT: Yale UP, 203): 80–90.]

2 [Editor William Kelly Simpson explains that square brackets are used for text that has been "restored when there is a gap in the manuscript" and parentheses indicate "phrases not in the original added as an aid to the reader" (8).]

was he who had to plow. It was he who reaped for him, and it was [he] who did for him every chore that was in the fields. Indeed, his younger brother [was] a perfect man: there was none like him in the entire land, for a god's virility was in him.

Now many days after this,[1] his younger brother /[2] [was tending] his cattle according to his daily habit, and he would [quit work] for his house every evening laden [with] all sorts of field vegetables, [with] milk, with wood, and [with] every [good produce of] the fields; he would place them before his [elder brother] while he was sitting with his wife, and he would drink and eat, and [he would leave to spend the night in] his stable among his cattle [daily].

Now after dawn and the next day had come about, [he would bring foods] which were cooked and would place them before his elder brother, [and he would] give him bread for the fields, and he would drive his cattle to let them graze in the fields while he followed behind his cattle. [And th]ey [would] tell him, "The herbage of such and such a place is good." And he would listen to all that they said and take them to the place / with good herbage which they were desiring so that the cattle which were in his charge became exceedingly fine, and they multiplied their offspring very much.

At plowing time his [elder] brother told him, "Have a team [of oxen] made ready for us for plowing, for the soil has emerged so that it is just right for plowing. Also, you are to come to the field with seed because we shall start plowing tomorrow,"[3] so he said to him. Then his / younger brother made all preparations that his elder brother had told him to [make]. And after dawn [and the next] day had come about, they went to the field carrying their [seed] and started [to] plow with [their hearts] very pleased with their project as [they] began working.

Now many [days] after this, while they were in the field, they needed seed. So he sent his younger brother, saying, "Go quickly and fetch us seed from the village." His younger brother found his elder brother's wife seated plaiting her hair.[4] He told her, "Get up and give me seed / so that I may hurry off to the field, because it's for me that my elder brother is waiting. Don't cause a delay." Then she told him, "Go, open the granary and fetch for yourself what you want. Don't make <me>[5] leave my hairdressing unfinished."

---

1 This and similar expressions marking the passage of time occur throughout the story as conventionalized formulas that are not always to be taken literally. In fact, this paragraph and the following one are not really part of the narrative proper but serve to provide the necessary background for the action of the story that begins following the statement about the increase in the size of the herd. See E.F. Wente, in *JNES* [*Journal of Near Eastern Studies*] 21 (1962): 308–10.

2 [Slashes are used here as they are in poetry: to indicate a line break.]

3 In ancient Egypt the sowing of the seed for cereal crops was performed simultaneously with the plowing of the soil.

4 As the text stands, the translation should be, "His younger brother found the wife of his elder brother while one was sitting plaiting her hair."

5 [Angle brackets indicate "words which the copyist erroneously omitted" (Simpson 8).]

Then the youth entered his stable and fetched a large vessel, since it was his wish to take a lot of seed. He loaded himself with barley and emmer and came out carrying it. Then she asked him, "How much is what is on your shoulder?" And he told her, "It is / three sacks of emmer and two sacks of barley, totaling five, that are on my shoulder," so he said to her. Then she [spoke with] him, saying, "There is [great] virility in you, for I have been observing your exertions daily," for it was her wish to know him through sexual intimacy. She got up, seized hold of him, and said to him, "Come, let's spend an hour lying together. Such is to your advantage: I will then make you fine clothes."

Then the youth became like an Upper Egyptian panther in ⸢furious⸣[1] rage over the wicked proposition she had made to him, and she became exceedingly fearful. He had words with her, saying, "Now look, you are just like a mother to me, and your husband is just like a father to me, for he who is older than I it is who has brought me up. What means / this great offense <you> have said to me? Don't say it to me again! But I will tell it to no one, nor will it escape my mouth to anybody." He picked up his load and went off to the field. Then he reached his elder brother, and they started to work <at> their project. Afterward, at evening time, his elder brother quit work for his house, while his younger brother was (still) tending his cattle and [would] load himself with all produce of the field and bring back his cattle / before him to let them spend the night (in) their stable, which was in the village.[2]

Now the wife of his elder brother was fearful <because of> the proposition she had made. So she got some fat and bandages and pretended to be an assaulted woman in order to tell her husband, "It's your young brother who has assaulted <me>." Her husband quit work in the evening according his daily habit. He reached his house and found his wife lying down, pretending to be sick. She did not pour water upon his hands as usual, nor had she lit up for his arrival, so that his house was in darkness as she lay vomiting.[3] Her husband said to her, "Who has quarreled with you?" She said to him, "No one has quarreled with me except your / young brother. When he returned to take seed to you, he found me sitting alone and said to me, 'Come, let's spend an hour lying together. You shall loosen your plaits,'[4] so he said

1 [Half brackets indicate words or phrases that Egyptologists have found to be "uncertain or imperfectly understood" in the process of deciphering and translating the original hieroglyphics (Simpson 8).]

2 This sentence, which is also not part of the narrative proper, serves to explain how Anubis would customarily return home before Bata, thus setting the stage for the episode at the barn door.

3 E. Rowínska and J.K. Winnicki, in *GM* [*Göttinger Miszellen*] 134 (1993): 85–89, argue that the verb here means "spilling," expressing contempt of Bata, rather than "vomiting," although in the Israel Stela, line 20, the same verb refers to disgorging after the manner of a crocodile.

4 On this passage and its sexual connotation, see E. Graefe, in *SAK* [*Studien zur Altägyptischen Kultur*] 7 (1979): 53–61, and P. Derchain, in *SAK* 7: 62–63.

to me, but I refused to obey him. 'Isn't it so that I am your mother, and that your elder brother is just like a father to you?' so I said to him. And he became afraid and assaulted <me> to prevent me from making a disclosure to you. Now if you let him live, I shall pass away. See, when he returns, don't [let him live any longer], because I curse this wicked proposition which he would have carried out yesterday."[1]

Then his elder brother became / like an Upper Egyptian panther, and he sharpened his spear and put it in his hand. His elder <brother> then stood behind the door <of> his stable in order to kill his younger brother as he was returning in the evening to let his cattle enter the stable. Now when the sun set, he loaded himself <with> all sorts of field vegetables according to his daily habit, and returned. The lead cow entered the stable and said to her herdsman, "Look, your elder brother is standing in wait for you holding his spear to kill you. You must get away from him." He heard what his lead cow said, and / the next one entered and said the same. He looked under the door of his stable and saw his elder brother's feet as he was standing behind the door with his spear in his hand. He set his load onto the ground and hastened to run off in flight, and his elder brother went in pursuit of him, carrying his spear.

Then his younger brother prayed to Pre-Harakhti, / saying, "My good lord, it is you who distinguishes wrong from right." Thereupon Pre heard all his petitions, and Pre caused a great (gulf of) water to come between him and his elder <brother>, infested with crocodiles, so that one of them came to be on one side and the other on the other (side). His elder brother struck twice upon (the back of) his hand because he had failed to kill him. Then his younger brother called to him on the (other) side, saying, "Wait there until dawn. As soon as the sun disk rises, I shall / contend with you in his presence, and he will deliver the culprit to the just, for I shall nevermore be with you, nor shall I be in a place where you are. I shall go to the Valley of the Cedar."

Now after dawn and the next day had come about, Pre-Harakhti arose, and they looked at each other. Then the youth had words with his elder brother, saying, "What's the meaning of your coming in pursuit of me in order to kill <me> unjustly without having heard what I have to say? For I'm still your young brother; and / you are just like a father to me, and your wife is just like a mother to me, isn't it so? When you sent <me> to fetch us seed, your wife said to me, 'Come, let's spend an hour lying together.' But see, it has been distorted for you into something otherwise." Then he informed him about all that had transpired between him and his wife. He swore by Pre-Harakhti, saying, "As for your <coming> to kill me unjustly, carrying your spear, (it was) because of a sexually aroused slut!" He got a reed knife, cut off his phallus, and threw it into the water. The catfish swallowed <it>, and he / grew

---

1 Or "I am suffering from this wicked proposition which he would have carried out yesterday," but the determinative of the verb favors "curse." The term "yesterday" is used because day was over at sunset, even though the Egyptian day began at dawn.

weak and became feeble. His elder brother became very grieved and stood weeping for him aloud. He could not cross over to where his younger brother was because of the crocodiles.

Then his younger brother called to him, saying, "If you have recalled a grievance, can't you recall a kindness or something that I have done for you? Now go to your home and take care of your cattle, for I shall not stay in a place where you are. I shall go off to the Valley of the Cedar. Now what you shall do on my behalf is to come and take care of me if <you> find out that something has happened to me <after> I extract my heart and put it on top of the blossom of the cedar tree. And if the cedar tree is cut down and falls to the ground, / you are to come to search for it. Even if you spend seven years searching for it, don't let your heart become discouraged, for if you do find it and put it into a bowl of cool water, then I will become alive in order that <I> may avenge the wrong done to me. Now you shall ascertain whether something (has happened) to me if a jar of beer is delivered to you in your hand and produces froth. Don't delay upon seeing that this comes to pass with you."

Then he went off to the Valley of the Cedar, and his elder brother went off to his home, his hands placed upon his head and his (body) smeared with dirt. Presently he reached his home, and he killed his wife, cast her <to> the dogs, and sat down in mourning over his younger brother.

Now many days after this, his younger brother was in the Valley of the Cedars with no one with him as he spent all day hunting desert game. He returned in the evening to sleep under the cedar tree on top of whose blossom his heart was. And / many days after this, he built for himself a country villa with his (own) hands <in> the Valley of the Cedar, filled with all sorts of good things, with the intention of establishing a household for himself.

Presently he went out from his country villa and encountered the Ennead[1] as they were walking (along) governing the entire land. The Ennead spoke in unison, saying to him, "Oh, Bata, Bull of the Ennead, are you alone here having abandoned your town before the face of the wife of Anubis, your elder brother? / See, (he) has killed his wife, and thus you will be avenged upon him <for> all wrong done against you." And they felt very sorry for him. Pre-Harakhti told Khnum,[2] "Please fashion a (marriageable) woman for Bata so that he does not (have to) live alone." Thereupon Khnum made for him a house companion who was more beautiful in her body than any woman in the entire land, for (the seed of) every god was in her. Then the seven Hathors[3] came (to) see her and said with one voice, "It is [by] an (executioner's) blade that she shall die."

1 The company of the major gods.

2 A creator god represented as shaping man on a potter's wheel.

3 The goddesses who determine an individual's fate.

So he coveted her intensely while she was dwelling in his house and he spent all day / hunting desert game, bringing (it) back and putting (it) down before her. He told her, "Don't go outside lest the sea carry you away, for I will be unable to rescue you from it, because I am a female like you and my heart lies on top of the blossom of the cedar tree. But if another finds it, I shall fight with him." Then he revealed to her all his inmost thoughts.

Now many days after this, while Bata went to hunt according to his daily habit, / the maiden[1] went out to stroll under the cedar tree which was next to her house. Then she beheld the sea surging up behind her, and she hastened to flee from it and entered her house. So the sea called to the cedar tree, saying, "Seize hold of her for me," and the cedar tree removed a tress from her hair. Then the sea brought it to Egypt and deposited it in the place of the launderers of Pharaoh, l.p.h.[2] So the scent of the tress of hair turned up in the clothes of Pharaoh, l.p.h., and the king wrangled with the launderers of Pharaoh, l.p.h., saying, "Scent of ointment is in the clothes of the Pharaoh, l.p.h.!" The king got to wrangling with them daily, but / they didn't know what to do. The chief launderer of Pharaoh, l.p.h., went to the bank, very worried as a consequence of the daily wranglings with him. Then <he> stopped short and stood on the seashore opposite the tress of hair that was in the water. He had someone go down, and it was brought to him. <Its> scent was found exceedingly fragrant, and he took it away to Pharaoh, l.p.h.

Then the learned scribes of Pharaoh, l.p.h., were brought. They told Pharaoh, l.p.h., "As for this tress of hair, / it belongs to a daughter of Pre-Harakhti in whom is the seed of every god. Now it is tribute to you <from> another country. Send envoys forth to every foreign country to search for her. As for the envoy who will go to the Valley of the Cedar, have many men go along with <him> to fetch her." Then His Majesty, l.p.h., said, "What you have said is very, very good." And (they) were sent off.

Now many days after this, the men who had gone abroad returned to render report to His Majesty, l.p.h., whereas those who had gone to the Valley of the Cedar failed to return, for Bata had killed them, leaving (only) one of them to render report to His Majesty, l.p.h. So His Majesty, l.p.h., sent forth many soldiers as well as chariotry in order to bring her back, / a woman being among them through whom all sorts of beautiful feminine adornments were presented to her (Bata's wife). The woman returned to Egypt with her, and there was jubilation for her in the entire land. His Majesty, l.p.h., loved her very much and appointed her to (the rank of) Chief Lady. Then he spoke with her in order to have her divulge the nature of her

---

1 Bata's wife was still a virgin.

2 [Simpson notes that the phrase "'may he live, prosper, and be in health,' frequently follows a royal name; following the usual custom, it is usually rendered in our texts as 'l.p.h.'" (8).]

husband, but she said to His Majesty, l.p.h., "Have the cedar tree cut down and chopped up." The king sent / soldiers carrying their tools to cut down the cedar tree, and they reached the cedar tree. They cut off the blossom upon which Bata's heart was, and he fell dead that very instant.

Now after dawn and the next day had come about and the cedar tree had been cut down, Anubis, Bata's elder brother, entered his house, and he sat down and washed his hands. He was handed a jar of beer, and it produced froth. Another of wine was handed him, and it turned bad. Then he took his / staff and his sandals as well as his clothes and his weapons, and he hastened to journey to the Valley of the Cedar. He entered the country villa of his younger brother and found his younger brother lying dead upon his bed. He wept when <he> saw <his> younger brother lying in death, and he went to search for his younger brother's heart beneath the cedar tree under which his younger brother slept in the evening. / He spent three years searching for it without finding it. Now when he had commenced the fourth year, his heart desired to return to Egypt, and he said, "I shall depart tomorrow," so he said in his heart.

Now after dawn and the next day had come about, he began walking under the cedar tree and spent all day searching for it. He quit in the evening. He spent time to search for it again, and he found a (cedar) cone.[1] He left home with it: it was indeed his younger brother's heart. And he fetched a bowl of cool water, dropped it into it, and sat down according to his daily <habit>.

After night had fallen, / his heart absorbed the water, and Bata shuddered over all his body and began looking at his elder brother while his heart was (still) in the bowl. Anubis, his elder brother, took the bowl of cool water in which his younger brother's heart was and <had> him drink it. His heart assumed its (proper) position, and he became as he used to be. So they embraced each other and conversed with one another. Then Bata said to his / elder brother, "Look, I shall transform (myself) into a large bull that has every beautiful color and whose sort is unparalleled, and you shall sit upon <my> back. By the time the sun rises, we shall be where my wife is that <I> may avenge myself. And you shall take me to where the king[2] is, for every sort of good thing shall be done for you and you shall be rewarded with silver and gold for taking me to Pharaoh, l.p.h., because I shall become a great marvel, and there shall be jubilation for me in the entire land. And (then) you shall depart to your village."

Now after dawn / and the next day had come about, Bata transformed (himself) into the form which he had mentioned to his elder brother. Then Anubis, his elder

1 Because of a cedar cone's similarity to a bunch of grapes, the Egyptian uses the word "grapes."

2 Here and following, the Egyptian uses the term "One" in reference to the king.

brother, sat down upon his back. At dawn he arrived at the place where the king was, and His Majesty, l.p.h, was informed about him. He saw him and became very joyful over him. He made a grand oblation for him, saying, "It is a great marvel that has come to pass." And there was jubilation for him in the entire land. Then / his weight was made up in silver and gold for his elder brother,[1] who (again) settled down in his village. The king gave him much personnel and many goods, for Pharaoh, l.p.h., loved him very much, more than anybody else in the entire land.

Now many days after this, he (the bull) entered the kitchen and stood in the place where the Lady was, and he began speaking with her, saying, "See, I'm still alive!" She asked him, "Who indeed are you?" And he told her, "I am Bata. I realize that when you caused the cedar tree to be chopped up for Pharaoh, l.p.h., it was on account of me, to keep me from staying alive. See, / I'm still alive, but as a bull." The Lady became very fearful because of the declaration her husband had made to her. Then he left the kitchen.

His Majesty, l.p.h., sat down and made holiday with her. She poured (drinks) for His Majesty, l.p.h., so that the king was very happy with her. Then she said to His Majesty, l.p.h., "Swear to me by God as follows, 'As for what <she> will say, I shall grant it to her.'" And he heard all that she said, "Let me eat of the liver of this bull, / for he will never amount to anything," so she said speaking to him. The king became very vexed over what she had said, and Pharaoh, l.p.h., felt very sorry for him.

Now after dawn and the next day had come about, the king proclaimed a grand oblation as an offering up of the bull, and he sent a chief royal butler of His Majesty, l.p.h., to sacrifice the bull. Thereupon he was sacrificed. While he was upon the men's shoulders, he twitched in his neck and shed two drops of blood beside the two doorposts of His Majesty, l.p.h., one chancing on one side of the great portal of Pharaoh, l.p.h., and the other on the other side. They grew into / two large Persea trees, each of which was exquisite. Then someone went to tell His Majesty, l.p.h., "Two large Persea trees have grown this night as a great marvel for His Majesty, l.p.h., beside the great portal of His Majesty, l.p.h." And there was jubilation for them in the entire land, and the king presented an offering to them.

Now many days after this, His Majesty, l.p.h., appeared at the audience window of lapis lazuli with a wreath of all sorts of flowers on <his> neck, and he <mounted> a chariot of electrum / and came out from the palace, l.p.h., to inspect the Persea trees. Then the Lady came out in a chariot following Pharaoh, l.p.h. His Majesty, l.p.h., sat down under one Persea tree <and the Lady under the other. And Bata> spoke with his wife, "Ha, you liar! I am Bata. I'm alive in spite of you. I realize that when you had

1 That is, the elder brother was rewarded with an amount of silver and gold equivalent to the weight of the bull.

<the cedar tree> cut down for Pharaoh, l.p.h., it was on account of me. I transformed (myself) into a bull, and you had me killed."

Now many days after this, the Lady stood pouring (drinks) for His Majesty, l.p.h., so that the king was happy with her. She told His Majesty, l.p.h., "Swear to me by God as follows, 'As for what the Lady will say to me, I shall grant it to her,' so you shall say." And he heard / all that she said. She said, "Have these two Persea trees cut down and made into fine furniture." So the king heard all that she said. After [a] little while His Majesty, l.p.h., sent skilled craftsmen, and the Persea trees of Pharaoh, l.p.h., were cut down. The queen, the Lady, watched this, and then a splinter flew up and entered the Lady's mouth. / She swallowed <it> and became pregnant in the completion of a brief moment, and the king made out of them (the Persea trees) whatever was her desire.

Now many days after this, she bore a son, and someone went to tell His Majesty, l.p.h., "A son has been born to you." Then he was brought, and nurse and maids were assigned to him. And there was jubilation <for him> in the entire land. The king sat down and made holiday, and they began to nurture him.[1] His Majesty, l.p.h., loved him very much from that moment, and he appointed him / Viceroy of Kush. And many days after this, His Majesty, l.p.h., made him crown prince of the entire land.

Now many days after this, when he had completed many [years] as crown prince in (the) entire land, His Majesty, l.p.h., flew up to the sky.[2] Then the king[3] said, "Have my high officials of His Majesty, l.p.h., brought to me that I may inform them regarding everything / that has happened to me." His wife [was] then brought to him, and he contended with her in their presence.[4] An affirmative (decision) was reached among them.[5] His elder brother was brought to him, and he made him crown prince in the entire land. He <spent> thirty years as king of Egypt. He departed from life, and his elder brother succeeded him on the day of death.

Thus it concludes happily and successfully.

---

1 The verb translated "nurture" refers basically to the physical act of nursing a child; its Semantic range also included child rearing in an extended sense.

2 A common expression used to refer to the death of the king.

3 I.e., Bata, the new king.

4 That is, Bata litigated with his wife. The expression cannot mean that Bata judged his wife, as is evident from the use of the same locution [above, p. 44: "Wait there until dawn. As soon as the sun disk rises, I shall / contend with you in his presence ..."].

5 The implication is the condemnation of Bata's unfaithful wife, whose death by execution had been fated by the seven Hathors.

2. Lucius Apuleius, *Metamorphoses* (mid-2nd century ACE; *translated by Jack Lindsay, 1960*[1])

Also known as The Golden Ass, *Apuleius's* Metamorphoses *contains one of the first references to a figure that has come down through history as a stock image of the teller: the old woman, or hag. She is the voice telling the story that has come to be known as "Cupid and Psyche." Jack Lindsay's lively translation demonstrates the extraordinary talent this figure possesses for weaving a narrative with romance, adventure, and caution. Significant in this early version of the tale is the level of physical detail offered—detail about décor, the character's beautiful bodies, and the trauma they frequently sustain. Such a wealth of detail could almost distract us from the heavy significance of the characters in this story. Many of these material details, such as the wedding procession, the contrast between crags and gem-paved floors, and the oil lamp that illuminates and wounds, can be explored for allegorical meanings that help us think through the great and tragic love affair depicted here between Psyche and Cupid.*

THE OLD WOMAN'S TALE (EXCERPT)

Once upon a time there lived in a certain city a king and queen, and they had three daughters remarkably beautiful. But though the two elder girls were as comely as you could wish, yet it didn't strike you dumb with despair to have a look at them—while as for the youngest girl, all man's praising words were too poor to touch (let alone becomingly adorn) a beauty so glorious, so victorious.

Citizens in crowds, and droves of pilgrims, were attracted by the fame of the extraordinary spectacle. They pressed about her, and stood moonstruck with wonder at her unapproachable loveliness. They raised their right hands to their lips, laying thumb and forefinger together and throwing her a kiss of reverence as though it were the goddess Venus herself that they adored. Already the word had gone abroad through the nearby cities and bordering countries that a goddess had been brought forth by the deep-blue womb of ocean, and nourished by the froth of the curling waves; and that she now dwelt among mortals, allowing them to gaze promiscuously on her divinity—or that, at the very least, Venus had had a Second Birth (this time from earth, not water): a Venus endowed with the flower of virginity, and germinated from a distillation of the stars.

Every day the tale drifted farther. Soon the neighbouring islands, most of the mainland, scores of provinces, were echoing with the news. Many were the hurrying men that made long journeys by land and over the deep seas, only to gaze upon

1 [Source: Jack Lindsay, trans. and ed., *The Golden Ass* (Bloomington, IN: Indiana UP, 1960): 105–21.]

this splendid product of the age. No one set sail for Paphos; no one set sail for Cnidos—no, not even for Cythera—to come into the presence of Venus. Her sacred rites were forgotten; her shrines were falling into ruin; her cushions were trampled on; her ceremonies were neglected; her images were ungarlanded; and the old ashes lay dirtying the desolate altar.

A young girl had supplanted her, and the divinity of the mighty goddess was worshipped in the shrine of a human face. In her morning walks the virgin was propitiated by the victims and food-offerings due to the missing Venus. When she strolled down the street, the people rushed out and presented her with votive tablets; or they strewed her way with flowers.

This intemperate attribution of divine rights and qualities to a mortal girl deeply incensed the actual Venus. Transported with indignation, and shaking her head in a towering rage, she uttered the following soliloquy:

"I the primal Mother of all living, I the elemental Source of energy, I the fostering Venus of the girdled earth—I am degraded to sharing my empire and honour with a mere wench. My name, engraved on the heavens, is defiled by the excrement of earth. I must forsooth be vaguely content with the remnants of another's worship and with the duties paid to a deputy. A girl that will one day die borrows the power of my name. It meant nothing then that shepherd Paris, whose good taste and integrity Love himself admitted, set me above the other great goddesses as the Queen of Beauty. But this giglot whoever she may be shall not smugly usurp my dignities. I shall take measures that she may soon be sorry for her charlatan charms."

So anon she summoned her son, that winged lad, the naughty child who has been so spoilt that he despises all social restraint. Armed with flames and arrows he flits in the night from house to house. He severs the marriage-tie on all sides; and unchastised he perpetrates endless mischief; and he does everything save what he ought to do. This lad, prone enough to harm on his own lewd initiative, Venus whetted-on with her words. She brought him to the city of our tale and pointed out Psyche—for that was the name given to the girl. Moaning and incoherent with wrath, Venus related the story of her rival's beauty and insolence.

"I beseech you," she said, "by the tie of mother-love, by the sweet wounds of your arrowhead, by the honeyed warmth of your torch, provide your parent with her revenge, her full revenge. Exact heavy retribution for these contumelious charms. And, above everything else, do your best to give her the fate that I ordain. Let the virgin be gripped with most passionate love for the basest of mankind—one that Fortune has stripped of his rank and estate, and almost of his skin—one so vile that his wretchedness has no parallel anywhere."

Thus she spoke. Whereupon with loose-lipped kisses she long and closely farewelled the lad, and then sought the margin of the tide-swept shore. She trod the spray-tips of the tossing waters with her rosy feet; and lo, the sea fell calm over all its glossy surface. At once, as if by pre-arranged signal, her marine retinue appeared. The daughters of Nereus rose, chanting in chorus, and with them Portunus[1] shaggy with his sea blue beard, Salacia[2] with her bosom full of fishes, dwarf Palaemon driving a dolphin-chaise, and troops of Tritons bounding out of every wave. One Triton gently wound his tuneful conch; another held a silken ombrelle to shade her from the sun's fierce heat; another floated ahead, holding a mirror up before his mistress's face; and others swam yoked to her car. This was the company attending Venus on her progress to the palace of Oceanus.

Meanwhile Psyche, for all her manifest beauty, reaped no benefit from her pre-eminence. She was gazed at by all, praised and mazed; but no man, king or prince or even commoner, raised any pretensions to her hand in marriage. They admired her as a sample of divinity, but only as men admire an exquisitely finished statue. Long before, the two elder sisters, whose ordinary beauty had made no noise among distant populations, had been wooed by kings of good standing; and now they were happily married. But Psyche, lonely lass, sat sad at home, mourning her forlorn fate, weak in body and sick at heart; and she hated the beauty that gave pleasure to all the world save herself.

Accordingly the sorrowing father of this ill-fated girl suspected the wrath of the gods; and dreading some visitation from heaven, he consulted the ancient oracle of the Milesian God.[3] With prayers and sacrifices he besought the powerful deity to bestow a marriage-bed and a husband on this slighted maid.

Apollo, though a Grecian and Ionic, yet (for love of the composer of this Milesian Tale) gave a Latin response which translates as follows:

King, stand the girl upon some mountain-top
adorned in fullest mourning for the dead.
No mortal husband, King, shall make her crop—
it is a raging serpent she must wed,
which, flying high, works universal Doom,
debilitating all with Flame and Sword.
Jove quails, the Gods all dread him—the Abhorred!
Streams quake before him, and the Stygian Gloom.

When the announcement of the holy oracle was delivered, the king, formerly so pleased with life, dragged himself sadly home and unfolded to his wife the

---

1 Portunus: Harbour-god, also called Palaemon.
2 Salacia: Sea-goddess with name derived from *salum* the "salt sea."
3 Milesian God: Apollo.

injunctions of this melancholy response. They all lamented, wept, groaned, for several days. But at last arrived the dread hour when the shocking oracle must be consummated. The procession was formed for the fatal wedding of the unfortunate girl. The torches burned dully, choked with ash and soot; and the tunes of the marriage-flute were replaced by plaintive Lydian melodies. The gay hymeneal-songs quavered away into doleful howls; and the bride wiped her tears with the nuptial veil itself.

The entire city turned out to show its mourning respect for the afflicted family. A day of public lamentation was at once sympathetically ordered. But the necessity of obeying the dictates of heaven demanded that the sad-faced Psyche should be surrendered to her fate. The death-marriage was sorrowfully solemnized; and the funeral of the living bride moved on, attended by the whole populace. Thus the weeping Psyche was present, not at her wedding, but at her funeral; and while the anguished parents, horrified unendurably, strove to delay the ghastly procession, the girl herself exhorted them to submit.

"Why rack your old and harrowed limbs forever on a cross of misery?" she cried. "Why waste your breath, dearer to me than my own, in this endless moaning? Why do you disfigure with ineffectual tears those faces that I honour so truly? Why do you destroy the light of my life in those sad eyes of yours? Why do you tear your grey hair? Why do you beat your breasts, hallowed with the milk of love? Are these torments to be the glorious guerdon that you win through my surpassing beauty?

"Too late you realize that the deadly shaft of envy has cruelly smitten you. When the tribes and the nations were hymning me with divine honours, when all their voices chimed in titling me the second Venus, that was the hour for grief and tears, that was the hour when you should have given me up for lost. Now I feel, now I realize, that Venus is my murderess, and none other. Lead forward, and stand me up on the rock to which the response devoted me. Why should I lag? Why should I shrink aside from the coming of Him that has been born to destroy the world?"

The virgin said no more. She took her place in the flocking procession and strode onwards resolutely. At length they arrived at the appointed crag on a precipitate mountain-top; and there they deposited the girl and left her. The nuptial torches, with which they had lighted their way, now spluttered out in the tears of the onlookers, and were dropped. With heads drooping, the procession turned back. As for the poor parents, demoralized by their loss, they barred themselves up in their darkened palace and abandoned their lives to an everlasting gloom.

But as Psyche lay trembling apprehensively and weeping on the top-shelf of the crag, a gentle breath of fondling Zephyrus fluttered and tweaked her dresses, and puffed them up. Gradually raised on the palm of a tranquil wind, she was smoothly wafted down the steep and rocky slope, and laid softly on the lap of the valley, on flower-sprinkled turf.

Book the Fifth

Psyche, pleasantly reposing in a tender verdant nook on a couch of dewy grasses, felt all her agitated limbs relax; and she drifted into a sweet sleep, from which she awoke fully refreshed. Her mind was now at peace. She saw a grove composed of tall and thick-boughed trees. She saw a fountain flashing with waters like glass in the middlemost of the grove.

Near to the plashing foot of the fountain there stood a palace built not by human hands but by divine power. You had but to give one glance into the hall to know that you stood before the gorgeous pleasure-house of a god. The lofty ceilings, delicately fretted out of citronwood and ivory, were upheld by pillars of gold. The walls were completely crusted with silver modelling, while shapes of wild beasts and of other animals flanked the entrance. A marvellous man it was (a demigod, a very god at least) that deftly savaged silver to such forms.

The pavement itself was a mosaic of gems splintered and fitted together so as to weld their colours and to represent various objects. O madly happy, more than happy, must be that man who can trample on jewels and carcancts! All the other parts of this extensive mansion were equally splendid beyond estimation. The walls, inlaid with ingots of gold, lighted the rooms with their own warm glow, so that even if the sun withdrew the house would still exude illumination—so effulgent were the rooms, the porticoes, the doors. The furniture too was constructed on the same lordly scale; and the place might easily have been reckoned a castle of heavenly masonwork, used by Jove during his visits to mankind.

Invited by this delightful outlook, Psyche approached nearer; and timidly affecting courage, she crossed the threshold. The lovely vista lured her on; and she wandered through the premises, wondering at all she saw. Farther in, she found magnificent storerooms crammed with every luxury. No wish but found its fulfilment there.

But more wonderful even than these vast riches was the total absence of all closures, all bars, all janitors. The treasure of a world lay before her, unforbidden.

While she was gazing round in rapture, a bodiless voice addressed her. "Why, lady," it asked, "do you stand astonished at this fine show? All that you see is yours. Hie therefore to the bedroom, and rest your wearied body on the couch; and when you so desire, arise and bathe yourself. We whose voices you hear are your handmaidens. It is our duty to obey all your wishes; and when we have attended to your bodily comforts, a banquet fit for a queen will be served."

Psyche felt herself happy and safe in these counsels of divine providence. She hearkened to the aerial Voices, and soothed away all her tiredness—first in sleep, and then in the bath. The moment this was done, she saw near by a half-moon dais with a raised seat and all the materials for a restorative meal. Joyously she seated herself.

Immediately cups of nectarous wine and relays of dishes garnished with every conceivable dainty were set before her by some spiritual agency; for not a servant appeared. And though she could see no human being, yet she heard people speaking around her; and these Voices were her only servants.

After she had sumptuously dined, One entered unseen and sang; and Another played on a lyre, and both lyre and lyrist were unseen. And then a rich harmony, like the sound of many interwoven Voices, was borne upon her ears; and though she could still see no human form, she seemed to stand in the midst of a mighty choir.

When these diversions were over, Psyche yielded to the suggestions of the dusk and retired to bed; and when the veils of night were drawn, an insinuating murmur floated into her ears. Then, afraid for her maidenhead in that lonely place, she quailed and was all the more shaken because she did not know what threatened.

But as she shuddered the anonymous bridegroom drew near, and climbed into bed, and made Psyche his bride, and departed hastily before sunrise. At once the waiting-voices entered the bedroom and solicitously tended the young bride with her ruptured virginity.

Thus her life went on, day after day; and habit brought its trails of pleasure, and the sound of the unknown Voices was the solace of her solitude. But meanwhile her parents were muddying the dregs of their existence with grief and lamentation; and the story, spreading far and wide, was carried at last to the ears of her elder sisters, who forthwith left their homes in mourning and hurried back, to console their parents.

On the night of their arrival Psyche's husband remarked—for she could feel and hear him, she could do all but see him—"Psyche, my precious, my darling wife, termagant Fortune has an ugly trick ready for you, which needs (I think) the shrewdest counterblast on our part. Your sisters, dismayed by the report of your death, are endeavouring to trace you. They will climb up yonder crag. If then you should chance to hear their outcry, make no answer, do not even look their way. If you act otherwise, you will bring on me a heavy misfortune and on yourself utter destruction."

Psyche promised, assuring him that she would be an obedient wife. But when he and the night drained away together, the poor girl spent the whole next day in weeping and moaning, exclaiming that she was now hopelessly lost; for not only was she confined in a heavenly dungeon, deprived of all human intercourse, but she was not allowed to relieve the minds of her sorrowing sisters or even to look at them from a distance. Without indulging in food, bath, or any other amusement, but copiously weeping, she lay down to rest. A little later, her husband (appearing at her side somewhat earlier than usual) embraced her as she wept, and thus expostulated:

"O Psyche, my love, is this what you promised me? What am I your husband to expect of you now? What am I to hope for? Daylong and nightlong you grieve, and you lie within my embrace as on a cross of torment. So be it. Do as you desire, and follow the destructive bias of your whims. When repentance comes, you will remember my warning—too late."

At this she begged and swore that she would kill herself, till she extorted from her husband the licence that she desired, to see her sisters, soothe their grief, and put her head together with theirs. At last the young beseeching bride gained her point, with a further concession: that she would give her sisters as much gold and jewels as she wished.

But one condition he emphasized so repeatedly as to scare her: never to let any guile of the sisters lure her into inquiries concerning her husband's identity—or by her sacrilegious curiosity she would cast herself down from her exalted height of Fortune and never again enjoy his embraces.

She thanked her husband gratefully. "O no," she said, restored to cheerfulness, "I'd rather die a hundred times than lose your darling caresses. I love you, desperately love you, whoever you are. I cherish you like my own soul. I would not exchange you for Love himself. But all the same I think you ought to grant my prayer. Bid Zephyrus this coachman of yours to fetch my sisters down—as I was fetched."

And she kissed him persuasively, and murmured endearments, and twined him with her arms and legs, and said in a wheedling whisper, "O my honey, O my husband, O you sweet sweet soul of your Psyche."

Unable to resist her coaxing compulsion, her husband felt his will reluctantly drown beneath her kisses. He promised that she should have all her wishes; and then at the first smudge of light he vanished from the arms of his wife.

The sisters had inquired the locality of the crag where Psyche had been left. They hurriedly climbed the slope; and standing on the rock they wept and beat their breasts till the boulders and scarps resounded with their inconsolable screams. They called on their hapless sister by name till the piercing echoes of their grief reached all the way down the valley. Psyche in her agitation ran wildly out of the palace.

"Hallo there!" she called back. "Why are you making yourselves so miserable, and all for nothing? Here is the person you mourn. Cease this wailing. Dry those tears that have wetted your cheeks for so long. In a moment you can hold in your arms the sister that you're lamenting."

Then she summoned Zephyrus and informed him of her husband's permission. Obeying her commands, in a jiffy he brought the sisters gliding unharmed down to Psyche upon the downiest blast. In a tangle of embraces, a flurry of kisses, the girls turned one to the other until the tears, sealed for a space, burst forth again—this time from excess of joy.

"Now come inside," said Psyche. "Come into our house and learn to smile again. You must cheer up with your Psyche now."

With this prologue she showed them all the resources of her house of gold, and introduced them to the household of attendant Voices. She gave them a tiptop entertainment—first, all the luxuries of the bath; then, the spirit-served delicacies of her table—till, at length satiated by the inexhaustible supply of god-sent riches, the elder sisters began to nourish a jealous hatred in the depths of their hearts. One of them was particularly tireless in interrogating Psyche minutely as to who was the master of this divine residence, what kind of man he was, and how he shaped as a husband.

Psyche however managed to follow out her husband's instructions and let nothing slip to betray her secret. But making the best of the situation she told them that he was a young man, extremely handsome, with cheeks just shaded by the downiest of beardlets—and that most of his time was employed in country-sports and mountain-hunting. Then, to save herself from any contradictory phrases that would expose the truth, she loaded her sisters with gold and jewelled necklaces; and calling Zephyrus she bade him convey them back to the summit.

When these orders had been obeyed, the excellent sisters returned home, burning with a rancorous jealousy that swelled at every step. Soon they were chattering with mutual indignation. One said to the other:

"So now you see how daft and cruel and unjust is Fortune! Did it overjoy you to find that we sisters, though we have the same parentage, have very different lots? Here are we, the elders by birth, delivered as bondsmaids to foreign husbands, packed far away from homeland and parents, like exiles. That's our life. And here is the youngest daughter, the end-product of our mother's decrepit womb, owning all that wealth and a god for a husband—and she doesn't even know how to make a proper use of her good fortune. You saw, sister, what a mass of necklaces lie about the house, and what value they are—what glistening stuff, what sparkling gems, what parquets of gold, she treads carelessly underfoot. If in addition to this she has the fine-looking husband that she describes, then there is no woman happier in the whole world. Perhaps when he is in the clutch of long habit and the ties of their affection are strengthened, this god of a husband will make her a goddess too.

"By Hercules, that's what he's done. That's the explanation of her airs and graces. Think of her. Think of her condescending pride. The woman breathes the goddess already, she with her attendant Voices and her ladyship over the very winds. But I (poor nothing) am fettered to a husband older than my father, a man who's balder than a pumpkin and as passionate as a peascod, a man who (to make matters worse) locks and bars up the whole house, the suspicious fool!"

"And I," answered the other, "I have to lie down tamely under a husband who's tortured and twisted with gout, and who consequently cultivates my venus-plot very sparsely. I spend most of the time in chafing his crippled chalky fingers and scalding my dainty white hands with stinking fomentations, filthy napkins, and horrid poultices. My role is not wife but nurse-of-all-works. You, sister, seem to tolerate your position with quite a deal of patience—I might say, low-spiritedness—for I believe in saying what I think. For my part I won't endure for another moment the good fortune that has dropped into the lap of one who doesn't deserve it. Recollect also how overbearingly, how sneeringly she behaved towards us; and how her puffed-up attitude peeped out of every boast that she couldn't control as she showed us round; and how she bundled on us against her will a few oddments of her huge wealth; and how then, bored with our company, she gave orders for us to be swept-up and blurted and whizzed away. I'm not a woman, I can't squeeze out another breath, unless I bring down this fine erection of her fortunes; and if these insults rankle in you too, as they certainly ought, then let us concert some workable plan. First of all, let us agree not to show these things we're carrying to anyone—not even our parents. In short, we must not admit that we know she's alive and well. It is quite enough to have had the vexation of seeing what we have seen, without scattering abroad the news of her glory among the family and the whole city. For there's no glory when nobody knows how rich she is. We'll teach her that we're not her slaves but her elder sisters. So for the present let's return to our husbands and our poor mediocre houses; and then after thoroughly digesting the situation let's return equipped to lessen her pride."

The two wicked sisters agreed on this wicked plan. They hid all the priceless gifts; they dishevelled their hair; they beat their faces (which deserved the blows); they redoubled their feigned lamentations. Then, having depressed their parents and reopened the sores of the old people's grief, they set off for their homes to finalize the schemes of harming (or rather murdering) their innocent sister.

Meanwhile Psyche's unknown husband once more warned her during his bedtime colloquies. "Do you see what great danger threatens you? On the horizon Fortune launches the stormcloud. Unless you take the most active measures, it will soon be thundering upon you. These vicious wolf-bitches are straining every sinew to catch you in an impious snare. Their aim is to persuade you to look upon my face—which as I have admonished you, if you once see, you will never see again.

"If then these bloodsucking harlots return daggered with their venomous thoughts—for they will return, I know—hold no communication with them. If you find that beyond you through your natural candour and your gentle inexperience, at least hear no inquiries that they make about your husband, and answer nothing. For before long our family is to be increased; and you, child as you are, yet bear a child in your womb. If you keep your peace concerning our secret, that child will be divine. If you profane our secret, it will be mortal."

Psyche glowed with happiness at the news. She abandoned herself to the comforting hope of divine offspring. She foretasted joyfully the glory of this future pledge and the dignity of a mother's name.

She counted the marching days, the lapsing months; and in her novitiate of gestation she wondered how her precious womb could swell so richly from so tiny a prickling. But those pestilent and repulsive Furies, breathing their viperous virulence and hurrying with damned zeal, set out once more; and once more Psyche was warned by her fleeting husband:

"The day of judgment comes, the awful danger. The malices of your sex, your own blood in hatred, have risen against you. Camp is struck; the battle-line is drawn up; the charge is sounded. Your wicked sisters have unsheathed the sword; the blade is at your throat. Alas my sweetheart Psyche, what agonies hem us in. Have mercy on yourself and on me; and by your inviolable silence save your home, your husband, yourself, and our baby from the dreadful ruin that menaces us. Refuse to see or hear these vile women who cannot claim the name of sister after this murderous hate, this severance of all the ties of blood. Leave them to stand like Sirens on that crag, making the rocks re-echo with their ominous voices."

Psyche replied with hesitant tears and sobs, "Already, I should have considered, I have provided you with clear proof that I was trustworthy and able to control my tongue; and you will be just as pleased at the firmness of mind that I'll show now. All you have to do is to tell Zephyrus to obey orders as before. You ought at least to let me see my sisters to compensate for not seeing your sacrosanct lineaments. By these aromatic tresses curling about your face, by these apple-cheeks tenderly like my own, by that breast pleasant with an indescribable warmth, by my hope of seeing your face at least mirrored in my unborn babe's! say yes to the loving prayers of your worried suppliant. Breathe into your devoted Psyche a new soul of joy. Never any more shall I beg to see your face. Henceforth the deep dark night will mean nothing to me. I clasp you, my only light."

Beguiled by her words and her yielding embraces, the husband wiped away her tears with his own hair, and promised that she should have her wish. Then he vanished the moment light was born.

But the brace of sisters, sworn in conspiracy, did not even visit their parents. They went straight from shipboard to the crag, made with haste. They did not even dawdle for the arrival of the carrier-wind, but leaped into the valley-depth with uncontrollable foolhardiness. Zephyrus however was mindful of the royal command. He reluctantly received them on the bosom of his soughing blast and bore them to the ground. With quickening steps the pair restlessly dashed into the house; and hiding behind the name of sisters they embraced their quarry. Then, strewing a smile upon the pit of their hoarded guile, they flattered her.

"Psyche, you're not as slim as you used to be. Soon you'll be a mother. Oh, you can't think what a joy for us all you're carrying in your reticule. The whole house will simply be wild with delight. Oh, how happy we will be to amuse your golden baby. For if he only matches his parents in beauty—and so he must—then he'll be a pure love."

Thus with a prattle that sounded like affection they won Psyche over. She at once made them seat themselves to recover from the fatigues of travel. She had them laved in warm flowing baths and entertained them at a choice repast where most-tasty dishes and concoctions marvellously came and went. She ordered the harp to twang, and it rippled sweetly—the flute to play, and its notes issued forth—the choir to sing, and they sang. The music ravished the souls of the hearers with its delicious cadences; but not a performer was to be seen.

But not all the honeyed song with its tempering sweetness mitigated one whit the wickedness of the scheming women. They guided the conversation towards the hidden snare and made deftly oblique inquiries as to the husband, what kind of a man he was, and where he was born, and what was his family.

Psyche in extreme artfulness forgot her former account and produced a fresh fiction. She said that her husband was a merchant from the adjoining province, a man of tremendous wealth, now middle-aged with a sprinkle of grey in his hair. Then again she abruptly changed the subject, loaded her sisters with presents, and sent them back on their wind-carriage. But while they were returning home, borne aloft on the tranquil breath of Zephyrus, they conferred as follows:

"What are we to say, sister, of the lurid lies of that idiot? One moment her husband is a young fellow that trims a beard of the softest down. The next moment he's a middle-aged man with hair showing silvery. Who can this be that in so brief a space suddenly becomes changed into an old man? There's only one explanation, my sister; and that is that this worthless woman is telling us a string of lies, or that she doesn't know herself what her husband looks like. But whichever supposition is true, she must as soon as possible have all these riches whipped away from her. And yet if she has never seen his face, it must be a god that she has married and a god that she is bearing us under her belt. If that's so, and if she does become the mother of a divine babe (which heaven forbid), I'll string myself up on the spot in a noose. Therefore let us go meanwhile to see our parents, and develop some scheme on the lines we have laid down in our discussion."

Thus inflamed, the sisters made a disdainful call on their parents, and tossed feverishly awake all night. Then, desperate in the morning, they rushed back to the crag, and by the usual vehicle of wind descended in frenzy. They squeezed out some tears from under their lids, and guilefully said to Psyche:

"Here you sit smiling when it's only blissful ignorance that stops you from seeing the terrible danger you're in. But we, who watch over your affairs so vigorously, are nailed on a cross of painful apprehension. We have discovered for an absolute fact something that in true sympathy with all sorrow and misfortune we cannot keep to ourselves any longer. We've discovered that it's a monstrous, twining, twisted, coiling, venomous, swollen-throated, ravenously gaping-jawed Serpent that reposes with you secretly in the night. Don't you recall the Pythian Responses that announced you the destined bride of a bloodthirsty beast? Besides, many of the country-folk who go hunting in these regions, and scores of the neighbours, saw him gliding home in the evening from his pasturage and swimming across the shoals of the river hard by.

"Everybody is saying that he won't long keep on pampering you with enticing complaisances in the way of food. But as soon as your womb is fully rounded with pregnancy he will gobble you up as an appetizing morsel in a prime state. So it's up to you to decide whether you want to listen to us, your sisters, who are thinking only of your best advantages—whether you want to escape death and to come to live with us, safe from all attacks; or whether you want to be engulfed in the bowels of a cruel beast.

"But if you're so keen on your rural solitude full of nothing but Voices—so attached to the filthy and dangerous embraces of clandestine lust, and the caresses of a poisonous serpent—at least we have discharged our duty like loving sisters."

Psyche (poor girl) so sincere herself and so tender-hearted was stiff with horror at this dreadful disclosure. Whirled out of all her senses, she took no heed of her husband's admonitions and of her own promises. She felt herself swept before an avalanche of anguish. Trembling, with all the blood shocked out of her face, she managed at last in a strangled voice to falter out a few words:

"O my dearest sisters, you're still as loving as ever. You've acted as you ought, as your sisterly duty dictated. I'm sure that all you've been told seems to me genuine. For I've never seen my husband's face, and I don't know where he comes from. I only hear him whispering at night. I have to accept a husband of unknown standing, a shape that flees the light. So I agree that you must have hit the truth. He is some monster. He spends his time in frightening me from looking at him, and in threatening me with some great evil for being curious about his face. So if you can bring a ray of hope to your poor misguided sister, don't lose a moment. For if you neglect that, you'll undo all the good which your care has done me so far."

The wicked women, having thus won the approaches to their sister's defenceless heart, emerged from their ambushes and frankly assaulted the simple girl's panic-stricken meditations with the drawn sword of craft.

Accordingly the first answered. "Since the bond of blood obliges us to consider no personal danger when your life is at stake, we will show you the only road which leads to safety. This plan is the result of our long, long thought. On the side of the bed where you usually lie, hide a very sharp razor, whetted on the palm of your hand to the finest edge. And hide a lamp, trimmed and full of oil, a lamp that burns with a steady flame, behind some of the bedroom-hangings. Make all these arrangements with the utmost precaution. When the Thing has slid into the chamber and climbed up on the bed, wait until he's stretched out and begun to breathe heavily inside the coils of sleep. Then slip out of the sheets and tiptoe on bare feet slowly along the floor. Rescue the lamp from its shroud, and by the light's direction find the moment for this glorious deed. Boldly lift up your right-hand. Slash the blade down with all your strength, and sever the head of the baneful Serpent at the nape of the neck. And don't think we'll be far. We shall be anxiously standing-by for the signal that your safety is secured. Then together we'll remove all this property; and and [*sic*] we'll soon see you married to a human being like yourself."

With all these arguments they poured flame into the vitals of their sister; and when they saw that she was fully kindled, they at once abandoned her. Afraid to be caught within the area of the approaching crisis, they were carried to the crag by the usual sudden blast; and hastening with brisk terror to the quay, they sailed away.

But Psyche, left alone (if a girl tormented by wild Furies can be considered alone), flooded and ebbed with sorrows like a stormy sea. She began to prepare for the ugly deed with assured intention and obdurate heart; but almost immediately she hesitated irresolute, distracted with wavering impulses and decisions. She hurried, then lagged. She was bold, then timid. She was doubtful, then furious. And (strangest of all) in the same person she hated the beast but loved the bridegroom. Yet as evening drew on the night, she made a last demented effort and prepared the scene for her wicked deed.

Night came; and her husband came; and after some amorous skirmishes he fell into a heavy sleep. Then drooping in body and mind, yet fed with unusual strength by the cruelty of fate, she brought forth the lamp and seized the knife, boldly shedding her sex.

But as soon as she raised the lamp and unbared the mystery of her bed, she saw the sweetest and gentlest of all wild creatures: Cupid himself, a beautiful god beautifully lying on the couch. At sight of him the flame burned cheerfully higher, and the razor dulled its sacrilegious edge.

But as for Psyche, she was terrified at the sight. She lost all self-control; and swooning, pallid, trembling, she dropped on her knees and sought to hide the knife—deep in her own bosom. And so she would have done, had it not been that the blade, shrinking from such an atrocity, fell to the floor out of her heedless hands.

And then, for all her faintness and fear, she felt her flagging spirits revive as she gazed at the beauty of the god's face. She saw the gay lovelocks of his golden head, drenched with ambrosia—the curls gracefully drifting over his milky breast and ruddied cheeks, some in front and some behind—while the very lamp-flame guttered before the flashing splendour.

On the shoulders of the flying god there bloomed dewy plumes of gleaming whiteness; and though the wings themselves were laid at rest, yet the tender down that fringed the feathers frisked in a continuous running flutter. The rest of his body was so smoothly warmly rounded that Venus could look on it and feel no pang at having borne such a child. At the foot of the couch lay his bow, his quiver, and his arrows: the gracious weapons of the mighty god.

While Psyche stood spellbound with insatiable delight and worship, impelled by wonder she began to handle her husband's weapons. She drew one of the arrows out of the quiver and tested its sharpness, on the tip of her thumb. But pressing unduly hard (for her hand still trembled) she pricked the skin and evoked some tiny drops of rose-red blood. Then, burning more and more with desire for Cupid, she laid herself broadly upon him; and opening her mouth with forward kisses she applied herself eagerly to the embrace, fearing only that he would wake too soon.

But while she stirred above him in the extremity of agonized joy, the lamp (actuated either by treachery, or by base envy, or by a desire to touch so lovely a body—to kiss it in a lamp's way) spewed a drop of glowing oil from the point of its flame upon the god's right shoulder.

O bold and reckless lamp! base officer of love! to burn the very god of Flame—you that some lover, inspired by the need to possess the beloved even at night, first devised.

The god, thus burnt, leaped out of bed; and spying the scattered evidences of Psyche's forfeited truth, he made to fly mutely out of the clasp of his unfortunate wife. But Psyche, as he rose into the air, caught hold of his right leg with both hands and clung there, a wailing drag upon his upward flight. Into the cloudy zones they soared, until her muscles gave way and she dropped to the earth.

The god her lover did not desert her as she lay upon the ground. He alighted upon a nearby cypress and gravely admonished her from its swaying top:

"O simple-hearted Psyche! Putting aside the commands of my mother Venus who had bidden me infatuate you with some base wretch and degrade you to his bed, I chose rather to fly to you myself as a lover. I acted rashly, well I know. I the world-famous archer stabbed myself with my own arrowhead. I took you for my wife—only to have you think me a wild bear and raise the blade to sever my head ... which bears those very eyes that loved you so fondly.

"This it was I bade you always to beware. This it was against which my loving-heart forewarned you. But as for those fine advisers of yours, they shall pay heavily for their pernicious interference. My flight is penalty enough for you."

As he ended, he spread his wings and soared out of sight. But Psyche lay prostrate on the ground and strained her eyes after her winging, vanishing husband, harassing her mind with most piteous outcries; and when his wings with sweeping strokes had rapt him out of her life into the vast distance, she crawled to a nearby river and threw herself from the bank into the waters. But the gentle stream, in horror and in reverent fear of the god who can heat even the dank water-deeps, took Psyche on the soft curl of a wave and laid her safe on the thick green turf of the bank.

It chanced that at this moment Pan the country-god was seated on the river-lip, embracing Echo, goddess of the mountainside. He was teaching her to sing all kinds of tunes. Near by, she-goats gambolled along the winding pasture of the banks, cropping the weedy tresses of the river. The goatfoot god, aware of Psyche's sad fate, compassionately called the sick and stricken girl to his side, and comforted her with friendly words:

"Pretty maiden, I am a country-fellow, a shepherd, but my mind is stored with much odd knowledge as the result of long experience. If I may hazard a guess (which among wise men goes by the title of a divination) I judge by these halting and stumbling steps, and by the extreme paleness of your face, and by the incessant sighs you heave, and by the sad look in your eyes, that you are madly in love. Hearken then to me. Seek no longer to lose your life by dashing yourself to pieces or by any other such recourse of despair. Lay grief aside. Cease your sorrow. Woo Cupid with adoring prayers. For he is the mightiest of the gods, a wanton lad and spoilt. Press him with grateful offers of compliance."

Thus spoke the shepherd-god; and Psyche, making no reply beyond an obeisance to his divinity, wandered on. And when she had dragged herself a little farther, she came at the dusk of day by some unmapped by-path to the gates of the very city over which the husband of one of her sisters was king. Discovering this, Psyche asked that her sister should be informed who had arrived. She was then quickly ushered in; and after an exchange of embraces and compliments, the sister inquired the causes of her visit. Psyche answered:

"I suppose you remember the advice you gave when you persuaded me that it was a beast lying with me under pretence of marriage, and that I ought to kill him with a sharp blade before he gulped poor me down into his greedy maw. Well, I followed out your suggestions until I got as far as holding up the lamp over his face to assist me. But what I saw was the most wonderful heavenly sight: the very son of goddess Venus, Cupid himself, I tell you, stretched in quiet sleep. I was wonderstruck before such a happiness and distraught with my excess of joy; and while I stood there not knowing what to do in my glory, by my cruel bad-luck a burning drop of oil spirited out of the lamp on to his shoulder. He was startled out of his sleep by the pain and opened his eyes to find me armed with flame and steel.

"'In punishment for your shocking conduct,' he said, 'get out of my bed immediately. Take away all your belongings, and I'll marry your sister instead'—and then he mentioned you by name. 'I'll marry her straightway with full marriage-ceremony.'

"And then he told Zephyrus to puff me away, past the precincts of the palace."

No sooner had Psyche finished speaking than the other, pricked-on by ravening rash lust and rankling jealousy, rushed out to tell her husband a story fabricated on the spur of the moment—something about a rumour of her parent's death—and then taking ship she proceeded with all speed to the crag as of old.

Although the wind was blowing from the wrong quarter, yet in her flustering hopes she screamed. "Receive me, Cupid, a wife that's worthy of you. And you, Zephyrus, buoy up your mistress."

Then she leaped out into the air, and fell headlong; and not even as a corpse was she able to find the landing that she desired—for her limbs were torn to pieces by the jutting rocks, and strewn down the face of the cliff, as she deserved; and her entrails provided nourishment for the birds and beasts that laired in the cliff; and thus she perished.

Nor was the punishment of the other sister long in fulfilment. For Psyche's wandering trail led her to another city, where that other sister dwelt. Psyche gave her the same misunderstanding; and the woman, lured by the hope of supplanting her sister, dashed off to the crag and fell into the same death.

Meanwhile Psyche travelled through many peoples, resolute in quest of Cupid; and Cupid, wounded by the lamp-spilth, lay moaning in his mother's bedroom. Then a white seagull, the bird that skims across the waves of the sea with its wings, dived down into the bosom of the waters. There, accosting Venus as she washed and swam, the bird informed her that her son was confined to bed, complaining of a severe burn; that his cure was doubted; and that gossip and insult of all kinds were being bandied about among mankind, involving the reputation of the whole Venus-family. "The lad has been whoring in the mountains," people were saying, "while Venus has given herself up to aquatic sports—and in consequence there is no Joy, no Grace, no Elegance anywhere, nothing but the Rude, the Rustic, and the Uncouth—no Marriage-bond, no Social Intercourse, no Love of Children; nothing but an utter Lack of Order, and an unpleasant Horror of anything so low as Nuptials."

Thus did the meddlesome chatterbox of a bird whisper into the ear of Venus, tearing Cupid's reputation to tatters. And Venus in a pet instantly exclaimed:

"So this fine son of mine has already set up a mistress, has he! Come now, you're the only true loving servant I have, what is the name of the wench that seduced my ingenuous-hearted son who's not yet in man's clothes? Is she one of the tribe of Nymphs, or of the company of the Hours, or of the choir of the Muses, or of my own train of Graces?"

The garrulous bird needed no second bidding. "I don't know, mistress," he said, "I'm not sure. I think the girl that he's so badly smitten with, is named ... let me see ... if my memory doesn't deceive me, her name's Psyche."

"Psyche!" Venus cried in a fury of indignation. "Surely he hasn't picked out Psyche, the pretender to my throne of beauty, the rival of my renown! And, insult added to injury, he has taken me as a bawd, for it was my finger that pointed the way to the trollop."

With this complaint she rose up out of the sea, and hurried to her Golden Chamber, where she found her sick son, just as she had been told. Before she was through the door, she began yelling at him. "Fine goings-on! so perfectly in accord with our position in the scheme of things and your good name! First of all, you trample on the express orders of your mother—your queen I should say. Next, you refuse to stretch my enemy on the cross of dirty embraces. More, at your age you, a mere boy, entangle yourself in a low lewd schoolboy affair—just to annoy me with a woman I hate for daughter-in-law. But no doubt you presume, you jokester, you profligate, you disgusting fellow, that you are my only high-born son, and that I'm past the age of bearing another. Well, I wish you to know that I do intend to have one, at once, a far better son than you've ever been. No, to make you feel your disgrace more keenly, I'll adopt one of the sons of my slave-girls; and I'll hand him your wings and flame and bow and arrows and every bit of your equipment, which you know I didn't give you to use like this. For there's not a single strap of it that was supplied at your father's expense.

"But from earliest childhood you've been naughtily inclined. You have ungovernable hands, and often have so far lacked respect for your elders as to beat them. And your mother herself, me, me I repeat, you daily expose before the world, you parricide. And often you've struck me and despised me as if I were a widow. You don't even fear your stepfather, brave and redoubtable warrior as he is. Not a bit of it. You're forever making him pledge wenches and make a fool of himself, all to torture me.

"However, I'll see that you're sorry for your games. You'll learn what a sour and bitter thing marriage is. But now that you've made a laughing-stock of me, what am I to do? Whither shall I wander? What snare will hold this slippery young scoundrel? Shall I seek help from mine enemy Sobriety whom I have so often offended for the sake of this wilful boy?

"No, I shrink from any contact with so coarse and unfashionable a woman. Yet the comfort of revenge is not to be spurned, whatever the instrument. I must consult with her forthwith. She is the one. She will castigate this good-for-nought soundly. She shall empty his quiver and blunt his arrows, unstring his bow and quench his torch. She will purge his body with the strongest medicines; and I shall believe that I have atonement for my injury when I have shorn those golden locks which my hands have so often dressed—when I have clipped those wings which I have dyed in my bosom's fount of nectar."

With these words she flung herself in rage out of the room, peevish with true venereal-bile. But she had hardly left ere she met Ceres and Juno, who perceiving her flushed countenance asked why she spoiled the charm of her sparkling eyes with such a sullen frown.

"Glad we've met," replied Venus. "I want you to help me to carry into action the purpose of my outraged breast. Make inquiry, I beg, with all your resources for that runagate vagabond Psyche. For the notorious scandal about my family must be known to you, as well as the villainy of the son that I disown."

The two goddesses, aware of all that had happened, did their best to soften the anger of Venus.

"What is there so terrible," they asked, "in your son's conduct that you should combat his pleasures so obstinately, and be so eager to destroy the girl he loves? Is it really such a crime to flash a smile at a pretty girl? Haven't you noticed that he's a male, and a young man at that? At least you must know how many years old he is—or does he bear his years so charmingly that you want to think of him as a child forever? Can it be that you (his mother and more, a woman-of-the-world) insist on scrutinizing all your handsome son's little pleasures, taxing him with his wild oats, scolding him for his love-affairs, and reproving his responses to the very arts and lewderies you inspire? What god, what man, who will not revolt when he finds that you, who scatter the seeds of desire on every side, would repress the loves of your own household and close the door of the workshop where female frailties are compounded?"

Thus did they through fear of his arrows espouse the cause of absentee Cupid, and graciously stand bail for him. But Venus, indignant that her injuries should be treated with levity, turned her back and in all haste set off again towards the open sea.

Book the Sixth

Meanwhile Psyche was wandering to and fro, day and night, searching restlessly for the track of her husband—all the more eager because, though she had provoked his wrath, and though he might still be unrelenting before the blandishments of a wife, yet he might be won by her offer to be his slave. At length she saw a temple on the summit of a tall mountain.

"How do I know," she cried, "that this may not be the mansion of my lord?"

Straightway she began to climb the steep slopes up which despite all her tiredness she struggled strenuously, goaded by hope and dedicated love. Under this stimulation she reached the lofty ridges and at last entered the divine residence. There she saw blades of wheat, some sheaved, others twisted into garlands; and she saw ears of barley. And there were scythes, and all the apparatus of harvestwork—lying haphazardly about as when they have been dropped from the lax hands of reapers in the sweltering heat. Psyche set to work sorting out and ordering all these objects in their proper places; for she reflected that it was wrong of her to show lack of reverence for the shrine and ceremonies of any god, and that the best course lay in courting the benevolent compassion of them all.

While she was diligently engaged in these chores, she attracted the notice of Ceres, Lady of Bounty, who called out from far away:

"O Psyche, sad one, are you there? Venus wanders in bitter quest over all the world, seeking fiercely for your trail. Her heart cries out for dreadful vengeance. She is gathering together all her divine energies to surround you with terror. Can you then pause to take my affairs under your wing or to consider anything but your own safety?"

Psyche cast herself before the goddess, wetting the holy feet with tears and sweeping the ground with her tresses.[1]

1 [*Editors' note: The story continues through the end of Book Six of* The Golden Ass *with Psyche wandering the world searching for Cupid and eventually surrendering herself to Venus, who welcomes her by imposing three dangerous tasks to test her "housewifery": 1) separating a pile of wheat, barley, millet, vetches, beans, and lentil grains into parcels by type, 2) collecting wool from gold-fleeced sheep on the other side of a treacherous river, 3) requesting a boxful of beauty from Proserpine in the Underworld. These she accomplishes with Cupid's help. The tale ends when the gods grant her immortality and she bears Cupid's son, Pleasure.*]

3. Marie de France, "Le Fresne" (c. 1160; *translated by Judith P. Shoaf, 1996*[1])

"Le Fresne" is one of a group of poems ascribed to Marie de France. Marie identifies herself as the poems' speaker/author in the prologue to one of them, but her identity largely remains a mystery except for what she tells us. These tightly rhymed lyric poems, or "lais," represent some of the earliest European literature, certainly the first attributed to a woman. Shoaf's translations perform the challenging task of reproducing the verse rhythm and rhyme. "Le Fresne" takes up themes of birth, identity, betrayal, and inheritance—all acute concerns for feudal culture, in which land titles and social class passed exclusively through family lines and alliances. Ash Tree's triumph comes when she is recognized and reaps the benefits of her social status—a theme that remained important to fairy-tale tellers and writers for centuries until the possibility of class mobility made inheritance a less inexorable factor in one's social success.

LE FRESNE

I'll tell you the lai of the Ash Tree now,
Le Fresne,[2] as a story goes I know.
In Brittany lived, yesteryear,
Two knights—they were neighbors, near,
Rich men, the sort who do what they want—
Noble knights, bold, proud, valiant.
They'd lived near each other all their life,
And each had married himself a wife.
Soon one lady grew big with child;
When her nine months was fulfilled,
In one birth she produced two boys.
Her good lord could not count his joys—
Then, to add to his joys' savor
He sent word to his good neighbor
His wife's had not one son, but two!

1 [Source: Judith P. Shoaf, 1996, <http://www.clas.ufl.edu/users/jshoaf/Marie/fresne.pdf>.]

2 Marie gives the title only in French (Le Fresne), not in English or Breton (compare the endings of Chevrefoil and Laustic). "Fresne" is simply a masculine noun, the name of the ash tree; I have retained the French form for the girl's name and included both English and French for the tree's name in my translation. Le Fresne's sister's name, La Codre, means "the hazel," and is (mostly) a feminine noun.... The grammatical/sexual gender contrast in Le Fresne's name extends an ambiguity that begins when she's born—throughout her infant adventures she's mostly referred to as "l'enfant" (the baby), a masculine noun requiring masculine pronouns; I've used "it" instead of "he" but in French the baby is "he" most of the time.

So many children inside her grew—
He'll give one boy to his friend to raise,
And with his own name to baptize.
At his table sits the rich man—
Look! here comes his friend's footman;
In front of the high table he kneels;
His message, word for word, he tells.
The lord thanked God for the news, of course,
And gave the messenger a fine horse.
The knight's wife smiled just a little
(She sat right beside him at table)
For she was full of envy and pride;
She loved saying cruel things; she lied.
This time she really lost her head:
Right in front of everyone, she said,
"So help me God, I do wonder
Where this gentleman found the advisor
Who told him to ask my lord to foster
A child born of shame and dishonor.
For his wife bore two boys, not one,
To his dishonor, and her own.
It's quite true, as we all know well,
That never was, nor will we hear tell,
Nor could it happen on this earth
That one woman in a single birth
Had two separate sons, except where
Two separate men had put them there."
Her lord looked her over, long and hard,
Then scolded her for what he'd heard:
"Lady," he said, "let it drop!
You shouldn't say such things, so stop!
The truth is that, all her life,
That lady's been a faithful wife."

Everyone in the house heard
And remembered every word.
It was talked about and repeated
Until all Brittany had heeded.
The lady was hated for her slur

(Later, worse will come to her)—
Poor wife or rich wife, every and each
Who heard it hated her for her speech.
The messenger went back to his lord
And told him the story, every word.
When he'd heard it told and explained,
He suffered, was confused and pained.
His good wife, his children's mother,
He mistrusted now altogether,
And he guarded her, almost in prison,
Though she had given him no reason.

The lady who'd come up with this smear
Got pregnant herself within the year,
And pregnant, in fact, with twins.
Now her neighbor, the good wife, wins!
She carried them until she was due,
And bore two daughters. It hurts too
Much—she suffers awful torments.
To herself now she laments:
"Alas!" she says, "What shall I do?
I'll never regain my honor, it's true!
My good name! No, shame thrives and lives.
My lord and all his relatives
Will never believe me now, for sure,
Once they hear of this adventure,
For I have judged myself a criminal;
I spoke ill of all women, all—
For didn't I say that it's never been
Nor have we ourselves ever seen
A woman who bore two children
Unless she had known two men?
Now I have two; it's plain to see,
The worst of it's turned back on me.
You can slander others and lie
But not know it'll hit you in the eye;
A person may speak ill of a person
Who's more worth praising than the first one.
Now, to avoid castigation

I must kill one of these children.
I'd rather make it up to God
Than live in shame, under a cloud."
The women in the room there with her
Comforted her but they told her
They couldn't let her act as she spoke—
Killing people is no joke.

The lady kept a damsel; she
Came from the best kind of family.
She'd brought her up with great care
And loved her and held her dear.
She heard how the lady cried,
Wept and mourned and piteously sighed.
This tormented the poor maid; she
Came to comfort her dear lady.
"Madame," she said, "Now there's no need—
Stop mourning so—listen, heed
Me! Give one of these babes to me—
I'll take it and you will be free.
I'll see you never feel shame or pain,
Or ever have to see her again.
I'll dump her somewhere on church ground
(I'll carry her there safe and sound).
Some holy man'll find her in the church;
God willing, he'll find her a nurse."
She spoke thus, and the lady heard
With greatest joy; she gave her word
If the girl carried this task forward
She'd give her a rich reward.
In a fine linen scarf they lapped
The noble babe, then gently wrapped
Her in a wheel-stitched silk brocade.
A gift from her lord, it was made
In Constantinople—he'd been there;
No-one ever saw a cloth so fair.
With a piece of bodice-string
She tied on Baby's arm a ring,
A big ring, pure gold, an ounce heavy,

Set with a fine rosy ruby,
And letters engraved all around.
Wherever the baby might be found,
Anyone would know, at once and truly,
She had been born to good family.

The damsel picked up the infant
And left the lady's room that instant.
That night, after the sun was down,
She slipped quietly out of town.
She took her way along a high road
Which led her into the wild wood.
She keeps to the path through the forest shade
To the other side, still holding the babe;
Off the main road she never veers.
Far away, to the right, she hears
Dogs bark, cocks crow to call the dawn.
That way, she knows, she'll find a town.
Quick as she can she makes her way
In the direction she heard dogs bay.
In a town of beauty and wealth
This young woman finds herself.
In the town is an abbey
Richly endowed in every way;
I happen to know, here live some nuns
And a prudent abbess runs
It. The maiden spots the steeple, tall,
Sees the abbey towers and wall.
She goes there at her quickest rate
And stops before the abbey gate.
She lays down the child she's borne all night
And kneels down, humble in God's sight.
She begins her prayer this way:
"God, by your holy name I pray
If it please you, please, dear Lord,
Protect this child, be its safeguard."
When she'd finished all her prayer
She happened to look behind her.
She saw an ash tree thick and wide

With boughs and branches on every side;
At its fork it branched in four.
Shade is what it was planted for.
She picked the baby up again
And ran to the ash tree—"fresne."
She put the child up, left her there;
God watch over you, was her prayer.
Now the maiden goes back home
To tell her lady what she's done.

In the abbey there was a porter
Who used to open the church door—
The gate through which the people pass
When they come to hear the Mass.
That night he was up betimes,
Lit lamps and candles, rang the chimes,
Opened the church, ready for Mass.
He glimpsed the cloth up in the ash.
He supposed it was some loot, seized
By a robber, hidden in the trees.
He had no other theory.
Quickly he went to the tree,
Felt around, and found the child.
Now he thanks God's mercy mild.
He doesn't leave the babe in the boughs,
But takes it right home to his house.
He has a daughter; she's a widow—
Her lord died leaving her a little
One in the cradle, still at her breast.
The good man calls her from her rest:
"Get up, get up, my dear daughter—
Light fire and candles, bring some water!
I've got a child, newborn, you see.
I found it outside, in the ash tree.
With your own milk you will nurse it.
Warm it up now, gently wash it!"
She does just as he commands—
Lights fire, takes the child in her hands,
Bathes the baby, gets it warm,

Nurses it with her own milk.[1]
She finds the ring tied on its arm;
They see the rich, fine piece of silk.
They understand and both agree
This child is of the nobility.

The next day, when the good abbess
Leaves church after hearing Mass,
The porter comes to speak to her.
He wants to tell the adventure
Of the baby he found in the tree.
The abbess commands that he
Bring this foundling child around
To her, just as it was found.
The porter goes home quickly,
Brings the baby back gladly,
Shows my lady abbess the child.
She looks it over for a while;
She herself will have someone raise
This child as her niece, so she says.
She sternly forbids the porter
Ever to tell just how he brought her.
So the abbess brings the girl up now.
Because she was found in the ash-tree bough
(Ash is "fresne"), they called her "Le Fresne,"
And Le Fresne is her name among men.

The lady tells folk she's her niece;
Thus a long time hidden, in peace,
Dwelling within the abbey close,
Gently brought up, the damsel grows.
When she reaches that age and stature
Where beauty is formed by nature,
There's no lovelier girl in Brittany,
No young lady more versed in courtesy.

---

1 In Marie's lai *Milun*, which is also the story of a baby abandoned at birth, she makes particular note of the provision of nurses for the baby as it is transported to the mother's sister's house. Here it is coincidence that provides little Fresne with milk.

Her noble nature was easy to teach
Good manners and gentleness of speech.
All who saw her loved this damsel,
Admired her, prized her as a marvel.

The lord of Dol was a noble prince—
No better lived before or since.
I'll tell you his name before I'm done:
His subjects called their lord Gurun.
He heard tell of this hidden maiden,
And began to love her unbidden.
He went jousting to a tourney,
And returned by way of the abbey.
He asked for the damsel fair;
The abbess showed her to him there.
He saw her, so beautiful, wisely ruled
By prudence, polite, well-bred and -schooled.
If he can't have her love, he mused,
He will curse Fate and feel abused.
He's lost; how to do it? If he went
Too often to visit the convent,
The abbess'd think what might occur,
And he'd never get to set eyes on her.
He comes up with one strategy:
He resolves to endow the abbey;
He'll give land with such generosity
The abbey will benefit in perpetuity.
As benefactor, his only request
Is a room there, just a place to rest.
To join their brother- and sisterhoods
He's donated plenty of worldly goods;
It seems his purpose ends and begins
With obtaining remission of his sins.
Often he goes there to stay,
Talking to the girl all day.
With prayers and promises he haunts
Her till she gives him what he wants.

When he's sure of her affection,
He one day makes this proposition:
"Beauty," he says, "before this is over
Truth will out you've made me your lover.
Now come live with me! Come, leave!
You know, as I think and believe,
If your aunt discovers our affair,
It'll be so hard for her to bear,
And if you should get pregnant here
She'd be so angry, having you near.
If you will just take my advice,
You'll come home with me—don't think twice.
For I will never fail or hurt you—
I will tell you what's best to do."
She, whose love always increases,
Gives in and does whatever pleases
Him. She goes off with him alone;
He takes her to his castle home.

She brings her ring and silk brocade,
Hoping they'll someday be of aid.
The abbess had given them to her,
Telling her the whole adventure
How she had been sent to the abbey,
How she was found lying in the ash tree.
The silk and ring were her only present
From whoever it was who first sent
Her; she had no other legacies;
But she had raised her as her niece.
The girl looked them carefully over,
Then shut them up in a little coffer.
Now she brings this coffer along;
To leave or forget it would be wrong.
The knight who took her from the abbey
Loves and cherishes her dearly,
And his servants and the men of his hall—
There isn't one, big man or small,
Who doesn't love her noble ways,
And honor her as worth all praise.

Long had she lived with him this way
When his vassal knights one day
Began to treat this as a grievance.
Often and often they spoke to advance
Their plan: he'll take some noble bride,
And send this other from his side;
If he had an heir, they'd be glad,
Who'd have from him, as he had had,
His title, lands, and property.
What a crime—what a pity
If, because of this concubine,
He had no child in the legal line.
From now on, he loses his feudal rights;
He won't be lord of his vassal knights
Unless he does what they want him to.
The knight grants them their due:
He'll take a wife, with their advice.
Have they looked into a likely choice?
"My lord," they said, "Near our manor
Lives a nobleman, your equal in honor;
His one daughter's his heir, as it stands—
With her you could get vast lands.
She's called La Codre, the Hazel Tree,
No damsel for miles is so lovely.
Leave the Ash now lying there,
And trade her for the Hazel fair.
The Hazel gives sweet nuts and pleasure;
Barren Ash, fruitless, is no treasure.
We'll try to arrange to get this bride
To give you, if God's on our side."
They do what they can to attract
This marriage; soon they have a contract.

Alas! fate strikes a cruel blow
For none of these good men even know
These two damsels' past adventure:
Each is the other one's twin sister!

Her sister's hidden from Le Fresne—
Her lover marries the other one.
When she learns another's in her place,
She never makes an ugly face,
But serves her lord[1] with sweet patience,
And treats his court with deference.
The knights of the lord's household,
Squires, servants young and old,
They all mourn for Le Fresne,
For now they'll never see her again.

The wedding day comes; her lord sends
Invitation to all his friends,
Dol's archbishop especially,
Who owes him feudal loyalty.
Now they present him with his bride.
Her mother's come there, at her side.
She fears that young girl, for her part,
Who, they say, holds this lord's heart;
She'd make mischief, surely, if she could,
Between her daughter and her lord.
They'll have to dump her, get her out,
She'll talk to her son-in-law about
Marrying her off to some gentleman—
He'll be free of her then. That's her plan.

The wedding feast was richly laid;
Music, games of all sorts were played.
The damsel had gone to the bedroom.
For all she'd seen, no sign of gloom

1 Another interesting ambiguity derives from Marie's use of the word "sire/seigneur" (here, "Her lord"). The word means "lord" but also "husband" and could certainly be translated "husband" many times—that is what it means in the opening story about Le Fresne's parents. But as Le Fresne's story develops, the double meaning gains force: Gurun is her "seigneur," her lord and master, yet he is not her legal husband. After leaving the abbey, she is no longer a "damoiselle" or young lady, but a "meschine" or servant-girl (translated just "girl"); she is certainly not his bride or wife, the role reserved for her sister. Her intensification of the master-servant relationship finally brings it about that her "seigneur" really becomes her "seigneur," and a wifely (!) attitude triumphs over the technicalities of marriage contracts. I might add that, as in the other lais, the lovers are called "ami-amie," friend or lover, as well as "her lord" and "that girl." But Le Fresne's mother also addresses her as "belle amie" ("Beauty, dear"), a loverlike phrase.

Hinted feelings deeply troubled,
Or, by a little anger, ruffled.
In the bride's entourage, sweetly,
She'd served everyone politely.
They marveled at her lack of venom,
All who saw her, men and women.
Her mother too had looked her over;
Her heart began to prize and love her.
She thought, and said, if she had known
What she was like, this other one,
She'd never have lost out to her daughter—
She'd not have taken her lord and master.
So, that night, to help prepare
The wedding bed for the bridal pair,[1]
The damsel went to the bridal chamber;
She doffed her cloak (to disencumber
Herself for work), called servants there,
Showed them exactly how and where
Her lord liked things done and set;
For she had often noticed it.
When they'd prepared the wedding bed
On top they tossed an old bedspread.
The cloth was just some thin, worn stuff;
The girl saw it—she'd seen enough
To know it's no good, not suitable;
It weighed down her heart with trouble.
She opened her coffer, took her brocade,
On her lord's bed this silk she laid.
She did this to honor the pair,
Since the archbishop would be there

---

1 The story is related to the "patient Griselda" legend (retold by Petrarch and then immortalized by Chaucer in his *Clerk's Tale*), in which a husband gets carried away playing God to his Job-like wife. Marie's Gurun, though, seems morally weak rather than tyrannical and cruel like Griselda's husband, Walter. [...] Despite the unfeminist (and, I think, unironic) message that humility triumphs and a good wife is a good slave, the lai depicts a world in which power—to legitimize children and to save or slay them, to slander, to confer social dignity and to educate, to solve the mystery and make all things right—is in the hands of women. Le Fresne's mother, who seems unpromising moral material at the outset, turns out to be a good mother after all; instead of being punished at her abused daughter's wedding like the stepmothers in many fairy tales, she is allowed to grow out of her youthful rage and spite, to reform and be forgiven.

To sign them with the cross and bless
Them—it's his job, he can't do less.

When everyone had left the chamber,
The lady brought in her daughter.
She wants to put her to bed; best
Begin, she says, by getting undressed.
She sees the silk brocade spread there;
She's never seen a cloth so fair
Except the one in which she wrapped her
Baby daughter when she hid her.
Now she remembers that lost child;
Her heart trembles, she grows wild.
She calls in the head chamberlain.
"Tell me, as you're a Christian, when
And where did you find this fine brocade?"
"Madame," he answered, "that's easily said;
The damsel brought it, for the bed;
She dumped it on top of the old spread,
An ugly one—she saw that in a wink.
The brocade belongs to her, I think."
Next the lady called her in;
She came and stood before her, then
Respectfully she doffed her cloak.
Finally the mother spoke.
"Beauty, dear, don't hide the truth!
Where did you find this fine silk cloth?
Where'd it come from? How'd you get it? Who,
If it was a gift, gave it to you?"
The girl answers, "Madame, please,
My aunt, the abbess—I'm her niece—
Who raised me, she gave this to me
And told me to keep it carefully.
I was given this and a golden ring
By those who sent me, a foundling."
"Beauty, may I see the ring?"
"Yes, ma'am, that's an easy thing."
She brought the ring to the mother,

Who very carefully looked it over.
Identification was easily made;
She knew the ring and the silk brocade.
She doubted no more, she knew, believed,
That this girl was her daughter indeed.
She can't hide it; so all can hear,
"You are my daughter, beauty dear!"
She cries. From pain and pity she fell
Back in a faint, and lay there a spell.
When she's revived from her swoon,
She calls her lord to the bedroom.
He comes, worried, full of fears.
The moment her husband appears,
He falls at his feet, clasps his knees,
Lets her kisses mix with her pleas,
Begging pardon for her sin.
He can't make out the case she's in.
"Lady," he said, "What do you mean?
There's only ever been good will between
Us. Whatever you did, I forgive it!
Say what you want; I will give it!"
"Lord, since you grant me pardon,
I'll tell you all, so now listen!
Once, long ago, my evil nature
Let me speak nonsense of my neighbor:
I vilified her for having twins—
I blackened myself, for my sins.
I gave birth; truth is, when I did,
I bore two daughters—one I hid,
Had her dumped in a church by my maid.
I sent with her our silk brocade
And the gold ring you gave to me
When first you spoke of love to me.
I can no longer hide anything:
I've found the brocade and the ring!
I recognize this girl, our daughter.
Through my folly we almost lost her!
And this is the same demoiselle
(Beautiful, wise and good as well)

Who was so loved by that knight
Who has married her sister tonight!"
The lord replied, "I am glad of this!
Never before have I known such bliss!
Now we've found our girl who was lost,
God has given us joy rejoiced,
Before we could double the treachery.
Daughter," he said, "Come here to me!"
The girl rejoiced at heart, for sure,
When she heard this adventure.
Her father won't wait; from the room
He goes himself to fetch the groom
(His son-in-law) and archbishop,
And tell the tale from start to finish.
Up the knight's heart rejoicing flew,
At this adventure, when he knew.
The archbishop said it'd be all right
To leave things as they were that night.
Tomorrow he'll divorce or divide
The knight from his espoused bride.
They all agreed on this good plan.
Thus separated was wife from man
And he married his dear, next day,
And her father gave the bride away,
For his heart was warm toward her;
He made her his half-inheritor.
He and his wife and their daughter
Stayed till the wedding-feast was over.
Then they returned to their own country,
Taking La Coudre, the Hazel Tree;
They found her a fine rich groom
And married her off nearer home.

When this story got around,
Just as it happened, people found
A lai of it, Le Fresne, the Ash Tree;
The[y] named the lai after the lady.

4. Anon., *Alf Layla wa Layla* (14th century; *translated by Husain Haddawy, 1990*[1])

Although contemporary readers may not recognize the title Alf Layla wa Layla, *this text has had a powerful presence in English-language literature and popular culture for over 300 years. Usually translated as either the* 1001 Nights *or the* Arabian Nights, *it is associated with such well-known stories as that of "Ali Baba and the Forty Thieves" and "Sindbad the Sailor." The text has a complex history, in both manuscript and published form: versions of tales included in this text have circulated for centuries in oral traditions (including Persian and Indian), and while there is evidence that a manuscript edition of* Alf Layla wa Layla *may have existed as early as the eighth century, the earliest extant manuscript dates to fourteenth-century Syria (and this is the one included here that has been edited by Muhsin Mahdi and translated by Husain Haddawy). Numerous other Arabic manuscript versions were produced in subsequent centuries. The history of English translation contributes to the sense of* Alf Layla wa Layla *as a complex and unstable textual phenomenon: English readers first experienced it in the early eighteenth century through translation from the French* Mille et Une Nuits, Contes Arabes *by Antoine Galland, and it was only in the nineteenth century that there were attempts at translation directly from Arabic to English. These nineteenth-century efforts to discover the "real"* Arabian Nights *were complicated by many factors, including not only the use of different source manuscripts as the basis for the translations but also the shaping influence of the interests and preoccupations of specific translators and the perceived tastes and sensibilities of their audiences. The results were as disparate as the bowdlerized but ethnographically oriented edition by Edward William Lane (1838–41), which reached an enormous audience, and the more sensationalistic and erotic edition of Sir Richard Burton, which was produced for a small number of private subscribers.*

One of the features that distinguishes Alf Layla wa Layla *is its structural and narrative complexity, which involves a frame story in which a well-read, determined, and skilled woman named Shahrazad is established as narrator, telling tales nightly in an effort to save her own life but also to quell the fury of her husband, a cuckolded and murderous king. The unit of narrative here is not the "chapter" or the individual story, but the "night," and each night ends at a provocative moment in the middle of a story, or a story-within-a-story, or even a story-within-a-story-within-a-story. Resisting narrative closure, the cycles of tales serve a very distinct function in relation to the frame story, maintaining King Shahrayar's interest, as he becomes enmeshed in the narrative webs spun by Shahrazad—an experience shared by the reader.*

1 [Source: Husain Haddawy, trans. *The Arabian Nights* (New York: W.W. Norton, 1990): 3–16.]

THE STORY OF KING SHAHRAYAR AND SHAHRAZAD, HIS VIZIER'S DAUGHTER

IT IS RELATED—BUT GOD KNOWS and sees best what lies hidden in the old accounts of bygone peoples and times—that long ago, during the time of the Sasanid dynasty[1] in the peninsulas of India and Indochina, there lived two kings who were brothers. The older brother was named Shahrayar, the younger Shahzaman. The older, Shahrayar, was a towering knight and a daring champion, invincible, energetic, and implacable. His power reached the remotest corners of the land and its people, so that the country was loyal to him, and his subjects obeyed him. Shahrayar himself lived and ruled in India and Indochina, while to his brother he gave the land of Samarkand to rule as king.

Ten years went by, when one day Shahrayar felt a longing for his brother the king, summoned his vizier[2] (who had two daughters, one called Shahrazad, the other Dinarzad) and bade him go to his brother. Having made preparations, the vizier journeyed day and night until he reached Samarkand. When Shahzaman heard of the vizier's arrival, he went out with his retainers to meet him. He dismounted, embraced him, and asked him for news from his older brother, Shahrayar. The vizier replied that he was well, and that he had sent him to request his brother to visit him. Shahzaman complied with his brother's request and proceeded to make preparations for the journey. In the meantime, he had the vizier camp on the outskirts of the city, and took care of his needs. He sent him what he required of food and fodder, slaughtered many sheep in his honor, and provided him with money and supplies, as well as many horses and camels.

For ten full days he prepared himself for the journey; then he appointed a chamberlain in his place, and left the city to spend the night in his tent, near the vizier. At midnight he returned to his palace in the city, to bid his wife good-bye. But when he entered the palace, he found his wife lying in the arms of one of the kitchen boys. When he saw them, the world turned dark before his eyes and, shaking his head, he said to himself, "I am still here, and this is what she has done when I was barely outside the city. How will it be and what will happen behind my back when I go to visit my brother in India? No. Women are not to be trusted." He got exceedingly angry, adding, "By God, I am king and sovereign in Samarkand, yet my wife has betrayed me and has inflicted this on me." As his anger boiled, he drew his sword and struck both his wife and the cook. Then he dragged them by the heels and threw them from the top of the palace to the trench below. He then left the city and going to the vizier ordered that they depart that very hour. The drum was struck, and they set out

1 A dynasty of Persian kings who ruled from c. 226 to 641 CE.

2 The highest state official or administrator under a caliph or a king (literally, "one who bears burdens").

on their journey, while Shahzaman's heart was on fire because of what his wife had done to him and how she had betrayed him with some cook, some kitchen boy. They journeyed hurriedly, day and night, through deserts and wilds, until they reached the land of King Shahrayar, who had gone out to receive them.

When Shahrayar met them, he embraced his brother, showed him favors, and treated him generously. He offered him quarters in a palace adjoining his own, for King Shahrayar had built two beautiful towering palaces in his garden, one for the guests, the other for the women and members of his household. He gave the guest house to his brother, Shahzaman, after the attendants had gone to scrub it, dry it, furnish it, and open its windows, which overlooked the garden. Thereafter, Shahzaman would spend the whole day at his brother's, return at night to sleep at the palace, then go back to his brother the next morning. But whenever he found himself alone and thought of his ordeal with his wife, he would sigh deeply, then stifle his grief, and say, "Alas, that this great misfortune should have happened to one in my position!" Then he would fret with anxiety, his spirit would sag, and he would say, "None has seen what I have seen." In his depression, he ate less and less, grew pale, and his health deteriorated. He neglected everything, wasted away, and looked ill.

When King Shahrayar looked at his brother and saw how day after day he lost weight and grew thin, pale, ashen, and sickly, he thought that this was because of his expatriation and homesickness for his country and his family, and he said to himself, "My brother is not happy here. I should prepare a goodly gift for him and send him home." For a month he gathered gifts for his brother; then he invited him to see him and said, "Brother, I would like you to know that I intend to go hunting and pursue the roaming deer, for ten days. Then I shall return to prepare you for your journey home. Would you like to go hunting with me?" Shahzaman replied, "Brother, I feel distracted and depressed. Leave me here and go with God's blessing and help." When Shahrayar heard his brother, he thought that his dejection was because of his homesickness for his country. Not wishing to coerce him, he left him behind, and set out with his retainers and men. When they entered the wilderness, he deployed his men in a circle to begin trapping and hunting.

After his brother's departure, Shahzaman stayed in the palace and, from the window overlooking the garden, watched the birds and trees as he thought of his wife and what she had done to him, and sighed in sorrow. While he agonized over his misfortune, gazing at the heavens and turning a distracted eye on the garden, the private gate of his brother's palace opened, and there emerged, strutting like a dark-eyed deer, the lady, his brother's wife, with twenty slave-girls, ten white and ten black. While Shahzaman looked at them, without being seen, they continued to walk until they stopped below his window, without looking in his direction, thinking that he had gone to the hunt with his brother. Then they sat down, took off their clothes, and suddenly there were ten slave-girls and ten black slaves dressed in the same clothes as the girls. Then the ten black slaves mounted the ten girls, while the lady called, "Mas'ud, Mas'ud!" and a black slave jumped from the tree to the ground, rushed to her, and, raising her legs, went between her thighs and made love to her. Mas'ud topped the lady, while the ten slaves topped the ten girls, and they carried on till noon. When they were done with their business, they got up and washed themselves. Then the ten slaves put on the same clothes again, mingled with the girls, and once more there appeared to be twenty slave-girls. Mas'ud himself jumped over the garden wall and disappeared, while the slave-girls and the lady sauntered to the private gate, went in and, locking the gate behind them, went their way.

All of this happened under King Shahzaman's eyes. When he saw this spectacle of the wife and the women of his brother the great king—how ten slaves put on women's clothes and slept with his brother's paramours and concubines and what Mas'ud did with his brother's wife, in his very palace—and pondered over this calamity and great misfortune, his care and sorrow left him and he said to himself, "This is our common lot. Even though my brother is king and master of the whole world, he cannot protect what is his, his wife and his concubines, and suffers misfortune in his very home. What happened to me is little by comparison. I used to think that I was the only one who has suffered, but from what I have seen, everyone suffers. By God, my misfortune is lighter than that of my brother." He kept marveling and blaming life, whose trials none can escape, and he began to find consolation in his own affliction and forget his grief. When supper came, he ate and drank with relish and zest and, feeling better, kept eating and drinking, enjoying himself and feeling happy. He thought to himself, "I am no longer alone in my misery; I am well."

For ten days, he continued to enjoy his food and drink, and when his brother, King Shahrayar, came back from the hunt, he met him happily, treated him attentively, and greeted him cheerfully. His brother, King Shahrayar, who had missed him, said, "By God, brother, I missed you on this trip and wished you were with me." Shahzaman thanked him and sat down to carouse with him, and when night fell, and food was brought before them, the two ate and drank, and again Shahzaman ate and drank with zest. As time went by, he continued to eat and drink with appetite, and became lighthearted and carefree. His face regained color and became ruddy, and his body gained weight, as his blood circulated and he regained his energy; he was himself again, or even better. King Shahrayar noticed his brother's condition, how he used to be and how he had improved, but kept it to himself until he took him aside one day and said, "My brother Shahzaman, I would like you to do something for me, to satisfy a wish, to answer a question truthfully." Shahzaman asked, "What is it, brother?" He replied, "When you first came to stay with me, I noticed that you kept losing weight, day after day, until your looks changed, your health deteriorated, and your energy sagged. As you continued like this, I thought that what ailed you was your homesickness for your family and your country, but even though I kept noticing that you were wasting away and looking ill, I refrained from questioning you and hid my feelings from you. Then I went hunting, and when I came back, I found that you had recovered and had regained your health. Now I want you to tell me everything and to explain the cause of your deterioration and the cause of your subsequent recovery, without hiding anything from me." When Shahzaman heard what King Shahrayar said, he bowed his head, then said, "As for the cause of my recovery, that I cannot tell you, and I wish that you would excuse me from telling you." The king was greatly astonished at his brother's reply and, burning with curiosity, said, "You must tell me. For now, at least, explain the first cause."

Then Shahzaman related to his brother what happened to him with his own wife, on the night of his departure, from beginning to end, and concluded, "Thus all the while I was with you, great King, whenever I thought of the event and the misfortune that had befallen me, I felt troubled, careworn, and unhappy, and my health deteriorated. This then is the cause." Then he grew silent. When King Shahrayar heard his brother's explanation, he shook his head, greatly amazed at the deceit of women, and prayed to God to protect him from their wickedness, saying, "Brother, you were fortunate in killing your wife and her lover, who gave you good reason to feel troubled, careworn, and ill. In my opinion, what happened to you has never happened to anyone else. By God, had I been in your place, I would have killed at least a hundred or even a thousand women. I would have been furious; I would have gone mad. Now praise be to God who has delivered you from sorrow and distress. But tell me what has caused you to forget your sorrow and regain your health?" Shahzaman replied, "King, I wish that for God's sake you would excuse me from telling you." Shahrayar said, "You must." Shahzaman replied, "I fear that you will feel even more troubled and careworn than I." Shahrayar asked, "How could that be, brother? I insist on hearing your explanation."

Shahzaman then told him about what he had seen from the palace window and the calamity in his very home—how ten slaves, dressed like women, were sleeping with his women and concubines, day and night. He told him everything from beginning to end (but there is no point in repeating that). Then he concluded, "When I saw your own misfortune, I felt better—and said to myself, 'My brother is king of the world, yet such a misfortune has happened to him, and in his very home.' As a result I forgot my care and sorrow, relaxed, and began to eat and drink. This is the cause of my cheer and good spirits."

When King Shahrayar heard what his brother said and found out what had happened to him, he was furious and his blood boiled. He said, "Brother, I can't believe what you say unless I see it with my own eyes." When Shahzaman saw that his brother was in a rage, he said to him, "If you do not believe me, unless you see your misfortune with your own eyes, announce that you plan to go hunting. Then you and I shall set out with your troops, and when we get outside the city, we shall leave our tents and camp with the men behind, enter the city secretly, and go together to your palace. Then the next morning you can see with your own eyes."

King Shahrayar realized that his brother had a good plan and ordered his army to prepare for the trip. He spent the night with his brother, and when God's morning broke, the two rode out of the city with their army, preceded by the camp attendants, who had gone to drive the poles and pitch the tents where the king and his army were to camp. At nightfall King Shahrayar summoned his chief chamberlain and bade him take his place. He entrusted him with the army and ordered that for three days no one was to enter the city. Then he and his brother disguised themselves and entered the city in the dark. They went directly to the palace where Shahzaman resided and slept there till the morning. When they awoke, they sat at the palace window, watching the garden and chatting, until the light broke, the day dawned, and the sun rose. As they watched, the private gate opened, and there emerged as usual the wife of King Shahrayar, walking among twenty slave-girls. They made their way under the trees until they stood below the palace window where the two kings sat. Then they took off their women's clothes, and suddenly there were ten slaves, who mounted the ten girls and made love to them. As for the lady, she called, "Mas'ud, Mas'ud," and a black slave jumped from the tree to the ground, came to her, and said, "What do you want, you slut? Here is Sa'ad al-Din Mas'ud." She laughed and fell on her back, while the slave mounted her and like the others did his business with her. Then the black slaves got up, washed themselves, and, putting on the same clothes, mingled with the girls. Then they walked away, entered the palace, and locked the gate behind them. As for Mas'ud, he jumped over the fence to the road and went on his way.

When King Shahrayar saw the spectacle of his wife and the slave-girls, he went out of his mind, and when he and his brother came down from upstairs, he said, "No one is safe in this world. Such doings are going on in my kingdom, and in my very palace. Perish the world and perish life! This is a great calamity, indeed." Then he turned to his brother and asked, "Would you like to follow me in what I shall do?" Shahzaman answered, "Yes. I will." Shahrayar said, "Let us leave our royal state and roam the world for the love of the Supreme Lord. If we should find one whose misfortune is greater than ours, we shall return. Otherwise, we shall continue to journey through the land, without need for the trappings of royalty." Shahzaman replied, "This is an excellent idea. I shall follow you."

Then they left by the private gate, took a side road, and departed, journeying till nightfall. They slept over their sorrows, and in the morning resumed their day journey until they came to a meadow by the seashore. While they sat in the meadow amid the thick plants and trees, discussing their misfortunes and the recent events, they suddenly heard a shout and a great cry coming from the middle of the sea. They trembled with fear, thinking that the sky had fallen on the earth. Then the sea parted, and there emerged a black pillar that, as it swayed forward, got taller and taller, until it touched the clouds. Shahrayar and Shahzaman were petrified; then they ran in terror and, climbing a very tall tree, sat hiding in its foliage. When they looked again, they saw that the black pillar was cleaving the sea, wading in the water toward the green meadow, until it touched the shore. When they looked again, they saw that it was a black demon, carrying on his head a large glass chest with four steel locks. He came out, walked into the meadow, and where should he stop but under the very tree where the two kings were hiding. The demon sat down and placed the glass chest on the ground. He took out four keys and, opening the locks of the chest, pulled out a full-grown woman. She had a beautiful figure, and a face like the full moon, and a lovely smile. He took her out, laid her under the tree, and looked at her, saying, "Mistress of all noble women, you whom I carried away on your wedding night, I would like to sleep a little." Then he placed his head on the young woman's lap, stretched his legs to the sea, sank into sleep, and began to snore.

Meanwhile, the woman looked up at the tree and, turning her head by chance, saw King Shahrayar and King Shahzaman. She lifted the demon's head from her lap and placed it on the ground. Then she came and stood under the tree and motioned to them with her hand, as if to say, "Come down slowly to me." When they realized that she had seen them, they were frightened, and they begged her and implored her, in the name of the Creator of the heavens, to excuse them from climbing down. She replied, "You must come down to me." They motioned to her, saying, "This sleeping demon is the enemy of mankind. For God's sake, leave us alone." She replied, "You must come down, and if you don't, I shall wake the demon and have him kill you." She kept gesturing and pressing, until they climbed down very slowly and stood before her. Then she lay on her back, raised her legs, and said, "Make love to me and satisfy my need, or else I shall wake the demon, and he will kill you." They replied, "For God's sake, mistress, don't do this to us, for at this moment we feel nothing but dismay and fear of this demon. Please, excuse us." She replied, "You must," and insisted, swearing, "By God who created the heavens, if you don't do it, I shall wake my husband the demon and ask him to kill you and throw you into the sea." As she persisted, they could no longer resist and they made love to her, first the older brother, then the younger. When they were done and withdrew from her, she said to them, "Give me your rings," and, pulling out from the folds of her dress a small purse, opened it, and shook out ninety-eight rings of different fashions and colors. Then she asked them, "Do you know what these rings are?" They answered, "No."

She said, "All the owners of these rings slept with me, for whenever one of them made love to me, I took a ring from him. Since you two have slept with me, give me your rings, so that I may add them to the rest, and make a full hundred. A hundred men have known me under the very horns of this filthy, monstrous cuckold, who has imprisoned me in this chest, locked it with four locks, and kept me in the middle of this raging, roaring sea. He has guarded me and tried to keep me pure and chaste, not realizing that nothing can prevent or alter what is predestined and that when a woman desires something, no one can stop her." When Shahrayar and Shahzaman heard what the young woman said, they were greatly amazed, danced with joy, and said, "O God, O God! There is no power and no strength, save in God the Almighty, the Magnificent. Great is women's cunning." Then each of them took off his ring and handed it to her. She took them and put them with the rest in the purse. Then sitting again by the demon, she lifted his head, placed it back on her lap, and motioned to them, "Go on your way, or else I shall wake him."

They turned their backs and took to the road. Then Shahrayar turned to his brother and said, "My brother Shahzaman, look at this sorry plight. By God, it is worse than ours. This is no less than a demon who has carried a young woman away on her wedding night, imprisoned her in a glass chest, locked her up with four locks, and kept her in the middle of the sea, thinking that he could guard her from what God had foreordained, and you saw how she has managed to sleep with ninety-eight men, and added the two of us to make a hundred. Brother, let us go back to our kingdoms and our cities, never to marry a woman again. As for myself, I shall show you what I will do."

Then the two brothers headed home and journeyed till nightfall. On the morning of the third day, they reached their camp and men, entered their tent, and sat on their thrones. The chamberlains, deputies, princes, and viziers came to attend King Shahrayar, while he gave orders and bestowed robes of honor, as well as other gifts. Then at his command everyone returned to the city, and he went to his own palace and ordered his chief vizier, the father of the two girls Shahrazad and Dinarzad, who will be mentioned below, and said to him, "Take that wife of mine and put her to death." Then Shahrayar went to her himself, bound her, and handed her over to the vizier, who took her out and put her to death. Then King Shahrayar grabbed his sword, brandished it, and, entering the palace chambers, killed every one of his slave-girls and replaced them with others. He then swore to marry for one night only and kill the woman the next morning, in order to save himself from the wickedness and cunning of women, saying, "There is not a single chaste woman anywhere on the entire face of the earth." Shortly thereafter he provided his brother Shahzaman with supplies for his journey and sent him back to his own country with gifts, rarities, and money. The brother bade him good-bye and set out for home.

Shahrayar sat on his throne and ordered his vizier, the father of the two girls, to find him a wife from among the princes' daughters. The vizier found him one, and he slept with her and was done with her, and the next morning he ordered the vizier to put her to death. That very night he took one of his army officers' daughters, slept with her, and the next morning ordered the vizier to put her to death. The vizier, who could not disobey him, put her to death. The third night he took one of the merchants' daughters, slept with her till the morning, then ordered his vizier to put her to death, and the vizier did so. It became King Shahrayar's custom to take every night the daughter of a merchant or a commoner, spend the night with her, then have her put to death the next morning. He continued to do this until all the girls perished, their mothers mourned, and there arose a clamor among the fathers and mothers, who called the plague upon his head, complained to the Creator of the heavens, and called for help on Him who hears and answers prayers.

Now, as mentioned earlier, the vizier, who put the girls to death, had an older daughter called Shahrazad and a younger one called Dinarzad. The older daughter, Shahrazad, had read the books of literature, philosophy, and medicine. She knew poetry by heart, had studied historical reports, and was acquainted with the sayings of men and the maxims of sages and kings. She was intelligent, knowledgeable, wise, and refined. She had read and learned. One day she said to her father, "Father, I will tell you what is in my mind." He asked, "What is it?" She answered, "I would like you to marry me to King Shahrayar, so that I may either succeed in saving the people or perish and die like the rest." When the vizier heard what his daughter Shahrazad said, he got angry and said to her, "Foolish one, don't you know that King Shahrayar has sworn to spend but one night with a girl and have her put to death the next morning? If I give you to him, he will sleep with you for one night and will ask me to put you to death the next morning, and I shall have to do it, since I cannot disobey him." She said, "Father, you must give me to him, even if he kills me." He asked, "What has possessed you that you wish to imperil yourself?" She replied, "Father, you must give me to him. This is absolute and final." Her father the vizier became furious and said to her, "Daughter, 'He who misbehaves, ends up in trouble,' and 'He who considers not the end, the world is not his friend.' As the popular saying goes, 'I would be sitting pretty, but for my curiosity.' I am afraid that what happened to the donkey and the ox with the merchant will happen to you." She asked, "Father, what happened to the donkey, the ox, and the merchant?" He said:

[The Tale of the Ox and the Donkey]

There was a prosperous and wealthy merchant who lived in the countryside and labored on a farm. He owned many camels and herds of cattle and employed many men, and he had a wife and many grown-up as well as little children. This merchant was taught the language of the beasts, on condition that if he revealed his secret to anyone, he would die; therefore, even though he knew the language of every kind of animal, he did not let anyone know, for fear of death. One day, as he sat, with his wife beside him and his children playing before him, he glanced at an ox and a donkey he kept at the farmhouse, tied to adjacent troughs, and heard the ox say to the donkey, "Watchful one, I hope that you are enjoying the comfort and the service you are getting. Your ground is swept and watered, and they serve you, feed you sifted barley, and offer you clear, cool water to drink. I, on the contrary, am taken out to plow in the middle of the night. They clamp on my neck something they call yoke and plow, push me all day under the whip to plow the field, and drive me beyond my endurance until my sides are lacerated, and my neck is flayed. They work me from nighttime to nighttime, take me back in the dark, offer me beans soiled with mud and hay mixed with chaff, and let me spend the night lying in urine and dung. Meanwhile you rest on well-swept, watered, and smoothed ground, with a clean trough full of hay. You stand in comfort, save for the rare occasion when our master the merchant rides you to do a brief errand and returns. You are comfortable, while I am weary; you sleep, while I keep awake."

When the ox finished, the donkey turned to him and said, "Greenhorn, they were right in calling you ox, for you ox harbor no deceit, malice, or meanness. Being sincere, you exert and exhaust yourself to comfort others. Have you not heard the saying 'Out of bad luck, they hastened on the road'? You go into the field from early morning to endure your torture at the plow to the point of exhaustion. When the plowman takes you back and ties you to the trough, you go on butting and beating with your horns, kicking with your hoofs, and bellowing for the beans, until they toss them to you; then you begin to eat. Next time, when they bring them to you, don't eat or even touch them, but smell them, then draw back and lie down on the hay and straw. If you do this, life will be better and kinder to you, and you will find relief."

As the ox listened, he was sure that the donkey had given him good advice. He thanked him, commended him to God, and invoked His blessing on him, and said, "May you stay safe from harm, watchful one." All of this conversation took place, daughter, while the merchant listened and understood. On the following day, the plowman came to the merchant's house and, taking the ox, placed the yoke upon his neck and worked him at the plow, but the ox lagged behind. The plowman hit him, but following the donkey's advice, the ox, dissembling, fell on his belly, and the plowman hit him again. Thus the ox kept getting up and falling until nightfall, when the plowman took him home and tied him to the trough. But this time the ox did not bellow or kick the ground with his hoofs. Instead, he withdrew, away from the trough. Astonished, the plowman brought him his beans and fodder, but the ox only smelled the fodder and pulled back and lay down at a distance with the hay and straw, complaining till the morning. When the plowman arrived, he found the trough as he had left it, full of beans and fodder, and saw the ox lying on his back, hardly breathing, his belly puffed, and his legs raised in the air. The plowman felt sorry for him and said to himself, "By God, he did seem weak and unable to work." Then he went to the merchant and said, "Master, last night, the ox refused to eat or touch his fodder."

The merchant, who knew what was going on, said to the plowman, "Go to the wily donkey, put him to the plow, and work him hard until he finishes the ox's task." The plowman left, took the donkey, and placed the yoke upon his neck. Then he took him out to the field and drove him with blows until he finished the ox's work, all the while driving him with blows and beating him until his sides were lacerated and his neck was flayed. At nightfall he took him home, barely able to drag his legs under his tired body and his drooping ears. Meanwhile the ox spent his day resting. He ate all his food, drank his water, and lay quietly, chewing his cud in comfort. All day long he kept praising the donkey's advice and invoking God's blessing on him. When the donkey came back at night, the ox stood up to greet him, saying, "Good evening, watchful one! You have done me a favor beyond description, for I have been sitting in comfort. God bless you for my sake." Seething with anger, the donkey did not reply, but said to himself, "All this happened to me because of my miscalculation. 'I would be sitting pretty, but for my curiosity.' If I don't find a way to return this ox to his former situation, I will perish." Then he went to his trough and lay down, while the ox continued to chew his cud and invoke God's blessing on him.

"You, my daughter, will likewise perish because of your miscalculation. Desist, sit quietly, and don't expose yourself to peril. I advise you out of compassion for you." She replied, "Father, I must go to the king, and you must give me to him." He said, "Don't do it." She insisted, "I must." He replied, "If you don't desist, I will do to you what the merchant did to his wife." She asked, "Father, what did the merchant do to his wife?" He said:

[The Tale of the Merchant and His Wife]

After what had happened to the donkey and the ox, the merchant and his wife went out in the moonlight to the stable, and he heard the donkey ask the ox in his own language, "Listen, ox, what are you going to do tomorrow morning, and what will you do when the plowman brings you your fodder?" The ox replied, "What shall I do but follow your advice and stick to it? If he brings me my fodder, I will pretend to be ill, lie down, and puff my belly." The donkey shook his head, and said, "Don't do it. Do you know what I heard our master the merchant say to the plowman?" The ox asked, "What?" The donkey replied, "He said that if the ox failed to get up and eat his fodder, he would call the butcher to slaughter him and skin him and would distribute the meat for alms and use the skin for a mat. I am afraid for you, but good advice is a matter of faith; therefore, if he brings you your fodder, eat it and look alert lest they cut your throat and skin you." The ox farted and bellowed.

The merchant got up and laughed loudly at the conversation between the donkey and the ox, and his wife asked him, "What are you laughing at? Are you making fun of me?" He said, "No." She said, "Tell me what made you laugh." He replied, "I cannot tell you. I am afraid to disclose the secret conversation of the animals." She asked, "And what prevents you from telling me?" He answered, "The fear of death." His wife said, "By God, you are lying. This is nothing but an excuse. I swear by God, the Lord of heaven, that if you don't tell me and explain the cause of your laughter, I will leave you. You must tell me." Then she went back to the house crying, and she continued to cry till the morning. The merchant said, "Damn it! Tell me why you are crying. Ask for God's forgiveness, and stop questioning and leave me in peace." She said, "I insist and will not desist." Amazed at her, he replied, "You insist! If I tell you what the donkey said to the ox, which made me laugh, I shall die." She said, "Yes, I insist, even if you have to die." He replied, "Then call your family," and she called their two daughters, her parents and relatives, and some neighbors. The merchant told them that he was about to die, and everyone, young and old, his children, the farmhands, and the servants began to cry until the house became a place of mourning. Then he summoned legal witnesses, wrote a will, leaving his wife and children their due portions, freed his slave-girls, and bid his family good-bye, while everybody, even the witnesses, wept. Then the wife's parents approached her and said, "Desist, for if your husband had not known for certain that he would die if he revealed his secret, he wouldn't have gone through all this." She replied, "I will not change my mind," and everybody cried and prepared to mourn his death.

Well, my daughter Shahrazad, it happened that the farmer kept fifty hens and a rooster at home, and while he felt sad to depart this world and leave his children and relatives behind, pondering and about to reveal and utter his secret, he overheard a dog of his say something in dog language to the rooster, who, beating and clapping his wings, had jumped on a hen and, finishing with her, jumped down and jumped on another. The merchant heard and understood what the dog said in his own language to the rooster, "Shameless, no-good rooster. Aren't you ashamed to do such a thing on a day like this?" The rooster asked, "What is special about this day?" The dog replied, "Don't you know that our master and friend is in mourning today? His wife is demanding that he disclose his secret—, and when he discloses it, he will surely die. He is in this predicament, about to interpret to her the language of the animals, and all of us are mourning for him, while you clap your wings and get off one hen and jump on another. Aren't you ashamed?" The merchant heard the rooster reply, "You fool, you lunatic! Our master and friend claims to be wise, but he is foolish, for he has only one wife, yet he does not know how to manage her." The dog asked, "What should he do with her?"

The rooster replied, "He should take an oak branch, push her into a room, lock the door, and fall on her with the stick, beating her mercilessly until he breaks her arms and legs and she cries out, 'I no longer want you to tell me or explain anything.' He should go on beating her until he cures her for life, and she will never oppose him in anything. If he does this, he will live, and live in peace, and there will be no more grief, but he does not know how to manage." Well, my daughter Shahrazad, when the merchant heard the conversation between the dog and the rooster, he jumped up and, taking an oak branch, pushed his wife into a room, got in with her, and locked the door. Then he began to beat her mercilessly on her chest and shoulders and kept beating her until she cried for mercy, screaming, "No, no, I don't want to know anything. Leave me alone, leave me alone. I don't want to know anything," until he got tired of hitting her and opened the door. The wife emerged penitent, the husband learned good management, and everybody was happy, and the mourning turned into a celebration.

"If you don't relent, I shall do to you what the merchant did to his wife." She said, "Such tales don't deter me from my request. If you wish, I can tell you many such tales. In the end, if you don't take me to King Shahrayar, I shall go to him by myself behind your back and tell him that you have refused to give me to one like him and that you have begrudged your master one like me." The vizier asked, "Must you really do this?" She replied, "Yes, I must."

Tired and exhausted, the vizier went to King Shahrayar and, kissing the ground before him, told him about his daughter, adding that he would give her to him that very night. The king was astonished and said to him, "Vizier, how is it that you have found it possible to give me your daughter, knowing that I will, by God, the Creator of heaven, ask you to put her to death the next morning and that if you refuse, I will have you put to death too?" He replied, "My King and Lord, I have told her everything and explained all this to her, but she refuses and insists on being with you tonight." The king was delighted and said, "Go to her, prepare her, and bring her to me early in the evening."

The vizier went down, repeated the king's message to his daughter, and said, "May God not deprive me of you." She was very happy and, after preparing herself and packing what she needed, went to her younger sister, Dinarzad, and said, "Sister, listen well to what I am telling you. When I go to the king, I will send for you, and when you come and see that the king has finished with me, say, 'Sister, if you are not sleepy, tell us a story.' Then I will begin to tell a story, and it will cause the king to stop his practice, save myself, and deliver the people." Dinarzad replied, "Very well."

At nightfall the vizier took Shahrazad and went with her to the great King Shahrayar. But when Shahrayar took her to bed and began to fondle her, she wept, and when he asked her, "Why are you crying?" she replied, "I have a sister, and I wish to bid her goodbye before daybreak." Then the king sent for the sister, who came and went to sleep under the bed. When the night wore on, she woke up and waited until the king had satisfied himself with her sister Shahrazad and they were by now all fully awake. Then Dinarzad cleared her throat and said, "Sister, if you are not sleepy, tell us one of your lovely little tales to while away the night, before I bid you goodbye at daybreak, for I don't know what will happen to you tomorrow." Shahrazad turned to King Shahrayar and said, "May I have your permission to tell a story?" He replied, "Yes," and Shahrazad was very happy and said, "Listen" ...

B: EARLY PRINT TRADITIONS

5. Giovan Francesco Straparola, ***Le Piacevoli notti*** **(1551, 1553;** ***translated by Nancy Canepa, 2011***[1]**)**

Known as the first published European collection of fairy tales, Giovan Francesco Straparola's Le Piacevoli notti *forms a bridge among several traditions. First, Straparola borrows the model for print groupings of stories popularized by Chaucer in* Canterbury Tales *and Boccaccio in* Il Decameron, *where an event inspires people who find themselves gathered together to recount stories to pass the time. In this case, it is no catastrophe, but a party on Murano, the island off Venice—the thriving commercial center Shakespeare would choose a generation later for his tale of the merchant. But when it comes to the nature of the tales they tell, Straparola draws on local Italian folklore, fable, literature, and science to produce bawdy characters ("Crazy Pietro") that resemble the seventeenth-century style of Basile and short adventures involving metamorphosis, marvel, and social ascent. An example of these three themes can be found in "King Pig." Together, they speak to the banality of marvel in the fairy-tale universe, a condition of the genre that carries through later print and performance traditions.*

CRAZY PIETRO, NIGHT THREE, TALE 1

Crazy Pietro becomes wise by virtue of a fish called tuna, which he catches and saves from death. He takes for his wife Luciana, daughter of King Luciano, who through an enchantment had previously been made pregnant.

1 [Source: Nancy Canepa, unpublished.]

I FIND EVIDENCE, MY LOVELY LADIES, both in ancient stories and modern ones, that the acts committed by a crazy man in the throes of his madness, whether they occur by nature or by chance, many times result in good. And so I have in mind to tell you a fairy tale about a crazy man who, in the throes of his madness, grew wise due to an action of his own, and took the daughter of a king for his wife, as you can hear from my account.

On the island of Capraia, located in the Ligurian Sea and ruled by King Luciano, there once lived a poor little widow named Isotta. She had a son who was a fisherman, but it was his misfortune to be crazy, and everyone who knew him called him Crazy Pietro. Every day he went off to fish, but fortune was so hostile to him that he never caught a thing. And every time he returned home, when he was still more than half a mile away from the house he would start shouting so loudly that everyone on the island could easily hear him. And this is what he shouted: "O Mother, bring big basins and little basins, big buckets and little buckets, big tubs and little tubs, for Pietro has a load of fish!" His poor mother had faith in her son's words and, believing what he said to be true, prepared everything for his arrival. But as soon as he got to his mother, the crazy fellow would jeer at her and make fun of her, sticking out his tongue a full palm's-length.

The house of this poor little widow faced the palace of King Luciano, who had the most lovely and graceful ten-year-old daughter, to whom, as his only child, her father had given his own name, calling her Luciana. As soon as Luciana would hear Crazy Pietro say, "O Mother, bring big basins and little basins, big buckets and little buckets, big tubs and little tubs, for Pietro has caught a lot of fish," she would run to the window, and the sight of him gave her so much amusement and delight that at times she felt that she would die laughing. When he saw her laughing so immoderately, the crazy fellow was most offended, and insulted her with inappropriate words. But the more he attacked her with insulting words, the harder she laughed and acted as if it were a game, as children of a tender age are wont to do.

And so Pietro continued to go fishing day in and day out, and to foolishly repeat to his mother the aforementioned words. One day it happened that the poor boy caught a big, fat fish, commonly called by the name of tuna. This gave him such great happiness that he began to jump up and down on the shore, shouting, "I'll be able to bring some dinner to my mother yet, I'll be able to bring some dinner to my mother yet!" And he repeated these words a number of times.

When the tuna saw that it had been caught and could in no way escape, it said to Crazy Pietro, "Pray, brother, out of courtesy I beg you to free me from this captivity and to give me my life. Pray, dear brother, what do you want with me? Once you've eaten me, what other benefit do you expect to obtain? But on the other hand, if you spare me from death, at another time I could easily be of use to you."

But the good Pietro, who was more in need of eating than of words, wanted all the same to throw the fish over his shoulder and take it home, so that he could enjoy it in happiness with his mother, who also suffered from great need. But the tuna did not cease to beg him with all of its heart, offering to provide him with all the fish he desired. And after that it promised to grant him whatever he asked for. However crazy he was, Pietro's heart was not made of diamond, and, moved to pity, he agreed to free the tuna from its death. And he pushed it so hard with his feet and his hands that he was able to throw it back into the sea.

When the tuna saw that it had received such a great favor, it did not want to appear ungrateful, and said to Pietro, "Get into your little boat, and with an oar and your body tip it over to one side so that the water may get in." Pietro got into the boat, and when he caused it to curve up and lean to one side above the sea, such an abundance of fish washed onto the boat that it was in the greatest danger of sinking. Upon seeing this, Pietro, who esteemed the danger to be but little, grew very happy. And gathering up as much of the fish as he was able to carry on his back, he set off toward home.

When he was not far from the house, he began, in his usual fashion, to shout loudly, "O Mother, bring big basins and little basins, big buckets and little buckets, big tubs and little tubs, for Pietro has caught a lot of fish!"

His mother, who thought she was being mocked and made fun of like the other times, resolved not to do anything. But the crazy fellow continued to shout even louder, at which his mother, fearing that he might commit some even greater act of madness if he did not find the receptacles ready, prepared everything. When Pietro reached home and his mother saw such an abundance of beautiful fish, she grew very happy, praising God that for once she had had good luck.

Hearing Pietro's loud shouts, the daughter of the king ran to the window and began to taunt and jeer at him, laughing raucously at his words. Not knowing what else to do, the poor boy, who was lit up with anger and fury, ran to the shore and called out loudly to the tuna, asking it for help. The tuna heard the voice, and when it recognized whose it was, it swam in close to shore and, extending its head from the briny waves, asked him what his wish might be. To which the crazy fellow said, "For the moment I want nothing more than for Luciana, daughter of King Luciano, to find herself pregnant."

In less than a blink of an eye everything that he had wished for was executed.

Before many days and months had gone by, the girl's virginal belly had begun to grow, so that although she had not yet reached her twelfth year, she showed all the telltale signs of being a pregnant woman. When the girl's mother saw this, she was most afflicted, and could not come to terms with the fact that a girl of eleven years, who did not yet show any sign of being a woman, could become pregnant. And thinking, instead, that as is wont to happen, she had fallen prey to some incurable disease, she insisted that she be seen by the women who are expert in such things, who, after diligently examining her in great secrecy, judged the girl to be, without a doubt, pregnant.

The queen could not bear the weight of this excessive ignominy, and decided to share the news with King Luciano, her husband, who when he heard it felt that he would die of grief. He conducted, by every honest and covert means, the investigation necessary to discover the identity of he who had violated the girl, but he got nowhere at all, and in order to avoid such a shameful humiliation, he resolved to have his daughter killed in secret. But her mother, who loved her daughter tenderly, begged the king to spare her until she gave birth, after which he could do what he wished. The king—who was, after all, her father—was moved to compassion for the girl, his only child, and acquiesced to the mother's wishes.

When the time arrived to give birth, the girl delivered a beautiful baby boy, and he was of such supreme beauty that the king could not bear that he be killed. Instead, he ordered the queen to have him nursed and well nourished until he was one year old.

When the baby arrived at the term of one year, he had so grown in beauty that there was no other baby who could equal him, and the king decided to conduct an experiment to find the man who had fathered him. He had a public proclamation issued in every corner of the city, ordering that, under penalty of having his head cut from his torso, every man over the age of fourteen must present himself to His Majesty, carrying in his hands a fruit or a flower or some other thing that might excite the baby's interest. According to the king's command, everyone came to the palace bearing a fruit, or a flower, or one thing or another in their hands. They passed in front of the king, and then sat according to their ranks.

It happened that as a certain youth was on his way to the palace, as all the others were, he ran into Crazy Pietro, and said to him, "Where are you going, Pietro? Why don't you go to the palace, like the others, and obey the king's orders?" To which Pietro answered, "Come on, what would I do in such a crowd? Don't you see that I'm poor and naked, that I don't even have the clothes to cover myself, and you want me to go and present myself among all those lords and courtiers? I certainly won't do that."

Then the youth said, joking, "Come with me and I'll give you some clothes; who knows, the baby might be yours!" So Pietro went off to the youth's house and was given some clothes, which he took. He put them on, and then went to the palace in the company of the youth. After going up the stairs of the palace, he placed himself behind a door, so that he could barely be seen. When everyone had been presented to the king and was seated, the king ordered the baby to be brought into the hall, thinking that if the father were present, the most visceral paternal feelings might be excited. The wet nurse took the baby in her arms and carried him into the hall, where everyone caressed him, giving him now a fruit, now a flower, now one thing and now another, but the baby pushed it all away with his hand.

The wet nurse, who had been walking up and down the hall, at one point passed close to the palace door, at which the child immediately burst out laughing, and his head and whole body were so doubled over that he almost fell out of his wet nurse's arms. But she did not notice anything, and continued her course around the room. When she got back to the door again, the child was beside himself with joy, laughing and pointing to the door with his finger. The king, who had already noticed the child's actions, called the wet nurse over and asked her who was behind the door. The wet nurse answered that it was a beggar, as this was what she thought. But when the king summoned the man into his presence, he recognized him as Crazy Pietro. The child, who was right there, opened his arms and threw them around Pietro's neck, hugging him tightly. Upon seeing this, the king grew more and more distressed, and once he had politely dismissed his company, he deliberated that Pietro, his daughter, and the baby must die.

But the queen, who possessed great prudence, most wisely considered that if they were beheaded and burnt alive by order of the king, this would result in no little insult and disgrace for the king. And so she persuaded him to order a barrel, the biggest that could be made, and to close the three of them inside it and have it thrown to sea, so that without too much suffering they might be left to their fate. The king was greatly pleased by this counsel. He ordered the barrel and had the three of them put inside it, with a basket of bread and a flask of good vernaccia, as well as a bushel of figs for the child. He then had the barrel thrown onto the high seas, imagining that sooner or later it would hit a reef and break open, and they would drown.

Things went differently than what the king and queen had expected, however. When Pietro's little old mother, already oppressed by her years, heard of the curious case of her son, she was overcome by grief, and in the course of a few days she died. The miserable Luciana, under the assault of tempestuous waves in the barrel, and able to see neither the sun nor the moon, wept over her misfortune without pause. And having no milk with which to quiet the child, who would also frequently cry, she sometimes put him to sleep by feeding him figs.

But Pietro paid no attention to any of this, and gave mind to nothing but the bread and the vernaccia. When Luciana saw this, she said, "Oh dear, Pietro! You see how I suffer this punishment innocently because of you, and you laugh, eat, and drink in that senseless way, not considering for a moment our common peril." To which he answered, "We find ourselves in this situation not through any fault of mine, but because you continually mocked me and made fun of me. But keep up your spirits," he said, "we'll soon leave our worries behind." "I think," said Luciana, "that you're right when you say that we'll soon leave our worries behind, since any time now the barrel will be split open by some rock, and we'll all drown."

Then Pietro said, "Be quiet now, for I have a secret, and if you knew what it was, you would be amazed, and it might even cheer you up." "What kind of secret do you have," said Luciana, "that could relieve us from all of our suffering?"

"I have a fish," said Pietro, "that does whatever I command, and it would deny me nothing even if it risked losing its life. It was that fish that made you pregnant." "That's a good thing," said Luciana, "if it's true. But what's this fish called?" To which Pietro replied, "It's called tuna." "Make it give me the same power you have," said Luciana, "and order it to do whatever I say." "May your will be done," said Pietro.

And he called the tuna right over and ordered that whatever Luciana obliged it to do, be done. Once she had the power to command the tuna, the young woman immediately ordered it to cast the barrel onto one of the loveliest and most secure cliffs that could be found in her father's kingdom. And after this, that he make Pietro leave his filthy and crazy state, and become the most handsome and wisest man in the world. And not yet content, she wished again that a sumptuously rich palace be built on that cliff, with loggias and grand halls and splendid chambers, and that in back it have a delightful and elegant garden, full of trees that produced gems and precious pearls, in the middle of which would be a fountain of icy cold water and a vault of precious wines. All of this was carried out generously and without ado.

The king and queen, remembering how miserably they had deprived themselves of their daughter and the baby, and imagining that their flesh had already been devoured by fish, were filled with regret and never found a moment of happiness or cheer. And in this state of affliction and mourning, they decided to go off to Jerusalem and visit the Sacred Lands as a means to comfort their distraught hearts. When a ship had been prepared and equipped with everything that was needed, they embarked and left, and sailed with prosperous and favorable winds.

They were not yet a hundred miles from the island of Capraia, when from off shore they saw a rich and superb palace high above the sea, on a little island. And since it was quite lovely, as well as subject to their dominion, they resolved to go and see it. They sailed in close to the island, landed, and got off the ship. They had not yet reached the palace when Crazy Pietro and the king's daughter Luciana recognized them, and descended the steps to meet them, cordially receiving them with the warmest of welcomes. The king and the queen did not recognize them, however, as they were completely transformed.

When they had entered the lovely palace, they looked it over closely and offered many compliments, and then they went down a secret ladder that led to the garden, which the king and queen found so pleasing that they swore that in all of their days they had never seen any other that they liked as much. In the middle of the beautiful garden there was a tree with three golden apples on one of its branches, and the caretaker, by Luciana's express command, watched over them so that they would not be stolen. But, and I'm not sure how, someone hid the most beautiful of the apples in the king's shirt, without him noticing anything. And when the king was preparing to leave, the caretaker said to Luciana, "Madam, one of the three apples—the most beautiful—is missing, and I don't know who stole it."

Luciana then ordered the caretaker to search each person present thoroughly, since it was not a matter to be taken lightly. When the caretaker had carefully searched everyone not once but twice, he returned to Luciana and told her that he had not found it. Upon hearing this, Luciana pretended to be very upset, and turning to the king, she said, "Holy Majesty, you must forgive me if I have you searched again, for the golden apple that I am missing is of the highest value, and I esteem it over all else."

The king, unaware of the plot and sure that he was not at fault, loosened his robes, and the apple immediately fell to the ground. At the sight of this, the king was amazed and bewildered, as he did not know how it had come to be in his clothes. Luciana, observing this reaction, said, "My lord, we have treated you most warmly and honored you, offering you the welcome and tributes that you worthily deserve, and in exchange for such a welcome you steal the fruit of our garden behind our backs. It appears that you show us great ingratitude."

The king, who was innocent, went to great efforts to make her believe that he had not stolen the apple. Luciana saw that the appropriate time to reveal herself and make her innocence known to her father had arrived. With a tearful countenance she said, "My lord, you should know that I am that Luciana whom you unhappily begot, and whom you cruelly condemned to death, together with Crazy Pietro and the little boy. I am that Luciana, your only child, whom you found pregnant, although I had known no man. And this is the innocent child whom I conceived without the stain of sin," and she presented the boy to him.

"And this is Crazy Pietro, who thanks to a fish called tuna became the wisest of men, and built this great and magnificent palace. It was he who, unbeknownst to you, placed the apple under your clothes. It was he by whom I became pregnant, not through carnal union but because of an enchantment. And just as you are innocent of having stolen the golden apple, I too am entirely innocent of the pregnancy."

Weeping with happiness, everyone then embraced, and great festivities ensued. After several days had gone by, they got on the ship and returned to Capraia, where there was a grand celebration and more festivities. And the king wed Luciana to Pietro, and awarded his son-in-law such status that he lived honorably and in comfort for a long time. And when the king arrived at the end of his life, he named Pietro his successor.

COSTANTINO FORTUNATO, NIGHT ELEVEN, TALE 1

Soriana comes to her death and leaves three sons, Dusolino, Tesifone, and Costantino Fortunato, the last of whom acquires a powerful kingdom thanks to a cat.

So often, my lovely ladies, you see the richest of men fall into great poverty, but also the most destitute rise to a high state. This is what happened to one poor little fellow, who started out as a beggar, and then attained royal status.

In Bohemia there once was a woman by the name of Soriana, who was extremely poor and had three sons, the first of whom was called Dusolino, the second Tesifone, and the third Costantino Fortunato. She had nothing of substance in the world but three things: a kneading chest that women use to prepare bread, a peel on which they bake bread, and a cat. Soriana was already heavy with years, and as she neared death, she made up her last will and testament. To Dusolino, her oldest son, she left the kneading chest; to Tesifone the peel; and to Costantino the cat.

When the mother had died and been buried, the neighboring women began asking to borrow the chest and the peel for their own needs, and since they knew that the boys were extremely poor, they would make them pizza, which Dusolino and Tesifone ate without sharing any part of it with their younger brother Costantino. And if Costantino asked them for something, they answered that he should go ask his cat to give it to him. And so poor Costantino, together with his cat, suffered greatly. But the cat, who was enchanted, felt compassion for Costantino and, angry with the two brothers who treated him so cruelly, said, "Costantino, don't be sad, for I intend to provide for both your and my own lives."

The cat left the house and went out to the country, where, pretending to be asleep, she caught a passing hare and killed it. Then she went to the royal palace, and when she saw some courtiers she told them that she wanted to speak with the king. The king, hearing that it was a cat who wanted to speak to him, had her summoned and asked her what sort of request she brought. The cat answered that her master, Costantino, was sending him a gift of a hare that he had caught, and she presented it to the king. The king accepted the gift, and asked the cat who this Costantino was. The cat answered that he was a man whose goodness, beauty, and power had no superiors. At this, the king gave the cat the warmest of receptions, offering him delectable things to eat and to drink. When the cat was well sated, with a sleight of paw and without being seen by anyone she filled her knapsack, which was next to her, with some of the fine victuals. Then she asked the king's permission to leave, and brought the food to Costantino.

When his brothers saw the food that Costantino was enjoying, they asked him to share it with them, but he returned their favor and refused. And this gave rise to a burning envy, which continuously gnawed at their hearts.

Although Costantino had a handsome face, on account of all his suffering he was infected with scabies and ringworm, which were of great annoyance to him. But then he went with his cat to the river and was diligently licked and smoothed, and in a few days he was completely free of disease.

The cat continued, as we have described, to present gifts at the royal palace, and in this way supported her master. But at a certain point the cat grew tired of going back and forth, and was afraid that she might be considered a nuisance by the king's courtiers, and she said to her master, "Sir, if you do what I order you to, I will make you rich in a short time." "And how will you do that?" asked her master. The cat replied, "Come with me; your search has ended, for I'm more than willing to turn you into a rich man."

And so they went together to a spot by the river that was close to the royal palace. The cat undressed her master and, by common consent, threw him in the river, after which she began to shout loudly, "Help, help, come quickly, come quickly, mister Costantino is drowning!"

When the king heard this, he considered how many times he had received gifts from this fellow, and sent his people to help. Mister Costantino got out of the water and was dressed in fine clothes, and then was brought before the king, who received him with great ceremony. When the king asked Costantino why he had been thrown into the river, his painful condition did not allow him to answer, but the cat, who was always there right next to him, said, "You must know, O king, that some thieves had been informed that my master was carrying a load of jewels that he planned to give to you. They stripped him of everything he had and, intending to put him to death, they threw him in the river. Only by the mercy of these gentlemen was he saved from death."

Upon hearing this, the king ordered that Costantino be cleaned and well taken care of. And since he saw that he was handsome and knew that he was rich, he determined to give him his daughter Elisetta for a wife, providing her with a dowry of gold and precious gems, as well as splendid garments.

When the marriage had been celebrated and the triumphal processions had ended, the king ordered ten mules to be loaded with gold, and five others with the most ornate of garments, and he sent his daughter off to her husband's home, accompanied by many of his own men. Costantino saw how respectable and rich he had become, and did not know where to take his wife. He conferred with his cat, who said, "No need to worry, master, we'll take care of everything."

As everyone was happily riding along, the cat hurried quickly ahead, and when she was at quite a distance from the rest of the group, she came across some knights, to whom she said, "What are you doing here, you poor men? Take your leave at once, for a great cavalcade is about to arrive, and they're planning to attack you; here they are, they're getting closer, you can hear the clamor of their whinnying horses."

The frightened knights said, "What shall we do, then?" To which the cat replied, "This is what you are to do. If you're asked whose knights you are, you must answer bravely, 'Mister Costantino's,' and you will not be bothered."

When the cat had advanced farther down the road, she came across an enormous herd of sheep and oxen, and did something similar with their owners. And to whomever else she encountered she told the same thing.

The people accompanying Elisetta asked, "Whose knights are you, and whose fine herds are these?" And everyone answered in unison, "Mister Costantino's." Those accompanying the bride said, "So, then, Mister Costantino, are we beginning to enter into your holdings?" And he nodded his head yes. And he answered yes in the same way to everything that was asked of him, so that the company judged him to be an immensely wealthy man.

The cat arrived at a magnificent castle, where she found a small party of people, and said, "What are you doing, honorable men? Aren't you aware of your impending ruin?" "What are you talking about?" said the residents of the castle. "In less than an hour a band of soldiers will arrive here, and they will cut you to pieces. Don't you hear the horses whinnying? Don't you see the dust in the air? If you don't want to perish, take my advice, and you will all be safe. If anyone asks you whose castle this is, you must say, 'It belongs to Mister Costantino Fortunato.'" And so they did.

When the noble company had reached the lovely castle, they asked the caretakers whom it belonged to and they replied, in spirited fashion, "To Mister Costantino Fortunato." And so they entered the castle, and were honorably lodged.

The lord of that castle was Sir Valentino, a valorous soldier, who a short time earlier had left the castle to bring his newly wedded wife home. But to his misfortune, before he arrived at the place where his beloved wife was waiting for him, he had a sudden and terrible accident on account of which he immediately died. And so Costantino Fortunato was left to be lord of the castle.

Not much time had elapsed before Morando, king of Bohemia, died. The people proclaimed their desire to have Costantino Fortunato become their king, since as the husband of Elisetta, daughter of the dead king, the succession to the throne was due him. And in this way Costantino went from being a pauper and a beggar to a lord and a king, and lived a long time with his Elisetta, and left many heirs to the throne.

KING PIG, NIGHT TWO, TALE 1

Galeotto, King of England, has a son who is born a pig. The son marries three times, and when he sheds his pigskin and becomes a magnificent young man, he is named King Pig.

My charming ladies, there is no language sufficiently terse or eloquent that could express, even in a thousand years, how indebted man is to his Creator for having been put in this world as a human being, and not a brute beast. This brings to mind, indeed, a tale that took place in our times, in which a boy who was born a pig later became a magnificent young man, and was called King Pig by all.

You must know, therefore, my dear ladies, that Galeotto, King of England, was a man no less rich in gifts of fortune than in those of spirit. His wife, named Ersilia, was the daughter of Mattias, King of Hungary, and surpassed all other matrons of her time in beauty, virtue, and refinement. Galeotto ruled his kingdom so prudently that there was not a person who could with any truth complain about him. Although the two of them had lived together for a long time, fate willed it that Ersilia had never become pregnant. And this displeased the one and the other very much.

One day Ersilia was walking through her garden and picking flowers, and since she was already quite weary, she eyed a spot full of tender green grasses, and went over and sat down; beckoned by her sleepiness and by the birds that sang sweetly up in the green limbs, she fell asleep. At that moment three splendid fairies came passing through the air, and when they saw the young woman asleep, they stopped. After considering her beauty and grace, they discussed rendering her inviolable and enchanted; at the end, all three fairies were in agreement. The first one said, "I wish that she may be inviolable, and that the first night she lies with her husband she may become pregnant and that from her be born a son whose beauties have no equals in the world."

The next one said, "And I wish that no one may offend her, and that the son born from her be endowed with every virtue and kindness that can be imagined."

The third said, "And I wish that she may be the wisest and richest of all women, but that the son she conceives be born completely covered with pigskin, and that his gestures and manners all be those of a pig, and that he never be able to leave that state unless he first takes three wives."

When the three fairies had left, Ersilia awoke and arose at once, gathered up the flowers that she had picked, and returned to the palace.

Before many days had passed Ersilia became pregnant, and when she reached the desired birth, she delivered a son whose limbs were not those of a human, but a pig. When this news reached the ears of the king and queen, they felt immeasurable grief. And so as to avoid the repercussions of such a birth resulting in the disgrace of the queen, who was a good and saintly woman, more than once the king resolved to have the pig killed and thrown into the sea. But then, after turning it over in his mind and thinking, with reason, that whatever this son was, he had been generated by the king and was his own blood, he lay to rest any fierce intentions that he had previously had, and, embracing pity mixed with pain, decided that his son should in all regards be brought up and nourished not as a beast, but as a rational animal. The child was thus diligently nourished, and would often come to his mother, rising on his hind legs and putting his little snout and trotters in her lap. His merciful mother, for her part, caressed him, putting her hands on his bristly back and hugging and kissing him no differently than if he had been a human creature. And the child curled his tail, and with very clear signs showed her how pleasing the maternal caresses were to him.

When the little piggy was more grown up, he began to speak like a human being, and to stroll around the city, and wherever there was garbage and filth, he plunged right in, as pigs do. Afterwards, he would return home filthy and stinking, and when he went up to his father and mother and rubbed against their clothes, he soiled them all over with muck. But because he was their only child, they put up with everything patiently.

One day the little pig came home, filthy and dirty as usual, and, jumping all over his mother's clothes, he grunted and said to her, "My dear mother, I would like to get married." When she heard this, his mother answered, "You've got to be crazy, who do you think would take you as a husband? You're stinky and dirty, and you think a baron or knight is going to give you his daughter?" To which he replied, grunting, that he wanted a wife by all means. The queen, not knowing how to deal with this, said to the king, "What should we do? You can see what sort of situation we are in. Our son wants a wife, but no woman will want him for her husband." The little pig then returned to his mother and said, grunting loudly, "I want a wife, and I will continue to want one until I have the girl that I saw today, for she was most pleasing."

This girl was the daughter of a poor little woman who had three daughters, each of whom was marvelously beautiful. When the queen heard this, she immediately sent for the poor woman together with her eldest daughter, and said to her, "Dearest mother, you are poor and laden with daughters; if you give your consent to what I ask, you will go away rich. I have a son who is a pig, and I'd like to marry him to your eldest daughter. I ask that you pay your respect not to him, since he's a pig, but to the king and me, for at the end our whole kingdom will be in her possession."

Upon hearing these words, the girl grew quite upset and, turning as red as a morning rose, said that she would not consent to such a thing under any condition. But the poor woman's pleas were so sweet that her daughter finally contented her.

When the pig returned home, all filthy, he ran to his mother, who said to him, "My son, we have found you a wife, and she will be to your satisfaction." After she had the bride dressed in the most splendid of royal clothing, she brought her in and she introduced her to the pig. When he saw her, so beautiful and full of grace, he rejoiced, and, stinky and dirty as he was, he circled around her, pushing with his snout and hooves and giving her the most ardent caresses a pig has ever given. But because he was soiling all her clothes, she pushed him away. Then the pig said to her, "Why are you pushing me away? Didn't I have that clothing made for you?" To which she, full of pride, scornfully answered, "Neither you nor your kingdom of pigs made it for me." And when it came time to go and rest, the young woman said, "What am I going to do with this stinky beast? Tonight, when he's in his first sleep, I'll kill him." The pig, who was not far off, heard these words but said nothing.

At the appointed hour the pig, all smeared with mud and other foul matter, arrived at the magnificent bed, lifted the feather-light sheets with his snout and hooves and soiled everything with fetid excrement, and then got into bed next to his bride. It wasn't long before she fell asleep. The pig, though, had only pretended to fall sleep, and with his sharp tusks he pierced her chest so violently that she immediately died.

After he arose the next morning at the usual time, he went off, according to his habit, to feed and dirty himself. The queen thought that she should go and visit her daughter-in-law, and when she found that she had been killed by the pig, she felt the greatest grief. Upon returning home and receiving a bitter reprimand from the queen, the pig replied to her that he had done to his bride what she had wanted to do to him. And he indignantly left.

Before many days had passed the pig began to goad his mother again about wanting to marry, this time the other sister. Although the queen was most contrary, he nevertheless wanted the girl at all costs, and threatened to bring everything to ruin if he could not have her. When the queen heard this, she went to the king and told him the whole story, and he said that it would be better to have the pig killed than for the pig to cause some great evil in the city. But the queen, who was his mother and nurtured a great love for him, could not suffer the thought of remaining without him, even if he was a pig. And so she summoned the poor little woman with her other daughter, discussed the matter at length with them, and after they had much deliberated about the marriage, the second daughter consented to accept the pig for her husband.

It did not work out as she desired, however, since the pig killed the second girl as he had done with the first, after which he left the house at once. When he returned to the palace at the appointed time covered with such filth and mud that it was impossible to get near him for the stench, he was severely rebuked by the king and queen for his excessive actions. But the pig boldly replied that he had done to his bride what she had intended to do to him.

Before long Mister Pig again began to prod his mother about wanting to marry and to take the third sister for his wife, who was even more beautiful than the first and the second. When this demand was flatly denied, he pleaded even more insistently to have her, and with fearful and boorish words he threatened the queen's death if he did not get the girl as his bride. Upon hearing his foul and shameful words, the queen felt such torment in her heart that she was close to going mad. And so she put aside every other thought and summoned the poor little woman and her third daughter, who was named Meldina, and said to her, "Meldina, my dear girl, I want you to take Mister Pig for your husband, not out of respect for him but for his father and me, for if you are able to be with him in the right way, you will be the happiest and most content woman there is."

Meldina replied with a serene and clear countenance that she was very happy, and thanked the queen very much for deigning to accept her as her daughter-in-law. And even if she had nothing else, it would be enough that she had gone in one instant from being a poor little girl to the daughter-in-law of a powerful king. When the queen heard this grateful and loving answer, she could not keep the tears from her eyes because of the sweetness that she felt. But she still feared that what had happened to the other two would happen to her.

The new bride was dressed in rich clothing and precious jewels, and waited for her dear bridegroom to come home. And when Mister Pig arrived, filthier and dirtier than he had ever been, his bride received him kindly, spreading her precious dress on the ground and begging him to lie next to her. The queen told her to push him away, but she refused to do this, and said the following words to the queen:

I have heard tell of three things
Sacred, venerable and pious crown.
For one, which is impossible to find,
The search is too great a folly.
Do not place your trust in the other,
As it leads neither to reason nor to the straight path.
The third, the precious and rare gift
That you have in your hands, make sure to hold dear.

Mister Pig, who was not sleeping but understood everything clearly, stood up and began to lick her face, throat, chest and shoulders, and she, in exchange, caressed him and kissed him, so that he was all aflame with love.

When it came time to rest, the bride went off to bed and waited for her dear bridegroom to come, and it wasn't long before he approached the bed, all filthy and stinking. She lifted up the blankets and invited him lie next to her, placing his head on the pillow. Then she covered him well and closed the bed curtains so that he would not suffer the cold.

At the break of day Mister Pig went off to pasture, leaving the mattress full of excrement. And in the morning the queen went to the bride's chamber, believing that she would see what she had already seen with the other two. But instead, she found her daughter-in-law cheerful and content, even if the bed was soiled with every sort of filth and foul matter. And she thanked the supreme God for this lovely gift, that her son had found a wife to his liking.

Before much time had gone by, one day, while exchanging pleasurable considerations with his lady, Mister Pig said to her, "Meldina, my darling wife, if I could believe that you would not reveal to anyone a great secret of mine, I would uncover to you, and not without your greatest happiness, something that until now I have kept hidden. Since I know that you are prudent and wise, and I see that you love me with perfect affection, I would like you to be privy to it." "Of course you may reveal your every secret to me," said Meldina, "I promise you that I will not disclose it against your wishes to anyone."

Reassured by his wife's words, Mister Pig took off his stinking and dirty skin, and a graceful and magnificently handsome young man remained, and that whole night he lay tightly embraced with his Meldina. After commanding that she not say a word about any of this, for the time was near for him to leave this miserable state, he got out of bed, collected his porcine covering, and went back to his garbage, just as he had done before. I leave it to each of you to imagine the nature and degree of Meldina's happiness at finding herself in the company of such a fair and exquisite young man.

Before long the young woman became pregnant, and when it came time to give birth, she was delivered of a beautiful baby boy. This brought great happiness to the king and the queen, and most of all because he had the form of a human being and not a beast. Keeping such a sublime and marvelous thing secret was, however, a great weight on Meldina, and thus she went to her mother-in-law and said, "Most prudent queen, I believed my companion to be a beast, but the husband you gave me is the most handsome, virtuous, and well-mannered young man that nature ever created. When he comes to my chamber to lie with me, he takes off his stinking skin and places it on the ground, and there stands an elegant and fair young man. And no one could possibly believe this if they did not see it with their own eyes."

The queen thought that her daughter-in-law spoke in jest, while in fact she told the truth. And when she asked her how she might see this, her daughter-in-law answered, "Come to my chamber in the early hours of the night and you will see that what I tell you is true."

Night came, and after waiting for the hour when everyone had gone to rest, the queen had torches lit, and together with the king she went to her son's chamber.

Upon entering, she found the pigskin on the ground in a corner of the chamber, and, nearing the bed, she saw that her son was a magnificent young man, and that his wife Meldina was holding him tightly in her arms. At this sight, the king and queen rejoiced greatly, and the king ordered that before anyone left the room the skin be torn into tiny shreds, and such was the happiness of the king and queen for their renewed son that they came close to dying of pleasure. And when King Galeotto saw that he had such a son, and a daughter-in-law besides, he removed his diadem and his royal cloak, and in his place his son was crowned with great ceremony, and was named King Pig. King Pig reigned much to the satisfaction of his people, and with Meldina, his beloved wife, he lived in great happiness for a long time.

R.I. [Richard Johnson], *The History of Tom Thumbe, the Little, for his small stature surnamed, King Arthur's Dwarfe* (1621) [website]

Published 70 years before the term "fairy tale" was even coined, and set in the time of the legendary King Arthur, this chapbook account of the adventures of Tom Thumb (provided as a web text; see http://sites.broadviewpress.com/marveloustrans/) includes many elements closely associated with fairy tales in later centuries—including its focus on a downtrodden but determined hero, armed with fairy gifts and aspiring to royal favor. While the history of the fairy tale in English is largely a history of translation (from Italian, French, German, Norwegian, and Russian, among other languages), this early text points to the role that British tale traditions played in this complex history.

6. Giambattista Basile, *Lo cunto de li cunti* (1634–36; *translated by Nancy Canepa, 2007*[1])

Basile's Tale of Tales *contains what are surely among the most inventive literary fairy tales. Written in Neapolitan dialect, which made their translation and circulation a challenge until quite recently, they mark the beginning of the European print tradition. Although this collection was not the first to circulate in written form—*Alf Layla wa Layla *and the* Panchatantra *are both earlier collections—Basile is the first self-identified author of such a grouping of stories. The striking originality of Basile's style—part bawdy street fair and part sophisticated literary salon—makes him unique in the early modern fairy-tale corpus. Marvel is a favorite theme, with metamorphoses happening across "seemingly insurmountable geographical, class and even species lines," in the words of translator Nancy Canepa. And such bodily experiences as rage, passion, and sex are described in lengthy, voluptuous detail abound. Basile achieves at least some*

1 [Source: Nancy Canepa, *The Tale of Tales, or Entertainment for Little Ones* (Detroit, MI: Wayne State UP, 2007), 83–89, 115–25, 163–68, 413–17.]

of the bawdiness and hilarity of his description with high-flying metaphors that relate foreheads to hammers and women to plagues. Such paradoxical couplings along with rambling strings of metaphors heaped one upon the other gives an earthiness to his characters and a surprisingly modern feel to his tales.

THE CINDERELLA CAT, SIXTH ENTERTAINMENT OF THE FIRST DAY[1]

Zezolla, incited by her teacher to kill her stepmother, believes that she will be held dear for having helped the teacher to marry her father; instead she ends up in the kitchen. But due to the power of some fairies, after numerous adventures she wins a king for her husband.

THE AUDIENCE LOOKED LIKE STATUES as they listened to the tale of the flea, and they gave a certificate of asininity to the boorish king, who had exposed his own flesh and blood and the succession of his state to such great risks, and all for a piddling matter. Once they had all corked their mouths, Antonella uncorked hers in the manner that follows: "In the sea of malice, envy always finds herself with a hernia[2] in the place of a bladder, and where she expects to see another drown, she finds herself either underwater or dashed against a reef, just as happened to certain envious girls that I have in mind to tell you about.

"You should know, then, that there once was a widowed prince who had a daughter so dear to him that he had eyes for no one else. He had taken on a first-rate sewing teacher for her, who taught her how to do the chain-stitch, openwork, fringes, and the hem-stitch, and showed her more affection than words can express. But the father had just remarried; he had taken a fiery, wicked, and demonic thing for his wife, and her stepdaughter soon began to make this accursed woman's stomach turn. She gave the girl sour looks, made awful faces at her, and knitted her eyebrows in such a

---

1 Basile's tale is the earliest literary version of Cinderella in Europe, preceding Perrault's "Cendrillon" (1697) by over sixty years. Norman Penzer comments on two motifs that do not commonly appear in other versions: "The unusual incident of Cennerentola murdering her mother-in-law by letting the lid of a chest fall on her neck reminds us of the Grimms' [tale "The Juniper Tree"], where the wicked stepmother shuts the lid of the apple-chest on the little boy as he stoops to get an apple." Norman Penzer, ed. and translated by, *The "Pentamerone" of Giambattista Basile* vol. 1 (London: John Lane and the Bodley Head, 1932) 62 . The other motif, "the stopping of the ship," appears also in … "The Little Slave Girl," and … Marie-Catherine d'Aulnoy, "Finette Cendron."

2 "It was popular belief that hernias, and especially strangulated hernias, were caused by envy, since one can 'die' from both" (81). Ruggero Guarini and Alessandra Burani, eds., *Il racconto dei racconti, ovvero Il Trattenimiento dei piccolo* (Milan: Adelphi, 1994).

frightful manner that the poor little thing was always complaining to the teacher of her stepmother's ill treatment, saying, 'Oh, God, couldn't you be my little mommy, you who give me so many smooches and squeezes?'

"She chanted this so incessantly that she planted a wasp in the teacher's ear, and one day, blinded by evil spirits, the teacher said to her, If you follow the advice of this madcap, I'll become your mother and you'll be as dear to me as the pupils of these eyes.' She was about to go on speaking when Zezolla (for that was the girl's name) said, 'Forgive me if I take the words out of your mouth. I know you love me dearly, so mum's the word, and *sufficit*; teach me the trade, for I'm new in town; you write and I'll sign.' 'All right, then,' replied the teacher, 'listen carefully; keep your ears open and your bread will come out as white as flowers. As soon as your father leaves, tell your stepmother you want one of those old dresses in the big chest in the storeroom so that you can save the one you're wearing. Since she likes to see you all patched up in rags, she'll open the chest and say, "Hold the lid up." And as you're holding it while she rummages around inside, let it bang shut, and she'll break her neck. Once that's done, you know that your father would coin counterfeit money to make you happy, so when he caresses you, beg him to take me for his wife and, lucky you, you'll become the mistress of my life.'

"After Zezolla heard this, every hour seemed like a thousand years to her. She followed her teacher's instructions to a tee, and once the mourning for the stepmother's accident was over, she began to play her father's keys to the tune of marrying the teacher. At first the prince thought it was a joke, but his daughter beat so hard that she finally broke the door down, and in the end he yielded to Zezolla's words. He took Carmosina, the teacher, for his wife, and held grand festivities.

"Now while the newlyweds were off carrying on and Zezolla was standing at one of the balconies[1] of the palace, a little dove flew down onto the wall and said to her, 'If ever you should wish for something, send your request to the dove of the fairies on the island of Sardinia, and you will be immediately satisfied.'

"The new stepmother smoked Zezolla with caresses for five or six days, seating her at the best place at the table, giving her the best morsels, dressing her in the best clothes. But in no time at all she annulled and completely forgot about the service rendered (oh, sad is the soul housed in a wicked mistress!), and began to raise to all heights six daughters of her own whom she had kept secret up until then. And she worked her husband over so well that as his stepdaughters entered into his graces, his own daughter fell from his heart, and from one day to the next Zezolla ended up being demoted from the royal chamber to the kitchen and from a canopied bed to the hearth, from sumptuous silks and gold to rags, from the scepter to the spit. And

1 *gaifo* (Neap.): "In Naples, a sort of small hanging terrace" (62). Benedetto Croce, intro. and notes, *Lo Cunto de li Cunti (Il Pentamerone) de Giambattista Basile* (Naples: V. Vecchi, 1891).

not only did her status change, but her name as well, for she was no longer called Zezolla but Cinderella Cat.

"It happened that the prince had to go to Sardinia for affairs of state, and, one by one, he asked Imperia, Calamita, Shiorella, Diamante, Colombina, and Pascarella, who were the six stepdaughters, what they wanted him to bring them on his return. One asked for luxurious clothing, one for ornaments for her hair, one for rouges for her face, one for toys to pass the time, one for one thing, and one for another. Finally he asked his daughter, almost scornfully, 'And you, what would you like?' And she: 'Nothing, except that you give my regards to the dove of the fairies and tell her to send me something; and if you forget, may you be unable to go forward or backward. Keep in mind what I say: your arm, your sleeve.'[1]

"The prince departed, did his business in Sardinia, and bought what his stepdaughters had requested; Zezolla slipped his mind. But after he embarked on his vessel and it was about to set sail, the ship was unable to leave port, just as if it had been blocked by a sea lamprey.[2] The captain of the ship, close to desperation, fell asleep out of fatigue and in his dreams saw a fairy, who said to him, 'Do you know why you cannot remove the ship from port? Because the prince who is with you broke a promise he made to his daughter, remembering everyone except his own flesh and blood.' The captain awoke and told his dream to the prince, who, confused about his failing, went to the fairies' grotto and, after giving them his daughter's regards, asked that they send her something.

"And lo and behold, a lovely young woman who was a banner to beauty came out of the cavern and told him that she thanked his daughter for remembering her so kindly, and that Zezolla should be happy, as a tribute of love for the fairy. With these words, she gave him a date tree, a hoe, a golden pail, and a silk cloth, and told him that the date tree was for planting and the other things for cultivating it. The prince, astonished by these gifts, took leave of the fairy and returned to his land, where when he had given all of the stepdaughters what they had requested, he at last gave his daughter the gift sent by the fairy.

"Nearly bursting out of her skin with joy, Zezolla planted the date in a fine pot, hoed it, watered it, and dried it with the silk cloth every morning and evening, so that after four days, when the plant had grown as tall as a woman, a fairy came out and said to her, 'What is your wish?' Zezolla answered that she wished to leave the house now and then but didn't want her sisters to know. The fairy replied, 'Whenever you like, go to the pot and say,

1 "Proverbial way of saying: 'If you don't keep your word, all the worse for you'" (Croce 63).

2 *remmora* (Neap.): marine or sea lamprey, "which attaches itself, by a sort of suction cup, to other fish or to ships; according to popular lore the lamprey could prevent or hinder navigation (Pliny, Natural History IX 25)" (138). Michele Rak, ed. and translated by, *Lo Cunto de li Cunti* (Milan: Garzanti, 1986).

Golden date of mine
I've weeded you with the little hoe of gold,
I've watered you with the little pail of gold,
I've dried you with the cloth of silk,
Now strip yourself and dress me!

And when you want to undress, change the last verse to: "Strip me and dress yourself.'"

"Now then, a feast day arrived and the teacher's daughters went out, all flowery, bedecked, and painted; all ribbons, little bells, and baubles; all flowers, scents, rosies, and posies. Zezolla immediately ran to the pot, uttered the words the fairy had taught her, and found herself fixed up like a queen, after which she was placed on a white thoroughbred with twelve trim and elegant pages in tow. Then she went to the place her sisters had gone, and they drooled over the beauty of that splendid dove.

"As fate willed it, the king showed up there, too, and when he saw Zezolla's extraordinary beauty he immediately fell under its spell, and he asked his most trusted servant to find out how he could get more information about this phenomenon of beauty—who she was and where she lived. Without a moment's delay the servant went after her; but having discovered the ambush, she threw out a handful of golden coins obtained from the date tree for this purpose. When he caught sight of those gleaming coins the servant forgot about following the horse, preferring to fill his claws with small change, while Zezolla dashed back and slipped into the house. Once she had undressed the way the fairy had instructed her to, those harpies of her sisters arrived and, just to make her boil, told her of all the fine things they had seen. In the meantime the servant went back to the king and told him about the coins, at which the king erupted in a great rage and told him that for four shitty beans he had sold off his pleasure and that on the next feast day he was at all costs to make sure he found out who the beautiful girl was and where the lovely bird had its nest.

"The next feast day arrived, and after the sisters went out, all decorated and elegant, and left the despised Zezolla at the hearth, she immediately ran to the date tree. Once she had said the usual words, a band of damsels came out: one held a mirror, one a little bottle of squash water,[1] one a curling iron, one a rouge cloth, one a comb, one some brooches, one the clothes, and one pendants and necklaces. They made her as beautiful as a sun and then put her in a coach drawn by six horses and accompanied by footmen and pages in livery, so that upon reaching the same place where the other party had been held, she only compounded the astonishment in her sisters' hearts and the fire in the king's breast.

1 *acqua de cocozze* (Neap.): "cosmetic and medicinal oil extracted from squash" (Croce 65).

"But when she left again and the servant followed after her, she threw out a handful of pearls and jewels so that he would not catch up with her, and while that worthy fellow stopped to peck at them, since they were not to be wasted, she had time to drag herself back home and undress in the usual fashion. With a face this long, the servant returned to the king, who said, 'I vow on the soul of my ancestors that if you don't find her, you'll get a fine beating and a kick in the ass for every hair in your beard!'

"The next feast day arrived, and after the sisters went out, Zezolla returned to the date tree and repeated the enchanted song, at which she was magnificently dressed and placed in a golden coach accompanied by so many servants that she looked like a whore arrested in the public promenade and surrounded by police agents.[1] She went, made her sisters' mouths water, and then left, with the king's servant tailing the coach as if he were stitched to it by a double thread. When she saw that he was still stuck to her side she said, 'Use your whip, coachman!' and the coach rushed forth at breakneck speed. Indeed, it raced along so fast that she lost one of her pattens,[2] the prettiest little thing you ever did see. The servant, who wasn't able to reach the flying coach, picked the patten up from the ground and brought it to the king, telling him what had happened.

"The king took the patten in his hand and said, 'If the foundations are so beautiful, what must the house be like? O lovely candlestick that held the candle that consumes me! O tripod of the charming cauldron in which my life is boiling! O beautiful corks, attached to the fishing line of Love used to catch this soul! There: I'll embrace and squeeze you; if I cannot reach the plant, I will adore its roots, and if I cannot have the capitals, I will kiss its base! You were once the memorial stone for a white foot, and now you are a snare for this black heart. You made the lady who tyrannizes this life a span and a half taller, and you make this life grow just as much in sweetness, as I contemplate and possess you.'

"As he was saying this the king called the scribe, summoned the trumpeter, and—toot toot toot!—issued a proclamation: all the women of the land were invited to come to the festivities and banquet that he had gotten the idea to hold. And when the appointed day came, oh, my goodness! What a spread, what merrymaking! Where

---

1 "Courtesans were prohibited from circulating in carriages in public streets or in gondolas along the Posillipo beach, the daily promenade of the viceroys and nobility. Those who transgressed the prohibition (and this was not infrequent) were apprehended and surrounded by police, and then taken to prison" (Croce 545).

2 *chianiello* (Neap.): "The *chianielli* were, at the time, more than simple mules: they were overshoes whose soles and heels—often of exaggerated height—were made of cork. When they were worn over ladies' shoes or slippers, they allowed their wearer to get out of a carriage and walk on the street without getting the hem of her dress dusty or muddy; during the sixteenth and seventeenth centuries in Naples, the use of *chianielli* also became popular among courtesans" (Guarini and Burani 87).

did so many pastries and casseroles[1] come from? And the stews[2] and meatballs? And the macaroni and ravioli?[3] There was enough to feed an entire army!

"Once the women had all arrived—noble and common, rich and ragged, old and young, beautiful and ugly—and polished off their due, the king made a toast and then tried the patten on each of his guests, one by one, to see whom it would fit like a glove and as neatly as a pin, in the hope that he might recognize the one he was seeking from the fit of the patten. But when he couldn't find a foot to match it, he began to despair. Nonetheless, after he had requested silence, he said, 'Come back tomorrow to do penance with me again; but if I am dear to you, leave no woman at home, whoever she may be.' The prince said, 'I have a daughter, but she looks after the hearth and is an unworthy wretch and does not deserve to sit at the same table at which you eat.' The king said, 'Let her be at the top of the list, for that is my wish.' And so they left and all came back the next day, and along with Carmosina's daughters came Zezolla. As soon as the king saw her she seemed to him to be the one he wanted, although he pretended not to notice.

"After they finished working their jaws it was time to try the patten on. And no sooner was it drawn close to Zezolla's foot than it hurled itself with no help at all onto the foot of that painted egg of Love,[4] just like iron runs to a magnet. When the king saw this he raced to clamp her in the press of his arms, and when he had seated her under the royal canopy he put a crown on her head and commanded that all the women present curtsy and show her their veneration, for she was their new queen. Upon seeing this the sisters nearly died of anger, and, not having the stomach to stand this heartbreak, they quietly stole away to their mother's house, confessing in spite of themselves that *those who oppose the stars are crazy*."

---

1 *pastiere e casatielle* (Neap.): "The *pastiera* is the famous Easter cake made with short pastry filled with ricotta, candied fruit, wheat berries, orange peel, and other flavorings. *Casatielli* are ring-shaped casseroles made with flour dough, lard, pepper, and unshelled hard-boiled eggs that decorate the borders; also an Easter dish" (Guarini and Burani 88).

2 *li sottestate* (Neap.): "*Sottestati* is composed of veal stewed in a sauce of plums, garlic, pine nuts, raisins, sugar, almonds, and cinnamon" (Guarini and Burani 88).

3 *li maccarune e graviuole* (Neap.): "That is, 'ravioli': not to be confused with 'gravioli,' which were a type of sweet made in monasteries"; *Maccaruni* had not yet, at this time, come to take first place in Neapolitan cuisine; Neapolitans were not yet called 'maccaroni-eaters,' but 'leaf-eaters' [because of their many vegetable dishes]. Macaroni are more often indicated as being Sicilian or Sardinian" (Croce 545).

4 Cupid, Venus's son. "G.B. Pino (in his *Ragionamento sovra del asino*, Naples, c. 1530) says of Cupid: 'He was the dear son, he was the painted egg of his mother, Venus.' It was the custom to send eggs painted various colors as holiday gifts" (Croce 27).

THE OLD WOMAN WHO WAS SKINNED, TENTH ENTERTAINMENT OF THE FIRST DAY[1]

The king of Strong Fortress falls in love with the voice of an old woman, and after he is tricked with a sucked-on finger, he gets her to sleep with him. But upon discovering her old hide, he has her thrown out the window, and when she remains hanging on a tree she is enchanted by seven fairies, after which she becomes a splendid young woman and the king takes her for his wife. But the other sister is envious of her fortune, gets skinned to make herself more beautiful, and dies.

THERE WASN'T ONE PERSON WHO didn't like Ciommetella's tale, and they derived a double-soled pleasure from seeing Canneloro freed and the ogre, who had done such a butcher job on the poor hunters, punished. And when the order was given to Iacova to seal the next letter of entertainment with her coat of arms, she began to speak in this manner: "The accursed vice, embedded in us women, of wanting to look beautiful reduces us to the point where to gild the frame of our forehead we spoil the painting of our face, to whiten our old and wizened skin we ruin the bones of our teeth, and to put our limbs in a good light we darken our eyesight, so that before it is time to pay our tribute to time we procure ourselves rheumy eyes, wrinkled faces, and rotten molars. But if a young girl who in her vanity gives in to such empty-headedness deserves reproach, even more worthy of punishment is an old woman who out of her desire to compete with young ladies becomes a laughingstock for others and the ruin of her own self, as I am about to tell you, if you will lend me a bit of your ears.[2]

"Two old women had retired to a garden facing the King of Strong Fortress's quarters. They were the summary of all misfortunes, the register of all deformities, the ledger of all ugliness: their tufts of hair were disheveled and spiked, their

1 See Penzer's discussion of the appearance of a number of the motifs in this tale in legend, religious traditions, folklore, and the literary fairy tale tradition. These include a man marrying a hag who then turns into a beautiful lady ("The Weddynge of Syr Gawayne," the legend of Perceval); the "false sybarite" motif; and the flaying of the sister. With regard to the latter, he notes that the "terrible end of the other sister is rather surprising when we remember that the lucky sister had been given gifts by the fairies to make her beautiful, noble, and virtuous. Yet as soon as she is married, she proceeds to treat her less lucky sister in the most heartless and cruel way imaginable." The similarities with Hans Christian Andersen's "Little Claus and Big Claus" and Grimm [sic], "Little Farmer," are also noted.... Croce mentions a similar tale by Pitrè ... and cites corresponding Sicilian, Venetian, Abbruzzese, and Tyrolean versions (287).

2 The introduction to the tale contains an antifeminist diatribe against the use of cosmetics and other instruments of false beautification that was common in disquisitions on the proper comportment of women, as well as in writings on rhetoric, where the celebration of what lies under the merely cosmetic—in body or words—was often linked to the topos of "naked truth." This passage, in particular, brings to mind the preamble to tale 1.10 of the *Decameron*, which criticizes the same female "vice."

foreheads lined and lumpy, their eyelashes shaggy and bristly, their eyelids swollen and heavy, their eyes wizened and seedy-looking, their faces yellowed and wrinkled, their mouths drooly and crooked; in short, they had beards like a billy goat's, hairy chests, round-bellied shoulders, withered arms, lame and crippled legs, and hooked feet. And to prevent even the Sun from catching a glimpse of their hideous appearance, they stayed holed up in a few ground-level rooms[1] under the windows of that lord.

"The king was reduced to such a state that he couldn't even fart without causing those old pains in the neck to wrinkle their noses, for they grumbled and threw themselves about like squid over the smallest thing. First they said that a jasmine flower fallen from above had given one of them a lump on her head, then that a torn-up letter had dislocated one of their shoulders, and then that a pinch of dust had bruised one of their thighs.

"Upon hearing of this monster of delicacy, the king concluded that underneath him lived the quintessence of softness, the prime cut of the most delectable of meats, and the flower of all tenderness, by reason of which he was overcome by a craving all the way down to the little bones in his feet and a desire straight through to his bone marrow to see this marvel and to get a clearer idea of the matter. And so he began to send down sighs, to clear his throat when there was nothing to clear, and, finally, to speak more expeditiously and with greater boldness, exclaiming, 'Where, oh where do you hide yourself, jewel, splendor, beautiful product of the world? "Come out, come out, Sun, warm up the emperor!"[2] Uncover those lovely graces, show those lamps of the shop of Love, stick out that dainty head, O counting house heaped with beauty's money! Don't be so stingy about letting yourself be seen! "Open your doors to the poor falcon!" "Give me an offering if you want to give me one!"[3] Let me see the instrument from which issues that sweet voice! Allow me to see the bell where that tinkling is formed! Let me catch a glimpse of that bird! Do not make me graze on absinthe like a sheep from Ponto[4] by refusing to allow me to look at and contemplate that beauty of all beauties!'

1 *no vascio* (Neap.): street-level apartments were usually inhabited by members of the lower classes and were "at this time already a phenomenon connected to the growth in population and lack of housing" (Rak 218).

2 A Neapolitan children's song, probably of ritual origin. The complete text of this song appears in the introduction to day 4, in which the company of tale-tellers and audience engages in song, dance, and merrymaking before the day's tales start. Recently (1976) this same song became the prologue to a musical based on Basile's "La gatta cenerentola" (Cinderella) created by Roberto de Simone and the Nuova Compagnia di Canto Popolare, a well-known group of Neapolitan "ethno-musicians."

3 Two more children's games: "Open the Doors" is a circle game, and "Give Me an Offering" is a song children sang on New Year's Eve as they went from door to door….

4 For this belief on Pontine sheep, Basile refers to Pliny's *Natural History* (book 27): "Absinthi genera plura … Ponticum, e Ponto, ubi pecora pinguescent illo, et ob id sine felle reperiuntur" (cit. Croce 100).

"The king said this and other words, but he might as well have been playing the Gloria, for the old women had stopped up their ears. This, however, only added wood to the king's fire: he felt himself heated up like an iron in the furnace of desire, squeezed by the tongs of deliberation, and pounded by the hammer of amorous torment, and all to forge a key that could open the little chest of jewels that was making him die of longing. And still he did not pull back, instead continuing to send forth entreaties and to strengthen his assaults, never taking a rest.

"The old women, who had begun to put on airs and grow cocky as a result of the king's offers and promises, resolved not to waste this opportunity to nab a bird that was about to fly into the snare all by himself. And so, one day when the king was ranting and raving[1] above their window, they told him through the keyhole in a tiny little voice that the greatest favor they could do would be to show him, in eight days, just one finger of their hand. The king, who as a practiced soldier knew that fortresses are won span by span, did not refuse this solution, hoping to conquer finger by finger the stronghold that he was keeping under siege, since he also knew that 'first take and then ask' was an ancient proverb. And thus, once he had accepted this ultimatum of the eighth day by which to see the eighth wonder of the world, the old women's sole activity became that of sucking their fingers like a pharmacist who has spilled some syrup, with the plan that when they reached the established day whoever had the smoothest finger would show it to the king.

"Meanwhile, the king was on tenterhooks as he waited for the agreed-upon hour to blunt his desire: he counted the days, he numbered the nights, he weighed the hours, he measured the moments, he made note of the seconds, and he probed the instants that had been meted out to him in anticipation of the desired good. Now he begged the Sun to take a shortcut through the celestial fields so that by gaining ground it would unhitch its fiery carriage and water its horses, tired after such a long trip, before the usual time; now he implored Night to sink the shadows so that he could see the light, which yet unseen was keeping him in the kiln of Love's flames; now he grew incensed with Time, who to spite him was wearing crutches and leaden shoes so as to delay the hour for liquidating the debt to the thing he loved and for respecting the contract stipulated between them.

"But as the Sun in Leo[2] would have it, the time came, and he went in person to the garden and knocked on the door, saying, 'Come out, come out, wherever you

1 *faceva ... lo sparpetuo* (Neap.): "playful deformation of the formula used in the mass for the dead: *luxperpetua eis;* a *sperpetua* is a whiny lament" (Guarini and Burani 129).

2 The "Sun in Leo" or *solleone* refers, of course, to the hottest period of the summer. Its disruptive effects were well documented, as we see, e.g., in these verses by the sixteenth-century satirist Nelli: "più tardi e qual più presto, / Secondo che quell sol trova I soggetti / Disposti" (cit. Croce 551).

are!'[1] Then one of the two old women—the one most laden with years, since the touchstone had shown her finger to be of greater carats than her sister's—stuck her finger through the keyhole and showed it to the king.

"Now this was no mere finger, but a sharpened stick that pierced the king's heart. Or rather, it was no stick, but a cudgel that stunned him on the head. But what am I saying, stick and cudgel? It was a match struck on the tinder of his desires, a fuse lit from the powder magazine of his longings. But what am I saying, stick, cudgel, match, fuse? It was a thorn under the tail of his thoughts—indeed, a cure of laxative figs that made him eliminate the gas of amorous affect in a mess of sighs.

"And as he held that hand and kissed that finger, which had been transformed from a shoemaker's rasp to a goldsmith's burnisher, he began to say, 'O archive of sweetness, O rubric of joys, O register of Love's privileges, by reason of which I have become a store of troubles, a warehouse of anguish, and a customhouse of torment! Is it possible that you wish to appear so obstinate and hard that my laments cannot move you? I beg you, my fair heart, if you have shown me your tail through this hole, now show me your snout, and let us make a gelatin[2] of happiness! If you have shown me your shell, O sea of beauty, now show me your sweet flesh; uncover those eyes of a peregrine falcon and let them feed on this heart! Who keeps the treasure of that beautiful face sequestered in a shithouse? Who quarantines that fair merchandise in a hovel? Who imprisons the forces of Love in that pigsty?[3] Come out of that ditch, flee that stable, abandon that hole! "Jump, little snail, and give Cola your hand";[4] spend me for what I'm worth! You know, after all, that I'm a king and not any old cucumber; you know that I can do and undo as I like. But that impostor of a blind boy, son of a cripple and a whore, who has free rein over scepters, has willed that I be your subject and that I beg you for the grace of what I could seize however and whenever I please.[5] And furthermore, I know, as a certain someone said, that caresses, and not bravado, sweeten up Venus.'

"The old woman knew where the old devil kept his tail, since she was a master fox, a big old cat, a shrewd, astute, and wily one, and she reflected that it's precisely when a superior begs for something that he's actually issuing a command, and that a vassal's stubbornness gets the choleric humors of the master's intestines moving, which then burst forth in a dysentery of ruin. And so she decided to act accordingly,

1 Another children's game, of the hide-and-seek variety.

2 Boiled pig snout, served in its own gelatin, was commonly sold by street vendors in Basile's time, as it still is today (Rak 218).

3 *mantrullo* (Neap.): "pigpen, also the cell of those condemned to death" (Guarini and Burani 131).

4 This is the first verse of a Neapolitan villanelle.

5 Love or Cupid, the son of Venus and Vulcan, is "one of the recurrent figures of Greco-Roman mythology in these tales, in which sexual relationships are, directly or indirectly, a basic plot element" (Rak 219).

and with the little voice of a skinned cat she said, 'My lord, since you are inclined to put yourself beneath one who is under you, having deigned to descend from the scepter to the distaff, from the royal halls to the stable, from lavish robes to rags, from greatness to misery, from the terrace to the cellar, and from a steed to an ass, I cannot, nor ought not, nor want not to contradict the will of so great a king. And since you desire this alliance between prince and servant, this mosaic of ivory and poplar, this inlay of diamonds and glass, here I am, ready and prepared to do your will. I beg of you only one favor, as a first sign of the love that you bear me: that I be received in your bed at night and without a candle, since my heart could not bear the burden of being seen naked.' The king, gurgling with delight, swore to her with one hand on the other that he would willingly do this. And so, after he sent a kiss of sugar to that fetid mouth, he left, and could hardly wait for the Sun to stop plowing and for the fields of the heavens to be sown with stars, so that he in turn could sow the field where he intended to harvest bushels of joy and heaps of delight.

"When Night arrived—and, finding itself surrounded by so many shop burglars and cloak thieves,[1] squirted out black ink like a squid—the old woman smoothed back all the wrinkles on her body and gathered them behind her shoulders in a knot, which she tied tightly with a piece of twine. A servant then led her by the hand in the darkness to the king's bedroom, where, once she had taken off her rags, she flung herself onto the bed. The king was more than ready to light the fuse on his artillery, and as soon as he heard her come and lie down he smeared himself all over with musk and civet and sprayed himself from head to toe with cologne water, and then raced to bed like a Corsican hound. And it was lucky for the old woman that the king was wearing so much perfume, on account of which he wasn't able to smell the fumes coming from her mouth, the stink of her little tickly areas, and the stench of that ugly thing.

"But no sooner had he lain down than, feeling around, he became aware of that business on the back of her neck and discovered the dried tripe and deflated bladders that the wretched old woman kept in the back of her shop. Keeping his composure, he decided not to say anything right then, since he needed to have a clearer idea on the matter. And so, pretending not to notice, he cast anchor at Mandracchio when he had believed he would be on the coast of Posillipo, and sailed forth on a barge when he had thought he would be charting his course on a Florentine galley.[2]

---

1 Common crimes of the time, in which Spaniards were considered to have the greatest expertise (Croce 103).

2 Mandracchio was an area of ill repute near the Dogana (Customs) in the port of Naples; the famous Neapolitan hill of Posillipo was, since ancient times, the site of aristocratic pastimes. A *permonara* (barge) was an "old, discarded ship that was kept at wet dock to house the crew, to hold prisoners, or for other uses"; the elegant Florentine galleys were often, at this time, used to guard the Mediterranean coasts against pirates (Croce 104).

But no sooner had the old woman dropped off into her first sleep than the king took a chamois bag containing a flint stone from his writing table of ebony and silver, and lit a little oil lamp. After conducting a search under the sheets and finding a harpy in the place of a nymph, a Fury in the place of a Grace, and a Gorgon in the place of a Cypriot, he flew into such a rage that he wanted to cut the towrope that had moored that ship. Snorting with fury, he yelled for all his servants, who when they heard the call to arms threw on their shirts[1] and came upstairs.

"Flailing about like an octopus, the king said to them, 'Look at the fine trick this old bogeyman's grandmother has played on me! I believed I was going to gobble up a milk-calf and instead I find myself with a buffalo placenta; I thought I had trapped a splendid dove and I end up with this owl in my hand; I imagined I had a morsel fit for a king and I find myself with this disgusting thing in my claws: taste it and spit it out! And yet when you buy a cat in the bag this and even worse happens! And yet it was she who arranged this affront, and it will be she who shits her penance! So go and get her right now, just as she is, and throw her out the window!'

"When the old woman heard this she began to defend herself with kicks and bites, saying that she appealed the sentence, since he was the one who had turned her like a winch until she came to his bed and that besides, she could call a hundred doctors to her defense along with, above all, the saying that goes, 'An old chicken makes a good broth,' and the other one, 'Don't leave the old road for the new.' But after all that they picked her straight up and hurled her down into the garden, and she had the luck not to break her neck, for she was left hanging by her hair on the branch of a fig tree.

"Early the next morning—before the Sun took possession of the territories it had been ceded by Night—some fairies came passing by the garden. Due to some irritation or other they had never spoken or laughed, and when they saw, hanging from the tree, the ugly shade who had caused the shadows to clear out before the usual time, they were overcome by such side-splitting laughter that they came close to getting a hernia, and once they set their tongues in motion they weren't able to close their mouths about that lovely spectacle for a good while. And such was their amusement and pleasure that in payment each of them cast a spell on her: one by one, they wished that she might become young, beautiful, rich, noble, virtuous, well loved, and blessed by good luck.

"When the fairies had left, the old woman found herself on the ground, sitting on a chair of rich velvet fringed in gold under the same tree as before, which had been transformed into a canopy of green velvet backed in gold. Her face had turned into that of a fifteen-year-old girl, so beautiful that by comparison all other beauties would have looked like worn-out house slippers alongside an elegant, perfect-fitting

1 *fatto na 'ncammisata* (Neap.): according to Croce, a reference to how, "during night-time attacks, soldiers would put shirts over their armor so that they could recognize each other in the dark" (104–05).

little pump; next to this enthroned grace all other graces would have been deemed worthy of Ferrivecchi or Lavinaro;[1] and where she played her chitchat and blandishments with a winning hand, all the others would have played a losing bank. And, furthermore, she was so primped up, fancified, and sumptuous that she looked like a royal majesty: her gold was blinding, her jewels dazzling, the bloom of her flowers stunning; and surrounding her were so many servants and ladies-in-waiting that it looked like the day of pardon.[2]

"In the meantime the king, who had thrown a blanket over his shoulders and a pair of old slippers on his feet, went to the window to see what had happened to the old woman. When he saw what he never would have imagined, he stood there with his mouth hanging open and looked that fine piece of a girl up and down from head to toe for a good long while, as if he were enchanted. Now he admired her hair, in part spread out over her shoulders and in part harnessed with a golden tie, which gave the Sun cause for envy; now he stared at her eyelashes, crossbows that took hearts as their targets; now he looked at her eyes, blind lanterns of Love's patrol;[3] now he contemplated her mouth, amorous winepress where the Graces squeezed out delight and obtained sweet Greco and savory Mangiaguerra wines.[4] He swung from side to side like a shaky rafter, and nearly went out of his mind when he saw the baubles and trinkets that were hanging at her neck and the magnificent clothes she was wearing. Talking to himself, he said, Am I asleep or am I awake? Am I in my right mind or am I going crazy? Am I myself or am I not myself? What kind of move[5] caused such a lovely ball to hit this king, so that I am sent to my ruin? I'll be done for, I'll be destroyed if I don't pull myself out of this! How has this sun risen? How has this flower blossomed? How was this bird hatched, so that she can pull my desires like a hook? What sort of boat brought her to these lands? What sort of cloud rained her down? What sort of torrents of beauty are carrying me straight to a sea of woes?'

"As he was saying this he flew down the stairs and ran into the garden, where he went before the renovated old woman and, nearly wiping the ground, said to her, 'O my dear little pigeon-face; O little doll of the Graces, splendid dove of the carriage of Venus, triumphal cart of Love! If you have set your heart to soak in the Sarno River,[6]

---

1 *grazia de sieggio* (Neap.): "Neapolitan nobility was divided into those 'with a seat' (i.e., assigned to one of six noble seats), and those 'without a seat.' The first, and more ancient group was of much greater prestige" (Croce 552). Ferrivecchi and Lavinaro were among the poorest streets in Naples.

2 *la perdonanza* (Neap.): "processions for the purchase of indulgences" (Rak 219).

3 *Lantern a bota* (Neap.): "'A small oil lamp, invented by the Brescians, that allowed one to cover and uncover the light at will; today their use is prohibited almost everywhere,' says Tomaso Garzoni [in his *Piazza universal*]. In fact, only the police were permitted to use them" (Croce 32).

4 Two famous wines from the area around Naples.

5 *trucco* (Neap.): "a game in which small balls (*ipalle*) were thrown and hit" (Rak 220).

6 Anything immersed in the waters of the Sarno River, it was said, would turn to stone; cane seeds were thought to have dangerous properties; sparrow feces was believed to cause blindness ... (Croce 107).

if cane seeds have not gotten into your ears and sparrow shit has not fallen into your eyes, I am sure that you can see and hear the pain and torment that, directly and on the rebound, those beauties of yours have cast into my chest. And if you cannot surmise from the ash cloth of this face the lye that boils inside this chest,[1] if you cannot imagine from the flames of these sighs the furnace that burns in these veins, then if you are sympathetic and of good judgment you can at least infer from that golden hair what sort of cord binds me, and from those black eyes what sort of coals roast me, and from the red arches of those lips what sort of arrow pierces me. Do not, then, bar the door of pity, do not lift the bridge of mercy, do not stop the duct of compassion! If you do not deem me worthy of obtaining a pardon from this lovely face, at least give me a safeguard of good words, a pass of a promise or two, and a pledge card of fair hopes, for otherwise I shall take my slippers far from here[2] and you shall never again see their shape.'

"These and a thousand other words issued forth from the depths of the king's heart and deeply moved the renovated old woman, who at the end accepted him as her husband. And so she rose from her seat and took him by the hand, and they went together to the royal palace, where in the wink of an eye a huge banquet was prepared. Since all the ladies of the land were invited, the old bride wanted her sister to be among them, but they had a lot to do and say before they were able to find her and drag her to the feast, because out of great fear she had gone and holed herself up and hidden away so that not a trace of her could be found. But God willed that she finally came, and once she was sitting next to her sister, whom it was no joke for her to recognize, they began the merrymaking.

"The wretched old woman had another hunger that was gnawing at her, though, since she was consumed with envy to see her sister's coat shine, and every few minutes she would pull her by the sleeve and say, 'What did you do, my sister, what did you do? Lucky you, you've got the chain!'[3] And her sister would answer, 'Just think about eating now, and we'll talk about it later.' The king kept on asking what was going on, and to cover things up his bride answered that her sister wanted a little green sauce. And the king immediately ordered that garlic paste, mustard, pepper sauce, and a thousand other relishes that stimulate the appetite be brought.

"But the old woman, to whom the grape relish tasted like cow bile, went back to nagging her sister, and asked her again, 'What did you do, my sister, what did you do? Tell me, or I'll make you the fig under my cloak.'[4] And her sister answered, 'Be

1 The "ash cloth" (*cennerale*) was used to cover laundry basins in order to contain the ash therein (which was used as a detergent); lye is also a common detergent.

2 Neapolitan idiom meaning "to pass on to the other world."

3 Words of another children's game, here used as an augury.

4 *fare nafico* (Neap.): "A gesture of contempt, known in Italy, France, Germany, Holland, England, etc., and consisting of placing the thumb between the index and middle fingers.... [It] is held by some to be a

quiet, for we have more time than money; eat now, and may it go down the wrong way, and then we'll talk.' The king, curious, asked what she wanted, and his bride, who felt as tangled up as a chick in a pile of tow and would have liked to do without that hammering at her temples, answered that she wanted something sweet. And then there came a blizzard of pastries, a bombardment of wafers and little doughnuts, a flood of blancmange, and a downpour of honey brittle.[1]

"But the old woman, who was as agitated as a squid and had a bad case of the runs, started up with the same music again until the bride could no longer stand it, and to get her off her back she answered, 'I skinned myself, sister.' When the envious sister heard this she said, under her breath, All right then, your words don't fall on deaf ears! I want to try my luck, too, for every spirit has a stomach, and if I come away with my hands full you won't be the only one having a good time. I want my part, too, right up to the fennel.'[2]

"As she was thus speaking, the tables were cleared. Pretending to go and satisfy a bodily need, she ran straight off to a barber's shop, where she found the master barber, took him aside in a back room, and said to him, 'Here are fifty ducats for you; skin me from head to toe.'[3] The barber, judging her to be crazy, answered, 'Go on, sister; you're talking funny and you're surely in need of someone to accompany you.'[4] And the old woman replied, with a face of marble, 'You're the one who's crazy, if you can't recognize your own good fortune. For if I win at a certain game, in addition to the fifty ducats I'll let you hold your basin under Fortune's beard. So, then, gather up your instruments and don't waste time; you're in for some good luck.'

"After arguing, fighting with her, and protesting for a good while, the barber was finally led by the nose, and behaved like the guy who 'ties up the ass wherever his master wants.' And when he had set her on a stool he started to hack away at that black bark, which drizzled and piddled blood all over and which every now and then, as steady as if he were giving her a shave, said, 'Ugh, she who wants to appear

---

sign-symbol of the vulva, and is used for example in Italy, as both an insulting gesture and a counter to the evil eye (a wish for good luck): one etymological theory holds that the expression originated in an Italian word meaning both the fruit and the *pudendum muliebre,* thus making of the gesture a punning symbol" (Leach and Fried 378). In this case, the potential ambivalence of the gesture (insult or wish for good luck), as well as the pun, are fully exploited by Basile. See also Giuseppe Pitrè, *Biblioteca delle tradizioni popolari siciliane* vol. 17 (Palermo: L. Pedone-Lauriel, 1875) 244–45.

1 All traditional Neapolitan sweets. *Pastidelle* (pastries) were made with eggs, sugar, and cinnamon; *neole* (wafers; from the Latin *nebulae)* from flour and boiled must; *tarallucce* were small doughnut-shaped cookies (made with sugar) or crackers (made with pepper, anise, or other spices); *iancomangiare* (blancmange) was another sweet, a gelatinous pudding made with milk or almond milk, and produced in monasteries; *franfellicche* were little pieces of sweet brittle made with honey and syrup (see Rak 220).

2 Up to the very end; fennel is served at the end of the meal.

3 Barbers of the time performed multiple roles: "in barber shops one could have more or less complex surgical procedures done, such as teeth extraction, the application of leeches, and more" (Rak 220).

4 As patients at an insane asylum are accompanied by nurses (Croce 109).

beautiful must suffer.' And as he continued to send her to her ruin and she repeated the same refrain, they kept up a counterpoint on the lute[1] of her body until he reached the rosette of her navel,[2] at which point her blood abandoned her and with it her strength, and she fired a departing shot from below, proving at her own risk the truth of Sannazaro's verse: *Envy, my son, destroys itself.*"[3]

CAGLIUSO, FOURTH ENTERTAINMENT OF THE SECOND DAY[4]

Due to the industry of a cat left to him by his father, Cagliuso becomes a gentleman. But when he shows signs of being ungrateful to the cat, it reproaches him for his ingratitude.

It is impossible to describe the great pleasure that everyone felt at the good fortune of Viola, who used her wits to construct such a fine destiny in spite of the vexations caused her by her sisters, enemies of their own flesh and blood, who tried so many times to trip her and break her neck. But since it was time for Tolla to pay the rent she owed, she coughed up the golden coins of lovely words and paid her debt in the following manner: "Ingratitude, my lords, is a rusty nail that when driven into the tree of courtesy causes it to dry up; it is a broken sewer that turns the foundations of affection into a sponge; it is a bit of soot that, falling into the pot of

1 *colascione* (Neap.): "A wide-necked lute with two or three strings, very popular in southern Italy in Basile's time" (Guarini and Burani 63).

2 The *rosa* is the circular opening in the body of stringed instruments, from which derives the expression *contrapuntiarefi' a la rosa,* or to take a long time with something.

3 The reference is to these verses from Iacopo Sannazaro's *Arcadia,* ed. Franceso Erspamer (Milan: Mursia, 1990) 6.4–6: "Nel mondo oggi gli amici non si trovano, / la fede e morta e regnano le invidie / e i mal costumi ognor piu si ri-novano." Rak comments that "envy was one of the most popular topics in court society, and was debated in numerous treatises" (220). One of the "authorities" frequently cited was Ovid, who in book 2 of the *Metamorphoses* describes Envy as an old hag not so dissimilar from Basile's old woman: "Eyes wild, teeth thick with mold, gall dripping green … / Envy is sleepless, her heart anxiety, / And at the sight of any man's success / She withers, is bitten, eats herself away" (Ovid 79).

4 This is, of course, the tale that will become better known in Charles Perrault's version, "The Master Cat, or Puss in Boots." Basile had a predecessor in Straparola (*Le piacevoli notti* 11.1, "Costantino Fortunato"), and popular variants can be found in Pitrè (*Fiabe, nov.* e *race. sic.* 88, "Don Giuseppi Birnbaum" and *Nov. tosc.* 12, "The Fox") and Imbriani 10 ("King Mes-sememi-gli-bocca-'l-fumo"). A version of this tale (largely derived from Perrault) also appeared in the 1812 edition of the Grimms' tales, though was later removed. Penzer comments that "Perrault was troubled about the ending to the tale and affixes a moral that is quite inapplicable. It has been repeatedly pointed out that the cat is an unscrupulous adventurer who indulges in a series of mean frauds to benefit a worthless youth who usually plays a very passive part in the tale […] we are still ignorant whence Straparola and Basile derived their tale—a curious tale that never seemed to have a satisfactory end. […] Thus in some cases the cat turns into a human being, in others he becomes prime minister" (1:158). The end of Basile's tale differs notably from Straparola's, since in the latter the cat merely disappears from the tale once its important work as a helper is done. Another notable difference between Straparola and Basile's and later versions is that the cat in the first two is female.

friendship, takes away its aroma and taste. And this can be formally seen and proved; you'll see a rough sketch of it in the tale that I am about to tell you.

"There once was, in my city of Naples, an old, wretchedly poor man, who was so full of withouts, so destitute, hungry, miserable, gaunt, and lacking even the smallest wrinkle in his purse, that he went around as naked as a louse.

"When he was about to shake out the sacks of his life he called Oraziello and Pippo, his sons, and said to them, 'I have already been convened according to contract for the debt I owe Nature. And believe me, if you are Christians, that it would be my great pleasure to sail out of this Mandracchio[1] of sorrows and escape from this pigsty of suffering, if it weren't for the fact that I'll be leaving you impoverished, as penniless as Saint Chiara,[2] stranded on the five roads of Melito[3] without a coin, as clean as a barber's basin, as light on your feet as a sergeant, and as dry as a prune pit. For you own as much as a fly can carry on its foot, and if you run for a hundred miles you won't drop a cent,[4] since my luck has driven me to where the three dogs shit;[5] life is no longer mine to have, and what you see is what you can write about, because I have always, as you know, been one for yawns and little crosses,[6] and I've always gone to bed without a candle. But despite all of this, I still want to leave you a sign of my love when I die; so you, Oraziello, my firstborn, take that sieve that's hanging on the wall, with which you'll be able to earn your bread; and you, Pippo, the nest shitter, take the cat. And remember your daddy.' As he was saying this he burst into tears, and a short while later he said, 'Farewell, night has come!'

"Oraziello had his father buried with the help of some charity, and then took his sieve and went running around from here to there trying to make a living, and the more he sifted the more he earned. But Pippo, upon taking the cat, said, 'Just look what a pathetic inheritance my father has left me! I don't know how to provide for myself and now I have to shop for two! Who ever heard of such a wretched legacy? Better if it had never been!' The cat, who heard this moaning, said to him, 'You complain too much! You've got more luck than brains, though you don't know your own luck, for I can make you rich if I try.' When he heard this Pippo thanked Her Royal Catness, petted her three or four times on the back, and warmly entrusted himself to

1 See "The Old Woman Who Was Skinned" [p. 125, note 2].

2 As poor as Saint Chiara (Claire), the founder of the order of the Clarisse, with its ideal of absolute poverty; "alternately, the reference might be to the church of Santa Chiara, one of the biggest in Naples, built by Robert of Anjou" (Rak 334).

3 "In Melito, on the road from Naples to Aversa, there is an area called 'the five roads,' where, in a spot called 'Fascenaro,' there are always great numbers of beggars" (Croce 564).

4 *na maglia* (Neap.): "ancient name for a coin of very low value" (Croce 168).

5 "I.e., in miserable conditions; the origin of the expression is unknown" (Croce 168).

6 "Made on the mouth to prevent evil spirits from taking advantage of that moment [the yawn] to enter into the body" (Croce 564).

her care. And then the cat, feeling sorry for poor Cagliuso,[1] showed up every morning—when the Sun went fishing for Night's shadows with its golden hook and bait of light—at either the Chiaia beach or the Rock of Fish,[2] and when she spotted a big mullet or a nice bream she grabbed it and brought it to the king, saying, 'Lord Cagliuso, slave to Your Highness from the ground floor up to the terrace, sends you this fish with his respect and says, "Great lord, small gift."' The king, with the happy face usually awarded to those who bring goods, answered the cat, 'Tell this lord whom I don't know that I send him infinite thanks.'

"Other times the cat would run off to the hunting grounds, either the swamps or the Astroni,[3] and when the hunters shot down an oriole or a great tit or a blackcap, she collected them and presented them to the king with the same message. And she employed this stratagem so often that one morning the king said to her, 'I feel so obliged to this lord Cagliuso that I would like to meet him in order to reciprocate the affection that he has shown toward me.' To which the cat answered, 'Lord Cagliuso's desire is to give his life and blood for your crown; and tomorrow morning—when the Sun sets the stubble of the aerial fields on fire—he will, without a doubt, come to pay homage to you.'

"And so when morning came, the cat went to the king and said to him, 'My lord, Lord Cagliuso sends his apologies, for he cannot come. Last night some servants of his ran off, and they didn't even leave him the shirt on his back.' Upon hearing this the king immediately had an armful of clothes and undergarments taken from his wardrobe and sent them to Cagliuso. And before two hours had gone by, Cagliuso, led by the cat, came to the palace, where he received a thousand compliments from the king, and after sitting him at his side the king gave orders that a magnificent banquet be prepared.

"But as everyone was eating, every now and then Cagliuso would turn to the cat and say to her, 'My little kitty, keep an eye on those rags of mine, for I wouldn't want anything bad to happen to them.' And the cat answered, 'Be quiet, shut your trap, don't talk about such trifles!' When the king wanted to know what Cagliuso needed, the cat answered that he had gotten the craving for a little lemon, and the king immediately sent someone to the garden to get a basket of them. And Cagliuso kept up with the same music about his tatters and shirttails and the cat kept on telling him to plug up his mouth and the king asked him again what he needed and the cat invented another excuse to make up for Cagliuso's pettiness.

1 At this point in the text Pippo's name changes to Cagliuso.

2 "Place where fish was distributed to fishmongers by the wholesale buyers, on via della Marina. There were 'fish stones' at Santa Lucia and Chiaia as well" (Croce 564).

3 "Hunting grounds, the Paduli (Ital. 'marshes') are in the eastern part of Naples; the Astroni are near the Agnano lake." The latter were a royal hunting reserve (Croce 564).

"Finally, after having eaten and chatted for a long time about this and that, Cagliuso took his leave. But that fox of a cat stayed with the king and described to him Cagliuso's valor, brains, good judgment, and above all his great riches in the countryside outside of Rome and in Lombardy, for which he would deserve to marry into the family of a crowned king. When the king asked what exactly there was, the cat answered that it was impossible to keep track of the furniture, buildings, and other furnishings of that moneybags, since even he did not know how much he had, and that if the king wanted to find out more about it he could send his people outside the kingdom with her, and they could see with their own eyes that his riches were without equal in the world.

"The king summoned some of his faithful men and ordered them to obtain detailed information on the matter, and they followed in the cat's footsteps. As soon as they had gotten beyond the borders of the kingdom the cat, with the excuse that she had to find refreshment for them along the way, at every turn ran ahead and for every flock of sheep, herd of cattle, stable of horses, and drift of pigs she came across, she said to the shepherds and guardians, 'Hey there, take heed! A bunch of bandits intends to sack everything they find in this land! But if you want to escape their fury and make sure your goods go unharmed, just say they belong to Lord Cagliuso, and no one will touch a hair on your head.' She said the same thing at the farms along the way, so that wherever the king's men arrived, they found a bagpipe tuned to the same key: everything they encountered was said to belong to Lord Cagliuso. And so, tired of asking, they returned to the king and praised Lord Cagliuso's riches from the sky to the sea. When the king heard this, he promised the cat a nice reward if she arranged the marriage between Cagliuso and his daughter, and the cat, shuttling back and forth, finally pulled off the deal.

"When Cagliuso arrived, the king delivered him a great dowry and his daughter, and after a month of festivities Cagliuso said that he wanted to take his bride to his estates. The king accompanied them to the border of his kingdom, and they set off for Lombardy, where, on the cat's recommendation, Cagliuso bought some properties and land, and became a baron.

"Cagliuso now found himself rolling in wealth, and he thanked the cat over and over again, saying that he owed his life to her and his greatness to her good offices, that a cat's devices had done him more good than his father's wits, and that she should therefore feel free to do and undo whatever she thought fit and pleased her with his possessions and his life. Finally, he gave her his word that as soon as she died—a hundred years from then!—he would have her stuffed and placed inside a golden cage in his own bedroom, so that he might always keep the memory of her before his eyes.

"The cat listened to this show of braggadocio, and before three days had gone by she pretended to be dead and stretched herself straight out in the garden. When Cagliuso's wife saw this she shouted, 'Oh, my husband, what a great tragedy! The cat is dead!' 'And may every evil accompany her,' answered Cagliuso. 'Better her than us.' 'What shall we do?' replied the wife. And he: 'Take her by her foot and throw her out the window!'

"Hearing of this fine reward when she would have least imagined it, the cat began to say, 'This is the great gratitude for the fleas that I picked off your neck? These are the thousand thanks for those rags I got you to throw away, so worn out that you could have hung them on spindles? This is what I get back, after having dressed you as elegantly as a spider and fed you when you were hungry, miserable, and threadbare? When you were in tatters, covered with shreds, all patched up, and coming apart at the seams, you corpse stripper? This is the fate of those who try to wash an ass's head! Get lost, and may everything I've done for you be damned; your throat doesn't deserve to be spit in![1] What a lovely golden cage you've prepared for me, what a fine burial you've planned for me! There you have it: you offer your services, you make sacrifices, you labor, you sweat, and all for this nice prize! Oh, miserable is he who fills up his pot with the hopes of someone else! That philosopher was right when he said, "If you go to bed an ass, you'll wake up one!" In short, the more you do, the less you should expect. Good words and wicked actions deceive only the wise and the mad.'

"So speaking and shaking her head, she headed out of there, and however much Cagliuso tried to lick her down with the lung[2] of humility, nothing could get her to come back. And as she ran off without once turning her head, she said, *May God save you from the rich who become poor and from the beggar who has worked his way up*."

1 "Reference to the popular custom of spitting in a newborn's mouth as a first sign of recognition and affection" (Guarini and Burani 209).

2 "Cat food that a street vendor, called *zpolmonaro* [lung seller] would bring to the houses of Naples in the morning; all the cats in the neighborhood would become agitated and meow as they heard their benefactor getting closer" (Croce 172).

SUN, MOON, AND TALIA, FIFTH ENTERTAINMENT OF THE FIFTH DAY [1]

Talia dies because of a little piece of flax and is left in a palace, where a king chances to pass by and causes her to have two children. The children fall into the hands of the king's jealous wife, who orders that they be cooked and served to their father and that Talia be burned. The cook saves the children and Talia is freed by the king, who has his wife thrown into the same fire that had been prepared for Talia.

ALTHOUGH THE STORY OF THE ogresses might have solicited a bit of compassion, instead it was the cause of pleasure, for everyone was happy that Parmetella's affairs had gone far better than expected. After this tale it was Popa's turn for deliberating, and since her feet were already in the stirrups she began to speak in this manner:[2]

"There once was a great lord who at the birth of a daughter named Talia summoned all the wise men and fortune-tellers of his kingdom to predict her future. After conferring a number of times, they concluded that she would find herself in great danger because of a little piece of flax. And so the king issued a prohibition aimed at avoiding that baleful encounter: in his house neither flax nor hemp nor anything of the sort was to enter.

"But when Talia came to be a big girl and was looking out the window one day, she saw an old woman who was spinning pass by. Since she had never seen a distaff or a spindle and was greatly pleased by all that winding, she became so curious that she had the woman come up and, taking the distaff in her hand, she began to draw the thread. But then, by accident, a little piece of flax got under her fingernail and she fell dead to the ground.

"At the sight of this the old woman started running, and she's still jumping down those stairs. And when the hapless father heard of the accident that had occurred,

1 This is an early version of the "Sleeping Beauty" tale, which was followed subsequently by Charles Perrault's "The Sleeping Beauty in the Wood," with which it bears close resemblance, and Grimms' 50 [tale "Brier Rose"], which eliminates the whole second part and ends with the heroine waking up to her prince.

2 This is one of the few tales missing a moralizing introduction, which typically follows the description of the reactions of the listeners to the preceding tale. Although there is not one in the original edition of 1636 and its reprint in 1644, in subsequent editions a new paragraph is added, which Croce includes in his 1925 translation. It reads: "It has been seen again and again that, for the most part, cruelty serves as an executioner to he who exercises it, nor has it ever been seen that he who spits at the heavens does not get it back on his own face. And the other side of this coin, innocence, is a shield made of the wood of the fig tree on which every sword of malice is broken and leaves its tip, so that just when a poor man believes himself to be dead and buried he finds himself being reborn in flesh and bones, as you will hear in the tale that I am about to tap from the barrel of memory with the spigot of this tongue" (cit. Croce 498).

he paid for that pail of bitter wine with a barrel of tears and had her placed inside that same palace, which was in the country, seated on a velvet chair under a brocade canopy. Then he closed the doors and abandoned forever the palace that had been the cause of such great sorrow, so as to thoroughly erase every memory of this misfortune.

"But some time later a king who was out hunting lost his falcon, which after it escaped flew in a window of that house. When it didn't respond to his call the king knocked at the door, since he thought people lived there. After knocking for a long time he had a harvester's ladder brought, intending to scale the house himself to see what was inside. He climbed up and looked all over the place and, not finding a living soul, just stood there awhile like a mummy. Finally he arrived at the room where Talia sat, as if enchanted, and when he saw her he thought she was asleep. He called to her, but no matter what he did and how loud he yelled she did not wake up, and since her beauty had enflamed him, he carried her in his arms to a bed and picked the fruits of love. Then he left her in the bed and returned to his kingdom, where he did not remember what had happened for a long time.

"After nine months Talia unloaded a pair of babies, one a boy and the other a girl, who looked like two bejeweled necklaces. They were cared for by two fairies that had appeared in the palace, who would place them at their mother's teats; one day, when they were trying to suck but couldn't find the nipple, they grabbed her finger and sucked so long that the piece of flax came out. Talia felt like she was awakening up from a long sleep, and when she saw those jewels beside her she offered them her tit and held them as dear as her own life.

"And while she did not know what had happened to her and how it was that she was alone in that palace with two children by her side and people who brought her things to eat without her being able to see them, the king, who had remembered her, found an occasion to go hunting and came to see her. Finding her awake and in the company of two painted eggs of beauty, he was stunned with joy and told Talia who he was and what had happened. They made friends and a strong bond was established, and after staying several days with her he took his leave with the promise that he would return and take her away with him. He then went back to his kingdom, where he mentioned Talia and the children at every chance he got, so that when he was eating he had Talia in his mouth and also Sun and Moon, for those were the names he had given the children, and when he went to bed he called for the one and the other.

"The king's wife had already become a little suspicious after her husband's delay in returning from the hunt, and when she heard all this talk of Talia, Moon, and Sun she felt burned by something other than the sun. And so she called her secretary and said to him, 'Listen here, my boy: you're between Scylla and Charybdis,[1] the jamb and the door, the club and the prison bars. If you tell me who my husband is in love with I'll make you rich, and if you hide it from me I'll make sure you're found neither dead nor alive.' Her crony was on the one hand all shaken up by fear and on the other fleeced by interest, which is a blindfold on honor's eyes, a veil on the face of justice, and a crowbar on words given. He thus gave her bread for bread and wine for wine, at which the queen sent the secretary to visit Talia on the king's behalf and tell her that he wanted to see the children. Talia sent them to him with great joy, and that heart of Medea ordered the cook to slit their throats, make various little dishes and delicacies out of them, and then serve them to her poor husband. The cook, however, was of tender lung, and when he saw those two lovely golden apples he took pity on them and gave them to his wife to hide, instead preparing two goat kids in a hundred different sauces.

"The king came home, and the queen had the food served with great gusto. While the king was eating with great gusto, too, and exclaiming, 'Oh, on the life of Lanfusa,[2] this dish is so good! Oh, on the soul of my grandpa, this other one is so tasty!' she kept on saying, 'Eat up, for you're eating what is yours.' The king paid no attention to this refrain two or three times, but finally, when he heard the music keeping up, he answered, 'I know that what I'm eating is mine, since you didn't bring a thing with you to this house!' and he got up angrily and went out to the nearby countryside to unleash his anger.

"In the meantime the queen, not yet satisfied with what she had done, called the secretary back and had him summon Talia with the excuse that the king was waiting to see her. Talia came the instant she heard this, eager to find her light without realizing that only fire awaited her, and she appeared before the queen, who with a face like Nero's, livid with rage, said to her, 'May you be welcome, madam slut![3] So you're that fancy piece of trash, that weed with whom my husband takes his pleasure! So you're that bitch who makes my head spin like a top! Go on, you've reached purgatory, and I'm going to make you pay for the pain you've caused me!'

---

1 *Sciglia e Scariglia* (Neap.): "Scylla was a maiden transformed into a monster, with the head and body of a woman and the tail of a fish, who devoured six of Ulysses's companions (Homer, *Odyssey* 12). After she was killed by Hercules she was reborn in the sea god Forco, of whom she was daughter, and lay in ambush in the Strait of Messina. Carybdis, which also appears in the myth of the Argonauts, was the whirlpool situated on the other shore of the strait" (Rak 954).

2 "In chivalric epics, Ferrau's oath on his mother's head (see, for example, Ludovico Ariosto, *Orlando Furioso* I.30). Here it is used with the meaning of swearing on the life of a stranger whose fate is of no interest" (Rak 270).

3 *Troccola* (Neap.): from the Neapolitan *trocula*, a rattle or clapper, and so by association a chatterbox, busybody, or woman of little consideration (Penzer 2:131)....

"When Talia heard this she began to apologize, saying that it wasn't her fault and that the king had taken possession of her territory when she was under a sleeping spell. But the queen, who had no intention of listening to excuses, had a huge fire lit right there in the courtyard of the palace and then ordered that Talia be thrown onto it. Seeing that things had taken a bad turn, Talia fell down on her knees before the queen and begged her to at least give her the time to take off the clothes she was wearing. Not so much out of pity for the poor girl as to retrieve those gold-and pearl-embroidered clothes, the queen said, 'Get undressed; that I will allow you to do.' Talia began to undress, letting out a shriek with every piece of clothing she took off. And when she had taken off her dress, her skirt, and her jacket, and was about to take off her petticoat, she let out the last shriek while they dragged her off to supply the ashes for the laundry tub where Charon[1] washed his breeches.

"At that very moment the king ran in and, discovering this spectacle, demanded to know the whole story. He then asked about his children and heard his own wife, who reproached him with betraying her, tell him of how she had gotten him to devour them. When the hapless king heard this he fell prey to desperation and began to cry, 'So I was the werewolf that attacked my own little sheep! Alas, why didn't my veins recognize the springs of their own blood? O renegade Turk, what kind of a ferocious thing did you do? Just wait; you're going to end up as compost in a broccoli plot, and I won't be sending this face of a tyrant to the Colosseum[2] for her penance!' And as he was saying this he ordered that she be thrown into the same fire lit for Talia, together with the secretary who had been an instrument in the bitter game and a weaver of the wicked plot. He was intending to do the same with the cook who he thought had chopped up his children, but the cook threw himself at the king's feet and said, 'Actually, my lord, the service I performed for you would deserve a pension[3] other than a furnace full of coals, a subsidy other than a pole in the ass, an entertainment other than to blacken and shrivel in a fire, and a profit other than to mix the ashes of a cook with those of a queen! This is certainly not the great thanks that I expect for having saved your children in spite of that sack of dog bile, who wanted to kill them so that what was part of your body would return to that same body.'

1 In Greek and Roman mythology, the ferryman who transported the souls of the dead across the River Styx to Hades.

2 *Culiseo* (Neap.): The Colosseum, Rome's great amphitheater, was begun by Emperor Vespasian and finished by his son Titus in 90; according to Christian legend, it was the site of barbarous cruelty. Basile also puns on *culo* (ass).

3 *chiazza morta* (Neap.): A sort of military pension that had been instituted by the viceroy Pedro de Toledo, "which called for one place in each company of Spanish or Italian soldiers to be left empty in order to provide for the subsistence of three invalid soldiers. One was given the lodging of the 'absent' soldier, and the other two the salary" (Croce 76). This, as well as *aiuto de costa* (subsidy) and *trattenemiento* (entertainment), are terms of Spanish origin, relative to military pensions and other forms of assistance.

"When he heard those words the king was beside himself and thought he was dreaming, nor could he believe his own ears. He finally turned to the cook and said, 'If it is true that you saved my children, you may rest assured that I will free you from turning the spit and that I will place you in the kitchen of this heart, where you can turn my desires as you please and claim for yourself a prize so great that you will consider yourself happy to be in this world!' While the king was speaking these words the cook's wife, who saw the state of need her husband was in, brought Moon and Sun before their father. And, playing the game of three with his wife and children, he sent out a whirlwind of kisses first to the one and then to the other, and when he had given the cook a large reward and named him his gentleman-in-waiting he took Talia for his wife. She enjoyed a long life with her husband and children, and recognized after all her ordeals that for those who are lucky, *good rains down even when they are sleeping.*"

7. Marie-Jeanne Lhéritier de Villandon, *Oeuvres meslées* (1696; *translated by Robert Samber, 1729*[1])

Lhéritier was celebrated in her lifetime as a writer and also because of her connection to her uncle, Charles Perrault, author of the famed Mother Goose tales. In fact, the first English translation of "The Discreet Princess," reproduced here, was included in the volume of Perrault translations published by Robert Samber in 1729. Highly educated for her time and proficient in a number of literary genres, Lhéritier was one of a select number of women writers inducted into literary academies in the seventeenth century: L'Académie des jeux floraux de Toulouse *(1696) and* La Academia des Ricovrati de Padoua *(1697). "The Discreet Princess" has come down to us as one her of most engaging and politically charged tales. She has her heroine outwit the craftiest man in the land, cross-dress, and pass herself off as a doctor. Widely acclaimed in her day for her piety, Lhéritier also railed in her literature against courtly habits that disempowered or allowed the mistreatment of women. This story (among others in her corpus) demonstrates her disdain for rogue noblemen and their abuse of vulnerable ladies. She also suggests a solution: educate women. Her heroine, Finetta, manifests extraordinary talents of the mind and the body. While she is not the only heroine in the French fairy-tale corpus to be so endowed, she is particularly cunning and ruthless in her vengeance.*

"The Discreet Princess" has the unique characteristic of referring frequently to its dedicatee, French fairy-tale author Henriette-Julie de Murat. Several times, the narrator directly addresses her to comment on the plot. Samber changed Lhéritier's dedicatee to Lady Mary Wortley Montagu, so that it is to her "Ladyship" that Samber's narrator speaks.

1 [Source: Robert Samber, *Histories or Tales of Past Times* (London: J. Pote, 1729): 137–214.]

Mary Montagu famously recorded her life as an ambassador's wife in Turkey through letters that are now hailed as an early example of travel narrative and a rare first-hand account of the Middle East as seen through a woman's experience.

THE DISCREET PRINCESS; OR THE ADVENTURES OF FINETTA. A NOVEL

In the time of the first Crusades, a certain King in Europe, where his kingdom was I cannot tell, resolved to make war against the Infidels in the Holy Land. Before he undertook so long a journey, he put his kingdom into such good order, and committed the care of the regency to so able a minister, that he was intirely [sic] easy upon that account.

What most disquieted this Prince, was the care of his family. His queen had not long been dead. She left him no son, but he saw himself father of three young princesses, all marriageable. My chronicle does not inform me what were their true names. I only know, that as in those happy times, the honest simplicity of the people gave very freely surnames to eminent persons, according to their good and bad Qualities; the eldest of these Princesses they called *Drone-illa*; the second they called *Babillarde*, which signifies, in modern Phrase, a perpetual talker; and the third *Finetta*; names which had all of them just relation to the characters of these three sisters.

Never was anything in the World known as indolent and unactive as *Drone-illa*. She waked every day at one o'clock in the afternoon: she was dragged along to church in the same condition, as when she got out of her bed; her night-clothes all tumbled, her gown loose, no girdle, and very often one slipper of one sort, and one of another. They used to rectify this mistake before night; but they could never prevail upon this Princess to go any otherwise than in slippers: it was an insupportable Fatigue to put on shoes. As soon as she had dined, she sat down to her *Toilette*, where she continued till the evening. The rest of her time, till midnight, she employed at play, and eating her supper: after that, they were almost as long in pulling off her clothes, as they had been in putting them on; she could never be persuaded to go to bed till it was broad Day.

Babillarde led quite another sort of Life; this Princess was very brisk and active, and employed very little time about her person; but she had such a strange itching to talk, that from the very moment she waked, till the time she went to sleep, her mouth never was quiet. She knew the history of everything, ill managements, tender compacts, the gallantries and intrigues not only of the whole Court, but of the meanest Cits.[1] She kept a register of all those wives who pinched their families

1 [Short for "citizen" and used for townsfolk/tradesmen as opposed to countryman/gentlemen in the eighteenth century.]

at home, to appear the finer abroad, and was exactly informed what gained such a Countess's woman, and such a Marquis's Valet de Chambre. The better to be instructed in all these little things, she gave audience to her nurse and mantua-maker with greater pleasure, than she would to an Ambassador and at last, her head could entertain nothing but these fine stories, with which it was so fluffed, that she knew every thing, from the King, her father, down to the footmen: for provided she could but talk, she did not care what was the subject. This terrible itch of talking, produced yet another bad effect upon this Princess: for notwithstanding her great rank, her too familiar airs gave encouragement to the pert sparks of the Court to talk of love to her. She heard their speeches without any ceremony, purely to have the pleasure of answering them; for from morning till night, whatever it might cost her, she must either hear others tattle, or tattle herself. *Babillarde* no more than her eldest Sister, ever employed herself in thinking, reflecting or reading. She never troubled herself about domestick affairs, or the amusements of her spindle or needle: for young ladies in those days were not above sewing and spinning. In short, these two sisters lived in a perfect idleness, in relation both to mind and body.

The youngest three of these Princesses was of a quite different character, she was continually employed as well about her mind as person: She was of surprising vivacity, and she applied it to good uses. She danced, sang and played upon musick to perfection, finished with wonderful address and skill all those little works of the hand, which generally amuse Persons of her sex. She put the King's household into exact regulation and order, and by her care and vigilance, hindered the pilferings of the lower officers: for in those days princes were cheated by those of their household.

These talents were not bounded here; she had a great deal of judgment, and such a wonderful presence of mind, that she immediately found the means of extricating herself out of the greatest difficulties. This young Princess had, by her penetration, discovered a dangerous snare a perfidious Ambassador had laid for the King her father, in a Treaty which that prince was going to sign. To punish the treachery of this Ambassador and his Master, the King altered the article of the Treaty, and by wording it in the terms his daughter dictated to him, he in his turn deceived the deceiver himself. The young Princess moreover discovered a vile piece of roguery that a certain Minister had a mind to play the King; and by the advice she gave her father, he so managed it, that the infidelity of that wretch fell upon his own head. The Princess gave, on several other occasions, such marks of her penetration and fine genius that the people on that account gave her the surname of *Finetta*.

The King loved her far above his other daughters, and depended so much upon her good sense, that if he had had no other child but her, he would have begun his journey with no manner of uneasiness; but he distrusted so much the conduct of his other daughters, that he relied entirely upon that of *Finetta*. And so, to be assured of the steps his family might take in his absence, as he was of those of his subjects, he took such measures as I am now going to relate.

I make no doubt, Madam, but you have heard a hundred times of the wonderful power of Fairies. The King I speak of, being a great friend of one of these able women, went to her, and acquainted her with the uneasiness he was in about his daughters. It is not, said he, that the two eldest, whom I am so uneasy about, have ever done the least thing contrary to their duty: but they have so little wit and judgment, are so imprudent, and live so unemployed, that I fear in my absence, to amuse themselves, they will engage in some foolish intrigue or other. As for *Finetta* I am secure of her virtue: however, I shall treat her as her sisters, to make no distinction for which reason, sage Fairy, I desire you to make three distaffs of glass for my daughters, to be made with that artfulness, that each of them may not fail to break, as soon as she, to whom it belongs, does anything against her honour.

As this Fairy was very able and expert, she gave that Prince three enchanted distaffs, which were so wrought, as to answer his design: but he was not content with this precaution; he put the Princesses into a very high tower, that was built in a very solitary and desert place. The King told his daughters, that he commanded them to take up their residence in that tower during his absence, and forbad them letting any person whatsoever into it. He took from them all their officers and servants of both sexes and after having presented them with the enchanted distaffs, the qualities of which he told them, he kissed the Princesses, locked the doors of the tower, of which he took himself the keys, and departed.

You will perhaps believe, Madam, that these Princesses were now in danger of dying with hunger: quite the contrary. There was care taken to fix a pully to one of the windows of the tower: there ran a rope through it, to which the Princesses tied a basket, which they let down every day. In this basket was put every day provisions, which when they had drawn up, they retired with the rope into their apartments.

Drone-illa and *Babillarde* led such a life of solitude, as filled them with despair, they fretted themselves to such a degree, as was beyond expression: but they were forced to have patience; for their distaffs were represented to them so terrible, that they were afraid the least step, though never is little awry or equivocal, might break them.

As for *Finetta* she was not in the least out of humour: her spindle, needle, and musick furnished her with Efficient amusement and besides this, by order of the minister that then governed the state, there was care taken to put into their basket letters, which informed the Princesses of everything that was done or transacted within and without the kingdom. The King granted it should be so, and the minister, to make his Court to the Princesses, did not fail of being very exact as to this article. *Finetta* read all this news with a great deal of attention, and diverted herself with it: but as for her two sisters, they took no manner of notice of it; they said, they were too much out of humour to amuse themselves with such trifles, they ought to have cards at least to divert their melancholy, during their father's absence.

Thus they past their time in great disquiet, murmurring continueally against their hard fortune; and I suppose they did not fail saying, That *it is much better to be born happy than to be born the son of a King*: they were frequently at the windows of the tower, to see at least what passed in the country. One day as *Finetta* was employed in her chamber about some pretty work, her sisters, who were at the window, saw at the foot of the tower a poor woman cloathed in rags and tatters, who cried out to them in a sorrowful tone, and in a very moving manner complained to them of her misery. She begged them, with her hands joined together, that they would let her come into the castle, telling them, that she was a most unfortunate and wretched stranger, that knew how to do a thousand things, and would serve them with the utmost fidelity. Upon this, the Princesses bethought themselves of their father's orders, not to let anyone come into the tower; but *Drone-illa* was so weary of serving herself, and *Babillarde* was so uneasy at having no body to talk to but her sisters, that the earnest desire that one had to be dressed piecemeal and by degrees, and the eagerness of the other to have somebody else to chat with, made them resolve to let this stranger in.

Do you think, said *Babillarde* to her sister, that the King's order extends to this poor wretch? I believe we may take her in without any consequence. You may do, sister, said *Drone-illa*, what you please. *Babillarde*, who only waited her consent, immediately let down the basket, the poor woman got into it, and the Princesses drew her up by help of the pully. When they viewed this woman more attentively, the horrible nastiness of her clothes turned their stomach: they would have given her others; but she told them she would change them the next day but at present, she would think upon nothing but her work. She was speaking these words, when *Finetta* came into the chamber: this Princess was strangely surprized to see this unknown creature with her sisters, who told her the reasons which had induced them to draw her up; but *Finetta*, who saw that all was over, dissembled her uneasiness at this juncture.

In the mean time this new servant of these Princesses took a hundred turns about the castle, under pretence of doing her work, but in reality to observe how everything was disposed in it; however, and I doubt not, Madam, but you will think so too, this pretended beggar-woman was as dangerous in this castle, as Count Ory was in the nunnery, where he entered, being disguised like a fugitive Abbess. To keep your Ladyship no longer in suspense, I shall tell you, Madam, that this creature in ragged clothes was the son of a powerful king, who was one of the most artful and designing persons of his time, govern'd entirely the king his father, and indeed that required not much address: for that Prince was of so sweet and easy a character, that he had the surname given him of *Moult-benign*, and the Prince, who always acted with artifice and cunning, the people surnamed *Riche-en-cautelle* but in shortness *Riche-cautelle*.

He had a younger brother, who was as full of good qualities as he was of bad: however, notwithstanding their different tempers, there was so strict an union between these two princes, that everybody was surprized at it. Besides the good qualities which the youngest prince was master of, the beauty of his face and the gracefulness of his person was so remarkable, that everybody called him *Bel-a-voir*. It was *Riche-cautelle,* who had put the ambassador of the king his father, upon that wicked turn in the Treaty which was frustrated by the address of *Finetta,* and fell upon themselves. *Riche-cautelle* who never had before that time any love for the King the Princesses' father, since then entertained for him the utmost aversion; so that when he was informed of the precautions which that Prince had taken in relation to his daughters, he took in himself a pernicious pleasure, in hoping to deceive the prudence of so suspicious a father: and accordingly *Riche-cautelle* obtained leave of the King his father, to travel upon some invented pretence, and took such measures as gained him entrance into the tower where these Princesses were confined, as you have heard.

In examining the castle, this Prince observed that it was very easy for the princesses to call out to passengers, and he concluded, that it was best for him to continue in his disguise all day, because they could, if they had a mind to it, call out to people, and chastise him for his rash enterprise. He remained then all day long in his rags, and counterfeited a professed beggar-woman; but at night, after the Princesses had supped, *Riche-cautelle* threw off his rags, and shewed himself dressed like a Cavalier in rich apparel, all covered with gold and diamonds. The poor Princesses were so much frightened at this sight, that they began to fly away with the utmost precipitation. *Finetta* and *Babillarde,* who were very nimble, soon got to their chambers; but *Drone-illa* who could scarce walk, was stopt by the Prince.

He immediately threw himself at her feet, declaring who he was, and told her, that the reputation of her beauty and her picture, had obliged him to leave a delightful court, to come and offer her his faith and vows. *Drone-illa* was so much at a loss, that she could not answer the Prince, who was still upon his knees, one word: but as by entertaining her with a thousand soft endearing expressions, and making as many protestations, he conjured her to receive him that very moment for her husband: her natural softness not suffering her to contend, she told *Riche-cautelle* in a very indolent and droning tone, that she believed him sincere, and accepted of his fidelity; they observed no greater formalities than those which are the conclusion of marriage. But immediately she lost her distaff; for it broke into a thousand pieces.

Babillarde and *Finetta* in the meanwhile, were in strange inquietudes, they had gotten separately into their apartments, and locked themselves in. These apartments were at a great distance one from another, and as each of these Princesses were ignorant of each other's fate, they did not sleep one wink all night long. The next morning the pernicious Prince led *Drone-illa* into a ground apartment, which was at the end of the garden, where this Princess signified the uneasiness she was in for her sisters, though she dared not see them, for fear they should blame her for her marriage. The Prince told her, he would undertake they should approve of it; and after some discourse, went out, and locked *Drone-illa* in before she could perceive it, and then looked about carefully to find out the Princesses. It was some time before he could discover in what chambers they had secured themselves: but at last, the strong inclination which *Babillarde* had to speak, causing this Princess to talk and bewail her cruel destiny to herself: the Prince heard her; and coming up to the door, saw her through the keyhole.

Riche-cautelle spoke to her through the door, and told her what he had told her sister, which was, that it was only to offer her his faith and heart, which had caused him to undertake the enterprise of entering the tower: he praised, not without excessive exaggeration, her wit and beauty; and *Babillarde* who was fully persuaded in herself, that she had the utmost merit, was foolish enough to believe every syllable that the Prince told her. She answered him with a torrent of words, which were not too disobliging. It is certain this Princess must have had a strange fury of speech, to acquit herself as she did; for she was in a terrible weakness, having not eaten anything all day, by reason she had nothing proper in her chamber. As she was extremely lazy, and had no manner of thought of anything but talking, she had not the least foresight: when she had occasion for anything, she had recourse to *Finetta*; and this aimable Princess, who was as laborious and provident as her sisters were the contrary, had always in her chamber, biskets, macaroons, and dried and wet sweetmeats of all sorts, and of her own making. *Babillarde,* who had not the like advantage, finding herself at that time very much pressed with hunger and the protestations which the Prince made on the other side of the door, opened it at last to that seducer, when he proved himself a perfect Comedian; for he had well studied his part.

After this, they went both of them out of this apartment, and came into the office of the castle, where they found all sorts of refreshments; for the basket furnished the Princess every day with more than enough. *Babillarde* could not help being still in pain for her sisters, and what might become of them; but it came into her head, I know not upon what foundation, that they were both of them without doubt, locked up in *Finetta*'s chamber, where they wanted for nothing. *Riche-cautelle* used all the arguments he could to confirm her in this opinion, and told her, that they would go and find out the Princesses towards the evening. She was not of his mind, but said, they should go and see after them as soon as they had done eating.

In short, the Prince and Princess fell both of them to very heartily; and when they had done, *Riche-cautelle* desired to see the best apartment of the castle: he gave his hand to the Princess, who led him thither, and when he was there, he began to exaggerate the tender Passion he had for her, and the advantages she would have in marrying him. He told her, as he had done her sister *Drone-illa,* that she ought to accept of his faith that very moment; because if she should see her sisters before she had taken him for her husband, they would not fail to oppose it; and being, without contradiction, one of the most powerful of the neighbouring Princes, he would most probably seem to them a person fitter for her eldest sister than her, who would never consent to a match she herself might desire with all imaginable ardour. *Babillarde,* after a great deal of discourse, which signified nothing, was as extravagant as her sister had been; she accepted the Prince for her husband, and never thought of the effects of her glass distaff, till after it was broken in pieces.

Towards evening, *Babillarde* returned to her chamber with the Prince; and the first thing she cast her eyes upon, was the glass distaff all broken to bits; she was very much troubled at this sight: the Prince asked her the reason of her uneasiness: as her passion for talking made her uncapable of holding her tongue, she very foolishly told *Riche-cautelle* the mystery of the distaff, at which this Prince was wickedly overjoyed, since the father of these Princesses would by this means be intirely convinced of the bad conduct of his daughters.

Babillarde in the mean time was no longer in the humour of going to look for her sisters, she had reason to fear they would not approve of her conduct: but Prince offered himself to do this Office, and told her, he should not want the means to perswade [sic] them to approve of it. After this assurance, the Princess, who had not slept all night, began to slumber; and while she slept, *Riche-cautelle* turned the key upon her, as he had done before to *Drone-illa.*

Is it not true, Madam, that this *Riche-cautelle* was a consummate villain, and these two Princesses loose and imprudent persons? I am very angry with such kind of people, and doubt not but you are so too in a high degree: but do not be uneasy, they will all be treated as they deserve, and no one triumph, but the sage and courageous *Finetta.*

When this perfidious Prince had locked up *Babillarde,* he went into all the rooms of the castle, one after another; and as he found them all open but one, which was fastened in the inside, he concluded for certain, that there it was where *Finetta* had retired. As he had composed a string of compliments, he went to retail out at *Finetta*'s door, the same things he had made use of to her sisters: but this Princess, who was not a *Dupe* as her sisters, heard him a long while, without giving him any answer. At last, finding that he knew she was in that room, she told him, if it was true that he had so strong and sincere a passion for her, as he would perswade [sic] her, she desired he would go down into the garden, and shut the door upon him, and after that she would talk to him as much as he pleased out of the window of that apartment which bore upon the garden.

Riche-cautelle would not accept of this; and as the Princess always resolutely persisted in not opening the door, this wicked Prince, mad with impatience, went and got a billet, and broke it open. He found *Finetta* armed with a great hammer, which had been accidentally left in a wardrobe near her chamber. Emotion raised *Finetta's* complexion, and tho' her eyes sparkled with rage, she appeared to *Riche-cautelle* of an inchanting beauty. He would have cast himself at her feet: but she said to him boldly, as she retired, Prince, if you approach me, this hammer sends you into the other world. What! beautiful Princess, cried out *Riche-cautelle* in his hypocritical tone, does the love I have for you inspire you with such cruel hate? He began to preach to her, but at one end of the room, (the Princess being at the other) of the violent ardour which the reputation of her beauty and wonderful wit had inspired him with. He added, that the only motive he had to put on such disguise, was only with respect to offer her his hand and heart: and told her, that she ought to pardon, on account of the violence of his passion, his boldness in breaking open her door. He ended, by endeavouring to persuade her, as he had her sisters, that it was her interest to receive him for her husband as soon as possible. He told her, moreover, he did not know where her sisters were retired; because he was not in any pain about them, having his thoughts wholly fixed upon her. The *adroite* Princess feigning herself entirely pacified, told him, that she must find out her sisters, and after that, they would take their measures all together: but *Riche-cautelle* answered, that he could by no means resolve upon that, till she had consented to marry him; because her sisters would not fail to oppose the match, on account of their right of eldership.

Finetta, who with good reason distrusted this Prince, found her suspicions redouble by this answer: she trembled to think what might have happened to her sisters, and resolved to revenge them with the lame stroke which might make her avoid a misfortune, like what she judged had befallen them. This young Princess then told *Riche-cautelle,* that she readily consented to marry him; but she was fully persuaded, that marriages which were made at night, were always unhappy; and therefore desired he would defer the ceremony of plighting to each other their mutual faith, till the next morning. She added, he might be assured she would not mention a syllable of all this to the Princesses her sisters, and begged him to give her only a little time to say her prayers; that afterwards she would bring him into an apartment, where he should have a very good bed, and then she would return to her own room till the morrow morning.

Riche-cautelle, who was not ove[r] and above courageous, seeing *Finetta* always with the hammer in her hand, which she played with like a fan, *Riche-cautelle,* I say, consented to what the Princess desired, and went away, to give her some time to meditate. He was no sooner gone, but *Finetta* hasted to make a bed over the hole of a sink in one of the rooms of the castle. This room was as handsome as any of the rest; but they cast into the hole of that sink, which was very large, all the ordures of the castle. *Finetta* put over the hole two weak sticks across, then very handsomely made the bed upon them and immediately returned to her chamber. A moment after came *Riche-cautelle* and the Princess brought him into the room where she had made his bed, and retired. The Prince, without undressing threw himself hastily upon the bed, and his weight having all at once broken the little sticks, he fell down to the bottom of the sink without being able to stop himself, breaking his head all round, and raising upon it a hundred bunches. The fall of the Prince made a great noise in the Pipe as it fell; and besides, being not far from *Finetta*'s chamber, she soon knew her artifice had had the promised success, and she felt a secret joy, which was extremely agreeable to her; it was impossible to describe the pleasure, when she heard him muttering in the sink. He very well deserved that punishment, and the Princess had reason to be pleased with it.

But her joy was not so great, as to make her forget her sisters; her chief care was to see after them. It was no hard matter to find out *Babillarde*. *Riche-cautelle*, after having double-locked that Princess into her chamber, had left the key in the door: *Finetta* went hastily in; and the noise she made awaked her sister in a start, who was in a very great confusion, when she saw her. *Finetta* related to her after what manner she had gotten rid of the wicked Prince who would have offered her violence, *Babillarde* was thunderstruck at this news; for in spite of her talkativeness she had so little sense, that she ridiculously believed every word *Riche-cautelle* had told her: there are such *Dupes* as she in the world. That Princess dissembling the excess of her sorrow, went out of her chamber with *Finetta* to look after *Drone-illa*. They went into all the rooms of the castle, but could not find her. At last, *Finetta* bethought herself, that she might be in the apartment of the garden, where indeed they found her half dead with despair and weakness; for she had eaten nothing all the day. The Princesses gave her all necessary assistance, after which they told each other their adventures, which affected *Drone-illa* and *Babillarde* with mortal sorrow: after this, they went all three to bed.

In the mean time *Riche-cautelle* passed the night very uneasily, and when it was day, he was not one jot the better. This Prince was in such a place, the utmost horror of which was, he could not see; because not the least glimpse of light could enter. However, at last, with a great deal of painful struggling, he came to the end of the drain, which ran into a river at a great distance from the castle. He found means to make the people who were fishing in the river hear him, by whom he was drawn out in such a pickle, as raised compassion in those good people.

He ordered himself to be carried to his father's court, to get cured, and this disgrace made him take such a strong hatred and aversion to *Finetta*, that he thought less of his cure than revenge.

That Princess passed her time but very sadly; honour was a thousend times more dear to her than life, and the shameful weakness of her sisters had thrown her into so great a despair, that she had much difficulty to get the better of it. At the same time, the ill state of health of those two Princesses, which was the consequences of their unworthy marriages, put moreover *Finetta*'s constancy to the proof. *Riche-cautelle,* who had a long while been an able cheat, summoned, since this adventure, all his wits, to make himself in the highest degree a tricking villain; neither the sink, nor the bruises, gave him so much vexation, as the spite he was in of having been outwitted. He surmised the effects of his two marriages; and to tempt the ailing Princesses, he caused to be carried under the windows of the castle great tubs full of trees, all laden with fine fruit. *Drone-illa* and *Babillarde* who were often at the windows, could not but see the fruit: immediately they had a violent desire to eat of it, and they pestered *Finetta* to go down in the basket to gather some. The complaisance of that Princess was so great, and being willing to oblige her sisters, she did as they desired her, and brought up the fruit, which they devoured with the utmost greediness.

The next day there appeared fruits of another kind. This was a fresh temptation for the Princesses, and a fresh instance of *Finetta*'s complaisance, and obliging temper. But immediately *Riche-cautelle*'s officers, who were in ambush, and had failed of their design the first time, were not wanting to complete it the second: They seized upon *Finetta* and carried her off in the sight of her sisters, who tore their hair for anguish and despair.

Riche-cautelle's guards executed so well their master's orders that they brought *Finetta* to a country house, where the Prince had retired for the recovery of his health. As he was transported with fury against this Princess, he said to her a hundred brutish things, which she answered always with a firmness and grandeur of soul, worthy a Heroine as she was. At last, after having kept her for some time prisoner, he had her brought to the top of a mountain extremely high, whither he followed immediately after. Here it was that he told her, they were going to put her to death, and after such a manner as would sufficiently revenge all the injuries she had done him. Then that Prince very barbarously shewed *Finetta* a barrel stuck in the inside all round with penknives, razors, and hooked nails, and told her, that in order to give her the punishment she deserved, they were going to put her into that vessel, and roll her down from the top of the mountain into the valley. Though *Finetta* was no *Roman,* she was no more afraid of the punishment than *Regulus* heretofore was at the sight of the like destiny: this young Princess kept up all her firmness, and presence of mind; *Riche-cautelle,* instead of admiring her heroick character, grew more enraged against her than ever, and resolved to hasten her death; and to that end bent himself down to look into the barrel, which was to be the instrument of his vengeance, to examine if it was well provided with all its murdering weapons.

Finetta, who saw her persecutor very attentive in looking into the barrel, lost no time, but very dexterously pushed him into it, and rolled it down the mountain, without giving the Prince any time to know where he was. After this, she ran away, and the Prince's officers, who had seen, with extreme grief, after what cruel manner this aimable Princess had treated their master, had not the presence of mind to stop her; besides, they were so much frightened at what happened to *Riche-cautelle,* that they thought of nothing else but stopping the barrel: but their endeavours were all in vain, he roll'd down to the bottom of the mountain, where they took him out all over wounded in a thousand places.

This accident of *Riche-cautelle* threw King *Moult-benin* and Prince *Bel-a-voir* into the utmost despair; but as for the people, they were not at all concern'd, *Riche-cautelle* was very much hated, and they were even astonished to think, that the young Prince, who had such noble and generous sentiments, could love this unworthy elder brother. But such was the good nature of this Prince, that he was very much attached to all that were of the family, and *Riche-cautelle* always had the address to shew him such tender marks of affection, that this generous prince could never pardon himself in not answering them with interest. *Bel-a-voir* was then touched with excessive grief at the wounds of his brother; and he tried all means to have him perfectly cured; but notwithstanding all the care that everybody took of him, nothing could do *Riche-cautelle* any good. On the contrary, his wounds seemed every day to grow worse, and prognosticate he would linger on in a great deal of misery and pain.

Finetta, after having disengaged herself from this terrible danger, had now got very happily to the castle, where she had left her sisters, and where it was not long before she had new troubles to encounter with. The two Princesses were brought to bed each of them of a son; at which *Finetta* was very much perplexed. However, the courage of this Princess did not abate: The desire she had to conceal the shame of her sisters, made her resolve to expose herself once more, though she very well knew the danger. To bring about her design, she took all the measures prudence could suggest. She disguised herself in man's clothes, put the children of her sisters into boxes, in which she had bored little holes over against the mouths of these little infants, that they might breathe: She got on horseback, and took along with her these boxes, and some others; and in this equipage, arrived at the capital city of King *Moult-benin,* where *Riche-cautelle* was.

As soon as *Finetta* came into the city, she was told after what noble manner *Bel-a-voir* paid for the medicines that were given his brother, which had brought to court all the Mountebanks of *Europe*: for at that time there were a great many adventurers without business or capacity, who gave themselves out for wonderful proficients, having received the gift from God to cure all manner of distempers. These people, whose whole science consists in nothing but to cheat impudently, found always a great deal of credit among the people; they knew how to impose upon them by their extraordinary exteriour, and by the odd names they went by. These kinds of doctors never stay in the place of their nativity and the prerogative of coming from a long way off often, with the vulgar, supplies the place of merit.

The ingenious Princess, who knew all this, took a name that was entirely strange to that kingdom, which was *Sanatio*. Then she gave it out, that the *Chevalier Sanatio* was come to town with wonderful secrets, to cure all sorts of wounds the most dangerous and inveterate. *Bel-a-voir* sent immediately for this pretended knight. *Finetta* came, made the best empirick[1] in the world, threw out five or six terms of art, with a Cavalier air; nothing was wanting. This Princess was surprised at the good mien, and agreeable carriage of *Bel-a-voir*; and after having discoursed some time with this Prince, about the wounds of *Riche-cautelle* she told him she would go and fetch a bottle of incomparable water, and in the meanwhile leave two boxes she had brought thither, which contained some excellent ointments, very proper for the wounded Prince.

Upon saying this, the pretended physician went out, and came no more. They were very impatient at his staying so long. At last, as they were going to send to him to hasten his coming, they heard the cryings of young children in Prince *Riche-cautelle*'s chamber. This surprised everybody: for there was no manner of appearance of any children: some listened attentively, and they found that these cries came from the doctor's boxes.

It was in reality *Finetta*'s little nephews. This Princess had given them a great deal to eat before she came to the palace; but as they had been there now a long time, they wanted some more, and explained their necessities, by singing this doleful tune. They opened the boxes, and were very much surprized to find in them actually two little babes very pretty. *Riche-cautelle* made no doubt immediately, but that this was a new trick of *Finetta*. He entertained such a fury against her, as was not to be expressed; and his pains increased to such a degree, that they concluded he must of necessity die very soon.

Bel-a-voir was penetrated with the most lively sorrow, but *Riche-cautelle* perfidious to his last moment, resolved to abuse the tenderness of his brother. You have always loved me, Prince, said he, and you lament your loss of me; I can have no greater proofs of your love, in relation to my life: I am dying, but if ever I have been dear to you, grant this one thing, I beg of you, which I am going to ask of you.

Bel-a-voir, who, in the condition he saw his brother in, found himself capable of refusing him nothing, promised him with the most terrible oaths, to grant him whatever he should desire. As soon as *Riche-cautelle* heard these oaths, he said to his brother, embracing him, I die contented, brother, since I am revenged; for that which I beg

1 [Early modern term for physicians who based their ideas on observation and experience rather than inherited wisdom. It could also mean quack. Both definitions seem operative here.]

of you to do for me, is to ask *Finetta* in marriage, as soon as I am dead; you will undoubtedly obtain this wicked Princess; and the moment she shall be in your power, plunge your poniard into her heart. *Bel-a-voir* trembled with horror at these words; he repented the imprudence of his oaths; but it was not now the time to unsay them; and he had no mind his brother should take notice of his repentance, who expired soon after. King *Moult-benin* was very sensibly troubled at his death, but the people, far from regretting *Riche-cautelle,* were extremely glad, that his death secured the succession of the crown to *Bel-a-voir,* whose merit was dear to all the world.

Finetta, who had once more happily returned to her sisters, heard soon after of the death of *Riche-cautelle* and some time after that, news came to the three Princesses, that the King their father was come home. This Prince came in a hurry to the tower; and his first care was, to ask to see the glass distaffs. *Drone-illa* went and brought that which belonged to *Finetta,* and shewed it to the King, then making a very low curtesy carried it back again to the place whence she had taken it. *Babillarde* did so too; and *Finetta* in her turn brought her distaff: but the King, who was very suspicious, had a mind to see them all three together; no one could shew hers but *Finetta* and the King fell into such a rage against his two eldest daughters, that he sent them that moment away to the Fairy who had given him the distaffs, desiring her to keep them with her as long as they lived, and punish them according to their deserts.

As a beginning of their punishment, the Fairy led these two Princesses into a gallery of her enchanted castle, where she had caused to be painted the history of an infinite number of illustrious women, who made themselves famous by their virtue and laborious life. By the wonderful effect of Fairy art, all these figures moved, and were in action from morning till night: there was seen everywhere trophies and devises to the honour of these virtuous ladies; and it was no light mortification for the two sisters, to compare the triumph of these heroines with the despicable situation, which their unhappy imprudence had reduced them to. As an addition to their Chagrin, the Fairy told them, with a great deal of gravity, that if they had been as well employed as those whom they saw in the picture, they had not fallen into the unworthy errors which ruined them; but that *Idleness was the mother of all vice* and the source of all their misfortunes. The Fairy added, that in order to hinder them from falling into the like misfortunes, she would give them thorough employment; and indeed she obliged the Princesses to employ themselves in the coarsest and meanest of work and without having any regard to their complexion, she sent them to gather peas in the garden, and pull up the weeds. *Drone-illa* could not help falling into despair, at leading a life that was so little conformable to her inclinations, and died with fatigue and vexation. *Babillarde,* who some time after found means to make her escape by night out of the Fairy's castle, broke her skull against a tree, and died in the arms of some country people.

Finetta's good nature made her very sensibly grieve for the sad destiny of her sisters, and in the midst of these troubles, she was informed that Prince *Bel-a-voir* had asked her of the King her father in marriage, who had consented to it, without giving her any notice of it: for in those days the inclination of parties was the least thing they considered in marriage. *Finetta* trembled at this news; she had reason to fear lest the hatred which *Riche-cautelle* had for her, might infect the heart of a brother who was so dear to him: and she had apprehensions that this young Prince only married her, to make her a sacrifice to his brother. Full of these disquiets the Princess went to consult the sage Fairy, who esteemed her as much as she despised *Drone-illa* and *Babillarde*.

The Fairy would reveal nothing to the Princess, she only said to her, Princess, you are sage and prudent, you would not hitherto have taken such just measures for your conduct, had you not always born in mind, that *Distrust is the mother of security*. Continue to think earnestly on the importance of this maxim, and you will come to be happy, without the assistance of my art. *Finetta* having not been able to get any further light out of the Fairy, returned to the Palace in extreme agitation.

Some days after, this Princess was married by an ambassador in the name of Prince *Bel-a-voir*, and she let out to go to her spouse in a magnificent equipage: she made in the same manner her entries into the two principal frontier towns of King *Moult-benin* and in the third she found *Bel-a-voir*, who was come to meet her, by order of his father. Everybody was surprised to see the sadness of this Prince at the approach of a marriage, for which he had shewn so great a desire: the king himself was forced to interpose, and sent him, contrary to his inclination, to meet the Princess.

When *Bel-a-voir* saw her, he was struck with her charms, he made her his compliments, but in so confused a manner that the two courts, who knew how much wit and gallantry this Prince was master of, believed he was so sensibly touched, that through the force of love he had lost his presence of mind. The whole town shouted for joy, and there were everywhere concerts of music and bonfires. In short, after a magnificent supper they were for conducting them to their apartments.

Finetta, who was always thinking of the maxim which the Fairy had revived in her mind, had her design in her head. This Princess had gained one of the women, who had the key of the closet that belonged to the apartment which was designed for her: and she had privately given orders to that woman to carry into the closet some straw, a bladder, sheep's blood, and the guts of some of those animals that had been dress'd for supper. The Princess, on some pretence, went into this closet, and made an Image of the straw, into which she put the guts, and the bladder full of blood: after that, she dress'd it up in women's night-clothes. When *Finetta* had finished this little puppet, she returned to her company: and some time after, they conducted the Princess and her spouse to their apartment. When they had allowed as much time at the *Toilette* as was necessary, the ladies of honour took away the Flambeaux [candles] and retired. *Finetta* immediately threw the Image of straw upon the bed, and went and hid herself in one of the corners of the chamber.

The Prince, after having sighed three or four times very loud, drew his sword, and ran it through the body of the pretended *Finetta*: at the same instant he felt the blood trickle all about, and the woman of straw without motion. What have I done, cried *Bel-a-voir*; what! after so many cruel conflicts! after having so much weighed with myself if I should keep my oaths at the expence of a crime! have I taken away the life of a charming Princess I was born to love! her charms ravished me the moment I saw her, and yet I had not the power to free myself from an oath which a brother, possessed with a fury, had exacted from me by an unworthy surprise! Ah! heavens! could anyone so much as dream to punish a woman for having too much virtue! Well! *Riche-cautelle* I have satisfied thy unjust vengeance, but now, I will revenge *Finetta* in her turn by my death. Yes, beautiful Princess, my sword shall—. By these words the Princess, who understood that the Prince, who in his transport had dropt his sword, was feeling for it, in order to thrust it through his body, was resolved he should not be guilty of such a folly, and therefore cried out, My Prince, I am not dead, the goodness of your heart made me devine your repentance, and by an innocent cheat I have hinder'd you from committing the worst of Crimes.

Upon which *Finetta* related to *Bel-a-voir* the foresight she had in relation to the Figure of straw. The Prince, all transported to find the Princess alive, admired the prudence she was mistress of on all occasions, had infinite obligations to her for preventing him from committing a crime, which he could not think on without horror, and did yet comprehend how he could be so weak not to see the nullity of those wicked oaths, which had been exacted from him by artifice.

However, if *Finetta* had not been ever persuaded, that *Distrust is the mother of security*, she had been killed, and her death been the cause of that of *Bel-a-voir*: and then afterwards, people would have reasoned at leisure upon the oddness of this Prince's sentiments. Happy prudence and presence of mind! which preserved this royal Pair from the most dreadful misfortunes in the world, for a destiny the most sweet and delightful. They always retained for each other an extreme tenderness, and passed through a long succession of happy days, in so much felicity and glory, as is impossible for the most able pen or tongue to describe.

Your Ladyship sees now an end of the history of the Adventures of the Princess *Finetta*, which is not only very famous, but, as Tradition informs us, also of very great antiquity, which assures us, that the *Troubadours*, or Storiographers of *Provence*, invented *Finetta* a long while before *Abelard*, or the celebrated Count *Thibaud* of *Champagne* obliged the world with their Romances.

It is certain that these kinds of fables contain a great deal of good morality, and for that reason ought to be told to little children in their very infancy, to inspire them betimes with Virtue so eminently brilliant in your Ladyship. I know not, Madam, whether you ever heard *Finetta* spoken of at that age: but for my part,

I.

A Hundred times and more to me of old,
Instead of fables made of beasts and fowl,
Of cocks and bulls, the bat and owl,
The morals of this tale, my nurse has told.
Here with one little glance we see
A Prince reduced to utmost misery:
A dangerous Prince, whose sable[1] mind
To perpetrate most horrid crimes inclin'd
O'erwhelm'd profoundly low
In endless shame irreparable woe.

II.

Here too, as in a magick glass, is shown,
How two imprudent ladies royal born,
Whom every princely virtue should adorn,
Of their high character unworthy grown;
By passing all their time in Indolence,
Lost to all honour's noble sense,
And to strict virtue having small regard,
Fell horribly to acts of foulest shame
And stain'd indelibly their royal name,
Retrying for their crimes a prompt and just reward.

III.

But if we see in this delightful tale
The Vicious punish'd, so we likewise see
Virtue triumphant, and prevail,
Loaded with glorious spoils of victory.
After a thousand incidents which none
Could e'er foresee, or in the least surmise
FINETTA, prudent, sage, discreet and wife,
And Bel-a-voir, that gen'rous Prince serene,

1 [From the language of heraldry, sable means black. Samber uses it metaphorically here to describe the prince's dark mind.]

Bless'd in the love of his beloved Queen,
In perfect glory mount the royal Throne.

IV.

In fact, these tales strike deeper on the mind,
Afford diversion and instruction more
Than those invented heretofore,
Or in the modern mint of fable coin'd,
Of beasts and birds, of gnats and Flies,
And all those inconsistent Reveries,
(A Gallimaufry strange, God knows,)
Of Monkey Barbers, Monkey Beaus,
The graduate Ass, and proud exalted Pie
With little Doctor Elephant so sly,
And all what else we Fabulists invent,
Retail'd in pretty sterile chiming Cant.

V.

I can't but own I take delight extreme,
And all young people do the same,
Reading or hearing of these kinds of Tales,
So much their sweet Simplicity prevails:
But more diffusive would their beauties rife
Of more extent their moral Virtues Prove,
Did noble Ladies in their Families
Admit them Audience, and their Lecture love.
The Mystick Meanings, which their Tour contains,
Like vital gold lock'd up in min'ral veins,
These in his tales by Aesope wrapped so well,
Certainly equal; and, Some say, excel.

FINIS.

8. Catherine Bernard, *Inès de Courdoue* (1696; *translated by Christine A. Jones, 2011*[1])

Catherine Bernard is not among the best known French fairy-tale writers today perhaps due to her relatively limited output of tales: "Riquet" is one of only two, and they are both intercalated into her novel, Inès de Courdoue (Inès of Cordoba)*. Bernard was acclaimed during her lifetime for poetry as well as prose and is best known today for her novels. Since the context of "Riquet" is a novel set in Spain, the fairy tale locates its action geographically in Granada. Although national allusion is not altogether uncommon in French tales of the seventeenth century, here it provides insight into character names that otherwise sound invented (in both French and English). Bernard writes in a remarkably economical and witty hand, and in "Riquet" contributed one of the least encouraging endings in the French fairy-tale corpus. Significantly, the tales in* Inès de Courdoue *are told by great (albeit fictional) women of the Spanish court whose explicit goal in the game of telling that they propose as entertainment is psychological realism set into fantastical action—as though psychological truth can only emerge in highly fictional landscapes. One "truth" that emerges here turns on the vexed relationship between beauty and intellect, on the one hand, and gender, on the other.*

RIQUET À LA HOUPPE [2]

A GREAT LORD IN GRANADA,[3] POSSESSED of immense wealth worthy of his title, had trouble at home that poisoned all the riches showered upon him by fate. His only daughter, born with all the features of a beautiful face, was so stupid that even beauty looked unpleasant on her. Her movement utterly lacked grace and her physique was heavy because, although her body was slender, there was no soul in it.

---

1 [Source: Christine A. Jones, unpublished.]

2 Emile Littré has argued based on Bernard's northern origins that "Riquet" comes from a Normand word for "deformed, hunchback." Other possible meanings of the word can be found through the Spanish word "riqueza" or wealth, and the root of "ric," "rex" or king, which describes the status of the gnome in the story. The family name Riquet belonged to the chief engineer of the Canal du Midi, arguably Louis XIV's most ambitious civic expansion project, which linked the north and south of the realm for the first time. There is a strange resonance with the story, which links the over- to the underworld through Riquet. The word "houppe" refers to something like a tassle in the seventeenth century: "Tuft, a sort of bouquet of wool or silk for decoration" (*Dictionnaire de l'Académie française*, 1694). Tuft does not conjure ugliness, but fashionable ornament. Given the ambiguity of both terms, I take them as the eponymous character's proper name and have not translated them as regular nouns. All subsequent definitions are taken from this edition of the *Dictionnaire*, identified henceforth as DAF: http://artfl-project.uchicago.edu/. Translations are my own.

3 The story has an historical setting: Granada, Spain. More than that, the names in the story are or derive from Spanish words: *arada* = husbandry, *mama* = breast, and *riqueza* = wealth.

Mama (that was the girl's name) did not have enough sense to know that she did not have any, but she could feel that people snubbed her even if she could not explain why. Walking alone one day (a common thing for her), she saw emerging from the earth a man so hideous that he could have been a monster. The sight of him made her want to run but his words called her back.

"Stop," he said to her. "I have some inconvenient truths to tell you, but I have pleasant ones to foretell. With such beauty, you yet have a certain something that makes people turn away from you. It's that you have no thoughts in your head, and without boasting I can say that this flaw makes you infinitely worse off than I am, as I am but the body to your mind. That's the cruel part of what I have to say to you, but by the stupid look on your face I'm guessing that I gave you too much credit thinking I would offend you. This makes me despair for the purpose of my proposal…but I will venture to make it: Do you want to be intelligent?"

"Yes," Mama answered, as if she were saying, "No."

"Alright then," he continued, "here's how. You must fall in love with Riquet à la Houppe—that's my name. You must marry me in one year. That's the condition I'm putting on you. Think about it if you can. Otherwise, repeat over and over the words I am about to tell you; they will eventually teach you to think. Good-bye for one year. Here are the words that will chase your insouciance away and at the same time heal your mental handicap.

Oh, giver of soul and life,
Cupid, if to stop being a twit,
I need only learn to love,
To this I submit.

As she said them, her figure relaxed, she looked more alive, her gait seemed freer. She repeated them.

She goes to her father's house, tells him logical things, shortly thereafter reasonable things, and eventually clever things.

Such a swift and considerable metamorphosis was not lost on the people most concerned. Suitors came in droves. Mama was no longer alone at balls or on walks. Soon men renounced God, became jealous—they were talking about her only and for her only.

With all the men who found her desirable, there was no chance that she was going to find her ideal in Riquet à la Houppe. The mind he gave her did its benefactor an ill turn. The words she repeated faithfully did inspire her to love someone, but with a result that thwarted the author's plan: that someone was not him.

She preferred the best looking man among the men who pined for her. He was not the best off financially, so her parents, who could see that they had wished her ill in wishing for intelligence and were now powerless to take it away, at least tried to talk her out of love. But forbidding a pretty young thing to love is like forbidding a tree to sprout leaves in May. It only made her love Arada all the more (that was her lover's name).

She was very careful not to betray to anyone how she happened to learn to think. Her vanity had an investment in keeping it secret; by then she had wit enough to understand the importance of concealing the mystery of how she came by it.

Meanwhile, the year Riquet à la Houppe had given her to learn to think and decide to marry him was nearly over. She watched in terrible distress as the end approached—her mind had become a double-edged sword that would not let her ignore a single painful scenario: losing her lover forever, living under the reign of a person she hardly knew except for his grotesquery,[1] which was perhaps the least of his flaws; that is, someone she agreed to marry while accepting his gifts, which she had no desire to return to him. Those were her thoughts.

One day when she was off on her own imagining her cruel destiny, she heard a loud noise and voices from below that were singing the words Riquet à la Houppe had taught her. She shuddered; it was the sound of her doom.

Suddenly, the ground opens up, she is brought down into it, and she sees Riquet à la Houppe surrounded by men that are grotesque like him.

What a vision for someone who had been courted by the most desirable men in the land! She was more distressed than shocked and cried a river of tears, which was at that point the only thing she could do with the mind Riquet à la Houppe had given her.

He watched her and it was his turn to be sad: "Madame," he told her, "I can see clearly that you find me more unpleasant now than the first time I appeared to you. I doomed myself when I gave you a mind. But after all, you are still free and you can choose to marry me or relapse into your previous condition.[2] I'll return you to

---

1 The word in French is "difformité." In the seventeenth century, *difformité* belongs to the lexicon of math and architecture and means lack of proportion. To the extent that art was meant to ennoble, move man closer to perfection, the word had moral overtones as well. A "difformité" rendered something ugly because it was asymmetrical and, therefore, not good art. The word "grotesquery" in contemporary English refers to something unnatural and distorted—ugly because it does not correspond to rules of proportion—which makes it an interesting translation of *difformité*. Furthermore, in the language of design, "grotesques" are fanciful creatures drawn into borders and garlands. Their use in the Renaissance was partially to render a design eclectic and asymmetrical. By the end of the seventeenth century, proportion dominated the arts as one of its primary requirements, and the "grotesque" became much less unruly and disproportionate. That gives nice subtext to the character of Riquet à la Houppe—an outdated artistic conceit, one that belongs underground.

2 The verb "retomber" (fall again, relapse), draws on the medical language of disease and the moral language of sin. It gives interesting subtext to the question of intelligence, as though lack thereof was some sort of disease.

your father's care in the state in which I found you, or will make you queen of this kingdom. I am the king of the gnomes and you will be their queen;[1] and if you can accept my physique and forego visual pleasure, all other pleasures will be yours. The treasures locked within the earth belong to me, you will command them. Anyone who can have gold and a mind and still be unhappy deserves to be. I worry that you may be a drama queen;[2] I worry that surrounded by my wealth I seem over the top to you. But if my treasures along with me are not to your liking, say so and I will send you far from this place; I want nothing to interfere with my happiness here. You have two days to get to know this place and to seal my fate and yours."

Riquet à la Houppe took his leave after bringing her to a sumptuous apartment where she was served by gnomes of her gender whose ugliness afflicted her less than that of the men. They served her a grand feast whose perfection wanted only for guests. The after-dinner entertainment was a play, but the actors' grotesquery stood in the way of any interest she might have taken in the subject. In the evening they threw a ball and she attended but without any desire to flirt. Afterwards she felt such mortal horror [at what was happening] that it would have prevented her from resolving to thank Riquet à la Houppe for the fortunes and the pleasures if the threat of idiocy had not overcome it.

She would readily have taken back her stupidity to free herself from the bonds of an odious husband were it not for her lover because that would mean losing this lover in the cruelest way. It is true on some level that in marrying the gnome she was already lost to the lover: she could never see or speak to Arada, not even send news; he might even suspect her of infidelity. In the end, she would belong to a husband who had taken from her the one thing she loved, which would forever make him odious to her, even when he was kind. What's more, he was a monster. Hence, the difficulty of the decision.[3]

---

1 Bernard's identification of Riquet as king of the gnomes grants him an important position in the cosmology of the marvelous universe. In the seventeenth century, the word was associated with Cabalism and denoted "certain genies or invisible peoples that are said to live within the earth where they are guardians of its treasures, mines, and gemstones. *Gnomes are known as friends of mankind*" (DAF). Riquet's power, while benevolent by tradition, is formidable, and Mama underestimates it at her peril.

2 The expression "avoir une fausse délicatesse"—to feign sensitivity—appears in Jean de La Bruyère's moralistic portraits of various social types, *Les Caractères* (1688), to describe the behavior featured in the essay "Affecté(e)," on men and women whose mannerisms seem overly affected. This is one of the rare social maladies covered in La Bruyère's *Caractères* that is shared by men and women, although men who succumb to it are invariably acting like women. Since these behaviors correspond to a way of interacting socially that distinguishes their practitioners as excessive and effeminate in La Bruyère, I opted in English for a popular moniker of excessive and effeminate sensitivity.

3 Although Mama's indecision could appear to be the sign of a foolish mind, she is exercising a capacity that René Descartes described as the definitive proof of the mind's existence: doubt. This capacity allows him to make the proof of his own existence via that of his mental faculties in *Meditations* (1641).

When the two days had passed, she was no less indecisive: she told the gnome that the choice was impossible.

"That's as good as deciding against me," he told her, "so I'll return you to the former condition you cannot bring yourself to choose."

She trembled; the thought of losing her lover to the disdain he would feel for her affected her deeply enough to make her give him up.

"Alright then," she said to the gnome, "that decides it. I must give myself to you."

Riquet à la Houppe did not play hard to get; he married her. Mama's mind expanded even more through this union, but her unhappiness increased in proportion to her intelligence. She was horrified that she had given herself to a monster and wondered every minute how she could spend another minute with him.

The gnome was well aware that his wife hated him and was afflicted by it, in spite of the pride he took in the power of his intellect. Her aversion to him was a constant judgment of his grotesquery and made him hate women, marriage, and the curiosity that drove him to venture away from home. He often left Mama alone. And since alone she was reduced to thinking, she thought that she had to make Arada see with his own eyes that she was not being unfaithful.[1] He could reach this place, since she got there safely. At least she had to send news to him and blame her absence on the gnome that had abducted her, the [mere] sight of which would speak to her fidelity. Nothing is impossible for a smart woman in love.

She conscripted a gnome to be her messenger to Arada; luckily this was still a time of faithful lovers. He tormented himself with the thought that Mama had forgotten him, but never resented her for it; vile suspicion never entered his head; he complained and he fell to pieces, but without a single offensive thought for his lover and without longing to be cured.

You can imagine that, feeling as he did, he hastened to Mama at risk of his life as soon as he knew where to find her and that she did not forbid him to come.

He came to the subterranean place where Mama was living, he saw her, and he threw himself at her feet. She spoke with words more affectionate than erudite. He got permission from her to give up the world and live underground, and she made him beg for it even though her sole desire was that he commit to this very plan.

Mama's humor returned little by little and it enhanced her beauty, but unnerved the gnome's love. His intellect was too great and he knew Mama's disgust too well to believe that the mere force of habit would ease her distress.

Then Mama made the foolish decision to dress up; he was too honest with

1 There is an interesting use of the verb here, which is normally reflexive. Typically, one convinces oneself by looking: seeing is believing. Mama says *she* will convince him with *his* own eyes, which gives her more agency than she should have in the equation. Her overblown sense of her power seems validated by the last sentence of the paragraph, "Nothing is impossible ...," but the ensuing plot does not support the aphorism.

himself to believe that he was the worthy cause of it; he searched, as he sensed that there was a good-looking man hiding in his palace—that was all it took. He plotted revenge that would be sweeter than simply getting rid of her. He summoned Mama.

"I don't bother with complaining or making reproachful remarks," he told her, "I leave that to mankind. When I gave you an intellect I hoped to benefit from it; you have used it against me; yet, I cannot completely take it from you since you submitted to the condition I imposed on you. But if you did not violate the contract, you did not strictly honor it either. Let's split the difference: you will be intelligent by night (I don't want anything to do with a stupid wife); but by day you can be stupid for anyone you want."

In that instant, Mama felt a heaviness in her mind that soon she no longer felt at all. That night her ideas came back to life and she thought about her misery; she cried but did not have the resolve to console herself or use her wits to find a creative solution.

The next night she noticed that her husband was sound asleep and put an herb under his nose that would deepen his slumber as long as she desired. She got up to get away from the object of her fury. Guided by her reveries, she made her way to the place where Arada was staying, not to look for him, but perhaps because she fancied that he was looking for her. She found him on a garden path where they would often meet to talk imploring heaven and earth to find her. Mama told him the tale of her woe, which was alleviated by the pleasure she took in describing it to him.

The next night, although it was unplanned, they met again in the same place and these illicit rendez-vous continued so long that even their shame eventually became a new kind of pleasure. Mama's mind and her love inspired her to many creative schemes for pleasing Arada and for helping him forget that she was mindless half the time.

When the lovers would see the light of day, Mama would go wake the gnome; she would carefully remove the soporific herb as soon as she was close to him. The day would arrive, she would become an idiot again, but she would spend the time sleeping.

Such tolerably happy times cannot last—the leaf that induced slumber also induced snoring. A servant gnome who was half asleep and half awake thought his master was whining, ran to him, saw the herb that was placed under his nose, and removed it, assuming it must be bothering him: one cure, three wretches. The gnome realized he was alone, went out of his mind, and pursued his wife; chance or his miserable fate guided him to the place where the two lovers sat swearing their eternal love to each other. He said nothing, but tapped the lover with a wand that gave him a face and figure just like the gnome's, and he switched places with him several times until Mama could not distinguish the lover from the husband. She found herself with two husbands instead of one and never knew who to complain to for fear of taking the object of her loathing for the object of her love. But maybe she lost little [in the bargain]: in the course of time lovers become husbands.

Charlotte-Rose de Caumont de La Force, "The Enchanter," ***Les Contes des Contes*** **(1697; translated by Lewis Seifert and Domna Stanton, 2010) [website]**

Charlotte-Rose de Caumont de La Force was one of the first fairy-tale writers to publish her stories without a frame story. In "The Enchanter" (provided as a web text; see http://sites.broadviewpress.com/marveloustrans/), La Force elaborates on an obscure episode from the Arthurian or "Grail" tradition, but she also takes inspiration from the fairy tales of Basile and her own contemporary Charles Perrault, including a sleeping beauty that she weaves into a complex tale of mistaken identities and familial betrayal. In this fairy tale La Force pushes the margin of acceptable subjects in seventeenth-century literature to its limits, particularly in its explicit sexuality and violence.

9. Charles Perrault, ***Histoires ou contes du temps passé*** **(1697;** ***translated by Christine A. Jones, 2011***[1]**)**

Charles Perrault's volume of stories was not the first of the French tales to gain popularity in the English language, but in the nearly 300 years since they were first translated they have become canonical. Perrault's Contes du temps passé *included one key illustration, positioned as the frontispiece: it depicted an older, humbly dressed woman at fireside, drop spindle in her hand, with a group of young aristocrats around her. Above this evocative, fictive scene of storytelling was a plaque that read "Contes de ma mere l'oye," or "Tales of my mother the goose"—and Perrault's tales became known as "Mother Goose tales." Although Perrault's tales likely had some parallels in contemporary oral traditions, they do not represent efforts to document popular storytelling (despite current misconceptions): they are literary tales, written for a courtly audience, and shaped by Perrault's distinctive voice—playful, ironic, and inventive. Perrault was writing not only in the midst of the fairy-tale vogue exemplified by the work of Lhéritier, La Force, Bernard, d'Aulnoy, and Murat, but also on the heels of the publication of the first official French dictionary. Perrault's use of language may appear simple in syntax and structure, but in fact his word choice and phraseology are erudite and also experimental: in his French text, Perrault invents names and seeks out uncommon words, which in many cases have become iconic.*

This slim volume includes early written versions of the most recognizable plots in fairy tale history: a sleeping beauty, an abused princess whose prince finds her slipper,

1 [Source: Christine A. Jones, unpublished.]

a young girl who ventures into the woods and meets her death. Yet, the reader will note that Perrault's tales do not correspond to the image we now have of these familiar plots. The four tales reproduced here in new translation offer a glimpse back into seventeenth-century concerns that motivated him to publish them. A particular aspect of Perrault that has often been lost in translation is the complex relationship between his plots and his morals. While we might assume that the moral supports the ostensible plot of the story with its nearly inevitable happy ending, in fact they often undermine the facile meaning we may be tempted to take from the stories. The most evident way they contravene the idea of singular message is when there are two morals instead of one, labeled "moral" and "another moral," as though there could be many more. Rereading Perrault's versions of these plots with this simple idea in mind—maybe the tales do not so clearly have "one" meaning—invites us to pay closer attention to the cultural markers that identify these stories with the courtly world of seventeenth-century France.

BLUE BEARD[1]

ONCE UPON A TIME A man had magnificent town homes and country estates, servingware in gold and silver, furniture covered in brocade fabrics, and carriages covered in gold. By some terrible misfortune, the man's beard was blue, which gave him such a horrid, nasty appearance that women and girls fled at the sight of him.

One of his neighbors, a noblewoman, had two daughters who were the perfection of beauty. He asked the woman for the hand of one of her daughters in marriage and let her decide which one she would offer him. Neither one willing to marry a blue-bearded man, they wanted no part of it, and each sent him back to the other. What sickened them even more was the fact that he had already married several women and it was unclear what had become of them.

To get to know them, Blue Beard invited them to one of his country estates for eight long days with their mother, three or four of their best friends, and some other neighbors. Their visit was filled with strolling, hunting and fishing, dancing and feasting, afternoon tea. They stayed up all night playing pranks on each other. In the end, it was all so enjoyable that the younger sister began to think that the man's beard was not all that blue and that he was a very courtly gentleman. Upon their return to the city, they decided to marry.

A month had passed when Blue Beard told his wife that he had important business in the countryside that would take him at least six weeks; that he hoped she

---

1 Like "The Little Red Riding Hood" this title is a metonymy: an object or attribute that comes to stand for the character, which seems to be a habit particular to Perrault in the French fairy-tale corpus. Cinderella's subtitle, "the little glass slipper," arguably functions in a similar way.

would amuse herself in his absence; that she should invite her friends; that she should take them to the country if she wanted to; and everywhere show her guests a good time.[1]

He told her: "Here are the keys to the two furniture attics, here are the keys to the buffet with the gold and silver services not for everyday use; keys to the safes with my bouillon and silver coin; keys to the boxes where I keep my jewels; and here is the master key to all the apartments. Now, this little key is the key to the office at the end of the great hall of the downstairs apartment.[2] Open everything, go everywhere, but as far as the little office goes, you may not go in there—and I am so serious about this that if you do end up opening it, my anger will know no bounds."

She promised to follow all the directives he had just given her and after he kissed her, he gets in his carriage and leaves for his trip.

The neighbors and good friends, who would not visit the young wife while the husband was around because his blue beard scared them, so badly wanted to see the splendor of her home that they showed up before being invited. There they were right away making their way through the bedrooms, offices, and dressing rooms, one more splendid and sumptuous than the next. After that, they climbed to the furniture attics where they could not believe the number of beautiful tapestries, beds, day beds, curios, pedestal tables, dressing tables and mirrors—mirrors long enough to reflect them from head to toe and with the most magnificent decorative edging you have ever seen; some in glass and others in silver or gold plate.[3] They went on and on with their exaggeration and jealousy of their friend's happiness. She, for her part, took no interest in all the splendor because she wanted so badly to go and open the office in the downstairs apartment.

Her curiosity got the better of her and without even considering how rude it was to leave her guests, she hurried down a private staircase, moving so fast that two or

---

1 "Faire bonne chère" refers etymologically to putting on a good face (a warm welcome), but evolved by the seventeenth century into something closer to a general sense of entertaining guests. Today it refers to a good time at the table, i.e., eating well or preparing a good meal.

2 The word *cabinet* (office), which refers generally in the seventeenth century to any room in the house where one retreats to work and keeps important documents and books, has a secondary meaning that seems pertinent here: "*Cabinet* also refers to the most closely guarded secrets and mysteries of the court" *Dictionnaire de l'Académie française*, 1694; hensforth DAF.

3 The first seventeenth-century definition of "sofa" identifies them as Turkish benches covered in rugs that would have been used by prime ministers of the Ottoman Empire when they gave audience. The more likely meaning, day bed, refers to a relatively new type of furniture in the 1690s: "We also call a *sofa* a kind of two-sided day bed, which has recently come into use in France" (DAF). "Curios" is my translation for another use of *cabinet* here, which could refer to a piece of furniture in which one kept papers and also curiosities: exotica and other expensive objects such as porcelain in which one would invest to demonstrate one's fashionability. Cabinets of this sort could also be entire rooms, especially at royal palaces.

three times she thought she would break her neck. She stood before the door for a while thinking about the restrictions her husband had placed on her and considering the misery that could befall her for disobeying, but the temptation proved strong enough that she could not overcome it. So she took out the little key and, shaking, opened the door to the office.

At first she could not see anything because the shutters were closed. Moments later, she began to see that the floor was covered with congealed blood wherein the corpses of several women that had been hung along the walls could forever see their reflection[1]—the very women Blue Beard had married and successively slit at the throat.

She thought she would die of fright and dropped the little key that she had just pulled out of the lock. When her wits came back to her, she picked up the key, locked the door, and went up to her room to rest a little. But she could not relax, she was too upset.

She saw that the key was spotted with blood and tried two or three times to rub it off, but the blood would not budge. She washed to no avail, and even when she scoured it with an abrasive and with sandstone the blood remained. You see, the key was enchanted and there was no way to clean it thoroughly. When you got rid of it on one side, it appeared on the other.

That very night Blue Beard came back from his trip saying that he had received word en route to the effect that the business for which he had set out had been resolved in his favor. His wife made every effort to show him that she was elated by his sudden return.

The next day he asked for the keys back and she gave them to him, but her hand shook so much that he readily guessed what had happened.

"How is it," he said to her, "that the key to the office is not with the other ones?"

"I guess I left it on my dressing table upstairs."

"Be sure to give it to me soon."

When he had asked several times, she had to deliver the key. After looking it over, Blue Beard said to her, "Why is there blood on this key?"

"I know nothing about that," replied the wife.

"You know nothing about that," repeated Blue Beard, "but *I* know all about it. You tried to get into the office! Alright, Madam, you will go in and you will take your place among the ladies you've seen there."

1 The verb for what is happening in the blood in this passage is *se mirer*, literally to see oneself reflected, but also to watch or contemplate oneself. The reflexivity of the verb suggests more active meaning in the passage than the transitive verb "to reflect." That is to say, Perrault appears to give the corpses a fantastical kind of agency, as though they see themselves in their own blood.

Wailing and begging for forgiveness, she threw herself at her husband's feet showing all the signs of sincere remorse for her failure to obey. Her beauty and pain would have softened even stone, but Blue Beard's heart was harder than stone.[1]

"You are going to die, Madam, and very soon."

Her eyes wet with tears, she replied, "Since I am going to die, give me some time to pray."

"You can have half of fifteen minutes," Blue Beard shot back, "and not one minute more."

When she was alone, she called to her sister and told her, "Anne, sister Anne (that was her name), please climb to the top of the tower to see if my brothers are not on their way. They promised to come see me today. If you spot them, signal to them to hurry."

Sister Anne climbed to the top of the tower and the poor thing cried out to her now and then, "Anne, sister Anne, is there nothing in sight?"

And sister Anne would reply, "I see nothing but the sun raining dust and the grass getting lush."[2]

In the meantime, Blue Beard gripped a wide blade in his hand and would scream to his wife, "Get down here now or I'll come up there!"[3]

"Just a second, please"[4] his wife would answer and quickly call out in a whisper to her sister, "Anne, sister Anne, is there nothing in sight?"

And sister Anne would answer, "I see nothing but the sun raining dust and the grass getting lush."

"I told you to get down here or I'll come up there!"

"I'm on my way!" his wife would say and call out, "Anne, my dear Anne, is there nothing in sight?"

Then sister Anne said, "I see a thick spray of dust approaching from this side."

"Is it my brothers?"

"I'm afraid not, sister, it's a herd of sheep."

---

1 The expression in French is "attendrir la roche"—to soften stone—and refers to a process used in mining in lieu of explosives: rock is heated with burning wood and the resulting caustic vapors render it more easily broken. It plays on the expression *attendrir le coeur*, "soften the heart."

2 In French, Perrault gives agency to the sun and grass, which "poudroie" (its rays make the dust visible) and "verdoie" (greens), respectively. The verb "poudroyer," suggests too that her vision is clouded by the dusty haze.

3 Blue Beard switches here from the formal "vous" to the informal "tu" with his wife, which changes the power dynamic between them in his favor. We can also see in this shift from "Madam," which he drops, to informal address that his anger is unhinged. The blade he holds is a cutlass: a compact, wide, single-edged sword used at the time by sailors. Because of its size, it would have been convenient to the task at hand.

4 In this, her last direct speech with him, the wife continues to use the formal "vous" with her husband, confirming her subordinate position.

"Are you coming down?" Blue Beard would scream.

"Just a second," his wife would answer and then call out, "Anne, sister Anne, is there nothing in sight?"

Then she said, "I see two cavalry soldiers arriving from this side but they are still very far away." In the next moment, she screamed, "Thank God! It's my brothers. I'm signaling as well as I can to tell them that they should hurry."

Blue Beard started screaming so loudly that the house shook. His miserable wife came down looking distraught and a mess, and was about to throw herself at his feet when he said, "That won't work. You are going to die."

Then he grabbed her by the hair with one hand and raised the blade with the other, ready to slash her throat. His miserable wife turned to him with cold, dead eyes and requested a brief moment to collect herself.

"No. No!" he said, "Commend your soul to God."

Just then, there was pounding so loud at the door that Blue Beard froze. It opened and in came two soldiers drawing swords and running straight for Blue Beard.

He knew they were his wife's brothers, one a dragoon and one a musketeer, which made him run for his life, but the two brothers followed him so closely that they overtook him before he could get out the door. They drove their swords through his body and left him for dead. The miserable wife was almost as dead as her husband and could not find the strength to get up and hug her brothers.

As it was, Blue Beard had no heirs and thus his wife retained possession of his entire fortune. She spent a large portion of it on the marriage of her sister Anne to a young nobleman who had been in love with her for a long time, some more buying the title of Captain for her two brothers,[1] and the rest she used to get married herself to a very courtly gentleman who helped her forget the miserable time she had had with Blue Beard.

Moral

Curiosity, in spite of all its mirth,
Often costs much more than it's worth.
Everywhere and always examples abound.
Sorry ladies, but it's an illusory crutch.
As soon as you seize it, it is nowhere to be found
And it always costs too much.

1 Under Louis XIV no system of promotion existed in the military. Soldiers aspiring to be officers paid for the position and the right to perform its duties. For the ranks of Captain and Colonel, money alone did not suffice—the appointment also had to be approved by the king.

Another Moral

Even a wit of the dimmest cast,
Who is not so very worldly,
Will discover anon that this story
Is a tale of times long past.
No more the terrible husband of old
Whose demands were impossibly bold.
Though he now be discontent and domineering
Still with his wife he's endearing.
The color of his beard no longer stands
To show among them who wears the pants.

CINDERELLA, OR THE LITTLE GLASS SLIPPER

ONCE UPON A TIME A nobleman married his second wife, the most conceited and arrogant woman you've ever seen. She had two daughters with the same disposition who were exactly like her. For his part, the husband also had a little girl, but she was sweet and kind beyond compare. She got that from her mother, who had the most charming personality in the world.

Hardly had the marriage ceremony ended than the stepmother let her ugly disposition explode. She could not stand the appealing qualities in this young child, which made her daughters seem even more odious. She gave her the most menial chores in the house: she was the one who cleaned the dishes and put them away; who scrubbed Madame's bedroom, as well as Mademoiselles her daughters'. She slept on the top floor of the house in the attic on a pathetic straw mattress, while her sisters had bedrooms with parquet floors, the most fashionable style of bed, and mirrors in which they could look at themselves from head to toe. The poor thing suffered it all patiently and could not even complain to her father, who was utterly controlled by his wife and would have punished her.

When she had finished her chores, she would go to the fireplace hearth and sit in the ashes, which made everyone call her Ashwipe.[1] The younger sister, who was not as mean as the older one, called her Cinderella. And yet, Cinderella with the ugly clothes managed still to be a thousand times prettier than her sisters, however splendidly dressed.

---

1 The cruel name Perrault invents for his heroine, "Cucendron," is a combination of *cu,* probably from *cul* (ass), and *cendron,* a deformation of *cendre* (ash). The word sounds vulgar and comical in French, as it identifies the girl with her habit of putting her ass in the ashes. My translation aims for similarly crude comedy. Cinderella, the standard translation of "Cendrillon," opts for the homophone cinder instead of ash.

It happened that the son of the king threw a ball and that he requested the presence of the nobility. Our two Mademoiselles were also invited thanks to their considerable celebrity in town. And so they were very pleased and very concentrated on choosing the clothes and hairdos that would best suit the occasion. More hardships for Cinderella, who was of course the one to iron her sisters' lingerie and flute their cuffs.[1] They went on and on about how they would dress.

"I," said the older one, "will wear my red velvet ensemble and my English lace."[2]

"I," said the younger one, "will have only my everyday skirt, but to make up for it, I will wear my brocade coat with the gold flowers and my diamond festoon,[3] which has a certain charm."

They brought in the best hair designer to create double-rowed hairpieces and commissioned beauty marks from the best craftswoman. The sisters called Cinderella in to ask her opinion. Cinderella gave them the most excellent advice—she had good taste—and even offered to do their coiffures, to which they agreed.[4]

While she was doing their hair, they said to her: "Cinderella, wouldn't you be delighted to go to the ball?"

"Ah, Mademoiselles! You are joking. I don't need that."

"That's true. People would have a good laugh if they saw an Ashwipe at the ball."

---

1 The expression "godronner les manchettes," which I have rendered "flute their cuffs," comes from the language of laundering, as it would have been the professional cleaner that performed this operation on collars—known as *collets* or ruffs—and cuffs (*manchettes*). Like ironing, it consisted of pleating the starched fabric around a heated metal cone (goffering iron) to give it a scalloped shape that would last through the evening.

2 A "garniture d'Angleterre" refers to lace made in Belgium and imported through England in the second quarter of the seventeenth century. Because "garniture" refers by the end of the seventeenth century to headpieces and ribbons, as well as the traditional lace trim, it could indicate fabric laced through the hair to create one of the elaborate coiffures popular during the period of Louis XIV's trend-setting mistress, Madame de Montespan. These hair-dos are discussed below, p. 170, note 4.

3 Diamond festoon is my translation of "barrière de diamants," an expression that no longer exists in French and may not have existed when Perrault wrote it. The historical expression for a bib diamond necklace is "rivière de diamants." "Barrière"—barricade, fence, barrier—gives a much less romantic image of the necklace than "river" of diamonds. Perrault may be suggesting that the sister's necklace is excessive and in bad taste—like some kind of body armor. There is an overall sense that the sisters' accessories are out of fashion.

4 "Cornettes," pleated ribbons worn in the hair, were in high vogue when the king's second mistress, Madame de Montespan, influenced fashion at court (roughly 1670–85). The names of the high hairdos worn by noblewomen had names that reflected their extravagant playfulness, such as "Hurluberlu" (literally unthinking or scatterbrained). In the later styles, which called for *cornettes*, the hair was swept up high on the head, done in stacks of curls, and ornamented with cascading pleated or bowed ribbons. These works of art were long out of fashion in 1697. By that time, Louis XIV had taken another mistress, whose piety and devotion to the Church legislated against excessive body ornament. The sisters, then, are over the top and outdated. Cinderella's beauty will be less ostentatious and more glamorous.

Someone else would have set their coiffures lopsided, but Cinderella was too good [for that] and she set them just right. They went two days without eating in a delirium of pleasure, more than a dozen laces broke tightening their corsets to make their waists look smaller, and they stood all day in front of their mirrors.

When at last the special occasion arrived, they set out and Cinderella followed them with her eyes as long as she could. When she could not see them anymore, she began to cry. Her godmother, who saw her in tears, asked what was the matter.

"I would really like ... I would really like ..."

She sobbed so hard that she could not finish. Her godmother, who was a fairy, said to her: "You would really like to go to the ball, right?"

"Well, yes," said Cinderella, heaving.

"So, then, will you be a good girl?" said the godmother. "I will help you go."

She took her into her bedroom and said, "Go to the garden and find me a pumpkin." Right away Cinderella went to cut the prettiest one she could find and carried it to her godmother, but could not imagine how this pumpkin was going to get her to the ball. Her godmother scraped the inside clean, leaving only the skin, and tapped it with her wand. The pumpkin suddenly turned into a magnificent gilded carriage. Next she went to look in her mousetrap, where she found six mice, all of them alive. She told Cinderella to lift the door of the mousetrap and as they scurried out, she tapped each one with her wand, which instantly turned it into a beautiful horse; together they made an impressive team of six horses with coats in dappled mousy gray.

She struggled with what to use for a coachman. "Let me see," said Cinderella, "if by any chance there is a rat in the rat trap. We will make a coachman out of him."

"Good idea," said the godmother, "Go see."

Cinderella brought the rat trap, which held three chubby rats. The fairy picked one among them for its commanding facial hair and, tapping it with her wand, turned him into a chubby coachman with one of the most dashing moustaches you've ever seen.

Next she said, "Go to the garden. You'll find six lizards behind the watering pot.[1] Bring them to me."

No sooner had she delivered them than the godmother turned them into footmen, who climbed on the back of the carriage in their livery and stood at the ready as though they had done this all their lives.

Then the fairy said to Cinderella: "Voila! Here is all you need to get to the ball. Aren't you just delighted?"

"Yes, but will I go like this, in my disgusting clothes?"

---

1 This portable garden technology was new in Perrault's day.

Her godmother so much as tapped her with the wand and at that moment her clothes turned to robes of gold and silver covered in precious gems; next she gave her a pair of glass slippers, the prettiest in the world. Once she was outfitted in finery, she got into the carriage, but her godmother advised her first and foremost not to stay out past midnight, warning that if she stayed at the ball one minute more, her carriage would again turn to a pumpkin, her horses to mice, her footmen to lizards, and that her old clothes would return to their usual state.

She promised her godmother that she would absolutely leave the ball before midnight. She leaves, giddy with happiness.

The son of the king, who had been alerted to the arrival of a grand princess that no one recognized, ran to receive her; he extended his hand as she stepped down from the carriage and led her to the room where the guests were gathered. Then there was total silence. They stopped dancing, the violins stopped playing; all attention turned to take in the many glorious splendors of this mystery woman. There was only brouhaha, "Ah, she is so beautiful!"

Old as he was, even the king could not stop watching her and telling the queen under his breath that it had been a while since he'd seen someone so attractive and appealing. The ladies turned their attention to studying her hair and clothes so they could look like that the next day—provided they could find fabric beautiful enough and artisans capable enough.

The son of the king gave her the most prominent seat at the table and then took her by the hand to lead her in a dance. She danced with such grace that the crowd admired her even more. A very fine meal was served that the young prince did not touch because he was fully occupied with taking her in. She sat down with her sisters and showed them every manner of courtesy. She even gave them some of the oranges and lemons[1] that the prince had given her, which shocked them because they had no idea who she was.

As they chatted away, Cinderella heard the clock strike eleven forty-five. Quickly she bowed to the guests with great ceremony and ran out as fast as she could. As soon as she got home, she went to find her godmother and, thanking her, told her that she hoped very much to go to the ball again the next day because the son of the king had requested her presence. She was caught up in telling her godmother everything that had happened at the ball when the two sisters banged on the door. Cinderella opened it.

"You certainly took your time getting back," she yawned, rubbing her eyes and stretching as though she had only just woken up, and even though she had had no desire to sleep since they left.

---

1 Expensive and rare, citrus fruits were cultivated at great expense in the gardens of Versailles to be enjoyed by royalty and the wealthiest courtiers.

"If you had been at the ball," one of the sisters told her, "you would never have tired of it. There was the most beautiful princess, the most beautiful you've ever seen. She was so polite and gracious toward us; she gave us oranges and lemons."

Cinderella was giddy with happiness: she asked the name of the princess, but they answered that no one knew who she was, that the son of the king was just sick about it, and that he would give everything in the world to know who she was. Cinderella smiled and said, "She was really beautiful, then? God, you are so lucky! Could I at least get a glimpse of her? What to do ... Mademoiselle Javotte, lend me the yellow ensemble that you wear all the time."

"That's just what I'll do," said Mademoiselle Javotte. "Honestly. Lend your clothes to a disgusting Ashwipe like that. I would have to be simply mad."

Cinderella naturally expected this refusal and was glad for it because she would have been in quite a bind if her sister had agreed to lend her the clothes.

The next day the sisters were at the ball, as was Cinderella, but even more finely dressed than the first time. The son of the king planted himself next to her and showered her nonstop with compliments. The young lady never tired of it and forgot how her godmother had cautioned her—to the point that when she heard the clock strike twelve she thought it had not yet struck eleven. She got up and dashed out, lithe as a deer.

The prince tracked her but could not catch her. She dropped one of her glass slippers, which the prince picked up gingerly. Cinderella arrived home mightily winded with no carriage, with no footmen, and in her ugly clothes—nothing left of all her splendor but one of her little slippers, the twin of the one she had dropped. People asked the guards at the palace gate if they hadn't seen a princess leave. They said that they had not seen anyone leave except a little girl who was very poorly dressed and looked more like a peasant than a young lady.

When her two sisters came home from the ball, Cinderella asked them if they had again amused themselves and if the beautiful woman had come. They said yes, but that she ran off when the clock struck midnight and so hastily that she dropped one of her little slippers, the prettiest in the world; that the son of the king had picked it up; that all he did for the rest of the ball was stare at it; and that, for certain, he was deeply in love with the charming someone to whom the slipper belonged.

They were right since a few days later the son of the king announced by trumpet blast that he would marry the woman whose foot was a perfect match for the slipper. They started trying it on princesses, then duchesses and the rest of the court, but it was futile. They brought it to the sisters, who tried everything in their power to get their foot into the slipper, but did not succeed. Cinderella was watching, recognized the slipper, and chuckled, saying, "Maybe I should see if it fits me."

Her sisters cracked up and made fun of her. The gentleman trying the slipper, who had looked carefully at her and found her very attractive, said that this seemed fair and that he had been ordered to try it on every girl. He directed Cinderella to the seat and drawing the slipper to her foot saw that it went in easily and that it fit like a hand in a glove.[1]

The sisters' shock was great, but it was greater still when Cinderella took the other little slipper out of her pocket and put it on her foot. That's when the godmother arrived and giving a little tap of her wand to Cinderella's clothes, dressed her even more magnificently than before.

Now the two sisters could see in her the charming someone they had seen at the ball. They threw themselves at her feet, apologizing for all the cruelty they had put her through. Cinderella helped them up, embraced them, told them that she forgave them willingly, and asked them to be her friends forever.

They brought her before the young prince dressed in her finery: he thought she looked more beautiful than ever and, just days later, married her.

Cinderella, who was as good as she was gorgeous, moved her sisters into the palace and married them that very day to two of the court's high ranking noblemen.

Moral

In the fair sex, beauty is a rare treasure
Its marvelous features we tirelessly praise
But to have what we call good grace
Is priceless and the greater pleasure.

Grace Cinderella's godmother gave her on loan.
Dressed her, taught her not to fail,
So much and so well that she grabbed a throne.
(For such is the moral we'll give this tale.)

Beauties, this talent is more precious than your hair's lift
To win his heart, to someday be crowned,
Good grace is the real fairy's gift.
Without it you are lost, with it you are found.

Another Moral

No doubt it gives a girl a strong lead
To have wit, bravery,
Breeding, good sense,

1 The expression "comme de cire" (like wax) refers to two surfaces that come together equally and with a perfect fit.

And other similarly fine talents
That the heavens dole out as meed.

But in you they will come to nothing
Will fail to help you thrive,
If you do not have the essential thing—
Godparents—that brings them to life.

THE LITTLE RED RIDING HOOD[1]

ONCE UPON A TIME THERE was a young country girl, the prettiest you ever did see. Her mother was crazy about her and her grandmother crazier still. The older woman had made-to-fit for her a tufted red bonnet with a short scarf attached that cloaked her shoulders. It suited her so well that everyone called her the little red riding hood.

One day after baking and making galettes, her mother told her, "I'd like you to go see how your grandmother is doing because I heard she was sick. Take her a galette and this small jar of butter."[2]

The little red riding hood left right away for her grandmother's house, where she lived in another village. When she crossed the woods, she ran into the neighborhood wolf, who very much wanted to eat her, but didn't dare because of the woodsmen in the forest. He asked her where she was going. The poor girl, who didn't know that it is dangerous to stop and listen to wolves, told him: "I'm going to see my grandmother and bring her a galette with a small jar of butter from my mother."

"Does she live far?" said the wolf. "Oh, yes," said the little red riding hood, "it's further than that mill you see way over there. There, the first house in the village."

"You know what?" said the wolf, "I'd like to go see her, too. I'll set out on this path and you take that one. We'll see who gets there faster."

The wolf raced down the short path, while the young girl set out on the long one, happily picking hazelnuts, running after butterflies, and making bouquets with tiny flowers she found.

---

1 Like "Blue Beard" this title is a metonymy: an object or attribute that comes to stand for the character. I have kept the article in the title and in the text (as Perrault does) when it becomes her identifying feature because it is never capitalized in the 1697 edition. That is to say, unlike the name Blue Beard, "little red riding hood" does not become her proper name. The girl under the garment thus remains nameless. While it is not uncommon for characters in French fairy tales to be called only by their title or salient feature (Princess, Father, Queen, Beauty, Beast Ogress, Woodsman, etc.), it is rare that a heroine should have a descriptor that is not capitalized. This omission is particularly striking in a literary genre where any noun can be capitalized for emphasis.

2 A "galette" is a flat cake that was made in the oven when it was being used to bake bread, which is one explanation for the two verbs in the sentence. Today *galette* refers to a buckwheat crêpe, which is served savory, not sweet like a regular crêpe.

It did not take the wolf long to arrive at the grandmother's house. He knocked: Knock, knock.

"Who's there?"

"It's your granddaughter, the little red riding hood," said the wolf, imitating her voice, "with a galette and a small jar of butter from my mother."

The old grandmother, who stayed in her bed because she did not feel well, called out, "Pull the pin, loose the latch."[1]

The wolf pulled the pin and the door opened. He threw himself at the old woman and devoured her in a flash because he had not eaten for three days. Next he closed the door and lay down in the grandmother's bed to wait for the little red riding hood. A little while later, she came knocking at the door: Knock, knock.

"Who's there?"

The little red riding hood heard the wolf's gruff voice and was afraid at first, but she figured her grandmother must have gotten the flu and answered, "It's your granddaughter, the little red riding hood with a galette and a small jar of butter from my mother."

Softening his voice a little, the wolf called out, "Pull the pin, loose the latch."

The little red riding hood pulled the pin and the door opened. Watching from under the covers as she entered, the wolf said to her, "Put the galette and small jar of butter on the hutch and come, lie down with me."

The little red riding hood takes off her clothes and goes to get into bed[2]—where she was shocked to see how her grandmother looked undressed for bed.[3] She said to her,

"Grandmother, you have such big arms!" "That's to hug you better, my girl."

"Grandmother, you have such big legs!" "That's to run better, my dear."

"Grandmother, you have such big ears!" "That's to hear better, my dear."

"Grandmother, you have such big eyes!" "That's to see better, my dear."

"Grandma, you have such big teeth!" "That's to eat you up."

And with that, the wolf threw himself at the little red riding hood and ate her.

---

1 Although translators often opt for "had stayed in bed," the tense in Perrault matches the rest of the sentence, which suggests that she does not get up to open the door *this time*, although normally she would.

2 Perrault shifts to the present for a line or two in several of his tales. Catherine Bernard does the same in "Riquet à la Houppe" (see my translation in this volume). The present marks a significant moment in the narrative and puts the reader into the time of the action, as though we bear witness to it. This usage may also suggest the expectation of reading aloud.

3 The expression "en son déshabillé" refers to the clothes one wears when staying at home or to sleep, which, in the seventeenth century, were far less binding and concealing than those one wore to go out. My choice of "undressed" rather than dressed for bed picks up on the past participle in the French expression to emphasize that the wolf is revealed, not concealed in these clothes.

Moral[1]

Here we see how young children,
Especially young girls,
Beautiful, attractive, and sweet,
Get into trouble giving their attention to all sorts of people.
And it is not surprising if so many fall prey to the wolf.
I say *the* wolf because not all wolves are alike.
There are those with courteous personalities,
Not loud or nasty or hotheaded,
But reserved, compliant, and calm,
Who follow young ladies into their homes,
all the way to their bedrooms.
And yet! Who among us does not know
that the saccharine[2] wolf, of all wolves,
is the most treacherous?

SLEEPING BEAUTY

ONCE UPON A TIME A king and a queen were so upset about not having any children, so upset that there are no words to describe it. They tried thermal baths all over the world, wishes, pilgrimages, everyday prayers—they spared no effort and nothing worked. But eventually the queen got pregnant and gave birth to a girl. They gave her a fitting baptism and made all the fairies to be found in the kingdom—they found seven—godmothers so that each one of them might grant her a blessing, as fairies customarily did in those days. Thus, the princess was endowed with every exceptional talent imaginable.[3]

After the baptismal rites, everyone went back to the king's palace where he hosted a sumptuous banquet for the fairies. Each one of them received a magnificent service in a solid gold box; it contained a spoon, a fork, and a diamond- and ruby-encrusted knife made of fine gold. But as they took their places at the table, in walked an old fairy whom no one had thought to invite because it had been fifty years since she left her tower and everyone assumed she was dead or under a spell. The king had a place set for her but

1 Although Perrault wrote this moral in verse, as he does with all the Tales of Times Past, rhyming the translation would have resulted in the loss of cultural specific language, which I have retained here.

2 *Doucereux*: "Sweet without being agreeable. Used figuratively for people [...] who appear too sweet and too affected. We say, 'To be saccharine with a woman' to mean 'Act so as to make her believe that you are in love with her' ..." (DAF).

3 This detail seems premature since the next two paragraphs describe the scene in which the princess receives their blessings. We can take the second and third paragraphs as explanations of this introductory remark.

could not give her the solid gold box he had given the others because he had had only seven made for the seven fairies. The old fairy took it as an insult and mumbled some threatening remarks. One of the young fairies near her heard them. Sensing that she might grant the tiny princess a sinister blessing, [the young fairy] got up quickly when they left the table and hid behind a wall tapestry to make sure that she could speak last and be able to remedy as best she could any harm the old fairy might do.

Meanwhile, the fairies began granting the princess blessings. The youngest declared that she would be the most charming person in the world; the next that she would have the mind of an angel; the third that she would do everything with exemplary grace; the fourth that she would be a fine dancer; the fifth that she would sing like a nightingale, and the sixth that she would play an assortment of instruments to the highest perfection.

When it was the old fairy's turn she said, with her head shaking more out of spite than old age, that the princess would puncture her own hand with a spindle and die from it. This unholy blessing sent shivers through the assembly and no one could hold back the tears. Just then the young fairy came out from behind the tapestry and said loudly and clearly,

"Take heart, king and queen, your daughter will not die. I'm afraid my limited powers cannot completely undo what my superior has done. The princess will have to puncture her own hand with a spindle. But instead of dying, she will only fall into a deep sleep for 100 years, and when they have elapsed, the son of a king will arrive to wake her up."

In an attempt to escape the misfortune pronounced by the old fairy, the king issued an edict forbidding anyone to spin yarn on a spindle and even to have spindles around the house, under penalty of death.

Fifteen or sixteen years went by, and the king and queen had moved the family to their country estate where the young princess was going from room after room exploring. She went all the way up to the small room at the top where an aged woman was alone spinning at her distaff. This old girl had not heard a word about the king's prohibition against spinning.

"What are you doing, old woman?"

"I'm spinning, sweet thing," she replied, not recognizing the princess.

"Wow! That's really something," said the princess in response, "How do you do it? Let me have it to see if I can do it as well as you."

The minute she grabbed the spindle (she was very energetic and a bit impulsive, and besides, the Fairies' Decree[1] mandated it), she punctured her own hand and passed out. The old girl was at a loss and called for help.

---

1 "Arrêt des Fées" (Fairies' Decree) appears capitalized in the 1697 text. While other important nouns are also capitalized, here the combination creates what looks like a title and I have retained it. The word "arrêt"

They come from every direction,[1] throw water on the princess' face, untie her corset, slap her hands, massage her temples with the magical water that preserved the Queen of Hungary[2]—

But nothing brought her back.

In the meantime, the king, who had followed the noise up the stairs, remembered the fairies' prophesy. He deemed the incident inevitable because fairies called for it and had the princess set up in the most elegant apartment in the palace on a bed cover embroidered with gold and silver. You would have taken her for an angel, she looked so beautiful. Fainting had not drained her face of its warm color. She had rosy cheeks and lips like coral. She did have her eyes shut, but her gentle audible breathing proved she was not dead.

The king instructed everyone to let her sleep in peace until it was time for her to wake up. At the moment of the princess's mishap the good fairy that had saved her by condemning her to sleep for a hundred years was 12,000 leagues [or 40,000 miles] away in the Kingdom of Mataquin. But she learned of it instantly from a little dwarf wearing seven-league boots—those were boots that moved you seven leagues with every step. The fairy left as soon as possible in a blazing chariot pulled by dragons and arrived within the hour. The king extended his hand as she stepped down from the carriage. She appreciated everything he had done, but her gift of incredible foresight made her realize that it would be alarming for the princess to wake up all alone in the château. So here's what she did:

She tapped everything in the château with her wand: governesses, maids of honor, ladies-in-waiting, courtiers, the king's attendants, butlers, chefs, the kitchen help, security guards, gatekeepers, pages, and footmen.[3] She also tapped all the horses in the stable with their groomers, the guard dogs, and little Puff, the princess's pet dog that was with her on the bed. As she tapped them, they all fell asleep to wake up only

---

refers generally to a biding decision made by an authority figure and specifically in the jurisprudence of 1690 to decrees published by Louis XIV's court, which expressed his law in final legal decisions. It suggests that like kings, fairies have a binding authority. Since this reads like a title, it seems furthermore that these laws are disseminated officially through print or public announcement. Calling the enunciation an "arrêt" raises the fairy's baptismal blessing to a political act. It is further contrasted in the text with the word "edit" (edict), or proclamation, which is what the king issues to stop the practice of spinning in the kingdom. In political terms, the "arrêt" expresses a final ruling, whereas the "edit" issues an order (DAF).

1 As we have seen above (p. 176, note 2), Perrault shifts to the present for a line or two in several of his tales.

2 *L'eau de la reine d'Hongrie*: curative astringent and perfume made from macerated rosemary. It was named for Elisabeth of Poland, Queen Consort of Hungary (1320–42), who credited its rejuvenating properties with preserving her beauty and strength throughout her life. She lived to be 75. Important women at the court of Louis XIV, the letter writer Madame de Sévigné among them, used it as perfume.

3 Note that for noble houses, the number of hired help attached to the prince could be staggering. Louis XIV had 1,500 people concerned with his meals alone. And lest these positions appear menial, many were jobs of privilege. The managerial positions were held by nobility, with a prince of the blood (*Grand Maître*) overseeing the whole operation.

when their mistress did and be ready to tend to her needs. Even the spits over the fire pit, heavy with partridges and pheasants, fell asleep. The fire, too. All of it happened in an instant. Fairies don't waste time.

Then the king and queen kissed their precious child without waking her up, left the château, and had prohibitions issued preventing anyone and everyone from coming near it. These prohibitions proved unnecessary because fifteen minutes later such an impressive number of big and small trees and brambles and thorns wove themselves in and around the château grounds that neither man nor mouse could get through. They were woven in such a way that you could only see the top of the château's towers, and only from very far away. No one doubted that the fairy had once again worked her art to ensure that while the princess slumbered, she was safe from inquiring minds that wanted to know.[1]

At the end of the hundred years, the son of the reigning king, from a different family than the slumbering princess, was out that way for a hunt. He asked about two towers he could see above a tall, thick forest. Each person told him the story he had heard. Some said it was a castle haunted by spirits; others that all the wizards of the land gathered there for their midnight Sabbath. Popular opinion had it that the château belonged to an ogre who brought all the children he could catch there to eat them at his leisure where no one could follow him because he alone had the cunning to forge a path through such a dense woodland.

The prince did not know what to think, but then an old farmer spoke up and told him, "Your highness, more than fifty years ago I heard someone tell my father that in this château lay the most beautiful princess in the world, that she would be woken up by the son of a prince, and that she was promised to him."

The prince felt all hot and bothered after this speech and knew without even thinking that he would be the one to end this marvelous adventure. Impelled by love and glory he resolved right then and there to see who was in there.

Barely had he stepped towards the woodland when all the big trees and brambles and thorns moved aside on their own to let him pass. He walked towards the château at the end of the long majestic avenue that led to it. It did unsettle him a bit to see that none of his men had been able to follow him because the trees wove themselves back together as soon as he came through. He continued on his path all the same—young princes in love always find their courage. He came to a grand courtyard and

1 The word "curieux" in the seventeenth century referred to a disposition among the elite: to be curious was to be fashionably interested in the exotic. The "curieux" was a gentleman who sought out novelty and was probably a collector. If it sounds negative in this context, as though the public has prying eyes, it is because the trait was unsavory in everyone besides the gallant nobleman, namely, women and townspeople who might be prone to curiosity out of inappropriate or prurient desire. The colloquial turn of phrase I've used here refers to such a nosey personality. On the feminine manifestation of curiosity as dangerous desire, see "Blue Beard" (p. 164).

everything he saw there could make the blood run cold. The silence was terrible, death masks everywhere, and it was strewn with bodies of men and animals that looked dead. But he could tell from the pimpled nose and ruddy cheeks of the porters that they were just sleeping, and the drops of wine at the bottom of their glasses gave away the cause of their slumber.

He crosses a marble courtyard,[1] climbs a staircase and walks into the guards' quarters where they were all lined up in formation, rifles on their shoulders and snoring like champions. He crosses several bedrooms full of sleeping courtiers and ladies, some standing, some sitting. He enters a gilded room—

And there on the bed, curtains drawn on every side, was the most exquisite vision he had ever seen: a princess that was probably about fifteen or sixteen years old, so radiantly beautiful that she had a divine glow. Trembling and in awe he dropped to his knees before her.

Since the end of the enchantment had come, the princess woke up. She looked at him with more feeling in her eyes than is really appropriate for a first encounter and said,

"Is that you, prince? You certainly took your time."

Enchanted by these words and even more by the manner in which she expressed them, the prince was at a loss to communicate his joy and thanks. He swore that he loved her more than he loved himself. His language was clumsy, but all the more charming for it. He was more flustered than the princess, which should be no surprise since she had had time to think about what she wanted to say to him. It would seem—although this detail is missing from the story—that the good fairy allowed her to have pleasant dreams during her very long slumber.

After talking together for four hours, they still had not said half of what they wanted to say to each other.

In the meantime, the whole palace had woken up with the princess. Everyone readied themselves to work, but as they had not fallen in love, they were dying of hunger. The maid of honor, no less affected by it than the others, lost patience and loudly told the princess that the meat was ready. The prince helped the princess get up—she was fully and sumptuously dressed—but he kept silent on the subject of her high collar, which made her look like my grandmother. It did not make her less attractive.

They came into a hall of mirrors and ate a meal served by the queen's attendants. Violins and oboes played old tunes; they were excellent even though it had been a hundred years since anyone played them. Right after dinner and without delay, the family chaplain married them in the chapel of the château and the maid of honor

---

1 On the use of the present tense, see p. 176, note 2.

opened the bed curtains.[1] They hardly slept. The princess didn't really need it and the prince left bright and early to return to the village and his father, who was no doubt concerned about him.

The prince told him that while he was out hunting, he got lost in the forest and slept the night at the cabin of a coal-maker who fed him black bread and cheese. His father the king, who was good-natured, believed it, but his mother did not find the story compelling. He hunted almost every day and always had an excuse ready. Once when he slept two or three nights away from home, she became convinced that he was having an illicit love affair. In truth, he lived that way with the princess for two full years and had two children with her: the first, a daughter named Aurora and the second a son named Daylight because he was even lovelier than his sister.

Several times the queen attempted to get an explanation out of her son, telling him that he should be satisfied with the life he had, but he never could trust her with his secret. She descended from ogres and the king had only married her for her vast fortune. People at court even declared under their breath that she had an ogre's desires and when she saw little children walk by it was all she could do not to throw herself at them. So the prince never said anything.

Now, when the king died, which happened two years later, and the prince found himself sovereign of the realm, he publicly announced his marriage and, with great pomp and circumstance, brought his wife and children to the château. A spectacular ceremony attended his entrance into the capital city flanked by his children.

Some time later, the king left to make war on Emperor Catalabutte. He designated his mother the queen regent and entrusted his wife and children to her care. The war was to last all summer and as soon as he left the Queen Mother sent her daughter-in-law and the children to a country house in the woods to be able more easily to sate her violent desire. She visited there a few days later and one night told the butler, "I want to eat young Aurora for lunch tomorrow."

"No, Madame!"

"I want to," said the queen—and she said it in the drawl of an ogre hankering for young flesh—"and I want her in a *Robert* sauce."[2]

Seeing very well that it does not pay to fool with an ogress, the poor man grabbed

---

1 Pulling the curtains on the poster bed of the seventeenth century would be the equivalent today of turning down the sheets. In other words, she prepared the bed for them.

2 "Sauce Robert" dates from the birth of modern French culinary technique in the seventeenth century and is one of only a few early modern recipes that are still used in modern France. A basic roux (browned butter with flour) combines with onion and spices and simmers in a demi-glace, a veal-based wine reduction. The preparation of demi-glace alone takes hours, which makes this rich sauce time-consuming to make. The Ogress's desire for *sauce Robert* attests the refinement of her taste in spite of her monstrous birth. But her sudden demand for French gastronomy as though it were fast food betrays her savagery and would tax even a seasoned chef.

his knife and went up to young Aurora's room. She was four years old then and, jumping gleefully, she threw her arms around his neck and begged for candy. He began to cry, the knife fell from his hand, and he went down to the barnyard to kill a young lamb instead. The sauce he made was so good that his mistress swore she had never eaten anything so delicious.

At the same time, he had taken young Aurora to his wife with instructions to hide her in the little room they occupied at the back of the barnyard. Eight days later the evil queen said to the butler, "I want to eat young Daylight for dinner."

He did not respond, resolved to trick her as he had before. He went to look for young Daylight and found him with a miniature foil in his hand playing at fencing with a large monkey. He was only three. The butler brought him to his wife who hid him with young Aurora. In his place, he prepared a small and tender young goat that the ogress found absolutely delicious.

Things had gone smoothly so far, but one evening the evil queen told the butler, "I want to eat the queen in the same sauce you made for her children." At that point, the butler despaired of tricking her again. The young queen was over twenty, to say nothing of the hundred years she had been asleep: her skin was a bit tough, even if smooth and white, and who could find an animal as tough-skinned as that in the menagerie? He resolved to save his own life by taking the life of the young queen and went up to her room intent on getting it over with. He worked himself into a fury and burst into the queen's room with the knife drawn. And yet, he did not want to catch her off guard, so conveyed with utmost respect that he had received the order from the Queen Mother.

"Do what you have to do," she told him, offering him her neck, "Execute the order you were given. I will go to my children, my poor babies, that I so loved." She believed they were dead since they had disappeared without explanation.

"No. No, Madame," responded the weary butler. "You will not die and you will go to your precious children, but at my home where I hid them. I will trick the Queen Mother again and serve her a young doe in your place."

He showed her to his room where she could embrace and cry with her children, and went to prepare a doe. The queen ate it for dinner, savoring it as though it were the young queen. She was very pleased with her cruelty and was prepared to tell the king upon his return that the rabid wolves in the area had eaten his wife and his two children.

One evening as she paced the courtyards and barnyard to sniff out fresh meat, which she did routinely, she heard the sound of young Daylight crying coming from a room below—his mother the queen wanted him whipped because he had been bad—and she heard young Aurora plead for mercy on her brother's behalf.

The ogress recognized the voices of the queen and her children. Furious that she had been tricked, she *demands* first thing the next day—in a dreadful voice that terrified everyone—that they bring a big tub to the center of the courtyard and fill it with toads, vipers, water snakes, and serpents. She ordered the queen and her children, the butler, his wife, and her maid to be taken by force with their hands tied behind their backs and thrown in.

There they stood with the executioners poised to throw them into the tub when the king, who arrived home earlier than expected, trotted in on horseback. In complete and total shock, he demanded that someone explain this terrible vision. No one seemed willing to apprise him of the situation, when suddenly, the ogress, enraged by this turn of events, threw herself head-first into the tub and was devoured by the very creatures she had put there. The king could not help but be vexed by the scene. She was his mother. But he took comfort in his beautiful wife and his children.

Moral

Waiting a time for a husband to find
Rich, dashing, elegant, and kind
That's the traditional way.
But wait a hundred years for him … asleep?
You won't find a female today
Whose slumber is so deep.
The fable also tries to make us see
That a strong marriage bond
May be differed, long postponed
And not for that reason be less happy.
But the fair sex does so desire
The promise of conjugal bliss
That I've neither the strength nor the fire
To force upon them this premise.

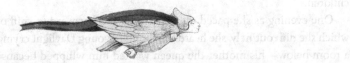

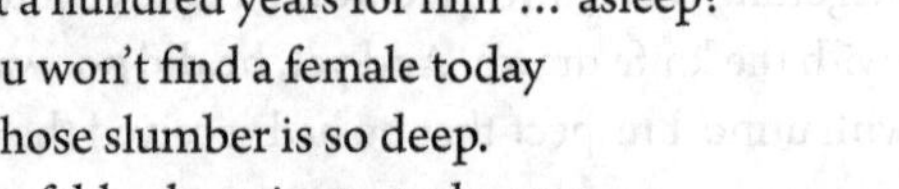

10. Marie-Catherine d'Aulnoy, *Les Contes des fées* (1698)

Marie-Catherine d'Aulnoy penned more fairy tales than any other writer in the 1690s and also wrote novels, inventive travel narratives (set in Spain), and fictional memoires. Her tales were the first of the French contes des fées to gain notoriety in English popular print culture, and it was through translation of her work that the term "fairy tale" entered the English language. "The Fairies' Tales" is unique in the corpus, as it serves as a frame tale to her first collection and depicts an elusive scene of sharing written stories among the nobility. Many writers, including famed letter writer Madame de Sévigné, mention the habit of sharing written work in Parisian salons—or literary gatherings—but few describe the scene. D'Aulnoy's setting seems realistic: the Château at Saint-Cloud belonged to Louis XIV's young brother Philippe d'Orléan and its elaborate gardens played host to aristocratic visits throughout the reign. And in it, the author reads from her own book, rather than telling stories in spontaneous performance—a phenomenon also illustrated in the images that accompany her first editions and that feature a learned or sophisticated woman reading from a book before an audience. Nevertheless, the presence of woodland fairies makes this reading a fantastical event that also serves as an allegory for writerly inspiration. It also not so subtly establishes D'Aulnoy as the most envied writer of her entourage. "Finette Cendron," which follows, takes up a favorite theme in her work in the unlikely plot of a Cinderella story: the resourceful heroine. D'Aulnoy's stories feature strong fairies and able heroines who are worthy of their help. A particular cultural allusion is worthy of note: the red velvet and pearl encrusted slipper she wears and loses, unlike Perrault's fantastical glass slipper, has its basis in the elaborate aristocratic dress of 1690s France.

THE FAIRIES' TALES, TRANSLATED BY CHRISTINE A. JONES, 2011[1]

AFTER A BOUT WITH THE worst of everything a long winter can do, the return of warm weather inspired many of the witty and refined to go out to Saint-Cloud. They admired everything; they praised it all; Madame D…, who wore out more quickly than the rest of the group, sat down on the edge of a fountain. "Leave me alone here," she said, "on the chance that a sylvan or druid might deign to pay me a visit and chat." Everyone gave her trouble for being lazy; but they grew impatient and the desire to see a thousand beautiful things that opened up before their eyes prevailed over any they may have had to stay with her. "Since this conversation you imagine having with the keepers of these woodlands is by no means assured," Monsieur de Saint P… said to her, "I will give you the [book of] Fairy's Tales to keep you pleasurably occupied." "If I had not written them," smiled Madame D…, "their

1 [Source: Christine A. Jones, unpublished.]

striking originality might have made an impression.... but don't worry about me, I will not be the least bit bored."

She insisted so firmly that the delightful group went on its way; and after they had seen everything, they came back to the shaded grove where Madame D... sat waiting for them. "Well, you certainly missed out!" cried the Countess of F... as she approached her. "What we just saw is fantastic." "And what just happened to me is, too," she replied. "Just imagine that as I looked all around and perceived a thousand different things to admire, I suddenly saw a nymph close to me. Her bright and gentle eyes, lively and sophisticated air, and gracious and affable disposition made me just as happy as I was surprised to see her. The delicate fabrics that she wore revealed a shapely figure; a knot of ribbon gathered her long braided hair at her waist; and the elegance of her features left nothing to be desired. I was about to say something to her when she interrupted me with these verses:

'When an exalted prince retreats here for sport,
When this sumptuous palace and its tranquil rockery,
Become a welcoming sanctuary
To host his magnificent court,
Of everything the eye commands,
Shouldn't we ponder,
Is it no wonder,
That so much treasure enriches its beautiful lands?
Here, the happy days of Rhea are alive
Sorrow trembles when they arrive
To banish it forever.
Innocence, games, pleasure, and laughter
Everywhere spell its doom;
These charming groves, these parterres in flower,
Fear not the chill of winter's icy tomb;
Look at the sky so serene,
Never does a cloud of woe,
Deny this land the sun's warm glow,
Blooms in a thousand colors enhance the scene,
Look how the emerald stems
Brighten the color of the floral gems,
In this enchanted wood, listen to the birds,
Watch in these fertile plains,
Gentle animals graze in herds,

And through the shimmering fields winds a path of
fountains;
Look at their spray soaring up to the
Gods.
On these shadowy promenades,
That snake under the pines,
Shepherds are more refined,
Shepherdesses more courteous.
In this beautiful place we forget to adore,
The havens, so sumptuous,
Where the Gods lived before.
Cradled in peace and quietness,
Majesty reigns here,
Exalted goodness is peer,
Of Grandeur in excess;
Yet though it impress
Nothing can be seen
That equals the Princess
For whom these habitats preen.'

"The nymph talked as much as I listened," continued Madame D…, "then she seemed to be startled by the noise you made as you walked up. 'Adieu,' she said to me, 'I thought you were alone, but since you are with others, I'll come see you another time.' As she finished saying these words, she disappeared; and I'll admit that I was not particularly upset to see you approach because the whole adventure was beginning to spook me." "You are so fortunate," retorted the Marquise de…, "to have such a wonderful relationship, now with the Muses, now with the Fairies—you could never tire of it. And if I knew as many tales as you do, I would consider myself a very great lady." "These gems," replied Madame D…, "lack much of the necessary luster; all of my good friends the fairies have, until now, been stingy with their favors; and I assure you that I intend to neglect them the way they neglect me." "Oh no!" cried the Contesse de F…, interrupting her, "I beg forgiveness on their behalf; we were expecting you to share more of their adventures, and this is the perfect place to do it. No one has ever been as attentive to you as we will be today." "It seems," said Madame D…, "as though I guessed right about some of your expectations: Here is a book [of stories] just waiting to be read; and to heighten your pleasure, I've included a Spanish novella, which is absolutely true and which I learned in the original."

FINETTE CENDRON, TRANSLATED BY ELIZABETH LEE AND ANNIE MACDONELL, 1892[1]

THERE WAS ONCE UPON A time a king and a queen who managed their affairs very badly. They were driven out of their kingdom, and had to sell first their crowns, then their clothes, their linen, their laces, their furniture, bit by bit, in order that they might have bread to eat. The pawnbrokers were tired of buying, for every day something new was sold. When at last they were stripped of nearly everything they possessed, the king said to his wife: "Here we are exiled from our kingdom, with nothing left us to live on. We must therefore earn our own and our poor children's bread. Think, then, what we shall do, for till now I have only followed kingcraft, which is very easy." The queen, who was very clever, asked eight days to think about the matter. At the end of that time, she said: "There is no reason why we should be miserable, your majesty. All you have to do is to make nets to catch birds in the woods and fish in the sea. While the lines are wearing out I shall make others for you. As for our three daughters, they are lazy minxes, and no mistake, who think they are still great ladies, and play at being such. They must be sent away, so far away that they will never come back; for it would be impossible for us to give them the fine clothes they would desire."

The king began to weep when he saw he must part from his children, for he was a kind father; but the queen was mistress. He agreed, therefore, to all her proposals, and said: "Tomorrow morning rise early, and take your three daughters wherever you think suitable." While they were planning this, Princess Finette, the youngest girl, was listening through the keyhole. When she had found out the intention of her father and mother, she ran off as fast as ever she could to a large grotto, a long way from home, where the Fairy Merluche, her god-mother lived.

Finette took with her two pounds of fresh butter, some eggs, milk, and some flour to make a nice cake for her god-mother, so that she might get a good welcome from her. Very merrily did she set out on her journey, but the farther she went the more tired she grew. The soles of her shoes were quite worn through, and her pretty little feet were so torn that it was pitiful to see them. At last she had to give up, and sitting down on the grass, she began to cry.

A beautiful Spanish jennet passed by, saddled and bridled, with more diamonds on its saddle-cloth than would buy three whole towns. On seeing the princess, it began feeding quietly by her side, and bending its knee, it seemed to bow before her. "Pretty one," she said, taking hold of the bridle, "will you carry me to my god-mother, the fairy? I shall be so grateful if you will, for I am so tired that I am like to die. And

---

1 [Source: Anne Thackeray Ritchie, intro., Elizabeth Lee and Annie Macdonell, trans., *The Fairy Tales of Madame d'Aulnoy, Newly Done into English* ([1892; 1895] Honolulu, HI: UP of the Pacific, 2003): 188–202.]

if you help me now, I will give you nice oats, and hay, and fresh straw to lie on." The horse bent down almost to the ground before her, and little Finette jumped on its back, whereupon it set off running as lightly as a bird. At the entrance of the grotto, it stopped as if it had known the way, as indeed it did; for it was Merluche, knowing that her god-daughter was coming to see her, who had sent this beautiful horse.

When she was inside, she made three low bows to her god-mother, and taking the hem of her dress, she kissed it, saying: "Good-day, god-mother, how are you? Here is some butter, some milk, some flour, and some eggs, which I have brought to make a nice cake for you, just as we do at home." "Welcome, Finette," said the fairy; "come till I give you a kiss." So saying, she kissed her twice, which made Finette very happy, for Madam Merluche was not a common fairy. "Now, god-daughter," said she, "I want you to be my little maid. Take down my hair and comb it." The princess undid it, and combed it, in the cleverest possible way. "I know quite well," said Merluche, "why you came here. You overheard the king and the queen, who want to lead you away and lose you, and you wish that no such evil thing may happen to you. Well, you have only to take this ball of thread. It will never break. Fasten one end to the door of your house, and keep it in your hand. When the queen has left you, it will be easy to return by following the thread."

The princess thanked her god-mother, who filled a bag for her with beautiful dresses all of gold and silver, and after kissing her, mounted her again on the beautiful horse, and in two or three minutes she was landed at the door of their majesties' hut. "My little friend," said Finette to the horse, "you are very pretty, and very good, and you run faster than the sun. I thank you for your trouble, and now go back to where you came from." She entered the house very quietly, and hiding her bag under her pillow, went to her bed as if nothing had happened.

As soon as day dawned, the king awoke his wife, saying: "Come, madam, come, get ready for the journey." She got up immediately, put on her thick shoes, a short skirt, a white camisole, and took a stick in her hand. Then she called her eldest daughter, whose name was Fleur d'Amour; her second, Belle-de-Nuit; and her third, Fine-Oreille, or Finette, as she was usually called. "I learnt in a dream last night," said the queen, "that we must go and see my sister. She will entertain us well, and we can eat and laugh as much as ever we like." Fleur d'Amour, who was miserable at living in this lonely place, said to her mother: "Very well, madam, let us go wherever you please. Provided that I get away from here, it doesn't matter to me." The two others said the same. So after bidding good-bye to the king, all the four set off.

They went such a very long way that Fine-Oreille began to be much afraid she would not have thread enough, for they had gone nearly a thousand leagues. She used always to walk behind her sisters, passing the thread deftly through the bushes. When the queen thought that her daughters would not be able to find their way back, she went into a large wood, and said: "My little lambs, go to sleep now. I shall be the shepherdess who watches round her flock, for fear the wolf should eat them." So lying down on the grass they fell asleep, and the queen left them there, thinking she should never see them again. Finette had shut her eyes, but was not asleep. "If I were a wicked girl," she said, "I should go away at once, leaving my sisters here to die, for they beat me and scratch me till the blood comes. But in spite of all their cruelty, I will not leave them." So she awoke them, and told them the whole story. They began to cry, and begged her to take them along with her, and said they would give her lovely dolls, and their little silver dolls' house, and their other toys, and their sugar-plums. "I know well enough that you will do nothing of the kind," said Finette, "but all the same, I will be a kind sister to you." And getting up, she followed her thread, and the princesses did so too, so that they got home almost as soon as the queen.

Stopping at the door, they heard the king saying: "My heart is very sore at seeing you coming back by yourself." "Well, but we didn't know what to do with our daughters," said the queen. "Yet, if you had brought my Finette back," replied the king, "I should not mind about the others, for they care for nobody." Tap, tap, came their knock. "Who is there?" said the king. "Your three daughters," they answered, "Fleur d'Amour, Belle-de-Nuit, and Fine-Oreille." The queen was all of a tremble. "Do not open the door," she said; "it must be their ghosts, for they themselves could not have come back." And the king, who was just as great a coward as his wife, said: "You are deceiving me; you are not my daughters." But Fine-Oreille, who was quickwitted, said to him: "Father, I am going to bend down. Look at me through the cat's hole, and if I am not Finette, I'll let you beat me." The king looked as she had told him, and as soon as he recognized her, he opened the door to them. The queen pretended that she was very glad to see them, and told them she had forgotten something, and that she came to fetch it, but assuredly she would have found them again. And they made as if they believed her, and went up to their sleeping-place in a pretty little garret for the night.

"Well, sisters," said Finette, "you promised me a doll; give it me then." "And how can you expect it, you little monkey?" said they. "It is all on account of you that the king does not love us." Thereupon they took their distaffs and beat her without mercy. When they had chastised her well, she went to bed, but with so many scars and swellings that she could not sleep. So she heard the queen saying to the king, "I shall take them in another direction, still further off, and I am sure they will never return." When Finette heard this plan, she got up very quietly, meaning to pay another visit to her god-mother. Going into the poultry-house, she took two chickens and a fine cock, and wrung their necks, then two little rabbits that the queen was feeding up with cabbage against the next time they should be having a feast; and putting them all in a basket, she set off. But she had not gone a league, groping all the way, and in terror of her life, when the Spanish jennet galloped up to her, snorting and neighing. She thought it was all up with her, and that soldiers were coming to capture her, but when she saw the pretty horse all by itself, she mounted, delighted to go on her way in this comfortable fashion; and very soon she was at her god-mother's house.

After the usual greetings, she gave her the chickens, the cock, and the rabbits. Then she begged Merluche to help her by good counsel, making known to her how the queen had sworn to take them away to the end of the world. Merluche told her god-daughter not to be miserable, and giving her a sack full of ashes, she said: "You will carry the bag in front of you, and shake it as you go. You will walk on the ashes, and when you want to return, you need only look for your footprints. But do not bring your sisters back. They are too wicked, and if you bring them, I will never see you any more." Finette took leave of her, taking with her by Merluche's orders some thirty or forty millions of diamonds in a little box which she put in her pocket. The horse was quite ready, and carried her off as before.

When day broke the queen called the princesses, and when they came she said to them: "The king is not very well. Last night I dreamt that I must go and gather flowers and herbs in a certain country where they are very good. They will make him young again, therefore let us set out at once." Fleur d'Amour and Belle-de-Nuit, who could not believe their mother was anxious to get rid of them, were very sorry to hear this. However they had to set off; and they went so far that never was such a long journey made before. Finette, who did not say a word all the while, kept behind the others, shaking the ashes very cleverly, not letting the wind or the rain spoil any of them.

The queen, fully persuaded they could never find the way again, noticed one evening that her three daughters were fast asleep, so she took advantage of this to leave them and return home. When daylight came, and Finette knew that her mother was no longer with them, she awoke her sisters. "We are alone," she said; "the queen has gone away." Fleur d'Amour and Belle-de-Nuit began to cry, to tear their hair, and to beat their faces with their fists. "Alas!" they exclaimed; "what shall we do?" Finette was the kindest girl in the whole world, and again she took pity on her sisters. "Think what risk I am running," she said; "for when my god-mother gave me the means of returning, she forbade me to tell you the way, and said if I disobeyed her she would never see me again." Belle-de-Nuit threw herself on Finette's neck, and so did Fleur d'Amour, caressing her so tenderly that before long they all three returned together to the king and the queen.

Their majesties were very much astonished at seeing the princesses again, and spoke of it all night long. And the youngest girl, who was not called Fine-Oreille[1] for nothing, heard them making up a fresh plot for the queen on the morrow to take

1 Sharp ear.

them again into the wilds. She ran and awoke her sisters. "Alas!" she said to them, "we are lost. The queen is determined to take us to some desert and leave us there. It is your fault that my god-mother is angry, and that I dare not go and find her as I always did before." They were very much troubled, and one said to the other, "What shall we do, my sister, what shall we do?" At last Belle-de-Nuit said to the others, "There is no need to distress ourselves. Old Merluche hasn't the whole stock of cleverness in the world. We need only take peas with us and sow them along the road, and by the traces of their growth we can come back." Fleur d'Amour thought this a capital plan, so they took a large quantity of peas, and filled their pockets. But Fine-Oreille, instead of carrying peas, took the bag with the pretty clothes, and the little box of diamonds, and as soon as the queen called them to be off, they were quite ready.

"I dreamt last night," she said to them, "that in a country which I need not name there are three handsome princes waiting to marry you. I am going to take you there to see if my dream is true." The queen walked on in front, and her daughters after her, sowing their peas, and quite easy in their minds, having no doubt but that they would return home again. This time the queen travelled farther than she had ever done before; but one dark night she left them, and came back to the king. Very tired was she when she reached home, but very glad not to have the cares of such a large household on her shoulders.

The three princesses, after sleeping till eleven o'clock in the morning, woke up. It was Finette that first perceived the queen's absence, and though she expected it, she could not help crying, having, so far as getting back was concerned, more confidence in her god-mother's help than in her sisters' cleverness. In a great fright, she told them the queen had gone, and that they must follow her as soon as possible. "Hold your tongue, you little monkey," said Fleur d'Amour; "we'll be able to find the road whenever we like. We don't want you to interfere unless your opinion is asked." Finette did not dare to answer, but when they tried to find the way, not a mark or a footpath could be found. The pigeons, of which there are a great number in that country, had eaten up the peas, and so the princesses began to cry and howl. After being two days without food, Fleur d'Amour said to Belle-de-Nuit, "Sister, have you nothing to eat?" "No," she answered. She asked Finette the same thing. "No more have I," she replied, "but I have just found an acorn." "Ah! give it to me," said one. "Give it to me," said the other; and each of them wanted to have it. "One acorn would hardly satisfy three of us," said Finette; "let us plant it; another will grow out of it for our use." They agreed, though there seemed little likelihood that a tree would grow in a country where there were none, and where only cabbages and lettuces were to be seen. The princesses ate of these, and if they had been very delicate, they would have died a hundred times. Nearly every night they lay down under the stars, and every morning and every evening went in turns to water the acorn, saying, "Grow, grow, pretty acorn!" And it began to grow visibly. When it had grown to some height, Fleur d'Amour wished to climb up on it, but it was not strong enough to bear her, and feeling it bend under her weight, she got down. The same thing happened to Belle-de-Nuit. Finette, lighter than the others, stopped longer, and they asked her, "Do you see nothing, sister?" "No, I see nothing," she answered. "That is because the oak is not high enough," said Fleur d'Amour; so they went on watering it, and saying, "Grow, grow, pretty acorn!" Finette never failed to climb up twice a day, and one morning when she was there, Belle-de-Nuit said to Fleur d'Amour: "I have found a bag our sister has hidden. What can be in it?" Fleur d'Amour said Finette had told her it was old lace she was mending. "Well, I think there are sugar plumbs in it," said Belle-de-Nuit. She was greedy, and wanted to see what was in it. She did find the laces of the king and the queen, but they served to hide Finette's beautiful clothes and the box of diamonds. "Well, was there ever such a wicked little creature?" she cried. "Let us take them all and put stones in their place." This they did without delay. When Finette came back, she did not notice what her sisters had done, for she did not think of ornaments in a desert. Her one thought was of the oak, which was growing to be the finest ever seen.

One time when she had climbed up and her sisters as usual asked her if she saw nothing, "I see," she cried, "a large house, so beautiful—so very, very beautiful, that I cannot describe it to you. The walls are of emeralds and rubies, the roof of diamonds, and it is all covered with golden bells; the weathercocks turn and turn with the wind." "That is not true," they said; "it is not so beautiful as you say." "Believe me, it is," replied Finette; "I don't tell lies. Come and see for yourselves, for my eyes are quite dazzled." Fleur d'Amour climbed up into the tree, and when she saw the castle, she could speak of nothing else. Belle-de-Nuit, who was very curious, would not be behind-hand, and climbing up, she was just as delighted as her sisters. "Certainly," they said, "we must go to that palace; perhaps we shall find handsome princes there who will only be too happy to marry us." All the evening long they spoke of nothing but their plan. Then they lay down in the grass, and when Finette seemed to be asleep, Fleur d'Amour said to Belle-de-Nuit, "Do you know what must do, sister? Get up and let us dress ourselves in the rich dresses Finette has brought." "You are right," said Belle-de-Nuit; so they got up, curled their hair, powdered their faces, stuck on beauty spots, and dressed themselves in gold and silver gowns, all covered with diamonds. Never was seen such a magnificent sight.

Finette, not knowing that her wicked sisters had robbed her, took her bag with the intention of dressing, and she was in great distress at only finding pebbles. At the same time she saw her sisters decked out like suns. She wept, and reproached them with their breach of faith to her, but they only laughed and mocked at her. "Would you really dare," she said, "to take me to the castle without any pretty dresses or ornaments at all?" "We have not too many for ourselves," replied Fleur d'Amour, "and we'll beat you if you talk any more about it." "But," Finette went on, "these dresses are mine. My god-mother gave me them. You have no part in them." "If you speak another word," they said, "we shall kill you, and bury you, and nobody will know anything about it." And poor Finette, afraid to anger them, followed them quietly, walking some steps behind, just as if she were their servant.

The nearer they came to the house, the more wonderful it seemed. "Hi!" said Fleur d'Amour and Belle-de-Nuit, "what a good time we are going to have! What good cheer we shall partake of as we sit at the king's table. But as for Finette, she will wash the dishes in the kitchen, for she is just like a scullion, and if any one asks who she is, let us take care not to call her our sister, but rather the little village herd." Finette, who was full of intelligence, and very pretty, was in great distress at such ill-treatment. When they went up to the gate of the castle they knocked, and at once a hideous old woman came to open the door to them. She had only one eye, in the middle of her forehead, but it was bigger than five or six ordinary eyes; her nose was flat, her complexion dark, and her mouth was so horrible that it made everyone afraid to look at it; she was fifteen feet high, and thirty feet in girth. "Oh, you miserable girls," she said, "what brings you here? Do you not know that this is the ogre's castle, and that all of you together would hardly be enough for his breakfast? But I am better than my husband. Come in, I shall not eat you up all at once. You may have the comfort of living two or three days more." When they heard the ogress speaking in this fashion, they ran away, thinking they could escape, but one of her strides was as good as fifty of theirs, and running after them, she caught them by their hair or by the skin of their necks. Bundling them under her arm, she threw all three of them into the cellar, which was full of toads and adders, and where you walked on the bones of those that had already been eaten.

As she wanted to crunch up Finette on the spot she ran to fetch vinegar and salt to eat her as a salad, but hearing the ogre coming, and thinking the princesses' skin white and delicate, she made up her mind to eat them all by herself. So she hastily put them into a large tub where they could only see out through a hole.

The ogre was six times as tall as his wife. When he spoke the house shook; when he coughed you would have thought it was claps of thunder. He had only one eye, a large, ugly one, his hair stood all on end, and he leant on a log which he used for a stick. In his hand he held a covered basket out of which he drew fifteen little children that he had stolen on the road, and whom he swallowed as if they had been fifteen fresh eggs. When the three princesses saw him, they shook with terror under the tub, and dared no longer cry aloud for fear he should hear them. But low to themselves they said, "He'll eat us all alive; how can we escape?" The ogre said to his wife, "I smell fresh meat, give me some." "Indeed," said the ogress, "you always think you smell fresh meat. It is four sheep that passed by." "Oh, I make no mistake," said the ogre. "I smell fresh meat for certain. I am going to look everywhere for it." "Look for it, then," she said, "but you won't find any." "If I find it," answered the ogre, "and if you are hiding it, I shall cut off your head to make me a ball." In terror at this threat she said to him, "Don't be angry, my little ogre, I am going to tell you the truth. To day there came here three young maidens whom I kept, but it would be a pity to eat them, for they know how to do everything. As I am now old I need rest; our beautiful house, as you see, is in very bad order; our bread is not baked properly; our soup no longer tastes good to you, and I don't look so beautiful in your eyes since I have been killing myself with work. They will, therefore, be my servants, so I beg of you not to eat them just now. If you wish to at some future time you can do as you like."

The ogre found it very hard to promise not to eat them up at once. "Let me have my own way," he said; "I shall only eat two of them." "No, you shall not eat any of them." "Very well; I shall only eat the little one." But she answered, "No, you shall not eat one of them." At last, after quarrelling for a long time, he promised not to eat them; while the ogress thought to herself, "When he goes to the hunt I shall eat them and tell him they have run away."

The ogre came out of the cellar and ordered them to be brought before him. The poor girls were nearly dead with fright; but the ogress reassured them. When he saw them he asked them what they could do, and they told him they could sweep and sew and spin perfectly; that their stews were so delicious that you would like to eat the plate even on which they were served; and as for their bread, cakes, and pies—why, people came for them from a thousand miles round. The ogre was greedy, and so he said, "Now, then, set these fine cooks to work at once." "But," said he, turning to Finette, "when you have lit the fire, how can you tell if the oven be hot enough?" "My lord," she answered, "I throw butter in, and then I taste it with my tongue." "Very well," he said, "light the fire then." The oven was as big as a stable, for the ogre and ogress ate more bread than two armies. The princess made an enormous fire, which blazed like a furnace; and the ogre, who was standing by, ate a hundred lambs and a hundred sucking pigs while waiting for the new bread. Fleur d'Amour and Belle-de-Nuit kneaded the dough. "Well," said the great ogre, "is the oven hot?" "My lord," replied Finette, "you will see presently." And so saying she threw a thousand pounds of butter into the oven. "I should try it with my tongue," she said, "but I am too little." "I am big enough," said the ogre, and bending down he went so far into the oven that he could not draw back again, so that he was burned to the bones. When the ogress came to the oven she was mightily astonished to find a mountain of cinders instead of her husband.

Fleur d'Amour and Belle-de-Nuit, who saw that she was in great distress, comforted her as they could, but they feared lest her grief should be consoled only too soon, and that regaining her appetite she would put them in a salad, as she had meant to do before. So they said to her, "Take courage, madam; you will find some king or some marquis who will be happy to marry you." At that she smiled a little, showing her teeth, which were longer than your finger. When they saw she was in a good humour, Finette said, "If you would but leave off wearing those horrible bearskins, and dress a little more fashionably! We could arrange your hair beautifully, and you would be like a star." "Come then," she said, "let us see what you can do; but be sure that if I find any ladies more beautiful than myself I shall hack you into little bits." Thereupon the three princesses took off her cap, and began to comb and curl her hair, entertaining her all the while with their chatter. Then Finette took a hatchet, and with a great blow from behind, severed her head from her body.

Never was there such joy. They climbed up to the roof of the house to amuse themselves by ringing the golden bells; they ran through all the rooms, which were of pearls and diamonds, and furnished so richly that they nearly died of joy. They laughed, they sang. Nothing was lacking. They had wheat, and sweetmeat, fruits, and dolls, as many as they liked. Fleur d'Amour and Belle-de-Nuit slept in beds hung with brocade and velvet, and they said to each other, "Here we are richer than was our father in his kingdom, but we want husbands. No one will come here, for this house is certainly looked on as a death-trap, and nobody knows of the death of the ogre and his wife. We must go to the nearest town to show ourselves off in our fine clothes, and it will not be long before we find honest merchants who will be glad enough to wed with princesses." As soon as they were dressed they told Finette that they were going for a walk, and that she must stop at home to look after the house and the washing, so that when they came back everything might be neat and clean; that if it were not they would beat her soundly. Poor Finette, stricken with grief, stopped alone in the house, sweeping, cleaning, washing, without a moment's rest, and always crying. "How unhappy I am," she said "to have disobeyed my god-mother! All kinds of evils happen to me. My sisters have stolen my beautiful clothes to dress themselves in. Without me the ogre and his wife would still be alive and well; and of what benefit is it to me that I killed them? It would have been as good to have been eaten by them as to live as I live now." When she had said this she was almost choked with her tears. Then her sisters came back, loaded with Portuguese oranges, preserves, and sugar, saying to her: "Oh, what a fine ball we have been to! And what a crowd was there! The king's son was dancing; we had a great many attentions paid us. But come now, pull off our shoes, and wash us. That's all you are good for." Finette did as she was told, and if by any chance a word of complaint escaped her, they threw themselves on her, beating her till she was senseless.

Next day they went again, and returned to tell of all the wonders they had seen. One evening, when Finette was sitting near the fire on a little heap of cinders, for want of anything else to do, she peered into the crevices of the chimney, and as she looked she found a little key, so old, and so rusty, that it gave her a great deal of trouble to clean it. When it was polished, she found it was gold, and she thought that a golden key must be for opening some beautiful little chest. So she began to run through the whole house, trying the key in all the locks, till at last she found it fit a casket of perfect workmanship. Opening this, she found in it dresses, diamonds, lace, linen, and very costly ribbons. She said nothing about her good fortune to her sisters, but waited impatiently till they should go out next day, and as soon as they had gone out of her sight, she dressed herself in such a way that she was more beautiful than the sun or the moon.

Thus decked out, she went to the same ball where her sisters were dancing, and though she wore no mask, she was so changed for the better that they did not recognize her. As soon as she made her appearance in the assembly a murmur of voices arose, some expressing their admiration, some their jealousy. She was asked to dance, and she excelled all the ladies in that as she did in beauty. The mistress of the house coming up to her and making her a deep bow, begged to know what she was called, so that she might ever keep in remembrance the name of so distinguished a lady. With much courtesy she answered that she was called Cendron. Not a lover was there but forgot his mistress for Cendron: not a poet but made verses to her. Never did a name make such a sensation in such a short time, and the echoes brought nothing back but Cendron's praises. No one had eyes enough to look on her, or voice enough to sing her praises.

Fleur d'Amour and Belle-de-Nuit, who at first had made a great noise wherever they appeared, now seeing the reception given to the new-comer, were bursting with rage. But Finette kept clear of all their spite with the most perfect grace possible. To look at her you would have said she was born to rule, and Fleur d'Amour and Belle-de-Nuit who never saw their sister but with soot on her face and grimier-looking than a little dog, had so forgotten all about her beauty that they did not recognise her at all, and paid court to Cendron like the others. As soon as the ball was nearly over she set off quickly, reached home, undressed in haste, and put on her rags again. When her sisters came back they said, "Ah! Finette, we have just been seeing a young princess who is quite charming. She is not an ugly ape like you. She is white as snow, and redder than roses. Her teeth are of pearl and her lips of coral. Her dress must weigh more than a thousand pounds, for it is all of gold and diamonds. Ah, how beautiful! how lovely she is!" And Finette would answer between her teeth, "I was like that, I was like that." "What are you muttering?" they said. And Finette answered still lower, "I was like that." This little entertainment lasted for a long time. Hardly a day passed but Finette put on new clothes, for it was a fairy casket, and the more you took from it, the more there was in it, and the clothes that came out of it were so fashionable that ladies took her for their model.

One evening when Finette had danced more than usual, and had stopped rather late, in her desire to make up for lost time and to get home before her sisters, she walked as fast as ever she could, and let fall one of her slippers, which was of red velvet embroidered with pearls. She did all she could to find it again on the road, but the night was so dark that her trouble was in vain, and she had to go in with only one foot shod.

Next day, Prince Chéri, the eldest son of the king, on his way to the chase, found Finette's slipper. He ordered them to pick it up, looked at it, turned it this way and that, kissed it, cherished it, and bore it away with him. From that day he would not eat. He grew thin and changed, was as yellow as a quince, melancholy, and spiritless. The king and queen, who loved him to distraction, sent in all directions for fine game and preserves for him. But to him these seemed less than nothing, and he only looked at them all, and would not answer the queen when she spoke to him. They sent to fetch doctors from all parts, even from Paris and Montpellier.[1] When they arrived they were shown the prince, and having watched him three days and three nights without once leaving him, they came to the conclusion that he was in love, and that he would die if a remedy were not provided.

The queen, who loved him tenderly, wept oceans of tears because she could not find out whom he loved and so arrange for his marriage. She brought the most beautiful ladies to his room, but he would not even look at them. At last she said to him one day, "My dear son, you will kill us with grief, for you are in love, and you hide your feelings from us. Tell us whom it is you long for, and she shall be yours even were she but a simple shepherdess." The prince, assured by the queen's promises, drew the slipper out from below his pillow, and showed it to her. "Madam," he said, "this is the cause of my illness. I found this dear little pretty slipper when I was going to the chase, and I shall never marry any but the lady whom it fits." "Very well, my son," said the queen, "do not grieve, we will send in search of her." And she went to tell the news to the king, who was very much astonished. Without delay he ordered that an announcement should be made with drums and trumpets that all the girls and all the women should come and try on the slipper, and that whosoever it should fit should wed with the prince. When all the ladies had heard the announcement they washed their feet with all sorts of waters, pastes, and pomades. There were some who peeled their feet, so that the skin should be more beautiful, others pared them, or fasted, to make them smaller. In crowds they set out to try on the slipper,

1 A famous French school of medicine.

but not one would it fit, and the more unavailing attempts were made the greater was the prince's distress.

Fleur d'Amour and Belle-de-Nuit one day dressed themselves so fine that they were a wonder to see. "Where are you going?" said Finette. "We are going to the great city," they answered, "where the king and the queen dwell to try on the slipper which the king's son found; for if it fits one of us, the prince will marry her and she shall be a queen." "And might I go too?" said Finette. "You, in truth!" said they. "You are a silly little goose. Be off and water the cabbages, you good-for-nothing."

Finette at once thought of putting on her finest clothes to go and try her luck with the others, for she had some idea that she would have a good chance. But what troubled her was that she did not know the way, for the ball they had danced at was not in the great town. She dressed in all her splendour, in a gown of blue satin covered with stars of diamonds, a sun made of them on her head, a full moon on her back, and all shining so brilliantly that you could not look at her without flinching. When she opened the door to go out she was very much astonished to find the beautiful Spanish jennet that had carried her to her god-mother. She caressed him, saying: "Welcome, little one; for you I am obliged to my god-mother, Merluche." Then it bent down, and she rode on it like a nymph. It was all covered with golden bells and ribbons, and its saddle cloth and bridle were priceless. As for Finette, she was far more beautiful than the fair Helen.

The jennet trotted lightly along to the music of the bells, cling, cling, cling. Fleur d'Amour and Belle-de-Nuit hearing the sound, turned and saw her coming. But what was their surprise at that moment, when they recognised that it was Finette Cendron! They themselves were all draggled, and their fine clothes covered with mud. "Sister," said Fleur d'Amour to Belle-de-Nuit, "I declare to you that that is Finette Cendron." The other said the same; and Finette passing close by at the moment, they were bespattered by her horse's hoofs, and their faces splashed with mud. And Finette laughed as she said, "Your highnesses, Cinderella despises you as much as you deserve"; then riding past them like an arrow she was gone. Belle-de-Nuit and Fleur d'Amour looked at each other. "Are we dreaming?" they said. "Who could have given Finette her fine clothes and the horse? What an astonishing thing! She is in luck. She will put the slipper on, and our journey will be in vain."

While they were mourning over their disappointment, Finette reached the palace, and as soon as she came in sight, everyone thought she was a queen. The soldiers presented arms, the drums began to beat, the trumpets sounded, and all the doors were flung open. Those who had seen her at the ball ran in front of her, calling out, "Room, make room for the fair Cendron, the wonder of the world!" With such pomp, she entered the dying prince's room, who, casting his eyes on her, was enchanted, and full of desire that her foot might be small enough to fit the slipper.

Without delay, she put it on, and showed the other one which she had brought on purpose. "Long live Princess Chéri!" they burst out. "Long live the princess who will be our queen!" The prince rose from his bed, and came forward to kiss her hands, and she thought him handsome and full of wit as he poured his compliments upon her. The king and queen, who had been told the news, hastened to the spot, and the queen taking Finette in her arms, called her her daughter, her darling, her little queen. She gave her beautiful gifts, and the generous king added more. The cannons were fired, there was music of violins, and of pipes, and all kinds of instruments, and nothing was heard but the sounds of dancing and merriment.

The king, the queen, and the prince begged Cendron to give her consent to the marriage. "No," she said, "I must first of all tell you my story," which she did very shortly. When they heard that she was born a princess, they were still more delighted, and almost besides themselves with joy. But when she told them the names of the king and queen, her father and mother, they knew that it was they themselves who had conquered their kingdom, and told her so. Then she swore she would not consent to the marriage till they gave back her father's estates. This they promised, for having more than a hundred kingdoms, one more or less was of very little consequence.

In the meanwhile Belle-de-Nuit and Fleur d'Amour arrived, and the first news they heard was that Cendron had put on the slipper. They did not know what to say or to do, and would have liked to have gone back without seeing her, but when she heard they were come, she ordered them to appear before her, and instead of scowling at them, and of punishing them as they deserved, she rose and came forward to embrace them tenderly. Then presenting them to the queen, she said, "Madam, these are my sisters, who are very amiable; I beg that you will love them." So astounded were they at Finette's goodness, that they could not utter a word. She promised them that they should return to their own kingdom, which the prince wished to restore to their family. At these words they threw themselves on their knees before her weeping for joy.

Never was there such a wedding-feast. Finette wrote to her god-mother, and put her letter along with magnificent gifts on the beautiful jennet. In the letter she begged her to find the king and queen, to tell them of her good fortune, and to say they might return to their kingdom when they liked. Merluche, the fairy, carried out these instructions perfectly, and Finette's father and mother went back to their own estates, and her sisters became queens like herself.

11. Henriette-Julie de Murat, *Histoires sublimes et allégoriques* (1699; *translated by Allison Stedman, 2011*[1])

Henriette-Julie de Castelnau, Comtesse de Murat (1668–1716) wrote much over a short period of time at the height of the interest in fairy tales. Her prodigious output during 1697–99 culminated in the publication of three collections of fairy tales: Contes de fées *(1698), whose name closely resembles Marie-Catherine d'Aulnoy's title of the same year,* Nouveaux Contes des fées *(1698), and* Histoires sublimes et allégoriques *(1699). Part of the salon circle that produced d'Aulnoy and Lhéritier, Murat seemed to revel in the success of the genre. Her contributions are among the last in this brief heyday of marvelous literature in France. "The Savage" picks up a plot scheme popularized by Straparola ("Costanza/Costanzo") and puts it to use as a critique of arranging marriages between very young women and much older men. This aristocratic social practice was particularly prevalent at the end of the seventeenth century as the monarchy's expensive wars and elaborate court rituals brought many noble families to the brink of financial ruin. Although in the context of the fairy tale these ill-matched unions are averted with the help of fairy magic, the constant parallel that the tale draws between the world of the fairy tale and that of contemporary France—Louis XIV appears in the story in a vignette that humanizes him—sends the message that real monarchs in European countries also have the power to put an end to such practices and safeguard the happiness of their (female) subjects.*

THE SAVAGE, A STORY

A LONG TIME AGO THE TERCIAN Islands[2] were governed by a king named Richardin.[3] He had married a beautiful princess, daughter of the King of the Cataracts of the Nile.[4] Her name was Corianthe. Richardin had been passionately in love with her, and as the king her father did not want to marry her to him, because he had promised her to the King of Bitter Fountains whom she did not love, he was forced to wage harsh wars in order to take possession of her; finally all ended to the great

1 [Source: Allison Stedman, unpublished.]

2 The Tercian Islands, more commonly known as the Azores, are a group of nine volcanic islands situated in the middle of the North Atlantic Ocean approximately 1,500 kilometers (930 miles) west of Lisbon, Portugal.

3 "Richard" was an old and inelegant word to designate a rich man. A social-climbing bourgeois family by the name of "Richardin" also appears in an experimental novel that Murat published the same year as "The Savage" (1699). See further Perry Gethner and Allison Stedman, *A Trip to the Country by Henriette-Julie de Castelnau, Comtesse de Murat* (Detroit: Wayne State UP, 2011), 96–107, 119–21.

4 The cataracts of the Nile are a series of six waterfalls or rapids caused by the protrusion of boulders and small rocks from the water. The First Cataract is located in modern Egypt and the rest are in Sudan.

happiness of both: for if Corianthe was beautiful, Richardin was the most handsome prince in the world. One year after their marriage, Corianthe gave birth to a princess as ugly as a beast. This did not please her or the king either, as he was persuaded that a beautiful girl costs less to marry off than an ugly one: she was named Disgrace. The following year the queen once again gave birth to another girl at least as ugly as the first one, another new sorrow for the king and the queen, but they had to have patience: they named her Pain. A few months later Corianthe became pregnant once again and the king, who was afraid that in the end she would only have another monster, took pains to surround her with only beautiful people, and had placed in her apartments the portraits of the most beautiful women that he could find: he even had some painted from imagination for lack of originals; finally and in spite of all these precautions, the queen once again gave birth to a princess even more horrible than the others. The king, in the throes of sorrow, named her Despair. There he was, the father of the three most frightening monkey-faced[1] girls in his kingdom. He told the queen that they should stop there, as he did not wish to populate the earth with monsters. So it was said, so it was done; the princesses lived on and grew into adolescence. They had as little wit as they did beauty: What to do with such merchandise? Poor Richardin was quite ashamed of it; he took it upon himself to announce with the sound of the trumpet and to post everywhere in his kingdom that if any princes, knights, barons or gentlemen wanted to marry his daughters, that he would give to each one of them upon their marriage one of his islands and the title of king.

Some time passed without anyone presenting himself; finally, one day, three knights were seen to arrive at court as disgraced by nature as the three princesses were: one was hump-backed and named Magotin;[2] the other was one-eyed and limping, and his name was Gambille;[3] as for the third, he had only one arm and one leg, they called him Trotte-mal.[4] These disfigured figures added to the sorrow of the poor father, but he could do no better; these knights had a lot of wit, and they had accomplished some fine feats. "Alas!" the queen would say to her husband, "you were afraid of populating the earth with monsters, it will surely be worse when these six people are united." "Not necessarily, Madame," replied the king, "one sees every day well-formed people having very badly turned children, as it happened to us, and on the contrary one sees monkey-faced people producing ones who are very agreeable looking." "So much the better," replied the queen. Finally Richardin married off

---

1 The daughters are referred to as *mâgottes*, the feminine of *mâgot*, meaning "fat monkey," a common insult during the early modern period.

2 "Magotin," a derivative of "magot." See note above.

3 Derived from the middle French verb "gambiller," referring to the thrashing leg movements of a fidgety child.

4 Literally, one who has trouble walking short distances.

his three daughters without great ceremony, and after having parted with his three islands in their favor, he retired to a country house with a mediocre income and a similar entourage. He was living in repose and without ambition when he forgot that he no longer wanted to have any children; it happened, I am not sure how, that Corianthe found herself pregnant; when she was certain of it, she felt a cruel distress over it. "Alas," she would say to the king, "what will become of this unfortunate child whose mother I will be? If again it's a girl as ugly as the others, what will we do about it, having nothing left to give her? If it's a prince, what consternation will not come to him when he will want, justifiably so, to take possession of his father's states, and he will chase his brothers-in-law out of it?" Richardin saw well that she was right and did not know how to argue against a speech so full of verisimilitude.[1] He only told her that the gods would bring order to it and that it was not necessary to aggrieve herself before the time had come. Finally, the distressed Corianthe gave birth to a princess who had never met her match in beauty. She consoled herself somewhat, hoping that the child's beauty would compensate for her [lack of] wealth. She was right to think this way, for never has there ever been a person more perfect: the more she grew, the more her charms increased, but her wit was even greater; all her inclinations were elevated and noble, she rode a horse perfectly, shot arrows, and wielded a sword with marvelous skill; she loved all types of knowledge; and what is most admirable of all is that these heroic occupations did not prevent her from excelling in all the occupations of her sex: she embroidered, she drew, she made decoupages,[2] and all of it to perfection; never has anyone sung better, played instruments better, or danced better. In the end what a prodigy of perfection was the divine Constantine,[3] for it was in this way that she was named.

Richardin and Corianthe would have well wished to see her married off, but there was no one to be found to ask for her hand. She was already eighteen years old, and their worries were mounting. The king, who always furnished himself with fine expedients, took it upon himself to have the charming Constantine marry one of his officers, who was a man without wealth, without good looks and without wit, and to whom he could not offer any other advantage than to leave to him, after his death,

1 Verisimilitude, or "the appearance of truth," was a criterion for literary fiction advanced by the conservative literary establishment during the second half of the seventeenth century. Novelists whose characters behaved in radical or original ways were consequently often criticized for falling short in this category. See, for example, the Abbé de Charnes' important 1679 critique of the Countess de Lafayette's famous historical novel *The Princess of Clèves*. Jean-Antoine Charnes, *Conversations sur la critique de la Princesse de Clèves*, ed. François Weil et al. (Tours: Université de Tours, 1973).

2 A craft that entailed cutting different fabrics into small pieces and reassembling them, either on etched wood or against another background, to create decorative objects.

3 Derived from the adjective *constant*, meaning "consistent, steadfast and firm," often used to describe fidelity in amorous relationships.

the small bit of wealth that remained in his possession. He talked to the queen about it, who did everything in her power to make him change his mind, telling him that it was better to leave the small wealth to Constantine alone than to have her share it with a family that could not be anything but miserable with so few resources; that she was not yet beyond the age of making some acquaintance according to her merit. But she gained nothing, the obstinacy of the king prevailed over her reasons; he made his intentions known to Constantine, who told him with respect that she would have rather remained unmarried than to misally[1] herself in this manner, but he remained unappeasable. The day came for the consummation of such an ill-matched union: the poor princess dissolved in tears, and begged the queen her mother to give her the means of avoiding a wrong that seemed to her more horrible than anything; the queen, who saw herself as being powerless to rescue her, added her tears to those of her daughter. Finally, after having cried quite a bit, Constantine said to the queen, "Madame, give me permission to flee and to give myself over to the will of the gods, give me a man's outfit, and in this disguise, I will seek out an honorable death in a faraway country, which I will always prefer over a shameful life." Corianthe was very pained to make use of this expedient, but not seeing any other way available, the queen consented to it. The very next night word was received of a merchant ship that was scheduled to set sail the following day. The queen had Constantine take one of the king's outfits, and giving her everything that she could, which was not much at all, she embraced her tenderly and had her leave under cover of darkness. The poor princess embarked, and sailed off to Sicily with the merchant.

When Richardin no longer found his daughter, he erupted in fire and flames against the queen, fearing well that she knew what had become of her, but she said nothing to him. In the meantime Constantine, under the name of Constantin, arrived in Sicily: when she got off the boat, she did not know which way to turn; what the queen her mother had given her was so little, that it was incapable of furnishing her with even the most mediocre of equipment.[2] As she was in this predicament, she fell asleep in a wood that she was passing through. She was awakened by something nudging her; upon opening her eyes she saw a beautiful woman dressed as Diana[3] is painted: she had on a morning dress of flowing gold and green fabric, leather

1 "Misalliance," also known as "derogation," was a popular theme in fairy tales of the time. For more on this, see Anne E. Duggan, *Salonnières, Furies and Fairies: The Politics of Gender and Cultural Change in Absolutist France* (Newark: U of Delaware P, 2005), especially Chapter 5.

2 When traveling, a person of the high-ranking nobility would typically have been accompanied by a sizable retinue of servants, mules, horses, and valets to secure the safe transportation of jewelry and fine clothes and to protect them from bandits. This ensemble was referred to as *equipage,* here translated as "equipment."

3 In Roman mythology Diana figures as the goddess of the hunt and the moon. Nicknamed "the virgin goddess," she was also believed to protect virgins and women.

buskins[1] the color of fire embroidered with gold and fastened with diamond buckles, her blond hair was tied behind her back with a ribbon of corn poppies and gold, an ebony quiver decorated with gold and filled with arrows fell upon her hip supported by a magnificent scarf; she held in her hand a bow in the same pattern, a small Greek-style helmet shaded her hairstyle with feathers the color of fire. The princess was agreeably surprised, but she was even more so when this charming person said to her in a cheerful tone: "Beautiful Princess, I have come here to offer you my succor; you have need of it, and it will not fail you: here is a horse," she continued, showing her one of the most beautiful tethered to a tree, "you only need to mount it and let it take the lead, it will bring you to a place where you will find asylum." "Madame," replied the princess with an air of surprise, "permit me to ask you who could have told you that I am in a country where I am unknown?" "Do not take any trouble over that, dear Constantine, I know as much about your situation as you yourself do, that is all I can tell you." As she said this she embraced her tenderly, and having untethered the horse, she said to him while touching him on the throat, "Embletin,[2] do your duty." The princess jumped up into the saddle with marvelous skill, and after having taken leave of her benefactress with as much civility as possible, she set off, and Embletin advanced with a stride so gentle, and at the same time so quick, that in no time at all she left the wood; and having crossed over a great plain, she saw the gates of a city that she believed she would enter, but Embletin, having turned to the right, guided her to the banks of a river where she saw a great number of knights and ladies who were out for a stroll, some on foot and others on horseback, in the middle of whom was a lord with a handsome face, magnificently dressed, and who held the hand of a young lady richly dressed and of unusual beauty.

Constantine or rather Constantin, since from here on we will refer to her by that name, asked a page who this lord and this lady were. He told him that it was the King of Sicily and the princess, his sister. Constantin made his way a bit further beyond the mounted guards, such that he could be seen by the king. He did not fail to be noticed by him; his beauty, his fine figure and his foreign clothes made [the king] curious to find out who he was, he commanded one of his officers to have [Constantin] come forward; once the officer made [Constantin] aware of what the king wanted, he dismounted his horse with a lot of grace, and presented himself before His Majesty in a manner so noble that the king was charmed by it. "Who are you, dear stranger?" this prince asked him, "and what matter brings you to this country?" "My lord," Constantine replied to him, "I am a gentleman from the Tercian Islands, who not having sufficient wealth to support my rank, due to the great number of

1 A Greco-Roman boot, calf-length, open in the front and typically fastened from toe to knee with laces. In Murat's time, the word was also used to designate a fashionable half boot.

2 Likely derived from the expression *d'emblée*, meaning "right away."

my brothers, has been obligated to seek among foreigners that which fortune refuses me in my own country." "She is very unjust, this fortune," replied the king, "to refuse her favors to someone with so much merit. What is your name?" "My name is Constantin," he replied. "Well then, Constantin," replied the prince, "if you would like to remain with me, you will find here all the protection that you deserve." "You do me much honor, great Prince," replied the fake Constantin. "I accept your proposal with pleasure, and I will try through my zeal and my loyalty to merit some part of the grace you honor me with." The king put him in the hands of his Grand Chamberlain,[1] and gave him orders to equip [Constantin] with everything necessary for him to take his place among his attendants; this was done, and by evening he appeared before the prince in this capacity. The magnificent attire in which he had been dressed accentuated his beauty and his fine features, the king was charmed by the refined manners of this new gentleman, but the princess Fleurianne, his sister, did not grow tired of admiring him. Constantin did not fail to go and pay his respects to this princess at her apartments; there he made more than one conquest,[2] but the most considerable among them was that of the princess herself, who felt for this handsome stranger something that surpasses ordinary esteem, but as she was sensible, she hid her feelings.

The King of the Canaries[3] had recently sent a magnificent diplomatic mission to the court of the King of Sicily to ask him for his sister's hand in marriage to the Prince Carabut, his only son. This prince was hump-backed and quite disagreeable, and the princess had no reason to be happy about it. He had sent her magnificent gifts, for he was one of the richest princes in the world; among other things he had two hundred serins[4] of every color in cages of gold filigree inlaid with precious stones. These birds sung and whistled divinely well, and what was most marvelous of all is that they spoke all sorts of languages, and told the princess the most beautiful things in the world on behalf of their master, who had a lot of wit and gallantry, but this did not diminish his ugliness. He arrived at the court, and the sight of his faults, set against the charms of the handsome Constantin, put the princess in a cruel state

1 During the reign of Louis XIV, the Grand Chamberlain was in charge of serving the king at table, presenting the king with a shirt during the royal waking ceremony, and assisting at ambassadorial receptions. Although Grand Chamberlains had played key roles in state affairs during the Renaissance, and had even managed the royal treasury during the Middle Ages, by the end of the seventeenth century the distinction had become almost entirely honorific.

2 This refers to Constantin's ability to capture the hearts of the princess's ladies in waiting and of the other female members of the nobility who frequent her apartments.

3 The Canaries are a group of 13 islands located 100 kilometers west of the border of Morocco and the Western Sahara. Colonized by Spain during the late 1400s, the islands were under Spanish control in the late 1600s and remain a Spanish territory today.

4 A small grey, green, yellow, and white streaked finch prevalent in the Mediterranean regions of Europe and closely related to the canary.

of indecision. She became very melancholy and the king, who took notice of it and who had little doubt that the prince's unpleasant attributes were the cause, did not want anything to do with it. He regretted having heard out the terms of this marriage proposal, finding it quite disproportionate; however the wit of the prince spoke out in his favor, he pressed for the fulfillment of his happiness, for he was very much in love with Fleurianne, but the king kept eluding and causing a thousand difficulties to be born.

Nonetheless the festivities at the court were grand; races were taking place there of which Constantin always won the prize. If a hunt took place, he took all the honors, if he danced at a ball, he eclipsed the best dancers; sometimes concerts were held at the princess's apartments, his fine voice and the graceful manner in which he played instruments earned him the admiration of everyone; the princess had her ladies in waiting work on embroideries to be used for her wardrobe and furniture, Constantin was always showing them new inventions, and worked alongside them, which surprised everyone, but the Princess Fleurianne felt her passion increase because of it. She said so many good things about him to the king on so many different occasions, that one day he said to her, "My sister, I see that you have so much esteem for Constantin, that even though I take great pleasure in having him in my retinue, I would prefer to deprive myself of him to make a gift to you; you have need of a squire, I will give him to you in this capacity." The princess blushed from a rush of joy that she was unable to control, [but] she regained her composure promptly and thanked the king in a manner designed to let him know that this pleased her a very great deal.

Constantin was brought into the princess's entourage in a capacity that made him almost inseparable from her. He was very happy about this, and his sex was less subject to suspicion with the princess than with the king, but it was not long at all before he began to notice that she had feelings for him that would lead to troubles of a different variety: he continued to dissimulate with a lot of skill. Meanwhile the king found himself at the end of his ability to procrastinate, and Prince Carabut was pressuring him so much to finalize his marriage with the princess, that [the king] was constrained to tell him that his natural deformities were distasteful to Fleurianne and, since he was not in the mood to force her will, he advised Carabut to wait a little bit longer; during which time he could be twice as attentive to [the princess] and could try to see new ways to please her to the greatest possible degree. The prince accepted this proposal, although it was against his wishes. He had noticed the princess's esteem for Constantin, and to ally him with his own interests, he gave him magnificent presents; one day when the princess was walking in the palace gardens some distance away from her ladies in waiting, she saw on Constantin's finger, as he was holding her hand, a diamond of admirable beauty. "What a beautiful jewel you have there," she said to him. "Where did you get it?" "From Prince Carabut, Madame," he replied to her. "He is very generous," said the princess, "and if nature had given him an appearance equal to his wit, one could say that this would have made a perfect prince." "Madame, the beauty of one's soul is always preferable to that of one's body," Constintin replied, "the former is often fleeting, but the latter remains eternally." "It is quite true," said Fleurianne, "but when one is obliged to spend one's life with a monster, regardless of what other fine qualities he may have, one is to be most pitied: I could love Carabut as a friend, but I know well that I will never love him as my spouse: how unjust nature is," she continued, throwing a languishing look over to Constantin, "and that a prince would find himself happy[1] to have received from [nature, the same] beauty that becomes useless in a subject that has been supplied with such a profusion of it!"[2] She stopped speaking, lowering her eyes. Constantin well understood her meaning, and he responded to her: "Madame, I wish it were in my power to pass along to Prince Carabut that which would make him agreeable to your eyes." "Oh, it would be much easier to join to so many charms the quality[3] that they lack," replied the princess. "Being chosen by a princess can make a prince out of a man to whom only this quality is lacking for him to be worthy of her, but she cannot give that which nature refuses to a subject whom she has deprived of her favors. I have said too much about it," she continued, blushing: "I have said too much about it, it is no longer in my power to dissimulate feelings that I have just brought to light in spite of myself. Yes, dear Constantin, you have all of my tenderness, and if I were the master of my destiny, I would not hesitate for a moment to take you for my husband, but since I cannot do this without failing in my duty, I am resolved never to marry another."

As she finished these words, and as Constantin was going to respond to her, they heard a rustling behind a hedge quite nearby them. The princess thought that it was her ladies in waiting, but having turned around, she saw them a few steps away from her. At that moment the ladies in waiting joined her, the conversation became general, but rather listless on her part. Carabut joined them as well, and he seemed fairly disconcerted; everyone went back to the palace, and the princess retired to her apartments. Prince Carabut remained there only a very short time; Constantin was in the antechamber when he came out. He approached him and said to him in a low voice, "Constantin, I have something to tell you, follow me." He obeyed him; together they crossed a gallery at the end of which was a stair that led down to one of the outer reaches of the gardens, where there was a door that led into a fairly isolated

---

1 That is, happy in his love affairs by marrying the woman he loves.

2 Although contemporary rules of decorum force the princess to couch her words in vague language, Constantin understands that the "prince" in question is Carabut, while he is being referred to as "subject."

3 The "quality" referred to is that of a noble title, as Fleurianne believes Constantin is a squire.

place. Carabut opened it, and when he had passed through it with Constantin, he closed it and seeing that they were alone, he said to him, "You must give me the reason for the feelings that the princess has for you, of which you are unworthy, I heard the conversation that you just had with her in the gardens." "My lord, if you heard the entire conversation, then you are well aware of my innocence," replied Constantin. "I am not guilty if...." "It is useless to justify yourself," interrupted the Prince, "I heard enough of it to be convinced that you occupy in Fleurianne's heart a place that she refuses to me. Your blood must avenge me of this preference." In saying this, he drew his sword; he was short, and Constantin's stature gave him a great advantage over him. No matter what he did to try to avoid engaging in this combat, it was impossible for him, yet it became even more fateful for poor Carabut, for in no time at all he was stabbed with two thrusts of a sword and fell dead. Constantin found himself in a difficult quandary, but seeing that the best option for him was to flee, he reentered the palace by another way, and running to the stables, he saddled Embletin, climbed on, and promptly left the city.

While Constantin was fleeing, Princess Fleurianne was having everyone look everywhere for him, but it was useless: his absence and the death of the prince made everyone believe that he was guilty. The king, who passionately loved Constantin, wished to ignore it, and although he was not angry that [Constantin] was nowhere to be found, he sent some of his men to look for him anyway, but they had secret orders to hide him if they came upon him. As for Fleurianne, she was in despair, and to hide her pain she pretended to be sick and took to her bed. The king hastened to send a diplomatic mission to the King of the Canaries, to return to him the body of the prince his son, and to attempt to make amends to him, which was turning out to be fairly difficult. During this whole time, Constantine was fleeing with Embletin without knowing where she was headed. Quite a bit of time had already passed as she was riding day and night, almost without resting or eating, when she entered into a thick forest; the more she advanced, the darker the forest became; night fell on her in this place, she rode a long time in the dark, crying out: "Alas, unfortunate princess, such is your destiny to be reduced to letting yourself be led by a beast."

With these reflections and other similar ones, she found herself in a place a little less dense and near a magnificent château. The door opened on its own, and Embletin, upon entering, had her cross a great courtyard and stopped at the foot of a flight of steps; Constantine dismounted, and Embletin, who knew this place, went promptly off to the stables. The princess went up the staircase, she crossed through a vestibule that seemed to her very beautiful from what she could judge in the darkness. Next she climbed a great staircase, and when she had only taken a few steps, she saw a young man who was holding a candle on a vermillion stand. He was handsome and very gallantly dressed: "Princess," he said to her while saluting her, "the Fairy

Obligeantine,[1] mistress of this house, having been apprised of your arrival, has sent me before you to take you to her apartment." The princess, although very surprised to see that she was known in this place, made her gratitude known to him. She was led through a succession of several rooms, which seemed to her to be of surprising magnificence. Her guide opened a door for her and let her enter it alone: it was a bedroom very brightly lit and quite magnificent, it was full of great mirrors, all the frames of which were inlaid in precious stones, the floor was strewn with carnations, jasmines and tuberoses.[2] A lady among the most finely dressed and among the most beautiful was lying on a bed of silver and green linen, the bed was strewn all over with flowers. As soon as this lady saw the princess, she held out her arm to her, saying to her, "Come closer charming princess, come and enjoy in my company the rest that you deserve, and which fate has refused you up until now." The princess approached her, and was agreeably surprised to see that this lady was the same one who had given her Embletin as a present. "Ah Madame," exclaimed Constantine receiving her embrace, "I see that it is to you alone that I owe all the good fortune of my life!" Obligeantine informed her that she knew about everything that had happened to her at the King of Sicily's court, and told her that she would be waiting in this château at the end of all her troubles. "Go and rest," said the fairy. "Tomorrow we will discuss everything at our leisure." She showed her a door and told her to push it open, this she did; she entered into a bedroom gallantly furnished, two very beautiful maidens dressed in very expensive clothing received her with much civility, they presented her with fruits and jams, she ate some, then they helped her into her bedclothes and into her bed.

When she awoke, the same two maidens came to help her dress in rich and gallant clothes appropriate for a woman; when she had finished getting ready, she went to Obligeantine's bedroom and found [the fairy] at her dressing table; she received her with great warmth. After dinner[3] several fairies of the first order came to call, [Obligeantine] introduced them to the princess and acquainted her with all the beauty of the château and its marvelous gardens. The next day she told her that she wanted to show her all of the marvelous things that fairy art can do, and to this end she led her into a gallery filled with cabinets, mirrors, tables, pedestals, candelabras, and chandeliers of infinite richness, at the end of which she opened a door of polished bronze, which led them into a large private study of which the floor one walked upon, the vault and the paneling were composed of clouds the color of a sunset on a fine day. "This is Destiny's private study," Obligeantine said to the princess, "and here you will see things that will be both astonishing and pleasing to you. Here," she continued,

1 Derived from the adjective *obligeant,* meaning "obliging, pleasing, and kind."

2 A white, sweet-smelling flower similar in appearance to the trumpet lily.

3 Refers to the main meal of the day, which would have been taken at noon.

touching one of the sides with a wand of antique bronze, "is where one can see everything that takes place in the realm of a king the whole world knows as Louis the Great;[1] on this other side is contained the general fate of the whole earth, and this one here is concerned with the fate of someone in particular." After that, she touched the side containing the general fate of mankind three times and distinct figures immediately began to emerge out of the clouds representing the most extraordinary events: battles, sieges of cities, kings massacred, [kings] dying of natural causes and dethroned, marriages both happy and unhappy, cities burnt to the ground, buildings overturned by earthquakes or struck down by lightning, the overflowing of rivers and streams, battles at sea and shipwrecks, the changing of the seasons, the end of the present century where the frailty of stars and planets creates widespread imbalances of weather,[2] and the horoscope of the century to come. After having specified all these things, she touched [her wand] to the fate of France, and the figures who emerged there represented all the marvels of the reign of Louis the Great, his numerous conquests, his army and navy regiments, the portraits of all the great captains commanding them and their individual exploits, his immense and inexhaustible riches, his palaces whose beauty verges on enchantment, the magnificence of his court, his beautiful and numerous family almost three generations of which are already apparent, the fine manners of his subjects, the sublime knowledge they possess in both the sciences and arts, the grandeur of his cities, the beauty and the abundance of his provinces, the flowering commercialism that he supports with all the nations of the earth, and above all his generosity beyond measure which makes him the protector of the innocent and oppressed. But this was nothing in comparison with the agreeable spectacle that appeared next: it was a young and beautiful princess coming forth from the middle of a mass of steep mountains,[3] she was glistening all over with precious stones, and wearing a crown of myrtle[4] on her head and [carrying] an olive branch[5] in her hand. A lady, whose air and demeanor seemed divine, held out a hand to her and with the other presented her to the King of France who received her with open arms and presented her in turn a young prince more or less her age,[6] handsome as Cupid and grandson of this great monarch, whom he was

1 Louis XIV, king of France from 1643 to 1715.

2 This is consistent with meteorological reports of the time.

3 Princess Marie-Adélaïde of Savoy who married Louis XIV's grandson, Louis, Duke of Burgundy and Petit Dauphin of France, at Versailles on December 6, 1697. The duchy of Savoy was located in the western Alps on land that today is shared between France and Italy.

4 Associated with Venus, a crown of myrtle symbolized love in the same way that a crown of laurel symbolized victory. The Princess of Savoy and the Duke of Burgundy were in love with each other, a rarity among aristocratic marriages of the time.

5 A symbol of the peace that was expected to result from this arranged marriage. [See p. 212, note 1, on the marriage as a contract for peace.]

6 On their wedding day, the Princess of Savoy and the Duke of Burgundy were twelve and fifteen, respectively.

destining to her as her husband, the union of whom was putting an end to a cruel war by bringing peace to an infinite number of powers united by jealousy against this flowering empire.[1] "There you have it," said the fairy to the princess, "the greatest event of our time."[2]

After she had finished these words, she touched the third side: "Here is the part that involves you, Princess," she said to her. Immediately she saw the Tercian Islands appear, the king her father and the queen her mother distressed with the loss of her, her three sisters and their husbands burdened by civil wars and domestic sorrows. Constantine, who was kindhearted, was touched by it and shed a few tears. Next the fairy showed her the Kingdom of Sicily, and in the palace of the king the princess Fleurianne, whom one wanted to betroth to a horrible lecher. "Alas!" cried the princess, "I spared her a monster by killing Carabut, but here is another suitor even more terrible! Oh Madame, is there no other way to rescue this kind princess?" "That is up to you," replied the fairy, laughing, "you will be able to get her out of this predicament as well, but the time has not yet come." The last figure to present itself to Constantine was that of herself. She was seated on an elevated throne, and the King of Sicily was placing a crown at her feet. "What does this mean, Madame?" asked the princess. "This you will learn in due time," replied the fairy, "after which everything will be restored to its rightful place." With that, they left the private study, which was closed behind them.

A few days later, the fairy told Constantine that she would like to show her all the courts of the world and that she would begin with that of France, where the most superb party known to mortals was about to be celebrated. For this endeavor, Obligeantine had a carriage prepared composed of the skull of a giant who had wandered onto her land, and whom she had exterminated by the power of her magic. This giant was ninety-six feet tall: she had his skull reworked in such an agreeable manner that everything necessary could be found in it from the undercarriage to the wheels, and as she only wanted to travel by night, she had it painted with a black veneer; she had harnessed to it two great mastiffs to whom she attached the wings of Indian bats who are, in that country, as large as cows. She dressed both herself and the princess in a black crape[3] lined with gold linen, and having placed in their mouths an herb that made them invisible, and of which they carried a large supply, they left with their

1 The wedding was stipulated by the Treaty of Turin and put an official end to the Nine Years' War (1688–97), a major war fought between Louis XIV and a European coalition seeking to protect their own territories from the Sun King's imperialism.

2 In referring to the marriage of the Princess of Savoy and the Duke of Burgundy as "the greatest event of our time," the fairy subtly undermines Louis XIV's other political achievements, most of which strengthened the power of the monarchy at the expense of the nobility.

3 A gauzy fabric made of silk or wool, usually used for mourning attire.

entourage and arrived a short time later at Versailles, precisely on the eve of the marriage of Madame the Princess of Savoy.[1] They were present at the ceremony without being as well dressed as they were at the wedding feast, and they ate the fruits and jams that were served to them. The fairy shoved the officers who were bringing out the dessert baskets, and while they were turning around to see who had dared to do this, she took out whatever she pleased without anyone noticing it. They saw the prince and the princess get dressed, get undressed, and go to bed,[2] they saw her dressing table and all her precious stones. As they were leaving the bedroom, the king was also coming out of it, and as Constantine was running to tell something to Obligeantine, she bumped into the king without realizing it. He was even more surprised to see no one nearby him, and after having looked around him with some worry, he continued on his way. Next they went to the ball and to the opera *Issé*,[3] which they found very beautiful, as beautiful as the [court] apartments. In the end, they participated in all the festivities surrounding this period of rejoicing. The fairy swore that only fairy magic could surpass the magnificence of this court. Every night they retired to the home of the fairy Marline, who lives in an invisible palace near the Château de Marly.[4]

After having seen the court of France, they continued on to Spain where they saw nothing worthy of their curiosity; the same happened in Germany and at the courts of the northern countries, but they had been satisfied enough with the magnificence of the Great Lord,[5] and with the riches of the Seraglio,[6] where they delved into court intrigue and discovered everyone's secrets. They went to Siam, to China, to Mongolia, to Persia, and finally they returned by way of England to see King William, who is famous for so many different things. They were curious to see the Parliament in session, but the gibberish of the laws, the copied bills, the taxes on tea, chocolate and coffee, the tons and pounds,[7] as well as [the English] way of counting everything in

---

1 [See p. 211, notes 4–6, on the Savoy-Burgundy marriage.]

2 Refers to the rising ceremony or *lever* and retiring ceremony or *coucher*. Inclusion in these traditional court ceremonies would have been reserved for high-ranking members of the nobility, which is why Constantine and Obligeantine must attend them invisibly.

3 A heroic, pastoral opera composed by André-Cardinal Destouches (1672–1749) in honor of the petit dauphin's marriage. It was performed for the first time at Fontainebleau in early October 1697 and for the second time at the Trianon of Versailles on December 17 of the same year. If Obligeantine and Constantine did in fact arrive on the eve of the petit dauphin's wedding, then their attendance at this opera would have coincided with their eleventh day at court.

4 A small royal residence located on the edge of the royal park at Versailles. As the king often went to Marly to escape the formal rigors of court, an invitation to Marly was considered highly exclusive.

5 Louis XIV.

6 Reference to the palace of the Turkish Emperor in Constantinople (modern Istanbul).

7 Refers to taxes levied against merchandise entering and leaving England. These taxes were informally referred to as *tonnage* and *poundage* because the weight of the merchandise was measured in tons and pounds.

sterling, frightened them so much that they left quite quickly, and to relax they came to Paris, where the Tuileries, the opera and the theatre amused them for a time. They realized that they had not yet been to Venice; they went there, and they spent a good part of Carnival[1] there, after which they returned to the fairy's château. Although they had moved quickly, they had nonetheless spent almost two months[2] on their travels. The beauty of the château relieved them of their fatigue, in this beautiful place pleasant things came one after the other.

While Constantine was leading such a pleasant and peaceful life, the same was not true at the court of the King of Sicily. He had endured a savage war with the King of the Canaries, who was galled by the death of the prince his son; [this king] added so many serins[3] to his troops that all the subjects of the King of Sicily thought they would be suffocated by them, but fortunately [the King of Sicily] thought to make use of the ashes of Mount Vesuvius,[4] and by this means he charred them all like pigs. What pained him the most in all of this were the two hundred talking serins that Carabut had given to Princess Fleurianne as a present; they had escaped from their cages, and having dispersed themselves throughout the whole kingdom, they had spread such wicked rumors that they had ignited a civil war that had been quite difficult to extinguish. The king was just beginning to be able to breathe again when he was brought word that coming out of the mountains, not far from the capital city, were some sort of men, or rather monsters, hideous and cruel, half man and half goat, who were causing frightful damage to the neighboring places, carrying off children, eating livestock, and spoiling crops, after which they retreated to inaccessible places. The king was resolved to go in person to exterminate this mob. He took with him his guards on foot and on horseback, his gentlemen in waiting, and all who were willing to follow him. The mountains into which these monsters had retreated were on the outer reaches of a great forest; the king sent for the roads to be cleared, and to attract them he had several flocks of sheep dispersed, along with vessels full of milk and wine, which they liked a lot; then, hiding himself behind the trees along with his men, he waited for them to come down from the mountains, which they did in little time. When they were well immersed in their meal, [the king's men] threw themselves upon them, and taking them by surprise they were able to kill quite a

1 A public celebration of several days immediately preceding the season of Lent. The festival is observed by Roman Catholic and Eastern Orthodox societies and usually combines parades, street parties, and masquerades with other circus-like activities.

2 Since Carnival generally takes place in early to mid-February, the women would have had to spend slightly more than two months traveling in order to see both the royal wedding and the Venetian carnival.

3 See p. 206, note 4 on "serins."

4 A tall, cone-shaped volcano located on the west coast of southern Italy, approximately nine miles from the Bay of Naples. Famous for its destruction of the Roman city of Pompeii in 79 CE, the volcano had last erupted in 1631.

few; but having rallied themselves together, [the monsters] threw themselves on the king's men with so much fury and agility that they killed several of them in turn; they threw themselves on the hinds of the horses and strangled them with their claws, or scratched their eyes out. This scared [the king's men] so much that they fled without giving a thought to the king, who found himself abandoned and surrounded by a herd of monsters. Fortunately they did not throw themselves on the hind of his horse as they had done to the others. [Instead] they howled all around him in a frightening manner and tried to trap him with the branches of trees that they had torn down; but the king, who was extremely clever, and who was riding a marvelous horse, killed a great number of them with his sword and his javelin, and the rest fled into the mountains.

When he found himself free, he considered turning back, and as night was falling he sounded a small horn to see whether his men would hear him, but no one responded. He was beginning to ride off when he saw one of these savage monsters coming out from behind a tree; [the monster] threw himself with surprising swiftness onto the hind of his horse, and clinging to it, prevented it from using its legs. The king was doing what he could to shake him off, when he heard this monster say to him, "Prince, have no fear, I won't do you any harm as long as you promise to do as I tell you." The king, surprised to hear an animal of this sort speak, responded to him, "As long as you don't ask me to do something impossible, I promise to do it." "I only ask that you bring me with you to your palace, and that you put me in a place where I can only be seen by you," replied [the monster], "and after I'll have been there for some time, I'll tell you some things that you won't find disagreeable." "I'm willing," said the king, "I promise you." Right then the monster let go of him and sat on the hind of his horse and the king set off on his way to the city. As night had fallen, they passed through it without being seen. His men were all going around saying that he was dead, he found the doors of his palace without guards, and when he came into the courtyard, some of his officers who caught a glimpse of him fled from fear or fright. He took advantage of this solitude to continue on to his apartments without being seen, he entered them with the savage, whom he was holding by the arm, and having opened a small private study where he kept locked up rare and precious gems, he left the savage in there, saying to him that he would make sure he had everything he needed. After this he went to the apartment of the princess his sister where all the most important figures of the court had assembled upon news of his death. He found her dissolved into tears; she cried out when she saw him enter. "Do not be afraid, Madame," he said to her, "the news of my death is a figment of the cowardice of my officers, the heavens have protected my life and I pardon them their lack of devotion to me." The princess embraced him tenderly and passed from a state of great sorrow to one of great joy; all the officers, very ashamed of themselves, came up to him to ask forgiveness, and he gave it to them. He did not say anything about the savage; he had food and drink brought to him in his room on other pretexts, and when he was alone he brought him what he needed to live on. He received a thousand embraces from this animal, who thanked him in admirable terms.

This monster had already been at the palace for some time when one day, when the king brought him something to eat, he said to him, "My lord, it is time for me to tell you what you must do to become the happiest prince on earth. You must tell your subjects that you are ready to be married, you will make all the necessary preparations for this kind of party; each one will be surprised not to know whom you wish to marry, your sister the princess will pressure you to tell her, but you will not open up to anyone. When everything is ready, and the day arrives, you will close up the apartment that you will have prepared for the queen your wife, you will take the key, then you will come and get me here, I will enter it with you and the princess, and you will see what the heavens have in store for you."

The king was as surprised as one can be, and did not know what he should do; but the savage, who saw his hesitation, reassured him, saying to him, "Do not be afraid, Prince, leave your fate to Destiny, who decreed a long time ago that these things should take place." The king promised him that everything would be promptly executed as he had said, and that very day he began to make preparations for his marriage. The princess was dumbfounded by the secret the king was keeping from her regarding whom he wished to marry, but he told her that she would find out everything when the time was right. Everyone at court and in the city thought that the king had fallen in love with the daughter of one of his subjects, and that he did not want to say anything for fear that the high-ranking members of the court would disapprove. There was no beautiful girl who did not secretly flatter herself as being the fortunate person in whose favor the prince would declare himself. Finally the day came: the night before, the king took the key to the apartment of the future queen, the next day he had himself dressed in his ceremonial clothes and ordered the princess his sister to dress herself in her most magnificent fittings. All the officers and ladies in waiting to the queen were under orders to stand at attention. The king, after having gotten dressed in his private study and from there gone into the one where the savage was, took him by the arm and in this way crossed through his apartment followed by his sister the princess. She was quite frightened to see the king leading in this monster. Everyone remained deep in silence, not knowing how this extraordinary behavior would turn out. The king opened the queen's apartment and crossed it all the way to the antechamber. The savage said to him in a low voice that everyone should remain here except for the princess; this was done. The three of them entered the bedroom and the savage closed the door behind them. The king was quite astonished to see the furniture of this room transformed into an unheard-of state of magnificence. There were, among other things, twelve large baskets made of gold, and inlaid with precious stones, filled with the finest jewels and the most beautiful clothes that anyone could imagine.

A few moments had passed since their entrance when a door that led into a private study opened on its own, and out came two ladies whose beauty and attire defied imagination; but the king was even more surprised when he recognized in the more beautiful of the two the features of the handsome Constantin. He was not mistaken, for he was indeed seeing the Princess Constantine, and she and Constantin were one and the same. The Fairy Obligeantine was accompanying her, and after she had greeted the King of Sicily, she said to him, "My lord, I present to you the beautiful Princess Constantine, daughter of the King of the Tercian Islands, who has been at your court under the name of Constantin, and for whom you had conceived so much friendship. It is she whom the gods have destined to be your wife; but this is not the only wonder that will take place today; the savage that you see here must become the husband of the charming Princess Fleurianne. Do not be afraid, Madame," [the fairy] said to her, seeing her surprise, "beneath this horrible appearance is a prince worthy of you, he is the King of the Loving Islands who, because of the rage of an unjust fairy, who wanted to make him love her against his will, has been kept in this form for several years, and he can only relinquish it upon the marriage of Princess Constantine with the King of Sicily. My lord," she said to the king, "nothing more than your happiness is necessary to release this prince from the terrible state to which he is reduced." The king who had had time to emerge from his shock, as had the princess, responded to the fairy, "I consent to everything you wish, Madame, and provided that the beautiful Constantine wants to make me happy, I have nothing left to wish for." The princess indicated her agreement with great delicacy and modesty, and once the fairy touched the savage with her golden wand, he became the most handsome prince that anyone has ever seen. He threw himself at the feet of the beautiful Fleurianne; and at that moment they conceived for one another the most tender of all passions. The king embraced Constantine, and the princess, who had been very much in love with Constantin, did not love her any less as Constantine. She assured her of her tenderness with a bit of confusion; Obligeantine told the king in a few words the story of the beautiful princess whom he was going to marry, and when she had finished, [she said to him]: "My lord, we must go and welcome King Richardin and Queen Corianthe, who are just now arriving at the palace to take part in their daughter's wedding, as are her three sisters the queens, and their husbands the kings, who have been summoned by my orders."

Princess Constantine blushed; her family's deformities caused her much consternation. The fairy, who was watching her, noticed this. "I have taken care of everything, beautiful princess," she said to her, "I never do things halfway, and even if the queens your sisters are not as beautiful as you are, they are beautiful enough at this very moment to ornament this party; and mother nature, aided by powerful magic, has also included the kings their husbands in their transformation." Upon saying these final words, she walked in front of them, the king followed her taking the hand of Constantine, and the King of the Loving Islands took the hand of Fleurianne. They crossed the apartment to the great astonishment of the whole court, and they arrived in the great hall of the palace where all the lords and ladies were assembled, to whom the king introduced the princess as their future queen.

Everyone was enchanted by her beauty and remained surprised by her resemblance to Constantin. This enigma was explained, along with that of the savage. Next, one saw enter the King and the Queen of the Tercian Islands, their three daughters and their husbands, who were as handsome and well-formed as they had previously been ugly and deformed, but their names remained the same. They could not stop embracing and admiring one another. The ceremony of this double marriage took place to the great happiness of everyone. The beautiful and obliging fairy presided over it and received thanks from everyone who had benefitted from her munificent provisions. She gave magnificent presents to Queen Corianthe and her daughters; the party was spectacular, and the fairy oversaw it all. She, herself put the newlyweds to bed,[1] and as the King of the Loving Islands had no equipment,[2] she had some assembled for him, which he found the next morning when he awoke. The jousts and tournaments lasted for several days, during which time Mâgotin, Gambille, and Trotte-mal accomplished fine feats: the prizes were distributed by the fairy, and they were found to be of infinite richness.

After all of this entertainment, which lasted several months, the King of the Loving Islands returned to his kingdom with his charming wife, a sumptuous retinue and immense riches; the three kings of the Tercian Islands [also] returned home, but King Richardin and the Queen his wife remained in Sicily with Queen Constantine until the end of their days; the fairy returned to her magnificent château.

1 See p. 213, note 3.

2 See p. 204, note 2.

12. Anne-Claude Phillip de Tubière-Grimoard de Pestels Levieux de Lévis, Comte de Caylus, Marquis d'Esternay, Baron de Bransac, *Féeries nouvelles* (1741; *translated by Roswell M. Field, 1917*[1])

As his titles—count, marquis, and baron—suggest, the Comte de Caylus had the pedigree of an Old Regime nobleman. Yet, he possessed the vast curiosity of the modern, iconoclastic intellectual of his day and devoted his time to learning. His pursuits ranged from engraving, amateur painting, and Greco-Roman archeology, to the study of the Middle Ages, the history of fairy tales, and a taste for the Orient. A celebrity in his own lifetime, Caylus has long been among the understudied writers of the eighteenth century. It is largely through the work of fairy-tale scholars that he has resurfaced. His first published fiction was fairy tales in the tradition of the French contes de fées, and he went on to publish "Oriental tales"—stories set in the Middle East that had become very popular in the wake of Antoine Galland's publication in French of the Thousand and One Nights *(1704–17)—and humorous satires. "Sylvain and Jocosa" nicely illustrates the paradox of traditionalism and iconoclasm that critics find prevalent in Caylus's writing. For one thing, the fairy appears as a traditional gift-giving entity but also plays a role she is rarely ascribed: that of tale teller. In this detail, Caylus appears to draw on the tradition of the French women writers (Lhéritier, d'Aulnoy, Murat) who associated themselves as writers with the power of fairies to alter history. The story has an excessively didactic undertone, delivered through the fairy's words and then explicated in the moral she gives to her own story (rather than leaving the interpretation up to her young listeners). Finally, eighteenth-century Orientalism—a fascination with and suspicion of the East—that marks Caylus's later literary production makes an appearance here in the tale told by the fairy, which is set in a Baghdad ruled by an insatiable sovereign and in a "large city in Asia" where a fowler's son unexpectedly becomes emir.*

SYLVAIN AND JOCOSA

Once upon a time there lived in the same village two children, one called Sylvain and the other Jocosa, who were both remarkable for beauty and intelligence. It happened that their parents were not on terms of friendship with one another, on account of some old quarrel which had taken place so long ago that they had quite forgotten what it was all about, and only kept up the feud from force of habit. Sylvain and Jocosa for their parts were far from sharing this enmity, and indeed were never

1 [Source: Roswell M. Field, *A Book of Famous Fairy Tales* ([1938] Chicago, IL: Auxiliary Educational League, 1953): 124–33.]

happy when apart. Day after day they fed their flocks of sheep together, and spent the long sunshiny hours in playing or resting upon some shady bank.

It happened one day that the fairy of the meadows passed by and saw them, and was so much attracted by their pretty faces and gentle manners that she took them under her protection, and the older they grew the dearer they became to her. At first she showed her interest by leaving in their favorite haunts many little gifts such as they delighted to offer one to the other, for they loved each other so much that their first thought was always, "What will Jocosa like?" or "What will please Sylvain?" And the fairy took a great delight in their innocent enjoyment of the cakes and sweetmeats she gave them nearly every day.

When they were grown up she resolved to make herself known to them, and chose a time when they were sheltering from the noonday sun in the deep shade of a flowery hedgerow. They were startled at first by the sudden apparition of a tall and slender lady dressed all in green and crowned with a garland of flowers. But when she spoke to them sweetly and told them how she had always loved them, and that it was she who had given them all the pretty things which it had so surprised them to find, they thanked her gratefully and took pleasure in answering the questions she put to them. When she presently bade them farewell, she told them never to tell anyone else that they had seen her. "You will often see me again," added she, "and I shall be with you frequently, even when you do not see me." So saying she vanished, leaving them in a state of great wonder and excitement. After this she came often, and taught them numbers of things and showed them many of the marvels of her beautiful kingdom, and at last one day she said to them:

"You know that I have always been kind to you. Now I think it is time you did something for me in your turn. You both remember the fountain I call my favorite? Promise me that every morning before the sun rises you will go to it and clear away every stone that impedes its course and every dead leaf or broken twig that sullies its clear waters. I shall take it as a proof of your gratitude to me if you neither forget nor delay this duty, and I promise that so long as the sun's earliest rays find my favorite spring the clearest and sweetest in all my meadows you two shall not be parted from one another."

Sylvain and Jocosa willingly undertook this service, and indeed felt that it was but a very small thing in return for all that the fairy had given and promised to them. So for a long time the fountain was tended with the most scrupulous care and was the clearest and prettiest in all the country round. But one morning in the spring, long before the sun rose, they were hastening toward it from opposite directions, when, tempted by the beauty of the myriads of gay flowers which grew thickly on all sides, they paused each to gather some for the other.

"I will make Sylvain a garland," said Jocosa, and "How pretty Jocosa will look in this crown!" thought Sylvain.

Hither and thither they strayed, led ever further and further, for the brightest flowers seemed always just beyond them, until at last they were startled by the first bright rays of the rising sun. With one accord they turned and ran toward the fountain, reaching it at the same moment, though from opposite sides. But what was their horror to see its usually tranquil waters seething and bubbling, and even as they looked down rushed a mighty stream, which entirely ingulfed [sic] it, and Sylvain and Jocosa found themselves parted by a wide and swiftly rushing river.

All this had happened with such rapidity that they had only time to utter a cry and each to hold up to the other the flowers they had gathered; but this was explanation enough. Twenty times did Sylvain throw himself into the turbulent waters, hoping to be able to swim to the other side, but each time an irresistible force drove him back upon the bank he had just quitted, while as for Jocosa, she even essayed to cross the flood upon a tree which came floating down torn up by the roots, but her efforts were equally useless. Then with heavy hearts they set out to follow the course of the stream, which had now grown so wide that it was only with difficulty they could distinguish each other.

Night and day, over mountains and through valleys, in cold or in heat, they struggled on, enduring fatigue and hunger and every hardship, and consoled only by the hope of meeting once more, until three years had passed, and at last they stood upon the cliffs where the river flowed into the mighty sea.

And now they seemed further apart than ever, and in despair they tried once more to throw themselves into the foaming waves. But the fairy of the meadows, who had really never ceased to watch over them, did not intend that they should be drowned at last, so she hastily waved her wand, and immediately they found themselves standing side by side upon the golden sand. You may imagine their joy and delight when they realized that their weary struggle was ended, and their utter contentment as they clasped each other by the hand. They had so much to say that they hardly knew where to begin, but they agreed in blaming themselves bitterly for the negligence which had caused all their trouble; and when she heard this the fairy immediately appeared to them. They threw themselves at her feet and implored her forgiveness, which she granted freely, and promised at the same time that now their punishment was ended she would always befriend them.

Then she sent for her chariot of green rushes, ornamented with May dew-drops, which she particularly valued and always collected with great care; and ordered her six short-tailed moles to carry them all back to the well-known pastures, which they did in a remarkably short time; and Sylvain and Jocosa were overjoyed to see their dearly loved home once more after all their toilful wanderings. The fairy, who had set her mind upon securing their happiness, had in their absence quite made up the quarrel between their parents and gained their consent to the marriage of the faithful lovers; and now she conducted them to the most charming little cottage that can be imagined, close to the fountain, which had once more resumed its peaceful aspect and flowed gently down into the little brook which inclosed [sic] the garden and orchard and pasture which belonged to the cottage. Indeed, nothing more could have been thought of, either for Sylvain and Jocosa or for their flocks; and their delight satisfied even the fairy who had planned it all to please them. When they had explored and admired until they were tired they sat down to rest under the rose-covered porch, and the fairy said that to pass the time until the wedding-guests whom she had invited could arrive she would tell them a story. This is it:

The Yellow Bird

Once upon a time a fairy, who had somehow or other got into mischief, was condemned by the high court of Fairyland to live for several years under the form of some creature, and at the moment of resuming her natural appearance once again to make the fortune of two men. It was left to her to choose what form she would take, and because she loved yellow she transformed herself into a lovely bird with shining golden feathers such as no one had ever seen before. When the time of her punishment was at an end the beautiful yellow bird flew to Bagdad and let herself be caught by a fowler at the precise moment when Badi-al-Zaman was walking up and down outside his magnificent summer palace. This Badi-al-Zaman—whose name means "Wonder-of-the-World"—was looked upon in Bagdad as the most fortunate creature under the sun because of his vast wealth. But really, what with anxiety about his riches and being weary of everything, and always desiring something he had not, he never knew a moment's real happiness. Even now he had come out of his palace, which was large and splendid enough for fifty kings, weary and cross because he could find nothing new to amuse him. The fowler thought that this would be a favorable opportunity for offering him the marvellous bird, which he felt certain he would buy the instant he saw it. And he was not mistaken, for when Badi-al-Zaman took the lovely prisoner into his own hands, he saw written under its right wing the words, "He who eats my head will become a king," and under its left wing, "He who eats my heart will find a hundred gold-pieces under his pillow every morning." In spite of all his wealth he at once began to desire the promised gold, and the bargain was soon completed. Then the difficulty arose as to how the bird was to be cooked; for among all his army of servants not one could Badi-al-Zaman trust. At last he asked the fowler if he were married, and on hearing that he was he made him take the bird home with him and tell his wife to cook it.

"Perhaps," said he, "this will give me an appetite, which I have not had for many a long day, and if so your wife shall have a hundred pieces of silver."

The fowler with great joy ran home to his wife, who speedily made a savory stew of the yellow bird. But when Badi-al-Zaman reached the cottage and began eagerly to search in the dish for its head and its heart he could not find either of them, and turned to the fowler's wife in a furious rage. She was so terrified that she fell upon her knees before him and confessed that her two children had come in just before he arrived, and had so teased her for some of the dish she was preparing that she had presently given the head to one and the heart to the other, since these morsels are not generally much esteemed; and Badi-al-Zaman rushed from the cottage vowing vengeance against the whole family.

The wrath of a rich man is generally to be feared, so the fowler and his wife resolved to send their children out of harm's way; but the wife, to console her husband, confided to him that she had purposely given them the head and heart of the bird because she had been able to read what was written under its wings. So, believing that their children's fortunes were made, they embraced them and sent them forth, bidding them get as far away as possible, to take different roads, and to send news of their welfare. For themselves, they remained hidden and disguised in the town, which was really rather clever of them; but very soon afterward Badi-al-Zaman died of vexation and annoyance at the loss of the promised treasure, and then they went back to their cottage to wait for news of their children.

The younger, who had eaten the heart of the yellow bird, very soon found out what it had done for him, for each morning when he awoke he found a purse containing a hundred gold-pieces under his pillow. But, as all poor people may remember for their consolation, nothing in the world causes so much trouble or requires so much care as a great treasure. Consequently, the fowler's son, who spent with reckless profusion and was supposed to be possessed of a great hoard of gold, was before very long attacked by robbers, and in trying to defend himself was so badly wounded that he died.

The elder brother, who had eaten the yellow bird's head, travelled a long way without meeting with any particular adventure, until at last he reached a large city in Asia, which was all in an uproar over the choosing of a new emir. All the principal citizens had formed themselves into two parties, and it was not until after a prolonged squabble that they agreed that the person to whom the most singular thing happened should be emir. Our young traveller entered the town at this juncture, with his agreeable face and jaunty air, and all at once felt something alight upon his head, which proved to be a snow-white pigeon. Thereupon all the people began to stare and to run after him, so that he presently reached the palace with the pigeon upon his head and all the inhabitants of the city at his heels, and before he knew where he was they made him emir, to his great astonishment.

As there is nothing more agreeable than to command, and nothing to which people get accustomed more quickly, the young emir soon felt quite at his ease in his new position; but this did not prevent him from making every kind of mistake, and so misgoverning the kingdom that at last the whole city rose in revolt and deprived him at once of his authority and his life—a punishment which he richly deserved, for in the days of his prosperity he disowned the fowler and his wife and allowed them to die in poverty.

"I have told you this story, my dear Sylvain and Jocosa," added the fairy, "to prove to you that this little cottage and all that belongs to it is a gift more likely to bring you happiness and contentment than many things that would at first seem grander and more desirable. If you will faithfully promise me to till your fields and feed your flocks, and will keep your word better than you did before, I will see that you never lack anything that is really for your good."

Sylvain and Jocosa gave their faithful promise, and as they kept it they always enjoyed peace and prosperity. The fairy had asked all their friends and neighbors to their wedding, which took place at once with great festivities and rejoicings, and they lived to a good old age, always loving one another with all their hearts.

13. Jeanne-Marie Leprince de Beaumont, *The Young Misses Magazine, Containing Dialogues between a Governess and Several Young Ladies of Quality Her Scholars* (1759) [1]

The fate of Jeanne-Marie Leprince de Beaumont as a fairy-tale writer was to be immortalized as the author of "Beauty and the Beast," but her contributions add up to a lasting influence far greater than the celebrity of this tale. To be sure, she wrote other fairy tales in the Young Misses Magazine *that she published first in French, then in English. With this publication, she put the fairy-tale tradition to an innovative use in her capacity as governess in Britain's high society. Her particular skill as a writer lay in tailoring stories from the French print tradition to her mid-eighteenth-century audience of elite young women. The* Magazine *gathered stories within a new type of frame: a dialogue between a teacher and her students, which was a model borrowed from the tradition of philosophical writings beginning with Plato's Socratic dialogues. In the portion reproduced here, an "affable" governess engages in witty exchange with her scholars, all "ladies of quality" who range in age from five to 12. Storytelling is contrasted to "lessons" as a pastime that goes easier on the body than learning; yet, the savvy reader quickly*

1 [Source: Jeanne-Marie Leprince de Beaumont, *The Young Misses Magazine, Containing Dialogues between a Governess and Several Young Ladies of Quality Her Scholars*, 3rd ed. ([1759] London: J. Nourse, 1776): vol. I, 45-67.]

understands that each story told by Mrs. Affable contains myriad instructions on life and love that challenge the traditional pillars of the nobility in Europe: lineage, luxury, rank. Leprince de Beaumont did not simply educate girls in the ways of their courtly world, she also sought through the fairy tale to change those ways. "Beauty and the Beast" offers Beauty as an exemplar of complementary attributes that seem paradoxical in "persons of quality," exemplified by her sisters. She is educated but capable of hard physical work, appreciative of natural beauty but respectful of the power that attends wealth, beautiful but humble. It may be no accident that the adjective used to describe Beauty's personality, affable, aligns her genteel character with the wisdom of the governess who tells the story.

Leprince de Beaumont first published "La Belle et la Bête" in the French Magazin des Enfants *in 1756. The translation of 1759, included here, is her own.*

BEAUTY AND THE BEAST

Dialogue V, The Third Day

Mrs. Affable. You are come very soon today, ladies: we have but just this moment got up from table.

Lady Witty. Mrs. Affable, I dined with these ladies, and we were so impatient to see you, that we were not above ten minutes at dinner.

Mrs. Affable. Then I must chide you, dear children, nothing is worse for your health than to eat too quick. To punish you, there shall be stories before tea, but we will go and walk in the garden.

Lady Mary. I like walking in the garden very well, but I like stories still better; pray, Mrs. Affable, forgive us this time; upon my conscience, I did not know it was a fault to eat so quick.

Mrs. Affable. And it is another fault to swear upon your conscience, you must not say so again. I will not let you repeat your lessons now, ladies, lest it should hurt you to think of your lessons so soon after dinner.

Lady Charlotte. Well, Mrs. Affable, we will say nothing, but you will tell us something; you promised us a pretty tale, will it hurt us to hear it?

Mrs. Affable. I see I must do as you would have me: when you are good children, I have not the heart to deny you anything: come, we will go and sit in the garden, and I will tell you the tale I promised you last time.

Beauty and the Beast; a Tale

THERE WAS ONCE A VERY rich merchant, who had six children, three sons, and three daughters; being a man of sense, he spared no cost for their education, but gave them all kinds of matters. His daughters were extremely handsome, especially the youngest; when she was little everybody admired her, and called her "*The little Beauty*"; so that, as she grew up, she still went by the name of *Beauty*, which made her sisters very jealous. The youngest, as she was handsomer, was also better than her sisters. The two eldest had a great deal of pride, because they were rich. They gave themselves ridiculous airs, and would not visit other merchants' daughters, nor keep company with any but persons of quality. They went out every day upon parties of pleasure, balls, plays, concerts, &c. and laughed at their youngest sister, because she spent the greatest part of her time in reading good books. As it was known that they were great fortunes, several eminent merchants made their addresses to them; but the two eldest said, they would never marry, unless they could meet with a duke, or an earl at least. Beauty very civily thanked them that courted her, and told them she was too young yet to marry, but chose to stay with her father a few years longer.

All at once the merchant lost his whole fortune, excepting a small country house at a great distance from town, and told his children with tears in his eyes, they must go there and work for their living. The two eldest answered, that they would not leave the town, for they had several lovers, who they were sure would be glad to have them, tho' they had no fortune; but the good ladies were mistaken, for their lovers slighted and forsook them in their poverty. As they were not beloved on account of their pride, everybody said, they do not deserve to be pitied, we are very glad to see their pride humbled, let them go and give themselves quality airs in milking the cows and minding their dairy. But, added they, we are extremely concerned for Beauty, she was such a charming, sweet-tempered creature, spoke so kindly to poor people, and was of such an affable, obliging behaviour. Nay, several gentlemen would have married her, tho' they knew she had not a penny; but she told them she could not think of leaving her poor father in his misfortunes, but was determined to go along with him into the country to comfort and attend him. Poor Beauty at first was sadly grieved at the loss of her fortune; but, said she to herself, were I to cry ever so much, that would not make things better, I must try to make myself happy without a fortune. When they came to their country-house, the merchant and his three sons applied themselves to husbandry and tillage; and Beauty rose at four in the morning, and made haste to have the house clean, and dinner ready for the family. In the beginning she found it very difficult, for she had not been used to work as a servant, but in less than two months she grew stronger and healthier than ever. After she had done her work, she read, played on the harpsichord, or else sung whilst she spun. On the contrary, her two sisters did not know how to spend their time; they got up at ten, and did nothing but saunter about the whole day, lamenting the loss of their fine cloaths and acquaintance. Do but see our youngest sister, said they, one to the other, what a poor, stupid, mean-spirited creature she is, to be contented with such an unhappy dismal situation. The good merchant was of a quite different opinion; he knew very well that Beauty outshone her sisters, in her person as well as her mind, and admired her humility and industry, but above all her humility and patience; for her sisters not only left her all the work of the house to do, but insulted her every moment.

The family had lived about a year in this retirement, when the merchant received a letter with an account that a vessel, on board of which he had effects, was safely arrived. This news had like to have turned the heads of the two eldest daughters, who immediately flattered themselves with the hopes of returning to town, for they were quite weary of a country life; and when they saw their father ready to set out, they begged of him to buy them new gowns, headdresses, ribbands, and all manner of trifles; but Beauty asked for nothing, for she thought to herself, that all the money her father was going to receive, would scarce be sufficient to purchase everything her sisters wanted. What will you have, Beauty? said her father. Since you have the goodness to think of me, answered she, be so kind to bring me a rose, for as none grows here abouts, they are a kind of rarity. Not that Beauty cared for a rose, but she asked for something, lest she should seem by her example to condemn her sisters' conduct, who would have said she did it only to look particular. The good man went on his journey, but when he came there, they went to law with him about the merchandize, and after a great deal of trouble and pains to no purpose, he came back as poor as before.

He was within thirty miles of his own house, thinking on the pleasure he should have in seeing his children again, when going through a large forest he lost himself. It rained and snowed terribly; besides, the wind was so high, that it threw him twice off his horse, and night coming on, he began to apprehend being either starved to death with cold and hunger, or else devoured by the wolves, whom he heard howling all round him, when, on a sudden, looking through a long walk of trees, he saw a light at some distance, and going on a little farther perceived it came from a place illuminated from top to bottom. The merchant returned God thanks for this happy discovery, and hasted to the place, but was greatly surprized at not meeting with anyone in the out-courts. His horse followed him, and seeing a large stable open, went in, and finding both hay and oats, the poor beast, who was almost famished, fell to eating very heartily; the merchant tied him up to the manger, and walking towards the house, where he saw no one, but entering into a large hall, he found a good fire, and a table plentifully set out with but one cover laid. As he was wet quite through with the rain and snow, he drew near the fire to dry himself. I hope, said he, the master of the house, or his servants, will excuse the liberty I take; I suppose it will not be long before some of them appear.

He waited a considerable time, till it struck eleven, and still nobody came: at last he was so hungry that he could stay no longer, but took a chicken and eat it in two mouthfuls, trembling all the while. After this he drank a few glasses of wine, and growing more courageous he went out of the hall, and crossed through several grand apartments with magnificent furniture, till he came into a chamber, which had an exceeding good bed in it, and as he was very much fatigued, and it was past midnight, he concluded it was best to shut the door, and go to bed.

It was ten the next morning before the merchant waked, and as he was going to rise he was astonished to see a good suit of clothes in the room of his own, which were quite spoiled; certainly, said he, this palace belongs to some kind fairy, who has seen and pitied my distress. He looked through a window, but instead of snow saw the most delightful arbours, interwoven with the beautifullest flowers that ever were beheld. He then returned to the great hall, where he had supped the night before, and found some chocolate ready made on a little table. Thank you, good Madam Fairy, said he aloud, for being so careful as to provide me a breakfast; I am extremely obliged to you for all your favours.

The good man drank his chocolate, and then went to look for his horse, but passing thro' an arbour of roses, he remembered Beauty's request to him, and gathered a branch on which were several; immediately he heard a great noise, and saw such a frightful beast coming towards him, that he was ready to faint away. You are very ungrateful, said the Beast to him, in a terrible voice; I have saved your life by receiving you into my castle, and, in return, you steal my roses, which I value beyond anything in the universe; but you shall die for it; I give you but a quarter of an hour to prepare yourself, and say your prayers. The merchant fell on his knees, and lifted up both his hands: My lord, said he, I beseech you to forgive me, indeed I had no intention to offend in gathering a rose for one of my daughters, who desired me to bring her one. My name is not My Lord, replied the monster, but Beast; I don't love compliments, not I; I like people should speak as they think; and so do not imagine, I am to be moved by any of your flattering speeches: but you say you have got daughters; I will forgive you, on condition that one of them come willingly and suffer for you. Let me have no words, but go about your business, and swear that if your daughter refuse to die in your stead, you will return within three months. The merchant had no mind to sacrifice his daughters to the ugly monster, but he thought, in obtaining this respite, he should have the satisfaction of seeing them once more; so he promised, upon oath, he would return, and the Beast told him he might set out when he pleased; but, added he, you shall not depart empty handed; go back to the room where you lay, and you will see a great empty chest; fill it with whatever you like best, and I will send it to your home, and at the same time Beast withdrew. Well, said the good man to himself, if I must die, I shall have the comfort, at least, of leaving something to my poor children.

He returned to the bedchamber, and finding a great quantity of broad pieces of gold, he filled the great chest the Beast had mentioned, locked it, and afterwards took his horse out of the stable, leaving the palace with as much grief as he had entered it with joy. The horse, of his own accord, took one of the roads of the forest, and in a few hours the good man was at home. His children came round him, but instead of receiving their embraces with pleasure, he looked on them, and holding up the branch he had in his hands, he burst into tears.

Here, Beauty, said he, take these roses; but little do you think how dear they are like to cost your unhappy father, and then related his fatal adventure: immediately the two eldest set up lamentable outcries, and said all manner of ill-natured things to Beauty, who did not cry at all. Do but see the pride of that little wretch, said they; she would not ask for fine clothes, as we did; but no truly, Miss wanted to distinguish herself, so now she will be the death of our poor father, and yet she does not so much as shed a tear. Why should I, answered Beauty, it would be very needless, for my father shall not suffer upon my account, since the monster will accept of one of his daughters, I will deliver myself up to all his fury, and I am very happy in thinking that my death will save my father's life, and be a proof of my tender love for him. No sister, said her three brothers, that shall not be, we will go find the monster, and either kill him, or perish in the attempt. Do not imagine any such thing, my sons, said the merchant, Beast's power is so great, that I have no hopes of your overcoming him: I am charmed with Beauty's kind and generous offer, but I cannot yield to it; I am old, and have not long to live, so can only lose a few years, which I regret for your sakes alone, my dear children. Indeed father, said Beauty, you shall not go to the palace without me, you cannot hinder me from following you. It was to no purpose all they could say, Beauty still insisted on setting out for the fine palace, and her sisters were delighted at it, for her virtue and amiable qualities made them envious and jealous.

The merchant was so afflicted at the thoughts of losing his daughter, that he had quite forgot the chest full of gold; but at night when he retired to rest, no sooner had he shut his chamber-door, than, to his great astonishment, he found it by his bed-side; he was determined, however, not to tell his children, that he was grown rich, because they would have wanted to return to town, and he was resolved not to leave the country; but he trusted Beauty with the secret, who informed him, that two gentlemen came in his absence, and courted her sisters; she begged her father to consent to their marriage, and give them fortunes, for she was so good, that she loved them, and forgave heartily all their ill usage. These wicked creatures rubbed their eyes with an onion to force some tears when they parted with their sister, but her brothers were really concerned. Beauty was the only one who did not shed tears at parting, because she would not increase their uneasiness.

The horse took the direct road to the palace, and towards evening they perceived it illuminated as at first: the horse went of himself into the stable, and the good man and his daughter came into the great hall, where they found a table splendidly served up, and two covers. The merchant had no heart to eat, but Beauty, endeavouring to appear chearful [sic], sat down to table, and helped him. Afterwards, thought she to herself, Beast surely has a mind to fatten me before he eats me, since he provides such a plentiful entertainment. When they had supped they heard a great noise, and the merchant, all in tears, bid his poor child, farewel [sic], for he thought Beast was coming. Beauty was sadly terrified at his horrid form, but she took courage as well as she could, and the monster having asked her if she came willingly; y—e—es, said she, trembling: you are very good, and I am greatly obliged to you; honest man, go your ways tomorrow morning, but never think of coming here again. Farewel Beauty, farewel Beast, answered she, and immediately the monster withdrew. Oh, daughter, said the merchant, embracing Beauty, I am almost frightened to death; believe me, you had better go back, and let me stay here; no, father, said Beauty, in a resolute tone, you shall set out tomorrow morning, and leave me to the care and protection of providence. They went to bed, and thought they should not close their eyes all night; but scarce were they laid down, than they fell fast asleep, and Beauty dreamed a fine lady came, and said to her, I am content, Beauty, with your good will; this good action of yours in giving up your own life to save your father's shall not go unrewarded. Beauty waked, and told her father her dream, and though it helped to comfort him a little, yet he could not help crying bitterly, when he took leave of his dear child.

As soon as he was gone, Beauty sat down in the great hall, and fell a crying likewise; but as she was mistress of a great deal of resolution, she recommended herself to God, and resolved not to be uneasy the little time she had to live; for she firmly believed Beast would eat her up that night.

However, she thought she might as well walk about till then, and view this fine castle, which she could not help admiring; it was a delightful pleasant place, and she was extremely surprised at seeing a door, over which was wrote, "BEAUTY'S APARTMENT." She opened it hastily, and was quite dazzled with the magnificence that reigned throughout; but what chiefly took up her attention, was a large library, a harpsichord, and several music books. Well, said she to herself, I see they will not let my time hang heavy upon my hands for want of amusement. Then she reflected, "Were I but to stay here a day, there would not have been all these preparations." This consideration inspired her with, fresh courage; and opening the library she took a book, and read these words in letters of gold:

"Welcome Beauty, banish fear,
You are queen and mistress here:
Speak your wishes, speak your will,
Swift obedience meets them still."

Alas, said she, with a sigh, there is nothing I desire so much as to see my poor father, and know what he is doing; she had no sooner said this, when casting her eyes on a great looking glass, to her great amazement she saw her own home, where her father arrived with a very dejected countenance; her sisters went to meet him, and notwithstanding their endeavours to appear sorrowful, their joy, felt for having got rid of their sister, was visible in every feature: a moment after, everything disappeared, and Beauty's apprehensions at this proof of Beast's complaisance.

At noon she found dinner ready, and while at table, was entertained with an excellent concert of music, though without seeing anybody: but at night, as she was going to sit down to supper, she heard the noise Beast made, and could not help being sadly terrified. Beauty, said the monster, will you give me leave to see you sup? That is as you please, answered Beauty trembling. No, replied the Beast, you alone are mistress here; you need only bid me be gone, if my presence is troublesome, and I will immediately withdraw: but, tell me, do not you think me very ugly? That is true, said Beauty, for I cannot tell a lie, but I believe you are very good-natured. So I am, said the monster, but then, besides my ugliness, I have no sense; I know very well that I am a poor, silly, stupid-creature. 'Tis no sign of folly to think so, replied Beauty, for never did fool know this, or had so humble a conceit of his own understanding. Eat then, Beauty, said the monster, and endeavour to amuse yourself in your palace, for everything here is yours, and I should be very uneasy, if you were not happy. You are very obliging, answered Beauty; I own I am pleased with your kindness, and, when I consider that, your deformity scarce appears. Yes, yes, said the Beast, my heart is good, but still I am a monster. Among mankind, says Beauty, there are many that deserve that name more than you, and I prefer you, just as you are, to those who, under a human form, hide a treacherous, corrupt, and ungrateful heart. If I had sense enough, replied the Beast, I would make a fine compliment to thank you, but I am so dull, that I can only say, I am greatly obliged to you. Beauty eat a hearty supper, and had almost conquered her dread of the monster; but she had like to have fainted away, when he said to her, Beauty, will you be my wife? She was some time before she durst answer, for she was afraid of making him angry, if she refused. At last, however, she said, trembling, No, Beast. Immediately the poor monster went to sigh, and hissed so frightfully that the whole palace echoed. But Beauty soon recovered her fright, for Beast having said, in a mournful voice, then farewel, Beauty, left the room; and only turned back, now and then, to look at her as he went out.

When Beauty was alone, she felt a great deal of compassion for poor Beast. Alas, said she, 'tis a thousand pities, any thing, so good-natured should be so ugly.

Beauty spent three months very contentedly in the palace: every evening Beast paid her a visit, and talked to her during supper, very rationally, with plain good common sense, but never with what the world calls wit; and Beauty daily discovered some valuable qualifications in the monster, and seeing him often had so accustomed her to his deformity, that, far from dreading the time of his visit, she would often look on her watch to see when it would be nine, for the Beast never missed coming at that hour. There was but one thing that gave Beauty any concern, which was, that every night, before she went to bed, the monster always asked her if she would be his wife. One day she said to him, Beast, you make me very uneasy, I wish I could consent to marry you, but I am too sincere to make you believe that will ever happen: I shall always esteem you as a friend, endeavour to be satisfied with this. I must, said the Beast, for, alas! I know too well my own misfortune, but then I love you with the tenderest affection: however, I ought to think myself happy, that you will stay here; promise me never to leave me. Beauty blushed at these words; she had seen in her glass, that her father had pined himself sick for the loss of her, and she longed to see him again. I could, answered she, indeed promise never to leave you intirely [sic], but I have so great a desire to see my father, that I shall fret to death, if you refuse me that satisfaction. I had rather die myself, said the monster, than give you the least uneasiness: I will send you to your father, you shall remain with him, and poor Beast will die with grief. No, said Beauty, weeping, I love you too well to be the cause of your death. I give you my promise to return in a week: you have shewn me that my sisters are married, and my brothers gone to the army; only let me stay a week with my father, as he is alone. You shall be there tomorrow morning, said the Beast, but remember your promise: you need only lay your ring on a table before you go to bed, when you have a mind to come back: farewel, Beauty. Beast sighed as usual, bidding her good night, and Beauty went to bed very sad at seeing him so afflicted. When she waked the next morning, she found herself at her father's, and having rang a little bell, that was by her bedside, she saw the maid come, who, the moment she saw her, gave a loud shriek, at which the good man ran upstairs, and thought he should have died with joy to see his dear daughter again. He held her fast locked in his arms above a quarter of an hour. As soon as the first transports were over, Beauty began to think of rising, and was afraid she had no clothes to put on; but the maid told her, that she had just found, in the next room, a large trunk full of gowns, covered with gold and diamonds. Beauty thanked good Beast for his kind care, and taking one of the plainest of them, she intended to make a present of the others to her sisters. She scarce had said so, when the trunk disappeared. Her father told her, that Beast insisted on her keeping them herself, and immediately both gowns and trunk came back again.

Beauty dressed herself, and in the mean time they sent to her sisters, who hasted thither with their husbands. They were both of them very unhappy. The eldest had married a gentleman, extremely handsome indeed, but so fond of his own person, that he was full of nothing but his own dear self, and neglected his wife. The second had married a man of wit, but he only made use of it to plague and torment every body, and his wife most of all. Beauty's sisters sickened with envy, when they saw her dressed like a princess, and more beautiful than ever, nor could all her obliging affectionate behavior stifle their jealousy, which was ready to burst when she told them how happy she was. They went down into the garden to vent it in tears; and said one to the other, in what is this little creature better than us, that she should be so much happier? Sister, said the oldest, a thought just strikes my mind; let us endeavour to detain her above a week, and perhaps the silly monster will be so enraged at her for breaking her word, that he will devour her. Right, sister, answered the other, therefore we must shew her as much kindness as possible. After they had taken this resolution, they went up, and behaved so affectionately to their sister, that poor Beauty wept for joy. When the week was expired, they cried and tore their hair, and seemed so sorry to part with her, that she promised to stay a week longer.

In the meantime, Beauty could not help reflecting on herself, for the uneasiness she was likely to cause poor Beast, whom she sincerely loved, and really longed to see again. The tenth night she spent at her father's, she dreamed she was in the palace garden, and that she saw Beast extended on the grass-plat,[1] who seemed just expiring, and, in a dying voice, reproached her with her ingratitude. Beauty started out of her sleep, and bursting into tears; am I not very wicked, said she, to act so unkindly to Beast, that has studied so much, to please me in everything? Is it his fault if he is so ugly, and has so little sense? He is kind and good, and that is sufficient. Why did I refuse to marry him? I should be happier with the monster than my sisters are with their husbands; it is neither wit, nor a fine person, in a husband, that makes a woman happy, but virtue, sweetness of temper, and complaisance, and Beast has all these valuable qualifications. It is true, I do not feel the tenderness of affection for him, but I find I have the highest gratitude, esteem, and friendship. Beauty having said this, rose, put her ring on the table, and then laid down again; scarce was she in bed before she fell asleep, and when she waked the next morning, she was overjoyed to find herself in the Beast's palace. She put on one of her richest suits to please him, and waited for evening with the utmost impatience, at last the wished-for hour came, the clock struck nine, yet no Beast appeared. Beauty then feared she had been the cause of his death; she ran crying and wringing her hands all about the palace, like one in despair; after having sought for him every where, she recollected her dream and flew to the canal in the garden, where she dreamed she saw him. There she found poor Beast stretched out, quite senseless, and, as she imagined, dead. She threw herself upon him without any dread, and finding his heart beat still, she fetched some water from the canal and poured it on his head. Beast opened his eyes, and said to Beauty,

1 [A piece of ground covered with grass, sometimes a flower bed.]

you forgot your promise, and I was so afflicted for having lost you, that I resolved to starve myself, but since I have the happiness of seeing you once more, I die satisfied. No, dear Beast, said Beauty, you must not die; live to be my husband; from this moment I give you my hand, and swear to be none but yours. Alas! I thought I had only a friendship for you, but the grief I now feel convinces me, that I cannot live without you. Beauty scarce had pronounced these words, when she saw the palace start to sparkle with light; and fireworks, instruments of music, everything seemed to give notice of some great event: but nothing could fix her attention; she now turned to her dear Beast, for whom she trembled with fear; but how great was her surprise! Beast was disappeared, and she saw, at her feet, one of the loveliest princes that eye ever beheld; who returned her thanks for having put an end to the charm under which he had so long resembled a Beast. Though this prince was worthy of all her attention, she could not forbear asking where Beast was. You see him at your feet, said the prince, a wicked fairy had condemned me to remain under that shape till a beautiful virgin should consent to marry me; the fairy likewise enjoined me to conceal my understanding; there was only you in the world generous enough to be won by the goodness of my temper, and in offering you my crown I can't discharge the obligations I have to you. Beauty, agreeably surprized, gave the charming prince her hand to rise; they went together into the castle, and Beauty was overjoyed to find, in the great hall, her father and his whole family, whom the beautiful lady, that appeared to her in her dream, had conveyed thither.

Beauty, said this lady, come and receive the reward of your judicious choice; you have preferred virtue before either wit or beauty, and deserve to find a person in whom all these qualifications are united: you are going to be a great queen, I hope the throne will not lessen your virtue, or make you forget yourself. As to you, ladies, said the fairy to Beauty's two sisters, I know your hearts, and all the malice they contain: become two statues, but, under this transformation, still retain your reason. You shall stand before your sister's palace gate, and be it your punishment to behold her happiness; and it will not be in your power to return to your former state, till you own your faults, but I am very much afraid that you will always remain statues. Pride, anger, gluttony, and idleness are sometimes conquered, but the conversion of a malicious and envious mind is a kind of miracle. Immediately the fairy gave a stroke with her wand, and in a moment all that were in the hall were transported into the prince's dominions: his subjects received him with joy; he married Beauty, and lived with her many years and their happiness as it was founded on virtue was compleat.

C: ROMANTICISM TO THE *FIN DE SIÈCLE*

Johann Ludwig Tieck, "The Elves," *Phantasus* vol. 1 (1812; translated by Thomas Carlyle, 1827) [website]

The fairy tales of the German Romantic poet Johann Ludwig Tieck vary widely in their form and themes, and in the "The Elves" (provided as a web text; see http://sites.broadviewpress.com/marveloustrans/) Tieck overlays a social class critique with a story of an alternative reality where children glitter and flowers abound and where the problems of class and ethnic division do not apply. Significantly, everyone in the story can see this place, but they do not see it the same way. Known for his symbolic elements and descriptions of nature, Tieck paints his contrasting realms of understanding with darkness and light, work and play, and insightful youth against blind maturity.

14. Wilhelm and Jacob Grimm, *Kinder- und Hausmärchen* (1812 and 1815, 1819, 1857; *translated by Jack Zipes* [1987] 2002[1])

Jacob and Wilhelm Grimm published a number of important works (both individually and in collaboration) on German language and narrative forms, but they are best remembered for the tales now known simply as "Grimms' fairy tales"—the volumes published in multiple editions between 1812 and 1857 as Kinder- und Hausmärchen. *Inspired by the movement known as German Romantic Nationalism, and especially by the*

1 [Source: Jack Zipes, *The Complete Fairy Tales of the Brothers Grimm*, 3rd ed. (New York, NY: Bantam, 2002): 53–58, 432–34, 181–88, 109–12, 168–71.]

writings on folk culture and folk expression by the philosopher Johann Gottfried Herder, the Grimms sought a narrative heritage that was imagined to be purely and essentially German—free from foreign influence and reflective of Germanic national character. One of the Grimms' important contributions to the history of tale publishing was their establishment of principles of field-based collection, which would inspire scores of collectors in other national contexts and would eventually develop into modern folklore fieldwork practices. In point of fact, the Grimms did not follow the principles they espoused: many of the tales they collected did not actually represent the living oral traditions of peasants far removed from urban life and print culture, but rather stories contributed by urban, literate friends and neighbors. The Grimms also made very significant changes to story texts, evident in comparisons of their 1810 manuscript to the first published volumes of the tales (1812, 1815) and what has come to be known as the "final edition" of the collection (1857)—elaborating on characters' motivations and exaggerating characteristics that mark figures as good and evil, for example (see Jack Zipes, Fairy Tales and the Art of Subversion, *2nd ed. [New York: Routledge, 2006]). The versions included here are translations from the final edition and reflect the Grimms' attempts to recreate (some may say invent) a distinctive German folk style and set of values. In these tales, as compared to the earlier literary fairy-tale tradition, there is an emphasis both on quoted speech and direct discourse and on extreme rewards and punishments.*

HANSEL AND GRETEL

A POOR WOODCUTTER LIVED WITH HIS wife and his two children on the edge of a large forest. The boy was called Hansel and the girl Gretel. The woodcutter did not have much food around the house, and when a great famine devastated the entire country, he could no longer provide enough for his family's daily meals. One night, as he was lying in bed and thinking about his worries, he began tossing and turning. Then he sighed and said to his wife, "What's to become of us? How can we feed our poor children when we don't even have enough for ourselves?"

"I'll tell you what," answered his wife. "Early tomorrow morning we'll take the children out into the forest where it's most dense. We'll build a fire and give them each a piece of bread. Then we'll go about our work and leave them alone. They won't find their way back home, and we'll be rid of them."

"No, wife," the man said. "I won't do this. I don't have the heart to leave my children in the forest. The wild beasts would soon come and tear them apart."

"Oh, you fool!" she said. "Then all four of us will have to starve to death. You'd better start planing the boards for our coffins!" She continued to harp on this until he finally agreed to do what she suggested.

"But still, I feel sorry for the poor children," he said.

The two children had not been able to fall asleep that night either. Their hunger kept them awake, and when they heard what their stepmother said to their father, Gretel wept bitter tears and said to Hansel, "Now it's all over for us."

"Be quiet, Gretel," Hansel said. "Don't get upset. I'll soon find a way to help us."

When their parents had fallen asleep, Hansel put on his little jacket, opened the bottom half of the door, and crept outside. The moon was shining very brightly, and the white pebbles glittered in front of the house like pure silver coins. Hansel stooped down to the ground and stuffed his pocket with as many pebbles as he could fit in. Then he went back and said to Gretel, "Don't worry, my dear little sister. Just sleep in peace. God will not forsake us." And he lay down again in his bed.

At dawn, even before the sun began to rise, the woman came and woke the two children: "Get up, you lazybones! We're going into the forest to fetch some wood." Then she gave each one of them a piece of bread and said, "Now you have something for your noonday meal, but don't eat it before then because you're not getting anything else."

Gretel put the bread under her apron because Hansel had the pebbles in his pocket. Then they all set out together toward the forest. After they had walked awhile, Hansel stopped and looked back at the house. He did this time and again until his father said, "Hansel, what are you looking at there? Why are you dawdling? Pay attention, and don't forget how to use your legs!"

"Oh, Father," said Hansel, "I'm looking at my little white cat that's sitting up on the roof and wants to say good-bye to me."

"You fool," the mother said. "That's not a cat. It's the morning sun shining on the chimney."

But Hansel had not been looking at the cat. Instead, he had been taking the shiny pebbles from his pocket and constantly dropping them on the ground. When they reached the middle of the forest, the father said, "Children, I want you to gather some wood. I'm going to make a fire so you won't get cold."

Hansel and Gretel gathered together some brushwood and built quite a nice little pile. The brushwood was soon kindled, and when the fire was ablaze, the woman said, "Now, children, lie down by the fire, and rest yourselves. We're going into the forest to chop wood. When we're finished, we'll come back and get you."

Hansel and Gretel sat by the fire, and when noon came, they ate their pieces of bread. Since they heard the sounds of the ax, they thought their father was nearby. But it was not the ax. Rather, it was a branch that he had tied to a dead tree, and the wind was banging it back and forth. After they had been sitting there for a long time, they became so weary that their eyes closed, and they fell sound asleep. By the time they finally awoke, it was already pitch black, and Gretel began to cry and said, "How are we going to get out of the forest?"

But Hansel comforted her by saying, "Just wait awhile until the moon has risen. Then we'll find the way."

And when the full moon had risen, Hansel took his little sister by the hand and followed the pebbles that glittered like newly minted silver coins and showed them the way. They walked the whole night long and arrived back at their father's house at break of day. They knocked at the door, and when the woman opened it and saw it was Hansel and Gretel, she said, "You wicked children, why did you sleep so long in the forest? We thought you'd never come back again."

But the father was delighted because he had been deeply troubled by the way he had abandoned them in the forest.

Not long after that the entire country was once again ravaged by famine, and one night the children heard their mother talking to their father in bed. "Everything's been eaten up again. We only have half a loaf of bread, but after it's gone, that will be the end of our food. The children must leave. This time we'll take them even farther into the forest so they won't find their way back home again. Otherwise, there's no hope for us."

All this saddened the father, and he thought, It'd be much better to share your last bite to eat with your children. But the woman would not listen to anything he said. She just scolded and reproached him. Once you've given a hand, people will take your arm, and since he had given in the first time, he also had to yield a second time.

However, the children were still awake and had overheard their conversation. When their parents had fallen asleep, Hansel got up, intending to go out and gather pebbles as he had done the time before, but the woman had locked the door, and Hansel could not get out. Nevertheless, he comforted his little sister and said, "Don't cry, Gretel. Just sleep in peace. The dear Lord is bound to help us."

Early the next morning the woman came and got the children out of bed. They each received little pieces of bread, but they were smaller than the last time. On the way into the forest Hansel crumbled the bread in his pocket and stopped as often as he could to throw the crumbs on the ground.

"Hansel, why are you always stopping and looking around?" asked the father. "Keep going!"

"I'm looking at my little pigeon that's sitting on the roof and wants to say goodbye to me," Hansel answered.

"Fool!" the woman said. "That's not your little pigeon. It's the morning sun shining on the chimney."

But little by little Hansel managed to scatter all the bread crumbs on the path. The woman led the children even deeper into the forest until they came to a spot they had never in their lives seen before. Once again a large fire was made, and the mother said, "Just keep sitting here, children. If you get tired, you can sleep a little.

We're going into the forest to chop wood, and in the evening, when we're done, we'll come and get you."

When noon came, Gretel shared her bread with Hansel, who had scattered his along the way. Then they fell asleep, and evening passed, but no one came for the poor children. Only when it was pitch black did they finally wake up, and Hansel comforted his little sister by saying, "Just wait until the moon has risen, Gretel. Then we'll see the little bread crumbs that I scattered. They'll show us the way back home."

When the moon rose, they set out but could not find the crumbs, because the many thousands of birds that fly about in the forest and fields had devoured them.

"Don't worry, we'll find the way," Hansel said to Gretel, but they could not find it. They walked the entire night and all the next day as well, from morning till night, but they did not get out of the forest. They were now also very hungry, for they had had nothing to eat except some berries that they had found growing on the ground. Eventually they became so tired that their legs would no longer carry them, and they lay down beneath a tree and fell asleep.

It was now the third morning since they had left their father's house. They began walking again, and they kept going deeper and deeper into the forest. If help did not arrive soon, they were bound to perish of hunger and exhaustion. At noon they saw a beautiful bird as white as snow sitting on a branch. It sang with such a lovely voice that the children stood still and listened to it. When the bird finished its song, it flapped its wings and flew ahead of them. They followed it until they came to a little house that was made of bread. Moreover, it had cake for a roof and pure sugar for windows.

"What a blessed meal!" said Hansel. "Let's have a taste. I want to eat a piece of the roof. Gretel, you can have some of the window, since it's sweet."

Hansel reached up high and broke off a piece of the roof to see how it tasted, and Gretel leaned against the windowpanes and nibbled on them. Then they heard a shrill voice cry out from inside:

"Nibble, nibble, I hear a mouse.
Who's that nibbling at my house?"

The children answered:

"The wind, the wind; it's very mild,
blowing like the Heavenly Child."

And they did not bother to stop eating or let themselves be distracted. Since the roof tasted so good, Hansel ripped off a large piece and pulled it down, while Gretel pushed out a round piece of the windowpane, sat down, and ate it with great relish. Suddenly the door opened, and a very old woman leaning on a crutch came slinking out of the house. Hansel and Gretel were so tremendously frightened that they dropped what they had in their hands. But the old woman wagged her head and said, "Well now, dear children, who brought you here? Just come inside and stay with me. Nobody's going to harm you."

She took them both by the hand and led them into her house. Then she served them a good meal of milk and pancakes with sugar and apples and nuts. Afterward she made up two little beds with white sheets, whereupon Hansel and Gretel lay down in them and thought they were in heaven. The old woman, however, had only pretended to be friendly. She was really a wicked witch on the lookout for children, and had built the house made of bread only to lure them to her. As soon as she had any children in her power, she would kill, cook, and eat them. It would be like a feast day for her. Now, witches have red eyes and cannot see very far, but they have a keen sense of smell, like animals, and can detect when human beings are near them. Therefore, when Hansel and Gretel had come into her vicinity, she had laughed wickedly and scoffed, "They're mine! They'll never get away from me!"

Early the next morning, before the children were awake, she got up and looked at the two of them sleeping so sweetly with full rosy cheeks. Then she muttered to herself, "They'll certainly make for a tasty meal!"

She seized Hansel with her scrawny hands and carried him into a small pen, where she locked him up behind a grilled door. No matter how much he screamed, it did not help. Then she went back to Gretel, shook her until she woke up, and yelled, "Get up, you lazybones! I want you to fetch some water and cook your brother something nice. He's sitting outside in a pen, and we've got to fatten him up. Then, when he's fat enough, I'm going to eat him."

Gretel began to weep bitter tears, but they were all in vain. She had to do what the wicked witch demanded. So the very best food was cooked for poor Hansel, while Gretel got nothing but crab shells. Every morning the old woman went slinking to the little pen and called out, "Hansel, stick out your finger so I can feel how fat you are."

However, Hansel stuck out a little bone, and since the old woman had poor eyesight, she thought the bone was Hansel's finger. She was puzzled that Hansel did not get any fatter, and when a month had gone by and Hansel still seemed to be thin, she was overcome by her impatience and decided not to wait any longer.

"Hey there, Gretel!" she called to the little girl. "Get a move on and fetch some water! I don't care whether Hansel's fat or thin. He's going to be slaughtered tomorrow, and then I'll cook him."

Oh, how the poor little sister wailed as she was carrying the water, and how the tears streamed down her cheeks!

"Dear God, help us!" she exclaimed. "If only the wild beasts had eaten us in the forest, then we could have at least died together!"

Early the next morning Gretel had to go out, hang up a kettle full of water, and light the fire.

"First we'll bake," the old woman said. "I've already heated the oven and kneaded the dough." She pushed poor Gretel out to the oven, where the flames were leaping from the fire. "Crawl inside," said the witch, "and see if it's properly heated so we can slide the bread in."

The witch intended to close the oven door once Gretel had climbed inside, for the witch wanted to bake her and eat her too. But Gretel sensed what she had in mind and said, "I don't know how to do it. How do I get in?"

"You stupid goose," the old woman said. "The opening's large enough. Watch, even I can get in!"

She waddled up to the oven and stuck her head through the oven door. Then Gretel gave her a push that sent her flying inside and shut the iron door and bolted it. *Whew!* The witch began to howl dreadfully, but Gretel ran away, and the godless witch was miserably burned to death.

Meanwhile, Gretel ran straight to Hansel, opened the pen, and cried out, "Hansel, we're saved! The old witch is dead!"

Then Hansel jumped out of the pen like a bird that hops out of a cage when the door is opened. My how happy they were! They hugged each other, danced around, and kissed. Since they no longer had anything to fear, they went into the witch's house, and there they found chests filled with pearls and jewels all over the place.

"They're certainly much better than pebbles," said Hansel, and he put whatever he could fit into his pockets, and Gretel said, "I'm going to carry some home too," and she filled her apron full of jewels and pearls.

"We'd better be on our way now," said Hansel, "so we can get out of the witch's forest."

When they had walked for a few hours, they reached a large river.

"We can't get across," said Hansel. "I don't see a bridge or any way over it."

"There are no boats either," Gretel responded, "but there's a white duck swimming over there. It's bound to help us across if I ask it." Then she cried out:

"Help us, help us, little duck!
We're Hansel and Gretel, out of luck.
We can't get over, try as we may.
Please take us across right away!"

The little duck came swimming up to them, and Hansel got on top of its back and told his sister to sit down beside him.

"No," Gretel answered. "That will be too heavy for the little duck. Let it carry us across one at a time."

The kind little duck did just that, and when they were safely across and had walked on for some time, the forest became more and more familiar to them, and finally they caught sight of their father's house from afar. They began to run at once, and soon rushed into the house and threw themselves around their father's neck. The man had not had a single happy hour since he had abandoned his children in the forest, and in the meantime his wife had died. Gretel opened and shook out her apron so that the pearls and jewels bounced about the room, and Hansel added to this by throwing one handful after another from his pocket. Now all their troubles were over, and they lived together in utmost joy.

My tale is done. See the mouse run. Catch it, whoever can, and then you can make a great big cap out of its fur.

THE WORN-OUT DANCING SHOES

ONCE UPON A TIME THERE was a king who had twelve daughters, one more beautiful than the next. They slept together in a large room, where their beds stood side by side, and in the evening, when they went to sleep, the king shut and locked the door. However, when he opened it in the morning, he would see that their shoes were worn out from dancing, and nobody could discover how this kept happening. Finally, the king had it proclaimed that whoever could find out where his daughters danced during the night could choose one of them for his wife and be king after his death. But anyone who came and failed to uncover everything after three days and nights would lose his life.

Not long after this proclamation a prince came and offered to undertake the venture. He was well received, and in the evening he was conducted to a room adjoining the bedchamber of the king's daughters. His bed was set up there, and he was told to watch and find out where they went dancing. And, just to make sure they could not do anything in secret or go out anywhere else, the door of their room that led to his was kept open. Still, the prince's eyes became as heavy as lead, and he fell asleep. When he awoke the next morning, all twelve of them had been to a dance, for their shoes were standing there with holes in their soles. The same thing happened the second and third night, and his head was cut off without mercy. After that there were many who came to try their luck, but they were all destined to leave their lives behind them.

Now, it happened that a poor soldier, who had been wounded and could longer serve in the army, headed toward the city where the king lived. Along the way he met an old woman, who asked him where he was going.

"I really don't know myself," he said, and added jokingly, "but I'd certainly like to find out where the king's daughters go dancing and where they wear out their shoes so I could become king."

"That's not so difficult," said the old woman. "Just don't drink the wine that's brought to you in the evening, and then pretend that you've fallen asleep." Then she gave him a little cloak and said, "When you put this cloak on, you'll be invisible, and you'll be able to follow all twelve of them."

After receiving such good advice, the soldier now became serious about the entire matter and plucked up his courage to present himself in front of the king as a suitor. He was welcomed just as cordially as the others had been and was given royal garments to put on. In the evening, at bedtime, he was led to the antechamber, and as he was preparing to go to bed the oldest daughter brought him a beaker of wine, but he had tied a sponge underneath his chin and let the wine run into it and did not drink a single drop. Then he lay down, and after lying there a little while, he began to snore as if in a very deep sleep.

When the princesses heard his snoring, they laughed, and the oldest said, "He too could have done better things with his life." After this they stood up, opened the closets, chests, and boxes, and took out splendid clothes. They groomed themselves in front of their mirrors and hurried about, eager to attend the dance. But the youngest said, "I don't know. You're all happy, yet I have a strange feeling. I'm sure that something bad is going to happen to us."

"You're a silly goose," said the oldest. "You're always afraid. Have you forgotten how many princes have already tried in vain? I didn't really need to give the soldier a sleeping potion. The lout would never have awakened even without it."

When they were all ready, they first took a look at the soldier, but he had shut his eyes tight, and since he neither moved nor stirred, they thought they were definitely safe. So the oldest went to her bed and knocked on it. Immediately it sank into the ground, and they climbed down through the opening, one after another, with the oldest in the lead. The soldier, who had seen everything, did not hesitate long. He put on his little cloak and climbed down after the youngest. Halfway down the stairs he stepped on her dress lightly, causing her to become terrified and cry out, "What's that? Who's holding my dress?"

"Don't be so stupid," said the oldest. "You've just caught it on a hook."

They went all the way down, and when they were at the bottom, they stood in the middle of a marvelous avenue of trees whose leaves were all made of silver and glittered and glimmered. You'd better take a piece of evidence with you, the soldier thought, and broke off a branch, but the tree cracked and made a tremendous sound. Again the youngest called out, "Something's wrong! Didn't you hear the noise?"

But the oldest said, "That was just a burst of joy because we'll soon be setting our princes free."

Then they came to another avenue of trees, where all the leaves were made of gold, and finally to one where all the leaves were made of pure diamond. The soldier broke off branches from each kind, and each time there was such a cracking sound that the youngest sister was terrified. But the oldest maintained that they were just bursts of joy. They went on and came to a large lake with twelve boats on it, and in each boat sat a handsome prince. They had been waiting for the twelve princesses, and each one took a princess in his boat, while the soldier went aboard with the youngest princess. Then her prince said, "I don't understand it, but the boat is much heavier today. I'll have to row with all my might to get it moving."

"It's probably due to the warm weather," said the youngest. "I feel quite hot too."

On the other side of the lake stood a beautiful, brightly lit palace, and sounds of merry music with drums and trumpets could be heard from it. They rowed over there, entered the palace, and each prince danced with his sweetheart. The invisible soldier danced along as well, and whenever a princess went to drink a beaker of wine, he would drain it dry before it could reach her lips. The youngest sister was terribly concerned about this too, but the oldest continued to soothe her. They danced until three in the morning, when all the shoes were worn through and they had to stop. The princes rowed them back across the lake, and this time the soldier sat in the first boat with the oldest sister. The princesses took leave of their princes on the bank and promised to return the following night. When they reached the stairs, the soldier ran ahead of them and got into bed, and by the time the twelve princesses came tripping slowly and wearily up the stairs, he was again snoring so loudly that they could all hear it, and they said, "We don't have to worry about him." Then they took off their beautiful clothes, put them away, placed the worn-out shoes under their beds, and lay down to sleep.

The next morning the soldier decided not to say anything but rather to follow and observe their strange life for the next two nights. Everything happened just as it had on the first night: they danced each time until their shoes fell apart. However, the third time he took a beaker with him for evidence. When the time came for him to give his answer, he took along the three branches and beaker and went before the king. The twelve princesses stood behind the door and listened to what he said. When the king asked, "Where did my daughters spend the night?" he answered, "With twelve princes in an underground palace." Then he reported what had taken place and produced the evidence. The king summoned his daughters and asked them whether the soldier had told the truth. When they saw that they had been exposed and that denying would not help, they had to confess everything. Then the king asked the soldier which princess he would like for his wife.

"I'm no longer so young," he answered, "so I'll take the oldest."

The wedding was held that same day, and the king promised to make him his successor to the kingdom after his death. The princes, however, were compelled to remain under a curse for as many nights as they had danced with the princesses.

SNOW WHITE

ONCE UPON A TIME, IN the middle of winter, when snowflakes were falling like feathers from the sky, a queen was sitting and sewing at a window with a black ebony frame. And as she was sewing and looking out the window, she pricked her finger with the needle, and three drops of blood fell on the snow. The red looked so beautiful on the white snow that she thought to herself, If only I had a child as white as snow, as red as blood, and as black as the wood of the window frame!

Soon after she gave birth to a little daughter who was as white as snow, as red as blood, and her hair as black as ebony. Accordingly, the child was called Snow White, and right after she was born, the queen died. When a year had passed, the king married another woman, who was beautiful but proud and haughty, and she could not tolerate anyone else who might rival her beauty. She had a magic mirror and often she stood in front of it, looked at herself, and said:

"Mirror, mirror, on the wall,
who in this realm is the fairest of all?"

Then the mirror would answer:

"You, my queen, are the fairest of all."

That reply would make her content, for she knew the mirror always told the truth.

In the meantime, Snow White grew up and became more and more beautiful. By the time she was seven years old, she was as beautiful as the day is clear and more beautiful than the queen herself. One day when the queen asked her mirror:

"Mirror, mirror, on the wall,
who in this realm is the fairest of all?"

The mirror answered:

"You, my queen, may have a beauty quite rare,
but Snow White is a thousand times more fair."

The queen shuddered and became yellow and green with envy. From that hour on, her hate for the girl was so great that her heart throbbed and turned in her breast each time she saw Snow White. Like weeds, the envy and arrogance grew so dense in her heart that she no longer had any peace, day or night. Finally, she summoned a huntsman and said, "Take the child out into the forest. I never want to lay eyes on her again. You are to kill her and to bring me back her lungs and liver as proof of your deed."

The huntsman obeyed and led Snow White out into the forest, but when he drew his hunting knife and was about to stab Snow White's innocent heart, she began to weep and said, "Oh, dear huntsman, spare my life, and I'll run into the wild forest and never come home again."

Since she was so beautiful, the huntsman took pity on her and said, "You're free to go, my poor child!" Then he thought, The wild beasts will soon eat you up. Nevertheless, he felt as if a great weight had been lifted off his mind, because he did not have to kill her. Just then a young boar came dashing by, and the huntsman stabbed it to death. He took out the lungs and liver and brought them to the queen as proof that the child was dead. The cook was ordered to boil them in salt, and the wicked woman ate them and thought that she had eaten Snow White's lungs and liver.

Meanwhile, the poor child was all alone in the huge forest. When she looked at all the leaves on the trees, she was petrified and did not know what to do. Then she began to run, and she ran over sharp stones and through thorn bushes. Wild beasts darted by her at times, but they did not harm her. She ran as long as her legs could carry her, and it was almost evening when she saw a little cottage and went inside to rest. Everything was tiny in the cottage and indescribably dainty and neat. There was a little table with a white tablecloth, and on it were seven little plates. Each plate had a tiny spoon next to it, and there were also seven tiny knives and forks and seven tiny cups. In a row against the wall stood seven little beds covered with sheets as white as snow. Since she was so hungry and thirsty, Snow White ate some vegetables and bread from each of the little plates and had a drop of wine to drink out of each of the tiny cups, for she did not want to take everything from just one place. After that she was tired and began trying out the beds, but none of them suited her at first: one was too long, another too short, but at last, she found that the seventh one was just right. So she stayed in that bed, said her prayers, and fell asleep.

When it was completely dark outside, the owners of the cottage returned. They were seven dwarfs who searched in the mountains for minerals with their picks and shovels. They lit their seven little candles, and when it became light in the house, they saw that someone had been there, for none of their things was in the exact same spot in which it had been left.

"Who's been sitting in my chair?" said the first dwarf.

"Who's been eating off my plate?" said the second.

"Who's been eating my bread?" said the third.

"Who's been eating my vegetables?" said the fourth.

"Who's been using my fork?" said the fifth.

"Who's been cutting with my knife?" said the sixth.

"Who's been drinking from my cup?" said the seventh.

Then the first dwarf looked around and noticed that his bed had been wrinkled and said, "Who's been sleeping in my bed?"

The others ran over to their beds and cried out, "Someone's been sleeping in my bed too!"

But when the seventh dwarf looked at his bed, he saw Snow White lying there asleep. So he called the others over to him, and when they came, they were so astounded that they fetched their seven little candles to allow more light to shine on Snow White.

"Oh, my Lord! Oh, my Lord!" they exclaimed. "What a beautiful child!"

They were so delirious with joy that they did not wake her up. Instead, they let her sleep in the bed, while the seventh dwarf spent an hour in each one of his companions' beds until the night had passed. In the morning Snow White awoke, and when she saw the seven dwarfs, she was frightened. But they were friendly and asked, "What's your name?"

"My name's Snow White," she replied.

"What's brought you to our house?" the dwarfs continued.

She told them how her stepmother had ordered her to be killed, how the huntsman had spared her life, and how she had run all day until she had eventually discovered their cottage.

Then the dwarfs said, "If you'll keep house for us, cook, make the beds, wash, sew, and knit, and if you'll keep everything neat and orderly, you can stay with us, and we'll provide you with everything you need."

"Yes," agreed Snow White, "with all my heart."

So she stayed with them and kept their house in order. In the morning they went to the mountains to search for minerals and gold. In the evening they returned, and their dinner had to be ready. During the day Snow White was alone, and the good dwarfs made sure to caution her.

"Beware of your stepmother," they said. "She'll soon know that you're here. Don't let anybody in!"

Since the queen believed she had eaten Snow White's liver and lungs, she was totally convinced that she was again the most beautiful woman in the realm. And when she went to her mirror, she said:

"Mirror, mirror, on the wall,
who in this realm is the fairest of all?"

The mirror answered:

"You, my queen, may have a beauty quite rare,
but beyond the mountains, where the seven dwarfs dwell,
Snow White is thriving, and this I must tell:
Within this realm she's still a thousand times more fair."

The queen was horrified, for she knew that the mirror never lied, which meant that the huntsman had deceived her and Snow White was still alive. Once more she began plotting ways to kill her. As long as Snow White was the fairest in the realm, the queen's envy would leave her no peace. Finally, she thought up a plan. She painted her face and dressed as an old peddler woman so that nobody could recognize her. Then she crossed the seven mountains in this disguise and arrived at the cottage of the seven dwarfs, where she knocked at the door and cried out, "Pretty wares for sale! Pretty wares!"

Snow White looked out of the window and called out, "Good day, dear woman, what do you have for sale?"

"Nice and pretty things! Staylaces in all kinds of colors!" she replied and took out a lace woven from silk of many different colors.

I can certainly let this honest woman inside, Snow White thought. She unbolted the door and bought the pretty lace.

"My goodness, child! What a sight you are!" said the old woman. "Come, I'll lace you up properly for once."

Snow White did not suspect anything, so she stood in front of the old woman and let herself be laced with the new staylace. However, the old woman laced her so quickly and so tightly that Snow White lost her breath and fell down as if dead.

"Well, you used to be the fairest in the realm, but not now!" the old woman said and rushed off.

Not long after, at dinnertime, the dwarfs came home, and when they saw their dear Snow White lying on the ground, they were horrified. She neither stirred nor moved and seemed to be dead. They lifted her up, and when they saw that she was laced too tightly, they cut the staylace in two. At once she began to breathe a little, and after a while she had fully revived. When the dwarfs heard what had happened, they said, "The old peddler woman was none other than the wicked queen! Beware, don't let anyone in when we're not with you!"

When the evil woman returned home, she went to her mirror and asked:

"Mirror, mirror, on the wall,
who in this realm is the fairest of all?"

Then the mirror answered as usual:

"You, my queen, may have a beauty quite rare,
but beyond the mountains, where the seven dwarfs dwell,
Snow White is thriving, and this I must tell:
Within this realm she's still a thousand times more fair."

When the queen heard that, she was so upset that all her blood rushed to her heart, for she realized that Snow White had recovered.

"This time I'm going to think of something that will destroy her," she said, and by using all the witchcraft at her command, she made a poison comb. Then she again disguised herself as an old woman and crossed the seven mountains to the cottage of the seven dwarfs, where she knocked at the door and cried out, "Pretty wares for sale! Pretty wares!"

Snow White looked out the window and said, "Go away! I'm not allowed to let anyone in."

"But surely you're allowed to look," said the old woman, and she took out the poison comb and held it up in the air. The comb pleased the girl so much that she let herself be carried away and opened the door. After they agreed on the price, the old woman said, "Now I'll give your hair a proper combing for once."

Poor Snow White did not give this a second thought and let the old woman do as she wished. But no sooner did the comb touch her hair than the poison began to take effect, and the maiden fell to the ground and lay there unconscious.

"You paragon of beauty!" said the wicked woman. "Now you're finished!" And she went away.

Fortunately, it was nearly evening, the time when the seven dwarfs began heading home. And, when they arrived and saw Snow White lying on the ground as if she were dead, they immediately suspected the stepmother and began looking around. As soon as they found the poison comb, they took it out, and Snow White instantly regained consciousness. She told them what had happened, and they warned her again to be on her guard and not to open the door for anyone.

In the meantime, the queen returned home, went to the mirror, and said:

"Mirror, mirror, on the wall,
who in this realm is the fairest of all?"

Then the mirror answered as before:

"You, my queen, may have a beauty quite rare,
but beyond the mountains, where the seven dwarfs dwell,
Snow White is thriving, and this I must tell:
Within this realm she's still a thousand times more fair."

When she heard the mirror's words, she trembled and shook with rage. "Snow White shall die!" she exclaimed. "Even if it costs me my own life!"

Then she went into a secret and solitary chamber where no one else ever went. Once inside she made a deadly poisonous apple. On the outside it looked beautiful—white with red cheeks. Anyone who saw it would be enticed, but whoever took a bite was bound to die. When the apple was ready, the queen painted her face and dressed herself up as a peasant woman and crossed the seven mountains to the cottage of the seven dwarfs. When she knocked at the door, Snow White stuck her head out of the window and said, "I'm not allowed to let anyone inside. The seven dwarfs have forbidden me."

"That's all right with me," answered the peasant woman. "I'll surely get rid of my apples in time. But let me give you one as a gift."

"No," said Snow White. "I'm not allowed to take anything."

"Are you afraid that it might be poisoned?" said the old woman. "Look, I'll cut the apple in two. You eat the red part, and I'll eat the white."

However, the apple had been made with such cunning that only the red part was poisoned. Snow White was eager to eat the beautiful apple, and when she saw the peasant woman eating her half, she could no longer resist, stretched out her hand, and took the poisoned half. No sooner did she take a bite than she fell to the ground dead. The queen stared at her with a cruel look, then burst out laughing and said, "White as snow, red as blood, black as ebony! This time the dwarfs won't be able to bring you back to life!"

When she got home, she asked the mirror:

"Mirror, mirror, on the wall,
who in this realm is the fairest of all?"

Then the mirror finally answered, "You, my queen, are now the fairest of all." So her jealous heart was satisfied as much as a jealous heart can be satisfied.

When the dwarfs came home that evening, they found Snow White lying on the ground. There was no breath coming from her lips, and she was dead. They lifted her up and looked to see if they could find something poisonous. They unlaced her, combed her hair, washed her with water and wine, but it was to no avail. The dear child was dead and remained dead. They laid her on a bier, and all seven of them sat down beside it and mourned over her. They wept for three whole days, and then they intended to bury her, but she looked so alive and still had such pretty red cheeks that they said, "We can't possibly bury her in the dingy ground."

Instead, they made a transparent glass coffin so that she could be seen from all sides. Then they put her in it, wrote her name on it in gold letters, and added that she was a princess. They carried the coffin to the top of the mountain, and from then on one of them always stayed beside it and guarded it. Some animals came also and wept for Snow White. There was an owl, then a raven, and finally a dove. Snow White lay in the coffin for many, many years and did not decay. Indeed, she seemed to be sleeping, for she was still as white as snow, as red as blood, and her hair as black as ebony.

Now it happened that a prince came to the forest one day, and when he arrived at the dwarfs' cottage, he decided to spend the night. Then he went to the mountain and saw the coffin with beautiful Snow White inside. After he read what was written on the coffin in gold letters, he said to the dwarfs, "Let me have the coffin, and I'll pay you whatever you want."

But the dwarfs answered, "We won't give it up for all the gold in the world."

"Then give it to me as a gift," he said, "for I can't go on living without being able to see Snow White. I'll honor her and cherish her as my dearly beloved."

Since he spoke with such fervor, the good dwarfs took pity on him and gave him the coffin. The prince ordered his servants to carry the coffin on their shoulders, but they stumbled over some shrubs, and the jolt caused the poisoned piece of apple that Snow White had bitten off to be released from her throat. It was not long before she opened her eyes, lifted up the lid of the coffin, sat up, and was alive again.

"Oh, Lord! Where am I?" she exclaimed.

The prince rejoiced and said, "You're with me," and he told her what had happened. Then he added, "I love you more than anything else in the world. Come with me to my father's castle. I want you to be my wife."

Snow White felt that he was sincere, so she went with him, and their wedding was celebrated with great pomp and splendor.

Now, Snow White's stepmother had also been invited to the wedding celebration, and after she had dressed herself in beautiful clothes, she went to the mirror and said:

"Mirror, mirror, on the wall,
who in this realm is the fairest of all?"

The mirror answered:

"You, my queen, may have a beauty quite rare,
but Snow White is a thousand times more fair."

The evil woman uttered a loud curse and became so terribly afraid that she did not know what to do. At first she did not want to go to the wedding celebration. But, she could not calm herself until she saw the young queen. When she entered the hall, she recognized Snow White. The evil queen was so petrified with fright that she could not budge. Iron slippers had already been heated over a fire, and they were brought over to her with tongs. Finally, she had to put on the red-hot slippers and dance until she fell down dead.

THE MAIDEN WITHOUT HANDS

A MILLER HAD BEEN FALLING LITTLE by little into poverty, and soon he had nothing left but his mill and a large apple tree behind it. One day, as he was on his way to chop wood in the forest, he met an old man whom he had never seen before.

"There's no reason you have to torture yourself by cutting wood," the old man said. "I'll make you rich if you promise to give me what's behind your mill."

What else can that be but my apple tree, thought the miller, and he gave the stranger his promise in writing.

"In three years I'll come and fetch what's mine," the stranger said with a snide laugh, and he went away.

When the miller returned home, his wife went out to meet him and said, "Tell me, miller, how did all this wealth suddenly get into our house? All at once I've discovered our chests and boxes are full. Nobody's brought anything, and I don't know how it's all happened."

"It's from a stranger I met in the forest," he said. "He promised me great wealth if I agreed in writing to give him what's behind our mill. We can certainly spare the large apple tree."

"Oh, husband!" his wife exclaimed in dread. "That was the devil! He didn't mean the apple tree but our daughter, who was behind the mill sweeping out the yard."

The miller's daughter was a beautiful and pious maiden who went through the next three years in fear of God and without sin. When the time was up and the day came for the devil to fetch her, she washed herself clean and drew a circle around her with chalk. The devil appeared quite early, but he could not get near her, and he said angrily to the miller, "I want you to take all the water away from her so she can't wash herself anymore. Otherwise, I have no power over her."

Since the miller was afraid of the devil, he did as he was told. The next morning the devil came again, but she wept on her hands and made them completely clean.

Once more he could not get near her and said furiously to the miller, "Chop off her hands. Otherwise, I can't touch her."

The miller was horrified and replied, "How can I chop off the hands of my own child!"

But the devil threatened him and said, "If you don't do it, you're mine, and I'll come and get you myself!"

The father was so scared of him that he promised to obey. He went to his daughter and said, "My child, if I don't chop off both your hands, the devil will take me away, and in my fear I promised I'd do it. Please help me out of my dilemma and forgive me for the injury I'm causing you."

"Dear Father," she answered, "do what you want with me. I'm your child."

Then she extended both her hands and let him chop them off. The devil came a third time, but she had wept so long and so much on the stumps that they too were all clean. Then he had to abandon his game and lost all claim to her.

Now the miller said to his daughter, "I've become so wealthy because of you that I shall see to it you'll live in splendor for the rest of your life."

But she answered, "No, I cannot stay here. I'm going away and shall depend on the kindness of people to provide me with whatever I need."

Then she had her maimed arms bound to her back, and at dawn she set out on her way and walked the entire day until it became dark. She was right outside a royal garden, and by the glimmer of the moon she could see trees full of beautiful fruit. She could not enter the garden though, because it was surrounded by water. Since she had traveled the entire day without eating, she was very hungry. Oh, if only I could get in! she thought. I must eat some of the fruit or else I'll perish! Then she fell to her knees, called out to the Lord, and prayed. Suddenly an angel appeared who closed one of the locks in the stream so that the moat became dry and she could walk through it. Now she went into the garden accompanied by the angel. She caught sight of a beautiful tree full of pears, but the pears had all been counted. Nonetheless, she approached the tree and ate one of the pears with her mouth to satisfy her hunger, but only this one. The gardener was watching her, but since the angel was standing there, he was afraid, especially since he thought the maiden was a spirit. He kept still and did not dare to cry out or speak to her. After she had eaten the pear, and her hunger was stilled, she went and hid in the bushes.

The next morning the king who owned the garden came and counted the pears. When he saw one was missing, he asked the gardener what had happened to it, for the pear was not lying under the tree and had somehow vanished.

"Last night a spirit appeared," answered the gardener. "It had no hands and ate one of the pears with its mouth."

"How did the spirit get over the water?" asked the king. "And where did it go after it ate the pear?"

"Someone wearing a garment as white as snow came down from heaven, closed the lock, and dammed up the water so the spirit could walk through the moat. And, since it must have been an angel, I was afraid to ask any questions or to cry out. After the spirit had eaten the pear, it just went away."

"If it's as you say," said the king, "I shall spend the night with you and keep watch."

When it became dark, the king went into the garden and brought a priest with him to talk to the spirit. All three sat down beneath the tree and kept watch. At midnight the maiden came out of the bushes, walked over to the tree, and once again ate one of the pears with her mouth, while the angel in white stood next to her. The priest stepped forward and said to the maiden, "Have you come from heaven or from earth? Are you a spirit or a human being?"

"I'm not a spirit, but a poor creature forsaken by everyone except God."

"You may be forsaken by the whole world, but I shall not forsake you," said the king.

He took her with him to his royal palace, and since she was so beautiful and good, he loved her with all his heart, had silver hands made for her, and took her for his wife.

After a year had passed, the king had to go to war, and he placed the young queen under the care of his mother and said, "If she has a child, I want you to protect her and take good care of her, and write me right away."

Soon after, the young queen gave birth to a fine-looking boy. The king's mother wrote to him immediately to announce the joyful news. However, on the way the messenger stopped to rest near a brook, and since he was exhausted from the long journey, he fell asleep. Then the devil appeared. He was still trying to harm the pious queen, and so he exchanged the letter for another one that said that the queen had given birth to a changeling. When the king read the letter, he was horrified and quite distressed, but he wrote his mother that she should protect the queen and take care of her until his return. The messenger started back with the letter, but he stopped to rest at the same spot and fell asleep. Once again the devil came and put a different letter in his pocket that said that they should kill the queen and her child. The old mother was tremendously disturbed when she received the letter and could not believe it. She wrote the king again but received the same answer because the devil kept replacing the messenger's letters with false letters each time. The last letter ordered the king's mother to keep the tongue and eyes of the queen as proof that she had done his bidding.

But the old woman wept at the thought of shedding such innocent blood. During the night she had a doe fetched and cut out its tongue and eyes and put them away. Then she said to the queen, "I can't let you be killed as the king commands.

However, you can't stay here any longer. Go out into the wide world with your child and never come back."

She tied the child to the queen's back, and the poor woman went off with tears in her eyes. When she came to a great wild forest, she fell down on her knees and prayed to God. The Lord's angel appeared before her and led her to a small cottage with a little sign saying "Free Lodging for Everyone." A maiden wearing a snow white garment came out of the cottage and said, "Welcome, Your Highness," and took her inside. She untied the little boy from her back and offered him her breast so he could have something to drink. Then she laid him down in a beautifully made bed.

"How did you know that I'm a queen?" asked the poor woman.

"I'm an angel sent by God to take care of you and your child," replied the maiden in white.

So the queen stayed seven years in the cottage and was well cared for. By the grace of God and through her own piety her hands that had been chopped off grew back again.

When the king finally returned from the wars, the first thing he wanted to do was to see his wife and child. However, his old mother began to weep and said, "You wicked man, why did you write and order me to kill two innocent souls?" She showed him the two letters that the devil had forged and resumed talking. "I did as you ordered," and she displayed the tongue and eyes. At the sight of them the king burst into tears and wept bitterly over his poor wife and little son. His old mother was aroused and took pity on him.

"Console yourself," she said. "She's still alive. I secretly had a doe killed and kept its tongue and eyes as proof. Then I took the child and tied him to your wife's back and ordered her to go out into the wide world, and she had to promise me never to return here because you were so angry with her."

"I shall go as far as the sky is blue, without eating or drinking, until I find my dear wife and child," the king said. "That is, unless they have been killed or have died of hunger in the meantime."

The king wandered for about seven years and searched every rocky cliff and cave he came across. When he did not find her, he thought she had perished. During this time he neither ate nor drank, but God kept him alive. Eventually, he came to a great forest, where he discovered the little cottage with the sign "Free Lodging for Everyone." Then the maiden in white came out, took him by the hand, and led him inside.

"Welcome, Your Majesty," she said, and asked him where he came from.

"I've been wandering about for almost seven years looking for my wife and child, but I can't find them."

The angel offered him food and drink, but he refused and said he only wanted to rest awhile. So he lay down to sleep and covered his face with a handkerchief. Then the angel went into the room where the queen was sitting with her son, whom she was accustomed to calling Sorrowful, and said, "Go into the next room with your child. Your husband has come."

So the queen went to the room where he was lying, and the handkerchief fell from his face.

"Sorrowful," she said, "pick up your father's handkerchief and put it over his face again."

The child picked the handkerchief up and put it over his face. The king heard all this in his sleep and took pleasure in making the handkerchief drop on the floor again. The boy became impatient and said, "Dear Mother, how can I cover my father's face when I have no father on earth. I've learned to pray to 'our Father that art in heaven,' and you told me that my father was in heaven and that he was our good Lord. How am I supposed to recognize this wild man? He's not my father."

When the king heard this, he sat up and asked her who she was.

"I'm your wife," she replied, "and this is your son, Sorrowful."

When the king saw that she had real hands, he said, "My wife had silver hands."

"Our merciful Lord let my natural hands grow again," she answered.

The angel went back into the sitting room, fetched the silver hands, and showed them to him. Now he knew for certain that it was his dear wife and dear son, and he kissed them and was happy.

"A heavy load has been taken off my mind," he said.

After the Lord's angel ate one more meal with them, they went home to be with the king's old mother. There was rejoicing everywhere, and the king and queen had a second wedding and lived happily ever after.

SIX SWANS

Once there was a king who was hunting in a vast forest, and he began chasing a deer so intensely that none of his men could follow him. When evening drew near, he stopped, looked around him, and realized he was lost. He searched for a way out of the forest but was unable to find one. Then he caught sight of an old woman, nodding her head back and forth and heading toward him. She was, however, a witch.

"Dear woman," he said to her, "can you show me the way out of the forest?"

"Oh, yes, Your Majesty," she answered. "I certainly can, but on one condition, and if you don't fulfill it, you'll never find your way out of the forest, and you will starve to death."

"What kind of condition?" asked the king.

"I have a daughter," said the old woman, "who is as beautiful as any maiden in the world. Indeed, she is worthy to be your wife, and if you make her your queen, I'll show you the way out of the forest."

The king was so tremendously frightened that he consented, and the old woman led him to her little hut, where her daughter was sitting by the fire. The maiden greeted the king as though she had been expecting him, and he observed that she was very beautiful. Nevertheless, he did not like her, and he could not look at her without secretly shuddering. After he had lifted the maiden onto his horse, the old woman showed him the way, and once the king reached the royal palace again, the wedding was celebrated.

The king had already been married before this, and he had seven children by his first wife, six boys and a girl, whom he loved more than anything in the world. Since he now feared that the stepmother might not treat them well and might even harm them, he brought them to a solitary castle in the middle of a forest. It lay so well concealed and the way to it was so hard to find that he himself would not have found it if a wise woman had not given him a ball of yarn with magic powers. When he threw the ball before him, the yarn unwound itself and showed him the way.

Now, the king went out to visit his dear children so often that the queen began to notice his absences. Since she was curious and wanted to know what he was doing out in the forest all alone, she gave his servants a great deal of money, and they revealed the secret. They also told her about the ball of yarn that alone could show the way. For a while she had no peace of mind, but she finally discovered where the king kept the ball. Then she made small white silk shirts, and she used the witchcraft that she had learned from her mother to sew a magic spell into them.

One day when the king had gone hunting, she took the little shirts, went out into the forest, and let the ball of yarn show her the way. When the children saw someone coming in the distance, they thought their dear father was coming to see them and ran joyfully out to greet him. But she threw a shirt over each one of them, and as soon as they were touched by the shirts, they were turned into swans and flew away over the forest. The queen went home delighted with herself, thinking that she was rid of her stepchildren. However, the girl had not run outside with her brothers, and the queen knew nothing about the girl.

The following day the king went to visit his children, but he found only the girl.

"Where are your brothers?" the king asked.

"Oh, dear Father," she answered, "they've gone away and left me alone." And she told him how, from her window, she had seen her brothers turn into swans, and how they had flown away over the forest. Then she showed him the feathers that they had dropped in the yard and left for her to gather.

The king mourned for his sons but had no idea that the queen had done this evil deed. Yet, he did fear that his daughter might also be stolen from him, and he wanted to take her with him. However, she was afraid of the stepmother and begged the king to allow her to spend one last night in the forest castle. I can't stay here any longer, the poor girl thought. I shall go and search for my brothers.

When night came, she fled the castle and went straight into the forest. She walked the whole night long and the entire next day without stopping, until she became so exhausted that she could go no farther. Then she saw a hut, and after entering it, she found a room with six small beds. Since she was afraid to lie down in any of the beds, she crawled underneath one and lay down on the hard floor, intending to spend the night there. However, just when the sun was about to set, she heard a rustling sound and saw six swans come flying through the window. They landed on the floor and blew at each other until all their feathers were blown off. After that their swan skins slipped off like shirts. The maiden observed all this, and when she recognized her brothers, she rejoiced and crawled out from under the bed. Her brothers were delighted to see their little sister, but their joy was short-lived.

"You can't stay here," they said to her. "This is a robbers' den. When they come home and find you here, they'll kill you."

"Can't you protect me?" asked their sister.

"No," they replied. "You see, we can take off our swan skins for only a quarter of an hour every evening. During this time we assume our human form, but after that we're changed back into swans."

Their sister wept and asked, "Can't you be set free?"

"We don't think so," they said. "The conditions are too hard. You'd have to go six years without speaking to anyone or laughing, and during this time you'd have to sew six little shirts for us made of asters. If just one single word were to fall from your lips, then all your work would be for naught."

Nevertheless, the maiden decided to set her brothers free, even if it might cost her her life. She left the hut, went into the middle of the forest, climbed a tree, and spent the night there. The next morning she got down, gathered asters, and began to sew. She could not talk to anyone, nor did she have a desire to laugh: she just sat there and concentrated on her work.

After she had spent a long time there, the king of the country happened to go hunting in the forest, and his huntsmen came to the tree where the maiden was perched. They called to her and said, "Who are you?"

She did not answer.

"Come down to us," they said. "We won't harm you."

She merely shook her head. When they continued to bother her with questions, she threw them her golden necklace and thought that would satisfy them. Yet, they persisted. Then she threw them her girdle, and when this did not work either, she threw down her garters and little by little everything that she had on and could do without until she had nothing left but her little shift. Still the huntsmen did not let themselves be deterred by all this. They climbed the tree, carried her down, and led her to the king, who asked, "Who are you, and what were you doing in that tree?"

She did not answer. He tried questioning her in all the languages he knew, but she remained as silent as a fish. Eventually, her beauty moved the king's heart, and he fell deeply in love with her. He covered her with his cloak, lifted her onto his horse, and brought her to his castle. There he had her dressed in rich garments, and her beautiful features were as radiant as the day is bright. Still, it was impossible to get her to utter a single word. He had her sit next to him at the table, and her modest ways and her polite manners pleased him so much that he said, "This maiden is the one I shall marry and no other woman in the world except her."

Within a few days he married her, but the king had an evil mother, who was dissatisfied with this marriage and spoke ill of the young queen.

"That wench! Why won't she speak?" she said. "Where does she come from? She's not worthy of a king."

A year later, when the queen gave birth to her first child, the old woman took the child away from her and smeared the queen's mouth with blood while she was asleep. Then the old woman went to the king and accused the young queen of being a cannibal. The king refused to believe this and would not tolerate anyone harming his wife. Meanwhile, the queen continued to sit and sew the shirts, and did not pay attention to anything else.

The next time, she gave birth to another handsome boy, and her wicked mother-in-law tried the same deception, but the king could not bring him-self to believe the charges brought against his wife.

"She's too pious and good," he said. "She'd never do anything like that. If she could talk, she could defend herself, and her innocence would come to it."

However, when the old woman stole the third newborn baby and accused the queen, who did not say one word in her own defense, the king could do nothing but hand her over to a court, which condemned her to death by fire.

The day came for the sentence to be carried out, but it was also the last day of the six years during which she had not been allowed to speak or laugh. Indeed, this meant that she had set her brothers free from the power of the magic spell. The six shirts were finished except for the left sleeve of the last shirt. When the queen was led to the stake, she carried the shirts over her arm, and as she stood on the stack of wood and the fire was about to be lit, she looked up and saw the six swans come flying through the air. Now she knew that her rescue was near at hand, and her heart jumped for joy. The swans swooped down and landed close by so that she could throw the shirts over them. As soon as the shirts touched them, the swan skins fell off, and her brothers stood before her in the flesh. They looked handsome and vigorous. Only the youngest was missing his left arm, and he had a swan's wing on his shoulder instead. They embraced and kissed each other, and the queen went up to the king, who was quite stunned by all this.

"Dearest husband," she said. "Now I may speak and tell you that I'm innocent and was unjustly accused."

She told him how the old woman had been deceiving him and had taken away her three children and hidden them. Then, to the king's great joy, the children were brought to him, and as a punishment the wicked mother-in-law was tied to the stake and burned to ashes. Thereafter, the king and queen, along with her six brothers, lived for many years in peace and happiness.

15. Thomas Crofton Croker, *Fairy Legends and Traditions of the South of Ireland* (1823)[1]

T. Crofton Croker was an Anglo Irishman living in England when he took on the project of collecting and publishing Fairy Legends and Traditions of the South of Ireland. *This early example of collection drew the attention of Jacob and Wilhelm Grimm in Germany (they translated it into German and commented on the perceived relationships between German and Irish oral traditions). Although Croker's work predates technological recording by half a century, it already bears the signs of ethnography to come: Croker names the performer, situates his reader in the scene of the telling, and comments on the audience reaction to the event. In fact, in some sense it is the storytelling event itself that is the "story" here, with Croker himself serving as narrator (and Peggy Barrett's quoted tale of supernatural encounter embedded within). Several elements of Barrett's performance style—explored by Croker in his comments—are worthy of note. Barrett takes a personal tragedy and turns it into an etiological tale, which Croker identifies as her "fireside" tendency. Neither collector nor performer marvel at the conflation of natural and supernatural, memory and imagination—and the degree to which teller and audience take this tale to be true remains ambiguous. Finally, the detail about Barrett looking first at her adult audience members and then down at her grandson adds a layer to this story. Croker has overlaid Barrett's performance with a framing device of his own that paints a complex picture of this old woman teller. He characterizes Barrett's life as "low and simple," even as he extols her superior narrative abilities. In light of her virtuosity, we are perhaps meant to question the apparent simplicity of her story and consider its possible ironies.*

1 [Source: T. Crofton Croker, *Fairy Legends and Traditions of the South of Ireland* ([1823] London: William Tegg, 1859): 145–51.]

THE CROOKENED BACK, PERFORMED BY PEGGY BARRETT

PEGGY BARRETT WAS ONCE TALL, well-shaped, and comely. She was in her youth remarkable for two qualities, not often found together, of being the most thrifty housewife, and the best dancer in her native village of Ballyhooley. But she is now upwards of sixty years old; and during the last ten years of her life, she has never been able to stand upright. Her back is bent nearly to a level; yet she has the freest use of all her limbs that can be enjoyed in such a posture; her health is good, and her mind vigorous; and, in the family of her eldest son, with whom she has lived since the death of her husband, she performs all the domestic services which her age, and the infirmity just mentioned, allow. She washes the potatoes, makes the fire, sweeps the house (labours in which she good-humouredly says "she finds her crooked back mighty convenient"), plays with the children, and tells stories to the family and their neighbouring friends, who often collect round her son's fireside to hear them during the long winter evenings. Her powers of conversation are highly extolled, both for humour and in narration; and anecdotes of droll or awkward incidents, connected with the posture in which she has been so long fixed, as well as the history of the occurrence to which she owes that misfortune, are favourite topics of her discourse. Among other matters, she is fond of relating how, on a certain day, at the close of a bad harvest, when several tenants of the estate on which she lived concerted in a field a petition for an abatement of rent, they placed the paper on which they wrote upon her back, which was found no very inconvenient substitute for a table.

Peggy, like all experienced story-tellers, suited her tales, both in length and subject, to the audience and the occasion. She knew that, in broad daylight, when the sun shines brightly, and the trees are budding, and the birds singing around us, when men and women, like ourselves, are moving and speaking, employed variously in business or amusement; she knew, in short (though certainly without knowing or much caring wherefore), that when we are engaged about the realities of life and nature, we want that spirit of credulity, without which tales of the deepest interest will lose their power. At such times Peggy was brief, very particular as to facts, and never dealt in the marvellous. But round the blazing hearth of a Christmas evening, when infidelity[1] is banished from all companies, at least in low and simple life, as a quality, to say the least of it, out of season; when the winds of "dark December" whistled bleakly round the walls, and almost through the doors of the little mansion, reminding its inmates, that as the world is vexed by elements superior to human power, so it may be visited by beings of a superior nature:—at such times would Peggy Barrett give full scope to her memory, or her imagination, or both; and upon one of these

1 [Croker uses infidelity here as a synonym of disbelief.]

occasions, she gave the following circumstantial account of the "crookening of her back."

"It was, of all days in the year, the day before May-day, that I went out to the garden to weed the potatoes. I would not have gone out that day, but I was dull in myself, and sorrowful, and wanted to be alone; all the boys and girls were laughing and joking in the house, making goaling-balls and dressing out ribands for the mummers next day. I couldn't bear it. 'Twas only at the Easter that was then past (and that's ten years last Easter—I won't forget the time), that I buried my poor man; and I thought how gay and joyful I was, many a long year before that, at the May-eve before our wedding, when with Robin by my side, I sat cutting and sewing the ribands for the goaling-ball I was to give the boys on the next day, proud to be preferred above all the other girls of the banks of the Blackwater, by the handsomest boy and the best hurler in the village; so I left the house and went to the garden. I staid there all the day, and didn't come home to dinner. I don't know how it was, but somehow I continued on, weeding, and thinking sorrowfully enough, and singing over some of the old songs that I sung many and many a time in the days that are gone, and for them that never will come back to me to hear them. The truth is, I hated to go and sit silent and mournful among the people in the house, that were merry and young, and had the best of their days before them. 'Twas late before I thought of returning home, and I did not leave the garden till some time after sunset. The moon was up; but though there wasn't a cloud to be seen, and though a star was winking here and there in the sky, the day wasn't long enough gone to have it clear moonlight; still it shone enough to make everything on one side of the heavens look pale and silvery-like; and the thin white mist was just beginning to creep along the fields. On the other side, near where the sun was set, there was more of daylight, and the sky looked angry, red, and fiery through the trees, like as if it was lighted up by a great town burning below. Everything was as silent as a churchyard, only now and then one could hear far off a dog barking, or a cow lowing after being milked. There wasn't a creature to be seen on the road or in the fields. I wondered at this first, but then I remembered it was May-eve, and that many a thing, both good and bad, would be wandering about that night, and that I ought to shun danger as well as others. So I walked on as quick as I could, and soon came to the end of the demesne wall, where the trees rise high and thick at each side of the road, and almost meet at the top. My heart misgave me when I got under the shade. There was so much light let down from the opening above, that I could see about a stone-throw before me. All of a sudden I heard a rustling among the branches, on the right side of the road, and saw something like a small black goat, only with long wide horns turned out instead of being bent backwards, standing upon its hind legs upon the top of the wall, and looking down on me. My breath was stopped, and I couldn't move for near a minute. I couldn't help, somehow, keeping my eyes fixed on it; and it never stirred, but kept looking in the same fixed way down at me. At last I made a rush, and went on; but I didn't go ten steps, when I saw the very same sight, on the wall to the left of me, standing in exactly the same manner, but three or four times as high, and almost as tall as the tallest man. The horns looked frightful; it gazed upon me as before; my legs shook, and my teeth chattered, and I thought I would drop down dead every moment. At last I felt as if I was obliged to go on—and on I went; but it was without feeling how I moved, or whether my legs carried me. Just as I passed the spot where this frightful thing was standing, I heard a noise as if something sprung from the wall, and felt like as if a heavy animal plumped down upon me, and held with the fore feet clinging to my shoulder, and the hind ones fixed, in my gown, that was folded and pinned up behind me. 'Tis the wonder of my life ever since how I bore the shock; but so it was, I neither fell, nor even staggered with the weight, but walked on as if I had the strength of ten men, though I felt as if I couldn't help moving, and couldn't stand still if I wished it. Though I gasped with fear, I knew as well as I do now what I was doing. I tried to cry out, but couldn't; I tried to run, but wasn't able; I tried to look back, but my head and neck were as if they were screwed in a vice. I could barely roll my eyes on each side, and then I could see, as clearly and plainly as if it was in the broad light of the blessed sun, a black and cloven foot planted upon each of my shoulders. I heard a low breathing in my ear; I felt, at every step I took, my leg strike back against the feet of the creature that was on my back. Still I could do nothing but walk straight on. At last I came within sight of the house, and a welcome sight it was to me, for I thought I would be released when I reached it. I soon came close to the door, but it was shut; I looked at the little window, but it was shut too, for they were more cautious about May-eve than I was; I saw the light inside, through the chinks of the door; I heard 'em talking and laughing within; I felt myself at three yards' distance from them that would die to save me;—and may the Lord save me from ever again feeling what I did that night, when I found myself held by what couldn't be good nor friendly, but without the power to help myself, or to call my friends, or to put out my hand to knock, or even to lift my leg to strike the door, and let them know that I was outside it! 'Twas as if my hands grew to my sides, and my feet were glued to the ground, or had the weight of a rock fixed to them. At last I thought of blessing myself; and my right hand, that would do nothing else, did that for me. Still the weight remained on my back, and all was as before. I blessed myself again: 'twas still all the same. I then gave myself up for lost: but I blessed myself a third time, and my hand no sooner finished the sign, than all at once I felt the burthen spring off of my back; the door flew open as if a clap of thunder burst it, and I was pitched forward on my forehead, in upon the middle of the floor. When I got up my back was crookened, and I never stood straight from that night to this blessed hour."

There was a pause when Peggy Barrett finished. Those who had heard the story before had listened with a look of half-satisfied interest, blended, however, with an expression of that serious and solemn feeling, which always attends a tale of supernatural wonders, how often soever told. They moved upon their seats out of the posture in which they had remained fixed during the narrative, and sat in an attitude which denoted that their curiosity as to the cause of this strange occurrence had been long since allayed. Those to whom it was before unknown still retained their look and posture of strained attention, and anxious but solemn expectation. A grandson of Peggy's, about nine years old (not the child of the son with whom she lived), had never before heard the story. As it grew in interest, he was observed to cling closer and closer to the old woman's side; and at the close he was gazing stedfastly at her, with his body bent back across her knees, and his face turned up to hers, with a look, through which a disposition to weep seemed contending with curiosity. After a moment's pause, he could no longer restrain his impatience, and catching her gray locks in one hand, while the tear of dread and wonder was just dropping from his eyelash, he cried, "Granny, what was it?"

The old woman smiled first at the elder part of her audience, and then at her grandson, and patting him on the forehead, she said, "It was the Phooka."

16. Hans Christian Andersen, *Eventyr, fortalte for børn* (1835–45; *translated by Tiina Nunnally, 2004*[1])

Hans Christian Andersen is one of the best known writers of fairy tales, and he was a literary celebrity both in his native Denmark—where he is still regarded as an important cultural figure—and beyond. His fairy tales have been popular in English print and popular culture from their first translation in the 1840s to the present day, but rereading his tales with a fresh perspective can help to reveal the layers of complexity in his approach to the genre. Many of Andersen's tales have elements of both sentimentality and an unyielding Christian moralism, but many can also be read as cynical commentaries on social relations, class, courtship, and sex. Andersen himself rose from extremely humble and unhappy beginnings, and his tales repeatedly return to a notion of "natural nobility": the belief that certain individuals are destined for greatness but that inherited class status does not necessarily correspond with nobility of character. The three tales included here are ones that helped to establish Andersen as a pre-eminent fairy-tale writer. "The Tinderbox" is a strikingly subversive and even amoral tale, in which a soldier finds his fortune and gains social

1 [Source: Tiina Nunnally, *Hans Christian Andersen, Fairy Tales* ([2004] New York, NY: Penguin, 2006): 5–11, 29–30, 207–12.]

position—ultimately becoming King—through trickery, murder, and kidnapping. On the other hand, "The Red Shoes" is one of Andersen's most explicitly Christian tales, featuring a heroine who must suffer to gain her ultimate reward—entry to heaven—and a moral clearly directed to children articulated by the figure of an angel. Many readers will be surprised to discover how tongue-in-cheek, satirical, and short Andersen's well-known story "The Princess on the Pea" really is. In the span of a single page, Andersen pokes fun at notions of ideal femininity, the world of the court, and even the conventions of the fairy-tale genre.

THE TINDERBOX

A SOLDIER CAME MARCHING ALONG THE road: one, two! left, right! left, right! He had his knapsack on his back and a sword at his side, because he had been off to war, and now he was on his way home. Then he met an old witch on the road. She was so hideous, her lower lip hung all the way down to her breast. She said, "Good evening, soldier. What a nice sword and big knapsack you have—you must be a real soldier! Now you shall have you all the money you could ask for!"

"Well, thanks a lot, you old witch," said the soldier.

"Do you see that big tree?" said the witch, pointing at a tree right next to them. "It's completely hollow inside. Climb up to the top and you'll find a hole that you can slip into and slide all the way down inside the tree. I'll tie a rope around your waist so I can hoist you back up when you call me."

"Why would I go inside that tree?" asked the soldier.

"To get the money!" said the witch. "You see, when you reach the bottom of the tree, you'll be in a huge passageway that's very bright because it's lit by more than a hundred lamps. Then you'll see three doors, and you'll be able to open them because the keys are in the locks. If you go inside the first chamber you'll see a big chest in the middle of the room, and on it sits a dog. He has eyes as big as a pair of teacups, but never mind that. I'll give you my blue-checked apron that you can spread on the floor. Go right over and pick up the dog and set him on my apron. Then open the chest and take as many *skillings*[1] as you like. They're all made of copper, but if you'd rather have silver, then go into the next room. In there is a dog with eyes as big as a pair of mill wheels, but never mind that. Set him on my apron and take the money. But if it's gold you want, you can have that too, and as much as you can carry, if you go into the third chamber. But the dog sitting on the money chest has two eyes that are each as big as the Round Tower. Now that's a real dog,

1 [The "skilling" is a Scandinavian coin (akin to the shilling) used in the old Danish currency system before the introduction of the krone in 1873. They were minted in all three metals.]

believe me! But never you mind. Just set him on my apron and he won't harm you. Then take from the chest as much gold as you like."

"Not bad," said the soldier. "But what do I have to give you in return, you old witch? Because I imagine there must be something you want."

"No," said the witch. "I don't want a single *skilling*. All you have to bring me is an old tinderbox that my grandmother left behind when she was down there last."

"Fine. Then let's have that rope around my waist," said the soldier.

"Here it is," said the witch. "And here is my blue-checked apron."

So the soldier climbed up the tree, tumbled down the hole, and stood, and then, just as the witch had said, he stood inside the huge passageway where hundreds of lamps were burning.

He opened the first door. Ooh! There sat the dog with eyes as big as teacups, staring at him.

"You're a handsome fellow!" said the soldier and set him on the witch's apron. Then he took as many copper *skillings* as his pockets would hold, closed the chest, put the dog back, and went into the second room. Eeek! There sat the dog with eyes as big as mill wheels.

"You shouldn't look at me so hard," said the soldier. "You might hurt your eyes!" And then he set the dog on the witch's apron, but when he saw all the silver coins inside the chest he threw away the copper coins he was carrying and filled his pocket and his knapsack with nothing but silver. Next he went into the third chamber. Oh, how hideous! The dog in there really did have eyes as big as round towers, and they were spinning around in his head like wheels.

"Good evening," said the soldier and doffed his cap, for he had never seen a dog like that before. But after he'd looked at him for a while, he thought to himself, "All right, that's enough." And he lifted him onto the floor and opened the chest. Good Lord, there was a lot of gold! Enough to buy all of Copenhagen and every single sugar pig sold by the cake-wives, and all the tin soldiers, whips, and rocking horses in the whole world! Yes, there was certainly plenty of money! So the soldier threw away all the silver that filled his pockets and knapsack and took the gold instead. Yes, all his pockets, his knapsack, his cap, and his boots were so full that he could hardly walk. Now he had money! He put the dog back on the chest, slammed the door shut, and called up through the tree:

"Hoist me up now, you old witch!"

"Do you have the tinderbox?" asked the witch.

"Oh, that's right," said the soldier. "I forgot all about it." And he went over and picked it up. The witch hoisted him up and he once again stood on the road, with his pockets, boots, knapsack and cap full of money.

"What do you want the tinderbox for?" asked the soldier.

"That's none of your business," said the witch. "You've got the money. Now just give me the tinderbox."

"Pish posh!" said the soldier. "Tell me right now what you want it for or I'll pull out my sword and chop off your head!"

"No," said the witch.

So the soldier chopped off her head. There she lay! But he wrapped up all his money in her apron, slung it in a bundle over his shoulder, stuffed the tinderbox in his pocket, and headed straight for the city.

It was a lovely city, and he went inside the loveliest of inns and demanded the very best rooms and his favorite food, because now he had so much money that he was rich.

The servant who was supposed to polish his boots thought that they were rather strange old boots for such a rich gentleman to be wearing, but he hadn't yet bought himself new ones. By the next day he had a good pair of boots and fine clothes to wear. The soldier was now a distinguished gentleman, and people told him about all the splendid things to be found in their city, and about their king and what a charming princess his daughter was.

"Where might I catch a glimpse of her?" asked the soldier.

"It's impossible to catch a glimpse of her," they all said. "She lives in an enormous copper palace surrounded by dozens of walls and towers. No one but the king dares visit her, because it was foretold that she would marry a simple soldier, and that certainly did not please the king."

"She's someone I'd like to see," thought the soldier, but that wasn't possible.

He was now leading a merry life, going to the theater, taking drives in the king's gardens, and giving away a great deal of money to the poor, which was a very nice gesture. No doubt he remembered from the old days how miserable it was not to have even a *skilling*. He was now rich and wore fine clothes, and had so many friends who all said he was a pleasant fellow, a real gentleman, and that certainly pleased the soldier. But since he was spending money each day and not taking any in, he finally had no more than two *skillings* left and had to move out of the beautiful rooms where he had been living and into a tiny little garret room right under the roof. He had to brush his own boots and mend them with a darning needle, and none of his friends came to see him because there were too many stairs to climb.

It was a very dark evening, and he couldn't even afford to buy a candle, but then he remembered there was a little stump of one in the tinderbox he had taken from the hollow tree when the witch had helped him inside. He took out the tinderbox and candle stump, but the minute he struck fire sparks leaped from the flint, the door flew open and the dog that he had seen inside the tree, the one with eyes as big as two teacups, stood before him and said, "What is my master's command?"

"What's this?" said the soldier. "What an amusing tinderbox, if I can wish for whatever I want! Bring me some money," he said to the dog, and zip, he was gone; zip, he was back, holding a big sack of *skillings* in his mouth.

Now the soldier realized what a wonderful tinderbox it was. If he struck it once, the dog who sat on the chest of copper coins came; if he struck it twice, the one with the silver coins came; and if he struck it three times, the one with the gold came. Now the soldier moved back downstairs to the beautiful rooms, dressed in fine clothing, and all his friends recognized him again, because they were so fond of him.

One day he thought, "how odd that no one is allowed to see that princess. Everyone says she's supposed to be so lovely. But what good is it if she's always kept inside that enormous copper palace with all those towers? Couldn't I possibly have a look at her? Where's my tinderbox?" And then he struck fire and zip, the dog with eyes as big as teacups appeared.

"I know it's the middle of the night," said the soldier, "but I have such a great desire to see the princess, if only for a moment."

The dog was out the door at once, and before the soldier knew it, he was back with the princess. She was sitting on the dog's back, asleep, and she was so lovely that anyone could see she was a real princess. The soldier couldn't resist, he had to kiss her, because he was a real soldier.

Then the dog ran back with the princes, but when morning came and the king and queen were pouring their tea, the princess said that she'd had a strange dream in the night about a dog and a soldier. She was riding on the dog's back, and the soldier had kissed her.

"That's certainly a fine story!" said the queen.

One of the old ladies-in-waiting was then ordered to keep watch at the bedside of the princess on the following night, to see if it was really a dream, or what else it might be.

The soldier was longing terribly to see the lovely princess once more, so the dog appeared in the night, picked her up, and ran as fast as he could, but the old lady-in-waiting put on her wading boots and ran just as swiftly right behind. When she saw them disappear inside a large building, she thought to herself: Now I know where it is. And with a piece of chalk she drew a big cross on the door. Then she returned home and went to bed, and the dog cam back too, bringing the princess. But when he saw that a cross had been drawn on the door where the soldier lived, he took another piece of chalk and put a cross on all the doors in the whole city. That was a clever thing to do, because now the lady-in-waiting wouldn't be able to find the right door, since there were crosses on all of them.

Early the next morning the king and the queen, the old lady-in-waiting, and all the officers went out to see where the princess had been.

"There it is!" said the king when he saw the first door with a cross on it.

"No, it's over there, my dear husband" said the queen, who saw another door with a cross on it.

"But there's one there, and one there!" they all said. Wherever they looked, there was a cross on every door. Then they realized it was no use to go on searching.

But the queen was a very clever woman who was capable of more than just riding around in a coach. She took her big golden scissors, cut a large piece of silk into pieces, and then stitched together a charming little pouch, which she filled with fine grains of buckwheat. She tied it to the back of the princess, and when that was done, she cut a tiny hole in the pouch so the grains would sprinkle out wherever the princess went.

That night the dog appeared once again, put the princess on his back, and ran off with her to the soldier, who loved her so much and wanted dearly to be a prince so that he could make her his wife.

The dog didn't notice the grain sprinkling out all the way from the palace to the soldier's window, as he ran along the wall, carrying the princess. In the morning the king and queen could see quite well where their daughter had been, and they seized the soldier and threw him into jail.

And there he sat. Oh, how dark and dreary it was, and then they told him, "Tomorrow you will hang." That was not a pleasant thing to hear, and he had left his tinderbox behind at the inn. In the morning he could see through the iron bars on the little window that people were hurrying to the outskirts of the city to watch him hang. He heard the drums and saw the marching soldiers. Everyone was in a great rush, including a shoemaker's apprentice wearing a leather apron and slippers. He was moving along at such a gallop that one of his slippers flew off and struck the wall right where the soldier was sitting, peering out through the iron bars.

"Hey, shoemaker's apprentice! You don't have to be in such a rush," said the soldier. "Nothing's going to happen until I get there. But if you run over to the place where I was staying and bring me my tinderbox, I'll give you four *skillings*. But you have to be quick about it!" The shoemaker's apprentice wanted those four *skillings*, so he raced off to get the tinderbox, brought it to the soldier, and ... well, let's hear what happened.

Outside the city, a huge gallows had been built, and around it stood the soldiers and many hundreds of thousands of people. The king and queen sat on a lovely throne right across from the judges and the entire council.

The soldier was already standing on the ladder, but as they were about to put the rope around his neck, he said that before a sinner faced his punishment he was always allowed one harmless request. He dearly wanted to smoke a pipe of tobacco; it would be the last pipe he had in this world.

Now, that was not something the king could refuse, and so the soldier took out his tinderbox and struck fire, one, two, three! And there stood all three dogs: the one with eyes as big as teacups, the one with eyes like mill wheels, and the one with eyes as big as the Round Tower.

"Help me now, so I won't be hanged!" said the soldier, and then the dogs rushed at the judge and the entire council, seizing one by the leg and one by the nose, and flinging them high into the air so they fell back down and were crushed to bits.

"Not me!" said the king, but the biggest dog seized both him and the queen and tossed them after all the others. The soldiers were afraid, and all the people shouted, "Little soldier, you shall be our king and wed the lovely princess!"

They put the soldier into the king's coach, and all three dogs danced before it, shouting "Hurrah!" The boys whistled through their fingers, and soldiers presented arms. The princess came out of her copper palace and became queen, and that certainly pleased her! The wedding celebration lasted for a week, and the dogs sat at the table too, making big eyes.

THE PRINCESS ON THE PEA

ONCE UPON A TIME THERE was a prince. He wanted a princess, but she had to be a real princess. So he traveled all over the world to find one, but wherever he went there was something wrong. There were plenty of princesses, but he wasn't quite sure if they were real princesses. There was always something that wasn't quite right. Then he went back home and was so sad because he dearly wanted to have a real princess.

One evening there was a terrible storm. Lightning flashed and thunder roared, the rain poured down, it was simply dreadful! Then there was a knock at the town gate, and the old king went to open it.

There was a princess standing outside. But good Lord how she looked because of the rain and the terrible weather! Water was streaming from her hair and her clothes, running into the toes of her shoes and out of the heels. Then she said that she was a real princess.

"Well, we'll see about that," thought the old queen, but she didn't say a word. She went into the bedroom, took off all the bedclothes, and placed a pea at the bottom of the bed. Then she took twenty mattresses and put them on top of the pea, and another twenty eiderdown quilts on top of the mattresses.

That's where the princess was to sleep that night.

The next morning they asked her how she had slept.

"Oh, dreadfully!" said the princess. "I hardly closed my eyes all night. Lord knows what there was in my bed. I was lying on something hard, and I'm black and blue all over! It's simply dreadful!"

Then they could see that she was a real princess, since she had felt the pea through those twenty mattresses and those twenty eiderdown quilts. No one else could have such tender skin except for a real princess.

And so the prince took her as his wife, because now he knew that he had a real princess. And the pea was placed in the Royal Curiosity Cabinet, where it can still be seen today, as long as no one has taken it.

Now you see, that was a real story!

THE RED SHOES

THERE WAS A LITTLE GIRL so delicate and charming, but in the summer she always had to go barefoot because she was poor. In the winter she wore big wooden clogs that made her little ankles turn quite red, and that was awful.

In the middle of the village lived Old Mother Shoemaker. She sat and sewed as best she could, using old strips of red cloth to make a little pair of shoes. Quite clumsy they were, but well-intended, and the little girl was to have them. The little girl's name was Karen.

On the very day that her mother was buried, Karen was given the red shoes, and she wore them for the first time. Now, it's true that they weren't the proper shoes for mourning, but she didn't have any others, and so she wore them on her bare feet, walking behind the humble coffin made of straw.

All at once a grand old carriage appeared, and inside sat a grand old woman. She looked at the little girl and felt sorry for her. Then she said to the pastor, "Listen here, give me that little girl and I will be kind to her!"

Karen thought she said this because of her red shoes, but the old woman said they were awful, and they were burned, while Karen was dressed in nice, clean clothes. She had to learn to read and sew, and people said that she was charming, but the mirror said, "You are much more than charming, you're lovely!"

Then the queen happened to travel through the land, and she brought along her little daughter, who was a princess. People came flocking to the palace, and Karen was there too. The little princess stood in a window for all to see dressed in fine white clothes. She wore neither a train nor a gold crown, but she had lovely, red kidskin shoes. Of course they were much prettier than the ones that Mother Shoemaker had sewn for little Karen. But nothing in the world could compare with red shoes!

Then Karen was old enough to be confirmed. She was given new clothes and she was also to have new shoes. The rich shoemaker in town measured her little foot. This was at home in his own parlor, where big glass cupboards stood filled with elegant shoes and shiny boots. Everything looked charming, but the old woman did not see well, so it gave her no pleasure. In the midst of all the shoes stood a pair of red ones just like the ones the princess had worn. How beautiful they were! The shoemaker said that they had been sewn for the child of a count, but they didn't fit properly.

"They must be made of the finest leather," said the old woman. "How they shine!"

"Yes, how they shine!" said Karen. And they fit, so they were bought. But the old woman didn't know that they were red, because she would never have allowed Karen to be confirmed wearing red shoes, and yet she did.

Everyone looked at her feet. When she walked up the church aisle toward the chancel doorway, she thought even the old paintings on the crypts, those portraits of pastors and their wives wearing stiff collars and long black gowns, had fixed their eyes on her red shoes. And that was all she could think of when the pastor placed his hand on her head and spoke of the holy baptism, of the pact with God, and the fact that she should now be a good Christian. The organ played so solemnly, the children sang so beautifully, and the old cantor sang too, but Karen thought only of her red shoes.

By that afternoon the old woman had heard from everyone that the shoes were red, and she said how dreadful that was. It wasn't the least bit proper. From that day on, whenever Karen went to church, she would always wear black shoes, even if they were old.

The following Sunday was her first communion, and Karen looked at the black shoes, she looked at the red ones—and then she looked at the red ones again and put them on.

It was lovely sunny weather. Karen and the old woman walked along the path through the grain fields where it was rather dusty.

At the church door stood an old soldier with a crutch and a long, odd-looking beard that was more red than white; in fact, it was red. He bowed all the way to the ground and asked the old woman whether he might wipe off her shoes. Karen stretched out her little foot too. "Oh look, what lovely dancing shoes!" said the soldier. "Stay on tight when you dance!" Then he slapped his hand on the soles.

The old woman gave the soldier a little *skilling* and then went with Karen into the church.

Everyone inside looked at Karen's red shoes; all the paintings looked at them too. And when Karen knelt before the altar and put the golden chalice to her lips, she thought only of the red shoes. They seemed to be swimming around in the chalice before her, and she forgot to sing the hymn, she forgot to say the Lord's Prayer.

Then everyone left the church, and the old woman climbed into her carriage. As Karen lifted her foot to climb in after her, the old soldier who was standing close by said, "Oh look, what lovely dancing shoes!" And Karen couldn't help herself, she had to take a few dance steps. As soon as she started, her feet kept on dancing. It was as if the shoes had taken control. She danced around the corner of the church, she couldn't stop herself. The coachman had to run after and grab her, and he lifted her into the carriage, but her feet kept on dancing and she kicked hard at the kind old woman. Finally they managed to take off the shoes, and her feet stopped moving.

At home the shoes were put in a cupboard, but Karen couldn't help looking at them.

Then the old woman fell ill, and they said she wouldn't live long. She needed someone to nurse and tend her, and who should do it but Karen? But over in town there was to be a great ball, and Karen was invited. She looked at the old woman, who didn't have long to live, after all. She looked at the red shoes, and didn't think there was any sin in that. She put on the red shoes. Why shouldn't she? And then she went to the ball and began to dance.

But when she wanted to turn right, the shoes danced to the left, and when she wanted to move up the floor, the shoes danced down the floor, down the stairs, along the street, and out the town gate. Dance she did, and dance she must, right out into the dark forest.

Then she saw a light overhead among the trees, and she thought it must be the moon, because it had a face, but it was the old soldier with the red beard. He sat there nodding and said, "Oh look, what lovely dancing shoes!"

Then Karen was horrified and tried to take off the red shoes, but they wouldn't come off. She tore off her stockings, but the shoes had grown onto her feet; dance she did and dance she must, over field and meadow, in rain and in sunshine, night and day, but nighttime was the most terrible of all.

She danced into the open churchyard, but the dead weren't dancing. They had better things to do than dance. She wanted to sit down on the pauper's grave, where bitter tansy[1] grew, but for her there was no peace or rest. And when she danced toward the open church door, she saw an angel there in long white robes, with wings that reached from his shoulders to the ground. His expression was stern and solemn, and in his hand he held a sword, gleaming and wide.

"Dance you shall!" he said. "Dance in your red shoes until you turn pale and cold! Until your skin shrivels up like a mummy's! Dance from door to door. And wherever proud and vain children live, you will knock so they hear and fear you! Dance you shall, dance—!"

"Have mercy!" cried Karen. But she didn't hear what the angel replied, because her shoes carried her through the gate, out to the field, across the road, and along the path, and always she had to keep dancing.

Early one morning she danced past a door she knew quite well. Inside a hymn

---

1 [Tansy, a bitter herb, is a yellow flowering plant. From the late Middle Ages onwards, tansy was associated with the Lenten meal, whether baked into cakes or cooked with eggs.]

could be heard, and they carried out a coffin that was adorned with flowers. Then she knew that the old woman was dead, and she felt as if she had now been forsaken by everyone and cursed by the angel of God.

Dance she did, and dance she must, dance into the dark night. Her shoes carried her over thickets and stumps, her feet were worn bloody. She danced across the heath to a lonely little house. She knew that this was where the executioner lived. She tapped her finger on the windowpane and said, "Come out! Come out! I can't come inside, because I'm dancing!"

And the executioner said, "Don't you know who I am? I chop off the heads of evil people, and I can feel my axe is trembling!"

"Don't chop off my head!" Karen cried. "Because then I won't be able to repent my sin. But chop off my feet with the red shoes!"

Then she confessed to her sin, and the executioner cut off her feet with the red shoes. But the shoes kept dancing with the little feet across the fields and into the deep forest.

And he carved wooden feet and crutches for her, taught her a hymn that sinners always sing, and she kissed the hand that had wielded the ax and set off across the heath.

"Now I've suffered enough for those red shoes," she said. "Now I'm going to church so they can see me." And she walked as fast as she could toward the church door, but when she got there, the red shoes were dancing in front of her. She was horrified and turned away.

All week long she was sad and wept many bitter tears, but when Sunday came, she said, "All right! Now I've suffered and struggled enough! I should think I'm just as good as many of those people sitting so proudly inside the church." Then she set off quite boldly, but she got no farther than to the gate when she saw the red shoes dancing in front of her. She was horrified and turned away, repenting her sin with all her heart.

She went over to the parsonage and asked if she might be taken into service there. She would work hard and do everything she could. She had no wish for wages; all she asked for was a roof over her head and permission to stay with good people. The pastor's wife felt sorry for her and gave her a position. And she was hardworking and thoughtful. Quietly she would sit and listen when the pastor read aloud from the Bible in the evening. All the children were very fond of her, but whenever they spoke of adornments and finery and being as lovely as a queen, she would shake her head.

The next Sunday they all went to church and they asked if she would like to come along, but with tears in her eyes she looked sadly at her crutches. Then the others went to hear God's Word while she went alone into her tiny room. It was only big enough for a bed and a chair. Then she sat with her hymnbook. As she began reading with a pious heart, the wind carried the tones of the organ from the church to her. She raised her tear-stained face and said, "Oh, help me, God!"

Then the sun shone so bright, and right in front of her stood the angel of God in the white robes, the one she had seen that night at the church door. He was no longer holding a sharp sword but a lovely green bough that was covered with roses. He touched it to the ceiling, which raised up high, and at the spot he had touched shone a golden star. He touched the walls and they moved outward. She saw the organ that was playing; she saw the old paintings of the pastors and their wives. The congregation was sitting in the carved pews and singing from their hymnals.

The church itself had come home to the poor girl in the tiny, cramped room, or perhaps she had gone to the church. She was sitting in a pew with the others from the parsonage. When they finished the hymn and looked up, they nodded and said, "It was right for you to come, Karen."

"It was God's mercy," she said.

The organ soared, and the children's voices in the choir sounded gentle and lovely. The bright, warm sunshine streamed through the window, reaching the church pew where Karen sat. Her heart was so filled with sunlight, with peace and joy, that it burst. Her soul flew on the sunlight to God, and no one asked about the red shoes.

17. Peter Christen Asbjørnsen and Jørgen Engebretsen Moe, *Norske Folkeeventyr* (1845–48; *translated by George Webbe Dasent, 1858*[1])

Peter Asbjørnsen and Jørgen Moe are best known for their collection of Norwegian tales, Norske Folkeeventyr. *Inspired by the Grimms'* Kinder- und Hausmärchen, *but also critical of what they saw as liberties taken with the German texts, Asbjørnsen and Moe published their first pamphlet of collected tales in 1841, without title, author, or introduction. In 1851 they published the greatly expanded volume, which included a lengthy introduction and a 115-page appendix of comparative notes, and it was on this volume that George Webbe Dasent based his 1858 translations, included here. One of the notable features in* Norske Folkeeventyr *is the stylistic and formal consistency of the volume: the tales have a very distinctive narrative style, employing popular idioms and avoiding literary language, and are unified by the formulaic opening, "Der ver engang"—translated by Dasent as "Once on a time." Although the volume was criticized by some Norwegian readers for its "low" style and occasionally raunchy content, it has come to be considered a national classic—and Dasent's translation, with its playful narrative style and with the more risqué stories (including "Little Annie the Goose Girl," in this volume) exiled to an appendix, was very popular in the English-speaking world.*

1 [Source: George Webbe Dasent, *Popular Tales from the Norse* (Edinburgh: Edmonston and Douglas, 1859: 25–40, 397–406, 478–82).]

Although these Norwegian stories are not prominent in current North American popular culture, tales like "East o' the Sun and West o' the Moon" and "Tatterhood" contain models of female strength, cunning, and determination that challenge assumptions about "typical" fairy-tale heroines and can prove very appealing to modern readers.

EAST O' THE SUN AND WEST O' THE MOON

ONCE ON A TIME THERE was a poor husbandman who had so many children that he hadn't much of either food or clothing to give them. Pretty children they all were, but the prettiest was the youngest daughter, who was so lovely there was no end to her loveliness.

So one day, 'twas on a Thursday evening late at the fall of the year, the weather was so wild and rough outside, and it was so cruelly dark, and rain fell and wind blew, till the walls of the cottage shook again. There they all sat round the fire busy with this thing and that. But just then, all at once something gave three taps on the window-pane. Then the father went out to see what was the matter; and, when he got out of doors, what should he see but a great big White Bear.

"Good evening to you!" said the White Bear.

"The same to you," said the man.

"Will you give me your youngest daughter? If you will, I'll make you as rich as you are now poor," said the Bear.

Well, the man would not be at all sorry to be so rich; but still he thought he must have a bit of a talk with his daughter first; so he went in and told them how there was a great White Bear waiting outside, who had given his word to make them so rich if he could only have the youngest daughter.

The lassie said "No!" outright. Nothing could get her to say anything else; so the man went out and settled it with the White Bear, that he should come again the next Thursday evening and get an answer. Meantime he talked his daughter over, and kept on telling her of all the riches they would get, and how well off she would be herself; and so at last she thought better of it, and washed and mended her rags, made herself as smart as she could, and was ready to start. I can't say her packing gave her much trouble.

Next Thursday evening came the White Bear to fetch her, and she got upon his back with her bundle, and off they went. So, when they had gone a bit of the way, the White Bear said,—

"Are you afraid?"

"No! she wasn't."

"Well! mind and hold tight by my shaggy coat, and then there's nothing to fear," said the Bear.

So she rode a long, long way, till they came to a great steep hill. There, on the face of it, the White Bear gave a knock, and a door opened, and they came into a castle, where there were many rooms all lit up; rooms gleaming with silver and gold; and there too was a table ready laid, and it was all as grand as grand could be. Then the White Bear gave her a silver bell; and when she wanted anything, she was only to ring it, and she would get it at once.

Well, after she had eaten and drunk, and evening wore on, she got sleepy after her journey, and thought she would like to go to bed, so she rang the bell; and she had scarce taken hold of it before she came into a chamber, where there was a bed made, as fair and white as anyone would wish to sleep in, with silken pillows and curtains, and gold fringe. All that was in the room was gold or silver; but when she had gone to bed, and put out the light, a man came and laid himself alongside her. That was the White Bear, who threw off his beast shape at night; but she never saw him, for he always came after she had put out the light, and before the day dawned he was up and off again. So things went on happily for a while, but at last she began to get silent and sorrowful; for there she went about all day alone, and she longed to go home to see her father and mother, and brothers and sisters. So one day, when the White Bear asked what it was that she lacked, she said it was so dull and lonely there, and how she longed to go home to see her father and mother, and brothers and sisters, and that was why she was so sad and sorrowful, because she couldn't get to them.

"Well, well!" said the Bear, "perhaps there's a cure for all this; but you must promise me one thing, not to talk alone with your mother, but only when the rest are by to hear; for she'll take you by the hand and try to lead you into a room alone to talk; but you must mind and not do that, else you'll bring bad luck on both of us."

So one Sunday the White Bear came and said now they could set off to see her father and mother. Well, off they started, she sitting on his back; and they went far and long. At last they came to a grand house, and there her brothers and sisters were running about out of doors at play, and everything was so pretty, 'twas a joy to see.

"This is where your father and mother live now," said the White Bear; "but don't forget what I told you, else you'll make us both unlucky."

"No! bless her, she'd not forget;" and when she had reached the house, the White Bear turned right about and left her.

Then when she went in to see her father and mother, there was such joy, there was no end to it. None of them thought they could thank her enough for all she had done for them. Now, they had everything they wished, as good as good could be, and they all wanted to know how she got on where she lived.

Well, she said, it was very good to live where she did; she had all she wished. What she said beside I don't know; but I don't think any of them had the right end of the stick, or that they got much out of her. But so in the afternoon, after they had done dinner, all happened as the White Bear had said. Her mother wanted to talk with her alone in her bed-room; but she minded what the White Bear had said, and wouldn't go up stairs.

"Oh! what we have to talk about, will keep," she said, and put her mother off. But somehow or other, her mother got round her at last, and she had to tell her the whole story. So she said, how every night, when she had gone to bed, a man came and lay down beside her as soon as she had put out the light, and how she never saw him, because he was always up and away before the morning dawned; and how she went about woeful and sorrowing, for she thought she should so like to see him, and how all day long she walked about there alone, and how dull, and dreary, and lonesome it was.

"My!" said her mother; "it may well be a Troll you slept with! But now I'll teach you a lesson how to set eyes on him. I'll give you a bit of candle, which you can carry home in your bosom; just light that while he is asleep, but take care not to drop the tallow on him."

Yes! she took the candle, and hid it in her bosom, and as night drew on, the White Bear came and fetched her away.

But when they had gone a bit of the way, the White Bear asked if all hadn't happened as he had said?

"Well, she couldn't say it hadn't."

"Now, mind," said he, "if you have listened to your mother's advice, you have brought bad luck on us both, and then, all that has passed between us will be as nothing."

"No," she said, "she hadn't listened to her mother's advice."

So when she reached home, and had gone to bed, it was the old story over again. There came a man and lay down beside her; but at dead of night, when she heard he slept, she got up and struck a light, lit the candle, and let the light shine on him, and so she saw that he was the loveliest Prince one ever set eyes on, and she fell so deep in love with him on the spot, that she thought she couldn't live if she didn't give him a kiss there and then. And so she did, but as she kissed him, she dropped three hot drops of tallow on his shirt, and he woke up.

"What have you done?" he cried; "now you have made us both unlucky, for had you held out only this one year, I had been freed. For I have a stepmother who has bewitched me, so that I am a White Bear by day, and a Man by night. But now all ties are snapt between us; now I must set off from you to her. She lives in a Castle which stands EAST O' THE SUN AND WEST O' THE MOON, and there, too, is a Princess, with a nose three ells long, and she's the wife I must have now."

She wept and took it ill, but there was no help for it; go he must.

Then she asked if she mightn't go with him?

No, she mightn't.

"Tell me the way, then," she said, "and I'll search you out; that surely I may get leave to do."

"Yes, she might do that," he said; "but there was no way to that place. It lay EAST O' THE SUN AND WEST O' THE MOON, and thither she'd never find her way."

So next morning, when she woke up, both Prince and castle were gone, and then she lay on a little green patch, in the midst of the gloomy thick wood, and by her side lay the same bundle of rags she had brought with her from her old home.

So when she had rubbed the sleep out of her eyes, and wept till she was tired, she set out on her way, and walked many, many days, till she came to a lofty crag. Under it sat an old hag, and played with a gold apple which she tossed about. Her the lassie asked if she knew the way to the Prince, who lived with his step-mother in the Castle, that lay EAST O' THE SUN AND WEST O' THE MOON, and who was to marry the Princess with a nose three ells long.

"How did you come to know about him?" asked the old hag; "but maybe you are the lassie who ought to have had him?"

Yes, she was.

"So, so; it's you, is it?" said the old hag. "Well, all I know about him is, that he lives in the castle that lies EAST O' THE SUN AND WEST O' THE MOON, and thither you'll come, late or never; but still you may have the loan of my horse, and on him you can ride to my next neighbour. Maybe she'll be able to tell you; and when you get there, just give the horse a switch under the left ear, and beg him to be off home; and, stay, this gold apple you may take with you."

So she got upon the horse, and rode a long long time, till she came to another crag, under which sat another old hag, with a gold carding-comb. Her the lassie asked if she knew the way to the castle that lay EAST O' THE SUN AND WEST O' THE MOON, and she answered, like the first old hag, that she knew nothing about it, except it was east o' the sun and west o' the moon.

"And thither you'll come, late or never, but you shall have the loan of my horse to my next neighbour; maybe she'll tell you all about it; and when you get there, just switch the horse under the left ear, and beg him to be off home."

And this old hag gave her the golden carding-comb; it might be she'd find some use for it, she said. So the lassie got up on the horse, and rode a far far way, and a weary time; and so at last she came to another great crag, under which sat another old hag, spinning with a golden spinning-wheel. Her, too, she asked if she knew the way to the Prince, and where the castle was that lay EAST O' THE SUN AND WEST O' THE MOON. So it was the same thing over again.

"Maybe it's you who ought to have had the Prince?" said the old hag.

Yes, it was.

But she, too, didn't know the way a bit better than the other two. "East o' the sun and west o' the moon it was," she knew—that was all.

"And thither you'll come, late or never; but I'll lend you my horse, and then I think you'd best ride to the East Wind and ask him; maybe he knows those parts, and can blow you thither. But when you get to him, you need only give the horse a switch under the left ear, and he'll trot home of himself."

And so, too, she gave her the gold spinning-wheel. "Maybe you'll find a use for it," said the old hag.

Then on she rode many many days, a weary time, before she got to the East Wind's house, but at last she did reach it, and then she asked the East Wind if he could tell her the way to the Prince who dwelt east o' the sun and west o' the moon. Yes, the East Wind had often heard tell of it, the Prince and the castle, but he couldn't tell the way, for he had never blown so far.

"But, if you will, I'll go with you to my brother the West Wind, maybe he knows, for he's much stronger. So, if you will just get on my back, I'll carry you thither."

Yes, she got on his back, and I should just think they went briskly along.

So when they got there, they went into the West Wind's house, and the East Wind said, the lassie he had brought was the one who ought to have had the Prince who lived in the castle EAST O' THE SUN AND WEST O' THE MOON; and so she had set out to seek him, and how he had come with her, and would be glad to know if the West Wind knew how to get to the castle.

"Nay," said the West Wind, "so far I've never blown; but if you will, I'll go with you to our brother the South Wind, for he's much stronger than either of us, and he has flapped his wings far and wide. Maybe he'll tell you. You can get on my back, and I'll carry you to him."

Yes! she got on his back, and so they travelled to the South Wind, and weren't so very long on the way, I should think.

When they got there, the West Wind asked him if he could tell her the way to the castle that lay EAST O' THE SUN AND WEST O' THE MOON, for it was she who ought to have had the prince who lived there.

"You don't say so! That's she, is it?" said the South Wind.

"Well, I have blustered about in most places in my time, but so far have I never blown; but if you will, I'll take you to my brother the North Wind; he is the oldest and strongest of the whole lot of us, and if he don't know where it is, you'll never find anyone in the world to tell you. You can get on my back, and I'll carry you thither."

Yes! she got on his back, and away he went from his house at a fine rate. And this time, too, she wasn't long on her way.

So when they got to the North Wind's house, he was so wild and cross, cold puffs came from him a long way off.

"BLAST YOU BOTH, WHAT DO YOU WANT?" he roared out to them ever so far off, so that it struck them with an icy shiver.

"Well," said the South Wind, "you needn't be so foul-mouthed, for here I am, your brother, the South Wind, and here is the lassie who ought to have had the Prince who dwells in the castle that lies EAST O' THE SUN AND WEST O' THE MOON, and now she wants to ask you if you ever were there, and can tell her the way, for she would be so glad to find him again."

"YES, I KNOW WELL ENOUGH WHERE IT IS," said the North Wind; "once in my life I blew an aspen-leaf thither, but I was so tired I couldn't blow a puff for ever so many days after. But if you really wish to go thither, and aren't afraid to come along with me, I'll take you on my back and see if I can blow you thither."

Yes! with all her heart; she must and would get thither if it were possible in any way; and as for fear, however madly he went, she wouldn't be at all afraid.

"Very well, then," said the North Wind, "but you must sleep here to-night, for we must have the whole day before us, if we're to get thither at all."

Early next morning the North Wind woke her, and puffed himself up, and blew himself out, and made himself so stout and big, 'twas gruesome to look at him; and so off they went high up through the air, as if they would never stop till they got to the world's end.

Down here below there was such a storm; it threw down long tracts of wood and many houses, and when it swept over the great sea, ships foundered by hundreds.

So they tore on and on,—no one can believe how far they went,—and all the while they still went over the sea, and the North Wind got more and more weary, and so out of breath he could scarce bring out a puff, and his wings drooped and drooped, till at last he sunk so low that the crests of the waves dashed over his heels.

"Are you afraid?" said the North Wind.

"No!" she wasn't.

But they weren't very far from land; and the North Wind had still so much strength left in him that he managed to throw her up on the shore under the windows of the castle which lay EAST O' THE SUN AND WEST O' THE MOON; but then he was so weak and worn out, he had to stay there and rest many days before he could get home again.

Next morning the lassie sat down under the castle window, and began to play with the gold apple; and the first person she saw was the Long-nose who was to have the Prince.

"What do you want for your gold apple, you lassie?" said the Long-nose, and threw up the window.

"It's not for sale, for gold or money," said the lassie.

"If it's not for sale for gold or money, what is it that you will sell it for? You may name your own price," said the Princess.

"Well! if I may get to the Prince, who lives here, and be with him tonight, you shall have it," said the lassie whom the North Wind had brought.

Yes! she might; that could be done. So the Princess got the gold apple; but when the lassie came up to the Prince's bed-room at night he was fast asleep; she called him and shook him, and between whiles she wept sore; but all she could do she couldn't wake him up. Next morning as soon as day broke, came the Princess with the long nose, and drove her out again.

So in the daytime she sat down under the castle windows and began to card with her golden carding-comb, and the same thing happened. The Princess asked what she wanted for it; and she said it wasn't for sale for gold or money, but if she might get leave to go up to the Prince and be with him that night, the Princess should have it. But when she went up she found him fast asleep again, and all she called, and all she shook, and wept, and prayed, she couldn't get life into him; and as soon as the first gray peep of day came, then came the Princess with the long nose, and chased her out again.

So, in the daytime, the lassie sat down outside under the castle window, and began to spin with her golden spinning-wheel, and that, too, the Princess with the long nose wanted to have. So she threw up the window and asked what she wanted for it. The lassie said, as she had said twice before, it wasn't for sale for gold or money; but if she might go up to the Prince who was there, and be with him alone that night, she might have it.

Yes! she might do that and welcome. But now you must know there were some Christian folk who had been carried off thither, and as they sat in their room, which was next the Prince, they had heard how a woman had been in there, and wept and prayed, and called to him two nights running, and they told that to the Prince.

That evening, when the Princess came with her sleepy drink, the Prince made as if he drank, but threw it over his shoulder, for he could guess it was a sleepy drink. So, when the lassie came in, she found the Prince wide awake; and then she told him the whole story how she had come thither.

"Ah," said the Prince, "you've just come in the very nick of time, for to-morrow is to be our wedding-day; but now I won't have the Long-nose, and you are the only woman in the world who can set me free. I'll say I want to see what my wife is fit for, and beg her to wash the shirt which has the three spots of tallow on it; she'll say yes, for she doesn't know 'tis you who put them there; but that's a work only for Christian folk, and not for such a pack of Trolls, and so I'll say that I won't have any other for my bride than the woman who can wash them out, and ask you to do it."

So there was great joy and love between them all that night. But next day, when the wedding was to be, the Prince said,—

"First of all, I'd like to see what my bride is fit for."

"Yes!" said the step-mother, with all her heart.

"Well," said the Prince, "I've got a fine shirt which I'd like for my wedding shirt, but somehow or other it has got three spots of tallow on it, which I must have washed out; and I have sworn never to take any other bride than the woman who's able to do that. If she can't, she's not worth having."

Well, that was no great thing they said, so they agreed, and she with the long nose began to wash away as hard as she could, but the more she rubbed and scrubbed, the bigger the spots grew.

"Ah!" said the old hag, her mother, "you can't wash; let me try."

But she hadn't long taken the shirt in hand, before it got far worse than ever, and with all her rubbing, and wringing, and scrubbing, the spots grew bigger and blacker, and the darker and uglier was the shirt.

Then all the other Trolls began to wash, but the longer it lasted, the blacker and uglier the shirt grew, till at last it was as black all over as if it had been up the chimney.

"Ah!" said the Prince, "you're none of you worth a straw: you can't wash. Why there, outside, sits a beggar lassie, I'll be bound she knows how to wash better than the whole lot of you. COME IN LASSIE!" he shouted.

Well, in she came.

"Can you wash this shirt clean, lassie, you?" said he.

"I don't know," she said, "but I think I can."

And almost before she had taken it and dipped it in the water, it was as white as driven snow, and whiter still.

"Yes; you are the lassie for me," said the Prince.

At that the old hag flew into such a rage, she burst on the spot, and the Princess with the long nose after her, and the whole pack of Trolls after her,—at least I've never heard a word about them since.

As for the Prince and Princess, they set free all the poor Christian folk who had been carried off and shut up there; and they took with them all the silver and gold, and flitted away as far as they could from the Castle that lay EAST O' THE SUN AND WEST O' THE MOON.

TATTERHOOD

Once on a time there was a king and a queen who had no children, and that gave the queen much grief; she scarce had one happy hour. She was always bewailing and bemoaning herself, and saying how dull and lonesome it was in the palace.

"If we had children there'd be life enough," she said.

Wherever she went in all her realm she found God's blessing in children, even in the vilest hut; and wherever she came she heard the Goodies scolding the bairns, and saying how they had done that and that wrong. All this the queen heard, and thought it would be so nice to do as other women did. At last the king and queen took into their palace a stranger lassie to rear up, that they might have her always with them, to love her if she did well, and scold her if she did wrong, like their own child.

So one day the little lassie whom they had taken as their own, ran down into the palace yard, and was playing with a gold apple. Just then an old beggar wife came by, who had a little girl with her, and it wasn't long before the little lassie and the beggar's bairn were great friends, and began to play together, and to toss the gold apple about between them. When the Queen saw this, as she sat at a window in the palace, she tapped on the pane for her foster-daughter to come up. She went at once, but the beggar-girl went up too; and as they went into the Queen's bower, each held the other by the hand. Then the Queen began to scold the little lady, and to say—

"You ought to be above running about and playing with a tattered beggar's brat."

And so she wanted to drive the lassie down stairs.

"If the Queen only knew my mother's power, she'd not drive me out," said the little lassie; and when the Queen asked what she meant more plainly, she told her how her mother could get her children if she chose. The Queen wouldn't believe it, but the lassie held her own, and said every word of it was true, and bade the Queen only to try and make her mother do it. So the Queen sent the lassie down to fetch up her mother.

"Do you know what your daughter says?" asked the Queen of the old woman, as soon as ever she came into the room.

No; the beggar-wife knew nothing about it.

"Well, she says you can get me children if you will," answered the Queen.

"Queens shouldn't listen to beggar lassies' silly stories," said the old wife, and strode out of the room.

Then the Queen got angry, and wanted again to drive out the little lassie; but she declared it was true every word that she had said.

"Let the Queen only give my mother a drop to drink," said the lassie; "when she gets merry she'll soon find out a way to help you."

The Queen was ready to try this; so the beggar-wife was fetched up again once more, and treated both with wine and mead as much as she chose; and so it was not long before her tongue began to wag. Then the Queen came out again with the same question she had asked before.

"One way to help you perhaps I know," said the beggar-wife. "Your Majesty must make them bring in two pails of water some evening before you go to bed. In each of them you must wash yourself, and afterwards throw away the water under the bed. When you look under the bed next morning, two flowers will have sprung up, one fair and one ugly. The fair one you must eat, the ugly one you must let stand; but mind you don't forget the last."

That was what the beggar-wife said.

Yes; the Queen did what the beggar-wife advised her to do; she had the water brought up in two pails, washed herself in them, and emptied them under the bed; and lo! when she looked under the bed next morning, there stood two flowers; one was ugly and foul, and had black leaves; but the other was so bright, and fair, and lovely, she had never seen its like; so she ate it up at once. But the pretty flower tasted so sweet, that she couldn't help herself. She ate the other up too, for, she thought, "It can't hurt or help one much either way, I'll be bound."

Well, sure enough, after a while the Queen was brought to bed. First of all, she had a girl who had a wooden spoon in her hand, and rode upon a goat; loathly and ugly she was, and the very moment she came into the world, she bawled out "Mamma."

"If I'm your mamma," said the Queen, "God give me grace to mend my ways."

"Oh, don't be sorry," said the girl, who rode on the goat, "for one will soon come after me who is better looking."

So, after a while, the Queen had another girl, who was so fair and sweet, no one had ever set eyes on such a lovely child, and with her you may fancy the Queen was very well pleased. The elder twin they called "Tatterhood," because she was always so ugly and ragged, and because she had a hood which hung about her ears in tatters. The Queen could scarce bear to look at her, and the nurses tried to shut her up in a room by herself, but it was all no good; where the younger twin was, there she must also be, and no one could ever keep them apart.

Well, one Christmas eve, when they were half grown up, there rose such a frightful noise and clatter in the gallery outside the Queen's bower. So Tatterhood asked what it was that dashed and crashed so out in the passage.

"Oh!" said the Queen, "it isn't worth asking about."

But Tatterhood wouldn't give over till she found out all about it; and so the Queen told her it was a pack of Trolls and witches who had come there to keep Christmas. So Tatterhood said she'd just go out and drive them away; and in spite of all they could say, and however much they begged and prayed her to let the Trolls alone, she must and would go out to drive the witches off; but she begged the Queen to mind and keep all the doors close shut, so that not one of them came so much as the least bit ajar. Having said this, off she went with her wooden spoon, and began to hunt and sweep away the hags; and all this while there was such a pother out in the gallery, the like of it was never heard. The whole Palace creaked and groaned as if every joint and beam were going to be torn out of its place. Now, how it was, I'm sure I can't tell; but somehow or other one door did get the least bit ajar, then her twin sister just peeped out to see how things were going with Tatterhood, and put her head a tiny bit through the opening. But, POP! up came an old witch, and whipped off her head, and stuck a calf's head on her shoulders instead; and so the Princess ran back into the room on all fours, and began to "moo" like a calf. When Tatterhood came back and saw her sister, she scolded them all round, and was very angry because they hadn't kept better watch, and asked them what they thought of their heedlessness now, when her sister was turned into a calf.

"But still I'll see if I can't set her free," she said.

Then she asked the King for a ship in full trim, and well fitted with stores; but captain and sailors she wouldn't have. No; she would sail away with her sister all alone; and as there was no holding her back, at last they let her have her own way.

Then Tatterhood sailed off, and steered her ship right under the land where the witches dwelt, and when she came to the landing-place, she told her sister to stay quite still on board the ship; but she herself rode on her goat up to the witches' castle. When she got there, one of the windows in the gallery was open, and there she saw her sister's head hung up on the window frame; so she leapt her goat through the window into the gallery, snapped up the head, and set off with it. After her came the witches to try to get the head again, and they flocked about her as thick as a swarm of bees or a nest of ants; but the goat snorted, and puffed, and butted with his horns, and Tatterhood beat and banged them about with her wooden spoon; and so the pack of witches had to give it up. So Tatterhood got back to her ship, took the calf's head off her sister, and put her own on again, and then she became a girl as she had been before. After that she sailed a long, long way, to a strange king's realm.

Now the king of that land was a widower, and had an only son. So when he saw the strange sail, he sent messengers down to the strand to find out whence it came, and who owned it; but when the king's men came down there, they saw never a living soul on board but Tatterhood, and there she was, riding round and round the deck on her goat at full speed, till her elf locks streamed again in the wind. The folk from the palace were all amazed at this sight, and asked, were there not more on board. Yes, there were; she had a sister with her, said Tatterhood. Her, too, they wanted to see, but Tatterhood said "No,"—

"No one shall see her, unless the king comes himself," she said; and so she began to gallop about on her goat till the deck thundered again.

So when the servants got back to the palace, and told what they had seen and heard down at the ship, the king was for setting out at once, that he might see the lassie that rode on the goat. When he got down, Tatterhood led out her sister, and she was so fair and gentle, the king fell over head and ears in love with her as he stood. He brought them both back with him to the Palace, and wanted to have the sister for his queen; but Tatterhood said "No"; the king couldn't have her in any way, unless the king's son chose to have Tatterhood. That you may fancy the prince was very loath to do, such an ugly hussy as Tatterhood was; but at last the king and all the others in the palace talked him over, and he yielded, giving his word to take her for his queen; but it went sore against the grain, and he was a doleful man.

Now they set about the wedding, both with brewing and baking; and when all was ready, they were to go to church; but the prince thought it the weariest churching he had ever had in all his life. First, the king drove off with his bride, and she was so lovely and so grand, all the people stopped to look after her all along the road, and they stared at her till she was out of sight. After them came the prince on horseback by the side of Tatterhood, who trotted along on her goat with her wooden spoon in her fist, and to look at him, it was more like going to a burial than a wedding, and that his own; so sorrowful he seemed, and with never a word to say.

"Why don't you talk?" asked Tatterhood, when they had ridden a bit.

"Why, what should I talk about?" answered the prince.

"Well, you might at least ask me why I ride upon this ugly goat," said Tatterhood.

"Why do you ride on that ugly goat?" asked the prince.

"Is it an ugly goat? why, it's the grandest horse bride ever rode on," answered Tatterhood; and in a trice the goat became a horse, and that the finest the prince had ever set eyes on.

Then they rode on again a bit, but the prince was just as woeful as before, and couldn't get a word out. So Tatterhood asked him again why he didn't talk, and when the Prince answered, he didn't know what to talk about, she said,—

"You can at least ask me why I ride with this ugly spoon in my fist."

"Why do you ride with that ugly spoon?" asked the prince.

"Is it an ugly spoon? why, it's the loveliest silver wand bride ever bore," said Tatterhood; and in a trice it became a silver wand, so dazzling bright, the sunbeams glistened from it.

So they rode on another bit, but the Prince was just as sorrowful, and said never a word. In a little while, Tatterhood asked him again why he didn't talk, and bade him ask why she wore that ugly grey hood on her head.

"Why do you wear that ugly grey hood on your head?" asked the Prince.

"Is it an ugly hood? why, it's the brightest golden crown bride ever wore," answered Tatterhood, and it became a crown on the spot.

Now, they rode on a long while again, and the Prince was so woeful, that he sat without sound or speech just as before. So his bride asked him again why he didn't talk, and bade him ask now, why her face was so ugly and ashen-gray?

"Ah!" asked the Prince, "why is your face so ugly and ashen-gray?"

"I ugly," said the bride; "you think my sister pretty, but I am ten times prettier"; and lo! when the Prince looked at her, she was so lovely, he thought there never was so lovely a woman in all the world. After that, I shouldn't wonder if the Prince found his tongue, and no longer rode along hanging down his head.

So they drank the bridal cup both deep and long, and, after that, both Prince and King set out with their brides to the Princess's father's palace, and there they had another bridal feast, and drank anew, both deep and long. There was no end to the fun; and, if you make haste and run to the King's palace, I dare say you'll find there's still a drop of the bridal ale left for you.

LITTLE ANNIE THE GOOSE GIRL

Once on a time there was a King who had so many geese, he was forced to have a lassie to tend them and watch them; her name was Annie, and so they called her "Annie the Goose-girl." Now you must know there was a King's son from England who went out to woo; and as he came along Annie sat herself down in his way.

"Sitting all alone there, you little Annie?" said the King's son.

"Yes," said little Annie, "here I sit and put stitch to stitch and patch on patch. I'm waiting today for the King's son from England."

"Him you mustn't look to have," said the Prince.

"Nay, but if I'm to have him," said little Annie, "have him I shall after all."

And now limners were sent out into all lands and realms to take the likenesses of the fairest Princesses, and the Prince was to chose [sic] between them. So he thought so much of one of them, that he set out to seek her, and wanted to wed her, and he was glad and happy when he got her for his sweetheart.

But now I must tell you this Prince had a stone with him which he laid by his bedside, and that stone knew everything, and when the Princess came little Annie told her, if so be she'd had a sweetheart before, or didn't feel herself quite free from anything which she didn't wish the Prince to know, she'd better not step on that stone which lay by the bedside.

"If you do, it will tell him all about you," said little Annie.

So when the Princess heard that she was dreadfully downcast, and she fell upon the thought to ask Annie if she would get into bed that night in her stead and lie down by the Prince's side, and then when he was sound asleep, Annie should get out and the Princess should get in, and so when he woke up in the morning he would find the right bride by his side.

So they did that, and when Annie the goose-girl came and stepped upon the stone the Prince asked,—

"Who is this that steps into my bed?"

"A maid pure and bright," said the stone, and so they lay down to sleep; but when the night wore on the Princess came and lay down in Annie's stead.

But next morning, when they were to get up, the Prince asked the stone again,—

"Who is this that steps out of my bed?"

"One that has had three bairns," said the stone.

When the Prince heard that he wouldn't have her, you may know very well; and so he packed her off home again, and took another sweetheart.

But as he went to see her, little Annie went and sat down in his way again.

"Sitting all alone there, little Annie, the goose-girl," said the Prince.

"Yes, here I sit, and put stitch to stitch, and patch on patch; for I'm waiting today for the king's son from England," said Annie.

"Oh! you mustn't look to have him," said the king's son.

"Nay, but if I'm to have him, have him I shall, after all"; that was what Annie thought.

Well, it was the same story over again with the Prince; only this time, when his bride got up in the morning, the stone said she'd had six bairns.

So the Prince wouldn't have her either, but sent her about her business; but still he thought he'd try once more if he couldn't find one who was pure and spotless; and he sought far and wide in many lands, till at last he found one he thought he might trust. But when he went to see her, little Annie the goose-girl had put herself in his way again.

"Sitting all alone there, you little Annie, the goose-girl," said the Prince.

"Yes, here I sit, and put stitch to stitch, and patch on patch; for I'm waiting today for the king's son from England," said Annie.

"Him you mustn't look to have," said the Prince.

"Nay, but if I'm to have him, have him I shall, after all," said little Annie.

So when the Princess came, little Annie the goose-girl told her the same as she had told the other two, if she'd had any sweetheart before, or if there was anything else she didn't wish the Prince to know, she mustn't tread on the stone that the Prince had put at his bedside; for, said she,—

"It tells him everything."

The Princess got very red and downcast when she heard that, for she was just as naughty as the others, and asked Annie if she would go in her stead and lie down with the Prince that night; and when he was sound asleep, she would come and take her place, and then he would have the right bride by his side when it was light next morning.

Yes! they did that. And when little Annie the goose-girl came and stepped upon the stone, the Prince asked,—

"Who is this that steps into my bed."

"A maid pure and bright," said the stone; and so they lay down to rest.

Farther on in the night the Prince put a ring on Annie's finger, and it fitted so tight she couldn't get it off again; for the Prince saw well enough there was something wrong, and so he wished to have a mark by which he might know the right woman again.

Well, when the Prince had gone off to sleep, the Princess came and drove Annie away to the pigsty, and lay down in her place. Next morning, when they were to get up, the Prince asked—

"Who is this that steps out of my bed?"

"One that's had nine bairns," said the stone.

When the Prince heard that he drove her away at once, for he was in an awful rage; and then he asked the stone how it all was with these Princesses who had stepped on it, for he couldn't understand it at all, he said.

So the stone told him how they had cheated him, and sent little Annie the goose-girl to him in their stead.

But as the Prince wished to have no mistake about it, he went down to her where she sat tending her geese, for he wanted to see if she had the ring too, and he thought, "if she has it, 'twere best to take her at once for my queen."

So when he got down he saw in a moment that she had tied a bit of rag round one of her fingers, and so he asked her why it was tied up.

"Oh! I've cut myself so badly," said little Annie the goose-girl.

So he must and would see the finger, but Annie wouldn't take the rag off. Then he caught hold of the finger; but Annie, she tried to pull it from him, and so between them the rag came off, and then he knew his ring.

So he took her up to the palace, and gave her much fine clothes and attire, and after that they held their wedding feast; and so little Annie the goose-girl came to have the king of England's son for her husband after all, just because it was written that she should have him.

George Cruikshank, "Cinderella and the Glass Slipper," ***George Cruikshank's Fairy Library*** **(1854) [website]**

George Cruikshank was famous as an illustrator, but he also published his own versions of well-known tales. They include a rendition of Charles Perrault's "Cinderella" (provided as a web text; see http://sites.broadviewpress.com/marveloustrans/), which reads as a kind of politically correct bedtime story for the nineteenth century. Cruikshank cast the stories through the lens of his ideological concerns and agendas, including his condemnation of alcohol and gambling, and was remarkably astute in his understanding that every telling is shaped by ideological biases of one kind or another.

18. Aleksandr Afanas'ev, ***Narodnye russkie skazki*** **(1855–64;** ***translated by Helena Goscilo, 2005*** **[1])**

"Narodnye skazki," popular tales, the expression Aleksandr Afanas'ev used to describe the Russian stories he published in the mid-nineteenth century, referred to stock plotlines and fantastical characters that appeared in a host of genres ranging from brief anecdote to legend to narrative poetry. Though the stories he published have come to be known in English as "fairy tales," their most memorable elements (Baba Yaga, Prince Ivan) belong to the wider world of Russian folklore. Afanas'ev modeled his collection on the Grimms' Kinder- und Hausmärchen *(1812–57), both in the number of tales collected and in the way his volumes brought Russian folklore to the attention of learned society as a subject of study. In the spirit of the Grimms, who identified the preservation of stories as a practice vital to a culture's linguistic survival, Afanas'ev came to story gathering through a concern about the Russian language, which had long been replaced by French among the nobility. As a teacher of Russian with no formal training in ethnography, he relied heavily on the fieldwork of others (especially Vladimir Dahl) and sometimes created a composite version from several variants of a tale. While these practices were not uncommon among folklorists of his day, they serve to highlight his role as literary editor, not merely collector, of Russian tales. Many of the stories in* Narodnye russkie skazki *became the templates upon which Vladimir Propp based his* Morphology of the Folktale *(1928, translated into English in 1958), a formal analysis of the basic building blocks of narrative structure. Afanas'ev's print versions not only preserved as they forged the folklore of his own society, but also exerted vicarious influence upon the evolution of fairy-tale studies in the late twentieth century. If these stories can be described as simple in language and tone, they are also elegant, provocative narratives that passed through many mouths and learned hands before reaching us in this form.*

---

1 [Source: Marina Balina, Helena Goscilo, and Mark Lipovetsky, eds., *Politicizing Magic: An Anthology of Russian and Soviet Fairy Tales* (Evanston, IL: Northwestern UP, 2005: 23–27, 32–33, 91–95, 79–84).]

THE FROG PRINCESS

Long, long ago, in ancient times, there was a king with three sons, all of them full grown. And the king said to them, "Sons! I want each of you to make a bow for yourself and to shoot it. Whichever woman brings back your arrow will be your bride. Whoever's arrow isn't brought back is not meant to marry." The oldest son shot his arrow, which was brought back by a prince's daughter. The middle son shot his arrow, which was brought back by a general's daughter. But the arrow of the youngest, Prince Ivan, was brought back by a frog, who gripped it in her teeth. The two older brothers were happy and jubilant, but Prince Ivan grew pensive and burst into tears. "How can I live with a frog? To live one's whole life isn't like wading a river or crossing a field!" He cried and cried and cried some more, but there was nothing to be done—he married the frog. Their wedding observed traditional rites; the frog was held on a dish.

And so they lived until one day the king wanted to find out what gifts the brides could make, which one was the most skilled at sewing. He gave the order. Prince Ivan again grew pensive and cried, "What can my frog make! Everybody'll laugh!" The frog only hopped on the floor, only croaked. As soon as Prince Ivan fell asleep, she went outside, shed her skin, turned into a beautiful maiden, and cried, "Nurses-purses! Make such and such!" The nurses-purses instantly brought a shirt of the finest workmanship. She took it, folded it, and placed it beside Prince Ivan, and once again turned into a frog, as if she'd never been anything else! Prince Ivan awoke, was overjoyed, took the shirt, and brought it to the king. The king accepted it, and examined it. "Well, this is quite a shirt—made to wear on special holidays!" The middle son brought a shirt, and the king said, "The only thing it's good for is to wear in the bathhouse!" And he took the shirt the oldest brother brought and said, "The only thing it's good for is to wear in a poor peasant's hut!" The king's sons went their separate ways. The two oldest agreed. "We had no cause to laugh at Prince Ivan's wife. She's not a frog, but a cunning witch!"

Once again the king gave an order—that his daughters-in-law bake some bread and bring it to show him who could bake best. At first the other two brides laughed at the frog; but when the time came they sent the chambermaid to spy on how she baked. The frog realized this, and she went and mixed some dough, rolled it, made a hollow in the top of the stove, and tossed the dough directly into it. The chambermaid saw this and ran to tell her mistresses, the royal brides, and they did exactly the same. But the cunning frog had fooled them. She immediately dug the dough from the stove, cleaned and greased everything as though nothing had happened, went out onto the porch, shed her skin, and cried, "Nurses-purses! This very minute bake me the kind of bread that my father ate only on Sundays and holidays!" The nurses-purses instantly brought her the bread. She took it, placed it beside Prince Ivan, and turned into a frog. Prince Ivan awoke, took the bread, and brought it to his father. Just then his father was accepting the older brothers' bread: their wives had dropped theirs into the stove just as the frog had, and so it had come out any which way. The king accepted the oldest brother's bread first, looked at it, and sent it back to the kitchen; he took the middle son's, and did the same. When Ivan's turn came, he handed over the bread. His father took it, looked at it, and said, "Now, this is bread—fit to eat on special occasions! Not like the older daughters-in-law's, which is like stone!"

Next the king decided to hold a ball, to see which of his daughters-in-law danced best. All of the guests and the daughters-in-law assembled, except for Prince Ivan. He thought, "How can I turn up with a frog?" And our Prince Ivan sobbed uncontrollably. The frog said to him, "Don't cry, Prince Ivan! Go to the ball. I'll be there in an hour." Prince Ivan cheered up a little when he heard the frog's words. He left, and the frog went, shed her skin, and dressed up in wonderful clothes! She arrived at the ball. Prince Ivan was overjoyed and everyone applauded: what a beauty she was! The guests started to eat; the princess would pick a bone and toss it in her sleeve, drink something, and toss the rest in her other sleeve. The other sisters-in-law saw what she was doing and also started putting their bones in their sleeves and pouring the remnants of their drinks in their other sleeves. The time came for dancing, and the king ordered the older daughters-in-law to dance, but they let the frog go first. She instantly took Prince Ivan's arm and headed for the floor: she danced and danced, whirled and whirled, to everyone's wonder! She waved her right hand, and forests and lakes appeared; she waved her left hand, and various birds appeared in flight! Everyone was awed. When she finished dancing, everything vanished. The other sisters-in-law took their turn dancing, and tried to do the same: whenever they waved their right hands, bones came flying out right at the guests; they'd wave their left hands, and water would spray, also onto the guests. The king was displeased, and shouted, "That's enough!" The daughters-in-law stopped dancing.

The ball was over. Prince Ivan left first, found his wife's skin somewhere, took it, and burned it. She came home, looked for the skin, but it was gone, burned! She went to bed with Prince Ivan, and before morning said to him, "Well, Prince Ivan, you should have waited a bit longer. I'd have been yours, but now God knows! Goodbye! Search for me beyond the thrice-ninth lands, in the thrice-tenth kingdom." And the princess vanished.

A year passed. Prince Ivan missed his wife. During the second year he got ready, received his father's and his mother's blessing, and set off. He walked for a long time and suddenly came upon a little hut, with its front facing the forest, its back to him. And he said, "Little hut, little hut! Stand as you used to of old, the way your mother stood you—with your back to the forest, and your front facing me." The little hut turned around. He entered the hut. An old woman sat there, and said, "Fie, fie! There was no whiff of a Russian bone to be sniffed, no sight to be seen, and now a Russian bone has actually come to my house! Where are you off to, Prince Ivan?" "First give me food and drink, old woman, and then ask questions." The old woman gave him food and drink and put him to bed. Prince Ivan said to her, "Granny! I've set off to find Elena the Beautiful." "Oh, my dear child, you took so long to come! At first she often used to mention you, but now she doesn't any longer, and she hasn't visited me for a long time. Go along to my middle sister, she knows more."

Next morning Prince Ivan set off, and came to another little hut, and said, "Little hut, little hut! Stand as you used to of old, the way your mother stood you—with your back to the forest, and your front facing me." The little hut turned around. He entered, and saw an old woman sitting there, who said, "Fie, fie! There was no whiff of a Russian bone to be sniffed, no sight to be seen, and now a Russian bone has actually come to my house! Where are you off to, Prince Ivan?" "I'm here, Granny, in search of Elena the Beautiful." "Oh, Prince Ivan," said the old woman. "You took so long to come! She's started to forget you, and is marrying someone else. Their wedding is soon! She lives with my older sister now. Go there, but watch out: as soon as you come near, they'll sense it, and Elena will turn into a spindle, and her dress will become golden thread. My sister will start winding the golden thread: when she's wound it around the spindle and put it in a box and locked the box, you have to find the key, open the box, break the spindle, throw the top back over your shoulder, and the bottom in front of you. Then she'll appear before you."

Prince Ivan set off, came to the third old woman, and entered the hut. She was winding golden thread, wound it around the spindle, and put it in a box, locked it, and put the key somewhere. He took the key, opened the box, took out the spindle, and, as said and as written, broke the top and threw the top over his shoulder, and the bottom in front of him. Suddenly Elena the Beautiful appeared, and greeted him. "Oh, you took so long to come, Prince Ivan! I almost married another." And the new groom was supposed to arrive soon. Elena the Beautiful took a flying carpet from the old woman, sat on it, and they took off, flew like the birds. The bridegroom suddenly appeared and found out that they'd left. He also was cunning! He followed in pursuit, and chased and chased them, and was only ten yards short of catching up with them. They flew into Russia on the carpet, and for some reason he wasn't allowed in Russia, and he returned. But they flew home, all were overjoyed, and they started to live and prosper, to everyone's glory at the end of the story.

BABA YAGA

Once there lived a peasant and his wife and they had a daughter. The wife died. The husband married again, and had a daughter with the new wife. The wife conceived a dislike for her stepdaughter and made the girl's life miserable. The peasant thought and thought and finally drove his daughter into the forest. As they rode through the forest he looked around and saw a little hut standing on chicken legs. And the peasant said, "Little hut, little hut! Stand with your back to the forest, and your front facing me." And the little hut turned around.

The peasant entered the little hut, and there was Baba Yaga, her head in front, a leg in one corner, and the other in another. "I smell a Russian smell!" said Yaga. The peasant bowed. "Baba Yaga the Bony-Legged! I've brought you my daughter to serve you." "Fine! Serve me. Serve me," said Yaga to the girl, "and I'll reward you for it."

The father said his farewells and drove off home. And Baba Yaga gave the girl the tasks of spinning a basketful of thread, heating the stove, and preparing everything for dinner, while she herself left. The girl bustled around the stove, crying bitterly. The mice ran out and said to her, "Maiden, maiden, why are you crying? Give us some kasha, and we'll tell you something useful." She gave them some kasha. "Here's what you should do," they said. "Stretch a thread on each spindle." Baba Yaga returned. "Well," she said, "is everything ready?" Everything was. "Now come and wash me in the bathhouse." Yaga praised the girl and gave her all sorts of beautiful outfits. Yaga left again and gave the girl even more difficult tasks. The girl cried again. The mice ran out and said, "Why are you crying, beautiful maiden? Give us some kasha, and we'll tell you something useful." She gave them some kasha, and they again told her what to do and how. Once again Baba Yaga returned and praised her and gave her some more beautiful outfits ... Meanwhile the stepmother sent her husband to find out whether his daughter was still alive.

The peasant set off. He came and saw that his daughter had become rich, very rich. Yaga wasn't home, and he took his daughter with him. As they approached their village, their dog barked, "Woof, woof, woof! The lady's coming, the lady's coming!" The stepmother ran out and hit the dog with a rolling pin. "You're lying," she said. "Say: 'The bones are rattling in the box!'" But the dog kept barking the same thing. They arrived. The stepmother kept plaguing her husband to take her daughter to Baba Yaga. He did.

Baba Yaga gave her various tasks, and left. The girl was wild with anger and cried. The mice ran out. "Maiden, maiden! Why are you crying?" they said. But she didn't let them finish, and hit first one, then the other with a rolling-pin. She spent her time chasing them and didn't get the tasks done. Yaga returned and got angry. The same thing happened again. Yaga broke her into pieces, and put the bones in a box.

And the girl's mother sent her husband to fetch their daughter. The father came and drove back with just the bones. As he approached the village, the dog on the porch once again barked, "Woof, woof, woof! The bones are rattling in the box!" The stepmother ran out with the rolling-pin. "You're lying," she said. "Say: 'The lady's coming!'" But the dog kept barking the same thing, "Woof, woof, woof! The bones are rattling in the box!" The husband arrived, and the wife wailed aloud! Here's a tale for you, for me—butter, too!

THE MAIDEN TSAR

IN A CERTAIN LAND, IN a certain kingdom, there was a merchant. His wife died, and he was left with a son, Ivan. He put a tutor in charge of the son, and after a certain while he himself married another woman. When Ivan the merchant's son grew of age and was very handsome, his stepmother fell in love with him. One day Ivan the merchant's son was on a raft at sea fishing with the tutor, when suddenly they saw thirty ships sailing toward them. On these ships was sailing a maiden tsar, with thirty maidens whom she called her sisters. When the raft drew close to the ships, all thirty ships dropped anchor. Ivan the merchant's son and the tutor were invited aboard the best ship, and there the maiden tsar, accompanied by the thirty maidens she called her sisters, greeted them and told Ivan the merchant's son that she'd fallen deeply in love with him and had come to see him. They became engaged on the spot.

The maiden tsar told Ivan the merchant's son to be in the same place at the same time the following day, and she said good-bye to him and sailed off. And Ivan the merchant's son returned home, had supper, and went to bed. The stepmother summoned the tutor to her room, got him drunk, and started asking him whether anything had happened while they'd been fishing. The tutor told her everything. She listened to the end, then gave him a pin, and said, "Tomorrow, when the ships approach, stick this pin into Ivan the merchant's son's clothes." The tutor promised to carry out her order.

The next morning Ivan the merchant's son got up and went fishing. As soon as the tutor saw the ships sailing in the distance, he instantly stuck the pin in Ivan's clothes. "Ah, I'm so sleepy!" said the merchant's son. "Listen, tutor, I'll lie down and sleep a bit, and as soon as the ships come close, please wake me up." "Fine! Of course I'll wake you." The ships drew close and dropped anchor. The maiden tsar sent for Ivan the merchant's son, asking that he hurry to see her, but he was dead to the world. They started trying to get him up, shook him, poked him, but no matter what they did they couldn't wake him, and so they gave up.

The maiden tsar told the tutor to have Ivan the merchant's son come to the same place again the next day, and ordered the crew to lift anchor and set sail. As soon as the ships left, the tutor took out the pin and Ivan the merchant's son awoke, leaped to his feet, and began shouting for the maiden tsar to come back. But she was already far away and didn't hear him. He came home sad and disappointed. The stepmother led the tutor to her room, got him drunk, asked him about everything that had happened, and ordered him to stick the pin into Ivan again the following day. Next day Ivan the merchant's son went fishing, again slept through the visit, and didn't see the maiden tsar. She told the tutor that he should turn up once more.

On the third day Ivan set off fishing with the tutor. As they approached the usual place and saw the ships sailing in the distance, the tutor immediately stuck the pin in, and Ivan the merchant's son fell into a deep sleep. The ships arrived and dropped anchor. The maiden tsar sent for her fiancé, inviting him to come aboard her ship. They tried everything they could to wake him, but no matter what they did he slept on. The maiden tsar learned of the stepmother's trickery and the tutor's disloyalty, and she wrote to Ivan the merchant's son that he had to cut off the tutor's head and, if he loved his fiancée, to seek her beyond the thrice-ninth lands in the thrice-tenth kingdom.

As soon as the ship set sail and made for the open sea, the tutor took the pin out of Ivan the merchant's son's clothes and he awoke, began shouting loudly and calling to the maiden tsar, but she was far away and didn't hear him. The tutor handed him the maiden tsar's letter. Ivan the merchant's son read it, drew his sharp sword, cut off the tutor's head, made with all haste for the shore, went home, said good-bye to his father, and set off to search for the thrice-tenth kingdom.

He walked where his eyes led, for a long time or a short time, neither near nor far, for quickly can a tale be spun, but slowly is a real deed done, and he came to a hut, a hut standing in an open field, turning around on chicken legs. He entered the hut, and there found Baba Yaga the bony-legged. "Fie, fie!" she said. "There wasn't sight or sound of a Russian smell before, and now here he is. Are you here of your own free will or by force, fine youth?" "A bit of free will, and twice as much by force! Do you know the thrice-tenth kingdom, Baba Yaga?" "No, I don't!" said Yaga and told him to go to her middle sister and ask her.

Ivan the merchant's son thanked her and went on. He walked and walked, not near and not far, not a long time or a short time, and came to an identical hut. He entered and found Baba Yaga. "Fie, fie!" she said. "There wasn't sight or sound of a Russian smell before, and now here he is. Are you here of your own free will or by force, fine youth?" "A bit of free will, and twice as much by force! Do you know where to find the thrice-tenth kingdom?" "No, I don't!" replied Yaga and told him to see her younger sister, who might know. "If she gets angry at you and wants to eat you, take the three trumpets she has and ask to play them. Play the first softly, the second louder, and the third loudest of all." Ivan the merchant's son thanked Yaga and went on.

He walked and walked, for a short time or a long time, neither near nor far, and finally saw a hut standing in an open field, turning around on chicken legs. He entered and found Baba Yaga. "Fie, fie! There wasn't sight or sound of a Russian smell before, and now here he is!" said Yaga and rushed to sharpen her teeth so as to eat her uninvited guest. Ivan the merchant's son asked her for the three trumpets, and played the first softly, the second louder, and the third loudest of all. Suddenly all kinds of birds came swooping down from all directions, the firebird among them. "Sit on me quickly," said the firebird, "and we'll fly wherever you need to go, or else Baba Yaga will eat you!" No sooner had he sat on it than Baba Yaga rushed back, seized the firebird by the tail, and pulled out quite a few feathers.

The firebird flew off with Ivan the merchant's son, and for a long time it soared high in the skies, until finally it arrived at the broad sea. "Well, Ivan the merchant's son, the thrice-tenth kingdom lies beyond this sea. I'm not strong enough to carry you over to the other side. Try to get there as best you can!" Ivan the merchant's son got down from the firebird, thanked it, and went off along the shore.

He walked and walked, came upon a hut, and entered. An old, old woman greeted him, gave him food and drink, and asked where he was going, why he was journeying so far. He told her that he was going to the thrice-tenth kingdom in search of the maiden tsar, his true love. "Ah!" said the old woman. "She no longer loves you. If she catches sight of you, the maiden tsar will tear you apart. Her love is hidden far, far away!" "How can I get it?" "Wait a bit! My daughter is living at the maiden tsar's and today she promised to visit me. Maybe we can find out from her." And the old woman changed Ivan the merchant's son into a pin and stuck him in the wall. In the evening her daughter flew in. Her mother asked whether she knew where the maiden tsar's love was hidden. "I don't know," replied the daughter and promised to find out from the maiden tsar herself. Next day she flew in again and told her mother, "On the other side of the sea there's an oak, and in the oak there's a chest, and in the chest there's a hare, and in the hare there's a duck, and in the duck there's an egg, and in the egg is the maiden tsar's love!"

Ivan the merchant's son took some bread and set off for the place she'd described. He found the oak, took the chest from it, pulled the hare out of the chest, the duck out of the hare, the egg out of the duck, and returned with the egg to the old woman. It was the old woman's name day soon, and she invited the maiden tsar and her thirty maidens whom she called sisters. She baked the egg, decked Ivan the merchant's son in holiday finery, and hid him.

At noon the maiden tsar and her thirty maidens suddenly flew in, sat down at table, and started to eat dinner. After dinner the old woman gave each of them a regular egg, but gave the maiden tsar the one that Ivan the merchant's son had obtained. The maiden tsar ate it and instantly fell passionately in love with Ivan the merchant's son. The old woman led him out from his hiding place. What joy there was, what happy celebration! The maiden tsar left with her fiancé, the merchant's son, for her kingdom. They married and really started to thrive, and prospered while they were both alive.

DANILO THE LUCKLESS

IN THE CITY OF KIEV our Prince Vladimir had many servants and peasants at court, and also the nobleman Danilo the Luckless. On Sundays Vladimir would give everyone a glass of vodka, but Danilo would get only a whack or two on the back of his neck. On big holidays some would get gifts, but he'd get nothing at all! On Saturday evening before Easter Sunday Prince Vladimir summoned Danilo the Luckless, handed him forty times forty sables, and ordered him to sew a fur coat before the holiday. The sables were not skinned, the buttons not made, and the loops not braided. He was ordered to press the shapes of forest animals into the buttons and to embroider the shapes of exotic birds into the loops.

Danilo the Luckless found the work hateful, tossed it aside, went outside the city gates, and wandered aimlessly, crying. He encountered an old, old woman going in the opposite direction. "Now, Danilo, don't split your sides with those sobs! Why are you crying, Luckless?" "Ah, you empty old bag, you silly ass, all patches and tatters, with eyes like platters! Leave me alone, I'm not in the mood!" He went on a little, and thought, "Why was I so nasty to her!" And he went back to her, and said, "Granny, dear heart! Forgive me. Here's why I'm so miserable: Prince Vladimir gave me forty times forty un-skinned sables from which to make a fur coat by tomorrow morning. He wants a lot of buttons made, silk loops braided, and the buttons must have golden lions on them, and the loops must have exotic birds on them, trilling and singing! And where am I to get all this? It's easier to stand behind a counter holding a cup of vodka!"

The old woman, Patched Belly, said, "Ah, so now it's 'Granny, dear heart!' Go to the blue sea, stand by the damp oak. At exactly midnight the blue sea will swell, and Chudo-Yudo will appear, a sea monster with a gray beard, without arms and legs. Seize him by the beard and beat him until Chudo-Yudo asks, 'Why are you beating me, Danilo the Luckless?' And you answer, 'I want the beautiful Swan Maiden to appear before me, to have her body show through her feathers, her bones to show through her body, to see her marrow flow from bone to bone, like pearls being poured from cone to cone.'" Danilo the Luckless went to the blue sea, stood by the damp oak. At exactly midnight the sea swelled, and Chudo-Yudo appeared, a sea monster without arms and legs, and nothing but a gray beard! Danilo seized him by the beard and started beating him against the damp earth. Chudo-Yudo asked,

"Why are you beating me, Danilo the Luckless?" "Here's why: give me the beautiful Swan Maiden. I want her body to show through her feathers, her bones through her body, and to see her marrow flow from bone to bone, like pearls being poured from cone to cone."

In a few moments the beautiful Swan Maiden appeared, swam up to the shore, and said, "So, Danilo the Luckless, are you avoiding great deeds for fun, or are you trying to get them done?" "Ah, beautiful Swan Maiden! Sometimes I avoid, other times I try, and now I'm doubling my efforts, hoping to get by. Prince Vladimir has ordered me to make him a fur coat: the sables are not skinned, the buttons not made, the loops not braided!" "Will you take me in marriage? Then everything will be done in time!" He thought, "How can I take her in marriage?" "Well, Danilo, what do you think?" "There's nothing I can do! I'll take you!" She shook her wings, she tossed her head, and twelve sturdy men rose from the seabed. They were all carpenters, woodcutters, and masons, and they set to work immediately: a house was built in an instant! Danilo took her right hand, kissed her sweet lips, and led her to the princely chambers. They sat down at the table, ate and drank, refreshed themselves, and then and there got engaged.

"Now, Danilo, lie down and rest, don't worry about a thing! I'll get it all done."

She put him to bed, went out onto the crystal porch, shook her wings, and tossed her head. "My own dear father! Give me your craftsmen." Twelve fine fellows appeared and asked, "Beautiful Swan Maiden! What are your orders?" "Sew me a fur coat right away: the sables are not skinned, the buttons not made, the loops not braided." They set to work; some got the skins ready and did the sewing, others forged and shaped the buttons, and the rest braided the loops. In an instant a dazzling coat was made. The beautiful Swan Maiden went and awakened Danilo the Luckless. "Get up, my dear! The coat's ready and the church bells are sounding in Prince Vladimir's city of Kiev. It's time for you to get up and get ready for the morning service." Danilo got up, put on the fur coat, and left the house. She looked out of the window, stopped him, gave him a silver cane, and instructed, "As you're leaving the church, strike your chest with this: birds will start singing their song, and lions will then roar along. Take off the fur coat and without any fuss give it to Prince Vladimir, so that he won't forget about us. He'll invite you to visit and dine, and will offer a cup of wine. Don't empty the cup, though you may drink gladly, for if you empty it, things will end badly! And, above all, don't boast about me, about building a house in one night, one, two, three." Danilo look the cane and set off. She again made him come back, and gave him three eggs—two silver, one gold—and said, "Give the silver ones to the prince and princess when you offer them Easter greetings, and the gold one give to the one with whom you'll live forever."

Danilo the Luckless said good-bye to her and went to the morning service. Everyone was surprised, "What about that Danilo the Luckless! He's managed to get the fur coat ready for the holiday." After the morning service he approached the prince and princess, offered them seasonal greetings, and accidentally took out the gold egg. Alyosha Popovich, a ladies' man, saw him do it. People started leaving the church, Danilo the Luckless struck his chest with the silver cane—and the birds sang their song, and the lions roared along. And Alyosha Popovich the ladies' man disguised himself as a crippled beggar and asked for holy alms. Everyone gave him something; only Danilo the Luckless stood there, thinking, "What can I give? I don't have anything!" And because it was a great holiday, he gave him the gold egg. Alyosha Popovich the ladies' man took the gold egg and changed back into his regular clothes. Prince Vladimir invited everyone for a bite to eat. And they ate and drank, refreshed themselves, and boasted. Danilo, who had drunk enough to be drunk, in his drunkenness began to boast of his wife. Alyosha Popovich the ladies' man started to boast about knowing Danilo's wife. But Danilo said, "If you know my wife, let my head be cut off, and if you don't know her, then you should have your head cut off!"

Alyosha went off, simply following his nose. He walked and cried. He encountered an old, old lady going in the opposite direction. "Why are you crying, Alyosha Popovich?" "Leave me in peace, you empty old bag! I'm not in the mood."

"Fine, but I can be useful to you!" And he asked her, "Granny, my dear! What did you want to tell me?" "Ah, now it's 'Granny, my dear!'" "You see, I boasted that I knew Danilo's wife ..." "Phew! How on earth could you know her? Not even a tiny bird could get into her domain. Go to such and such a house, and ask her to dine at the prince's. She'll start bathing and getting ready, and will put her chain on the windowsill. Take this chain and show it to Danilo the Luckless." Alyosha Popovich went up to the wood-carved window and invited the beautiful Swan Maiden to dinner at the prince's. She started bathing, dressing, and getting ready for the feast. As she did so Alyosha Popovich took her chain and ran to the palace and showed it to Danilo the Luckless. "Well, Prince Vladimir," said Danilo the Luckless. "I now see that my head should be cut off. Let me go home and say good-bye to my wife."

He went home and said, "Ah, my beautiful Swan Maiden! What have I done! In my drunkenness I boasted about you, my wife, and now must pay for it with my life!" "I know all about it, Danilo the Luckless! Go and invite the prince and princess and all the citizens to our house. And if the prince tries to refuse, saying it's dusty and dirty, and the roads are poor, and the sea has risen and slippery swamps have appeared, you tell him, 'Never fear, Prince Vladimir! There are snowball-wood bridges and oak planks built over the swamps and over the rivers, with crimson cloth spread over the bridges, all fastened down with nails of cast iron. No dust will touch the fine fellows' boots, no mud will cling to their horses' hooves.'" Danilo the Luckless left so as to invite the guests, while the beautiful Swan Maiden went out onto the porch, shook her wings, tossed her head, and created a bridge from her house to Prince Vladimir's palace. It was covered with crimson cloth and fastened down with nails of cast iron. On one side of it flowers bloomed and nightingales sang, and on the other apples ripened and fruit trees flourished.

The prince and princess set out for the visit with all their brave warriors. They approached the first river—wonderful beer flowed in it, and many soldiers fell near it. They approached the second river—wonderful mead flowed in it, and more than half of the brave troops paid their respects to the mead and tumbled on their sides. They approached the third river—wonderful wine flowed in it, and the officers rushed to it and drank till they were drunk. They approached the fourth river—strong vodka flowed in it, kin to that very wine, and the prince glanced around and saw his generals flat on their backs. The prince remained with only three companions: his wife, Alyosha Popovich the ladies' man, and Danilo the Luckless. The guests arrived, entered the high-ceilinged chambers, and in the chambers stood maple tables covered by silken tablecloths, and painted chairs. They sat down at table—there were many various dishes, and foreign drinks not in bottles, not in jugs, but flowing in entire rivers! Prince Vladimir and the princess didn't drink anything, didn't eat, but simply looked, waiting to see when the beautiful Swan Maiden would appear.

They sat at table for a long time, for a long time they waited, until the time came to return home. Danilo the Luckless called her once, twice, three times—but she didn't come out to join the guests. Alyosha Popovich the ladies' man said, "If my wife did this, I'd teach her to listen to her husband!" The beautiful Swan Maiden heard this, came out onto the porch, and said, "And here's how I teach husbands!" She shook her wings, tossed her head, and flew off, and the guests were left in the mud on the hillocks: on one side was the sea, on another grief, on the third was moss, and on the fourth no relief! Prince, better put your pride aside, mount Danilo for your ride! By the time they reached home they were covered in mud from head to toe! I wanted to see the prince and princess, but it was hard because they chased me from the yard. I ducked beneath the gate, and whack!—I banged against it, hurt my back!

19. John Francis Campbell, *Popular Tales of the West Highlands* (1860)[1]

John Francis Campbell was a friend of George Webbe Dasent, the English translator of Asbjørnsen and Moe's collection of Norwegian tales and author of a lengthy and influential essay on the "Origin and Diffusion of Popular Tales." Campbell credited Dasent with inspiring him to collect tales of the West Highlands of his native Scotland. As both a nationalist project and a collection that sought to document oral traditions, Campbell's Popular Tales of the West Highlands, Orally Collected *is a direct heir to the legacy established by Jacob and Wilhelm Grimm. Campbell coordinated a team of fieldworkers (an enterprise he was able to fund himself), employing a team of collectors fluent in Gaelic and native to the area. Unlike his predecessors, Campbell did not promote a vision of the "anonymous folk," but instead sought to document information about the tellers of particular tales, including their names, ages, occupations, and locations; Campbell also included each tale text in both Gaelic and English. In "The Story of the White Pet," included here, one finds echoes of the Grimms' work, not only in Campbell's general claim to be representing oral narrative, but also in the tale's plot: as a story of a pack of outcast animals who manage to outwit and gain the riches of a gang of human thieves, "White Pet" recalls the Grimms' famous version of that tale type, usually referred to as "The Musicians of Bremen." In the notes following the tale, Campbell explains that Mrs. MacTavish "got this story from a young girl in her service, November 1859, who learned it [...] when she was employed in herding cattle" (199). As a story told in an agricultural setting, "The Story of the White Pet" is interesting because it valorizes and rewards farm animals, casting its human characters as villains (the farmers) and fools (the thieves).*

THE STORY OF THE WHITE PET, PERFORMED BY MRS. MACTAVISH

From Mrs. MacTavish, widow of the late minister of Kildalton, Islay

THERE WAS A FAMER BEFORE now who had a White Pet (sheep), and when Christmas was drawing near he thought that he would kill the White Pet. The White Pet heard that, and he thought he would run away; and that is what he did.

He had not gone far when a bull met him. Said the bull to him, "All hail! White Pet, where art thou going?" "I," said the White Pet, "am going to seek my fortune; they were going to kill me for Christmas, and I thought I had better run away." "It

---

1 [Source: John Francis Campbell, ed. and trans., *Popular Tales of the West Highlands*, Vol. 1 (Edinburgh: Edmonston and Douglas, 1860): 194–97.]

is better for me," said the bull, "to go with thee, for they were going to do the very same with me."

"I am willing," said the White Pet; "the larger the party the better the fun."

They went forward till they fell in with a dog.

"All hail! White Pet," said the dog. "All hail! thou dog." "Where art thou going?" said the dog.

"I am running away, for I heard that they were threatening to kill me for Christmas."

"They were going to do the very same to me," said the dog, "and I will go with you." "Come then," said the White Pet.

They went then, till a cat joined them. "All hail! White Pet," said the cat. "All hail! oh cat."

"Where art though going?" said the cat. I am going to seek my fortune," said the White Pet, "because they were going to kill me at Christmas."

"They were talking about killing me too," said the cat, "and I had better go with you."

"Come on then," said the White Pet.

Then they went forward till a cock met them, "All hail! White Pet," said the cock. "All hail to thyself! oh cock," said the White Pet. "Where," said the cock, "art thou going?" "I," said the White Pet, "am going (away), for they were threatening my death at Christmas."

"They were going to kill me at the very same time," said the cock, "and I will go with you."

"Come, then," said the White Pet.

They went forward till they fell in with a goose. "All hail! White Pet," said the goose.

"All hail to thyself! oh goose," said the White Pet. "Where art thou going?" said the goose.

"I" said the White Pet, "am running away because they were going to kill me at Christmas."

"They were going to do that to me too," said the goose, "and I will go with you."

The party went forward till the night was drawing on them, and they saw a little light far away; and though far off, they were not long getting there. When they reached the house, they said to each other that they would look in at the window to see who was in the house, and they saw thieves counting money; and the White Pet said, "Let every one of us call his own call. I will call my own call; and let the bull call his own call; let the dog call his own call; and the cat her own call; and the cock his own call; and the goose his own call." With that they gave one shout—GAIRE![1]

1 ["Gaire" is Gaelic for laugh (the noun).]

When the thieves heard the shouting that was without, they thought the mischief was there; and they fled out, and they went to a wood that was near them. When the White Pet and his company saw that the house was empty, they went in and they got the money that the thieves had been counting, and they divided it amongst themselves; and then they thought that they would settle to rest. Said the White Pet, "Where wilt thou sleep tonight, oh bull?" "I will sleep," said the bull, "behind the door where I used" (to be). "Where wilt thou sleep thyself, White Pet?" "I will sleep," said the White Pet, "in the middle of the floor where I used" (to be). "Where wilt thou sleep, oh dog?" said the White Pet. "I will sleep beside the fire where I used" (to be). "Where wilt thou sleep, oh cat?" "I will sleep," said the cat, "in the candle press, where I like to be." "Where wilt thou sleep, oh cock?" said the White Pet. "I," said the cock, "will sleep on the rafters where I used" (to be). "Where wilt thou sleep, oh goose?" "I will sleep," said the goose, "on the midden, where I was accustomed to be."

They were not long settled to rest, when one of the thieves returned to look in to see if he could perceive if anyone at all was in the house. All things were still, and he went on forward to the candle press for a candle, that he might kindle to make him a light but when he put his hand in the box the cat thrust her claws into his hand, but he took a candle with him, and he tried to light it. Then the dog got up, and he stuck his tail into a pot of water that was beside the fire; he shook his tail and put out the candle. Then the thief thought that the mischief was in the house, and he fled; but when he was passing the White Pet, he gave him a blow; before he got past the bull, he gave him a kick; and the cock began to crow; and when he went out, the goose began to belabour him with his wings about the shanks.

He went to the wood where his comrades were, as fast as was in his legs. They asked him how it had gone with him. "It went," said he, "but middling; when I went to the candle press, there was a man in it who thrust ten knives into my hand; and when I went to the fireside to light the candle, there was a big black man lying there, who was sprinkling water on it to put it out; and when I tried to go out, there was a big man in the middle of the floor, who gave me a shove; and another man behind the door who pushed me out; and there was a little brat on the loft calling out CUIR-A-NEES-AN-SHAW-AY-S-FONI-MI-HAYN-DA—Send him up here and I'll do for him; and there was a GREE-AS-ICH-E, shoemaker, out on the midden belabouring me about the shanks with his apron."

When the thieves heard that, they did not return to seek their lot of money; and the White Pet and his comrades got it to themselves; and it kept them peaceably as long as they lived.

20. Christina Rossetti, *Goblin Market and Other Poems* (1862)[1]

Goblin Market and Other Poems *is considered the first book of Pre-Raphaelite poetry to achieve popular success. Christina Rossetti grew up in the circle of artists known as the Pre-Raphaelites, so named for their desire to reform nineteenth-century art by infusing it with the medieval mysticism that had been lost to the Classical ideals of Raphael in art history. Her brother, Dante Gabriel Rossetti, was a founding member of their "Brotherhood," in which she participated. The word brotherhood implies something of Rossetti's exceptional status in this group as a woman writer. Her popularity in the 1860s also made her the most widely read female poet of her day. Critics describe the settings of Rossetti's poems as dreamscapes: perhaps spiritual, perhaps psychological, but always magical. Her particular interest in goblins and fairies owes something to the mid-century European fascination with myth, legend, and tale encouraged in part by the Grimms and Andersen, and in part by early Romanticism and its emphasis on subterranean worlds. Many consider "Goblin Market" Rossetti's best work. It is certainly one of the most complex, both technically and thematically. On the one hand, it exhibits a formal tension between idealism and sensuality, where the pleasing abundance of the fruit (berries, berries, and more berries) is contrasted to Laura's wild sucking on its addictive juice. On the other hand, the story resists simple reduction to parable (as a story about temptation and the triumph of good over evil) or psychological portrait (of a fractured psyche that becomes whole). While the story responds to these readings, it offers much more, particularly in the way it ends with the transformation of the sisters' youthful experiences into a tale about sisterhood, told to their own children.*

GOBLIN MARKET

Morning and evening
Maids heard the goblins cry:
"Come buy our orchard fruits,
Come buy, come buy:
Apples and quinces,
Lemons and oranges,
Plump unpecked cherries,
Melons and raspberries,
Bloom-down-cheeked peaches,
Swart-headed mulberries,
Wild free-born cranberries,

1 [Source: Christina Rosetti, *Goblin Market and Other Poems*, 2nd ed. (London: Macmillan, 1865), 1–30.]

Crab-apples, dewberries,
Pine-apples, blackberries,
Apricots, strawberries;—
All ripe together
In summer weather,—
Morns that pass by,
Fair eves that fly;
Come buy, come buy;
Our grapes fresh from the vine,
Pomegranates full and fine,
Dates and sharp bullaces,
Rare pears and greengages,
Damsons and bilberries,
Taste them and try:
Currants and gooseberries,
Bright-fire-like barberries,
Figs to fill your mouth,
Citrons from the South,
Sweet to tongue and sound to eye,
Come buy, come buy."

Evening by evening
Among the brookside rushes,
Laura bowed her head to hear,
Lizzie veiled her blushes:
Crouching close together
In the cooling weather,
With clasping arms and cautioning lips,
With tingling cheeks and finger-tips.
"Lie close," Laura said,
Pricking up her golden head:
"We must not look at goblin men,
We must not buy their fruits:
Who knows upon what soil they fed
Their hungry thirsty roots?"
"Come buy," call the goblins
Hobbling down the glen.
"O!" cried Lizzie, "Laura, Laura,
You should not peep at goblin men."

Lizzie covered up her eyes
Covered close lest they should look;
Laura reared her glossy head,
And whispered like the restless brook:
"Look, Lizzie, look, Lizzie,
Down the glen tramp little men.
One hauls a basket,
One bears a plate,
One lugs a golden dish
Of many pounds' weight.
How fair the vine must grow
Whose grapes are so luscious;
How warm the wind must blow
Through those fruit bushes."
"No," said Lizzie, "no, no, no;
Their offers should not charm us,
Their evil gifts would harm us."
She thrust a dimpled finger
In each ear, shut eyes and ran:
Curious Laura chose to linger
Wondering at each merchant man.
One had a cat's face,
One whisked a tail,
One tramped at a rat's pace,
One crawled like a snail,
One like a wombat prowled obtuse and furry,
One like a ratel[1] tumbled hurry-scurry.
Lizzie heard a voice like voice of doves
Cooing all together:
They sounded kind and full of loves
In the pleasant weather.

Laura stretched her gleaming neck
Like a rush-imbedded swan,
Like a lily from the beck,
Like a moonlit poplar branch,
Like a vessel at the launch
When its last restraint is gone.

---

1 [A honey badger.]

Backwards up the mossy glen
Turned and trooped the goblin men,
With their shrill repeated cry,
"Come buy, come buy."
When they reached where Laura was
They stood stock still upon the moss,
Leering at each other,
Brother with queer brother;
Signalling each other,
Brother with sly brother.
One set his basket down,
One reared his plate;
One began to weave a crown
Of tendrils, leaves, and rough nuts brown
(Men sell not such in any town);
One heaved the golden weight
Of dish and fruit to offer her:
"Come buy, come buy," was still their cry.
Laura stared but did not stir,
Longed but had no money:
The whisk-tailed merchant bade her taste
In tones as smooth as honey,
The cat-faced purr'd,
The rat-paced spoke a word
Of welcome, and the snail-paced even was heard;
One parrot-voiced and jolly
Cried "Pretty Goblin" still for "Pretty Polly";
One whistled like a bird.

But sweet-tooth Laura spoke in haste:
"Good folk, I have no coin;
To take were to purloin:
I have no copper in my purse,
I have no silver either,
And all my gold is on the furze
That shakes in windy weather
Above the rusty heather."
"You have much gold upon your head,"
They answered altogether:

"Buy from us with a golden curl."
She clipped a precious golden lock,
She dropped a tear more rare than pearl,
Then sucked their fruit globes fair or red:
Sweeter than honey from the rock,
Stronger than man-rejoicing wine,
Clearer than water flowed that juice;
She never tasted such before,
How should it cloy with length of use?
She sucked and sucked and sucked the more
Fruits which that unknown orchard bore,
She sucked until her lips were sore;
Then flung the emptied rinds away,
But gathered up one kernel stone,
And knew not was it night or day
As she turned home alone.

Lizzie met her at the gate
Full of wise upbraidings:
"Dear, you should not stay so late,
Twilight is not good for maidens;
Should not loiter in the glen
In the haunts of goblin men.
Do you not remember Jeanie,
How she met them in the moonlight,
Took their gifts both choice and many,
Ate their fruits and wore their flowers
Plucked from bowers
Where summer ripens at all hours?
But ever in the moonlight
She pined and pined away;
Sought them by night and day,
Found them no more, but dwindled and grew gray;
Then fell with the first snow,
While to this day no grass will grow
Where she lies low:
I planted daisies there a year ago
That never blow.
You should not loiter so."
"Nay hush," said Laura:

"Nay hush, my sister:
I ate and ate my fill,
Yet my mouth waters still;
Tomorrow night I will
Buy more": and kissed her:
"Have done with sorrow;
I'll bring you plums tomorrow
Fresh on their mother twigs,
Cherries worth getting;
You cannot think what figs
My teeth have met in,
What melons, icy-cold
Piled on a dish of gold
Too huge for me to hold,
What peaches with a velvet nap,
Pellucid grapes without one seed:
Odorous indeed must be the mead
Whereon they grow, and pure the wave they drink,
With lilies at the brink,
And sugar-sweet their sap."

Golden head by golden head,
Like two pigeons in one nest
Folded in each other's wings,
They lay down, in their curtained bed:
Like two blossoms on one stem,
Like two flakes of new-fall'n snow,
Like two wands of ivory
Tipped with gold for awful kings.
Moon and stars beamed in at them,
Wind sang to them lullaby,
Lumbering owls forbore to fly,
Not a bat flapped to and fro
Round their rest:
Cheek to cheek and breast to breast
Locked together in one nest.

Early in the morning
When the first cock crowed his warning,
Neat like bees, as sweet and busy,

Laura rose with Lizzie:
Fetched in honey, milked the cows,
Aired and set to rights the house,
Kneaded cakes of whitest wheat,
Cakes for dainty mouths to eat,
Next churned butter, whipped up cream,
Fed their poultry, sat and sewed;
Talked as modest maidens should
Lizzie with an open heart,
Laura in an absent dream,
One content, one sick in part;
One warbling for the mere bright day's delight,
One longing for the night.

At length slow evening came:
They went with pitchers to the reedy brook;
Lizzie most placid in her look,
Laura most like a leaping flame.
They drew the gurgling water from its deep;
Lizzie plucked purple and rich golden flags,
Then turning homeward said: "The sunset flushes
Those furthest loftiest crags;
Come, Laura, not another maiden lags,
No wilful squirrel wags,
The beasts and birds are fast asleep."
But Laura loitered still among the rushes
And said the bank was steep.
And said the hour was early still,
The dew not fallen, the wind not chill:
Listening ever, but not catching
The customary cry,
"Come buy, come buy,"
With its iterated jingle
Of sugar-baited words:
Not for all her watching
Once discerning even one goblin
Racing, whisking, tumbling, hobbling;
Let alone the herds
That used to tramp along the glen,

In groups or single,
Of brisk fruit-merchant men.

Till Lizzie urged, "O Laura, come,
I hear the fruit-call, but I dare not look:
You should not loiter longer at this brook:
Come with me home.
The stars rise, the moon bends her arc,
Each glowworm winks her spark,
Let us get home before the night grows dark;
For clouds may gather
Though this is summer weather,
Put out the lights and drench us through;
Then if we lost our way what should we do?"

Laura turned cold as stone
To find her sister heard that cry alone,
That goblin cry,
"Come buy our fruits, come buy."
Must she then buy no more such dainty fruits?
Must she no more such succous[1] pasture find,
Gone deaf and blind?
Her tree of life drooped from the root:
She said not one word in her heart's sore ache;
But peering thro' the dimness, naught discerning,
Trudged home, her pitcher dripping all the way;
So crept to bed, and lay
Silent till Lizzie slept;
Then sat up in a passionate yearning,
And gnashed her teeth for balked desire, and wept
As if her heart would break.

Day after day, night after night,
Laura kept watch in vain,
In sullen silence of exceeding pain.
She never caught again the goblin cry:
"Come buy, come buy,"
She never spied the goblin men

1 [Juicy or succulent.]

Hawking their fruits along the glen:
But when the noon waxed bright
Her hair grew thin and gray;
She dwindled, as the fair full moon doth turn
To swift decay, and burn
Her fire away.

One day remembering her kernel-stone
She set it by a wall that faced the south;
Dewed it with tears, hoped for a root,
Watched for a waxing shoot,
But there came none;
It never saw the sun,
It never felt the trickling moisture run:
While with sunk eyes and faded mouth
She dreamed of melons, as a traveller sees
False waves in desert drouth
With shade of leaf-crowned trees,
And burns the thirstier in the sandful breeze.

She no more swept the house,
Tended the fowls or cows,
Fetched honey, kneaded cakes of wheat,
Brought water from the brook:
But sat down listless in the chimney-nook
And would not eat.

Tender Lizzie could not bear
To watch her sister's cankerous care,
Yet not to share.
She night and morning
Caught the goblins' cry:
"Come buy our orchard fruits,
Come buy, come buy":—
Beside the brook, along the glen,
She heard the tramp of goblin men,
The voice and stir
Poor Laura could not hear;
Longed to buy fruit to comfort her,

But feared to pay too dear,
She thought of Jeanie in her grave,
Who should have been a bride;
But who for joys brides hope to have
Fell sick and died
In her gay prime,
In earliest Winter time,
With the first glazing rime,
With the first snow-fall of crisp Winter time.

Till Laura, dwindling,
Seemed knocking at Death's door:
Then Lizzie weighed no more
Better and worse;
But put a silver penny in her purse,
Kissed Laura, crossed the heath with clumps of furze
At twilight, halted by the brook,
And for the first time in her life
Began to listen and look.

Laughed every goblin
When they spied her peeping:
Came towards her hobbling,
Flying, running, leaping,
Puffing and blowing,
Chuckling, clapping, crowing,
Clucking and gobbling,
Mopping and mowing,
Full of airs and graces,
Pulling wry faces,
Demure grimaces,
Cat-like and rat-like,
Ratel and wombat-like,
Snail-paced in a hurry,
Parrot-voiced and whistler,
Helter-skelter, hurry-skurry,
Chattering like magpies,
Fluttering like pigeons,
Gliding like fishes,—

Hugged her and kissed her:
Squeezed and caressed her:
Stretched up their dishes,
Panniers and plates:
"Look at our apples
Russet and dun,
Bob at our cherries
Bite at our peaches,
Citrons and dates,
Grapes for the asking,
Pears red with basking
Out in the sun,
Plums on their twigs;
Pluck them and suck them,
Pomegranates, figs."—

"Good folk," said Lizzie,
Mindful of Jeanie:
"Give me much and many":—
Held out her apron,
Tossed them her penny.
"Nay, take a seat with us,
Honor and eat with us,"
They answered grinning:
"Our feast is but beginning.
Night yet is early,
Warm and dew-pearly,
Wakeful and starry:
Such fruits as these
No man can carry;
Half their bloom would fly,
Half their dew would dry,
Half their flavor would pass by.
Sit down and feast with us,
Be welcome guest with us,
Cheer you and rest with us."—
"Thank you," said Lizzie: "but one waits
At home alone for me:
So, without further parleying,
If you will not sell me any

Of your fruits though much and many,
Give me back my silver penny
I tossed you for a fee."—
They began to scratch their pates,
No longer wagging, purring,
But visibly demurring,
Grunting and snarling.
One called her proud,
Cross-grained, uncivil;
Their tones waxed loud,
Their looks were evil.
Lashing their tails
They trod and hustled her,
Elbowed and jostled her,
Clawed with their nails,
Barking, mewing, hissing, mocking,
Tore her gown and soiled her stocking,
Twitched her hair out by the roots,
Stamped upon her tender feet,
Held her hands and squeezed their fruits
Against her mouth to make her eat.

White and golden Lizzie stood,
Like a lily in a flood,—
Like a rock of blue-veined stone
Lashed by tides obstreperously,—
Like a beacon left alone
In a hoary roaring sea,
Sending up a golden fire,—
Like a fruit-crowned orange-tree
White with blossoms honey-sweet
Sore beset by wasp and bee,—
Like a royal virgin town
Topped with gilded dome and spire
Close beleaguered by a fleet
Mad to tear her standard down.

One may lead a horse to water,
Twenty cannot make him drink.
Though the goblins cuffed and caught her,

Coaxed and fought her,
Bullied and besought her,
Scratched her, pinched her black as ink,
Kicked and knocked her,
Mauled and mocked her,
Lizzie uttered not a word;
Would not open lip from lip
Lest they should cram a mouthful in:
But laughed in heart to feel the drip
Of juice that syrupped all her face,
And lodged in dimples of her chin,
And streaked her neck which quaked like curd.
At last the evil people,
Worn out by her resistance,
Flung back her penny, kicked their fruit
Along whichever road they took,
Not leaving root or stone or shoot;
Some writhed into the ground,
Some dived into the brook
With ring and ripple,
Some scudded on the gale without a sound,
Some vanished in the distance.

In a smart, ache, tingle,
Lizzie went her way;
Knew not was it night or day;
Sprang up the bank, tore through the furze,
Threaded copse and dingle,
And heard her penny jingle
Bouncing in her purse,—
Its bounce was music to her ear.
She ran and ran
As if she feared some goblin man
Dogged her with gibe or curse
Or something worse:
But not one goblin skurried after,
Nor was she pricked by fear;
The kind heart made her windy-paced
That urged her home quite out of breath with haste
And inward laughter.

She cried "Laura," up the garden,
"Did you miss me?
Come and kiss me.
Never mind my bruises,
Hug me, kiss me, suck my juices
Squeezed from goblin fruits for you,
Goblin pulp and goblin dew.
Eat me, drink me, love me;
Laura, make much of me:
For your sake I have braved the glen
And had to do with goblin merchant men."

Laura started from her chair,
Flung her arms up in the air,
Clutched her hair:
"Lizzie, Lizzie, have you tasted
For my sake the fruit forbidden?
Must your light like mine be hidden,
Your young life like mine be wasted,
Undone in mine undoing,
And ruined in my ruin,
Thirsty, cankered, goblin-ridden?"—
She clung about her sister,
Kissed and kissed and kissed her:
Tears once again
Refreshed her shrunken eyes,
Dropping like rain
After long sultry drouth;
Shaking with anguish, fear, and pain,
She kissed and kissed her with a hungry mouth.

Her lips began to scorch,
That juice was wormwood to her tongue,
She loathed the feast:
Writhing as one possessed she leaped and sung,
Rent all her robe, and wrung
Her hands in lamentable haste,
And beat her breast.
Her locks streamed like the torch
Borne by a racer at full speed,

Or like the mane of horses in their flight,
Or like an eagle when she stems the light
Straight toward the sun,
Or like a caged thing freed,
Or like a flying flag when armies run.
Swift fire spread through her veins, knocked at her heart,
Met the fire smouldering there
And overbore its lesser flame;
She gorged on bitterness without a name:
Ah! fool, to choose such part
Of soul-consuming care!
Sense failed in the mortal strife:
Like the watch-tower of a town
Which an earthquake shatters down,
Like a lightning-stricken mast,
Like a wind-uprooted tree
Spun about,
Like a foam-topped water-spout
Cast down headlong in the sea,
She fell at last;
Pleasure past and anguish past,
Is it death or is it life?

Life out of death.
That night long Lizzie watched by her,
Counted her pulse's flagging stir,
Felt for her breath,
Held water to her lips, and cooled her face
With tears and fanning leaves:
But when the first birds chirped about their eaves,
And early reapers plodded to the place
Of golden sheaves,
And dew-wet grass
Bowed in the morning winds so brisk to pass,
And new buds with new day
Opened of cup-like lilies on the stream,
Laura awoke as from a dream,
Laughed in the innocent old way,
Hugged Lizzie but not twice or thrice;

Her gleaming locks showed not one thread of gray,
Her breath was sweet as May
And light danced in her eyes.

Days, weeks, months, years
Afterwards, when both were wives
With children of their own;
Their mother-hearts beset with fears,
Their lives bound up in tender lives;
Laura would call the little ones
And tell them of her early prime,
Those pleasant days long gone
Of not-returning time:
Would talk about the haunted glen,
The wicked, quaint fruit-merchant men,
Their fruits like honey to the throat,
But poison in the blood;
(Men sell not such in any town):
Would tell them how her sister stood
In deadly peril to do her good,
And win the fiery antidote:
Then joining hands to little hands
Would bid them cling together,
"For there is no friend like a sister,
In calm or stormy weather,
To cheer one on the tedious way,
To fetch one if one goes astray,
To lift one if one totters down,
To strengthen whilst one stands."

21. Anne Thackeray Ritchie, *Bluebeard's Keys and Other Stories* (1874)[1]

Anne Thackeray Ritchie found fame early when she published her first novel, The Story of Elizabeth, *in 1862 at the age of 25. By that time, she had already been steeped in the world of Victorian letters. The oldest daughter of novelist William Thackeray, she grew up around literati and came to know many of the luminaries of mid-century English literature, including Elizabeth Barrett, Alfred Lord Tennyson, and George Eliot. Her engagement with literary history was rich and varied, and included essays on major women writers (including Jane Austen) published under the title* Book of Sibyls *(1883), memoires, biographical prefaces to her father's work, and an important introduction to an 1892 collection of Madame d'Aulnoy's fairy tales in English (one of which is reprinted in this volume, see above, p. 188). The decade immediately preceding the publication of* Bluebeard's Keys *(1874) marks a period of intense focus on fairy tales in Thackeray Ritchie's career. Between 1866 and 1874, she published rewritings of what had by then become classic stories: "Little Red Riding Hood," "Cinderella," and "Beauty and the Beast," among others. These efforts culminated in her novella "Bluebeard's Keys," which appeared together with "Riquet à la Houppe" "Jack and the Beanstalk," and "The White Cat." In the 1874 volume, each rewrite begins with a verse poem called "Argument" in which Thackeray Ritchie retells the main twists and turns of the well-known version of the story. These arguments become a foil for her transposition of the older version into a Roman villa with neo-classical garden architecture and her total transformation of the plot into a chaptered novella. "Bluebeard's Keys" immediately shifts the focus from the man onto the object of curiosity, temptation, and secrecy in the narrative: the keys. The story of Fanny incorporates themes drawn from Cinderella, Greek mythology, and mystical Catholicism that together create an ominous atmosphere made tangible for the reader in sensual details such as the click of Fanny's heels on the silent, luxurious marble floor as she surveys the Marchioness's palace. Critics note the subversive elements of this Bluebeard read against Perrault's seventeenth-century version, which comes at least in part from the intimate relationship we build through the course of the chapters with the protagonist and, by extension, her fate.*

BLUEBEARD'S KEYS (EXCERPT)

Argument

Bluebeard spoke to his wife in tones of tender affection:
"Barbara, take these keys: thine husband goes on a journey,
"Such a necessity drives me to go; unwilling I leave thee;

1 [Source: Anne Thackeray Ritchie, *Bluebeard's Keys and Other Stories* (London: Smith, Elder & Co, 1874): 1–21.]

"Be thou keeper of all while Bluebeard mourns in his absence:
"All these household keys, one golden—key of a chamber
"Into the which thou mayst not look, since evil awaits her,
"Curious, who shall look: so Barbara leave it unopened."
Bluebeard parted.—At once her friends rushed all thro' the castle,
Into the chambers peered, tossed shawls and laces about them,
Saw great piles of gold, gold suits of wonderful armour,
Helmets, velvets, silks, gems, bracelets, necklaces, ermine,
Gaudy brocades, and silver spears, and gorgeous hauberks.
Meanwhile that gold key grew warm in her ivory fingers;
Ah, what vast ill on earth is caused by curious wifehood!
Quickly she leapt as a hunted deer through gallery windings
Straight to the chamber door: unlocked it, saw thro' the doorway
Nine fair wives in a heap of helpless de-capitation.
(These had Bluebeard slain for spying into the chamber.)
Seized with affright she shrieked, and falling fainted in horror:
Far from her hand in among those headless, beautiful Houris[1]
Glided, alas! the glitt'ring key: but Barbara bending
Picked it in anguish up: ran forth and carefully wiped it,
Stained as it was with a mark of murder, a horrible gore-spot;
Gore unwipable, gore unwashable, not to be cleansed.
Hearken! a noise in the hall, the strong portcullis ascending!
Bluebeard strode to his bride, and kissed his Barbara fiercely,
Thundering, "Where's my key?" but waiting long for an answer.
His blue beard grew dark and writhed in an indigo blackness;
Barbara turned very pale, and all red again in an instant,
Handed him his strange key. He roaring, "Here is a gore-spot,
"Gore unwipable, gore unwashable, not to be cleansed,
"Gore of my late wives' hearts: die thou too, Barbara—join them,"
Straight strode out for a sword. She called upon Anna her sister,
"Anna, my sister, go up to the tower, and scream for assistance:
"Come brothers, oh, come quick, bring swords and smite and avenge us!"
Anna returned with streaming eyes and woefully sighing,
"Fie upon all that long, bare highway, no man approaches";
So they wept and knelt and prayed for a speedy deliv'rance:
"Come brother Osman, come brother Alee, come to the rescue."
All in a wink those two, like wild cats, sprang thro' the casement,
Caught Bluebeard by the beard, and dyed it a dolorous crimson,

---

1 [Virgin nymphs that dwell in paradise in the Qur'an. By extension it refers to voluptuous beauty. Both meanings are invoked here because these beauties are dead.]

Making his head two halves. Then … Barbara dropped 'em a curtsey,
Clapped her white little hands with a laugh, and whirled pirouetting.—
Thus doth a vengeful Fate o'ertake all human oppressors.

Chapter I. Fanny's Work-Basket

Old keys have always had a strange interest for me. There are many places where they may be found, hidden away, or openly put up for sale. They are of every size and substance. There are dream keys and real ones. We have most of us crossed the shadow of the great keys of St. Peter's. We have heard of the key of the street, a dismal possession. Some of us have held the key of the mystery that puzzled us so long. There is the key of a heart's secret, too (for hearts come into the world, some locked, some flapping wide; and day by day the keys are forged that are to open them, or close them up forever); and the key of the cupboard, where the skeleton is hidden—and, besides all these ghost keys, there are the real keys in the iron, and if they belong to dreamland, it is by association only. You may see them rusting in any old second-hand dealer's shop among cracked china and worm-eaten furniture, and faded stuff and torn lace. You may buy them for a few pence to dream over, to jingle, to melt away: to do anything with but to lock and unlock the doors and caskets to which they once belonged. Here is the key of the old house that was burnt down long ago, and the key of the spinet, where such sweet music lived and streamed out at the touch of the ladies' white fingers. The music is circling still in distant realms, philosophers tell us; the lady is dead; the spinet, too, has vanished, but here is the key! It means nothing now—no more does the key of the casket where the letters used to be locked away, that were afterwards published for a certain sum of money; or the key of the empty cellar where the good wine was once kept, or the ring of old keys in a heap in a work-basket once....

Some one had picked them up and put them away there. These happened to be the keys of a home once warm with firelight and sunlight and loving looks. The sun still shone upon the walls, the fires still burnt upon the hearth, but the home was cold, for all the hot summer's sun, and the love seemed turned to dry tears and bitter salt. The keys lie in the work-basket, covered over with many shreds of tangled silk, with half-finished tattings and trimmings, with half-strung beads, scraps of rhyme jotted down on stray fly-leaves, or card-bobbins; a half-finished fillet of a silken purse; a Roman medal and a ribbon; a flower stitched on a great big bit of canvas, large enough for a whole parterre of flowers; some rosewater in an eastern bottle; some charms; and underneath everything the keys in a bunch. Did the owner lose them among the enemonies[1] of the Borghese gardens? Did not the lady of the

1 [Early spelling of anemone.]

work-basket spy them shining in the grass, and bring them safe away to the silken nest where they have been lying for many a day? Sometimes two soft brown hands come feeling at the half-open basket, pulling but long threads of coloured silk from the tangle: they are Fanny Travers' curious little hands, with gentle quick fingers. The work-basket stands in a recess, where all day long Fanny Travers' bird has been chirping, piping, whistling in a cage, hanging high up above the great city, from a window cut deep in the thickness of the palace wall.

The red frill of an old damask curtain catches the light, the shutters are closed, in bars of grey and gloom against the outside burning sun. In the window a couple of plants are growing: they stand on the stone ledge, dark against the chequered light and shade. A worn marble step leads up into the recess, where old Olympia has put ready a bit of carpet and two straw chairs for Fanny and her sister, who sometimes come and sit there, Roman fashion, resting their arms on the stone ledge, in the cool of the evening, looking out across tiles and countless casements and grey house-tops; across walled gardens and stone-yards, beyond the spires and domes of the great city to the great dome of all, that rises like a cloud against the Campagna and the distant hills: the flowing plash of a fountain sounds from below, so does the placid chip of the stone-workers under their trellis of vine, and a drone of church-bells from the distant outer world, bells that jangle like those Irish Sunday bells that Fanny and her sister can remember when they were little girls at home at Barrowbank, near Ballymoran Green. Now they are grown up young ladies, while these Italian chimes come echoing along the sunny sloping streets and broad places and stone-yards and garden-walls that lead to the old palace on the hill. Their window is high up in the palace; they live with their mother and old Olympia in a small side wing, to which they climb by a marble staircase leading from the great landing. Sometimes Fanny and her sister, seeing the doors ajar down below, peep in at a lofty marble hall where veiled statues seem to keep watch; everything is cool and dark and silent, though all day long the burning sun has been beating outside against the marble rocks of the old palace.

Fanny and her sister sit in a vaulted room with windows towards the front—windows that you could scarcely distinguish from the piazza, so hidden are they among the marble wreaths and columns which ornament the old palace, if it were not for the birdcage and for Anne's tall lily-pots flowering in the sun—the two girls' heads are bending over their work. They are busy with harmless magic, weaving themselves into elegant young ladies out of muslin shreds and scraps and frills. The little impetuous Fanny cuts and snips and runs along the endless breadths of tarlatan; Anne stitches on more demurely. The elegant young ladies who will come floating into the ball-room in their mother's train that evening are sitting at work in little shabby white morning-gowns. Their evening's magnificence is concocted of very simple materials—muslins washed and ironed by their own hands, ribbons turned and re-turned. Once, poor Anne, having nothing else at hand, trimmed her old dress with bunches of parsley....

Anne Travers was a sweet young creature. Fanny was very pretty, but not to compare to her; she was smaller, darker, more marked in feature: she looked like a bad photograph of her beautiful elder sister.

Nature is very perverse. She will give to one sister one hair's breadth more nose, that makes all the difference, one inch more height, one semitone more voice, one grain more colouring. Here was Anne, with beautiful dark eyes and beautiful black hair, lovely smiles, picturesque frowns, smooth gliding movements, and a voice that haunted you long after it had ceased to utter; and there was Fanny, stitching away on the marble step, surrounded by white scraps, and with black hair on end, and smaller eyes, shorter limbs, paler cheeks. She was nothing particular, most people said; not beloved, like Anne; she did not hope for much to brighten her toilsome life; she despaired and lost her temper at times; and yet there was a spirit and pathos of impetuosity about the little woman, that, so one person once said, outweighed all the suave charm of her sister's grace. Everyone loved Anne, she was so soft, so easily pleased, and so sure of pleasing. The life she led was not a wholesome one, but it did not spoil her. The twopenny cares that brought the purple to her mother's hair, and the sulky frown to Fanny's brow, only softened Anne's eyes to a gentle melancholy.

Poor little Fanny! how she hated the stealings and scrapings of fashionable life that fell to their share—the lifts in other people's carriages, the contrivances and mortifications. "Mamma, what *is* the good of it all?" she would say. "Let us go and live in a cottage, and Anne shall stand by the fountain and sell roses and violets."

Mrs. de Travers had not much humour for an Irishwoman.

"No children of mine, with my consent, shall ever give up appearances," she said, testily. "Is this the language, Fanny, you use after the many many sacrifices I have made? If Lord Tortillion had behaved as common decency might have suggested, we should have been spared all this. But his conduct shall make no difference in ours; and we will do our duty in our state of life."

Lord Tortillion was Fanny and Anne's grandfather, a stern Orangeman, who happening to hear of his son's marriage and conversion to Catholicism immediately cut off the young man's allowance. When Mr. de Travers died, he left his widow and daughters the price of his commission and an insurance on his life, which, with a small inheritance of Anne's, gave them something to live upon. The widow struggled valiantly on this slender raft to keep up her head in the fashionable whirlpool, to which she had been promoted by marriage. She acted honestly according to her lights. She thought it was her duty for her children's sake, and she worked away without ever asking herself to what it all tended.

People's duties are among the most curious things belonging to them. The South Kensington Museum might exhibit a collection of them. They are all-important to each of us, though others would be puzzled enough to say what they mean, or what good they are to anyone else. There might be glass cases with catalogued specimens of disciplines, of hair-shirts, and boiled fish, for some; then for others a sort of social Jacob's ladder, with one foot on earth and the other in Belgrave Square, to be clambered only by much pains, by vigils, by mortifications, by strainings and clutchings, and presence of mind. Some people feel that a good dinner is their solemn vocation; others try for poor soup, cheap flannel, and parochial importance; some feel that theirs is a mission to preach disagreeable truths; while others have a vocation for agreeable quibbles; there are also divisions, and sermons, and letters, and protests; some of us wish to improve ourselves, others prefer improving their neighbours. Mrs. de Travers had no particular ambition for herself, poor soul! She was a lazy woman, and would have contentedly dozed away the quiet evenings by the smouldering log, but a demon of duty came flitting up the palace stairs. "Get up," it whispered to her, "get up, put on your wedding-garment" (it was a shabby old purple dyed satin that had once been bought in hopes of an invitation to Tourniquet Castle); "never mind the draught, never mind the pain in your shoulder," says duty, "send old Olympia for a hack-cab, shiver down the long marble flight and be off, or Lady Castleairs won't ask you again." Can one blame the poor shivering martyr as she enters Lady Castleairs' drawing-room, followed by her two votive maidens? Anne took things placidly, accepted kindness and patronage with a certain sweet dignity that held its own; but poor little Fanny chafed and fumed, and frowned at the contrivances and scrapings and disputings of their makeshift existence. How she longed sometimes to forget the price of earth, air, fire, and water, of fish, flesh, and fowl. She would have liked silver pieces to give to the pretty little black-pated children who come running and dancing along the sunny streets, and peeping out of darkened doorways. She would have liked to buy the great bunches of roses that the girl with the sweet beseeching eyes would hold up to her by the fountain in the street below: great pale pink heads and white sprays flowering; and golden and yellow buds among leaves of darkest emerald, with purple and shining stems. But it was no use wishing; even roses mean money: it is only thistles and briers that we may gather for nothing.

So Fanny and Anne stitch on in the darkened room, while Olympia glides about in the passage outside, and Mrs. de Travers dozes in a birdcage-like little boudoir opening out of the sitting-room, among many quaint splendours fading away, mirrors with dim garlands painted on their surfaces, reflecting poor Mrs. de Travers' nodding head, she seems all crowned with roses and emblems of delight; also lyre-backed chairs, little miniatures hanging to faded ribbons, and hooks in the trellis wall, and an old tapestry carpet with Rebecca at the well and brown straggling camels coming up to drink. All is quite hot and silent: Mrs. de Travers snores loudly.

"Come, Nancy," says Fanny, in the outer room, "let us go for a turn in the garden."

"My head aches," says Anne; "I should like it. I suppose there will be time to finish our work."

"Everything is so tiresome," says Fanny, impetuously, "and I hate Lady Castleairs. O dear, how I wish,—I wish I was enormously rich."

Chapter II. The Terrace Opposite the Church

A closed gateway led to the old palace garden. The girls boldly jangled the cracked bell for admittance, and one of the gardeners came down the steps of a terrace, and unlocked the bars and let them in. This was old Angelo, who was not only head-gardener, but porter and keeper of the palace. He looked very portentous, and his nose was redder than usual. "They had received the news that his Highness the Marquis was expected," he said, "and after today he could no longer admit the young ladies to delight themselves in the grounds. 'When the master comes,'" said he, quoting an old Italian proverb, "'the keys turn in the lock.'"

"But he won't eat us up," says Fanny, pertly.

Old Angelo smiled as he shook his head.

"No," he said; "and yet the Lady Marchioness was as young and as pretty as you." Then he hastily added, "Now I will tell the men to put a *sgabella* for the young ladies in the shade."

The girls gratefully accepted, though they did not in the least know what he meant by a *sgabella*. It was a low wooden bench, which the under-gardener placed under the Spanish chestnut tree at the end of the avenue, just opposite the little rocky fountain. An Apollo stood over the fountain, with one arm outstretched against the blue waterfalls; green, close-creeping wreaths fell over the rocks; also many violets and ferns sprouting spring-like, and the iris stems of a few faint yellow flowers starting from the side of an old stone, and then a little wind stirs the many branches....

"This is nicer than that endless tucking," says Fanny. "I wish one's dresses grew like leaves and flowers."

"But what should we wear in winter?" says Anne, looking about. "Hush! what is that?"

"That" was a strange soft commotion in the air—a flapping, crooning murmur, and two doves, flying white through the sunshine, alighted by the rocky fountain, and began to drink. But Fanny jumped up to admire, and though she was no very terrible personage, the doves flew away.

"Silly creatures!" says Fanny, throwing a chestnut-leaf after them.

Then she started off, and went to walk on the terrace, from whence she could see the people in the street.

Anne followed slowly. How sweet and bright the fountain flowed! How quietly the shadows shook in time to the triumphal burst of spring light. Over the wall of the garden she caught sight of an ancient church front; rows of oleanders stood upon the terrace; and from all the bushes and branches came a sweet summer whistle of birds, and the pleasant dream and fresh perfume of branches swaying in the soft wind.

Also along the terrace a colony of gods had assembled in a stony Olympus: Venus, and Ceres, and Mercury, and Theseus, the mighty hunter—ancient deities, whose perennial youth had not saved them from decay. Their fair limbs were falling off, mouldy stains were creeping along the folds and emblems and torches. Theseus's lion's skin was crumbling away....

"How horrid it must be to die young!" said Fanny, stopping for an instant to look at fair Ceres, one of whose hands had fallen off, whose nose was gone, whose bountiful cornucopia was broken in the middle, scattering plaster flowers and morsels on the ground. "I wonder what Angelo meant by what he said about the Marchioness," said Fanny.

"I never listen to him," said Anne, walking on with a light step to a great pink stem studded with a close crop of flowers.

Some painter might have made a pretty picture of the girl bending in her white dress to admire the flower as it grew at the crumbling feet of the goddess of the forsaken altars.

Meanwhile, Fanny had sat down on the ledge of the low wall, and was peeping with her bright open eyes into the street below. The flower-girl was at her place by the fountain; the old women were at their doors; the great porches of the opposite church were thrown wide open at the close of some religious ceremony: there was a vague cloud of incense issuing with the people, who were coming from behind the heavy curtains: some monks, some Italian peasants, a soldier or two, and some of those Brothers of Pieta who follow the funerals and pray for the souls of the dead. Six of them came out of the church, following each other two by two, with long blue silk masks veiling their faces, as they walked away down the street; but a seventh, who seemed waiting for somebody or something, stood upon the step of the church, looking up and down the street.

"Fanny," cried Anne, who had been exploring the end of the terrace, "here is a staircase up into the house."

Fanny did not answer.

When Anne rejoined her sister, she found her sitting motionless on the stone wall just where she had left her, looking at something across the road.

"What is it? What are you waiting for?" cried Anne. "Come away, Fanny. How that horrible figure stares at us."

As she spoke, a monk came out of the church, and laid one hand on the shoulder of this blue-bearded figure (for the long pointed blue mask looked like nothing else). The man started, and withdrew his burning eyes, which had been fixed on Fanny, and the two walked away together down the sloping street. No one, except the sisters, looked after the strange-looking pair: such a sight was common enough in Rome. The monk's brown skirts flapped against his heels; the brother walked with long straight strides. He wore spurs beneath his black robe.

Fanny was quite pale. "Oh, Anne! I was too frightened to move," said she. "What is the little staircase? How horrid those people look."

The little staircase disappeared into the wall which abutted at the end of the terrace; there was a small door, which had always been closed hitherto, leading to it. Halfway up a small window stood open, with a balcony (iron-fenced, with an iron coronet woven into the railing). It was just large enough for one person to stand. This person was old Angelo, waiting for them with his keys and a duster under his arm. "This leads into the grand apartment," he said. "You may come if you like. I am going to see that all is in order for the coming of the Marquis. In the Marchioness's time it was full of company," he explained as he unlocked the heavy doors. "Now there are only the spiders and mice that we chase away."

Fanny and her sister liked nothing better than being allowed to go over the great rooms. They gladly accepted Angelo's offer; even though the elegant young ladies should have to appear mulcted[1] of their proper number of flounces that evening. They sprang up the narrow stairs two and three at a time, and came at once into a great bedroom, furnished with sumptuous blue satin hangings, with splendid laces covering the bed and the dressing-table, with beautiful china upon the mantelshelf—all silent, abandoned, magnificent. The toilet-glass was wreathed with lace, the pincushion must have cost as much as Fanny's whole year's allowance. This room was more newly furnished than the rest of the suite, and yet it was more melancholy and deserted looking than any other. Angelo took off his cap when he told them the Marchioness had died there.

"In that splendid bed?" said Fanny, thoughtfully.

"Not in the bed," said Angelo, hurrying on to the next apartment.

The girls followed. Fanny's high heels echoed as they patted along the marble floor.

"Yes, Anne, I should like to be enormously rich. Oh! how I like satin and velvet!" And she sank into a great yellow satin chair.

1 [In this context, a synonym of deprived.]

"Ché! ché!" cries old Angelo; "not on the best chairs. Farther on the young ladies shall rest."

Farther on were great rooms with closed windows, and shutters within shutters. Fanny flew along the marble floor, tapping from room to room. Anne followed. The girls soon left old Angelo and his duster behind. He could hear their voices exclaiming as they travelled to the end of the long suite. Great vases stood on the mosaic tables: faded hangings, with scripture subjects, waved from the panels. They passed room after room, and they came at last to one lofty hall, bigger than any they had passed through. It was unfurnished, but straight stone seats ran all round the wall, and at one end uprose a shadowy throne, raised beneath a daïs, where great plumes and a coat-of-arms were waving. Although the glories of the house of Barbi had passed from the family to which they once belonged, the insignia of their bygone dignities still faded there in all solemnity.

Some ten years before, the palace and the estates near Rome and the title had passed to a distant cousin of the grand old family, a foreigner, so people said, in humble circumstances. He had married soon after he inherited the property, but his married life had been but short, and since his wife's death he had not been seen in Rome. She was Sibilla, of the great Mangiascudi family, and it was said the Marquis bought her of her brothers. This was old Angelo's story; but he was always winking and shaking his head.

Fanny did not trouble herself about bygone or present Barbis, although they had numbered cardinals and ambassadors among their members. She was sliding and dancing along the polished floor, in and out among the many tables. She was less even-tempered than her sister, and she would spring from all the depths to all the heights of excitement in a few minutes. The great audience-hall opened into another vista of rooms, through which the girls turned back. They passed old windows, cabinets, and picture-frames, the "English boudoir" crammed with patchwork cushions and cheap gimcracks, with a priceless plaid paper-knife lying on a cushion beneath a glass. Then came more Italy; bare and stately, dim and grandiose. The two girls ran on, sometimes stopping short, sometimes hurrying along. At the end of all things was a little yellow room, with a vaulted ceiling, where some Cupids were flitting round an old crystal chandelier, fluttering, head downwards, in a white stucco cloud. Old Angelo had unfastened the closed shutters—for the sun at midday had passed beyond the corner of the palace—and the tall window looked out in shade upon a faint burning city, that flashed into dazzling misty distance. Some dead flowers were standing on the little stone balcony. The adventurous Fanny, peeping out, declared that she could not only see St. Peter's, but her own birdcage and their old red curtains overhead.

"We ought to go back and finish our flounces," said Anne, remembering the unfinished frills heaped up on the work-table in the window.

"Horrid things! Anne, how can you always talk about work just when we are most happy!" said Fanny, stamping. "We haven't half seen the things. Look at that curious old oak chest."

There were many objects displayed upon the tables and cabinets of this little room, and Fanny's frills would never have been hemmed if she had waited to examine them all. The oak chest stood upon a carved stand, with handles worked into some fanciful representation of hearts entwined.

On the panel above hung a picture that took the girl's fancy. It was the head of a peasant woman, painted by some great modern artist. It seemed taken in imitation of a celebrated head in the public galleries below, that people came from far and near to see. A beautiful woman, with dark imploring eyes, with a tremulous mouth that seemed ready to speak. In her hair were massive silver pins. Round her neck she wore the heavy coral necklace of the Italian peasants, with the addition of a crystal heart. The beautiful eyes were pitiful, but very sad. While Fanny stood absorbed, old Angelo appeared at a little door which led back into the blue bedroom—for they had come round the whole suite of rooms, and reached the place from whence they started.

"Come," said Angelo, "I have prepared the apartments for the Marquis. I shall let you young ladies out the other way."

"We could go back by the garden," said Fanny.

"I have locked the garden door," said Angelo. "The Marquis would be very angry if he chanced to see us there. He ordered it to be closed after the Lady Marchioness died."

"Angelo, is this the Marchioness?" said Fanny, pointing to the picture.

"No," said Angelo, gravely. "No one knows who it is. The Marquis bought the picture of Don Federigo, the great painter, who had taken her as she sat at the fountain. There was no such model in Rome. Poor little one! she came to a sad end: she fell into the river. Don Federigo and the Marquis would have saved her, but it was too late. He, some people say he has the evil eye, our Marquis! Come, come!"

Old Angelo, who had a way of suddenly losing his temper, stumped off; the girls followed, then went back to have another look at the picture.

"What is that noise? He will lock us in," said Anne, suddenly setting off running.

Fanny lingered one instant: as she looked, the pictured face seemed to change, the eyes to flash resentfully. It was a fancy, but it frightened her to be alone, and she, too, ran away.

22. Mary de Morgan, *On a Pincushion, and Other Fairy Tales* (1877)[1]

Mary de Morgan is best known for her three collections of literary fairy tales, the first of which was On a Pincushion and Other Fairy Tales, *published in 1877 and illustrated with woodcuts by her brother, the artist and designer William de Morgan. In addition to her fairy tales, de Morgan wrote numerous articles (primarily for American periodicals) on such topics as English socialism, the Jewish community of East London, and the state of education in Victorian England. The de Morgan family counted William Morris as a close family friend, and they shared Morris's interests in craft, aesthetics, and politics. Like her mother, Sophia Elizabeth Frend, Mary de Morgan was an active proponent of women's rights; she was a member of the suffragist organization known as the "Women's Franchise League" and was overseeing the establishment of a girls' school in Egypt when she died in 1907. De Morgan's progressive political views can be detected in her playful and satirical tale, "A Toy Princess," which calls into question dominant ideals of femininity, social decorum, and materialism.*

A TOY PRINCESS

MORE THAN A THOUSAND YEARS ago, in a country quite on the other side of the world, it fell out that the people all grew so very polite that they hardly ever spoke to each other. And they never said more than was quite necessary, as "Just so," "Yes indeed," "Thank you," and "If you please." And it was thought to be the rudest thing in the world for anyone to say they liked or disliked, or loved or hated, or were happy or miserable. No one ever laughed aloud, and if anyone had been seen to cry they would at once have been avoided by their friends.

The King of this country married a Princess from a neighbouring land, who was very good and beautiful, but the people in her own home were as unlike her husband's people as it was possible to be. They laughed, and talked, and were noisy and merry when they were happy, and cried and lamented if they were sad. In fact, whatever they felt they showed at once, and the Princess was just like them.

So when she came to her new home, she could not at all understand her subjects, or make out why there was no shouting and cheering to welcome her, and why everyone was so distant and formal. After a time, when she found they never changed, but were always the same, just as stiff and quiet, she wept, and began to pine for her own old home.

Every day she grew thinner and paler. The courtiers were much too polite to

1 [Source: Mary de Morgan, *On a Pincushion, and Other Fairy Tales*, 2nd ed. (London: Seeley, Jackson, and Halliday, 1877): 153–76.]

notice how ill their young Queen looked; but she knew it herself, and believed she was going to die.

Now she had a fairy godmother, named Taboret, whom she loved very dearly, and who was always kind to her. When she knew her end was drawing near she sent for her godmother, and when she came had a long talk with her quite alone.

No one knew what was said, and soon afterwards a little Princess was born, and the Queen died. Of course all the courtiers were sorry for the poor Queen's death, but it would have been thought rude to say so. So, although there was a grand funeral, and the court put on mourning, everything else went on much as it had done before.

The little baby was christened Ursula, and given to some court ladies to be taken charge of. Poor little Princess! *She* cried hard enough, and nothing could stop her. All her ladies were frightened, and said that they had not heard such a dreadful noise for a long time. But, till she was about two years old, nothing could stop her crying when she was cold or hungry, or crowing when she was pleased.

After that she began to understand a little what was meant when her nurses told her, in cold, polite tones, that she was being naughty, and she grew much quieter.

She was a pretty little girl, with a round baby face and big merry blue eyes; but as she grew older, her eyes grew less and less merry and bright, and her fat little face grew thin and pale. She was not allowed to play with any other children, lest she might learn bad manners; and she was not taught any games or given any toys. So she passed most of her time, when she was not at her lessons, looking out of the window at the birds flying against the clear blue sky; and sometimes she would give a sad little sigh when her ladies were not listening.

One day the old fairy Taboret made herself invisible, and flew over to the King's palace to see how things were going on there. She went straight up to the nursery, where she found poor little Ursula sitting by the window, with her head leaning on her hand.

It was a very grand room, but there were no toys or dolls about, and when the fairy saw this, she frowned to herself and shook her head.

"Your Royal Highness's dinner is now ready," said the head nurse to Ursula.

"I don't want any dinner," said Ursula, without turning her head.

"I think I have told your Royal Highness before that it is not polite to say you don't want anything, or that you don't like it," said the nurse. "We are waiting for your Royal Highness."

So the Princess got up and went to the dinner-table, and Taboret watched them all the time. When she saw how pale little Ursula was, and how little she ate, and that there was no talking or laughing allowed, she sighed and frowned even more than before, and then she flew back to her fairy home, where she sat for some hours in deep thought.

At last she rose, and went out to pay a visit to the largest shop in Fairyland.

It was a queer sort of shop. It was neither a grocer's, nor a draper's, nor a hatter's. Yet it contained sugar, and dresses, and hats. But the sugar was magic sugar, which transformed any liquid into which it was put; the dresses each had some special charm, and the hats were wishing-caps. It was, in fact, a shop where every sort of spell or charm was sold.

Into this shop Taboret flew; and as she was well known there as a good customer, the master of the shop came forward to meet her at once, and bowing, begged to know what he could get for her.

"I want," said Taboret, "a Princess."

"A Princess!" said the shopman, who was in reality an old wizard. "What size do you want it? I have one or two in stock."

"It must look now about six years old. But it must grow."

"I can make you one," said the wizard, "but it'll come rather expensive."

"I don't mind that," said Taboret. "See! I want it to look exactly like this," and so saying she took a portrait of Ursula out of her bosom and gave it to the old man, who examined it carefully.

"I'll get it for you," he said. "When will you want it?"

"As soon as possible," said Taboret. "By tomorrow evening if possible. How much will it cost?"

"It'll come to a good deal," said the wizard, thoughtfully. "I have such difficulty in getting these things properly made in these days. What sort of a voice is it to have?"

"It need not be at all talkative," said Taboret, "so that won't add much to the price. It need only say, 'If you please,' 'No, thank you,' 'Certainly,' and 'Just so.'"

"Well, under those circumstances," said the wizard, "I will do it for four cat's footfalls, two fish's screams, and two swan's songs."

"It is too much," cried Taboret. "I'll give you the footfalls and the screams, but to ask for swans' songs!"

She did not really think it dear, but she always made a point of trying to beat tradesmen down.

"I can't do it for less," said the wizard, "and if you think it too much, you'd better try another shop."

"As I am really in a hurry for it, and cannot spend time in searching about, I suppose I must have it," said Taboret; "but I consider the price very high. When will it be ready?"

"By tomorrow evening."

"Very well, then, be sure it is ready for me by the time I call for it, and whatever you do, don't make it at all noisy or rough in its ways"; and Taboret swept out of the shop and returned to her home.

Next evening she returned and asked if her job was done.

"I will fetch it, and I am sure you will like it," said the wizard, leaving the shop as he spoke. Presently he came back, leading by the hand a pretty little girl of about six years old—a little girl so like the Princess Ursula that no one could have told them apart.

"Well," said Taboret, "it looks well enough. But are you sure that it's a good piece of workmanship, and won't give way anywhere?"

"It's as good a piece of work as ever was done," said the wizard, proudly, striking the child on the back as he spoke. "Look at it! Examine it all over, and see if you find a flaw anywhere. There's not one fairy in twenty who could tell it from the real thing, and no mortal could."

"It seems to be fairly made," said Taboret, approvingly, as she turned the little girl round. "Now I'll pay you, and then will be off"; with which she raised her wand in the air and waved it three times, and there arose a series of strange sounds.

The first was a low tramping, the second shrill and piercing screams, the third voices of wonderful beauty, singing a very sorrowful song.

The wizard caught all the sounds and pocketed them at once, and Taboret, without ceremony, picked up the child, took her head downwards under her arm, and flew away.

At court that night the little Princess had been naughty, and had refused to go to bed. It was a long time before her ladies could get her into her crib, and when she was there, she did not really go to sleep, only lay still and pretended, till everyone went away; then she got up and stole noiselessly to the window, and sat down on the window-seat all curled up in a little bunch, while she looked out wistfully at the moon. She was such a pretty soft little thing, with all her warm bright hair falling over her shoulders, that it would have been hard for most people to be angry with her. She leaned her chin on her tiny white hands, and as she gazed out, the tears rose to her great blue eyes; but remembering that her ladies would call this naughty, she wiped them hastily away with her nightgown sleeve.

"Ah moon, pretty bright moon!" she said to herself, "I wonder if they let you cry when you want to. I think I'd like to go up there and live with you; I'm sure it would be nicer than being here."

"Would you like to go away with me?" said a voice close beside her; and looking up she saw a funny old woman in a red cloak, standing near to her. She was not frightened, for the old woman had a kind smile and bright black eyes, though her nose was hooked and her chin long.

"Where would you take me?" said the little Princess, sucking her thumb, and staring with all her might.

"I'd take you to the sea-shore, where you'd be able to play about on the sands, and where you'd have some little boys and girls to play with, and no one to tell you not to make a noise."

"I'll go," cried Ursula, springing up at once.

"Come along," said the old woman, taking her tenderly in her arms and folding her in her warm red cloak. Then they rose up in the air, and flew out of the window, right away over the tops of the houses.

The night air was sharp, and Ursula soon fell asleep; but still they kept flying on, on, over hill and dale, for miles and miles, away from the palace, towards the sea.

Far away from the court and the palace, in a tiny fishing village, on the sea, was a little hut where a fisherman named Mark lived with his wife and three children. He was a poor man, and lived on the fish he caught in his little boat. The children, Oliver, Philip, and little Bell, were rosy-cheeked and bright-eyed. They played all day long on the shore, and shouted till they were hoarse. To this village the fairy bore the still sleeping Ursula, and gently placed her on the doorstep of Mark's cottage; then she kissed her cheeks, and with one gust blew the door open, and disappeared before anyone could come to see who it was.

The fisherman and his wife were sitting quietly within. She was making the children clothes, and he was mending his net, when without any noise the door opened and the cold night air blew in.

"Wife," said the fisherman, "just see who's at the door."

The wife got up and went to the door, and there lay Ursula, still sleeping soundly, in her little white nightdress.

The woman gave a little scream at sight of the child, and called to her husband.

"Husband, see, here's a little girl!" and so saying she lifted her in her arms, and carried her into the cottage. When she was brought into the warmth and light, Ursula awoke, and sitting up, stared about her in fright. She did not cry, as another child might have done, but she trembled very much, and was almost too frightened to speak.

Oddly enough, she had forgotten all about her strange flight through the air, and could remember nothing to tell the fisherman and his wife, but that she was the Princess Ursula; and, on hearing this, the good man and woman thought the poor little girl must be a trifle mad. However, when they examined her little nightdress, made of white fine linen and embroidery, with a crown worked in one corner, they agreed that she must belong to very grand people. They said it would be cruel to send the poor little thing away on such a cold night, and they must of course keep her till she was claimed. So the woman gave her some warm bread-and-milk, and put her to bed with their own little girl.

In the morning, when the court ladies came to wake Princess Ursula, they found her sleeping as usual in her little bed, and little did they think it was not she, but a toy Princess placed there in her stead. Indeed the ladies were much pleased; for when they said, "It is time for your Royal Highness to arise," she only answered, "Certainly," and let herself be dressed without another word. And as the time passed, and she was never naughty, and scarcely ever spoke, all said she was vastly improved, and she grew to be a great favourite.

The ladies all said that the young Princess bid fair to have the most elegant manners in the country, and the King smiled and noticed her with pleasure.

In the meantime, in the fisherman's cottage far away, the real Ursula grew tall and straight as an alder, and merry and light-hearted as a bird.

No one came to claim her, so the good fisherman and his wife kept her and brought her up among their own little ones. She played with them on the beach, and learned her lessons with them at school, and her old life had become like a dream she barely remembered.

But sometimes the mother would take out the little embroidered nightgown and show it to her, and wonder whence she came, and to whom she belonged.

"I don't care who I belong to," said Ursula; "they won't come and take me from you, and that's all I care about." So she grew tall and fair, and as she grew, the toy Princess, in her place at the court, grew too, and always was just like her, only that whereas Ursula's face was sunburnt and her cheeks red, the face of the toy Princess was pale, with only a very slight tint in her cheeks.

Years passed, and Ursula at the cottage was a tall young woman, and Ursula at the court was thought to be the most beautiful there, and every one admired her manners, though she never said anything but "If you please," "No, thank you," "Certainly," and "Just so."

The King was now an old man, and the fisherman Mark and his wife were grey-headed. Most of their fishing was now done by their eldest son, Oliver, who was their great pride. Ursula waited on them, and cleaned the house, and did the needlework, and was so useful that they could not have done without her. The fairy Taboret had come to the cottage from time to time, unseen by anyone, to see Ursula, and always finding her healthy and merry, was pleased to think of how she had saved her from a dreadful life. But one evening when she paid them a visit, not having been there for some time, she saw something which made her pause and consider. Oliver and Ursula were standing together watching the waves, and Taboret stopped to hear what they said,—

"When we are married," said Oliver, softly, "we will live in that little cottage yonder, so that we can come and see them every day. But that will not be till little Bell is old enough to take your place, for how would my mother do without you?"

"And we had better not tell them," said Ursula, "that we mean to marry, or else the thought that they are preventing us will make them unhappy."

When Taboret heard this she became grave, and pondered for a long time. At last she flew back to the court to see how things were going on there. She found the King in the middle of a state council. On seeing this, she at once made herself visible, when the King begged her to be seated near him, as he was always glad of her help and advice.

"You find us," said his Majesty, "just about to resign our sceptre into younger and more vigorous hands; in fact, we think we are growing too old to reign, and mean to abdicate in favour of our dear daughter, who will reign in our stead."

"Before you do any such thing," said Taboret, "just let me have a little private conversation with you"; and she led the King into a corner, much to his surprise and alarm.

In about half an hour he returned to the council, looking very white, and with a dreadful expression on his face, whilst he held a handkerchief to his eyes.

"My lords," he faltered, "pray pardon our apparently extraordinary behaviour. We have just received a dreadful blow; we hear on authority, which we cannot doubt, that our dear, dear daughter"—here sobs choked his voice, and he was almost unable to proceed—"is—is—in fact, not our daughter at all, and only a *sham*." Here the King sank back in his chair, overpowered with grief, and the fairy Taboret, stepping to the front, told the courtiers the whole story; how she had stolen the real Princess, because she feared they were spoiling her, and how she had placed a toy Princess in her place. The courtiers looked from one to another in surprise, but it was evident they did not believe her.

"The Princess is a truly charming young lady," said the Prime Minister.

"Has your Majesty any reason to complain of her Royal Highness's conduct?" asked the old Chancellor.

"None whatever," sobbed the King; "she was ever an excellent daughter."

"Then I don't see," said the Chancellor, "what reason your Majesty can have for paying any attention to what this—this person says."

"If you don't believe me, you old idiots," cried Taboret, "call the Princess here, and I'll soon prove my words."

"By all means," cried they.

So the King commanded that her Royal Highness should be summoned.

In a few minutes she came, attended by her ladies. She said nothing, but then she never did speak till she was spoken to. So she entered, and stood in the middle of the room silently.

"We have desired that your presence be requested," the King was beginning, but Taboret without any ceremony advanced towards her, and struck her lightly on the head with her wand. In a moment the head rolled on the floor, leaving the body standing motionless as before, and showing that it was but an empty shell. "Just so," said the head, as it rolled towards the King, and he and the courtiers nearly swooned with fear.

When they were a little recovered, the King spoke again. "The fairy tells me," he said, "that there is somewhere a real Princess whom she wishes us to adopt as our daughter. And in the meantime let her Royal Highness be carefully placed in a cupboard, and a general mourning be proclaimed for this dire event."

So saying he glanced tenderly at the body and head, and turned weeping away.

So it was settled that Taboret was to fetch Princess Ursula, and the King and council were to be assembled to meet her.

That evening the fairy flew to Mark's cottage, and told them the whole truth about Ursula, and that they must part from her.

Loud were their lamentations, and great their grief, when they heard she must leave them. Poor Ursula herself sobbed bitterly.

"Never mind," she cried after a time, "if I am really a great Princess, I will have you all to live with me. I am sure the King, my father, will wish it, when he hears how good you have all been to me."

On the appointed day, Taboret came for Ursula in a grand coach and four, and drove her away to the court. It was a long, long drive; and she stopped on the way and had the Princess dressed in a splendid white silk dress trimmed with gold, and put pearls round her neck and in her hair, that she might appear properly at court.

The King and all the council were assembled with great pomp, to greet their new Princess, and all looked grave and anxious. At last the door opened, and Taboret appeared, leading the young girl by the hand.

"That is your father!" said she to Ursula, pointing to the King; and on this, Ursula, needing no other bidding, ran at once to him, and putting her arms round his neck, gave him a sounding kiss.

His Majesty almost swooned, and all the courtiers shut their eyes and shivered.

"This is really!" said one.

"This is truly!" said another.

"What have I done?" cried Ursula, looking from one to another, and seeing that something was wrong, but not knowing what. "Have I kissed the *wrong person*?" On hearing which every one groaned.

"Come now," cried Taboret, "if you don't like her, I shall take her away to those who do. I'll give you a week, and then I'll come back and see how you're treating her. She's a great deal too good for any of you." So saying she flew away on her wand, leaving Ursula to get on with her new friends as best she might. But Ursula could not get on with them at all, as she soon began to see.

If she spoke or moved they looked shocked, and at last she was so frightened and troubled by them that she burst into tears, at which they were more shocked still.

"This is indeed a change after our sweet Princess," said one lady to another.

"Yes, indeed," was the answer, "when one remembers how even after her head was struck off she behaved so beautifully, and only said, 'Just so.'"

And all the ladies disliked poor Ursula, and soon showed her their dislike. Before the end of the week, when Taboret was to return, she had grown quite thin and pale, and seemed afraid of speaking above a whisper.

"Why, what is wrong?" cried Taboret, when she returned and saw how much poor Ursula had changed. "Don't you like being here? Aren't they kind to you?"

"Take me back, dear Taboret," cried Ursula, weeping. "Take me back to Oliver, and Philip, and Bell. As for these people, I *hate* them."

And she wept again.

Taboret only smiled and patted her head, and then went into the King and courtiers.

"Now, how is it," she cried, "I find the Princess Ursula in tears? and I am sure you are making her unhappy. When you had that bit of wood-and-leather Princess, you could behave well enough to it, but now that you have a real flesh-and-blood woman, you none of you care for her."

"Our late dear daughter," began the King, when the fairy interrupted him.

"I do believe," she said, "that you would like to have the doll back again. Now I will give you your choice. Which will you have—my Princess Ursula, the real one, or your Princess Ursula, the sham?"

The King sank back into his chair. "I am not equal to this," he said: "summon the council, and let them settle it by vote." So the council were summoned, and the fairy explained to them why they were wanted.

"Let both Princesses be fetched," she said; and the toy Princess was brought in with great care from her cupboard, and her head stood on the table beside her, and the real Princess came in with her eyes still red from crying and her bosom heaving.

"I should think there could be no doubt which one would prefer," said the Prime Minister to the Chancellor.

"I should think not either," answered the Chancellor.

"Then vote," said Taboret; and they all voted, and every vote was for the sham Ursula, and not one for the real one. Taboret only laughed.

"You are a pack of sillies and idiots," she said, "but you shall have what you want"; and she picked up the head, and with a wave of her wand stuck it on to the body, and it moved round slowly and said, "Certainly," just in its old voice; and on hearing this, all the courtiers gave something as like a cheer as they thought polite, whilst the old King could not speak for joy.

"We will," he cried, "at once make our arrangements for abdicating and leaving the government in the hands of our dear daughter"; and on hearing this the courtiers all applauded again.

But Taboret laughed scornfully, and taking up the real Ursula in her arms, flew back with her to Mark's cottage.

In the evening the city was illuminated, and there were great rejoicings at the recovery of the Princess, but Ursula remained in the cottage and married Oliver, and lived happily with him for the rest of her life.

Henriette Kühne-Harkort, *Snow White, Freely Adapted from the Grimms* (1877, theater script; translated by Shawn C. Jarvis, 2001) [website]

Very little is known about Henriette Kühne-Harkort, the German author of several puppet plays and children's plays—scripts intended for use in home and school performance, including her adaptation of the Grimms' tale "Snow White." Kühne-Harkort's script (provided as a web text, see http://sites.broadviewpress.com/marveloustrans/) includes some interesting choices: she adds a host of male suitors to the tale's initial situation, so that the jealousy felt by the Queen (or countess, in this case) towards young Snow White (only seven years old in the Grimms' tale, but 16 years old in this script) is based not only on her beauty but also on her ability to attract male attention—specifically that of Kunimund, who eventually rescues and marries her.

23. Luigi Capuana, *C'era una volta ... fiabe* (1882; *translated by Gina Miele, 2011*[1])

Luigi Capuana's fairy tales are the culmination of a long process begun when he was still a child. Born in 1839 to a wealthy family, the young boy felt stifled by traditional schooling, preferring to listen as villagers and his elderly aunts spun tales about kings, queens, dwarves, wildmen from the woods, and invisible merchants who lived in the hills outside of his town of Mineo, Sicily. He delighted in these "fantasticherie" (reveries) traditionally told by Sicilian farmers and village tellers. Captivated by the work of early ethnographers and the trove of stories in his own backyard, Capuana himself became an erudite researcher and collector of tales. His collaboration with two important folklorists, Lionardo Vigo and Giuseppe Pitrè, fostered a desire to study with a scholarly eye the rich patrimony of Sicilian tradition. Coinciding in time with the publication of Pinocchio, *Carlo Collodi's masterpiece of Italian children's literature, Capuana's first collection of fairy tales,* C'era una volta ... fiabe, *from which the story included here is taken, was soon followed by many others, making him one of the most prolific authors of Italian fairy tales since Straparola and Basile. In addition to publishing a large corpus of fairy tales, he edited several children's journals and penned three theatrical fairy tales as well as three novels for children. Although Capuana expected fairy tales to be his legacy, his vast collection of tales has received comparatively little recognition from modern scholars of Italian literature or folklore. Instead, critics have focused on an aspect of his writing that could appear to be at odds with fantasy: he was part of a new turn in Italian literature towards what would become known as "verisimo" (literary realism). We see this emerge in his fairy tales as what fellow literary realist, Giovanni Verga, called the "science of the human heart." "The Talking Tree" aptly demonstrates Capuana's exploration of the human condition. Repetition and circularity give the story a distinctive rhythm that places his style at*

1 [Source: Gina Miele, unpublished.]

the intersection of traditional print and performance modes of storytelling. Cycles that familiarize us with particular refrains both drive the plot and invite the reader into the fairy-tale event as a knowing participant.

THE TALKING TREE

ONCE UPON A TIME THERE was a king who believed that he had gathered in his palace all of the most precious things in the world.

One day there came a stranger who asked to see the King's collection. The stranger carefully observed every item and then said:

"Your Majesty, you are missing the best item of all."

"What am I missing?" asked the King

"The talking tree."

And indeed, amongst all those precious items, there was no talking tree.

With this bug in his ear, the King could no longer sleep. He sent messengers around the world in search of the talking tree, but the messengers returned empty-handed.

The King thought himself fooled by the stranger, and he ordered him to be arrested.

"Your Majesty," said the stranger, "if your messengers have not searched properly, how is that my fault? Let them search better."

"And have you seen the talking tree with your own eyes?" asked the King.

"I have seen it with my own eyes and heard it with my own ears."

"Where?"

"I don't remember anymore."

"And what did it say?"

"It said: 'To wait and not to come is a thing for which to die.'"

So it was true! The King again sent out his messengers. A year passed, and once more they returned empty-handed.

Then the indignant King ordered the stranger's head be cut off.

"Your Majesty," said the stranger, "if your messengers have not searched properly, how is that my fault? Let them search better."

This insistence struck the King. Summoning his ministers, he said that he himself wanted to go on a quest to find the talking tree.

As long as he did not have the talking tree in his palace, the King didn't feel like a king.

And so, disguising himself, he set off.

He walked and walked, and after many days, the night overtook him in a valley where no living soul existed. Laying himself upon the ground, he was about to fall asleep when he heard a voice that seemed to be weeping:

"To wait and not to come is a thing for which to die."

He shook himself and strained his ear. Had he dreamed it?

"To wait and not to come is a thing for which to die."

No! He hadn't been dreaming! And he immediately asked:

"Who are you?"

No one replied. When morning finally broke, he saw nearby a beautiful tree with branches drooping down to the ground.

"It must have been that tree."

And just to be sure, he reached out his hand and tore off two leaves.

"Ahhh! Why do you tear me?"

The King, despite all of his great courage, was terrified.

"Who are you? If you are a baptized soul, respond, in the name of God!"

"I am the daughter of the King of Spain."

"And just how did you find yourself here?"

"I saw a crystal clear fountain, and I thought I would bathe in it. No sooner had I touched that water than I was cast under an evil spell."

"What can I do to set you free?"

"You must find the charm and swear to marry me."

"I will swear to that this moment, and I shall find that charm, even if I have to go to the ends of the earth to do it. But you, why didn't you answer me last night?"

"The Witch was there ... Shhhh! Be quiet, and go away; I hear the Witch coming back. If by bad luck she finds you, she will cast you under an evil spell too."

The King ran to hide behind a little wall and saw the Witch arrive, riding on a broomstick.

"With whom were you speaking?" [the Witch asked the talking tree].

"With the wind of the air."

"I see here footprints."

"Perhaps they are yours."

"Oh! So they are mine, are they?"

The Witch grasped an iron club and started to beat the tree.

"Stop, for heaven's sake! I will never do it again!"

"Oh! So they are mine, are they?" And she beat the tree again.

The King, utterly distressed, decided it was useless to continue on there; he needed to find that charm. And he turned back.

But he took the wrong road. When he realized that he was lost in a great wood and could not find his way, he decided to climb up to the top of a tree; otherwise, the ferocious beasts were sure to swallow him in one big gulp.

And then, at midnight, a deafening noise was heard throughout the whole forest. It was an Ogre who was returning home with his hundred mastiffs growling behind him.

"Oh, what a delicious smell of human flesh!"

The Ogre stopped at the foot of the tree and started to sniff around:

"Oh, what a delicious smell!"

The King was shaking like a leaf while the growling mastiffs searched around the brush, scratching at the spot where they smelled his footprints. But as luck would have it, it was dark as night, and after searching without success for some time, the Ogre went on his way calling his mastiffs to follow him.

"Come! Come!"

When it was day, the King, still trembling with fear, came down from the tree and began to move forward very cautiously. Soon he met a beautiful maiden.

"Beautiful maiden, for heaven's sake, point me in the right direction. I am a wayfarer who has lost my way."

"Oh, poor man! How did you end up here? In a little while my father will pass by again, and he will eat you alive. Oh, you poor man!"

In fact, one could hear the mastiffs' howls and the Ogre's voice calling them to follow him: "Come! Come!"

"This time I'm a dead man!" thought the King.

"Come here," said the maiden, "and throw yourself down on your hands and knees. I will sit on your back so my skirt will cover you. Don't breathe a word!"

The Ogre, seeing his daughter, stopped.

"What are you doing here?" he said.

"I'm resting."

"Oh, what a delicious smell of human flesh!"

"A little boy just passed by, and I made a nice little snack of him!"

"Good girl! And the bones?"

"The dogs gnawed them."

The Ogre would not stop sniffing the air.

"Oh, what a delicious smell!"

"If you want to get to the seashore, you mustn't delay anymore," said the daughter.

Once the Ogre had left, the King told the maiden his whole story, word for word.

"Your Majesty, if you will marry me, I shall give you the charm."

The maiden was a beauty, and the king would have married her willingly.

"Alas, lovely maiden! I have pledged myself [to someone else]."

She led him to the house, took down a jar, and rubbed her father's ointment on the King's chest. The King fell under a charm.

"And now, lovely maiden, you must lend me an axe."

"Here you are."

"What is this grease on it?"

"It is the oil from the whetstone upon which it was sharpened."

Because the King was enchanted by the charm, in only a blink of an eye he found himself back at the talking tree.

The Witch wasn't there, and the tree said to him:

"Watch out! My heart is hidden within this trunk. When the time comes to chop me down, don't pay attention to the Witch. If she tells you to strike upward, you must strike down. If she tells you to strike downward, you must strike up; otherwise you shall kill me. Then you must chop off the Witch's head with a single blow, or you too will be lost; not even the magic charm shall save you."

The Witch came then.

"What are you looking for in these parts?" [she asked the King].

"I am searching for a tree to make charcoal, and I was looking at this one here."

"Would it make you happy? I will give it to you on one condition: when you are chopping it down, you must strike where I tell you."

"Very well," said the King.

The King brandished his axe, which cut better than a razor, and asked:

"Where?"

"Here."

And he, instead, chopped in a different spot.

"I made a mistake. Let's try that again. Where?"

"Here."

And he, instead, chopped in a different spot.

"I made a mistake. Let's try that again."

In the meantime, the King couldn't find a way to strike the Witch: she was on her guard. The King exclaimed:

"Oooh!"

"What do you see?" asked the Witch.

"A star."

"During the day? That's impossible."

"Up there, straight across from that branch: look!"

And while the Witch had turned her back to him to look across from the branch, the King landed a blow to her neck and neatly chopped off her head.

The evil spell broken, there stepped out from the tree trunk a damsel so beautiful, he could scarcely gaze at her!

Thrilled beyond belief, the King returned with her to the royal palace and ordered a magnificent wedding feast to be prepared immediately.

When the wedding day arrived, while the ladies of the court were dressing the Queen in her wedding gown, they noticed, with great astonishment, that the Queen's flesh was as hard as wood. One of the ladies flew quickly to the King:

"Your Majesty, the Queen has flesh as hard as wood!"

"How is that possible?" [he asked].

The King and his ministers went to have a look. What they found was most surprising. To the eye, her body seemed so much like flesh that it could fool anyone;

but when you touched it, it was made of wood! And in the meantime, the Queen was speaking and moving.

The ministers told the King that he could not possibly marry this wooden doll, however much she talked and moved, and they gave the order to cancel the wedding feast.

"There must be another spell at work here!" thought the King, who remembered the grease on the axe.

He took a little piece of meat and cut it up with the axe. He had guessed right! The little pieces, to the eye, seemed so much like real meat that they could fool anyone; but when you touched them, they were made of wood. The Ogre's daughter had betrayed him out of jealousy.

The King said to his ministers:

"I must go. I will be right back."

And he found himself in the blink of an eye back in the woods where he had met that maiden.

"Your Majesty, what are you doing in these parts? What good wind blows you here?"

"I came here to find you."

The Ogre's daughter couldn't believe her ears.

"Do you swear as King that you came here to find me?"

"I swear as King!"

And it was true; but the maiden was imagining that he had come to ask her hand in marriage.

They linked arms and entered the house.

"This is the axe that you lent to me."

As he handed it back to her, the King managed to wound her hand.

"Oh, Your Majesty, look what you've done! I've turned to wood!"

The King pretended to be sorry for the accident:

"And is there no remedy?" he asked.

"Open the cupboard, take down the pot, and rub me all over with the oil you'll find inside, and I shall be instantly healed."

The King took down the jar:

"Wait here until I return!" [he called].

The Ogre's daughter realized what was happening and began to shriek:

"Treason! Treason!"

And she sent off behind him her father's hundred mastiffs. But it was no use ... the King had disappeared.

With that oil, the Queen's flesh softened immediately and she and the King could finally celebrate their wedding.

They royal feast lasted eight days, but we, the rest of us, did not even get a crumb.

24. Flora Annie Steel and Richard Carnac Temple, *Wide Awake Stories, A Collection of Tales Told by Little Children, Between Sunrise and Sunset, in the Panjab and Kashmir* (1884)[1]

Wide Awake Stories *represents one of many efforts to remake colonial ethnography into folklore books suitable for the British household library. In this case, the tales had been collected "from the lips of the narrator" primarily by Flora Annie Steel, an English writer who was married to a member of the Indian civil service. Due to her husband's failing health, Steel took on many of his duties and in her 22 years in India she became well-connected with colonial administrators, including Captain R.C. Temple. The tales were first published in the colonial periodicals* Indian Antiquary *and* Calcutta Review, *but in book form, Steel and Temple explain, the stories were rendered in what they call "purely literary form, whereas previously the object aimed at was to give them in strict translation, however uncouth to English ears" (iii). Steel and Temple underscore the fact that while the tales themselves had been reworked (according to perceived standards of taste and a sense of the generic expectations of the "tale collection"), the book still included an analytical section in which "the origin and history of the collection" is detailed, and "full notes have been attached"—with analysis "made to strictly conform to the method adopted by the Folk-Lore Society of England" (iii-iv).* Wide Awake Stories *dances on this border between the popular and the scholarly—including both an introduction addressed "To the little Reader" and over 100 pages of notes and analyses—demonstrating just how pervasive interest in Folklore (specifically, nationally defined corpora of tales) was in late Victorian Britain, but also how deeply ingrained certain generic conventions had become, including the formulaic "Once upon a time" and "happily ever after."*

PRINCESS AUBERGINE

ONCE UPON A TIME THERE lived a poor Brahman and his wife, so poor, that often they did not know whither to turn for a meal, and were reduced to wild herbs and roots for their dinner.

Now one day, as the Brahman was gathering such herbs as he could find in the wilderness, he came upon an Aubergine, or egg-plant. Thinking it might prove useful by-and-by, he dug it up, took it home, and planted it by his cottage door. Every day he watered and tended it, so that it grew wonderfully, and at last bore one large fruit as big as a pear, purple and white and glossy—such a handsome fruit, that the

1 [Source: Flora Annie Steel and Richard Carnac Temple, *Wide Awake Stories, A Collection of Tales Told by Little Children, Between Sunrise and Sunset, in the Panjab and Kashmir* (London: Trübner and Co., 1884): 79–88.]

good couple thought it a pity to pick it, and let it hang on the plant day after day, until one fine morning when there was absolutely nothing to eat in the house. Then the Brahman said to his wife—"We must eat the egg-fruit; go and cut it, and prepare it for dinner."

So the Brahman's wife took a knife, and cut the beautiful purple and white fruit off the plant, and as she did so she thought she heard a low moan. But when she sat down and began to peel the egg-fruit, she heard a tiny voice say quite distinctly, "Take care!—oh, please take care! Peel more gently, or I am sure the knife will run into me!"

The good woman was terribly perplexed, but went on peeling as gently as she could, wondering all the time what had bewitched the egg-fruit, until she had cut quite through the rind, when—what do you think happened? Why, out stepped the most beautiful little maiden imaginable, dressed in purple and white satin!

The poor Brahman and his wife were mightily astonished, but still more delighted; for, having no children of their own, they looked on the tiny maiden as a godsend, and determined to adopt her. So they took the greatest care of her, petting and spoiling her, and always calling her the Princess Aubergine; for, said the worthy couple, if she was not a Princess *really*, she was dainty and delicate enough to be any king's daughter.

Now not far from the Brahman's hut lived a King, who had a beautiful wife, and seven stalwart young sons. One day, a slave girl from the palace happening to pass by the Brahman's cottage, went in to ask for a light, and there she saw the beautiful Aubergine. She went straight home to the palace, and told her mistress how in a hovel close by there lived a Princess so lovely and charming, that were the King once to set eyes on her, he would straightway forget, not only his Queen, but every other woman in the world.

Now the Queen, who was of a very jealous disposition, could not bear the idea of anyone being more beautiful than she was herself, so she cast about in her mind how she could destroy the lovely Aubergine. If she could only inveigle the girl into the palace, she could easily do the rest, for she was a sorceress, and learned in all sorts of magic. So she sent a message to the Princess Aubergine, to say that the fame of her great beauty had reached the palace, and the Queen would like to see with her own eyes if report said true.

Now lovely Aubergine was vain of her beauty, and fell into the trap. She went to the palace, and the Queen, pretending to be wonderstruck, said, "You were born to live in kings' houses! From this time you must never leave me; henceforth you are my sister."

This flattered Princess Aubergine's vanity, so, nothing loth, she remained in the palace, and exchanged veils with the Queen, and drank milk out of the same cup with her, as is the custom when two people say they will be sisters.

But the Queen, from the very first moment she set eyes on her, had seen that Princess Aubergine was no human being, but a fairy, and knew she must be very careful how she set about her magic. Therefore she laid strong spells upon her while she slept, and said,

"Beautiful Aubergine! tell me true—
In what thing does your life lie?"

And the Princess answered—"In the life of your eldest son. Kill him, and I will die also."

So the very next morning the wicked Queen went to where her eldest son lay sleeping, and killed him with her own hands. Then she sent the slave girl to the Princess's apartments, hoping to hear she was dead too, but the girl returned saying the Princess was alive and well.

Then the Queen wept tears of rage, for she knew her spells had not been strong enough, and she had killed her son for naught. Nevertheless, the next night she laid stronger spells upon the Princess Aubergine, saying—

"Princess Aubergine! tell me true—
In what thing does your life lie?"

And the sleeping Princess answered—"In the life of your second son. Kill him, and I too will die."

So the wicked Queen killed her second son with her own hands, but when she sent the slave girl to see whether Aubergine was dead also, the girl returned again saying the Princess was alive and well.

Then the Sorceress-queen cried with rage and spite, for she had killed her second son for naught. Nevertheless, she would not give up her wicked project, and the next night laid still stronger spells on the sleeping Princess, asking her—

"Princess Aubergine! tell me true—
In what thing does your life lie?"

And the Princess replied—"In the life of your third son. Kill him, and I must die also!"

But the same thing happened. Though the young Prince was killed by his wicked mother, Aubergine remained alive and well; and so it went on day after day, until all the seven young Princes were slain, and their cruel mother still wept tears of rage and spite, at having killed her seven sons for naught.

Then the Sorceress-queen summoned up all her art, and laid such strong spells on the Princess Aubergine that she could no longer resist them, and was obliged to answer truly; so when the wicked Queen asked—

"Princess Aubergine! tell me true—
In what thing does your life lie?"

the poor Princess was obliged to answer—"In a river far away there lives a red and green fish. Inside the fish there is a bumble bee, inside the bee a tiny box, and inside the box is the wonderful nine-lakh[1] necklace. Put it on, and I shall die."

Then the Queen was satisfied, and set about finding the red and green fish. Therefore, when her husband the King came to see her, she began to sob and to cry, until he asked her what was the matter. Then she told him she had set her heart on procuring the wonderful nine-lakh necklace.

"But where is it to be found?" asked the King.

And the Queen answered in the words of the Princess Aubergine—"In a river far away there lives a red and green fish. Inside the fish there is a bumble bee, inside the bee a tiny box, and in the box is the nine-lakh necklace."

Now the King was a very kind man, and had grieved sincerely for the loss of his seven young sons, who, the Queen said, had died suddenly of an infectious disease. Seeing his wife so distressed, and being anxious to comfort her, he gave orders that every fisherman in his kingdom was to fish all day until the red and green fish was found. So all the fishermen set to work, and ere long the Queen's desire was fulfilled—the red and green fish was caught, and when the wicked sorceress opened it, there was the bumble bee, and inside the bee was the box, and inside the box the wonderful nine-lakh necklace, which the Queen put on at once.

Now no sooner had the Princess Aubergine been forced to tell the secret of her life by the Queen's magic, than she knew she must die; so she returned sadly to her foster-parents' hut, and telling them of her approaching death, begged them neither to burn or bury her body. "This is what I wish you to do," she said; "dress me in my finest clothes, lay me on my bed, scatter flowers over me, and carry me to the wildest wilderness. There you must place the bed on the ground, and build a high mud wall around it, so that no one will be able to see over."

The poor foster-parents, weeping bitterly, promised to do as she wished; so when the Princess died (which happened at the very moment the wicked Queen put on the nine-lakh necklace), they dressed her in her best clothes, scattered flowers over the bed, and carried her out to the wildest wilderness.

1 [Nine-lakh is a value of 900,000. Here it likely refers to the fantastically great worth of the necklace.]

Now when the Queen sent the slave girl to the Brahman's hut to enquire if the Princess Aubergine was really dead, the girl returned saying, "She is dead, but neither burnt nor buried; she lies out in the wilderness to the north, covered with flowers, as beautiful as the moon!"

The Queen was not satisfied with this reply, but as she could do no more, had to be content.

Now the King grieved bitterly for his seven young sons, and to try to forget his grief he went out hunting every day; so the Queen, who feared lest in his wanderings he might find the dead Princess Aubergine, made him promise never to hunt towards the north, for she said, "some evil will surely befall you if you do."

But one day, having hunted to the east, and the south, and the west, without finding game, he forgot his promise, and hunted towards the north. In his wanderings he lost his way, and came upon a high enclosure, with no door; being curious to know what it contained, he climbed over the wall. He could scarcely believe his eyes when he saw a lovely Princess lying on a flower-strewn bed, looking as if she had just fallen asleep. He could not believe she was dead, and, kneeling down beside her, spent the whole day praying and beseeching her to open her eyes. At nightfall he returned to his palace, but with the dawning he took his bow, and, dismissing all his attendants on the pretext of hunting alone, flew to his beautiful Princess. So he passed day after day, kneeling distractedly beside the lovely Aubergine, beseeching her to rise; but she never stirred.

Now at the end of a year, he one day found the most beautiful little boy imaginable lying beside the Princess. He was greatly astonished, but taking the child in his arms, cared for it tenderly all day, and at night laid it down beside its dead mother. After some time the child learnt to talk, and when the King asked it if its mother was always dead, it replied, "No! at night she is alive, and cares for me as you do during the day."

Hearing this, the King bade the boy ask his mother what made her die, and the next day the boy replied, "My mother says it is the nine-lakh necklace your Queen wears. At night, when the Queen takes it off, my mother becomes alive again, but every morning, when the Queen puts it on, my mother dies."

This greatly puzzled the King, who could not imagine what his Queen could have to do with the mysterious Princess, so he told the boy to ask his mother whose son he was.

The next morning the boy replied, "Mother bade me say I am your son, sent to console you for the loss of the seven fair sons your wicked Queen murdered out of jealousy of my mother, the lovely Princess Aubergine."

Then the King grew very wroth at the thought of his dead sons, and bade the boy ask his mother how the wicked Queen was to be punished, and by what means the necklace could be recovered.

The next morning the boy replied, "Mother says I am the only person who can recover the necklace, so tonight, when you return to the palace, you are to take me with you." So the King carried the boy back to the palace, and told all his ministers and courtiers that the child was his heir. On this the sorceress-queen, thinking of her own dead sons, became mad with jealousy, and determined to poison the boy. To this end she prepared some tempting sweetmeats, and, caressing the child, gave him a handful, bidding him eat them; but the child refused, saying he would not do so until she gave him the glittering necklace she wore round her throat, to play with.

Determined to poison the boy, and seeing no other way of inducing him to eat the sweetmeats, the sorceress-queen slipped off the nine-lakh necklace, and gave it to the child. No sooner had he touched it than he fled away so fast that none of the servants or guards could stop him, and never drew breath till he reached the place where the beautiful Princess Aubergine lay dead. He threw the necklace over her head, and immediately she rose up lovelier than ever. Then the King came, and besought her to return to the palace as his bride, but she replied, "I will never be your wife till that wicked sorceress is dead, for she would only murder me and my boy, as she murdered your seven young sons. If you will dig a deep ditch at the threshold of the palace, fill it with scorpions and snakes, throw the wicked Queen into it, and bury her alive, I will walk over her grave to be your wife."

So the King ordered a deep ditch to be dug, and had it filled with scorpions and snakes. Then he went to the sorceress-queen, and bade her come to see something very wonderful. But she refused, suspecting a trick. Then the guards seized her, bound her, flung her into the ditch amongst the scorpions and snakes, and buried her alive with them. As for the Princess Aubergine, she and her son walked over the grave, and lived happily in the palace ever after.

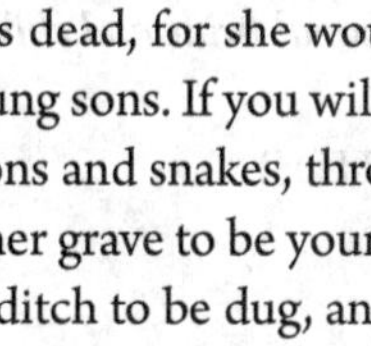

25. Rosamund Marriott Watson, *The Bird-Bride: A Volume of Ballads and Sonnets* (1889)[1]

Rosamund Marriott Watson was a prolific poet and critic who published largely under pseudonyms; her 1889 volume of fairy-tale influenced "ballads and sonnets"—from which the following poem is excerpted—was published under the name Graham R. Tomson. Watson was active in two important artistic and literary movements, aestheticism and decadence, but her fairy poems can also be read in intertextual dialogue with the wide range of field-based tale collections circulating in the late Victorian marketplace. Watson's attribution of "Ballad of the Bird-Bride" to the Eskimo signals her familiarity with both the tradition of British ballads lamenting lost love and non-European tale traditions—which were indeed becoming part of English print culture through the popularization of world folklore and ethnography and the rise of the English "folklore book"—including Henry Rink's popular Tales and Traditions of the Eskimo *published by Blackwood in 1875. This particular story of an animal transformed into a beautiful human bride has parallels in legends and tales about "selkies" (seal women), collected in Iceland, the Faroe Islands, and elsewhere. Watson's ballad gives voice to the lamentations of the grief-stricken husband, who has forever lost his animal-bride and children.*

BALLAD OF THE BIRD-BRIDE

(*ESKIMO*)

They never come back, though I loved them well;
  I watch the South in vain;
The snow-bound skies are blear and grey,
Waste and wide is the wild gull's way,
  And she comes never again.

Years agone, on the flat white strand,
  I won my sweet sea-girl:
Wrapped in my coat of the snow-white fur,
I watched the wild birds settle and stir,
  The grey gulls gather and whirl.

One, the greatest of all the flock,
  Perched on an ice-floe bare,
Called and cried as her heart were broke,
And straight they were changed, that fleet bird-folk,
  To women young and fair.

1 [Source: Graham R. Tomson [pseudonym for Rosamund Marriott Watson], *The Bird-Bride: A Volume of Ballads and Sonnets* (London: Longmans, Green and Co., 1889): 30–33.]

Swift I sprang from my hiding-place
  And held the fairest fast;
I held her fast, the sweet, strange thing:
Her comrades skirled, but they all took wing,
  And smote me as they passed.

I bore her safe to my warm snow house;
  Full sweetly there she smiled;
And yet, whenever the shrill winds blew,
She would beat her long white arms anew,
  And her eyes glanced quick and wild.

But I took her to wife, and clothed her warm
  With skins of the gleaming seal;
Her wandering glances sank to rest
When she held a babe to her fair, warm breast,
  And she loved me dear and leal.

Together we tracked the fox and the seal,
  And at her behest I swore
That bird and beast my bow might slay
For meat and for raiment, day by day,
  But never a grey gull more.

A weariful watch I keep for aye
  'Mid the snow and the changeless frost:
Woe is me for my broken word!
Woe, woe's me for my bonny bird,
  My bird and the love-time lost!

Have ye forgotten the old keen life?
  The hut with the skin-strewn floor?
O winged white wife, and children three,
Is there no room left in your hearts for me,
  Or our home on the low sea-shore?

Once the quarry was scarce and shy,
  Sharp hunger gnawed us sore,
My spoken oath was clean forgot,
My bow twanged thrice with a swift, straight shot,
  And slew me sea-gulls four.

The sun hung red on the sky's dull breast,
The snow was wet and red;
Her voice shrilled out in a woful cry,
She beat her long white arms on high,
"The hour is here," she said.

She beat her arms, and she cried full fain[1]
As she swayed and wavered there.
"Fetch me the feathers, my children three,
Feathers and plumes for you and me,
Bonny grey wings to wear!"

They ran to her side, our children three,
With the plumage black and grey;
Then she bent her down and drew them near,
She laid the plumes on our children dear,
'Mid the snow and the salt sea-spray.

"Babes of mine, of the wild wind's kin,
Feather ye quick, nor stay.
Oh, oho! but the wild winds blow!
Babes of mine, it is time to go:
Up, dear hearts, and away!"

And lo! the grey plumes covered them all,
Shoulder and breast and brow.
I felt the wind of their whirling flight:
Was it sea or sky? was it day or night?
It is always night-time now.

Dear, will you never relent, come back?
I loved you long and true.
O winged white wife, and our children three,
Of the wild wind's kin though ye surely be,
Are ye not of my kin too?

1 ["Full fain" is an archaic expression meaning well-pleased, full of joy.]

Ay, ye once were mine, and, till I forget,
  Ye are mine forever and aye,
Mine, wherever your wild wings go,
While shrill winds whistle across the snow
  And the skies are blear and grey.

Victor Stevens, *Little Red Riding Hood, or, The Saucy Squire of Sunnydale* (1900, pantomime script) [website]

Fairy tales have had an important place in British theaters from the eighteenth century to the present day. The rowdy, festive tradition of "pantomime" challenges contemporary visions of the fairy tale in many ways: for generations, fairy-tale pantomime has represented a form of popular family entertainment laced with topical reference and risqué humor. The full script (provided as a web text; see http://sites.broadviewpress.com/marveloustrans/) is a prime example of late Victorian pantomime and has much in common with current productions. It is a very loose adaptation of a well-known tale, "Little Red Riding Hood," featuring the requisite cross-dressed hero and "dame," a greedy and lecherous villain, music, dance, and plenty of slapstick humor.

D: MODERN/POSTMODERN TALES

26. Daniil Kharms, "A Children's Story" (c. 1920s-1930s; *translated by George Gibian, 1971*[1])

The experimental brand of humor and satire of Daniil Kharms (pen name of Daniil Ivanovich Yuvachov) flourished in the Soviet Union in the 1920s. First a poet, then a writer for children's magazines (one of them, Chizh, *is mentioned in the story below), he embraced literature of the absurd and co-founded a group of like-minded artists called OBERIU (an acronym for the Association of Real Art). Later, as the Stalinist government brought the arts fully under its direction, genres that did not promote a clear vision of social progress fell victim to censure or were pulled out of circulation, and their authors sanctioned or killed. Kharms's absurdist writing was at first banned; he was arrested in 1931 and again when the Nazis arrived in 1941, and died in prison in early 1942. George Gibian, a professor of Russian Literature at Cornell, rescued Kharms's children's stories from obscurity by translating them for the English-speaking world. "A Children's Story" represents an extraordinary reflection on the art of story-making and how writing exists at the intersection of creativity and imitation. Kharms then loops through an absurd logic that confounds the temporality and plot of the story. Ultimately, this avant-garde fantasy questions the temporal relationship we expect to see between experience (first) and writing (second), placing our role as readers into jeopardy. Who writes? Who is written? Where do we fit in?*

1 [Source: George Gibian, ed. and trans., *Russia's Lost Literature of the Absurd: A Literary Discovery* (Ithaca, NY: Cornell UP, 1971): 143–46.]

A CHILDREN'S STORY

"HERE," VANYA SAID, AND PUT a notebook on the table, "let's write a story."

"Let's," Lenochka said, and sat down in a chair.

Vanya took a pencil and wrote: "Once upon a time there lived a king."

Then Vanya started to think and to look up at the ceiling. Lenochka looked in the notebook and read what Vanya had written.

"There already is a story like that," Lenochka said.

"How do you know?" Vanya asked.

"I know because I read it," Lenochka said.

"How does the story go?" Vanya asked.

"A king was drinking tea with apples in it, and something stuck in his throat, and the queen pounded him on the back so the piece of apple would come out, and the king thought the queen was starting a fight, so he hit her over the head with a glass. The queen got mad and hit the king with a plate. The king hit the queen with a dish. The queen hit the king with a chair. The king jumped up and hit the queen with a table. The queen turned a cupboard over on the king. But the king crawled out from under the cupboard and smashed the queen with his crown. Then the queen caught the king by his hair and threw him out the window. But the king crawled back into the room through another window, grabbed the queen, and shoved her into the stove. But the queen crawled up through the chimney onto the roof and then climbed down the lightning conductor and into the garden and came back into the room through the window. The king was making a fire in the stove to burn up the queen. The queen sneaked up behind him and gave him a push. The king fell into the stove and burned up. That's the end of the story," Lenochka said.

"That's a very stupid story," Vanya said. "I wanted to write a completely different one."

"So go ahead and write it," Lenochka said.

Vanya took the pencil and wrote: "Once upon a time there lived a bandit."

"Wait a minute!" Lenochka shouted. "There already is a fairy tale like that."

"I didn't know that," Vanya said.

"Why, you know," Lenochka said, "a bandit was trying to run away from a guardsman and jumped on a horse, but jumped too hard and fell off the other side and dropped down on the ground. The bandit cursed and again jumped on the horse, but again he didn't figure his jump right, and fell over on the other side and fell on the ground. The bandit got up, shook his fist, jumped on the horse, and again jumped too far and fell down on the ground. At that point the bandit pulled a pistol from his belt, shot into the air, and again jumped on the horse, but with such force that he flew over it and hit the ground. Then the bandit tore his cap off his head, stomped on it with his feet, and again jumped up on the horse, and again jumped too far, fell on the ground, and broke his leg. The horse walked away a little. The bandit limped up to the horse and hit it on the head with his fist. The horse ran away. Guardsmen rode up, arrested the bandit, and took him to jail."

"I'm not going to write about a bandit," Vanya said.

"What are you going to write about?" Lenochka asked.

"I'm going to write a story about a blacksmith," Vanya said.

Vanya wrote: "Once upon a time there lived a blacksmith."

"There is a story like that already!" Lenochka shouted.

"Oh," said Vanya, and put his pencil down.

"Of course," Lenochka said. "Once upon a time there was a blacksmith. Once he was making a horseshoe, and he swung his hammer so hard that the hammer head flew off the handle, flew out the window, killed four pigeons, hit a fire tower, flew off to the side, broke a window in the fire chief's house, flew over the table where the fire chief and his wife were sitting, broke the wall in the fire chief's house, and flew out onto the street. There it knocked over a lamppost, knocked an ice-cream man off his feet, and hit Karl Ivanovich Shusterling on the head. He had taken his hat off for a moment to cool off the back of his head. After hitting the head of Karl Ivanovich Shusterling, the hammer head flew backward, again knocked the ice-cream man off his feet, knocked two fighting cats off the roof, knocked over a cow, killed four sparrows, again flew into the blacksmith shop, and flew back onto the handle which the smith was still holding in his right hand. All this happened so quickly that the smith didn't notice anything and kept on making a horseshoe."

"So that means a story has already been written about a smith; so I'll write a story about myself," Vanya said, and wrote: "Once upon a time there was a boy whose name was Vanya."

"There already is a story like that," Lenochka said. "Once upon a time there was a boy whose name was Vanya, and once he went up to ..."

"Wait a minute," Vanya said; "I wanted to write a story about myself."

"A story has already been written about you," Lenochka said.

"That's impossible," Vanya said.

"I tell you it's already been written," Lenochka said.

"Where has it been written?" Vanya asked, astonished.

"Buy Number 7 of the magazine *Chizh*, and you can read the story about yourself," Lenochka said.

Vanya bought *Chizh*, Number 7, and read in it the same story you have just finished reading.

27. Arkady Gaidar, "Skazka o voennoi taine, o Mal'chishe i ego tverdom slove" (1935; *translated by Helena Goscilo, 2005*[1])

Arkady Gaidar started his adult life early, age 14, when he enlisted as a soldier in the Red Army in 1918. Discharged later for medical reasons (shell-shock), he began to write—first novels, then tales, and then a career in journalism. The terrible experience of combat can be felt throughout his literary works, even in his stories for children. In "Skazka o voennoi taine," written shortly before World War II brought him back to a war zone as a journalist (he died on the Eastern Front in 1941), Gaidar situates his character Malchish-Kibalchish in the aftermath of a great war and on the doorstep of another bloody battle—with the same enemy. The "bourgeouins" (literally, the bourgeois people) will descend again to threaten the peace and prosperity of the boy and his village. Malchish-Kibalchish plays the role of hero, but also stands in for the never-revealed "military secret." Secrets play a curious role in narratives like this one, since they remain absent, yet as absences they constitute the pivot around which much of the story turns. In this tale, the secret and its keeper acquire force by virtue of their endurance, and intensify as symbols that develop from individual to collective and promise to action.

THE TALE OF THE MILITARY SECRET, MALCHISH-KIBALCHISH AND HIS SOLEMN WORD

LONG, LONG AGO, RIGHT AFTER the Big War ended, there lived a boy called Malchish-Kibalchish.

By then the Red Army had driven out the cursed bourgeouins' White troops and there was peace in the wide fields, in the green meadows where the rye grew, where the buckwheat flourished, where amid dense orchards and raspberry bushes stood the little house in which lived Malchish, nicknamed Kibalchish, and his father and his brother, but without a mother.

The father worked, mowing hay; the brother worked, carting hay. And Malchish helped, first his father, then his brother, or simply played with other boys and got into mischief.

Ahhhhh! How good life was! No whining bullets, no bursting shells, no burning villages. No need to get down on the floor to avoid bullets, no need to hide in the cellar from shells, no need to run into the forest to escape fires. No need to fear the bourgeouins. No one to bow down to. All you had to do was live and work—a good life!

And then one day—it was close to evening—Malchish-Kibalchish went out onto the porch. He looked around: the sky was clear, the wind warm, and the sun about

1 [Source: Marina Balina, Helena Goscilo, and Mark Lipovetsky, eds., *Politicizing Magic: An Anthology of Russian and Soviet Fairy Tales* (Evanston, IL: Northwestern UP, 2005): 123–30.]

to set behind the Black Mountains. And everything would have been fine, but something was wrong. And Malchish thought he heard something booming, something pounding. It seemed to Malchish as if the wind smelled not of orchard flowers, not of honey from the meadows, but either of smoke from fires or of powder from exploding shells. He told his father, but his father had come home tired.

"What're you talking about?" he said to Malchish. "That's the sound of a thunderstorm on the other side of the Black Mountains. That's the herdsmen's fires smoking behind the Blue River—they're tending their herds and cooking supper. You go to bed, Malchish, and sleep well."

Malchish left the room. He went to bed. But he couldn't sleep, no matter how he tried.

Suddenly he heard the sound of hoofs outside, then a knock at the window. Malchish-Kibalchish looked out and saw a rider by the window. The horse was coal black, the man's saber was shiny, his fur hat was gray, and the star on it was red.

"Hey! Get up!" the horseman shouted. "We've got trouble from where we least expected it. The cursed bourgeouins have attacked us from across the Black Mountains. It's flying bullets, exploding shells once again. Our units are fighting the bourgeouins, and our fastest messengers have galloped off to get help from the Red Army, which is far off."

His alarming announcement made, the horseman with the red star galloped off. And Malchish's father snatched his rifle from the wall, threw his bag over his shoulder, and put on his ammunition belt.

"Well," he told his older son, "I planted the rye thick, you'll clearly have a lot to harvest. Well," he told Malchish, "I've lived life under constant threat, and clearly you'll have to live it peacefully in my stead, Malchish."

With these words he soundly kissed Malchish and went off. And he had little time to spare for kissing, because by now everyone could hear and see how shells were bursting beyond the meadows and the dawn sky was burning from the glow of smoking fires beyond the mountains ...

A day went by, then another. Malchish went out onto the porch; no, no sign yet of the Red Army. Malchish climbed up onto the roof. He sat there all day. But there was nothing to see. Toward night he went to bed. Suddenly he heard hoofs again, a knock at the window. Malchish looked out: the same horseman was at the window. Only his horse was thin and tired, his saber bent and dark, his fur hat bullet-ridden, the star all torn, and his head bandaged.

"Get up!" shouted the horseman. "If it was a disaster before, it's now total disaster. There's a lot of bourgeouins, there are few of us. Nonstop bullets in the field, thousands of shells among the units. Hey, get up, you gotta help!"

The older brother got up and said to Malchish: "Good-bye, Malchish ... You're on your own now. There's cabbage soup in the pot, bread on the table, water in the spring, and your head on your shoulders. Live as best you can and don't wait for me."

A day went by, then another. Malchish sat on the roof by the chimney and in the distance saw a horseman racing toward him. The horseman galloped up, leaped from his horse, and said: "Give me a drink of water, good Malchish. I've not drunk for three days, not slept for three nights, and ridden three horses to death. The Red Army knows of our disaster. All the trumpets have sounded as loud as loud as can be. All the drums have sounded as loud as loud can be. All the war banners have been unfurled as far as far can be. All the Red Army is racing and galloping to help us. All we need, Malchish, is to hold out until tomorrow night."

Malchish climbed down from the roof, brought him water to drink. The messenger drank his fill and cantered off.

Evening arrived, and Malchish went to bed. But Malchish couldn't fall asleep—how could he possibly sleep?

Suddenly he heard footsteps on the street, rustling at the window. Malchish looked out and saw the same man standing at the window. The same, yet not the same: he had no horse—his horse was dead; no saber—his saber was broken; no fur hat—his hat had blown off; and he staggered where he stood.

"Hey, get up!" he shouted for the last time. "We've got shells, but the gunners have had it. We've got rifles, but few fighting men. And help is near, but we've no strength. Hey, whoever's left, get up! All we need is to make it through the night and hold out a day."

Malchish-Kibalchish looked down the street: the street was empty. The shutters weren't banging, the gates weren't creaking—there was no one to get up. The fathers had gone off, and the brothers had gone off—and no one was left.

All Malchish could see was an old man a hundred years old come out from behind a gate. The old man tried to lift a rifle, but he was so old he couldn't lift it. He tried to buckle on a saber, but he was so weak he couldn't buckle it. And the old man sat down on the ground, his head drooping, and he wept.

And it pained Malchish to see him. Malchish-Kibalchish went out into the street and shouted loud—loud enough for everyone to hear:

"Hey, you boys, boys big and small! Are we boys just to go on playing with wooden swords and skipping rope? Our fathers have gone, our brothers have gone. Are we boys just going to sit around waiting for the bourgeouins to come and carry us off to their cursed bourgeouinland?"

When they heard these words, boys big and small raised a great shout! Some ran out the door, some climbed out the window, and others jumped over the fence.

They all wanted to go and help fight. Only the bad boy called Malchish-Plokhish wanted to go to bourgeouinland. But he was so cunning, this Plokhish, that he didn't say anything; he only pulled up his breeches and ran off with the others, as though he intended to help.

And the boys fought through the dark night to the bright dawn. Only Plokhish didn't fight, but walked about looking for some way to help the bourgeouins. And behind a small hill Plokhish saw a pile of boxes, and in the boxes were hidden black bombs, white shells, and yellow cartridges. "Uh-uh," thought Plokhish. "This is just what I need."

Just then the Head Bourgeouin asked his bourgeouins: "So, bourgeouins, have you won the victory yet?" "No," the bourgeouins replied. "We trounced the fathers and the brothers, and we'd have been completely victorious, but Malchish-Kibalchish came to help them, and we can't beat him for the life of us."

The Head Bourgeouin was startled, grew furious, and shouted in a threatening voice: "How's it possible you can't beat Malchish? Akh, you useless yellow-belly bourgeois-nellies! How's it possible you can't trounce a kid like that? Get back there fast, and don't come back until you're victorious."

And the bourgeouins sat wondering what on earth they could do to defeat Malchish-Kibalchish. Suddenly they saw Malchish-Plokhish come crawling out of the bushes and making straight for them.

"Rejoice!" he shouted. "I, Plokhish, did it all myself. I chopped some logs, I got some hay, and set fire to all the boxes with the black bombs, the white shells, and the yellow cartridges. It'll all go up any minute!"

The bourgeouins were overjoyed at the news, enrolled Malchish-Plokhish instantly in their bourgeouin ranks, and gave him a whole barrel of jam and a whole basket of cookies.

Malchish-Plokhish sat there, stuffing himself and rejoicing.

All of a sudden the boxes he'd lit exploded! And the bang sounded like a thousand thunderbolts striking in one spot, and a thousand flashes of lightning bursting from a single cloud.

"Treason!" cried Malchish-Kibalchish.

"Treason!" cried all his faithful boys.

Then out of the smoke and fire poured the bourgeouin forces, and they overcame and seized Malchish-Kibalchish.

They put Malchish in heavy chains. They imprisoned Malchish in a stone tower. And they hurried off to ask what the Head Bourgeouin wanted to do with the captured Malchish.

The Head Bourgeouin thought long and hard, then he got an idea and said:

"We'll kill this Malchish. But first we'll make him tell us their Military Secret. You go to him, bourgeouins, and ask him: 'How is it that forty Tsars and forty Kings fought the Red Army, fought and fought, but only got trounced? How is it, Malchish, that all the prisons are full, that all the penal colonies are packed, and all the police are at their posts, and all our armies are on the go, yet we have no peace during the light of day or the dark of night? How is it, Malchish, cursed Kibalchish, that in my High Bourgeouinland, and in the Plains Kingdom, and in the Snow Realm, and in the Sultry State, everywhere on the same day in early spring and on the same day in late fall, they sing the same songs, though in different languages, carry the same banners, though in different hands, make the same speeches, think the same thoughts, and do the same things?' You ask him, bourgeouins, 'Does the Red Army, Malchish, have a military secret?' And have him tell you the secret. 'Do your workers have foreign aid?' And let him tell you where that aid comes from. 'Is there a secret passageway, Malchish, from your country to all the countries in the world, along which as soon as you call, our people here immediately respond; any time you burst into song, ours join in; anything you say, ours start to ponder?'"

The bourgeouins went off, but soon returned:

"No, Head Bourgeouin, Malchish-Kibalchish didn't reveal the Military Secret to us. He laughed right in our faces. 'The strong Red Army does have a powerful secret,' he said. 'And no matter when you attack, you'll not gain a victory.' He said, 'We have help beyond calculation, and however many people you throw in prison, you still won't succeed, and you'll have no peace during the light of day or the dark of night. There are profound secret passageways,' he said. 'But however hard you look, you won't find them. And even if you do find them, you won't be able to block them, close them, cover them. And that's all I'll tell you, and you cursed bourgeouins will never figure it out yourselves.'"

The Head Bourgeouin frowned at this and said:

"Put this secretive Malchish-Kibalchish to the most terrible torture known to man, and get the Military Secret from him, for we'll have neither life nor peace without this important Secret."

The bourgeouins left and this time returned after a long while, shaking their heads. "No," they said. "It didn't work, chief Head Bourgeouin. He stood pale, did Malchish, but proud, and he didn't tell us the Military Secret because he'd given his solemn word. And when we were leaving he got down and put his ear to the heavy stone of the cold floor, and, would you believe it, Head Bourgeouin, he smiled in such a way that all of us bourgeouins shuddered in fear, wondering if he'd heard our inevitable destruction marching along those secret passageways ..."

"What kind of country is this?" exclaimed the Head Bourgeouin in amazement. "What an inexplicable country, where even boys like this know the Military Secret and keep their solemn word so faithfully! Move quickly, bourgeouins, and kill this proud Malchish. Load the cannons, unsheathe your sabers, unfurl our bourgeouin banners, because I hear our signalmen sounding the alarm and our standard-bearers waving the flags. Looks like it'll be no light skirmish, but a heavy battle."

And Malchish-Kibalchish perished.

It was like a storm. Military guns rumbled like a peal of thunder. Exploding shells flashed like a streak of lightning. Men on horses swept in like the wind. And red banners sailed past like storm clouds. That's how the Red Army attacked.

Just as streams flowing down a dusty mountain unite in turbulent, loamy torrents, so at the first violent sound of war uprisings started seething in Mountainous Bourgeouinland, and thousands of angry voices joined them in the Plains Kingdom, and the Snow Realm, and the Sultry State.

And the defeated Head Bourgeouin fled in fear, loudly cursing the country with its amazing people, its invincible Red Army, and its undiscovered Military Secret.

They buried Malchish-Kibalchish on the green knoll by the Blue River. And they placed a big red flag above his grave.

Steamships sailing by hail Malchish!
Pilots flying by hail Malchish!
Locomotives racing by hail Malchish!
And Pioneers passing by salute him!

28. Sylvia Townsend Warner, *The Cat's Cradle-Book* (1940)[1]

The Cat's Cradle-Book *was published midway through a prolific writing career that spanned more than 50 years and that author Sylvia Townsend Warner nonetheless described as "accidental" (she had studied to be a musician). Warner wrote poetry, novels, and short stories and tales—many of which appeared in the* New Yorker *magazine. Her story of "Bluebeard's Daughter" belongs to a tradition in English of Orientalized "Bluebeard" tales that stretches back to the eighteenth century, when Orientalism first took hold in Europe. The trend may have begun in 1763 when a translator of Charles Perrault who signed his work G.M. (probably Guy Miège) changed the type of knife Bluebeard wields from a "cutlass" (Robert Samber's 1729 translation) to a "scimitar." Later, George Colman went further and set the story in Turkey for a 1798 melodramatic stage play,* Bluebeard, or Female Curiosity! *When Warner borrowed the idea of the Turkish setting, it had already been standard "Bluebeard" fare for over 150 years. Warner's unique twist on the story is that it does not follow the fate of the bearded man and his wife, but of their daughter. Djamileh bears the mark of genealogy in this exploration of curiosity and its effects on the marriage bond and the trust necessary to sustain it. In the twentieth-century extension of the Bluebeard family history, science appears as an acceptable outlet for the husband and wife's mutual curiosity that will "sublimate" it, in Djamileh's words, or prevent it from becoming a destructive force in the couple's personal lives.*

1 [Source: Sylvia Townsend Warner, *The Cat's Cradle-Book* (New York, NY: Viking P, 1940): 157–80.]

BLUEBEARD'S DAUGHTER

Every child can tell of his ominous pigmentation, of his ruthless temper, of the fate of his wives and of his own fate, no less bloody than theirs; but—unless it be here and there a Director of Oriental Studies—no one now remembers that Bluebeard had a daughter. Amid so much that is wild and shocking this gentler trait of his character has been overlooked. Perhaps, rather than spoil the symmetry of a bad husband by an admission that he was a good father, historians have suppressed her. I have heard her very existence denied, on the grounds that none of Bluebeard's wives lived long enough to bear him a child. This shows what it is to give a dog a bad name. To his third wife, the mother of Djamileh, Bluebeard was most tenderly devoted, and no shadow of suspicion rested upon her quite natural death in childbed.

From the moment of her birth Djamileh became the apple of Bluebeard's eye. His messengers ransacked Georgia and Circassia to find wet-nurses of unimpeachable health, beauty, and virtue; her infant limbs were washed in nothing but rosewater and swaddled in Chinese silks. She cut her teeth upon a cabochon emerald engraved with propitious mottoes, and all the nursery vessels, mugs, platters, ewers, basins, and chamber-pots were of white jade. Never was there a more adoring and conscientious father than Bluebeard, and I have sometimes thought that the career of this much-widowed man was inevitably determined by his anxiety to find for Djamileh an ideal stepmother.

Djamileh's childhood was happy, for none of the stepmothers lasted long enough to outwear their good intentions, and every evening, whatever his occupations during the day, Bluebeard came to the nursery for an hour's romp. But three days before her ninth birthday Djamileh was told that her father was dead; and while she was still weeping for her loss she was made to weep even more bitterly by the statement that he was a bad man and that she must not cry for him. Dressed in crape, with the Bluebeard diamonds sparkling like angry tears beneath her veils, and wearing a bandage on her wrist, Fatima came to Djamileh's pavilion and paid off nurses and governesses. With her came Aunt Ann, and a strange young man whom she was told to call Uncle Selim; and while the nurses lamented and packed and the governesses sulked, swooned, and clapped their hands for sherbet, Djamileh listened to this trio disputing as to what should be done with her.

"For she can't stay here alone," said Fatima. "And nothing will induce me to spend another night under this odious roof."

"Why not send her to school?"

"Or to the Christians?" suggested Selim.

"Perhaps there is some provision for her in the will?"

"Will! Don't tell me that such a monster could make a will, a valid will. Besides, he never made one."

Fatima stamped her foot, and the diamond necklace sidled on her stormy bosom. Still disputing, they left the room.

That afternoon all the silk carpets and embroidered hangings, all the golden dishes and rock-crystal wine-coolers, together with the family jewels and Bluebeard's unique collection of the Persian erotic poets, were packed up and sent by camel to Selim's residence in Teheran. Thither travelled also Fatima, Ann, Selim, and Djamileh, together with a few selected slaves, Fatima in one litter with Selim riding at her side, doing his best to look stately but not altogether succeeding, since his mount was too big for him, Ann and Djamileh in the other. During the journey Ann said little, for she was engaged in ticking off entries in a large scroll. But once or twice she told Djamileh not to fidget, and to thank her stars that she had kind friends who would provide for her.

As it happened, Djamileh was perfectly well provided for. Bluebeard had made an exemplary and flawless will by which he left all his property to his only daughter and named his solicitor as her guardian until she should marry. No will can please everybody; and there was considerable heartburning when Badruddin removed Djamileh and her belongings from the care of Fatima, Ann, and Selim, persisting to the last filigree egg-cup in his thanks for their kind offices towards the heiress and her inheritance.

Badruddin was a bachelor, and grew remarkably fine jasmines. Every evening when he came home from his office he filled a green watering-pot and went to see how they had passed the day. In the latticed garden the jasmine bush awaited him like a dumb and exceptionally charming wife. Now he often found Djamileh sitting beneath the bush, pale and silent, as though, in response to being watered so carefully, the jasmine had borne him a daughter.

It would have been well for Djamileh if she had owed her being to such an innocent parentage. But she was Bluebeard's daughter, and all the girl-babies of the neighbourhood cried in terror at her father's name. What was more, the poor girl could not look at herself in the mirror without being reminded of her disgrace. For she had inherited her father's colouring. Her hair was a deep butcher's blue, her eyebrows and eyelashes were blue also. Her complexion was clear and pale, and if some sally of laughter brought a glow to her cheek it was of the usual pink, but the sinister parental pigmentation reasserted itself on her lips, which were deep purple as though stained with eating mulberries; and the inside of her mouth and her tongue were dusky blue like a well-bred chow-dog's. For the rest she was like any other woman, and when she pricked her finger the blood ran scarlet.

Looks so much out of the common, if carried off with sufficient assurance, might be an asset to a modern miss. In Djamileh's time taste was more classical. Blue hair and purple lips, however come by, would have been a serious handicap for any young woman—how much more so, then, for her, in whom they were not only regrettable but scandalous. It was impossible for Bluebeard's badged daughter to be like other girls of her age. The purple mouth seldom smiled; the blue hair, severely braided by day, was often at night wetted with her tears. She might, indeed, have dyed it. But filial devotion forbade. Whatever his faults, Bluebeard had been a good father.

Djamileh had a great deal of proper feeling; it grieved her to think of her father's crimes. But she had also a good deal of natural partiality, and disliked Fatima; and this led her to try to find excuses for his behaviour. No doubt it was wrong, very wrong, to murder so many wives; but Badruddin seemed to think that it was almost as wrong to have married them, at any rate to have married so many of them. Experience, he said, should have taught the deceased that female curiosity is insatiable; it was foolish to go on hoping to find a woman without curiosity. Speaking with gravity, he conjured his ward to struggle, as far as in her lay, with this failing, so natural in her own sex, so displeasing to the other.

Djamileh fastened upon his words. To mark her reprobation of curiosity, the fault which had teased on her father to his ruin, she resolved never to be in the least curious herself. And for three weeks she did not ask a single question. At the end of the third week she fell into a violent fever, and Badruddin, who had been growing more and more disquieted by what appeared to him to be a protracted fit of sulks, sent for a doctoress. The doctoress was baffled by the fever, but did not admit it. What the patient needed, she said, was light but distracting conversation. Mentioning in the course of her chat that she had discovered from the eunuch that the packing-case in the lobby contained a new garden hose, the doctoress had the pleasure of seeing Djamileh make an instant recovery from her fever. Congratulating herself on her skill and on her fee, the old dame went off, leaving Djamileh to realize that it was not enough to refrain from asking questions, some more radical method of combating curiosity must be found. And so when Badruddin, shortly after her recovery, asked her in a laughing way how she would like a husband, she replied seriously that she would prefer a public-school education.

This was not possible. But the indulgent solicitor did what he could to satisfy this odd whim, and Djamileh made such good use of her opportunities that by the time she was fifteen she had spoilt her handwriting, forgotten how to speak French, lost all her former interest in botany, and asked only the most unspeculative questions. Badruddin was displeased. He sighed to think that the intellectual Bluebeard's child should have grown up so dull-witted, and spent more and more time in the company of his jasmines. Possibly, even, he consulted them, for though they were silent they could be expressive. In any case, after a month or so of inquiries, interviews, and drawing up treaties, he told Djamileh that, acting under her father's will, he had made arrangements for her marriage.

Djamileh was sufficiently startled to ask quite a number of questions, and Badruddin congratulated himself on the aptness of his prescription. His choice had fallen upon Prince Kayel Oumarah, a young man of good birth, good looks, and pleasant character, but not very well-to-do. The prince's relations were prepared to overlook Djamileh's origin in consideration of her fortune, which was enormous, and Kayel, who was of a rather sentimental turn of mind, felt that it was an act of chivalry to marry a girl whom other young men might scorn for what was no fault of hers, loved her already for being so much obliged to him, and wrote several ghazals expressing a preference for blue hair.

"What wouldn't I do, what wouldn't I do,
To get at that hair of heavenly blue?"

(the original Persian is, of course, more elegant) sang Kayel under her window. Djamileh thought this harping on her hair not in the best of taste, more especially since Kayel had a robust voice and the whole street might hear him. But it was flattering to have poems written about her (she herself had no turn for poetry), and when she peeped through the lattice she thought that he had a good figure and swayed to and fro with a great deal of feeling. Passion and a good figure can atone for much; and perhaps when they were man and wife he would leave off making personal remarks.

After a formal introduction, during which Djamileh offered Kayel symbolical sweetmeats and in her confusion ate most of them herself, the young couple were married. And shortly afterwards they left town for the Castle of Shady Transports, the late Bluebeard's country house.

Djamileh had not set eyes on Shady Transports since she was carried away from it in the same litter as Aunt Ann and the inventory. It had been in the charge of a caretaker ever since. But before the wedding Badruddin had spent a few days at the village inn, and under his superintendence the roof had been mended, the gardens trimmed up, all the floors very carefully scrubbed, and a considerable quantity of female attire burned in the stable yard. There was no look of former tragedy about the place when Djamileh and Kayel arrived. The fountain plashed innocently in the forecourt, all the most appropriate flowers in the language of love were bedded out in the parterre, a troop of new slaves, very young and handsomely dressed, stood bowing on either side of the door, and seated on cushions in stiff attitudes of expectation Maya and Moghreb, Djamileh's favourite dolls, held out their jointed arms in welcome.

Tears came into her eyes at this token of Badruddin's understanding heart. She picked up her old friends and kissed first one and then the other, begging their pardon for the long years in which they had suffered neglect. She thought they must have pined, for certainly they weighed much less than of old. Then she recollected that she was grown up, and had a husband.

At the moment he was not to be seen. Still clasping Maya and Moghreb, she went in search of him, and found him in the armoury, standing lost in admiration before a display of swords, daggers, and cutlasses. Djamileh remembered how, as a child, she had been held up to admire, and warned not to touch.

"That one comes from Turkestan," she said. "My father could cut off a man's head with it at a single blow."

Kayel pulled the blade a little way from the sheath. It was speckled with rust, and the edge was blunted.

"We must have them cleaned up," he said. "It's a pity to let them get like this, for I've never seen a finer collection."

"He had a splendid collection of poets, too," said Djamileh. "I was too young to read them then, of course, but now that I am married to a poet myself I shall read them all."

"What a various-minded man!" exclaimed Kayel as he followed her to the library.

It is always a pleasure to explore a fine old rambling country house. Many people whose immediate thoughts would keep them tediously awake slide into a dream by fancying that such a house has—no exact matter how—come into their possession. In fancy they visit it for the first time, they wander from room to room, trying each bed in turn, pulling out the books, opening Indian boxes, meeting themselves in mirrors.... All is new to them, and all is theirs.

For Kayel and Djamileh this charming delusion was a matter of fact. Djamileh indeed declared that she remembered Shady Transports from the days of her childhood, and was always sure that she knew what was round the next corner; but really her recollections were so fragmentary that except for the sentiment of the thing she might have been exploring her old home for the first time. As for Kayel, who had spent most of his life in furnished lodgings, the comfort and spaciousness of his wife's palace impressed him even more than he was prepared to admit. Exclaiming with delight, the young couple ransacked the house, or wandered arm in arm through the grounds, discovering fishponds, icehouses, classical grottoes, and rustic bridges. The gardeners heard their laughter among the blossoming thickets, or traced where they had sat by the quantity of cherry-stones.

At last a day came when it seemed that Shady Transports had yielded up to them all its secrets. A sharp thunderstorm had broken up the fine weather. The rain was still falling, and Kayel and Djamileh sat in the western parlour playing chess like an old married couple. The rain had cooled the air, indeed it was quite chilly; and Kayel, who was getting the worst of the game, complained of a draught that blew on his back and distracted him.

"There can't really be a draught, my falcon," objected Djamileh, "for draughts don't blow out of solid walls, and there is only a wall behind you."

"There is a draught," persisted he. "I take your pawn. No, wait a moment, I'm not sure that I do. How can I possibly play chess in a whirlwind?"

"Change places," said his wife, "and I'll turn the board."

They did so and continued the game. It was now Djamileh's move; and as she sat gazing at the pieces Kayel fell to studying her intent and unobservant countenance. She was certainly quite pretty, very pretty even, in spite of her colouring. Marriage had improved her, thought he. A large portrait of Bluebeard hung on the wall behind her. Kayel's glance went from living daughter to painted sire, comparing the two physiognomies. Was there a likeness—apart, of course, from the blue hair? Djamileh was said to be the image of her mother; certainly the rather foxlike mask before him, the narrow eyes and pointed chin, bore no resemblance to the prominent eyes and heavy jowl of the portrait. Yet there was a something ... the pouting lower lip, perhaps, emphasized now by her considering expression. Kayel had another look at the portrait.

"Djamileh! There *is* a draught! I saw the hangings move." He jumped up and pulled them aside. "What did I say?" he inquired triumphantly.

"Oh! Another surprise! Oh, haven't I a lovely Jack-in-the-Box house?"

The silken hangings had concealed a massive stone archway, closed by a green baize door.

Kayel nipped his wife's ear affectionately. "You who remember everything so perfectly—what's behind that door?"

"Rose-petal conserve," she replied. "I have just remembered how it used to be brought out from the cupboard when I was good."

"I don't believe it. I don't believe there's a cupboard, I don't believe you were ever good."

"Open it and see."

Beyond the baize door a winding stair led into a small gallery or corridor, on one side of which were windows looking into the park, on the other, doors. It was filled with a green and moving light reflected from the wet foliage outside. They turned to each other with rapture. A secret passage—five doors in a row, five new rooms waiting to be explored! With a dramatic gesture Kayel threw open the first door. A small dark closet was revealed, perfectly empty. A trifle dashed, they opened the next door. Another closet, small, dark, and empty. The third door revealed a third closet, the exact replica of the first and second.

Djamileh began to laugh at her husband's crestfallen air.

"In my day," she said, "all these cupboards were full of rose-petal conserve. So now you see how good I was."

Kayel opened the fourth door.

He was a solemn young man, but now he began to laugh also. Four empty closets, one after another, seemed to these amiable young people the height of humour. They laughed so loudly that they did not hear a low peal of thunder, the last word of the retreating storm. A dove who had her nest in the lime tree outside the window was startled by their laughter or by the thunder; she flew away, looking pale and unreal against the slate-coloured sky. Her flight stirred the branches, which shook off their raindrops, spattering them against the casement.

"Now for the fifth door," said Kayel.

But the fifth door was locked.

"Djamileh, dear, run and ask the steward for the keys. But don't mention which door we want unfastened. Slaves talk so, they are always imagining mysteries."

"I am rather tired of empty cupboards, darling. Shall we leave this one for the present? At any rate till after tea? So much emptiness has made me very hungry, I really need my tea."

"Djamileh, fetch the keys."

Djamileh was an obedient wife, but she was also a prudent one. When she had found the bunch of keys she looked carefully over those which were unlabelled. They were many, and of all shapes and sizes; but at last she found the key she had been looking for and which she had dreaded to find. It was a small key, made of gold and finely arabesqued; and on it there was a small dark stain that might have been a bloodstain.

She slipped it off the ring and hid it in her dress.

Returning to the gallery, she was rather unpleasantly struck by Kayel's expression. She could never have believed that his open countenance could wear such a look of cupidity or that his eyes could become so beady. Hearing her step, he started violently, as though roused from profound absorption.

"There you are! What an age you have been—darling! Let's see now. Icehouse, Stillroom, Butler's Pantry, Wine-cellar, Family Vault ... I wonder if this is it?"

He tried key after key, but none of them fitted. He tried them all over again, upside-down or widdershins. But still they did not fit. So then he took out his pocket-knife, and tried to pick the lock. This also was useless.

"Eblis take this lock!" he exclaimed. And suddenly losing his temper, he began to kick and batter at the door. As he did so there was a little click; and one of the panels of the door fell open upon a hinge, and disclosed a piece of parchment, framed and glazed, on which was an inscription in ancient Sanskrit characters.

"What the ... Here, I can't make this out."

Djamileh, who was better educated than her husband in such useless studies as calligraphy, examined the parchment, and read aloud: "CURIOSITY KILLED THE CAT."

Against her bosom she felt the little gold key sidle, and she had the unpleasant sensation which country language calls: "The grey goose walking over your grave."

"I think," she said gently, "I think, dear husband, we had better leave this door alone."

Kayel scratched his head and looked at the door.

"Are you sure that's what it means? Perhaps you didn't read it right."

"I am quite sure that is what it means."

"But, Djamileh, I do want to open the door."

"So do I, dear. But under the circumstances we had better not do anything of the sort. The doors in this house are rather queer sometimes. My poor father ... my poor stepmothers ..."

"I wonder," mused Kayel, "if we could train a cat to turn the lock and go in first."

"Even if we could, which I doubt, I don't think that would be at all fair to the cat. No, Kayel, I am sure we should agree to leave this door alone."

"It's not that I am in the least inquisitive," said Kayel, "for I am not. But as master of the house I really think it my duty to know what's inside this cupboard. It might be firearms, for instance, or poison, which might get into the wrong hands. One has a certain responsibility, hang it!"

"Yes, of course. But all the same I feel sure we should leave the door alone."

"Besides, I have you to consider, Djamileh. As a husband, you must be my first consideration. Now you may not want to open the door just now; but suppose, later on, when you were going to have a baby, you developed one of those strange yearnings that women at such times are subject to; and suppose it took the form of longing to know what was behind this door. It might be very bad for you, Djamileh, it might imperil your health, besides birth-marking the baby. No! It's too grave a risk. We had much better open the door immediately."

And he began to worry the lock again with his penknife.

"Kayel, please don't. *Please* don't. I implore you, I have a feeling—"

"Nonsense. Women always have feelings."

"—as though I were going to be sick. In fact, I am sure I am going to be sick."

"Well, run off and be sick, then. No doubt it was the thunderstorm, and all those strawberries."

"I can't run off, Kayel. I don't feel well enough to walk; you must carry me. Kayel!"—she laid her head insistently on his chest—"Kayel! I felt sick this morning, too."

And she laid her limp weight against him so firmly that with a sigh he picked her up and carried her down the corridor.

Laid on the sofa, she still kept a firm hold on his wrist, and groaned whenever he tried to detach himself. At last, making the best of a bad job, he resigned himself, and spent the rest of the day reading aloud to her from the erotic Persian poets. But he did not read with his usual fervour; the lyrics, as he rendered them, might as well have been genealogies. And Djamileh, listening with closed eyes, debated within herself why Kayel should be so cross. Was it just the locked closet? Was it, could it be, that he was displeased by the idea of a baby with Bluebeard blood? This second possibility was highly distressing to her, and she wished, more and more fervently, as she lay on the sofa keeping up a pretence of delicate health and disciplining her healthy appetite to a little bouillon and some plain sherbet, that she had hit upon a pretext with fewer consequences entailed.

It seemed to her that they were probably estranged forever. So it was a great relief to be awakened in the middle of the night by Kayel's usual affable tones, even though the words were:

"Djamileh, I believe I've got it! All we have to do is to get a stonemason, and a ladder, and knock a hole in the wall. Then we can look in from outside. No possible harm in that."

All the next day and the day after, Kayel perambulated the west wing of Shady Transports with his stonemasons, directing them where to knock holes in the walls; for it had been explained to the slaves that he intended to bring the house up to date by throwing out a few bow-windows. But not one of these perspectives (the walls of Shady Transports were exceedingly massy) afforded a view into the locked closet. While these operations were going on he insisted that Djamileh should remain at his side. It was essential, he said, that she should appear interested in the improvements, because of the slaves. All this while she was carrying about that key on her person, and debating whether she should throw it away, in case Kayel, by getting possession of it, should endanger his life, or whether she should keep it and use it herself the moment he was safely out of the way.

Jaded in nerves and body, at the close of the second day they had a violent quarrel. It purported to be about the best method of pruning acacias, but while they were hurrying from sarcasm to acrimony, from acrimony to abuse, from abuse to fisticuffs, they were perfectly aware that in truth they were quarrelling as to which of them should first get at that closet.

"Laterals! Laterals!" exclaimed Djamileh. "You know no more of pruning than you know of dressmaking. That's right! Tear out my hair, do!"

"No, thank you." Kayel folded his arms across his chest. "I have no use for *blue hair*."

Pierced by this taunt, Djamileh burst into tears. The soft-hearted Kayel felt that he had gone too far, and made several handsome apologies for the remark; but it seemed likely his apologies would be in vain, for Djamileh only came out of her tears to ride off on a high horse.

"No, Kayel," she said, putting aside his hand, and speaking with exasperating nobility and gentleness. "No, no, it is useless, do not let us deceive ourselves any longer.

I do not blame you; your feeling is natural and one should never blame people for natural feelings."

"Then why have you been blaming me all this time for a little natural curiosity?"

Djamileh swept on.

"And how could you possibly have felt anything but aversion for one in whose veins so blatantly runs the blood of the Bluebeards, for one whose hair, whose lips, stigmatize her as the child of an unfortunate monster? I do not blame you, Kayel. I blame myself, for fancying you could ever love me. But I will make you the only amends in my power. I will leave you."

A light quickened in Kayel's eye. So he thought she would leave him at Shady Transports, did he?

"Tomorrow we will go *together* to Badruddin. He arranged our marriage, he had better see about our divorce."

Flushed with temper, glittering with tears, she threw herself into his willing arms. They were still in all the raptures of sentiment and first love, and in the even more enthralling raptures of sentiment and first grief, when they set out for Teheran. Absorbed in gazing into each other's eyes and wiping away each other's tears with pink silk handkerchiefs, they did not notice that a drove of stampeding camels was approaching their palanquin; and it was with the greatest surprise and bewilderment that they found themselves tossed over a precipice.

When Djamileh recovered her senses she found herself lying in a narrow green pasture, beside a watercourse. Some fine broad-tailed sheep were cropping the herbage around, and an aged shepherdess was bathing her forehead and slapping her hands.

"How did I come here?" she inquired.

"I really cannot tell you," answered the shepherdess. "All I know is that about half an hour ago you, and a handsome young man, and a coachman, and a quantity of silk cushions and chicken sandwiches appeared, as it were from heaven, and fell amongst us and our sheep. Perhaps as you are feeling better you would like one of the sandwiches?"

"Where is that young man? He is not dead?"

"Not at all. A little bruised, but nothing worse. He recovered before you, and feeling rather shaken he went off with the shepherds to have a drink at the inn. The coachman went with them."

Djamileh ate another sandwich, brooding on Kayel's heartlessness.

"Listen," she said, raising herself on one elbow. "I have not time to tell you the whole of my history, which is long and complicated with unheard-of misfortunes. Suffice it to say that I am young, beautiful, wealthy, well born, and accomplished, and the child of doting and distinguished parents. At their death I fell into the hands of an unscrupulous solicitor who, entirely against my will, married me to that young man you have seen. We had not been married for a day before he showed himself a monster of jealousy; and though my conduct has been unspotted as the snow he has continually belaboured me with threats and reproaches, and now has determined to shut me up, forever, in a hermitage on the Caucasus mountains, inherited from a woman-hating uncle (the whole family are very queer). We were on our way thither when, by the interposition of my good genius, the palanquin overturned, and we arrived among your flocks as we did."

"Indeed," replied the aged shepherdess. "He said nothing of all that. But I do not doubt it. Men are a cruel and fantastic race. I too have lived a life chequered with many strange adventures and unmerited misfortunes. I was born in India, the child of a virtuous Brahmin and of a mother who had, before my birth, graced the world with eleven daughters, each lovelier than the last. In the opinion of many well-qualified persons, I, the youngest of her children, was even fairer—"

"I can well believe it," said Djamileh. "But, venerable Aunt, my misfortunes compel me to postpone the pleasure of hearing your story until a more suitable moment. It is, as you will see, essential that I should seize this chance of escaping from my tyrant. Here is a purse. I shall be everlastingly obliged if you will conduct me to the nearest livery-stables where I can hire a small chariot and swift horses."

Though bruised and scratched Djamileh was not much the worse for her sudden descent into the valley, and following the old shepherdess, who was as nimble as a goat, she scrambled up the precipice, and soon found herself in a hired chariot, driving at full speed towards the Castle of Shady Transports, clutching in her hot hand the key of the locked closet. Her impatience was indescribable, and as for her scruples and her good principles, they had vanished as though they had never been. Whether it was a slight concussion, or pique at hearing that Kayel had left her in order to go off and drink with vulgar shepherds, I do not pretend to say. But in any case, Djamileh had now but one thought, and that was to gratify her curiosity as soon as possible.

Bundling up a pretext of having forgotten her jewellery, she hurried past the house steward and the slaves, refusing refreshment and not listening to a word they said. She ran to the west parlour, threw aside the embroidered hangings, opened the green baize door, flew up the winding stair and along the gallery.

But the door of the fifth closet had been burst open.

It gave upon a sumptuous but dusky vacancy, an underground saloon of great size, walled with mosaics and inadequately lit by seven vast rubies hanging from the ceiling. A flight of marble steps led down to this apartment, and at the foot of the steps lay Kayel, groaning piteously.

"Thank heaven you've come! I've been here for the last half-hour, shouting at the top of my voice, and not one of those accursed slaves has come near me."

"Oh, Kayel, are you badly hurt?"

"Hurt? I should think I've broken every bone in my body, and I know I've broken my collar-bone. I had to smash that door in, and it gave suddenly, and I pitched all the way down these steps. My second fall today. Oh!"

As she leaned over him the little golden key, forgotten and useless now, slid from her hand.

"My God, Djamileh! You've had that key all this time. And so *that* was why you came back?"

"Yes, Kayel. I came back to open the door. But you got here before me."

And while that parry still held him she hastened to add:

"We have both behaved so shockingly that I don't think either of us had better reproach the other. So now let us see about your fracture."

Not till the collar-bone was mending nicely; not till the coverlet which Djamileh had begun to knit as she sat by her husband's bedside, since knitting is always so soothing to invalids, was nearly finished; not till they had solved the last of the acrostics sent to them by a sympathizing Badruddin, did they mention the affair of the closet.

"How could I have the heart to leave you—you, looking so pale, and so appealing?" said Kayel suddenly.

"And the lies I told about you, Kayel, the moment I came to ... the things I said, the way I took away your character!"

"We must have been mad."

"We were suffering from curiosity. That was all, but it was quite enough."

"How terrible curiosity is, Djamileh! Fiercer than lust, more ruthless than avarice ...."

"Insatiable as man-eating tigers ...."

"Insistent as that itching-powder one buys at low French fairs .... O Djamileh, let us vow never to feel curiosity again!"

"I made that vow long ago. You have seen what good it was."

They meditated, gazing into each other's eyes.

"It seems to me, my husband, that we should be less inquisitive if we had more to do. I think we should give up all our money, live in a village, and work all day in the fields."

"That only shows, my dearest, that you have always lived in a town. The people who work all day in the fields will sit up all night in the hopes of discovering if their neighbour's cat has littered brindled or tortoise-shell kittens."

They continued to interrogate each other's eyes.

"A man through whose garden flowed a violent watercourse," said Djamileh, "complained one day to the stream: 'O Stream, you have washed away my hollyhocks, swept off my artichokes, undermined my banks, flooded my bowling-green, and drowned my youngest son, the garland of my grey head. I wish, O Stream, that you would have the kindness to flow elsewhere.' 'That cannot be,' replied the stream, 'since Allah has bidden me to flow where I do. But if you were to erect a mill on your property, perhaps you would admit that I have my uses.' In other words, Kayel, it seems to me that, since we cannot do away with our curiosity, we had best sublimate it, and take up the study of a science."

"Let it be astronomy," answered Kayel. "Of all sciences, it is the one least likely to intervene in our private life."

To this day, though Bluebeard's daughter is forgotten, the wife of Kayel the astronomer is held in remembrance. It was she whose sympathetic collaboration supported him through his researches into the Saturnian rings, it was she who worked out the mathematical calculations which enabled him to prove that the lost Pleiad would reappear in the year 1963. As time went on, and her grandchildren came clustering round the telescope, Djamileh's blue hair became silver; but to the day of her death her arched blue brows gave an appearance of alertness to her wrinkled countenance, and her teeth, glistening and perfect as in her girlhood, were shown off to the best advantage by the lining of her mouth, duskily blue as that of a well-bred chow-dog's.

29. Gianni Rodari, *Venti storie più una* (1969; *translated by Nancy Canepa, 2011*[1])

Little known outside of his native land today, Gianni Rodari was hailed in Italy as the premier children's writer of his time. He was honored in 1970 with the Hans Christian Andersen Award given out by the Swiss-based International Board on Books for Young People for a lasting contribution to children's literature—that year Maurice Sendak received it for illustration. As a writer, Rodari had what we might call a socialist literary mission: to put the power of the word into every child's hands. And he believed that fantasy was an ideal vehicle for this project. The stories in Venti storie più una *collectively create a portrait of the social struggle of the poor. The family in "Nino and Nina" is too destitute to eat, but this long yarn finishes well, "just like what happens in a fairy tale." A familiar Hansel and Gretel plot has been taken out of the woods and written into a mid-century cityscape of streetcars and alleyways. Although it at first seems a "hostile forest of houses, amid the roar of the traffic," very similar to the terrors of the fairy-tale woods, the mid-twentieth-century urban version of the witch with a great oven—a baker—feeds them rather than feeding on them.*

1 [Source: Nancy Canepa, unpublished.]

NINO AND NINA

A POOR MAN LIVED WITH HIS family in a run-down hovel at the edge of the city. He was unemployed, his wife was ill, and the cupboard was often bare. One evening, he put his two children to bed very early, since he had nothing to give them for dinner, and he sat next to them, waiting for them to fall asleep. Nina, the younger of the two, dozed off almost immediately, and in her sleep she thrashed about as if she were having a bad dream. The older child, Nino, wasn't sleepy, but closed his eyes anyway, so that his father wouldn't see that he was hungry. The poor man sighed, went back to his wife, and said, "We can't go on like this. Those two little ones will get sick without anything to eat, and we won't even be able to have them treated because we have no money for the doctor. Tomorrow morning I'll bring the children to the city to see the Duomo, and I'll find a way to abandon them. Some good soul will take care of them."

The sick woman burst into loud tears. "Don't cry," said her husband, "or they'll wake up. Believe me, there's nothing else that we can do. It'll be for their own good."

But Nino wasn't sleeping, and he had heard everything. He waited for his parents to turn off the light, he waited for everything to grow still, and then he tiptoed out of the hovel, gathered some pebbles, and filled the pockets of his little jacket with them. "I'll plant a trail of pebbles on the road," he thought, "like children in fairy tales do when they're abandoned in the woods. That way me and Nina will be able to find the way back home, and Mama will be happy."

The next morning their father woke Nina and Nino up with a cheerful and festive face: "Come on, come on, hurry it up, we're going to the city to see the Duomo." The children got dressed quickly; Nino touched his pockets and felt the pebbles, and wasn't afraid.

But their father had decided, as a surprise before he abandoned them, that they would take the streetcar, and he spent his last money on the three tickets. It was a miserable day; there was a gelid drizzle and people were saying, "If the wind dies down, it's going to start snowing."

The windows of the streetcar were all closed, and Nino wasn't able to leave his trail of pebbles. "Never mind," he thought, "I'll just have to make sure Papa never gets out of my sight. I'll let him walk off a little way, and then I'll follow him without him seeing me."

"Look," their father was saying in the meantime, "look at all of these wonderful things: so many big buildings, so many cars. The city is beautiful!"

The city wasn't only beautiful, it was immense. It appeared to stop at the end of the street where the streetcar ran, with its cheerful rumble, but instead, at the end of that street another one began, and then another one, and wide, tree-lined avenues branched out in every direction, and in each avenue, in each street, in each square there were streetcars, automobiles, delivery trucks, and people, people, people everywhere. Was it possible that there were so many people in the world?

Nino and Nina looked out the window with their mouths open, enchanted.

Finally, their papa told them that it was time to get off, and the Duomo was right there in front of them. It was made entirely of marble, it was gray and shiny with rain, and at the top there was a forest of spires, strange spindly marble trees whose leaves were the clouds in the sky.

They went into the Duomo, holding hands, and walked in silence among the tall, mysterious columns. The columns, too, seemed to form a large forest, though it was nearly impossible for the eye to distinguish how their branches intersected, way up high, to support the ceiling.

Nino held his sister's hand on one side, his papa's on the other, and he felt his papa's hand squeezing his own, more and more tightly. Then his papa said, "Alright, wait for me here just a second; you can take a look at that pretty statue. Be good and don't be afraid, I'll come back right away."

"Yes, father," said Nina. Nino didn't say anything. He looked at his father, who was stroking his hair, and forced himself to smile at him. Then he saw him move off almost at a run, turn around, start walking again, hide behind a column.

"When he comes out from behind that column," Nino thought to himself, "we'll follow him." He waited, and waited, but his papa didn't reappear. Nino ran to the column, pulling his little sister behind him. Their papa was no longer there. "Maybe I had my eye on the wrong column," thought Nino. They wandered in vain from one column to another, up and down the immense naves. "I'm tired," said Nina at a certain point. "Why isn't papa coming back?"

Nino sat her down on a pew, and after a moment the little girl put her head down on his knees and closed her eyes. "I'll let her sleep a little," thought Nino, "then we'll go out and look for the way home." Instead, he was tired and overwrought, and fell asleep too.

They were awakened by someone shaking them rather roughly and by a voice that was saying, "What are you doing here? Do you think the Duomo is a dormitory?" They opened their eyes at the same time and saw a little old woman wrapped in a long black shawl. Her glasses sparkled frighteningly on her wrinkled face. Nina burst into tears. Nino got up, helped his sister to her feet, and then pulled her away by the arm.

"Where are you going? Come over here," the little old woman ordered, pointing a threatening finger at them. Or maybe she wasn't threatening them, maybe she was actually begging for alms. But in any case the two children were frightened and ran away, and the old woman couldn't run fast enough to catch up to them. She shook her head, puzzled, and looked around as if she were searching for help. But all she saw was a tourist reading his book. "Little tramps," the old lady thought. And she went off on her own business.

In the meantime, Nina was asking, "Was that the witch?" as they walked hand in hand through the crowds on the sidewalk. "No," said Nino, "witches don't live in cities." "Where are we going?" asked Nina again. "Home." "But we need to take the streetcar to go home," the little girl reasoned, "Why don't we take the streetcar?" "Because we don't have any money." "Can't we ask the owner of the streetcar to do us a favor and take us for free? We're such little children, we won't take up much room." "There are so many different streetcars, I'm not sure which to take." "But the owner of the streetcar must know!"

They wandered for hours and hours in the hostile forest of houses, amid the roar of the traffic, numbed by the cold and their confusion. Every now and then Nina would start to whine, complaining that she was hungry, cold, tired. Nino would let her rest for a few minutes against a wall, in a doorway, on the running board of a parked car. But the sight of a policeman in the distance or a suspicious look on the part of a passerby was enough to drive them out of their temporary refuge.

Towards evening it began to snow. Nino and Nina looked for shelter in a covered walkway, between two alleyways. There was a pile of wooden crates in there, under a portico of damp, dark stone. "We'll make ourselves a hut," said Nino. And in fact, they did. They moved some empty crates and found two that were bigger than the rest; they put them together, covered them with another crate, and ended up with a cozy little shelter. Nina got into one of the crates, Nino in the other. But they continued to hold hands in order to keep their courage up. No one passed by there, the sounds of the traffic were muffled by the snow, and it was just like being in a hut in the woods. And night was falling around them, in a sweet and maternal way in spite of everything. The two children whispered between themselves for a little while, and then slowly fell asleep.

Those crates belonged to a baker, and the door to his shop was right next to them. A few hours after midnight, the baker got up to make his first batch of bread. He was in a bad mood because his shop boy had quit and he had to do everything by himself: light the oven, mix and knead the bread, put the bread in the oven.

At a certain point he needed to go out under the portico to look for something. He thought he heard a strange noise, as if someone was snoring lightly. The noise was the sound of Nina breathing, for after roaming the streets all day, she had caught a nasty cold.

"What's this under here?" muttered the baker. In his sleep Nino must have heard the voice, because he began to toss and turn in his crate, knocking it with his shoes. "Who goes there?" said the baker, more loudly this time, picking up an iron bar.

He peered into the darkness without moving. Then he decided to look behind the crates, and he discovered the two children sleeping. He bent over them, curious. Nino was the first to wake up. In the semidarkness of the portico he saw, at a hands length from his own eyes, the baker's dark and severe eyes, his big moustache, his white apron. He let out a cry. Nina was awoken by his cry; terrified, she burst into tears and started shouting, "Mama! Mama!"

"Come on, come on," said the baker gruffly, "come out of there, now!" Nino was the first to obey, gently urging his sister, "Let's do what he says, and maybe he won't harm us." Nina was convinced that that big fat scary hulk of a man was the ogre in person, and she dared not even whisper.

The baker took them inside, sat them down on a half-empty flour sack, and turned around to check how hot the oven was. At the sight of the flames, Nina hugged her brother as tightly as she could and whispered in his ear, "I don't want him to stuff me in the oven!"

Nino didn't know how to reply to that; he patted her on the back and kissed her hair, as he had seen his mama and papa do so many times. Every so often the baker said something to them, but they were too terrified to reply. He opened and closed the oven door many times, and each time Nina thought her final hour had arrived. But then the baker continued to work, paying no attention to them. The room was warm and quiet, and little by little an extraordinary scent began to waft through the air, a warm and mysterious smell. Nino seemed to recognize that smell, that good, familiar fragrance, but he dared not give it a name. The two children had now calmed down a little and, with their arms still around each other, they watched the baker working.

Suddenly the big hulk of a man came toward them. He was carrying two golden, steaming forms of bread. "Are you hungry?" he asked. "Go on, take them. They're just two rolls; are you afraid they'll bite?" Nino took the two pieces of bread and gave one to his sister. They almost burnt his hands, but the fragrance was so intense that it gave him a headache.

They hadn't eaten for such a long time, and never in their lives had they tasted such delicious bread. They ate the two rolls, then another two, then another two. The big baker said nothing, but when he saw that they had finished, he went and got more rolls from a basket.

"When was the last time the two of you had something to eat?" he boomed, after bringing them their sixth roll each. And then Nina started to laugh; in fact, she sprung to her feet and started jumping around the shop as if she were crazy. Nino, too, smiled at the kind man, and thought to himself, "Imagine, we mistook him for an ogre!"

At around six in the morning the baker's wife came down to open up the shop. Her husband showed her the two children and she scolded him for not having called her right away. "Can't you see that they're feverish?" "Yes," said the baker, "they have the eating fever."

But the baker's wife would have none of this; she took the two children, brought them upstairs, and tucked them in bed. And they were still in bed when their papa arrived. After abandoning them he had returned to look for them, but he was too late, and after that he had gone from one police station to another, trying to get some word of them. He had finally been given the baker's address by an officer.

"Keep quiet, now," the baker's wife said to him, "don't wake them up. I called the police because it was my duty, but I didn't allow even the officers to wake them up. And now I think I have the right to hear the whole story. Out with it, then; come here and tell me what happened."

"What do you want me to tell you?" the poor man asked fearfully. "Everything," pronounced the baker's wife. The baker listened to the story, too, twisting his moustache. Then he said, "Well, I don't have an assistant at the moment, and I need someone to make deliveries to my customers. If you're happy with it, it's a job like any other."

Then the poor man started to cry, and he cried for all those days when he had had to swallow his tears so that his family wouldn't see. He accepted the position, and he always remembered that Nino and Nina had been the ones to find it for him, just like what happens in fairy tales, when abandoned children return home with a treasure.

30. Anne Sexton, *Transformations* (1971) [1]

Coming of age in the 1940s in comfortable middle-class America, Anne Sexton was restless. She rebelled at school, eloped at 19, tried modeling, battled depression, and attempted suicide. At the suggestion of a therapist, Sexton tried writing as a way to cope and took to it—an engagement with her mind through poetry that gave her work a shocking edge for its day. Her talent emerged in writing groups she joined among peers such as Robert Lowell and Sylvia Plath, and as she developed technically as a writer, recognition followed. In the wake of her first collection, To Bedlam and Back, *she won the National Book Award and a Pulitzer Prize and toured with a rock band that set her poems to music. In 1968 she became the Phi Beta Kappa poet at Harvard University. Today Sexton is often hailed as a "confessional" poet, though her poems are not necessarily autobiographical and the term misleadingly conflates the poet with her art. Instead, her poetry paints a world laid bare of its veneer of sociability, its mythic landscapes strewn with twentieth-century allusion—when her Sleeping Beauty pricks her finger, the king looks "like Munch's Scream"—and fantastical characters cut down*

1 [Source: Anne Sexton, *Transformations* ([1971] New York, NY: Mariner Books/Houghton Mifflin, 2001): 3–9.]

to everyday size—the Queen in her "Snow White" grows facial hair. Not surprisingly, fairy-tale themes appear frequently in Sexton's work, often as absurd representations of the very sociability she wrote to expose. Her provocative versions of classics such as Cinderella, Sleeping Beauty, and Snow White wrestle with passive models of femininity. In "Snow White," the virginal main character takes on the allure of a doll, emptied of human agency and fragile with porcelain limbs. She is the only character in the poem with no direct speech and ends the tale ambiguously, caught in the beauty trap she had hoped to escape.

SNOW WHITE AND THE SEVEN DWARFS

No matter what life you lead
the virgin is a lovely number:
cheeks as fragile as cigarette paper,
arms and legs made of Limoges,
lips like Vin Du Rhône,
rolling her china-blue doll eyes
open and shut.
Open to say,
Good Day Mama,
and shut for the thrust
of the unicorn.
She is unsoiled.
She is as white as a bonefish.

Once there was a lovely virgin
called Snow White.
Say she was thirteen.
Her stepmother,
a beauty in her own right,
though eaten, of course, by age,
would hear of no beauty surpassing her own.
Beauty is a simple passion,
but, oh my friends, in the end
you will dance the fire dance in iron shoes.
The stepmother had a mirror to which she referred—
something like the weather forecast—
a mirror that proclaimed
the one beauty of the land.

She would ask,
Looking glass upon the wall,
who is fairest of us all?
And the mirror would reply,
You are the fairest of us all.
Pride pumped in her like poison.

Suddenly one day the mirror replied,
Queen, you are full fair, 'tis true,
but Snow White is fairer than you.
Until that moment Snow White
had been no more important
than a dust mouse under the bed.
But now the queen saw brown spots on her hand
and four whiskers over her lip
so she condemned Snow White
to be hacked to death.
Bring me her heart, she said to the hunter,
and I will salt it and eat it.
The hunter, however, let his prisoner go
and brought a boar's heart back to the castle.
The queen chewed it up like a cube steak.
Now I am fairest, she said,
lapping her slim white fingers.

Snow White walked in the wildwood
for weeks and weeks.
At each turn there were twenty doorways
and at each stood a hungry wolf,
his tongue lolling out like a worm.
The birds called out lewdly,
talking like pink parrots,
and the snakes hung down in loops,
each a noose for her sweet white neck.
On the seventh week
she came to the seventh mountain
and there she found the dwarf house.
It was as droll as a honeymoon cottage
and completely equipped with

seven beds, seven chairs, seven forks
and seven chamber pots.
Snow White ate seven chicken livers
and lay down, at last, to sleep.

The dwarfs, those little hot dogs,
walked three times around Snow White,
the sleeping virgin. They were wise
and wattled like small czars.
Yes. It's a good omen,
they said, and will bring us luck.
They stood on tiptoes to watch
Snow White wake up. She told them
about the mirror and the killer-queen
and they asked her to stay and keep house.
Beware of your stepmother,
they said.
Soon she will know you are here.
While we are away in the mines
during the day, you must not
open the door.

Looking glass upon the wall ...
The mirror told
and so the queen dressed herself in rags
and went out like a peddler to trap Snow White.
She went across seven mountains.
She came to the dwarf house
and Snow White opened the door
and bought a bit of lacing.
The queen fastened it tightly
around her bodice,
as tight as an Ace bandage,
so tight that Snow White swooned.
She lay on the floor, a plucked daisy.
When the dwarfs came home they undid the lace
and she revived miraculously.
She was as full of life as soda pop.
Beware of your stepmother,

they said.
She will try once more.

Looking glass upon the wall ...
Once more the mirror told
and once more the queen dressed in rags
and once more Snow White opened the door.
This time she bought a poison comb,
a curved eight-inch scorpion,
and put it in her hair and swooned again.
The dwarfs returned and took out the comb
and she revived miraculously.
She opened her eyes as wide as Orphan Annie.
Beware, beware, they said,
but the mirror told,
the queen came,
Snow White, the dumb bunny,
opened the door
and she bit into a poison apple
and fell down for the final time.
When the dwarfs returned
they undid her bodice,
they looked for a comb,
but it did no good.
Though they washed her with wine
and rubbed her with butter
it was to no avail.
She lay as still as a gold piece.

The seven dwarfs could not bring themselves
to bury her in the black ground
so they made a glass coffin
and set it upon the seventh mountain
so that all who passed by
could peek in upon her beauty.
A prince came one June day
and would not budge.
He stayed so long his hair turned green
and still he would not leave.

The dwarfs took pity upon him
and gave him the glass Snow White—
its doll's eyes shut forever—
to keep in his far-off castle.
As the prince's men carried the coffin
they stumbled and dropped it
and the chunk of apple flew out
of her throat and she woke up miraculously.

And thus Snow White became the prince's bride.
The wicked queen was invited to the wedding feast
and when she arrived there were
red-hot iron shoes,
in the manner of red-hot roller skates,
clamped upon her feet.
First your toes will smoke
and then your heels will turn black
and you will fry upward like a frog,
she was told.
And so she danced until she was dead,
a subterranean figure,
her tongue flicking in and out
like a gas jet.
Meanwhile Snow White held court,
rolling her china-blue doll eyes open and shut
and sometimes referring to her mirror
as women do.

31. Robert Coover, *Briar Rose* (1996)[1]

American writer and Brown University professor Robert Coover has drawn on fairy-tale plots, themes, characters, and motifs in several of his works of postmodern fiction, including Pricksongs and Descants *(1969),* Stepmother *(2004), and* Briar Rose *(1996)—excerpted here. Coover has been acclaimed for his experiments with metafiction, including pioneering experiments with hypertext in the early 1990s before the advent of the World Wide Web and mainstream familiarity with what he called (in a 1992* New York Times *article) the "nonlinear or nonsequential space made possible by*

1 [Source: Robert Coover, *Briar Rose* (New York, NY: Grove P, 1996): 1–7.]

the computer." In Briar Rose, *Coover draws freely, creatively, and insightfully on a web of related texts: the Grimms' tale of the same name, but also Perrault's "Sleeping Beauty" and Basile's "Sun, Moon, and Talia." The result is a cast of characters and repertoire of motifs whose forms and meanings shift and alter as Coover repeatedly revisits the sleeping princess, her fairy attendant, and the questing prince in a series of nonlinear "lexia."*

BRIAR ROSE (EXCERPT)

HE IS SURPRISED TO DISCOVER how easy it is. The branches part like thighs, the silky petals caress his checks. His drawn sword is stained, not with blood, but with dew and pollen. Yet another inflated legend. He has undertaken this great adventure, not for the supposed reward—what is another lonely bedridden princess?—but in order to provoke a confrontation with the awful powers of enchantment itself. To tame mystery. To make, at last, his name. He'd have been better off trying for the runes of wisdom or the Golden Fleece. Even another bloody grail. As the briars, pillowy with a sudden extravagance of fresh blooms, their thorns decorously sheathed in the full moonlight, open up to receive him as a doting mother might, he is pricked only by chagrin. Yet he knows what it has cost others who have gone before him, he can smell their bodies caught in the thicket, can glimpse the pallor of their moon-bleached bones, tattling gently when the soft wind blows. That odor of decay is about the extent of his ordeal, and even it is assuaged by the fragrances of fresh tansy and camomile, roses, lilac and hyssop, lavender and savory, which encompass him affectionately—perhaps he has been chosen, perhaps it is his virtue which has caused the hedge to bloom—as he plunges deeper into the thicket, the castle turrets and battlements already visible to him, almost within reach, through its trembling branches.

She dreams, as she has often dreamt, of abandonment and betrayal, of lost hope, of the self gone astray from the body, the body forsaking the unlikely Self. She feels like a once-proud castle whose walls have collapsed, her halls and towers invaded, not by marauding armies, but by humbler creatures, bats, birds, cats, cattle, her departed self an unkempt army marauding elsewhere to a scatter of confused intentions. Her longing for integrity is, in her spellbound innocence, all she knows of rage and lust, but this longing is itself fragmented and wayward, felt not so much as a monstrous gnawing at the core as more like the restless scurry of vermin in the rubble of her remote defenses, long since fallen and benumbed. What, if anything, can make her whole again? And what is "whole"? Her parents, as always in her dreams, have vanished, gone off to death or the continent or perhaps to one of their houses of pleasure, and she is being stabbed again and again by the treacherous spindle, impregnated with a despair from which, for all her fury, she cannot awaken.

The pale moonlit turrets of the castle, glimpsed through the brambles, rise high into the black night above like the clenched fists of an unforgiving but stonily silent father, upon whose tender terrain below he is darkly trespassing, heralded by a soft icy clatter of tinkling bones. Unlike these others who ornament the briars, he has come opportunely when the hedge is in full bloom, or perhaps (he prefers to think) the hedge has blossomed tonight because it is he who has come, its seductive caresses welcoming him even as the cold castle overhead repels, the one a promise and a lure, showing him the way, the other the test he must undertake to achieve the object of his heroic quest. Which is? Honor. Knowledge. The exercise of his magical powers. Also love of course. If the old tales be true, a sleeping princess awaits him within. He imagines her as not unlike this soft dew-bedampened wall he is plunging through, silky and fragrant and voluptuously receptive. If she is the symbolic object of his quest, her awakening is not without its promise of passing pleasures. She is said, after all, to be the most beautiful creature in the world, both fair and good, musically gifted, delicate, virtuous and graceful and with the gentle disposition of an angel, and, for all her hundred years and more, still a child, innocent and yielding. Achingly desirable. And desiring. Of course, she is also the daughter of a mother embraced by a frog, and there has been talk about ogres in the family, dominion by sorcery, and congress with witches and wizards and other powers too dark to name. If there be any truth in these century-old rumors from benighted times, this adventure could end, not in love's sweet delirium, but in its pain, its infamous cruelty. This prospect, however, does not dissuade him. On the contrary. It incites him.

There is this to be said for the stabbing pain of the spindle prick. It anchors her, locates a self when all else in sleep unbinds and scatters it. When a passing prince asks who she is, she replies simply, having no reply other to offer, I am that hurts. This prince—if prince he be, and who can truly say as he/it drifts shapeshifting past, substantial as a fog at sea?—is but one of countless princes who have visited her in her dreams, her hundred years of dreams, unceasing, without so much as a day's respite. None remembered of course, no memory of her dreams at all, each forgotten in the very dreaming of them as though to dream them were to erase them. And yet, so often have her dreams revisited fragments and images of dreams dreamt before, a sort of recognizable architecture has grown up around them, such that, though each dream is, must be, intrinsically unique, there is an ambient familiarity about them all that consoles her as memory might, did she know it, and somewhat teaches her whereto to flee when terror engulfs her like a sudden wicked spell. One such refuge is what she sometimes supposes to be a kitchen or a servery, else a strange gallery with hearth and wooden tub, oft as not at ground level with a packed earthen floor and yet with grand views out an oriel's elevated bay. Sometimes there are walls, doors, ceilings, sometimes not. Sometimes she drifts in and out of this room alone, or it appears, in its drafty solitude, around her, but sometimes familiar faces greet her, if none she knows to name, like all else ever changing. Except for one perhaps: a loving old crone, hideously ugly and vaguely threatening, yet dearer to her in her dreams than any other, even courting princes.

Well, old crone. Ugly. Thank you very much. Has that smug sleeper paused to consider how she will look and smell after a hundred years, lying comatose and untended in an unchanged bed? A century of collected menses alone should stagger the lustiest of princes. The curse of the bad fairy, yes. She has reminded the forgetful creature of this in her dreams, has described the stagnant and verminous pallet whereon she idly snoozes and croned her indelible images of human decrepitude, has recounted for her the ancient legends of saints awaking from a hundred years of sleep, glimpsing with dismay the changes the world has suffered, and immediately crumbling into dust. Her little hearthside entertainments. Which are momentarily disturbing perhaps, causing her charge's inner organs to twitch and burble faintly, but nothing sticks in that wastrel's empty head, nothing except her perverse dream of lovestruck princes. Or maybe she knows, instinctively, about the bewitching power of desire, knows that, in the realm of first kisses, and this first kiss firstmost, she *is* beautiful, must be, the fairy herself will see to that, is obliged to, must freshen her flesh and wipe her bum, costume and coiffure her, sweep the room of all morbidity and cushion her for he who will come in lustrous opulence. Alone, the fragrances at her disposal would make a pope swoon and a saint cast off, his britches afore, eternity. No, all these moral lessons with which the fairy ornaments the century's dreaming are mere fancies invented for her own consolation while awaiting that which she herself, in her ingenerate ambivalence, has ordained.

32. Nalo Hopkinson, *Skin Folk* (2001)[1]

Jamaican-born, Toronto-based writer Nalo Hopkinson is the author of four novels and a short story collection; she has also edited anthologies of Caribbean fabulist fiction and postcolonial science fiction. Blending genres that have tended to be dominated by Euro-American (and frequently male) writers—science fiction, fantasy, magic realism, and horror—Hopkinson has infused her work with Caribbean imagery and diction. Her fiction has garnered tremendous critical acclaim, including Honorable Mention in Cuba's "Casa de las Americas" literary prize, the Warner Aspect First Novel Award, the Ontario Arts Council Foundation Award for emerging writers, the World Fantasy Award, and the Sunburst Award for Canadian Literature of the Fantastic.

"The Glass Bottle Trick" first appeared in a short story collection edited by Hopkinson, but it is also one of several stories in her book Skin Folk *that draws on and then re-imagines plots and motifs from classic European fairy tales. In this case, Hopkinson is responding to Perrault's "Blue Beard," reimagining the tale in terms of internalized racism, Caribbean belief systems (including the Jamaican "duppy," a malevolent ghost but also a term that is racialized in contemporary usage), and Creole-inflected language. Her plotline might itself be described as a "creole" of tradition and innovation. A significant change she makes in the telling is to relate the story from the young wife's perspective. Where in Perrault's version, the wife's behavior is as confusing and alienating as that of her domineering husband, Hopkinson's Beatrice is a very sympathetic figure: she works hard, has dreams for her future, and meets her husband-to-be while poring over* Gray's Anatomy. *This strength we continually see in her helps to float the narrative slowly towards its unexpected ending.*

THE GLASS BOTTLE TRICK

THE AIR WAS FULL OF storms, but they refused to break. In the wicker rocking chair on the front verandah, Beatrice flexed her bare feet against the wooden slat floor, rocking slowly back and forth. Another sweltering rainy season afternoon. The arid heat felt as though all the oxygen had boiled out of the parched air to hang as looming rainclouds, waiting.

Oh, but she loved it like this. The hotter the day, the slower she would move, basking. She stretched her arms and legs out to better feel the luxuriant warmth, then guiltily sat up straight again. Samuel would scold if he ever saw her slouching like that. Stuffy Sammy. She smiled fondly, admiring the lacy patterns the sunlight

1 [Source: Nalo Hopkinson, *Skin Folk* (New York, NY: Aspect/Warner Books, 2001): 83–101. "The Glass Bottle Trick" first appeared in Nalo Hopkinson, ed., *Whispers from the Cotton Tree: Caribbean Fabulist Fiction* (Montpelier,VT: Invisible Cities P, 2000).]

threw on the floor as it filtered through the white gingerbread fretwork that trimmed the roof of their house.

"Anything more today, Mistress Powell? I finish doing the dishes." Gloria had come out of the house and was standing in front of her, wiping her chapped hands on her apron.

Beatrice felt shyness come over her as it always did when she thought of giving the older woman orders.

Gloria quirked an eyebrow, crinkling her face like running a fork through molasses. "Then I go take the rest of the afternoon off. You and Mister Samuel should be alone tonight. Is time you tell him."

Beatrice gave an abortive, shamefaced "huh" of a laugh. Gloria had known from the start, she'd had so many babies of her own. She'd been made to run to Samuel with the news from since. But yesterday, Beatrice had already decided to tell Samuel. Well, almost decided. She felt irritated, like a child whose tricks have been found out. She swallowed the feeling. "I think you right, Gloria," she said, fighting for some dignity before the older woman. "Maybe ... maybe I cook him a special meal, feed him up nice, then tell him."

"Well, I say is time and past time you make him know. A pickney is a blessing to a family."

"For true," Beatrice agreed, making her voice sound as certain as she could.

"Later, then, Mistress Powell." Giving herself the afternoon off, not even a by-your-leave, Gloria headed off to the maid's room at the back of the house to change into her street clothes. A few minutes later, she let herself out the garden gate.

"That seems like a tough book for a young lady of such tender years."

"Excuse me?" Beatrice threw a defensive cutting glare at the older man. He'd caught her off guard, though she'd seen his eyes following her ever since she entered the bookstore. "You have something to say to me?" She curled the Gray's Anatomy *possessively into the crook of her arm, price sticker hidden against her body. Two more months of saving before she could afford it.*

He looked shyly at her. "Sorry if I offended, Miss," he said. "My name is Samuel."

Would be handsome, if he'd chill out a bit. Beatrice's wariness thawed a little. Middle of the sun-hot day, and he wearing black wool jacket and pants. His crisp white cotton shirt was buttoned right up, held in place by a tasteful, unimaginative tie. So proper, Jesus. He wasn't that much older than she.

"Is just ... you're so pretty, and it's the only thing I could think of to say to get you to speak to me."

Beatrice softened more at that, smiled for him and played with the collar of her blouse. He didn't seem too bad, if you could look beyond the stocious, starchy behaviour.

Beatrice doubtfully patted the slight swelling of her belly. Four months. She was shy to give Samuel her news, but she was starting to show. Silly to put it off, yes? Today she was going to make her husband very happy; break that thin shell of mourning that still insulated him from her. He never said so, but Beatrice knew that he still thought of the wife he'd lost, and tragically, the one before that. She wished she could make him warm up to life again.

Sunlight was flickering through the leaves of the guava tree in the front yard. Beatrice inhaled the sweet smell of the sun-warmed fruit. The tree's branches hung heavy with the pale yellow globes, smooth and round as eggs. The sun reflected off the two blue bottles suspended in the tree, sending cobalt light dancing through the leaves.

When Beatrice first came to Sammy's house, she'd been puzzled by the two bottles that were jammed onto branches of the guava tree.

"Is just my superstitiousness, darling," he'd told her. "You never heard the old people say that if someone dies, you must put a bottle in a tree to hold their spirit, otherwise it will come back as a duppy and haunt you? A blue bottle. To keep the duppy cool, so it won't come at you in hot anger for being dead."

Beatrice had heard something of the sort, but it was strange to think of her Sammy as a superstitious man. He was too controlled and logical for that. Well, grief makes somebody act in strange ways. Maybe the bottles gave him some comfort, made him feel that he'd kept some essence of his poor wives near him.

"That Samuel is nice. Respectable, hard-working. Not like all them other ragamuffins you always going out with." Mummy picked up the butcher knife and began expertly slicing the goat meat into cubes for the curry.

Beatrice watched the red lumps of flesh part under the knife. Crimson liquid leaked onto the cutting board. She sighed, "But, Mummy, Samuel so boring! Michael and Clifton know how to have fun. All Samuel want to do is go for country drives. Always taking me away from other people."

"You should be studying your books, not having fun," her mother replied crossly.

Beatrice pleaded, "You well know I could do both, Mummy." Her mother just grunted.

Is only truth Beatrice was talking. Plenty men were always courting her, they flocked to her like birds, eager to take her dancing or out for a drink. But somehow she kept her marks up, even though it often meant studying right through the night, her head pounding and belly queasy from hangover while some man snored in the bed beside her. Mummy would kill her if she didn't get straight A's for medical school. "You going have to look after yourself, Beatrice. Man not going do it for you. Them get their little piece of sweetness and then them bruk away."

"Two patty and a King Cola, please." The guy who'd given the order had a broad chest that tapered to a slim waist. Good face to look at, too. Beatrice smiled sweetly at him, made shift to gently brush his palm with her fingertips as she handed him the change.

A bird screeched from the guava tree, a tiny kiskedee, crying angrily, "Dit, dit, qu'est-ce qu'il dit!" A small snake was coiled around one of the upper branches, just withdrawing its head from the bird's nest. Its jaws were distended with the egg it had stolen. It swallowed the egg whole, throat bulging hugely with its meal. The bird hovered around the snake's head, giving its pitiful wail of, "Say, say, what's he saying!"

"Get away!" Beatrice shouted at the snake. It looked in the direction of the sound, but didn't back off. The gulping motion of its body as it forced the egg farther down its own throat made Beatrice shudder. Then, oblivious to the fluttering of the parent bird, it arched its head over the nest again. Beatrice pushed herself to her feet and ran into the yard. "Hsst! Shoo! Come away from there!" But the snake took a second egg.

Sammy kept a long pole with a hook at one end leaned against the guava tree for pulling down the fruit. Beatrice grabbed up the pole, started jooking it at the branches as close to the bird and nest as she dared. "Leave them, you brute! Leave!" The pole connected with some of the boughs. The two bottles in the tree fell to the ground and shattered with a crash. A hot breeze sprang up. The snake slithered away quickly, two eggs bulging in its throat. The bird flew off, sobbing to itself.

Nothing she could do now. When Samuel came home, he would hunt the nasty snake down for her and kill it. She leaned the pole back against the tree.

The light breeze should have brought some coolness, but really it only made the day warmer. Two little dust devils danced briefly around Beatrice. They swirled across the yard, swung up into the air, and dashed themselves to powder against the shuttered window of the third bedroom.

Beatrice got her sandals from the verandah. Sammy wouldn't like it if she stepped on broken glass. She picked up the broom that was leaned against the house and began to sweep up the shards of bottle. She hoped Samuel wouldn't be too angry with her. He wasn't a man to cross, could be as stern as a father if he had a mind to.

That was mostly what she remembered about Daddy, his temper—quick to show and just as quick to go. So was he; had left his family before Beatrice turned five. The one cherished memory she had of him was of being swung back and forth through the air, her two small hands clasped in one big hand of his, her feet held tight in another. Safe. And as he swung her through the air, her daddy had been chanting words from an old-time story:

Yung-Kyung-Pyung, what a pretty basket!
Margaret Powell Alone, what a pretty basket!
Eggie-law, what a pretty basket!

Then he had held her tight to his chest, forcing the air from her lungs in a breathless giggle. The dressing-down Mummy had given him for that game! "You want to drop the child and crack her head open on the hard ground? Ee? Why you can't be more responsible?"

"Responsible?" he'd snapped. "Is who working like dog sunup to sundown to put food in oonuh belly?" He'd set Beatrice down, her feet hitting the ground with a jar. She'd started to cry, but he'd just pushed her towards her mother and stormed out of the room. One more volley in the constant battle between them. After he'd left them Mummy had opened the little food shop in town to make ends meet. In the evenings, Beatrice would rub lotion into her mother's chapped, work-wrinkled hands. "See how that man make us come down in the world?" Mummy would grumble. "Look at what I come to."

Privately, Beatrice thought that maybe all Daddy had needed was a little patience. Mummy was too harsh, much as Beatrice loved her. To please her, Beatrice had studied hard all through high school: physics, chemistry, biology, describing the results of her lab experiments in her copy book in her cramped, resigned handwriting. Her mother greeted every A with a noncommittal grunt and anything less with a lecture. Beatrice would smile airily, seal the hurt away, pretend the approval meant nothing to her. She still worked hard, but she kept some time for play of her own. Rounders, netball, and later, boys. All those boys, wanting a chance for a little sweetness with a light-skin browning like her. Beatrice had discovered her appeal quickly.

"Leggo beast ..." Loose woman. The hissed words came from a knot of girls that slouched past Beatrice as she sat on the library steps, waiting for Clifton to come and pick her up. She willed her ears shut, smothered the sting of the words. But she knew some of those girls. Marguerita, Deborah. They used to be friends of hers. Though she sat up proudly, she found her fingers tugging self-consciously at the hem of her short white skirt. She put the big physics textbook in her lap, where it gave her thighs a little more coverage.

The farting vroom of Clifton's motorcycle interrupted her thoughts. Grinning, he slewed the bike to a dramatic halt in front of her. "Study time done now, darling. Time to play."

He looked good this evening, as he always did. Tight white shirt, jeans that showed off the bulges of his thighs. The crinkle of the thin gold chain at his neck set off his dark brown skin. Beatrice stood, tucked the physics text under her arm, smoothed the skirt over her hips. Clifton's eyes followed the movement of her hands. See, it didn't take much to make people treat you nice. She smiled at him.

Samuel would still show up hopefully every so often to ask her to accompany him on a drive through the country. He was so much older than all her other suitors. And dry? Country drives, Lord! She went out with him a few times; he was so persistent and she couldn't figure out how to tell him no. He didn't seem to get her hints that really she should be studying. Truth to tell, though, she started to find his quiet, undemanding presence soothing. His eggshell-white BMW took the graveled country roads so quietly that she could hear the kiskedee birds in the mango trees, chanting their query: "Dit, dit, qu'est-ce qu'il dit?"

One day, Samuel brought her a gift.

"These are for you and your family," he said shyly, handing her a wrinkled paper bag. "I know your mother likes them." Inside were three plump eggplants from his kitchen garden, raised by his own hands. Beatrice took the humble gift out of the bag. The skins of the eggplants had a taut, blue sheen to them. Later she would realize that that was when she'd begun to love Samuel. He was stable, solid, responsible. He would make Mummy and her happy.

Beatrice gave in more to Samuel's diffident wooing. He was cultured and well spoken. He had been abroad, talked of exotic sports: ice hockey, downhill skiing. He took her to fancy restaurants she'd only heard of, that her other, young, unestablished boyfriends would never have been able to afford, and would probably only have embarrassed her if they had taken her. Samuel had polish. But he was humble, too, like the way he grew his own vegetables, or the self-deprecating tone in which he spoke of himself. He was always punctual, always courteous to her and her mother. Beatrice could count on him for little things, like picking her up after class, or driving her mother to the hairdresser's. With the other men, she always had to be on guard: pouting until they took her somewhere else for dinner, not another free meal in her mother's restaurant, wheedling them into using the condoms. She always had to hold something of herself shut away. With Samuel, Beatrice relaxed into trust.

"Beatrice, come! Come quick, nuh!"

Beatrice ran in from the backyard at the sound of her mother's voice. Had something happened to Mummy?

Her mother was sitting at the kitchen table, knife still poised to crack an egg into the bowl for the pound cake she was making to take to the shop. She was staring in open-mouthed delight at Samuel, who was fretfully twisting the long stems on a bouquet of blood-red roses. "Lord, Beatrice; Samuel say he want to marry you!"

Beatrice looked to Sammy for verification. "Samuel," she asked unbelievingly, "what you saying? Is true?"

He nodded yes. "True, Beatrice."

Something gave way in Beatrice's chest, gently as a long-held breath. Her heart had been trapped in glass, and he'd freed it.

They'd been married two months later. Mummy was retired now; Samuel had bought her a little house in the suburbs, and he paid for the maid to come in three times a week. In the excitement of planning for the wedding, Beatrice had let her studying slip. To her dismay she finished her final year of university with barely a C average.

"Never mind, sweetness," Samuel told her. "I didn't like the idea of you studying, anyway. Is for children. You're a big woman now." Mummy had agreed with him too, said she didn't need all that now. She tried to argue with them, but Samuel was very clear about his wishes, and she'd stopped, not wanting anything to cause friction between them just yet. Despite his genteel manner, Samuel had just a bit of a temper. No point in crossing him, it took so little to make him happy, and he was her love, the one man she'd found in whom she could have faith.

Too besides, she was learning how to be the lady of the house, trying to use the right mix of authority and jocularity with Gloria, the maid, and Cleitis, the yardboy who came twice a month to do the mowing and the weeding. Odd to be giving orders to people when she was used to being the one taking orders, in Mummy's shop. It made her feel uncomfortable to tell people to do her work for her. Mummy said she should get used to it, it was her right now.

The sky rumbled with thunder. Still no rain. The warmth of the day was nice, but you could have too much of a good thing. Beatrice opened her mouth, gasping a little, trying to pull more air into her lungs. She was a little short of breath nowadays as the baby pressed on her diaphragm. She knew she could go inside for relief from the heat, but Samuel kept the air-conditioning on high, so cold that they could keep the butter in its dish on the kitchen counter. It never went rancid. Even insects refused to come inside. Sometimes Beatrice felt as though the house were really somewhere else, not the tropics. She had been used to waging constant war against ants and cockroaches, but not in Samuel's house. The cold in it made Beatrice shiver, dried her eyes out until they felt like boiled eggs sitting in their sockets. She went outside as often as possible, even though Samuel didn't like her to spend too much time in the sun. He said he feared that cancer would mar her soft skin, that he didn't want to lose another wife. But Beatrice knew he just didn't want her to get too brown. When the sun touched her, it brought out the sepia and cinnamon in her blood, overpowered the milk and honey, and he could no longer pretend she was white. He loved her skin pale. "Look how you gleam in the moonlight," he'd say to her when he made gentle, almost supplicating love to her at night in the four-poster bed. His hand would slide over her flesh, cup her breasts with an air of reverence. The look in his eyes was so close to worship that it sometimes frightened her. To be loved so much! He would whisper to her, "Beauty. Pale Beauty, to my Beast," then blow a cool breath over the delicate membranes of her ear, making her shiver in delight. For her part, she loved to look at him, his molasses-dark skin, his broad chest, the way the planes of flat muscle slid across it. She imagined tectonic plates shifting in the earth. She loved the bluish-black cast the moonlight lent him. Once, gazing up at him as he loomed above her, body working against and in hers, she had seen the moonlight playing glints of deepest blue in his trim beard.

"Black Beauty," she had joked softly, reaching to pull his face closer for a kiss. At the words, he had lurched up off her to sit on the edge of the bed, pulling a sheet over him to hide his nakedness. Beatrice watched him, confused, feeling their blended sweat cooling along her body.

"Never call me that, please, Beatrice," he said softly. "You don't have to draw attention to my colour. I'm not a handsome man, and I know it. Black and ugly as my mother made me."

"But, Samuel ... !"

"No."

Shadows lay between them on the bed. He wouldn't touch her again that night.

Beatrice sometimes wondered why Samuel hadn't married a white woman. She thought she knew the reason, though. She had seen the way that Samuel behaved around white people. He smiled too broadly, he simpered, he made silly jokes. It pained her to see it, and she could tell from the desperate look in his eyes that it hurt him too. For all his love of creamy white skin, Samuel probably couldn't have brought himself to approach a white woman the way he'd courted her.

The broken glass was in a neat pile under the guava tree. Time to make Samuel's dinner now. She went up the verandah stairs to the front door, stopping to wipe her sandals on the coir mat just outside the door. Samuel hated dust. As she opened the door, she felt another gust of warm wind at her back, blowing past her into the cool house. Quickly, she stepped inside and closed the door, so that the interior would stay as cool as Sammy liked it. The insulated door shut behind her with a hollow sound. It was air-tight. None of the windows in the house could be opened. She had asked Samuel, "Why you want to live in a box like this, sweetheart? The fresh air good for you."

"I don't like the heat, Beatrice. I don't like baking like meat in the sun. The sealed windows keep the conditioned air in." She hadn't argued.

She walked through the elegant, formal living room to the kitchen. She found the heavy imported furnishings cold and stuffy, but Samuel liked them.

In the kitchen she set water to boil and hunted a bit—where did Gloria keep it?—until she found the Dutch pot. She put it on the burner to toast the fragrant coriander seeds that would flavour the curry. She put on water to boil, stood staring at the steam rising from the pots. Dinner was going to be special tonight. Curried eggs, Samuel's favourite. The eggs in their cardboard case put Beatrice in mind of a trick she'd learned in physics class, for getting an egg unbroken into a narrow-mouthed bottle. You had to boil the egg hard and peel it, then stand a lit candle in the bottle. If you put the narrow end of the egg into the mouth of the bottle, it made a seal, and when the candle had burnt up all the air in the bottle, the vacuum it created would suck the egg in, whole. Beatrice had been the only one in her class patient enough to make the trick work. Patience was all her husband needed. Poor, mysterious Samuel had lost two wives in this isolated country home. He'd been rattling about in the airless house like the egg in the bottle. He kept to himself. The closest neighbours were miles away, and he didn't even know their names.

She was going to change all that, though. Invite her mother to stay for a while, maybe have a dinner party for the distant neighbours. Before her pregnancy made her too lethargic to do much.

A baby would complete their family. Samuel *would* be pleased, he would. She remembered him joking that no woman should have to give birth to his ugly black babies, but she would show him how beautiful their children would be, little brown bodies new as the earth after the rain. She would show him how to love himself in them.

It was hot in the kitchen. Perhaps the heat from the stove? Beatrice went out into the living room, wandered through the guest bedroom, the master bedroom, both bathrooms. The whole house was warmer than she'd ever felt it. Then she realized she could hear sounds coming from the outside, the cicadas singing loudly for rain. There was no whisper of cool air through the vents in the house. The air conditioner wasn't running.

Beatrice began to feel worried. Samuel liked it cold. She had planned tonight to be a special night for the two of them, but he wouldn't react well if everything wasn't to his liking. He'd raised his voice at her a few times. Once or twice he had stopped in the middle of an argument, one hand pulled back as if to strike, to take deep breaths, battling for self-control. His dark face would flush almost blue-black as he fought his rage down. Those times she'd stayed out of his way until he was calm again.

What could be wrong with the air conditioner? Maybe it had just come unplugged? Beatrice wasn't even sure where the controls were. Gloria and Samuel took care of everything around the house. She made another circuit through her home, looking for the main controls. Nothing. Puzzled, she went back into the living room. It was becoming thick and close as a womb inside their closed-up home.

There was only one room left to search. The locked third bedroom. Samuel had told her that both his wives had died in there, first one, then the other. He had given her the keys to every room in the house, but requested that she never open that particular door.

"I feel like it's bad luck, love. I know I'm just being superstitious, but I hope I can trust you to honour my wishes in this." She had, not wanting to cause him any anguish. But where else could the control panel be? It was getting so hot!

As she reached into her pocket for the keys she always carried with her, she realized she was still holding a raw egg in her hand. She'd forgotten to put it into the pot when the heat in the house had made her curious. She managed a little smile. The hormones flushing her body were making her so absent-minded! Samuel would tease her, until she told him why. Everything would be all right.

Beatrice put the egg into her other hand, got the keys out of her pocket, opened the door.

A wall of icy, dead air hit her body. It was freezing cold in the room. Her exhaled breath floated away from her in a long, misty curl. Frowning, she took a step inside and her eyes saw before her brain could understand, and when it did, the egg fell from her hands to smash open on the floor at her feet. Two women's bodies lay side by side on the double bed. Frozen mouths gaped open; frozen, gutted bellies, too. A fine sheen of ice crystals glazed their skin, which like hers was barely brown, but laved in gelid, rime-covered blood that had solidified ruby red. Beatrice whimpered.

"But Miss," Beatrice asked her teacher, "how the egg going to come back out the bottle again!"

"How do you think, Beatrice? There's only one way; you have to break the bottle."

This was how Samuel punished the ones who had tried to bring his babies into the world, his beautiful black babies. For each woman had had the muscled sac of her womb removed and placed on her belly, hacked open to reveal the purplish mass of her placenta. Beatrice knew that if she were to dissect the thawing tissue, she'd find a tiny foetus in each one. The dead women had been pregnant too.

A movement at her feet caught her eyes. She tore her gaze away from the bodies long enough to glance down. Writhing in the fast congealing yolk was a pin-feathered embryo. A rooster must have been at Mister Herbert's hens. She put her hands on her belly to still the sympathetic twitching of her womb. Her eyes were drawn back to the horror on the beds. Another whimper escaped her lips.

A sound like a sigh whispered in through the door she'd left open. A current of hot air seared past her cheek, making a plume of fog as it entered the room. The fog split into two, settled over the heads of each woman, began to take on definition. Each misty column had a face, contorted in rage. The faces were those of the bodies on the bed. One of the duppy women leaned over her own corpse. She lapped like a cat at the blood thawing on its breast. She became a little more solid for having drunk of her own life blood. The other duppy stooped to do the same. The two duppy women each had a belly slightly swollen with the pregnancies for which Samuel had killed them. Beatrice had broken the bottles that had confined the duppy wives, their bodies held in stasis because their spirits were trapped. She'd freed them. She'd let them into the house. Now there was nothing to cool their fury. The heat of it was warming the room up quickly.

The duppy wives held their bellies and glared at her, anger flaring hot behind their eyes. Beatrice backed away from the beds. "I didn't know," she said to the wives. "Don't vex with me. I didn't know what it is Samuel do to you."

Was that understanding on their faces, or were they beyond compassion?

"I making baby for him too. Have mercy on the baby, at least?"

Beatrice heard the *snik* of the front door opening. Samuel was home. He would have seen the broken bottles, would feel the warmth of the house. Beatrice felt that initial calm of the prey that realizes it has no choice but to turn and face the beast that is pursuing it. She wondered if Samuel would be able to read the truth hidden in her body, like the egg in the bottle.

"Is not me you should be vex with," she pleaded with the duppy wives. She took a deep breath and spoke the words that broke her heart. "Is … is Samuel who do this."

She could hear Samuel moving around in the house, the angry rumbling of his voice like the thunder before the storm. The words were muffled, but she could hear the anger in his tone. She called out, "What you saying, Samuel?"

She stepped out of the meat locker and quietly pulled the door in, but left it open slightly so the duppy wives could come out when they were ready. Then with a welcoming smile, she went to greet her husband. She would stall him as long as she could from entering the third bedroom. Most of the blood in the wives' bodies would be clotted, but maybe it was only important that it be warm. She hoped that enough of it would thaw soon for the duppies to drink until they were fully real.

When they had fed, would they come and save her, or would they take revenge on her, their usurper, as well as on Samuel?

Eggie-Law, what a pretty basket.

33. Neil Gaiman, "Instructions" (2000)[1]

As a testament to Neil Gaiman's immense notoriety at the printing of this anthology, on November 20, 2011 he appeared as a character on The Simpsons *in an episode entitled "The Book Job." Becoming an avatar of himself may have satisfied a particular desire of this fantasy and fairy-tale writer for adults and young readers. Gaiman works in a range of traditional and modern media, from comics to screenplays and fantasy horror novella to fairy tales. His multiple literary awards include in 2009 a Newbery Medal, recognizing the most distinguished contribution to children's literature, for* The Graveyard Book

1 [Source: Neil Gaiman, "Instructions," in *A Wolf at the Door and Other Retold Fairy Tales*, eds. Ellen Datlow and Terri Windling (New York, NY: Simon and Schuster, 2000): 30–34.]

(about a young boy who takes refuge from a killer in a cemetery and spends his formative years being raised by ghosts). The supernatural comic book series The Sandman *and the young adult fantasy* Coraline *(2002) have become classics in their genres. Gaiman tours with his wife, punk musician Amanda Palmer (of The Dresden Dolls), with a stage show of his poetry set to ukulele and piano.*

His 2007 film co-written with Roger Avary that turned Beowulf *into a 3-D fantasy thriller nicely illustrates Gaiman's relationship to the source material he adapts both through visual media and in his own creative voice. Rather than focus on the antiquity of the story, the film updates its epic grandeur in a lavish visual narrative that makes use of the latest technology (such as "performance capture") to create figures that appear post-human, not unlike RPG animations. Gaiman's novels and fairy tales are similarly postmodern in the way they send young protagonists into alternative realities where they go through a period of fear and longing only to be seduced by the strangeness of their new selves. Instead of overcoming their fears and their hybridity, they are mesmerized by them, learn to accept them as the new normal, and worry about moving comfortably in the apprehensible adult world. "Instructions" speaks directly to the reader, making each of us the protagonist that will walk through the fairy-tale plot. These could be the directives of a player moving his warrior avatar through a booby-trapped RPG castle. We learn how to navigate garden gates, the exact answer to the ferryman's question, and who to trust. A* Wizard of Oz *ending teaches us a new way to relate to fairy tales: how to digest them, not as exemplary narratives of behavior, but as mindscapes that reorient our perspective on the world to which we are bound to return when the story ends.*

INSTRUCTIONS

Touch the wooden gate in the wall you never saw before.
Say "please" before you open the latch,
go through,
walk down the path.
A red metal imp hangs from the green-painted front door,
as a knocker,
do not touch it; it will bite your fingers.
Walk through the house. Take nothing. Eat nothing.
However,
if any creature tells you that it hungers,
feed it.
If it tells you that it is dirty,
clean it.
If it cries to you that it hurts,

if you can,
ease its pain.

From the back garden you will be able to see the wild wood.
The deep well you walk past leads to Winter's realm;
there is another land at the bottom of it.
If you turn around here,
you can walk back, safely;
you will lose no face. I will think no less of you.

Once through the garden you will be in the wood.
The trees are old. Eyes peer from the undergrowth.
Beneath a twisted oak sits an old woman. She may ask for something;
give it to her. She
will point the way to the castle.
Inside it are three princesses.
Do not trust the youngest. Walk on.
In the clearing beyond the castle the twelve months sit about a fire,
warming their feet, exchanging tales.
They may do favors for you, if you are polite.
You may pick strawberries in December's frost.

Trust the wolves, but do not tell them where you are going.
The river can be crossed by the ferry. The ferryman will take you.
(The answer to his question is this:
If he hands the oar to his passenger, he will be free to leave the boat.
Only tell him this from a safe distance.)

If an eagle gives you a feather, keep it safe.
Remember: that giants sleep too soundly; that
witches are often betrayed by their appetites;
dragons have one soft spot, somewhere, always;
hearts can be well-hidden, and you betray them with your tongue.

Do not be jealous of your sister.
Know that diamonds and roses
are as uncomfortable when they tumble from one's lips as toads and frogs:
colder, too, and sharper, and they cut.
Remember your name.

Do not lose hope—what you seek will be found.
Trust ghosts. Trust those that you have helped to help you in their turn.
Trust dreams. Trust your heart, and trust your story.

When you come back, return the way you came.
Favors will be returned, debts be repaid.
Do not forget your manners.
Do not look back.
Ride the wise eagle (you shall not fall)
Ride the silver fish (you will not drown)
Ride the gray wolf (hold tightly to his fur).

There is a worm at the heart of the tower; that is why it will not stand.

When you reach the little house, the place your journey started
you will recognize it, although it will seem much smaller than you remember.
Walk up the path, and through the garden gate you never saw before but once.
And then go home. Or make a home.

Or rest.

34. Kelly Link, "Swans" (2000)[1]

Kelly Link is an important figure in the world of contemporary American fantasy as a writer, an editor, and the co-founder of the independent Small Beer Press in Easthampton, Massachusetts. Link's short fiction draws on the genres of fairy tale, science fiction, horror, and magic realism, and has earned her the Hugo award, multiple Nebula awards, and the World Fantasy Award. Link's forays into postmodern fairy tales reflect this interest in genre-bending, a fascination with the darker—and the darkly humorous—dimensions of the fairy-tale genre, and a long tradition of "cross-writing," or writing that blurs the categories of children's, young adult, and adult fiction. In the short story "Swans," Link draws on the Grimms' tales known as "Six Swans," in which a young girl must endure six painful years of silence and sew six shirts of asters in order to free her six swan brothers from the enchantment imposed by their beautiful and evil stepmother. In Link's creative reworking and recasting of the plot, the heroine is less than self-sacrificing, the stepmother is less than malicious, the brothers are noisy and

1 [Source: Kelly Link, "Swans," in *A Wolf at the Door and Other Retold Fairy Tales*, eds. Ellen Datlow and Terri Windling (New York, NY: Simon and Schuster, 2000): 74–92.]

annoying; and the needlework that promises to set them (and the rest of the community) free from enchantment is quilting—a form of creative expression connected with the children's dead mother, and taken up by the heroine at the end of the story.

SWANS

My name is Emma Bear, and I am eleven years old. I live on Black Ankle Road beside the Licking River. I live in a palace. My father is a king. I have a fairy godfather. This summer I read The True Confessions of Charlotte Doyle and learned how to make blue dye from a flower called woad. I have six brothers. My mother is dead. I'm in the seventh grade. My father remarried this summer. My favorite class is home ec. I love to sew. I make all my own clothes. My mother taught me how to sew. I can also knit, crochet, and quilt.

Yesterday my stepmother pointed her pinkie finger at my brothers and turned them all into swans. They were being too noisy. I'm never too noisy. I don't talk at all.

This year I was failing choir. I opened my mouth to sing, and nothing came out. I hadn't been able to say a word since my mother died. In my other classes, it was okay. Homework was okay. Math was okay, and English. Art was okay. I could write down answers on the blackboard. I carried around a pad of paper and a pen. You'd be surprised how often you don't actually have to say anything. Mostly if I just nodded, it was okay. But choir doesn't work that way. You can't sing by writing on a pad of paper. But nothing came out of my mouth when I opened it.

Last year I had lots of friends. This year I didn't have any. What happened in between? My mother died. I stopped talking. No more friends. Really, I've been too busy to have friends, I suppose.

When I first stopped talking, no one noticed. Not until Mom's funeral, when we were all supposed to stand up and say something. I stood up, but nothing came out when I opened my mouth. First my father sent me to see a psychologist. I just sat on her couch. I looked at pictures, and wrote down what they looked like. They all looked like flowers, or birds, or schnauzers. Then my fairy godfather came to the palace.

My fairy godfather is a little man with red hair. His name is Rumpelstiltskin. He was a friend of my mother's. He'd been away on business for a few months—he'd missed the funeral. His eyes were all red, and he cursed a lot. He'd loved my mother a lot. He sat with me for a long time, brushing my hair, and patting my hand.

Finally he said, "Well, you certainly don't have to talk until you want to. Kefflufrle. Excuse my French. What a mess this is, Emma."

I nodded. I wrote down on my pad of paper, *I miss her.*

"Fudge, I do, too," my godfather said. "Excuse the French."

He tapped me on the nose gently. "You know your father is going to have to get married again."

I wrote, *I'll have an evil stepmother*?

"That evil stepmother stuff is just a pile of horsepucky," he said, "excuse me. It's just baloney. Whoever he marries will be just as afraid of you and your brothers as you are of her. You keep that in mind."

To my father, he said, "Emma just needs a piece of time. When she needs to say something, she'll open her mouth and say it."

He hugged my father, and he hugged me. He said, "I have a commission for you, Emma. I have a godchild who is going to a ball. All she's got to wear are rags. She needs a fancy dress. Not pink, I think. It wouldn't match. She's got lovely red hair, just like me. Maybe a nice sea-foam green. Right down to the ankles. Lots of lace."

I wrote, *When do you need it*?

"When she turns seventeen," he said. "That's not for a bit. I'll send you her measurements. Okay?" *Okay*, I wrote and kissed him good-bye.

When my mother was young, she was famous. She could spin straw into gold. Her name was Cleanthea. A year ago, she went jogging in the rain, and then she caught cold, and then she died.

My mother's quilts were famous. Famous quilts have their own names. She made crazy quilts, which are just bits of scraps sewn together, and then decorated and embroidered with fancy stitches—wheat stitches, briar stitches, flowers, birds, little frogs, and snowflakes. She made Log Cabin quilts and Wedding Ring quilts, and she also made up her own patterns. Her quilts had names like Going Down to the River and Snakes Fall in Love and Watering the Garden. People paid hundreds of dollars for them. Every bed in the castle has a quilt on it that my mother made.

Each of my brothers had a quilt that my mother made just for them. She made my brother Julian a *Star Wars* quilt, with X-Wing Fighters and Death Stars. She made my oldest brother an Elvis quilt. Up close it's just strips and patches of purple cloth, all different patterns. But when you back away, you can see that all the bits of different colors of purple make up Elvis's face—his eyes, his lips, his hair. For my youngest brother, she made a Cats Eat Birds quilt. She sewed real feathers into the cats' mouths, and little red cloth-patch birds into their stomachs.

She never finished my quilt. We were working on it together. I'm still working on it now. I don't really want to finish it. In fact, it's gotten a little bit big for my bed. When I spread it out, it's almost as big as a swimming pool. Eventually, it will fill up my whole room, I guess. Every night now I sleep on a different bed in the castle, under a different quilt. I pretend that each quilt is a quilt that I have never seen before, that she has just finished making, just for me.

I should tell you about my father and my brothers. I should also tell you about my stepmother. My father is very tall and handsome, and also very busy with things like affairs of state and cutting ribbons at the grand openings of grocery stores and presenting awards to writers and musicians and artists and also going to soccer games and football games so that photographers can take his picture. That was how he met my stepmother. He was at the zoo, which had just been given a rare species of bird. He was supposed to be photographed with the bird on his shoulder.

When he arrived, however, the keepers were distraught. The bird had disappeared. Even worse, a naked woman had been found wandering around the grounds. She wouldn't say who she was, or where she came from. No one could find her clothes. The keepers were afraid that she might be a terrorist, or an anarchist, come to blow up the zoo, or kill my father. It would be bad publicity for everyone.

"Nonsense," my father said. He asked to meet the woman. The zookeepers protested, saying that this was a bad idea. My father insisted. And so my father's picture appeared in the papers, holding out his hand to a woman dressed in a long white T-shirt and a pair of flip-flops that one of the keepers got out of the lost and found. The picture in the paper was blurry, but if you looked closely you could see the look in my father's eyes. He looked like he'd been hit on the head. He looked like he was falling in love, which he was.

The woman, my stepmother, looked small and fragile in the photograph, like a Christmas tree ornament. She had long, feathered hair. The T-shirt hung on her like a tent, and the flip-flops were too big for her.

We still don't know much about my stepmother. She was from a faraway country, we thought, because she had a slight but unrecognizable accent. She was a little bit cross-eyed, like a Siamese cat. She never brushed her hair. It stuck up in points behind her ears, like horns. She was very beautiful, but she hated noise. My brothers made too much noise. That's why she turned them into swans.

They came and stood on the lawn this morning, and I fed them dried corn and bits of burnt buttered toast. They came back early, while my stepmother was still sleeping. They honked at me very quietly. I think they were afraid if they were loud, she'd turn them into something even worse. Snails, maybe, or toads.

Some of the other girls at school thought I was lucky to have so many brothers. Some of them said how handsome my brothers were. I never really thought so. My brothers used to pull my hair and short-sheet my bed, and they never helped with my homework unless I gave them my allowance. They liked to sit on top of me and tickle me until I cried. But when my mother died, they all cried. I couldn't.

My brothers' names are George, Theodore, Russell, Anthony, William, and Julian. George is the oldest. Theodore is the nicest. Anthony is the tallest. Russell has freckles, and he is allergic to milk. William and Julian are twins, and two years younger than me. They liked to wear each other's clothes and pretend that Julian was

William, and William was Julian. The thing is, all of them look alike now that they're birds. They all look like twins.

My father told us that my stepmother didn't like noise. They got married at the beginning of the summer. We got to throw rice. We'd only seen my stepmother twice before—once in the newspaper picture, and once when my father brought her home for dinner. There were a lot of important people at that dinner. We ate in the kitchen, but afterward we stood in the secret passageway and spied through the painting that has the eyes cut out.

My future stepmother didn't eat much dinner, but she had three helpings of dessert. This is when I first became suspicious that she was magic—a witch, or else under an enchantment. Witches and people under spells, magic people, always have sweet tooths. My fairy godfather carries around sugar cubes in his pockets and stirs dozens of them in his coffee, or else just eats them plain, like a horse. And he never gets cavities.

When my father and stepmother came back from their honeymoon, we were all standing on the palace steps. We had all just had baths. The palace steps had just been washed.

My father and stepmother were holding hands. When they saw us, my stepmother let go of my father's hand and slipped inside the palace. I was holding up a big sign that said, WELCOME HOME, DAD. There wasn't any room on the sign for STEPMOTHER.

"Hey," my brother George said, "what did you bring me?"

"Anthony stole my rocket launcher," Russell said.

"It wasn't me," Anthony said, "it was Theodore."

"It was NOT me," Theodore said, and William and Julian said, "Emma made us brush our teeth every night."

Everyone began yelling. My father yelled loudest of all.

"I'd really appreciate it if you all tried to be quiet and didn't yell all at once. Your stepmother has a bad headache, and besides, she's very shy, and not at all used to loud children," he said, looking at my brothers. Then he looked at me. "Emma," he said, "are you still not talking?"

I took out my notepad and wrote *yes* on it. He sighed. "Does that mean 'yes, you are talking now,' or 'yes, you still aren't talking'?"

I didn't say anything. I just smiled and nodded. "Maybe you'd like to show your new stepmother around the castle," he said.

My stepmother was in the library, reclining on a sofa with a damp cloth over her eyes. I stood there for a bit, and then I tapped my foot some. She didn't move. Finally I reached down and touched her shoulder. Her eyelids fluttered.

I held up my pad of paper. I wrote, *I'm Emma. I don't talk.*

She sat up and looked at me. She wasn't very big. When she stood up, I bet that we would have been the same height, almost, except she was wearing pointy black shoes with tall heels to make her look taller.

I wrote, *Dad asked me to show you the castle.*

I showed her around the castle. I showed her the kitchen with the roasting spit that the dogs turn, and the microwave, and the coffeemaker. I showed her the ballroom, which is haunted, and the dungeon, which my father had converted into an indoor swimming pool and squash court, and I showed her the bowling alley which is also haunted, and the stables, and the upstairs bathroom, which has modern plumbing. Then I took her to my mother's room. The quilt on the bed was Roses and Cabbages Growing Up Together, all pieced together from old green velvet hunting coats and rose-colored satin gloves.

My new stepmother sat down on the bed. She bounced experimentally, holding her head. She stared at me with her slightly crossed eyes. "A nice bed," she said in a soft, gravelly voice. "Thanks, Emma."

My mother made this quilt, I wrote. *Her quilts are very valuable. Please be careful when you are sleeping.* Then I left her there on my mother's bed. The next day she turned George into a swan. He was practicing his saxophone.

George is my father's heir. George doesn't want to be king. George wants to be a saxophonist in a heavy metal band. I was listening to him in the ballroom. He isn't very good yet, but he likes to have an audience. I sit and listen to him, and he pays me five dollars. He says someday it will be the other way round.

I was embroidering the back of a blouse with blue silk thread. I was trying to embroider a horse, but it looked more like a crocodile, or maybe a dachshund.

My stepmother had been swimming in the pool. She was still in her bathing suit. She came into the ballroom and left puddly footprints all over the waxed and polished black walnut floor. "Excuse me," she said. George ignored her. He kept on honking and tootling. He smirked at me. "Excuse me," our stepmother said, a little bit louder, and then she pointed her pinkie finger at him. She flicked her pinkie up at him, and he turned into a swan. The swan—George—honked. He sounded surprised. Then he spread out his wings and flew away through an open window.

I opened my mouth, but of course nothing came out. I stared at my stepmother, and she shrugged apologetically. Then she turned and left, still dripping. Later that afternoon when Anthony set off Russell's rocket over the frog pond, my stepmother turned him into a swan, too. I was up in the tree house watching.

You're probably wondering why I didn't tell someone. My dad, for instance. Well, for one thing, it was kind of fun. My brothers looked so surprised. Besides, at dinner no one missed Anthony or George. My brothers are always off somewhere, camping with friends, or else sleeping over at someone else's house, or else keeping vigil in the haunted bowling alley. The ghost always shows up in the bowling alley at midnight, with his head in his hand. The pins scream when he throws his head down the lane.

My stepmother had three helpings of pineapple upside-down cake. After dinner, she turned Theodore and Russell into swans. They were banging down the grand staircase on tin trays. I have to admit this is a lot of fun. I've done it myself. Not turning people into swans, I mean, sliding down on trays.

I had to open up a window for Theodore and Russell. They honked reproachfully at me as I pushed them out over the windowsill. But once they opened up their wings, they looked so graceful, so strong. They flew up into the sky, curving and diving and hanging on a current of air, dipping their long necks.

How do you do that? I wrote down on my pad. My stepmother was sitting down on the staircase, looking almost ashamed.

"I don't know," she said. "It just seems to happen. It's just so noisy."

Can you turn them back? I wrote.

"What an excellent inquiry," she said. "I do not know. Perhaps and we shall see."

William and Julian refused, as usual, to brush their teeth before bedtime. Loudly. I told them, *Be quiet, or else.*

"Or else what?" Julian screamed at me, his face red with temper.

New stepmother will turn you into a swan.

"Liar," William said loudly. He said it again, even louder, experimentally. My stepmother, wearing pink flannel pajamas, was standing there, just outside the bathroom door. She stuck her head in, looking pained. Julian and William pretended to be afraid. They screamed and giggled. Then they pretended to be swans, flapping their arms. My stepmother waved her finger at them, and they sprouted wings. They sprouted feathers and beaks, and blinked their black beady eyes at her.

I filled up the bathtub with water, and put them in it. It was the first time they ever seemed to enjoy a bath. Even better, they didn't have any teeth to brush.

Then I put them outside, because I wasn't sure if they were house-trained.

The next morning I woke under my favorite quilt, the Rapunzel quilt, with the gray tower, and the witch, and the prince climbing up the long yellow braids. I ate breakfast and then I went outside and fed my brothers. I'd never had pets before. Now I had six. I tried to decide what I liked better, birds or brothers.

When I went back to get more toast, my father was sitting in the kitchen, reading the morning paper. He was wearing the striped purple bathrobe I'd made him for Christmas three years ago. Mom had helped with the cuffs. The hem was a little bit frayed. "Good morning, Emma," he said. "Still not speaking? Where are the rest of you, anyway?"

I wrote down, *New stepmom turned them into swans.*

"Ha," he said. "You're a funny girl, Emma. Don't forget. Today I'm dedicating the new school gymnasium. We'll see you about two-ish."

First there were speeches. I sat with the rest of my grade, in the bleachers, and looked at my new stepmother. I was thinking that the smart thing would have been to buy her earplugs. Whenever my principal, Mr. Wolf, put his mouth too close to the microphone, there was a squeal of feedback. My stepmother was looking pale. Her lips were pressed tightly together. She sat behind Mr. Wolf on the stage, beside my father.

Sorley Meadows, who wears colored lip gloss, was sitting next to me. She dug her pointy elbow into my side. "Your stepmother is, like, tiny," she said. "She looks like a little kid."

I ignored her. My father sat with his back straight, and his mouth fixed in a dignified, royal smile. My father can sleep with his eyes open. That's what my mother used to say. She used to poke him at state occasions, just to see if he was still awake.

Mr. Wolf finished his speech, and we all clapped. Then the marching band came in. My father woke up. My stepmother put her hand out, as if she were going to conduct them.

Really, the band isn't very good. But they are enthusiastic. My stepmother stood up. She stuck out her pinkie finger, and instead of a marching band there was suddenly a lot of large white hissing swans.

I jumped down out of the bleachers. How mortifying. Students and teachers all began to stand up. "She turned them into birds," someone said.

My father looked at my stepmother with a new sort of look. It was still a sort of being hit on the head sort of look, but a different sort of being hit on the head. Mr. Wolf turned toward my father and my stepmother. "Your Royal Majesty, my dear mademoiselle," he said, "please do not be alarmed. This is, no doubt, some student prank."

He lifted the little silver whistle around his neck and blew on it. "Everyone," he said. "Please be quiet! Please sit back down."

My stepmother did not sit back down. She pointed at Mr. Wolf. Mrs. Heliotrope, the French teacher, screamed suddenly. Mr. Wolf was a swan. So was Mrs. Heliotrope. And as I watched, suddenly the new gymnasium was full of birds. Sorley Meadows was a swan. John Riley, who is someone I once had a crush on until I saw him picking his nose in the cloakroom, was a swan. Emma Valerie Snope, who used to be my best friend because we had the same name, was a swan. Marisa Valdez, the prettiest girl in the seventh grade, was a swan.

My father grabbed my stepmother's arm. "What is going on here?" he said to her. She turned him into a swan.

In that whole gymnasium, it was just me and my stepmother and a lot of swans. There were feathers floating all over in the air. It looked like a henhouse. I pulled out my pad of paper. I jumped up on the stage and walked over to her. She had just turned my whole school into a bunch of birds. She had just turned my father into a bird. She put her hand down absentmindedly and patted him on the top of his white feathery head. He darted his head away, and snapped at her.

I was so angry, I stabbed right through the pad of paper with my ballpoint. The tip of the pen broke off. I threw the pad of paper down.

I opened my mouth. I wasn't sure what was going to come out. Maybe a yell. Maybe a curse. Maybe a squawk. What if she turned me into a bird, too? "WHAT?" I said. "WHAT?"

It was the first word I had said in a whole year. I saw it hit her. Her eyes got so big. She threw her arm out, pointing her pinkie finger at me. I was pointing at her. "WHAT?" I said again. I saw her pinkie finger become a feather. Her arms got downy. Her nose got longer, and sharp. She flapped her wings at me.

She wasn't a swan. She was some other kind of bird. I don't know what kind. She was like an owl, but bigger, or maybe a great auk, or a kiwi. Her feathers looked fiery and metallic. She had a long tail, like a peacock. She fanned it out. She looked extremely relieved. She cocked her head to one side and looked at me, and then she flew out of the gymnasium.

"WHAT?" I screamed after her. "WAIT!" What a mess. She'd turned my family, my entire school into birds, and then she flew away? Was this fair? What was I supposed to do? "I want to be a swan, too! I want my mom!"

I sat down on the stage and cried. I really missed my mom.

Then I went to the school library and did a little research. A lot of the swans came with me. They don't seem to be house-trained, so I spread out newspaper on the floor for them.

My fairy godfather is never around when you need him. This is why it's important to develop good research skills, and know how to find your way around a library. If you can't depend on your fairy godfather, at least you can depend on the card catalog. I found the section of books on enchantments, and read for a bit. The swans settled down in the library, honking softly. It was kind of pleasant.

It seems that to break my stepmother's pinkie spell, I need to make shirts for all of the birds and throw the shirts over their necks. I need to sew these shirts out of nettle cloth, which doesn't sound very pleasant. Nettles burn when you pick them. Really, I think linen, or cotton is probably more practical. And I think I have a better idea than a bunch of silly shirts that no one is probably going to want to wear again, anyway. And how are you supposed to sew a shirt for a bird? Is there a pattern? Down in the castle storerooms, there are a lot of trunks filled with my mother's quilting supplies.

I miss my mother.

Excuse me. I just can't seem to stop talking. My voice is all hoarse and croaky. I sound like a crow. I probably wouldn't have gotten a good grade in choir, anyway. Mrs. Orlovsky, the choir teacher, is the swan over there, on top of the librarian's desk. Her head is tucked under her wing. At least I think it's Mrs. Orlovsky. Maybe it's Mr. Beatty, the librarian. My father is perched up on the windowsill. He's looking out the window, but I can't see anything out there. Just sky.

I think I'm going to finish the quilt that my mother and I started. It's going to be a lot bigger than either of us was planning on making it. When I finish, it should be big enough even to cover the floor of the gymnasium.

It's a blue quilt, a crazy quilt. Silk, corduroy, denim, satin, velvet. Sapphire, midnight blue, navy, marine, royal blue, sky blue. I'm going to patch in white birds with wide white wings on one side, and on the other side I'm going to patch in little white shirts. When I finish, I'm going to roll it up, and then throw it over all the swans I can find. I'm going to turn them back into people. This quilt is going to be as beautiful as sky. It's going to be as soft as feathers. It's going to be just like magic.

35. Marina Warner, "The Difference in the Dose" (2010) [1]

A self-proclaimed mythographer, Marina Warner has emerged as a leading figure in the study of fairy tales and, more precisely, their European history. With a long list of honorary doctorates, she has been a professor in the Department of Literature, Film and Theatre Studies at the University of Essex since 2004 and has long been a practitioner of what she calls "fabulism," on which she also teaches creative writing seminars. Two contributions to the academic field of fairy-tale studies are worthy of particular note. Her groundbreaking monograph, From the Beast to the Blond: On Fairy Tales and Their Tellers *(1995) undertakes a sweeping critical survey of the figure of the women teller in the West from the sibyl to Mother Goose to Angela Carter.* Wonder Tales: Six French Stories of Enchantment, *which she edited in 2004, presents new English translations of seventeenth-century tales with a view to recapturing their "wonder"—a term that she chooses against "fairy" to identify the genre with the experience of enchantment rather than a single element of its plot. Both of these texts reexamine tale history from a new perspective and bring it into contact with modern language that changes how we see it: the idea of the "blond" as a way to understand fairy-tale protagonists and the nineteenth-century German "Wundermärchen" as a way to describe writing from seventeenth-century France. Warner's approach to the fairy tale in her fiction follows a similar logic. "The Difference in the Dose: A Story after Rapunzel" recasts the Grimms' tale of the long-haired maiden locked in the tower as a modern story of towers and cravings, both physical and psychological, that connect even as they separate three generations of women.*

THE DIFFERENCE IN THE DOSE: A STORY AFTER RAPUNZEL

"OTHER CHILDREN HAVE A NANNA," says Daisy, "Why not me?

She turns her face up to her mother, who is combing her hair after washing it. It is curly and thick and tangles easily, so Bella combs it through before Daisy goes to bed, where she will wake the next morning with her hair in fiery spikes again. Bella's full name is Belladonna, the name of another flower, a different kind from lilies or roses, daisies or buttercups.

A flower that can be good for you, sometimes.

Bella's mother understands plants, and belladonna had a special significance for her, she used to say. She's a herbalist, she knows these things. She likes to say, "The only difference between a poison and a remedy is the dose."

1 [Source: Marina Warner, "The Difference in the Dose," *Marvels & Tales* 24.2 (2010): 317–28.]

Daisy is plucking at Bella's sleeve; she insists, her mouth beginning to twist into a cry, "Everyone in my class has a nanna. I'm—the—only—one—who—hasn't." She spells out each word as if learning to pronounce it for the first time.

"Your granny ..." Bella hesitates. Then she says, "Let me tell you a story, which will explain everything."

And she begins:

"Women sometimes discover they are having a baby only because they have a sudden craving. In Italian this urge is called, simply, *la voglia*. The want. The same word as will, but with the definite article added: *the* want. That makes it much more absolute. We call it a craving. When I was small, my mother told me *la voglia* is irresistible. It's a force that takes over and makes you ... quite irrational, quite uncontrollable. When *la voglia* comes over her, the future mother won't be refused; she'll stop at nothing—do you realise?—to get what she needs.

"Needs? Maybe. But maybe the substances she craves aren't helpful to the new life inside her ... Or maybe they're just caprices, the aberrant fancies of a mind unbalanced by endocrinal surges ..."

She's rushing on, talking to herself, she realises; she has lost Daisy's attention. So she changes direction, forgets the technical stuff, and says, "We might want all sorts of crazy things when someone like you is waiting to be born. Some not so crazy too. Our cravings can be an excuse for:

chocolate truffles
lavender pastilles
fried chips in strawberry jam
ice cream galore—pistachio, rum truffle, tutti frutti, raspberry swirl,
coconut candy, or any flavour you can think of. Haagen-Dazs Dulce
de Leche Mini-cups ... !"

"Cherrimisù!" cries Daisy.

"In some places they can all be bought in the middle of the night—imagine! Like a pizza, you can get them delivered!"

There's a pause as both picture this craziness. Then Daisy's mother goes on: "In some cases we want other things, we want:

coal dust from the scuttle
the colouring bits inside colouring crayons
mud and silt from puddles in the road
mustard and horseradish and ginger
soap powder and shampoo

beetles and eggshells
and ..."

She starts laughing.

Daisy giggles too. She begins to look around the room.

"Carpet," she shouts, "you might want to eat carpet!" She bangs on the table. "And wood! Nice tasty wood!"

"No," says the child's father, when he comes in and hears the stories his wife is telling their daughter. "No, those things would harm the baby inside."

He goes to the fridge and brings out a bottle of white wine and begins to look for the corkscrew.

"Even wine is forbidden to expecting mothers now," he says.

"But it wasn't when I was having you," says Bella to her daughter, cross with Piero because he has broken into their game. "And look at you, nothing wrong with you!"

The father pours out a glass for himself and another for Bella; Daisy settles herself against her mother and begins to draw with her finger in the misty veil forming on the bowl. Bella strokes her hair, which is almost dry now after her bath.

"Your nanna had cravings when she was having me."

Daisy looks up at her with excitement.

"What for?"

"Oh, ... spinach and carrots and things. Parsnips!" says Piero, her father, and leans over and kisses Bella firmly, to change the subject.

"Parsnips," giggles Daisy, and makes a face.

"She ate them raw!"

He grinds and snaps his teeth at Daisy, not to fail the general mood of jollity, because he realises how heavy he's been. But he can't help it, and adds, "That's how weird women get."

Belladonna can't remember her birth mother, the mother who had the cravings. She wouldn't ever have been able to remember her, because she was a tiny baby, only a few weeks old, when she was adopted, and she was never shown a photograph of her by the mother she knew, the one who brought her up, Charis Merryll, the beautiful lady gardener, best-selling author of several classic titles (*Orchids in the Penthouse; Urban Plots; Hanging Gardens for the Mostly Manicured*—and her most famous of all, *The Difference in the Dose*).

It's been ten years since Bella quarreled with Charis, a little longer than the length of time since Daisy was born. Charis found out that Bella was sleeping with Piero; she found them together in bed, in *her* bed, the one with the satin canopy bunched up into a cherub's fist, which was such bliss to sleep under. Charis was back from somewhere a day earlier than expected, and she'd come whooping into the lobby of the apartment block where they lived, thinking how it was so great; she'd finished the assignment ahead of time, and now she and her daughter could have a precious day together over the weekend, something that didn't happen often enough, something she treasured, better than usual weekend quality time, real time out from her busy life planning and planting gardens all over the world for architects, bringing greenery to the desert for hotels in the Gulf, and turning into new Edens the oil-rich Emirates' island Utopias that were rising up out of the swirling salt barrenness.

Charis was thinking all of this as she greeted the doorman of her Madison Avenue apartment block, the Golden Tower, as she went up in the elevator to the penthouse floor, as she pushed open the door, which was never locked, and found that it was, surprisingly, shut and bolted.

"Bella!" she cried out at the door. She never carried keys; she didn't need them, because the doorman and the janitor kept the tower quite safe.

"Bella!" Her heart contracted. Charis knew then something was wrong, terribly wrong.

She saw her child in peril. Images of horror jumped in her mind; interference storms jangled the stream of pixels from some terrible news bulletin: Bella sprawling, Bella drugged, Bella drunk, Bella damaged, abducted, gang raped, murdered.

The screaming inside her was already beginning as she went down again in the elevator to fetch the doorman to let her into her own home.

She was shaking as she asked him for his keys, and she didn't conceal her agitation from him. She began to form a different picture from her first terrors as she registered, with hindsight, that he had greeted her with a degree of surprise that was perhaps unexpected.

"Oh, you're back so early, Ms. Merryll," he'd said, before he had added with his more customary courtesy, "Have you had a good trip this time?"

Going back up in the elevator, her sense of ominousness gathered. The doorman opened the service door at the back, the one they never used, and she entered her apartment through the kitchen and began taking in the trail of tumbled glasses and dishes, the mulchy cocktail of smoke and booze and pizza, the drawn curtains and dropped blinds, the cushions tossed this way and that on the floor, the furniture moved out to the edges of the room, one lot of bodies sprawled on the couch, fast asleep, another heap of tangled limbs on the divan, the garden room window opened, her precious plants exposed to the night air. She started in her rage toward her daughter's bedroom: there she found more kids. Yes, kids, girls from Bella's class. Boys, too. She pulled off the covers to see where her daughter was. Not there. Not in the living room. She then realised, before she threw open the door to her own bedroom, where she would be.

She pulled off the sheets—and she saw Piero flung down on his front with nothing on (though she didn't yet know who he was, she saw only a man, a fully grown man with hair on his legs and his buttocks, too, and even on his back, an old man).

She realised that he was one of her circle of friends, a man she knew, a successful businessman with a string of wig makers, costumiers, and hire shops, a man almost her own age, someone she had found amusing, pleasant, clever at business, but not, absolutely not … not for her child, not like this, not to sleep with her. Rage began breaking her open, letting fly a swarm of demons.

He was lying with one arm over the body of her daughter. His right hand was plunged into her hair, and she was still in a party dress—and one of her own best outfits, Charis realised—though it was all undone and messed up around her. So without even knowing what she was doing, she grasped him by the shoulder and began hitting him as her tears started pouring down. He sprang up and hit her back, square on her left cheek with his right hand, and he was a vigorous man who weighed at least two stone more than Charis, and his blow sent her reeling to the floor.

Bella was awake now, screaming at them both, standing up in her mother's muddled dress, her hair bunched and knotted and sticking out in all directions.

"You don't deserve Bella," Piero was shouting. "You're a dried-up old bitch, and all your mothering is a big fucking lie."

"*Che stronza*," he bawled at her as he tied the sheet around himself like a smart beach sarong. "You've only ever wanted your big career and your big fucking credit card—you don't know anything about being a mother. Well, I love Bella. I am mother and father and lover and husband to her. I love her in ways your sort can never understand."

They raged at each other. And Bella took his side. Bella turned on her, said unheard-of terrible things to her, poured out a pent-up hatred on her, which had been harboured for years and years.

"You took me from my family. You stole me from my real mother. You thought you could buy me. Well, I am not someone you can buy anymore. I am not a slave."

Piero put his arm around her and tucked her in under his high shoulder, fastening her to him as if she were now his baby.

"Bella loves me," he said. "I am the best thing that ever happened to her. I love her more than you ever could. You selfish old bag, you wanted a trophy child. Another lifestyle accessory.

"Well, it's over. It's my turn now.

"You can buy yourself a puppy."

Charis thought:

In those days, I was so hoping for a child. The streets seemed to me to be crowded with nothing but women displaying their bumps, their navels pertly stuck out like a nipple, the parks teeming with young mothers with Walkmans dangling from their ears, pushing strollers, sometimes speeding on roller blades or, if the kids were a little older, sitting in the sun together chatting—by the playgrounds or the soccer pitch or the ice rink, where their offspring would be running about learning to be social.

But I, I had had abortions in earlier days when it seemed that every time I went to bed with someone it happened even if I was doing everything to prevent it. Then, when I wanted to have a baby, when I had established my business and had the books done and dusted and everyone wanted a Charis Merryll low-maintenance urban plot with every remedy and every herb you need, it stopped happening.

Alfred couldn't take my wanting one so much—it wore him out, my crying. It cut him out.

So I thought, I will find someone who is like I was then, someone who can have a baby very easily and then have another soon so won't miss the first one, and I'll persuade her to give me hers.

My plot—a different kind of plot—was quite clever, though I say so myself.

The fight in the main bedroom began to wake up the rest of the party, though not all. Some of the party guests began to rouse themselves and padded about in the apartment, trying to shake their lethargy and their hangovers and find their clothes and other belongings to make a getaway.

Gradually, the rest woke up, too, as their friends roused them with warning prods and whispers. At last Charis was alone with her daughter and her daughter's boyfriend, the man old enough to be her father.

"She is *seventeen,*" said Charis. "And you, how old are you? Forty?" She'd spat out the word.

"I'm old enough to get married," cried Bella. "My mother was my age when I was born. You told me so yourself. And Piero loves me, he says so. We're going to go and live far away from here, far away from you."

Weariness set in quickly. Charis was soon begging them to forgive and forget, as she would do, she promised. She'd experienced a terrible shock, but they could both work through it with time—and with love. They should live with her, or at least near her.

She was grubby with tears; she recognised that she couldn't command Bella's love exclusively. She knew she had to let go. But not now, not yet.

Piero had taken Bella with him to Italy, where they now live; Charis had tried to prevent him by making Bella a ward of the court, but he preempted her legal moves, and true to what he had sworn that terrible night ten years ago, he indeed married Bella on her eighteenth birthday, the day of her majority, when Charis could no longer exercise any jurisdiction over her daughter. Except love, and her love no longer equalled his in her daughter's needs.

Since then, Charis's letters have had no answer, and there is no point in her trying to telephone, since her calls to their mobiles are blocked, and in the house and in his offices Piero employs staff, and the staff have instructions not to take calls from Charis.

Yet Charis still moves through Bella's dreams, though she never tells Piero, because he always falls into a rage at the thought of her. Charis also appears to Bella by day: even though they are living far from Manhattan, where Charis still lives, Bella in Italy sees her mother's quick step in someone crossing a street in front of her, or in the lithe contours of a figure in the crowd passing by on the television in the background of some event. But it's an illusion; in fact they have not seen each other since that morning when Piero gathered her up with a few scraps of her things and planned everything—the honeymoon in Venice, the house in the hills outside Siena, and then the old *palazzone* in the country near Milan, where he had inherited from his dead parents an apartment with cracked frescoes on the high walls that told ancient stories of the gods, how they changed shape to make love to human girls who struggled to escape: changing their form, turning into trees, rivers, animals, flowers—and stars.

Then Daisy was born.

Now Daisy is ten years old and she wants to know her Granny.

"How much do you love me?" Daisy asks Bella. "Show me!" She holds her arms out wide. "I love you this much." She retracts them a little bit: "And I love Pappi this much."

"And I love you this much!" Bella imitates her daughter, throws her arms out as wide as she can and then brings them together around her and squeezes her tight.

Daisy gurgles and wriggles and squeals.

"It's too tight, you're crushing me too tight!"

Bella lets her go.

When she was a child, Bella began to realise that some of the other kids she knew had a father, and she only had a mother, and her mother was old, old enough to be her grandmother, or the mother of her school friends' mothers. Charis could look all haggard and witchy at the school gates, with her long white hair in a frizz and her dungarees and her grimy fingernails, so Bella ordered her not to come and stand near the exit but some way off, if she insisted on coming at all.

But once she began to pester Charis with questions, Charis told Bella that her birth mother had not been able to keep her, because she was ill and poor and tired, that she had wanted Bella to have a better life that she could give her, and had loved her too much not to want the very best for her.

But Charis never told Bella how it had come about; how she had plotted long and hard, how her need had rendered her lucid, rational, and resolute; how she had persevered, examining and reexamining the situation until the right candidate turned up, and she knew she had found the right woman to be the mother of the child that was going to be hers.

First Charis had taken the idea for the book to her agent, and then the agent had submitted the plan to a publisher, the right enterprising young publisher for such a strong marketing idea, one that combined so neatly two best-selling lines, "Gardening" and "Mind, Body, Spirit." Then, with the advance, Charis had leased a waste ground between two buildings on the Upper East Side in Spanish Harlem and brought in tons of earth to plant her Well Woman's Garden. Herbs and spices, teas and berries, flowers and bushes with properties that eased menstrual cramps and regulated cycles, that sweetened tension and lightened moods, that softened skin and strengthened nipples of nursing mothers: her garden had different geographical zones, some under cloches and glass frames to protect them against the New York frosts, some inside in two conservatories warmed by bulbs that glowed in the night like cat's eyes.

She studied monks' herbals and Caribbean wise women's manuals; she consulted the local *curanderas* from San Domingo and Dominica in the neighbourhood and traveled to Guadalajara and Mexico City to talk to the stall holders in the street markets there who sold remedies in coloured twists of paper.

In the Well Woman's Garden she planted saffron crocus and the spiky aloe; jojoba and echinacea; all the familiar culinary herbs and some not so familiar—alongside rosemary and parsley grew tansy and lovage and comfrey and sorrel and scabious. She scattered seeds of evening primrose by the wall facing west as the yellow trumpets drank in sunshine, and planted henbane in the crannies where it would cling to crumbs of earth. Queen Anne's lace, foxgloves, poppies were to grow wild, as if in a meadow.

All her plants were common, and all of them could be used to poison—as well as to heal.

She was greening the granite city.

In the more formal beds, she planted belladonna and vervain, rampion and rue—this was the part of the garden that was especially concerned with gynaecological troubles. She watched rampion begin to follow its name and climb vigorously up the wicker obelisks she provided: this was the king's cure-all, one of the most versatile of helpers, with a profound sway over the menstrual cycle. It was only one emmenagogue among several others: botany tuned in to biology. After all, plants were not so far from humans in their metabolism and their chemistry. Charis herself always felt brighter on clear days, and low cloud overhead made her droop.

The bed where belladonna and rampion grew was the part of the garden that was the heart of the project: her book *The Difference in the Dose* focussed on the principle that Charis had gleaned from the great Swiss physician Paracelsus, that sometimes the distance between boon and bane, between remedy and poison, between a comfortable pregnancy and a miscarriage, is a simple matter of a level teaspoon or a heaped one.

This part of the garden was controversial; rumours spread on the street (and Charis did nothing to discourage them) that what she grew there had power over babies growing in the womb.

She had assistants; she had sonar sensors to alert the presence of intruders, and a guard on duty at night as well.

Bella's mother was one of the visitors who came by one day, as others had done before her, and began to ask about the garden and that particular patch. She needed help, she said, help with morning sickness, which was making her life a torment. Charis saw her and understood her, felt the mixed fears of a young girl who was having a baby she hadn't thought to have, not yet, not now. She craved a medicine. Charis offered her an alternative, and as they talked, Charis recognised that at last she had found someone who would understand her craving. They would exchange their needs; one need for another. She would provide remedies (and something more besides) for the cramps and the nausea and the fear of what was coming; she, the younger woman, would give her, Charis, who had left it too late, the baby when she was born. Charis knew it was a girl: she used a herbal diagnostic from Trotula's famous book of recipes.

So when Daisy asked to meet her granny, Bella thought of Charis on the one hand and of the nameless mother on the other, and both of them haunted her day and night.

As Bella combed her daughter's hair before she put her to bed, maybe Daisy felt the lost mothers through her fingertips and was beginning to hum along to Bella's inward tune, amplifying her nascent yearnings in reciprocal exchange with her, and a song swelled up between them, about the rift in the past and a way to heal it.

Bella began to make inquiries, moving through knots and tangles. When Daisy first declared loudly and firmly that she was looking for her grandmother, the official in the United States consular office in Milan, whom she and Bella went to consult, assumed Bella must be searching for her birth mother. Bella realised the mistake and almost immediately understood that Daisy had divined her own curiosity, her own longing to fill the vacancy.

She was terrified but excited. Daisy was enraptured at the thought: they would find Bella's real mother and she would have a nanna of her own.

The process was complicated because they were now resident in Italy. But after toiling through mountains of documents, after a DNA test and paying out several expensive search fees to lawyers in America, a letter came with a name, an address—in Danville, California—and a photograph, a kind of mug shot, taken before Bella's birth, in which Bella saw nobody she knew or resembled: a thin-faced girl with a mutinous mouth and a back-combed bob, who could have been thirty years old, not the mere eighteen as the certificate declared.

It was looking at her mother's face that made Bella decide she must see Charis, too. The two women's meeting in that time before she was born and at the moment of her birth bound them together forever in the same story, and the story was theirs and couldn't be split in two.

Her resolve formed inside her like a flame; she felt her heart kindle and soar.

The blaze of her realisation gave her the force she needed to inform Piero and warn him that he could not oppose her in this enterprise.

"I am going to New York to see Charis again," she said. "It's been long enough."

He struggled against her; he poured vitriol on Charis. But he was passing his hands over his eyes, as if trying to rub out what he saw there at the same time as he summoned up all the rancour of his memories. And so, beneath all the sound and fury, quietness set in, and Bella understood with a lurch that he would not stop her going.

Not that she would have let him stop her, not now.

So she ran to Daisy's room and scooped her up and cried out to her child, "How much do I love you?" She was running from one side of the room to the other and all the way round and round—"Like this, like this!"—as Daisy jumped up and down, howling with laughter. "And you're going to meet your nanna. We're going to find her."

She had not dared admit to Piero that she had been searching for the other mother in her story, not Charis, not the one he knew, but the one with no name, the one who had given birth to her and then given her away.

She did not show him the copies of the documents she had procured, nor the tickets from New York to San Francisco that she had bought for herself and Daisy; she hid them in a wallet and tucked it into the inside pocket and then thrust it down deep inside the zipped-up lining of her suitcase, a part she never usually used.

She didn't tell Daisy either, not yet. It would depend on what happened when they reached Danville.

Scenes of their reunion danced in a frenzy before her eyes as she tried out the woman in the photograph in different settings:

—they would arrive at the door of a small house with a garden path, crazy paving, and a smoking chimney, and a street lantern haloed to one side. Bella and Daisy would skip toward her, hand in hand … there would be shock, astonishment, then bliss, bliss, bliss as they would fall into one another's arms.

Or:

(she was opening doors in the possible time ahead, doors with different scenes behind them)

—they would find the house empty because, yes, her mother, her real mother, would be at work. So they would knock at a neighbour's door and then go to another address, in downtown Danville, a shop or a bank or a business where she would be working, and they would wait in line for an appointment and then ... the same, the recognition that filled the heart to bursting.

Or:

—she would be living in squalor, in a doss-house, with drunken companions, a school of alkies falling among the debris of empty cans and bottles and roach ends or worse—needles, carbonized spoons, aluminium foil singed with smoke.

Bella would save her. She would appear in a glow at the door—Daisy would be sheathed in golden light, too. Together, they'd beam out love and warmth, cherishing and sustenance, and the years of separation would dissolve. The discovery of Daisy's existence would bring her hope and a reason to live. They would help her into rehab; they would bring her home with them.

In all of these scenes, Bella saw her own face slipping to eclipse the features of the woman in the photograph; she found she could not envisage her mother as she might have grown over the last twenty-seven years. She tried greying the dark hair of the woman in the picture; she tried adding lines around her mouth; she tried bowing her shoulders and tensing her neck till it turned scrawny.

The images tumbled through her mind as the plane crossed the world. Daisy fell asleep beside her in her seat, her furry lamb held close to her cheek, which lay against her mother's arm.

Across the cloud floor stretched Bella's dreams of their homecoming: her birth mother restored to them both, and she, Bella, restored to her—the dream was warm as a soft, sweet pudding straight from the oven, toasted sugar seeping from its fluffy edges; it was thrilling and made her tingle, creeping deliriously over her scalp and down her arms, like the times when Charis used to brush her hair before tucking her up and sometimes tease her by blowing softly on her neck and on her cheeks.

No, she told herself, Don't think of her, don't think of Charis.

Bella began to doze, but uneasily. The encounter that lay ahead loomed tall as a tall tower before them, a tower difficult to enter and hard to scale, a tower with no doors or windows.

They are driving along the freeway toward the address the bureau has given her after she sent them a sample of her DNA and proved she was who she was when she was born. The GPS map in the hired car is guiding them in a soft, motherly voice: "You are coming up to the exit. Two hundred yards, one hundred yards. Take the slipway. Take the next left, two hundred yards, one hundred yards."

The twists and turns continue; they are advancing deeper and deeper into the countryside without a sign of human habitation. On all sides of them the land sweeps up to the horizon in a thick, rough pelt of shrub and undergrowth, bristling, thorny; on the crest of the hills the pine trees stand serried, pointing blades into the cloud cover.

The gentle, persuasive voice keeps directing them. They keep following her instructions, turning, turning again.

Thank God for these systems, Bella thinks. She would never have been able to map-read her way to this place.

Now they are driving into the forest itself on the ridge; the light hangs in limp rags through the lattice of the pines. She can't hear them from inside the car with the A/C on but she knows they are soughing. She turns on her headlamps, even though it is still daytime.

Daisy begins to stir; Bella realises she doesn't want her to wake up and see what they are driving through, that she is not a little scared herself.

Then a sign appears by the side of the road; the name of the house in the address she has from the bureau comes into focus.

There is an intercom on the gate, angled down toward the driver's window. She presses the buzzer and realises it is mounted with a camera, into whose convex eye she stares, trying to smooth her face into pleasantness.

"Who is it?" says a voice, the sort of voice women used to have when women had smoked all their lives.

Gripes twist Bella's stomach. She does not recognise that voice. Yet she knows it.

"Mum," yells Daisy all of a sudden, "Mum, where are we?"

"I've come to see you. It's been a long time," begins Bella into the intercom.

"I don't know you," says the voice. "Come nearer the camera. Intruders aren't welcome here."

Daisy snuffles, twists anxiously; after an interval, the electronic arm of the gate slowly rises with a low whirr.

Bella murmurs to her reassuringly, "We're here," says Bella, "We've arrived—at your grandma's."

They drive over the rumble of a cattle grid and into a twisting drive, fringed with the same dense ranks of dark trees. The light has drained to a lemon tinge in the afternoon sky.

At the end of the drive they can now see the house: a house in the woods, encircled with a palisade, and in the doorway, a tall figure silhouetted against the room behind, holding a torch with the beam pointed toward them.

Bella takes Daisy tightly by the hand and walks toward the house, following the slice of light the beam cuts into the path.

E: CONTEMPORARY TRANSCRIPTIONS AND TRANSLATIONS

36. John Alden Mason, "Juan Bobo and the Riddling Princess: A Puerto Rican Folktale," translated by William Bernard McCarthy, 2005[1]

In his "translator's note," William Bernard McCarthy notes that this tale was one of many that the American anthropologist and linguist J. Alden Mason (1885–1967) collected during fieldwork in Puerto Rico in 1914–15 and that were later edited and published by Aurelio Espinosa. (Espinosa's own tale-collecting efforts pioneered the comparative study of Hispanic folklore and linguistics, and his son José Manuel has made his own contributions to tale scholarship; a text from José Manuel Espinosa's New Mexico fieldwork is included below, see pp. 433–35). Unlike many of his contemporaries, Mason did not record details about specific tellers and performances. Mason collected over 70 comic tales about "Juan Bobo," whom McCarthy describes as "a good-hearted but weak-brained lad who stumbles into good luck" (McCarthy 296). As McCarthy details, "the riddles of the princess and Juan are the centerpiece of the story. But they are not riddles in the conventional sense, since they do not actually describe the object that is the answer or pose a problem to be solved. They are rather some form of charade, providing the answer by burying the syllables of the required word, in correct order, within the wording of the verse" (McCarthy 297).

1 [Source: John Alden Mason and William Bernard McCarthy, trans., "Juan Bobo and the Riddling Princess: A Puerto Rican Folktale," *Marvels and Tales* 19.2 (2005): 299–302.]

JUAN BOBO AND THE RIDDLING PRINCESS: A PUERTO RICAN FOLKTALE, PERFORMER UNKNOWN (C. 1914–15)

All this has happened many times before, but this time it happened in that noble and faithful municipality, Rabid City, in the province of Cur, in the kingdom of Going-to-the-Dogs, in the reign of the great king Don Pedro Growl. There was in this kingdom a boy called Juan, a fool like many another, a bobo.

Now the king had a beautiful daughter who was blind in one eye and cross-eyed in the other. The king put out a notice telling the Rabid Citizens that he would give a handsome dowry and the hand of the most beautiful Princess Rabies (which in their language means *Rosebud*) to the man,

whoever he might be,
whether deaf in the knees, or squint-eared,
or lame-flanked:
he would give his gorgeous daughter as a bride to
whoever unriddled the riddle she posed,
and posed in turn a riddle she could not unriddle.
With Her Cleverness herself would he reward the one who entered and won.

"Ay, Madre," said Juan Bobo, "I'm going riddling."

"Where is it you think you're going, you donkey-brain? Are you tired of all the ways you used to worry me, and ready to start tormenting me in some new way? Let's see if you can go to bed!"

But the foolish boy made a bundle with his one nightshirt and headed off for the city where they were promising a princess. As there were no roads, he wandered over mountains and through wilderness until he came to the edge of the sea. There he saw a little fish flopping around on the beach. He picked it up and tossed it in the water.

"Thank you, Juan Bobo," said a husky voice. It was the fish's mother. "God preserve you from wolves and other wild animals."

He went on his way, well pleased with that good wish. Soon he came to the shore of a river, tried to ford it, and couldn't. Then he spotted an old horse standing high on the bank. He realized that it wanted a drink but couldn't get down to the water, so Juan filled his hat and gave it water to drink.

"Thank you, Bobo of all bobos," said the horse—and, by the way, it was all skin and bones. "Help me down to the river, and then get on my back."

Well, Juan, being a bobo, did exactly that, and the horse took off. It was going so fast that it would have trampled on some baby pigeons if that bobo on its back hadn't seen them in time. But Juan did see them and turned the horse aside.

"They've fallen out of their nest," said the horse. "There it is, up in that tree there, the one with its crown up there in the clouds. See, their mother's crying for them. Climb up and take them back to their mother."

So that's what the bobo did, climbing and climbing. He was gone on this difficult ascent for six days, feeding himself on fruit he picked from the tree. When he came down exactly six days later, he found the horse, all skin and bones, still waiting. He got on its back and it took off so fast that in the blink of an eye they came to the city ruled by the king who had promised his daughter in marriage. Juan noticed that inside the great gate of the city there was a wall of human heads. They were the ones who couldn't unriddle the riddles posed by the princess, nor pose a riddle that she couldn't unriddle.

Without a word to anybody, Juan Bobo headed straight for the palace. But before he got far he spotted a huge bonfire, a full league across, burning in front of the royal castle. It was fed with the bodies of those who had tried their hand at riddling.

Juan Bobo stuck his spurs in the bony flank of his horse and—oh, to have seen it—it jumped right across and landed in the courtyard, to the astonishment of everybody there.

"Whoosh, Whoosh," panted the horse.

"Here I am," said Juan, "to riddle and not be unriddled."

"Stranger, as you came through our fair city didn't you wonder about the piles of heads and bodies that you saw?" one of the guards asked him.

But he gave this guy an order: "I've come to riddle and not be unriddled."

They brought him to the king, who looked up and down in disdain at this bobo wearing a coat made of mattress ticking. Just then the princess came in. She lost no time in posing her riddle:

Though not from so high as a star,
Still I fall from on high,
And I am, for the man who finds me
The apple of his eye.
But you, with your foolish rashness,
Bold stranger at my door,
Will surrender your head to my father,
As wiser men have, before.

"I've got one in my pack," said Juan. "It's a *star apple*, a star apple, by God." And he pulled one of the delicious maroon-colored fruit out of his bag.

So the princess had lost the first round: star apple was indeed the answer to her riddle. So immediately Juan said,

You can pump me all you want,
Or go and ask your kin,

But the answer is so easy
To miss it is a sin.

They couldn't unriddle it. Juan Bobo, laughing all the while, gave them three days. They consulted the great wise men. They sent emissaries to all the countries, discovered and undiscovered. Nobody knew. They gave up and admitted defeat.

Then Juan Bobo told them: "If you make a mistake and eat a gourd instead, it'll kill you. It's *pumpkin*, by God, a pumpkin."

They all agreed that a pumpkin had to be the right answer. "The bobo is mine," said the princess.

"You're going to have to suck your thumbs a bit longer," said the king. And then to Juan: "The other day, while the princess was taking a walk on the beach, she lost a ring. And the winning riddler has to unriddle where it is and bring it back."

Figuring that he could escape on his horse, Juan said, "Give me a little time."

He went out into the courtyard, hopped on, and galloped away. He spurred the horse and it took off like a lightning.

When they came to the ocean the horse stopped dead, planting its hooves on the beach.

"Now is no time to stop. You can't be tired. Giddyap, horse."

But the horse said to him, "Look how you're talking. I'm no more horse than you are. Light down, foolish boy." And he turned into a caballero (the horse, that is: Juan already was one). He pulled out a long, strange-looking whistle and blew a long, ear-splitting blast on it. Suddenly all the fish were there at the edge of the beach.

"Please, Señores," said the horse-caballero, "which of you knows anything about the ring of the Biscay princess?"

"I don't know, I don't know," they all answered.

"We need the grouper," said the juey, the giant crab.

So the horse-caballero blew his whistle again. Immediately the grouper showed up with his huge, bulging stomach. "Do you know anything about the ring of the Biscay princess?"

"I was just about to get it when the porgy snapped it up right under my nose," said the grouper. "So I brought them both, the ring and the porgy. Here they are." And he spit them out on the spot.

Crazy with joy Juan Bobo ran to the palace and gave the ring to the king.

"There's still one little thing," said the king. "You will have to pick her out from a whole crowd of girls that I will show you." The king had set up a search for all the cross-eyed girls in his kingdom and in all others. He had taken such care in selecting them that they all looked exactly alike.

You can imagine what a tight spot Juan was in. But suddenly three young birds fluttered through the window and landed on one of the girls, settling on her head and on each shoulder. Juan recognized the three birds that he had helped to their nest.

"Oh, wonder of wonders, my darling," cried the king proudly. "Even the birds come to celebrate your beauty."

Nobody could deny that Juan had picked out the princess. There was nothing for the king to do but let Juan and her get married.

When the king died, Juan was chosen king. He ruled and governed his people with wisdom, without being absolutely absolute in his rule. What I am trying to say is, he was a model king. And he didn't forget his mother either. He had her come live in the castle!

37. J. Manuel Espinosa, *Cuentos de Cuanto Hay/Tales from Spanish New Mexico* (1931), translated and reworked by Joe Hayes, 1998[1]

This tale is one of 114 stories collected in 1931, from Spanish-speaking people in New Mexico, by José Manuel Espinosa—son of Aurelio Espinosa, the pioneering scholar of comparative Hispanic folklore and linguistics. Espinosa notes that when originally collecting these texts, he attempted to transcribe them "as closely as possible using standard Spanish orthography"; the text that follows has been translated and reworked by contemporary storyteller Joe Hayes. Collected before performance theory had reshaped folklore fieldwork, this text does not give us a sense of a specific storytelling event or of audience response, but it does offer an example of an animal bride story, reversing the roles of what are currently better known fairy tales in which a man is in animal form until marriage releases him from his enchantment.

THE ENCHANTED FROG, PERFORMED BY ALESNIO CHACÓN, 1931

ONCE A POOR MAN AND woman had three sons. The first son told his parents he wanted to go and find a life for himself, the second said the same, and the youngest also said he wanted to go find himself a life. The father and mother didn't want them to go, but finally they gave them permission and a blessing, and the sons set out.

The oldest went ahead of the others and he came to a resting place by a cottonwood tree, and a frog was singing there. He liked the song and shouted from below, "Why don't you come down here so that I can marry you?"

"No, no, I can't come down," the frog replied. "You couldn't make a life with me."

1 [Source: Joe Hayes, trans., *Cuentos de Cuanto Hay/Tales from Spanish New Mexico* (Albuquerque, NM: U of New Mexico P, 1998): 103–07.]

Finally, after the boy had tried for a long time to get her to come down, the frog jumped and fell into the boy's cape. When the boy saw her, he said, "What do I want with a frog?" And he threw her away and went on.

Later the second brother arrived there, and when he heard the frog singing so beautifully he said, "Come down so that I can marry you."

"No, sir," the frog said. "Yesterday a boy came by here and made me come down from my chamber, and when I came down he scorned me and threw me away."

The boy said he wouldn't do that. He said he really would marry her, and he spread out his cape for her to jump down. So the frog jumped down, but when he saw it he said, "Uy, how disgusting! What do I want with a frog?" And he threw her away just as his brother had done.

So then finally the youngest brother came along and like the others he heard the enchanted frog singing in the cottonwood tree. The boy told her to come down from the cottonwood because he wanted to meet her.

"No, I can't do that," the frog told him. "Two boys have come by here and both have asked me to come down, and then they scorned me and threw me away." But the boy keep begging for her to come down until the frog said, "All right, spread out your cape for me to jump down." The boy spread out the cape and the frog hopped and fell in the cape, and the boy took her and put her in his pocket. Then he went on down the road.

He came to the town where his two brothers were living. They were married now and were very proud, and the youngest brother was married too—to the frog. When they were all reunited, they wrote to their parents to tell them they were married and to send them presents. And wives of the older brothers also wrote, but not the frog. The frog couldn't write. And the parents wrote back saying they wanted to receive gifts from the wives. They told them to send them three embroidered kerchiefs.

The youngest brother was heartsick, and when he got home to his frog he told her what his parents had written. "Don't worry," the frog told him. "Throw me into the sea." So he went to the sea and threw her in, and the frog came out with a little cape made of a single cloth embroidered with pure gold.

"Send this little cape to your parents," she told him. The sons all sent their gifts and the parents were amazed by the gift the from the youngest son's wife—a little cape made of a single cloth embroidered with pure gold.

But then the parents sent word to say that they wanted to meet their sons' wives, told the sons to bring their wives for a visit. The sons all agreed to go to visit them with their wives, but the youngest was very worried and said to himself, "What am I going to do now? The frog doesn't even look like a woman." But when he went home and told the frog about it, she told him not to worry, that she would go too.

And since the frog knew that the wives of her brothers-in-law were spiteful, she went and started washing her hair with lye. The envious wives saw her and decided they were going to wash their hair with lye too. They washed their hair with lye and it all fell out and they were bald.

And then that night the frog told her husband, "Now take me and throw me into the deepest part of the sea. Leave me there and come for me in the morning."

The boy did that, but he was very sad because he didn't think he would see his frog ever again. The next day he got up very early and went to look for her at the place where he had thrown her into the sea, and there on the bank of the sea he found a princess in an elegant carriage.

"Here I am," she told him, "I'm free from my enchantment. Now let's go visit your parents." And they started out because the other brothers and their wives were already on their way.

They all arrived, and the parents were pleased to see their sons and their wives. The wives of the older two had their heads covered so no one could see they were bald. The parents were so pleased that they gave a banquet that night.

And when they were eating, the princess pretended she was stuffing garbanzos and eggs down the front of her dress, but she was really putting in money. But the bald-headed wives really did stuff garbanzos and eggs into their dresses.

After the banquet they all went to dance, and everyone's eye was on the beautiful princess and everyone said she was the prettiest woman they had ever seen. And with each turn she took as she was dancing she scattered pesos and silver coins. But the envious wives scattered the garbanzos and eggs they had stuffed into their bosoms when they were eating.

The people ran to get the money, and the dogs ran to get the garbanzos and eggs!

38. Linda Dégh, *Hungarian Folktales: The Art of Zsuzanna Palkó* (1995), translated by Vera Kalm, 1995[1]

Linda Dégh's extended fieldwork in one Hungarian village, and with one superbly talented tale-teller, represents one of the most focused and productive fieldwork endeavors of the twentieth century. Dégh's scholarly writing on folktales and contexts of performance brought national and international recognition to Zsuzanna Palkó, but Dégh's transcriptions of Palkó's tales (which she regularly told at wakes, entertaining mourners through the evening and night) have only recently been translated into English. As Dégh notes, the tale included here is one that Mrs. Palkó heard at the age of 14 "from Anna Petres, an older woman"; it became part of Mrs. Palkó's "standard repertoire pieces, well rehearsed, and refined by the inspiration of wake-audience commentators." Dégh recorded this performance of "The Serpent Prince" in 1950 at

1 [Source: Linda Dégh, ed. and Vera Kalm, trans., *Hungarian Folktales: The Art of Zsuzanna Palkó* (New York, NY: Garland, 1995): 77–92.]

Zsuzanna Palkó's home, "when she entertained the usual audience of neighbors after all the children were asleep." In her introductory notes to the English translation of this tale, Dégh notes that Palkó "identified with the heroine" in this female adventure story: this princess is less inclined to accept her fate as a beast's bride than the heroines of such tales as Dasent's translation of "East o' the Sun and West o' the Moon" (see p. 276) or Straparola's "King Pig" (see p. 109), and Palkó treats her "with particular fondness and compassion" (Dégh 77). Less compassion is shown to the Prince's second wife, who comes to a brutal end.

THE SERPENT PRINCE, PERFORMED BY ZSUZANNA PALKÓ, 1950

IT HAPPENED LONG AGO, BEYOND the beyond, even beyond the seven seas and beyond the glass mountain. There was a castle hill and below it an enormous willow tree. The willow tree had ninety-nine branches and on the ninety-nine branches sat ninety-nine crows, and if you don't listen to this story, they will peck your eyes out!

There was once a king and a queen. They were very sad for they had no offspring.

"Wife, it is your fault. You are at fault for you don't want us to have even one child."

"Don't say that, my heart is aching as much as yours that we have no children. But if God doesn't want to give us any, what can I do?"

Well, one day the king went to attend to his own affairs in parliament. The queen felt deeply distressed. It was bad enough that she was without child; to make matters worse, her husband spoke ill of her. She threw her arms up towards the sky:

"Dear God, why I am not worthy of having a child? If you don't want me to have a child, give me a snake son, so I can at least have one offspring."

As soon as she uttered the words, there was a snake son.

"My God, I must have offended you! Why did you bless me with this ugly beast? What will my husband say when he sees it? And the strangers, what will they say when they'll learn that a snake child was born to the king?"

Soon she telephoned her husband to call him home. He came running to find out what was wrong.

"Look," she said, "this is the boy we have. God gave him to us because I asked."

"Why did you ask for such a boy?" he said.

"In my bitterness I said to God that if I am not worthy of a child, at least he should let me have a snake son. He was born right away. Now what should we do?"

Said the king: "We will not have him baptized for I am ashamed, and I don't want even the priest to know the kind of offspring God gave us. We'll name him later. But you must not nurse him, just give him something and make sure that he eats it. Don't let him take your nipple in his mouth, lest some harm come to you."

Well, they made up a nice soft bed in a basket for the snake child and placed him into it. And they put the basket into the fanciest room, where usually no one entered. They put him in there. The queen brought him food and drink. He learned to eat and swallowed everything he was given. He developed and grew every day before their very eyes—still, as parents, how could they not have been grieving? They were grieving because they were ashamed. They could never take him out into the world, they thought, for fear that someone might see him. They would always have to keep him a secret.

When the snake grew to be as big as the axle of a carriage, he curled up in thick rings in the basket and held up his head, watching. His mother was loath to enter his room. She found him frightening, he was so large and repulsive. One day when she took the snake his midday meal and he had eaten his fill, he started to whistle, but he whistled so loud that the walls began to shake. He hadn't done anything like that before.

Said the queen to her husband: "Can you hear our son whistling so loud? I wonder what is wrong with him?"

"Go ask him. Something must be troubling him because until now he never whistled!"

So his mother went into his room: "Tell me, son, what is wrong with you? What do you want? What does this whistling mean?"

"It means, my dear mother, that I'd like to have a mate."

"Oh, my dear child, who would take you?"

"Well," he said, "I'll tell you whom to bring here. The king of the neighboring land has a very, very beautiful daughter. I want to take her for my wife. I am sending you as my emissary to ask for her hand in marriage. Say that a king's son has sent you and that he is waiting for a reply! And say no more, only that she should come with you for a trial visit and if she and the prince like each other, she should stay."

Who knows what kind of a world it was then, for the father let his daughter go with the queen to see the prince and if she liked him, she could stay. So the queen brought her home but instead of taking her straight to the snake, she led her into another chamber, which she and the king used as their sitting room.

"I went and brought the princess," she said to the king.

"All right, you brought the princess back but don't let her into our son's room; first give her something to eat and drink and then take her to our son. Don't show him to her until then!"

They set the table right away, but the princess said: "Where is the prince?"

"He'll come soon. You must rest now because you are tired, and have some food and drink. He'll be here by the time you have finished."

They sat down to eat and drink and talk. All the while the princess was trembling with excitement, wondering whether she would like the prince when she saw him. But the prince didn't appear.

Said the queen: "Come, let us surprise him, he may be in his room! Come, let's see!"

They entered the room and found it empty. The old queen went into the back, where there was a shelf installed in the corner, and there was the basket. As she approached, the serpent prince lifted his head and looked around.

Then the girl caught sight of him: "Oh dear! What is this snake doing here?"

"This is our son," said the queen.

The girl let out such a scream that she collapsed on the ground and fainted.

"God Almighty, don't abandon me!" she said. "Is this the kind of lad that I, a princess, deserve? Let me out of here!"

They helped her up, splashed some water on her, and she came to.

"My dear daughter," said the queen, "come, he won't hurt you. He is gentle, he'll do you no harm—he just loves you and wants you to be his wife."

"I'd rather have my head cut off," she said, "and be buried anywhere, than become his wife! Have you lost your senses? Do you want me to marry a snake? How could you take me away from my father's palace? Why did you take me and bring me here? And why didn't you tell me what your son was like?"

"Well, I didn't tell you, for I thought that if I told you, you wouldn't come. Now stay here," she said, "and be patient, you'll see, you won't regret it, he'll be very good to you."

"I don't care if he is a thousand times better, I don't want him! I detest looking at him, he is a wretched animal, a revolting, wretched animal!" she said. "And I should lie down in bed beside him? I'd rather kill myself!"

The queen begged her to have patience and not to be so upset and frightened. She locked the door behind her and left the girl in the room. The girl didn't know what to do. She ran from one window to another. They had bars on them, iron bars. There was no way out. The king and the queen left the house. She ran around in circles, she was about to *lose her mind in despair*. She ran around in circles weeping, kneading her hands in desperation, how to escape, what to do? Somehow the day would pass but what would happen at night? She screamed and cried bitterly, but no one had pity on her, no one let her out.

Well, when evening came the queen brought in the meal. The girl was watching the door, ready to slip out. But the queen immediately locked the door with a key so she couldn't get out. She was forced to stay. The queen had just put the food down, but found it again untouched in the morning. She couldn't eat one bite of it, she just couldn't take anything. All night long she was pacing up and down, screaming and lamenting, they could hear from the next room how she was crying. So, to avoid listening to her they went out, but they didn't release her. This went on for a week. The girl didn't eat, not even a single bite, didn't lie down to sleep, all she did was walk around in circles, while the snake kept trying to comfort her:

"Don't be afraid, my angel. I'll do you no harm. If you knew how much I love you, you wouldn't be afraid."

"You just keep your love from me! It would have been better if God had taken you the minute you saw the light of day! And now you dare to expect me to become your wife!"

The girl went on protesting and the snake kept trying to appease her with soothing words, tapping his tail.

After a week went by, the princess thought to herself: now she didn't care any more. She hadn't slept a wink all this time, nor had she anything to eat or drink. She was utterly exhausted, ready to die. So she decided to lie down and rest.

All the while the snake was lying on his stomach, blinking at her. Then he moved forward. The bed was ready, the queen had made it up for them when she got there. The girl fell asleep right away, she was so worn out. Suddenly she woke up feeling the snake creep up on her bare leg, slithering into bed. She let out such a scream that the king and the queen leaped out of bed: "Our son is killing the girl in there!"

They ran in to see and found nothing wrong except for the snake crawling into bed. The girl screamed and *screamed so hard that her eyes were popping out.*

"Get away from me you ugly beast! Go away you wretched animal, don't you come near me!"

And the snake spoke gently: "Please let me lie down beside you. I won't hurt you!"

The king and the queen having looked around, walked off and locked the door behind them. They left them there.

All night the crying and fighting continued. They woke up in the morning: "This night passed—I got away from him, but what will happen the next night? I wish I had a knife, or something," the girl said, "so that I could stab myself and die! I cannot stand to have him come near me in bed! I am so frightened of him that I *could die of despair.*"

Well, it was no use, the tools she could have used to kill herself had all been put away. The following night went the same way. The snake crawled up into her bed. By then the girl had started eating. The queen brought in the meal, the girl sat down at the table while they let the snake eat separately. "It is all the same now," she thought, "I am miserable but at least I shouldn't be miserable and hungry!" And so she began eating regularly.

One night, as she lay down, the snake slid into bed beside her. She grabbed a pillow and put it between them. She placed a pillow there to separate them, so the snake wouldn't touch her.

"It is no use for me to weep and cry; he sneaks into bed anyway, but at least he won't come near me," she thought. She put a pillow between them and went to sleep.

When she woke up, there was such a beautiful prince lying next to her, such a dazzling, regal-looking lad, that *one could sooner look at the sun than at him.* He was such a handsome, beautiful lad. She stared and stared at him. Was he a vision in her dreams or what? Such a handsome, beautiful lad, the likes of whom she had never seen *since her eyes had popped open.* She had never met a lad like this. She thought to herself:

Where has this prince come from?

She looked and the snake was nowhere to be seen. She put her arms around the lad and he woke up. She said to him:

"How did you come here, prince?"

"I didn't come, I am at home here. This is my home."

"How can this be?" she said. "Are you the snake?"

"I was, but now I am no longer," he said, "I have slipped out of the snakeskin."

"Well, don't slip back into it, for God's sake, I beg you! You are such a handsome lad, why did you put on that horrible animal skin? I was so repelled by it that I nearly *died of despair.* If you are a prince, why did you get into a snakeskin?"

"I had to do it."

He didn't say why or what had happened. All he said was that it had to be this way for a while. The girl was delighted. She gazed and gazed at him, so enchanted was she with her lover and one day she became pregnant.

Then the princess started grieving that her beloved was a prince by night and during the day he crawled back into the skin and became a snake again. He didn't show himself, not even his parents saw that he could transform himself. But the princess continued begging for him not to put on the snakeskin.

"Well, I have to," he said, "for it belongs to me, it is my cloak."

She went on thinking about it. Now she was able to lie down beside the snake and fall asleep because he could change and become a prince. And what a beautiful, handsome lad he was! But even if one day he came to shed the snakeskin for good, and even if this were soon, it would be too late.

The girl had heard that nearby lived a woman, a sorceress, who could perform all kinds of magic. So she went to see her one day when the old queen was not at home. She went over to the woman in the neighborhood.

The sorceress said to her: "What is wrong with you? Why are you so thin? Just skin and bones, you look like a skeleton. What is going on in your life? Don't you have enough to eat, or are you sick, or are you grieving? What is the matter?"

She said: "Don't even ask, my sorrow is so profound. Don't think that I am thin because I lack food. I am well off."

"Then why? How can a princess have such great troubles?"

She said: "Oh yes but I do! They have to do with my betrothed."

She told her, she related everything: how she came to the palace and why, and how she wasn't told that the royal son was a snake. The sorceress only heard about it then that the king had a snake son. Until then she hadn't heard it from anyone. No one had talked about it.

Said the princess: "At night he becomes such a beautiful prince that *one can sooner look at the sun than at him*, he is so dazzling, but at dawn he crawls back into his snakeskin. I am unhappy because he won't stop doing it, turning into a snake. And when he is a snake I am so frightened of him because he is so large, so huge that I could die, *fall into despair*."

"You know what, princess? I'll teach you what you must do, if you want him to be rid of his snakeskin," she said. "When you both go to bed and he falls asleep, you must get up, light a fire in the stove and once it is blazing, throw in the snakeskin and burn it. When he wakes and asks you where is the snakeskin, his cloak, you must answer that you haven't seen it. Then he will say: 'what is this bad odor that I smell?' And you must reply that you had combed your hair and tossed some into the stove. That is what caused the smell."

Well, the princess accepted the woman's advice. "If it is true that he will be freed of his snakeskin, I'll give you so much gold and silver that you'll never know poverty, or lack anything ever again," she promised.

"Just do what I told you and it will be all right, you'll see," she said.

The princess went home. Evening came and they went to bed. Once again the princess woke up at night with her husband next to her. He was beautiful, like a flower. If ever he had to leave her she would be heartbroken, she thought, he was so beautiful. The snakeskin was there, on his back. She slipped out of bed and lit a fire in the stove. When it was blazing, she gently removed the snakeskin, threw it into the flames and burned it.

Soon the prince woke up. He said: "Where is my cloak? And what is this bad smell in here?"

"Well," she said, "I was just combing my hair. I cast some into the stove and that causes the smell."

"Don't lie to me for I can see into your heart and I know that you burned it. But you'll be sorry, not I! All you needed to do was wait one more month," he said. "In one month, one week, one hour, one minute and one second, my time would have been up. There is a curse on me and I was to have worn the snakeskin until then. But now that you dared to burn it, that you did this without telling me, you'll have to suffer for it, and you'll be sorry! And now listen!"

The prince rose from his bed:

"You get up too," he said. "Let us see each other while I am still here."

He went out and brought back a dry hazel rod and a grain of wheat:

"Wife, I am telling you now I am leaving. I am leaving and you'll never hear from me and you'll never know where I am. I am giving you this dry hazel-rod so that you can plant it. You must plant it, nurture it and water it every day. You must watch over it so that nothing digs it up. Water it with your tears and with well-water and when the hazel-rod begins to sprout leaves and bear fruit, then you may set out to look for me. When you are ready to bring me some hazelnuts and bread made from the grain of wheat, then you may come after me!"

Next he put a band around her waist and a gold ring on her finger and said: "You will give birth to your child only when I put my arms around your waist, and you will remove this ring when I touch your finger with mine. And you must not come looking for me until you crack a nut from this dry hazel rod. You must sow this grain of wheat, care for it and let it multiply until you reap enough for baking a loaf of bread. Only then must you set forth to find me. Any sooner would be to no avail."

The woman wept bitterly, asking him to forgive her. What she did was not her own idea, she had followed someone's advice.

"Well, if someone advised you then ask that person to help you and comfort you now!"

"Don't leave me! Please forgive me! Aren't you sorry to leave me in my present condition, the way I am?"

"You are the way you are, but you will not be free of the child until I hold you, nor will the ring snap off your finger until my finger touches yours."

With these words the prince shook hands with her, kissed her and left. And the princess wept and wept so bitterly that her heart nearly broke.

The king and the queen asked her: "Why are you crying so?"

"The prince went into exile."

"Where has he gone?"

"He went into exile. He said to me that I would look for him in vain until this dry hazel rod took root and bore fruit, and until this single grain of wheat multiplied over the years so I could bake bread with it. Then, I should take the bread and the hazelnuts and go find him. And only when I find him and he puts his arms around my waist, may I give birth to my child. How can I stop crying," she said, "when will all this come to pass?"

"Look," said the king, "maybe you were up to some mischief and he got angry. Otherwise he wouldn't have left you here."

Well, she didn't have the courage to tell the king, her father-in-law, or her mother-in-law, what had happened. She didn't dare to say why the prince was so upset.

So she planted the hazel rod and watered it, watered it every day, with her tears or with well-water. She never stopped weeping. She planted the grain of wheat and built a small fence around it so that no chicken or other animal could scratch it out. By the following year the grain sprouted some stalks. She harvested the wheat and sowed it again at the right time and continued to water and care for it. With God's help the dry hazel rod took root and sprouted leaves. But by the time it was fully grown and in bloom, seven years had passed. And she, a mother-to-be, got so heavy that she could hardly move. She wept inconsolably.

"How can I bake a loaf of bread?" she said. "The wheat is plentiful and there are hazelnuts, but which way should I go looking for him? Well, I'll start out in God's name and keep going until somewhere I hear something about him."

So she packed some provisions for the road, took a little money with her along with the loaf of bread and set forth. She went on and on, crossing from one land into the next and into the one after that on her journey. And when she was barely able to walk, she reached an enormous open field.

"Dear God," she said, "it is getting dark and I see a big forest in the distance. Somehow I have to get through it. What will happen to me at night when I have to cross the woods? Please God, make a little cottage appear. Even if the devils live in it, I'd ask them for shelter, so as not to spend the night in the open under the skies."

As she reached the edge of the forest, she saw a light shining through the trees.

"I don't mind who lives there, I'll ask, maybe they'll take me in for the night."

She went and knocked at the door.

Someone cried out: "Come in."

An old woman was sitting by the fire. The hearth was large, the kind they used to have in the old days. She was stoking the cinders with an iron. Her nose was so long that its tip came down to her breasts.

"Good evening, grandma!"

"Good evening to you! What are you doing in this *god-forsaken place where not even a bird can fly*?"

"Misfortune brought me here. Would you kindly take me in, so I don't have to spend the night in the open? Wild beasts might attack me."

"I'd take you in, my girl, but I don't know if my son would get angry when he comes home. He is not here now. Perhaps he won't mind."

"If he's likely to get angry, I'd rather leave."

"What are you doing here? Why are you wandering about in these strange parts?"

"Where should I be wandering, dear grandma? I ask you because you are old, you have seen and heard a lot and been here and there. Have you ever heard of the serpent prince?"

"Well, my dear girl, I have grown old, most of my life is behind me—but I have never heard of him. I say to you, sleep here tonight, and start on your journey again tomorrow. By nightfall you will see another house like mine. My aunt lives in it. She might be able to tell you something about him, for she is older than I."

"Thank you kindly for your advice," she said.

She had dinner, made up her bed and lay down. In a little while the son came home. He burst in the door: "Mother dear, what is this strange smell? Who is sleeping here?"

"Don't be angry, my dear son, a poor woman wandering about asked for shelter and I let her in. She is searching for the serpent prince. Have you heard of him anywhere, son?"

"Well, my dear mother," he said, "I have been all over the world and peeped into every nook and cranny, even into the bottom of wells." (The old woman was the mother of the Moon.) "I have crossed forests and fields and streams, looked everywhere, but I have never heard of him."

The poor woman was very sad. She couldn't sleep, not even a wink. She wept so much during the night that the pillow under her head was soaking wet. She rose in the morning, washed and prepared to leave.

"I'll go now, dear grandma," she said, "I found no consolation for my great sorrow."

"Just do as I said, my girl. If you come upon my aunt, she may know something, she is older."

"All right, grandma, thank you very much."

"Look, my dear," she said, "I'll give you a gold bobbin—put it away for you may need it."

She thanked the old woman, put away the gold bobbin and started on her way. It happened that by evening she reached the other house and knocked at the door.

A faint voice answered: "Please, come in."

She entered the room. Once again she found an old woman, even older than the one before. She too, had a long nose, so long that it reached down to her navel, even farther. She looked up, but could barely see, her nose was in the way.

Said the girl: "Good evening, dear grandma!"

"Welcome, my girl. What are you doing here, in this *god-forsaken place where not even a bird can fly*?"

"Well, misfortune brought me here, my sad fate. I ask you, would you take me in? Would you be so kind and take me in for the night?"

"Sure," she said, "*this is God's shelter and man's resting place*. It is possible that my son will get angry but I'll placate him. I am the Sun's mother."

"May I ask you," she said, "you have been around a long time, you know much and have seen a lot—have you heard of the serpent prince anywhere?"

"No, I haven't, my child. Most of my life is behind me but I have never heard anything about him. Maybe my son knows. Come and eat while I make up your bed. I can see that you are tired." The poor girl was in tears and couldn't stop lamenting.

The old woman felt very sorry for her. As soon as she went to bed but was not yet asleep, in came the Sun:

"Oh dear," he said, "what is this bad smell here, mother?"

"Don't be angry, my son, a poor wandering woman had asked for shelter. I took her in," she said, "she is desperate."

"Why is she desperate?"

"Well," she said, "she wants to find the serpent prince. Did you hear of him anywhere, son?"

"My dear mother, I go around the whole world, I cross rivers and forests everywhere. I shine into every place, light up every corner, and look into every window," he said, "but I have never heard of him."

Said the old woman: "Poor woman. If she learns that you don't know anything either, she will be heartbroken. Maybe, if she looks up my old aunt on her way," she said, "she might have something to say about him."

When they rose in the morning, the old woman said to her: "My dear girl, my son couldn't say anything. He never heard of the serpent prince. But if you went to see my aunt, about the same hour you came here, she may be able to help. She is even older than we are. And if she cannot tell you, then I don't know what to say, how you'll find him."

Then she gave the young woman a reel:

"Well, my girl," she said, "my niece gave you a bobbin, so I'll give you a gold reel. Take good care of it, for you may need it!"

With those words she served the young woman breakfast and sent her on her way. She started on her journey and she walked and walked, although she did more weeping than walking. Eventually she reached the other house. By then it was evening and dark. She gathered up her courage and knocked at the door:

"Please," came the answer, "you may come in."

She entered and saw an old woman with a nose so long that it touched her knees. She looked up at her:

"What are you doing here, my dear girl?"

"I bid you a good evening, grandma!"

"A good evening to you too, my girl. What are you doing here, in this *godforsaken place where not even a bird can fly*?"

She said: "My misfortune brought me here, grandma. Would you give me shelter for the night?"

"*This is God's shelter and man's resting place, so do come in!*"

The old woman made her sit down and asked her why she came.

"Well, dear grandma," she said, "I see that you are old, you have seen a lot, heard a lot and learned a lot—tell me, have you heard of the serpent prince anywhere?"

"I haven't, my girl. Maybe my son can say something about him when he comes home, but I can't."

Right away she gave her something to eat, made up her bed and bid her to lie down to rest. So she lay down but couldn't fall asleep. She waited for the son, waited to find out whether he had any news for her.

Soon she heard a rustling sound. In came a light breeze, the kind that combs the wheatfields. It floated in through the door.

"Dear mother, what is this strange smell here?"

"My son," she said, "don't be upset. I took in this poor, wandering woman. Have you heard of the serpent prince anywhere? She is looking for him."

"Well, no, mother dear, I haven't," he said. "Yet I slip through the fields, the forests and the grassy meadows, I drift over everything, but I have never heard of him. Maybe my brother can say something, when he gets home."

The Breeze had a meal and went to bed. In a short while a loud noise started up outside, and there was such banging and cracking that they thought the roof of the little house was breaking asunder. There was such a strong windstorm!

Then the storm entered: "Good evening, dear mother!"

"Welcome, my son."

"What is this strange smell in here?"

"Don't be angry son, a poor, wandering woman came and asked for shelter, so I took her in," she said. "But before I give you your supper, let me ask you, have you ever heard of the serpent prince? She is looking for him."

"Maybe," he said, "I took off a corner of his castle yesterday."

The woman heard this from her bed and she became so overjoyed that her heart nearly burst from happiness. At last there was news about him!

"Son, then you know where he lives?"

"Sure I know," he said, "didn't I just say that I took a corner off his castle?" He was the Hurricane Wind.

"Well, son," said the old woman, "be so kind and take this poor woman there in the morning. She is in such a state that she can barely go on living."

"We'll see when the day breaks."

She served him a good meal and they all went to bed and fell asleep. When they rose in the morning, the old woman said: "Listen to me, my girl, I can bring you some comfort now."

But she already knew, she had heard it, for she had waited up for the Hurricane Wind.

"You see," the old woman continued, "he came home and said that he had taken a corner off the serpent prince's castle. So I asked him to take you there, for you would never find it on your own. He promised to do it."

They gave her some food, but in her excitement she couldn't eat or drink. She didn't want anything. She just waited, anxious to leave and to get there as quickly as possible.

The old woman handed her a gold spool and a ball of thread in pure gold:

"Look, my girl, I give these to you. Put them away carefully, you may need them."

She thanked her kindly and put the gold spool and thread away.

Said the Hurricane Wind: "Mount on my back and close your eyes!"

She climbed on the Hurricane's back, shut her eyes, and—"*one, two, three, take me where I want to be*"—they landed near the castle.

He set the woman down and said to her: "Ask the guards who are standing at the gate to let you in. Ask, and if they let you enter, walk in and the rest is your concern!" (I forgot something, but I won't add it now.)

So the woman entered the grounds and headed straight for the king's castle. She began strolling up and down in front of it, holding the gold bobbin in her hand. The queen, sitting at her window, saw her and thought she was a merchant selling a gold bobbin. Right away she sent down her maid to ask whether the gold bobbin was for sale. The maid came running and said:

"Is this bobbin for sale?"

"It is. I would sell it."

"Then follow me to the palace," she said.

She went, gladly, and the queen said to her: "What do you want for this bobbin?"

She said what the old woman had told her to say: "I don't want anything else, just let me spend one night in your husband's bedchamber, and you may have the bobbin."

The queen thought about it and decided that this was not a matter of great consequence. She said: "I don't mind. Meanwhile go to town for a walk, until he returns. He went hunting and won't be home until evening—then you may come back."

Well, the poor woman didn't feel like strolling about—she sat down in a corner and stayed there, weeping all day. What would happen next? Evening came and the king returned. They had their supper, ate and drank and he went to have his bath. They filled a big tub with water and helped him into it. And as the snake prince was having his bath, his valet brought in his drink that would lull him to sleep, and handed it to him. He gulped it down and fell asleep there in the tub. He dropped off right away and became limp, unconscious. His two bodyguards lifted him out and took him over to his bed all made-up in silk, and covered him. Then the old queen, the false queen, opened the door and pushed the young woman inside:

"Go," she said, "see if you can make him horny, go."

She shoved her inside and locked the door. The woman waited for the king's servants, his bodyguards, to fall asleep. They were in the adjoining room and there was not even a door separating them. Only a carpet was suspended in the opening, so that should something happen to the king they would be there to attend to him. But they were not yet asleep when she began: "I came, my dear husband. Wake up, put your arms around my waist so I can give birth to my child and put your finger on the gold ring, so I can take it off, for I am dying! I brought the bread made from the grain of wheat and the nuts borne by the hazel rod. Wake up, wake up, my dear husband!"

She carried on this way until dawn, but he didn't wake. He lay there as if he were dead. The woman wept bitterly.

She walked around the bed, who knows how many times, repeating: "Wake up, my dear husband! I have been looking for you. I came and brought with me all you have asked. Free me from my burden, or else I'll perish!" Morning came. Suddenly the queen flung the door open: "Get out, you beastly whore!"

She chased her out. The young woman left in great sadness. What should she do? She went down to the ground floor to think. One night had passed already and nothing had happened. What would become of her if the second night passed the same way? She took out the golden spool and started to unravel it. The queen caught sight of her from the window: "Run down, my girl, and ask the merchant whether she will sell the golden spool."

The girl went and asked: "Is it for sale?"

"It is," she said.

"Then please come with me to the palace, to see the queen."

She didn't have to be asked twice, she went.

Said the queen: "What do you want for the spool?"

"The same price as before," she said. "To be your husband's sweetheart for one night."

Oh, well, thought the queen, that doesn't amount to much. I'll give him a drink that will lull him to sleep and there will be nothing to worry about.

She said: "All right. Meanwhile, go out."

She asked the woman whether she was hungry, or whether she could offer her something. Nothing, she wanted nothing. Yet it had been a week since the poor woman had last eaten. She went out to a corner of the castle and there she stayed and lamented: "Dear God, I can only get in once more and if all I can achieve is what I have achieved so far, I'll die. My heart will break there, on the spot, for I cannot stand it any more." Even her hand began to swell. She couldn't grasp anything with it, it was so puffed up. When evening closed in again and the king returned from hunting, she went back to the castle.

"Wait," said the queen, "the king hasn't gone to bed yet." She pushed the woman into a small room and there she remained, weeping. All of a sudden the queen opened the door and let her out.

"Go," she said, "see if you can make him horny, go."

Once again they had given the king a drink to lull him to sleep, so they let her try her luck. She went in and this time didn't wait for the bodyguards to fall asleep. She didn't care either that the queen, whose chamber was next door, might also be awake.

She began again: "Oh dear, dear! Wake up, my husband! I came to you once more. Wake up my dear husband for I brought you the bread from the grain of wheat and the nuts from the hazel rod. Put your arms around my waist, so I can give birth to my child and touch my finger with yours, so I can take off this ring, or else my heart will break here and now!"

Then the third day arrived. The poor woman took out the ball of gold thread and strolled about with it in front of the castle. The queen saw her from her window and right away sent her maid to ask her to come up. She went.

"Is this ball of gold thread for sale?" she asked. "It is for sale."

"And what do you want for it?"

"No bargaining—what I want for it is that you let me spend one night with your husband."

"I'll let you," she said and bought the thread.

"And now you may go out into town and walk around until the evening. My husband will be back then, not before."

So the poor woman went out. She sank into a corner and wept bitterly. "Dear God, what will become of me if once more my efforts are of no avail tonight?"

Meanwhile the king was out hunting yet again.

On the road his valet said to him: "Your Majesty, I'd say something, but I don't dare."

"Go on," he said, "you started it, so go on!"

"My life is in your hands, Sir. Here is what happened," he said. "For two nights running, when we take you out of the bath and you lie down on your bed to rest, the queen lets a woman into your chamber. 'Go, see if you can make him horny, go,' she says and pushes her into the room. Then the woman waits for a while. I think she wants us and the queen to be asleep so we wouldn't hear anything. Then she begins: 'Wake up, my dear husband, wake up and touch my finger, let the gold ring fall off, for I am so swollen that I'll burst! I brought the bread from the grain of wheat and the nuts from the hazel rod. Wake up, wake up, my dear husband! Have pity on me!'"

That night the king stayed awake. He didn't fall asleep, for his valet had poured the sleep-inducing drink into the bath. He just pretended to be asleep. He went limp in the bathtub, his two servants lifted him out and placed him on the bed. Then the queen shoved the woman into his chamber.

"Go, see if you can make him horny, go" she said.

The king waited for her to say it three times, then he sat up. He was lying down until then. He recognized his wife at once. He put his arms around her waist and right away she gave birth to such a beautiful golden-haired child that *one could sooner look at the sun than at him*. There was no need for cloths, or for candles—the room was bright and shiny, bathed in light. They rejoiced, for not one child but twins were born to them. Two boys and both had golden hair. The king was happy. He touched the woman's finger with his, and the ring snapped off. He helped her lie down in his place, in the bed. He was overjoyed with his sons. He sent his bodyguard to bring a woman over to help. He went and brought back the emperor's midwife, who immediately set about to attend to them. She bathed them and swaddled them and placed them on either side of the table. The king was so happy that he walked around on tiptoe, so his steps wouldn't be heard and his wife could rest. That is how he got dressed. He offered her all kinds of fine things to eat and drink, but she felt ill—she couldn't take anything. Well, the king didn't close an eye all night—he just paced up and down by his wife's bedside. At daybreak, when it became light, the queen came at last. She flung the door open.

"Get out of here, you beast, you whore!" she said.

The king leapt in front of her.

"Whom are you calling a whore? Who is the whore here?"

The queen, the former queen, became so alarmed at this turn of events that she nearly collapsed. And right away the king called out: "Catch that woman, the former queen, and throw her into a cellar!"

They took the queen and thrust her into a cellar. Then the king summoned his advisers to counsel him on which woman was better, the wedded or the unwed. Which was better? Which one should he honor? Which one should he keep?

They said: "The wedded one, the one you had wed."

"How could you elevate the illegitimate one and discard the one you had wed?"

"It is right that you should respect your wedded wife."

"Well then," said the king, "I am ordering you now to bring two of the most unruly colts out of the stables and tie the wicked woman and even her old witch of a mother to their tails! She had covered up for her daughter all along, lest something be discovered, so she deserves no better."

They tied both women to the stallions' tails. Two lads, each with a whip in his hands, flogged the horses while they circled the fort twelve times, until the women's bodies, even their bones, were shattered to pieces. And those the king wanted destroyed, so he had them nailed to the walls of the fort and burnt so that not even dust would be left of them. Then they arranged a big baptism, a big feast. They invited the kings, princes, and barons from all over, and asked the godparents to come for the christening. They also brought in the bishop, renewed their marriage vows, and lived *as happily as two turtle doves*. They are alive to this day, if they haven't died.

39. A.K. Ramanujan, *Folktales of India: A Selection of Oral Tales from Twenty-Two Languages* (1991)[1]

The texts included in A.K. Ramanujan's ambitious collection Folktales of India: A Selection of Oral Tales from Twenty-Two Languages *are drawn from a variety of print sources, ranging from nineteenth-century colonial periodicals to Ramanujan's written accounts of tales he heard as a child. In the present context, it is important to underscore that, despite the book's subtitle, these texts do not directly represent oral tales themselves: as a reader, you are distanced from specific tale-telling events by many layers of editorial intervention, including (in many cases) the vagaries of field-based collection in the pre-recording technology era, the processes of transcription and translation, and Ramanujan's own efforts to "retell" and "adapt" his source material. The anthology itself—a print form with a long tradition—becomes the frame through which we read the tales. And if we feel as if we are reading rather than listening with our eyes, it may be due to the absence of real-time indicators of oral delivery. This collection and the tale "Hanchi" reprinted here are an excellent example of how "oral tale" continues to be a slippery term. It has been used historically to identify a wide range of print forms associated with orality, from heavily edited narratives to transcriptions of recorded performances. While no form of print can capture the vitality of live performance, we are reminded at these moments to interrogate the nature of a collector's relationship to her/his material.*

"Hanchi" has its roots in Ramanujan's own fieldwork: it is a Kannada tale, collected in Kittur in 1955 from a 65-year-old woman named Chennamma (a woman named after Kittur's famous nineteenth-century Queen, who led her people in armed rebellion against the British decades before the war of independence). The text Ramanujan has produced appears on the page much as a literary narrative would and does not attempt to capture the dynamics of Chennamma's performance. The story frames beauty as a potentially dangerous attribute—as a kind of burden and threat to familial stability. As in tales like Perrault's "Donkeyskin" or Dasent's translation of "Tatterhood" (see p. 284 in this volume) the heroine uses a disguise (in this case a mask from which she takes her name) to camouflage her beauty—necessary for her own self-protection and for the ultimate transformation of her fate. Even in name, "Hanchi" explores the relationship between people and possessions, and how we make sense culturally of the difference.

---

1 [A.K. Ramanujan, ed. *Folktales of India: A Selection of Oral Tales from Twenty-Two Languages* (New York, NY: Pantheon, 1991): 285–89. Translation of this tale first appeared as part of Ramanujan's essay "Hanchi: A Kannada Cinderella," in Alan Dundes, ed., *Cinderella: A Folklore Casebook* (New York, NY: Garland, 1983).]

HANCHI, PERFORMED BY CHENNAMMA, 1955

An old woman had two children, a son and a daughter. The girl had golden hair, but the brother had not been struck by it till one day, when both of them were grown up and the girl was a lovely young woman, he suddenly saw her hair of gold as if he had never seen it before and at once fell in love with her.

He went to his mother and begged her to give him his sister in marriage. The poor old woman was shocked and knew at once that disaster was ahead. But she hid her feelings and sent him to the nearby town to buy rice and flour and lentils for the wedding feast. As soon as he left the house, she went to her daughter and said to her, "Daughter, the time has come for you to leave me. You're as good as dead to me after this day. You're too beautiful to live here in safety. You have hair of gold; no one can look at it without desire. So I shall have a mask made for you; it will hide your face and hair and save you from future danger."

Then she ran to the potter and gave him a gold vessel to make a clay mask to fit her daughter's face. That very night she gave her daughter a bundle of food and sent her away with the parting words: "Never remove the mask from your face till your situation is better." When her daughter was gone, the poor woman poisoned herself in her grief. The son came home next day and found his sister gone and his mother dead. Searching in vain for his sister everywhere, he lost his mind and became a wandering madman.

The girl in the clay mask wandered from place to place as long as her mother's bundle of bread and rice lasted. Because her mask looked so much like a clay tile—*hanchu*—she changed her name to Hanchi. At noon and again by moonlight, she would stop by wayside brooks, untie her bundle of food, and eat. At last she came to a place very far from her hometown and struck up acquaintance with an old woman, who gave her food and shelter. One day the old woman came home and said that a *saukar*, a rich man, who lived nearby needed a maidservant, and that she had arranged to send Hanchi to his place. Hanchi agreed and went to the big house to work. She was an expert cook, and no one could equal her in making sweet rice dishes.

One day the *saukar* arranged for a banquet in his orchard and ordered Hanchi to make her special dishes of sweet rice. That day, everyone in the household went to the orchard for a grand meal—everyone, that is, except Hanchi and a younger son of the *saukar*, who had gone out somewhere. Hanchi thought she was alone, so she heated water for an oil bath. She wished to finish her bath before they all returned. She took off her mask, undid her splendid golden hair, applied oil all over her parched body, and started bathing. Meanwhile the young man who had gone out came back home, and shouted for the maid. Hanchi did not hear him in the bathhouse. Impatiently, he went in search of her, heard sounds in the bathhouse, and peeped in and saw her in all her beauty. He sneaked away before she saw him, but he had fallen deeply in love with the glowing beauty of her body and the glory that was her hair, and decided at once to make her his wife.

As soon as the family returned from the orchard, the son took his mother aside and told her of his desire. She was quite puzzled by her son's fascination with a black-faced maidservant. She asked him not to make a fool of himself over a dark lowborn wench, and promised to get him a really good-looking bride from a rich family if he would wait a little. But he would not hear of it. He was stubborn and they had a heated argument, at the end of which he dragged his mother to where Hanchi was, put his hand to the girl's face, snatched off her mask, and dashed it to the ground. There stood Hanchi in all her natural loveliness, crowned by her splendid tresses of gold. The mother was struck dumb by this extraordinary beauty and now found her son's infatuation quite understandable. Moreover, she had always liked the modest, good-natured Hanchi. She took the bashful young woman with her to an inner chamber and asked her a few questions, listened to her strange story, and liked her all the better for it. At the first auspicious moment, Hanchi was married to the young man.

The newlyweds were happy as doves, but their happiness didn't last long. There was a holy man whom everyone called Guruswami in the *saukar's* house. He was the rich man's chief counselor, and had a reputation for secret lore and black arts of many kinds. This man had long been casting lecherous glances at Hanchi and wanted her for himself. When Hanchi's mother-in-law told him one day of her eagerness to see a grandson by Hanchi, he had his plan ready. He told her that he could make Hanchi conceive with the help of his magic arts, and asked her to send the young woman to him. But first he asked for some plantains, almonds, betel leaves, and betel nuts to use in his magical rites.

On an auspicious day, Guruswami summoned Hanchi. He had before him all the fruits and nuts over which he had chanted his magical formulas. If she ate them, his love-magic would work on her and she would be irresistibly attracted to him. When she came in, he was chanting secret spells and praying that Hanchi would be his. But Hanchi was a clever girl and knew all about these wicked magicians. When he gave her a plantain, she secretly dropped the enchanted fruit into a trough and ate another she had brought with her. Guruswami went to his room that night, trusting that his magic would draw her to him and bring her into his arms. While he lay waiting for her, a she-buffalo ate the enchanted plantain in the trough and fell in love with Guruswami. She was in heat and came running to Guruswami's chamber and butted at his door with her horns. Thinking that Hanchi had come, he hastily opened the door and was badly mauled by the amorous buffalo.

But he did not give up. On several days he asked Hanchi's gullible mother-in-law to send her to him for certain rites. When she came, he gave her enchanted almonds and betel leaves. But clever Hanchi played the same old trick and ate the harmless almonds and leaves she had carefully brought with her, palmed away Guruswami's gifts and put them into various measures and bowls on her way back to her quarters. As Guruswami lay waiting for her that night, the measures and vessels came rolling towards his bedroom and knocked against the door. He hastily opened his door for the long-awaited Hanchi, and instead of her caresses, received hard blows from the inanimate vessels, which were irresistibly drawn to him. After the third visit, Hanchi threw the magic betel nuts at a broomstick that stood in a corner. When Guruswami opened his door and received a thorny broomstick into his arms, he had to accept failure. He changed his tactics.

He went to his old friend, Hanchi's father-in-law, and suggested they have another of his famous picnics in the orchard. The old man agreed. As before Hanchi prepared her fine sweet rice dishes, and like a good daughter-in-law stayed behind to look after the house while everyone else was away.

When the family were at the orchard picnic, Guruswami found an excuse to go home. He told everyone he had left something behind, and hurried back. On the way, he collected pieces of men's clothing such as coats and turbans. Then, while Hanchi was in the kitchen, he stole into her room and planted a man's coat and turban there, and threw bits of chewed betel and stubs of smoked cheroots under the bed and on the floor.

After planting all this false evidence in Hanchi's room, he ran breathlessly to the orchard where the family were enjoying themselves and cried, "Your daughter-in-law is a whore! I surprised her with a lover. She has forgotten the dignity of her family, her womanhood. This is sinful. It will bring misfortune to the whole clan! The slut!"

At these shocking words from their trusted family friend, they all ran to the house. With righteous indignation, Guruswami showed them the man's clothing, the tell-tale cheroot stubs and pieces of betel, as unquestionable evidence of Hanchi's adultery. Hanchi was as surprised as the rest of them, but her protests were just not heard. She accused Guruswami himself of being a bad man and told them of his black magic, but they all were so angry and suspicious that they beat her till she had blue welts. When she found that everyone was against her, she became silent and gave herself over to her fate. They shut her up in a room and starved her for three days, but they got no confession out of her. Her stubborn silence sent her husband and his father into fits of rage. Then Guruswami, finding that his plot was going well, suggested, "All this will not work with this wretched woman. We must punish her properly for her sin. Put her into a big box and give the box to me. I'll have it thrown into the river. You are too good to this sinner. We must punish her as she deserves!"

Anger and shame had made them blind, and they listened to him. Hanchi was dragged out, shut up in a box, and handed over to Guruswami. He had her carried out of the house, happy that his plot had succeeded.

Then he had to think of a way to get rid of the servants. He asked them to carry the box to an old woman's house outside town and leave it there till morning, as the river was still a long way off. Unknown to Guruswami, this old woman was none other than Hanchi's good friend who had helped her get a job and settle in the town. Guruswami told her there were ferocious mad dogs in the box; he was taking them to the river to drown them next day. He asked her to be very, very careful with it, not to meddle with it or open it lest the dogs should be let loose. When he left her, he had scared her more than he intended to. He promised he would soon come back to take the dangerous dogs away.

After he left, the old woman heard peculiar noises coming from the box and thought at first it was the dogs. But then she heard her own name being spoken: Hanchi in the box had recognized her old friend's voice and was calling for help. The old woman cautiously pried open the lid and found, to her great astonishment, Hanchi crouching inside the box! She helped the miserable girl out of her prison and gave her food and drink. Hanchi had eaten nothing for days and she was ravenous. She told her old friend all about her misfortunes and the villain Guruswami's plot to get her. The old woman listened carefully, and her mother wit soon found a way out. She hid Hanchi in an inner room, went into town, and found someone who was about to get rid of a mad dog. She had it muzzled, brought it home, and locked it up in the box. She took care to loosen the muzzle before she locked up the dog.

Guruswami was back very soon, eager to taste his new power over Hanchi. He came in perfumed and singing. When he examined the locks, the old woman assured him in a frightened voice that she was too scared even to touch the box. He asked her now to leave him alone in the room for his evening prayers.

He closed the door carefully and bolted it from the inside. Then, calling Hanchi's name lovingly, he threw open the lid of the box. His heart leaped to his mouth when he saw a hideous dog, foaming at the mouth, which sprang upon him and mangled him horribly with its bites. He cursed his own wickedness and cried that he was served right by all-seeing God, who had transformed a woman into a dog. Full of remorse, he called for mercy as he sank down under the dog's teeth. Neighbors, drawn by the cries of the wretched man, soon gathered and killed the dog. But they could not save Guruswami. He had been fatally infected with rabies.

Hanchi's husband and his family were shocked by what had happened to their friend Guruswami. Months later, the old woman invited them one day to her house. The good woman could not rest till she had seen justice done to Hanchi. When Hanchi's in-laws came, the old woman served them a delicious meal, with wonderful sweet rice dishes that no one could have prepared but Hanchi. Everyone who tasted them was reminded of her and felt sad. They naturally asked who this excellent cook was who equaled Hanchi. Instead of replying, the old woman presented Hanchi herself in the flesh. Her in-laws were amazed—they had believed Hanchi was dead and gone, drowned beyond return in the river. Guruswami had got rid of her for them, and the poor fellow had gone hopelessly mad soon after. The old woman cleared up the mystery of Hanchi's reappearance by telling them the true story about her and the villain Guruswami.

The husband and his family were full of remorse for what they had done to Hanchi and ashamed they had been taken in by such a viper as Guruswami. They cursed him at length and asked Hanchi to pardon them.

Hanchi's good days had begun. Her luck had turned, and brought her every kind of happiness from that day forward.

40. Marius Barbeau, *The Golden Phoenix and Other French-Canadian Fairy Tales* (1958), retold by Michael Hornyansky[1]

The French-Canadian tale "La princesse du tomboso" was originally collected in 1916 from Marcel Tremblay, Saint-Joseph des Éboulements, Charlevoix, Québec, by the prominent Canadian anthropologist and folklorist Marius Barbeau. The text presented here is one of the eight from Barbeau's extensive archive that were "retold" in English in the 1950s by the Canadian literary scholar Michael Hornyansky. Importantly, the text that follows does not directly represent a scholarly attempt to document a specific oral tale performance, as do those penned by Linda Dégh, Hasan El-Shamy, and Donald Braid, included in this volume. Nevertheless, this literary reworking of Tremblay's narrative is rooted in the history of French-Canadian folklore study—and it is a very amusing tale in its own right, reversing numerous generic expectations as the title character outwits the "youngest brother" Jacques who would have liked to claim the beautiful, clever Princess as his prize—and then is outwitted herself.

THE PRINCESS OF TOMBOSO, PERFORMED BY MARCEL TREMBLAY, 1916

THERE WAS ONCE A KING who had three sons. They did none of the things that princes are supposed to do, but stayed at home all day and ate their father out of house and home. When the old king lay dying, he called them to his bedside and said:

"My children, I have only one thing left to give you when I die. It is an old bowl. When you have buried me, go to the barn and you will find it behind the door. Pick it up and shake it, each of you in turn. Whatever falls out of it is your inheritance."

Then the old man breathed his last.

1 [Source: Marius Barbeau, *The Golden Phoenix and Other French-Canadian Fairy Tales, retold by Michael Hornyansky* (Toronto, ON: Oxford UP, 1958): 26–45.]

It was the custom in those days to keep the dead lying in state for a day and a night; but the king's sons were so anxious to see what the bowl held that they buried their father without delay. Then they ran to the barn and looked behind the door. Sure enough, the bowl was there.

The eldest son picked it up and shook it well. Presto! A silk purse fell into the air. Written on it in letters of gold were these words:

EVERY TIME I OPEN WIDE
A HUNDRED FLORINS ARE INSIDE.

He opened the purse wide, and—*cling, clang!*—a hundred shining florins tumbled to the ground. He closed the purse, opened it wide again, and found it still full to the brim.

"It works!" he exclaimed. "I'm rich!"

The second brother was growing impatient.

"Now it's my turn," he said.

He took the bowl, held it over his head, and shook it. This time a silver bugle fell out. Written on it in letters of gold were these words:

BLOW ONE END, AND YOUR TROOPS APPEAR;
THE OTHER, AND THE FIELD IS CLEAR.

The second prince lost no time. Putting the bugle to his lips, he blew a short blast. *Ta-rraa!* There in the field behind the barn stood an army of ten thousand soldiers waiting for his command.

Then he put the wide end of the bugle to his lips and blew again. Presto! In a twinkling the field was empty. "It works!" he exclaimed. "I'm powerful!" "Now it's my turn," said the youngest brother, whose name was Jacques.

He took the bowl and shook it. A leather belt fell out. Written on it in letters of gold were these words:

PUT ME ON AND TELL ME WHERE:
QUICK AS LIGHTNING YOU'LL BE THERE.

Jacques lost no time. Clasping the belt around his waist, he wished himself into the castle. *Whoosh!*—and there he stood inside the castle. He wished himself back into the barn. *Whoosh!* There he was back again. "Well, it works," he said. "Now I can travel cheap." "And just where do you propose to go?" asked his eldest brother.

"To Tomboso," said Jacques promptly. "With my belt it will be a simple thing to visit the Princess."

His brothers looked jealous. They had heard of the Princess of Tomboso, who was as beautiful as the moon. But they had never seen her, and they didn't have a magic belt.

"You'd better look out," they told him. "She'll play some trick on you."

"Oh, no fear of that."

"Anyway, the royal guards won't even let you into the castle."

"The guards won't trouble me," said Jacques. "I'll just wish myself into the Princess's chamber, and *whoosh!* I'll be there. Farewell, my brothers."

Clasping the belt around him, he made his wish. *Whoosh!* There he stood, in the finest room he had ever seen. And sitting on a velvet cushion by the window, eating a red apple, was the Princess of Tomboso, as beautiful as the moon.

When the Princess saw a man in her room, she gave a faint scream.

"Fair Princess," Jacques began, "do not be alarmed."

But it was too late. The Princess had fainted. Jacques sprang forward and caught her in his arms. He gazed at her in admiration. Never in his life had he seen such a lovely creature.

Presently the Princess opened her eyes.

"Are you a man from this world," she asked, "or an angel from heaven?"

"Princess, I'm a real man."

She sat up. "Then how did you arrive in my chamber? The doors are guarded, and the windows are high above the ground."

Jacques smiled modestly. "Ah, Princess, for me it was very simple. Do you see this belt I'm wearing? Well, it's no ordinary belt. I wished myself into your chamber, and *whoosh!* it brought me here."

"A magic belt? That's quite impossible," declared the Princess. "I don't believe you."

"Sweet Princess, you have something to learn. Watch me."

He wished himself down into the castle courtyard. *Whoosh!* There he was. The Princess stared down at him from her window. Then he wished himself back into her room and landed at the foot of the bed. The Princess was struck dumb with amazement.

"There," he said. "Now do you believe me?"

"What is your name?" asked the Princess.

"They call me Jacques."

"Well, Jacques, I think you are the most outrageous liar I've ever met."

"Princess, I have told you the plain truth."

She bit her lip in thought. "Perhaps it is true for you," she said. "But would it work for me too?"

"Certainly," said Jacques.

"Prove it, then. Let me see this marvellous belt of yours." Jacques took off the belt and showed it to her. She read the words written in letters of gold: *Put me on and tell me where: quick as lightning you'll be there.* Oh, Jacques!" she cried. "Lend it to me!"

"That I cannot do," he said firmly.

"Dear Jacques! *Please.*" And she held her arms out to him imploringly.

She looked so beautiful standing there before him that Jacques forgot his brothers' warning. He gave her the belt and watched her clasp it around her tiny waist.

"Now," she said, "I wish to be in my father's office."

Whoosh!—and there she stood, in her father's office. The king was startled, but she gave him no explanation.

"Father!" she cried. "There is a rascal in my chamber!"

At once the king sent his guard of honour to her room. Forty soldiers seized hold of Jacques and gave him a thorough beating. When he seemed half dead, they opened a window and threw him out of the castle.

Poor Jacques landed in the ditch by the roadside and lay there unconscious for three days and nights. When at last he came to his senses, he thought:

"I cannot go home now. When my brothers hear what has happened, they will finish me off."

But he had eaten nothing for days. He was starving.

"Ah, well," he said. "If I'm going to die, I might as well die at home."

When his brothers saw him stumbling up the path that evening, they knew that something must have happened to his belt. They came out of the castle shaking their fists, warning him what to expect if he came near.

But Jacques was too exhausted to care. He plodded into the castle while his brothers heaped reproaches and ridicule on his head.

"We ought to lock you up for the rest of your life," they said. "You can't be trusted on your own. Get in there under the stairs. We won't have anything more to do with you!"

For a whole month they kept him there, giving him nothing but bread and water. But one day Jacques said to his eldest brother:

"If you would lend me your purse, I could go and buy back my belt."

His brother sneered. "Do you think I would trust you with my purse after what happened to your belt?"

"But listen to my plan," said Jacques eagerly. "I'll go back to Tomboso and ask to speak to the Princess. When she asks what I want, I'll tell her the truth—that I want to buy back my belt. If she says I cannot pay for it, I shall open the purse wide and send a hundred florins rolling on the floor, *cling, clang!* If she wants more, I can fill her whole room with florins, right up to the ceiling. It won't cost you anything, for the purse is never empty. In the end I'll get my belt back."

His brother grumbled, but finally he agreed.

"But I warn you," he said, "if you come back without the purse, don't expect any mercy from me."

"No fear of that," said Jacques confidently.

And so he took the purse and made his way back to Tomboso. He asked to see the Princess. When she heard who it was, she had him shown up to her room. He found her eating a red apple and smiling.

"Why, hello, Jacques! And what can I do for you this fine day?"

"Fair Princess, I have come to buy back my belt."

"Your belt?" The Princess pretended not to understand. "My dear Jacques, what belt are you talking about?"

"Princess, I'll pay you a good price for it."

She laughed. "A young lad like you couldn't possibly afford to buy a valuable belt."

"I can fill this room with pieces of gold," said Jacques.

"How you boast, Jacques! Why, even my father the king hasn't enough gold florins to fill this room."

"I can fill it to the ceiling," said Jacques. "For me it's no trick at all."

The Princess shook her head. "Ah, Jacques, you never change. One simply can't believe a word you say."

"Very well, you shall see," said Jacques. "I have a little silk purse in my pocket. Open it wide, and a hundred florins tumble out. Open it wide again, and there are a hundred more."

He took the purse from his pocket and opened it wide, and—*cling, clang!*—a hundred shining florins fell to the floor. The Princess stared at them with round eyes.

"There," he said. "Now do you believe me?"

"Ah," she breathed. "With a purse like that, you can buy back any belt you like. But how can I be sure it will go on giving florins?"

"Look," said Jacques, "it's still full."

And—*cling, clang!*—he spilled another hundred gold pieces on the floor.

"Oh!" said the Princess. "Would it do that for me, too?"

"Certainly."

"Please let me try!"

"That I cannot do," said Jacques firmly.

"Dear Jacques! *Please.*" And she held out her arms as if to embrace him. She looked so beautiful that he forgot his resolutions and gave her the purse.

But she was still wearing the magic belt. At once she wished herself into her father's office. *Whoosh!*

The king looked up from his desk. "Terrible draught in here," he said. "Oh, it's you, my dear. What's the matter now?"

"Quick, Father! That rascal has come back to insult me."

The king's soldiers rushed to her room, captured Jacques, beat him nearly to death, and flung him out of the window.

For five days and nights he lay in the ditch unconscious. Finally he awoke and groaned.

"This time it's all over," he thought. "If I go back home, my brothers will finish me off for certain."

But he was so hungry that he had no choice. Once again he trudged wearily home.

His brothers had been searching for him for days. When they saw him approach, bruised and mud-stained, a pitiful sight, they guessed what had happened. They shook their sticks in the air, warning him what to expect if he came nearer. But poor Jacques didn't care. He stumbled into the castle and his brothers gave him another beating. Then they shut him up under the stairs with a jug of water and a bone to gnaw.

"That's all you'll get from us," they said. "When you finish that, there won't be any more."

For a whole month he stayed there, growing thinner and thinner. Then one day he spoke to his second brother, the one who had the silver bugle.

"If you lend it to me," said Jacques, "I'll go and get back the belt and the purse."

His brother sneered. "Do you think I would trust my bugle to a nitwit like you? You would only let it be stolen too."

"But I have a better plan. This time I won't even go to the Princess's room, so she won't have a chance to steal the bugle. I'll wait at the city gates until the king and the Princess drive out in their royal carriage. Then I'll seize the bridle, stop the horses, and command the Princess to return the belt and the purse, or else I'll besiege the city with my army and put the whole population to the sword."

His brother grumbled but finally agreed.

And so with the bugle under his arm Jacques once more took the road to Tomboso. By next morning he was ready, standing at the gates of the city. When the royal carriage came into sight, he blew the silver bugle. *Ta-rraa!* There stood an army of ten thousand men.

"General, we await your orders."

"Men," said Jacques, "surround the city."

The king of Tomboso was astonished to see so many soldiers, and the Princess was so frightened that she dropped the red apple she was eating. But when she saw who ran forward to hold the bridle of the horses, she smiled.

"So it's you again, Jacques! And what are you up to this time?"

"Fair Princess," said Jacques sternly, "if you do not return my belongings, I will give orders to sack the town."

"Good heavens!" cried the Princess. "This sounds serious. Of course I'll give everything back to you. I wasn't going to keep them anyway. But tell me first, brave general, where did you enlist this great army?"

"Fair lady, to raise an army like this is a very simple thing for me."

"A simple thing?" said the Princess. "Really, I can't believe that."

"Very well," said Jacques, "I'll tell you how it's done. Do you see this silver bugle? If I blow it at one end, ten thousand soldiers appear. Blow the other end, and they all vanish."

The Princess laughed. "A bugle does all that? Really, Jacques, I think you must be the prince of liars."

"You shall see," said Jacques. He blew the bugle at the wide end. Presto! In a twinkling the field was empty. Then he blew the other end and the whole army reappeared, ready to attack the town.

"Stop, stop!" cried the Princess. "I shall give you back what you asked for. But tell me, does the bugle obey you alone?"

"Why, no," said Jacques. "It obeys whoever blows it."

She unclasped the belt from her waist and pulled out the purse. But before handing them over to him, she said:

"What a wonderful bugle! May I try blowing it, just once?"

Jacques hesitated.

The Princess gave him an enchanting smile. "Dear Jacques," she said. "*Please.*"

"Can I trust you this time?" he demanded.

"I give you my word," said the Princess. "The word of Tomboso. If the bugle obeys me too, I shall return your belt and your purse."

And so poor Jacques forgot his promise and gave her the bugle. As soon as she had it she blew into the wide end. Presto! In a twinkling Jacques's army vanished. Then she blew at the other end. *Ta-rraa!* A new army appeared.

"Princess, we await your orders."

"Take this scoundrel," said the Princess, "and march over his body till he is seven times dead."

Two soldiers held Jacques down. Then the whole army marched over him until he was pounded flat into the ground.

For seven days and seven nights Jacques lay there without moving. But he must have had at least seven lives, for at last one morning he woke.

"This really is the end," he groaned. "I can never go home now."

Slowly he pulled himself out of the ground. His legs were so weak that he could hardly stand. Falling every few yards, he staggered away from Tomboso, following a little footpath that wound into the woods. He came to a marsh full of big green rushes, and there he lost the path. Several times he nearly drowned. Finally he fell exhausted in the hot sunshine at the edge of a clearing.

"Well," he thought, "I'll try to reach that apple tree. At least I'll be able to die in the shade."

Dragging himself along the ground, he got as far as the apple tree. Its branches were so laden with ripe shining fruit that they bent down within his reach. Nearby there was another tree, weighed down with plums.

"It must be an old orchard," said Jacques to himself. "I don't think I'll die just yet—not until I've had a little refreshment."

He ate one apple and a strange thing happened. His nose began to feel heavy, as if it was ready to drop off. He ate another, and his head began to bend forward with the weight. He ate a third apple, and by this time his nose had grown so long that it touched the ground.

"Thunderation!" cried Jacques. "Am I going to die with a nose like an elephant?"

He crawled on all fours to the plum tree. His nose was so heavy that he could not stand up. Rolling on his back, he kicked at the lowest branch. Plums fell all around him.

"Well," he thought, "they can't be any worse."

He ate one. It tasted sweet and juicy, and he felt better immediately. He ate another. Better still—now he could lift his head. At each mouthful he felt his nose shrinking, until by the time he had eaten three plums it was the finest nose you have ever seen.

"Let me see now. Eat apples, and your nose grows. Eat plums, and it shrinks. And I know someone who is very fond of fruit. Oho! My affairs are mending!"

Cheerfully he made his way back to the marsh where he cut down some rushes and plaited himself two baskets. The first he filled with apples, the second with plums. Then he set out towards Tomboso again.

In front of the castle he walked up and down, shouting like a pedlar:

"Apples for sale! Fresh apples!"

The Princess, who was very fond of apples, sent a servant downstairs to buy some. When she saw how delicious the fruit looked, she didn't worry about spoiling her dinner but began eating right away. She soon felt strange. She tried to stand up and fell forward on her face. Horrified, she stood up again and began running towards her bed. This time she tripped over her nose!

Feeling very sick indeed, she took to her bed and sent for the doctor. When he arrived she hid her face in the pillows so that he wouldn't see her nose. He felt her pulse and shook his head.

"Your highness," he said, "this is an odd kind of illness. You have no sign of a fever and your pulse is normal. Let me see your tongue."

The Princess shrieked so loudly that her servants came running.

"This doctor has insulted me!"

They threw the doctor out.

Jacques, who was waiting outside, said: "Good doctor, I think I can cure her. Be kind enough to lend me your cloak and your square cap. I will pay you well."

"No need to pay me," panted the doctor. "I've had enough of Tomboso." And flinging his cloak and cap at Jacques, he ran off.

Jacques picked up his basket of plums, which he had covered with green leaves and hidden by the roadside. Wearing the doctor's cap and gown and a very serious expression, and carrying the basket on his arm, he asked to be admitted to the castle. He was led to the Princess's room.

"It's another doctor," said the maid to the Princess. "This one looks like a medicine man. He's got no little black bag, only a basket of herbs."

"Show him in."

Jacques entered. He could not see the Princess's face, for she kept it hidden among her pillows.

"Your highness," he said, "how can I find out what is wrong with you if you won't let me see your tongue?"

She raised her head to shout for the servants. But Jacques seized her shoulders and turned her face up.

"Ah," he said. "So that's it! Why, Princess, you have a monster of a nose!"

"He's insulting me!" she shouted.

"Do you want to have me thrown out," asked Jacques, "or do you want to be cured?"

The Princess stopped shrieking. "Oh—can you cure me?"

Jacques took a plum from his basket. "Eat this," he said, "and we shall see."

The Princess ate the plum. Her nose grew a few inches shorter. She began to feel better. "Oh, you are a good doctor! Let me have another one."

"Not just yet." Jacques put down the basket and touched his fingers together. "You have another disease which we must cure first."

The Princess was astonished. "Another disease? What is that?"

"A naughty habit of taking things that don't belong to you."

"Why, Doctor, who could have told you a story like that?"

"Never mind how I know," said Jacques. "It is true, is it not?"

"Well," admitted the Princess, "I do happen to have a small belt here, but it's the merest trifle, hardly worth mentioning."

"Let me have that belt. Otherwise I am afraid I can do nothing for you."

"Certainly not," said the Princess. "I refuse to part with it."

"Very well. In that case I shall leave you here—with your nose." And Jacques picked up his basket, ready to depart.

"Wait, Doctor!" cried the Princess. She unclasped the belt and gave it to him. "Here it is. Now will you cure my nose?"

Jacques clasped the belt securely around his waist. "Your highness, are you sure there isn't some other trifle that doesn't belong to you?"

"No, nothing else ... well, only a little purse."

"Let me have that little purse, your highness."

"No. I would rather die than part with it."

"Very well," said Jacques. "If that is your decision, I shall leave you. Good day, Princess."

"Wait," said the Princess. "Here it is." And she gave him the purse. "Now will you cure my nose?"

"Not yet," said Jacques. "I think there is still one thing left."

"Oh, there is only a little bugle that I received from a certain young man. I really don't see what importance it could have."

"Nevertheless you must give it up. I must have the bugle too. Otherwise I cannot cure you completely."

The Princess burst into tears, but finally she had to give up the bugle. Then Jacques gave her plums to eat until her nose shrank. When he stopped, it was a very handsome nose, but it was exactly one foot long.

The Princess protested. "Surely you don't call this a complete cure?"

"It is more than you deserve," said Jacques. Stepping back, he took off his doctor's cap and gown and bowed to her. When she recognized him she gave a little scream.

"Yes," he said, "it is Jacques. You have treated me very badly, Princess."

She held out her arms. "Oh, Jacques, forgive me! Come, let me kiss you and make up for everything."

"No, thank you," said Jacques, picking up his basket. "I really don't care to kiss a Princess with a nose like yours. From now on, you know, they will call you the Princess with the Twelve-Inch Nose. Farewell, your highness!"

Since he was now wearing his belt again, he had only to wish himself home, and *whoosh!*—there he was. This time you may be sure that his brothers welcomed him with open arms. They praised his cleverness in recovering the belt and the purse and the bugle, and Jacques for his part resolved that he had learned his lesson. The three of them lived quite happily ever afterwards, and Jacques never went near Tomboso again.

41. Hasan M. El-Shamy, *Tales Arab Women Tell, and the Behavioral Patterns They Portray* (1999)[1]

In Hasan El-Shamy's introduction to his masterful collection of Tales Arab Women Tell, *he argues that readers' understandings of "Arab folktales as they are lived in real life" have been severely limited by the "scarcity of accurate texts, especially ones collected from females": for well over a century, books shaped by "writers' re-creative abilities" ("alterations, 'improvements,' and blatant forgeries and fabrications") have been framed as if they were direct representations of oral traditions. This tendency is very clear in the nineteenth-century texts that make a claim at representing oral storytelling—such as those of Jacob and Wilhelm Grimm, Thomas Crofton Croker, George Webbe Dasent, Flora Annie Steel, and others included in this volume—but the practice of reshaping and remaking orally collected tales for popular (and sometimes even scholarly) print consumption persists. In "The Daughters of the Bean Vendor" El-Shamy models a form of print entextualization that maintains a sense of the storytelling event: in this case, the narration of a tale about three sisters learning sewing from a local seamstress, told in 1971 by Lady Tahiyyah the Seamstress to her female apprentices, her youngest daughter, and Hasan El-Shamy. In El-Shamy's transcription, the narrator's tone, gestures, and asides are included, as are the reactions and responses of her audience. The tale may not include magic or the supernatural, but the youngest daughter's cheekiness to and one-upmanship of the Sultan's son—drawing on the materials and skills to which she has access in order to outwit a man who is her social superior—makes this tale truly "marvelous."*

THE DAUGHTERS OF THE BEAN VENDOR, PERFORMED BY TAHIYYAH M., 1971

STATE THE ONENESS OF GOD.

Once there was a man who was a bean vendor, one of those people who sell fava beans and cooked wheat for people to eat at breakfast; he had three daughters. One was the eldest, another was the middle, and one was the youngest.

Those three used to go to a seamstress in their neighborhood to learn sewing. Every morning while they were going to the seamstress they would find the sultan's son sitting on a chair in front of his father's palace and blocking their way in order to tease-flirt with them. That sultan's son would come to the eldest and would say to her, "Daughter of bean vendor, how are your father's beans?" She would reply [softly in a friendly tone],

1 [Source: Hasan M. El-Shamy, ed., *Tales Arab Women Tell, and the Behavioral Patterns They Portray* (Bloomington, IN: Indiana UP, 1999): 159–67.]

My father's beans were well cooked, well cooked;
family and close friends ate [some] from it.

So, he would say to her, "All right, you may kindly go ahead." Then he would come to the middle girl and would say to her, "Daughter of bean vendor, how are your father's beans?" She would reply [in a friendly tone],

My father's beans were well cooked, well cooked;
family and close friends ate from it!

So, he would say to her, "All right, you may kindly go ahead!" Then he would come to the youngest and would say [slyly and provocatively], "You, damned one, who are the youngest, how are your father's beans?" She would reply [firmly and with some anger]:

My father's beans were well cooked, well cooked;
family and close friends ate from it!
What concern of yours is it, you son of a clog!?

The sultan's son would hear this and would become vexed at her and would say [in a threatening tone], "By God, I'll show you!"

One day he went to the seamstress—(where the girls worked, I mean)—and said to her, "I would like you to keep the youngest girl at your house tonight!" and he gave her a pound, or something. She said to him, "Will do!"

At sunset when it was time for the girls to return home, their tutor (*'ublit-hum*) said, "Who would stay with me [overnight] for we need to bake [bread] tomorrow [at dawn]?"

The eldest girl said [with enthusiasm], "I would, my tutor!" She answered her, "No! You will not do." The middle girl said, "I would, my tutor." She answered her, "No! You will not do." The two [girls] said, "All right." So she looked toward the youngest. She [the youngest girl] said [without zeal], "I would stay overnight with you, tutor!" The tutor [readily] said, "Oh yes, you cutie! You sugar! You stay with your tutor and help her bake. You are the one who impresses me!"

The two elder sisters went home while she stayed with that tutor of hers. Whenever she asked, "Where is the flour?" the tutor would say, "We've got it!"

"Where is the yeast?"

"We've got it."

"Let us start early so that we can finish early."

"O sister, there is plenty of time; it is still too early."

Things kept on going like this until the girl fell asleep. Naturally she was tired and she did not feel anything around her. After a little while, her tutor put out the light (one of those No. 10 kerosene lamps of older times). The sultan's son came—for that was the sign they had agreed on. She had told him, "When it gets dark, come to my place when the light is turned off." He cleared his throat at the door, and she opened the door for him.

When he got inside, he kept on hugging and kissing the girl. She would wake up and see nothing. She would say to her tutor, "'Tutor of mine, what is this that hugs and kisses?" The tutor would say, "Sleep, sleep, there is nothing; it is [only] a nightmare!" After a while the sultan's son went home. In the morning, when the girl woke up, she asked the seamstress, "We haven't done any baking, tutor." She answered her, "We changed our mind, maybe tomorrow."

The following day, as she and her sisters were going to the seamstress's house, they found the sultan's son, as he was used to, in front of his father's palace. He asked the eldest girl, "Daughter of bean vendor, how are your father's beans?"

She answered him, "My father's beans were well cooked, well cooked, and family and close friends ate some."

He would say to her, "All right, you may kindly go on."

Then he asked the middle one, "Daughter of bean vendor, how are your father's beans?"

She answered him, "My father's beans were well cooked, well cooked, and family and close friends ate some."

"All right, you may kindly go on!"

[Narrator speaks emphatically] Then, what next? He came to the youngest. He said to her [with a hint of sarcasm], "Daughter of bean vendor, how are your father's beans?"

She [defiantly] answered,

My father's beans were well cooked, well cooked;
family and close friends ate from it!
What concern of yours is it, you son of a clog!

He said to her [in a twitting manner, and imitating a female's voice], "'O my tutor, what is this that hugs and kisses?' 'O [girl], sleep, sleep! There is nothing, it is only a nightmare!'"

That was it!! She said [in anger], "That was you!!"

He replied, "Yes! [It was] I."

She said to herself, "Well, well, well. I must get even!" She thought and thought; she went to the tinsmith and said to him, "I want you to make me ten cones to fit my fingers, [at the end of each cone there should be a holder for] a needle." He said to her, "Will do! And come back at such and such a time!"

She waited until midnight [narrator speaks in a low tone denoting secrecy]; she put on a black outer-garment (*galabiyyah*), covered her face and head with a black shawl, with two holes for her to see through. She fitted ten candles into the candlesticks at [the end of the tin] cones and lighted them. She went to the sultan's palace, where the sultan's son happened to be. As soon as the gatekeeper saw her, he became frightened and asked [in a fearful, trembling tone], "Who is there?"

She answered [in a husky, eerie tone], "I am Little Azrael [angel of death]; Big Azrael sent me ahead of him, and he will follow, in order to seize the soul of the sultan's son."

As soon as the guard heard this, he placed his tail between his teeth and flew away [thus fleeing in a hurry, like a scared dog is thought to do]. The same thing happened with every guard and doorkeeper; they all ran away. She, finally, reached his room and found him asleep on the bed. [She hissed at him a quivering tone:] "I am Little Azrael! Big Azrael has sent me ahead of him to seize the soul of the sultan's son!!" He [the sultan's son] opened his eyes like this [narrator opens her own eyes slowly in a slumbering manner]. He bounded up from his sleep; naturally he saw those ten flaming fingers and the black thing. He was about to—(may God protect your status)—wet the bed! [Laughter.] She said to him, "Prepare yourself for death!" He replied [in an imploring tone], "I am too young to die. Take my money; take my belongings; take my father's palace! Take everything!! Just let me be!" She said, "No! Utter the [death] Testimony over your soul: prepare yourself for death!"

He kept on begging her for mercy, and she kept on saying, "No!" until finally, he plucked off his own beard—(from fright, he pulled his own whiskers out). Whether he fainted or passed out, I don't know what; when she left, he was finished. His servants came and revived him. His condition was very bad and he kept on [mumbling], "Little Azrael is here and Big Azrael is following him! Little Azrael is here and Big Azrael is following him." They soothed him until he was calm again. But, still, he did not change.

The following day he sat in front of his father's house. When the bean vendor's daughters passed by, he stopped them and asked, "How are your father's beans, you eldest?"

She answered him, "My father's beans were well cooked, well cooked; and [our] family and close friends ate some!"

He asked the middle one, "How are your father's beans?"

She answered him, "My father's beans were well cooked, well cooked, and [our] family and close friends ate some!"

He asked the youngest, "How are your father's beans, you damned one, who are the youngest?"

She replied,

My father's beans were well cooked, well cooked;
family and close friends ate from it!
What concern of yours is it, you son of a clog!

He retorted [sarcastically, in a girl's voice], "'O my tutor, what is this that hugs and kisses!?' 'Oh, sleep, sleep; it is a nightmare!'"

She retorted [in an eerie voice], "'I am Little Azrael; Big Azrael will follow. I've come to seize the soul of the sultan's son.' [In an imploring, frightened tone,] 'I am too young to die! Take my money, take my belongings ...'"

The sultan's son [interrupted and] exclaimed [with considerable bitterness], "*'Â-â-â-kh-kh-kh!* Was that you!!?"

[She answered defiantly,] "Yes, that was I!"

He realized that he will not be able to get anywhere with her. So he decided to get to her through her father. He sent a messenger to the bean vendor to say to him, "The sultan's son wants you." When he [the bean vendor] went to him at the palace, he [the sultan's son] said to him, "Tomorrow I want you to come here, riding-walking. If you do not, I will do to you—(distant one: *el-bi¿îd)*—such and such [evil things]."

The man became very confused, and he returned to his home saddened. The girls asked him, "[May it turn out to be] a good thing! What is the matter, Father? Why are you sad?" He told them the story, and that the sultan said to him—the sultan's son (I mean) said to him, "'You must come here tomorrow, riding-walking!'"

The youngest said, [in an unconcerned tone], "Don't be afraid, father! Our neighbor has a burro that has just given birth to a little one; get it from him and ride it. Your feet will be dragging on the ground [while] you will be seated on its back; you will be 'riding-walking!'"

He did as his daughter, the youngest, told him to do and went to the sultan's son: riding the little donkey, with his feet dragging on the ground. When he (the sultan's son] saw him coming in this manner, he said to him [in a disappointed tone], "'*Â-â-â-h* [I see]! This [idea] is not of your own doing; it is your youngest daughter's!" [Pause.] [The sultan's son continued in a commanding voice,] "Since this is the case, tomorrow you must come here attired-naked!"

The man, saddened, returned home to his daughter. She said to him, "What happened, Father? Didn't the little ass work out?" He answered [in despair], "Daughter, it worked out, but the sultan's son said, 'This [solution] is not yours! Tomorrow I want you to come here attired-naked!'"

She said [in a reassuring tone], "Is that all? Go to our neighbor So-and-so, the fisherman; borrow his net and wear it like a mantle. You will be dressed and you will be naked!" (Narrator giggles and adds, "May God's name protect your status.")

The man did as his [youngest] daughter told him to do; he went to his neighbor the fisherman and said, "Father of So-and-so, by God, lend me an old net of yours." The man said, "More than gladly!" The bean vendor wore the net and went to the sultan's son "attired-naked." The sultan's son became extremely vexed, for he knew that it was all the work of the bean vendor's young[est] daughter. He said to him [angrily], "Tomorrow I want you to bring me your three daughters: pregnant!" He [the bean vendor, in a pleading tone] said, "Sire, how can that be! They are virgins!" He [the sultan's son] said [in an uncompromising tone], "This is no concern of mine. Bring them here pregnant, tomorrow!"

The man returned home to his daughters saddened, more [so] than before. They asked him, "What is the matter, Father?" He said to them, "Nothing!" (Of course he was ashamed to tell them that the sultan's son told him, "I want you to bring me your three daughters pregnant.") The youngest asked, "Didn't the net work out?" He replied, "[Yes], it worked out. But now the sultan's son is saying to me, 'I want you to bring to me your three daughters: pregnant!'"

She thought for a while and said, "Simple! Go buy lots of lentil, and we will cook it with lots of fried minced onions (*taqliyyah*)." [Narrator laughs repeatedly and interrupts her story until she is able to continue.] "And you know ..., after we drink that lentil soup our stomach[s] will get inflated and bloated (*batninâ titnifikh witibangar*), ... and we will be ... pregnant-and-virgins!!" [Laughter.]

The man did as his daughter had told him. They bought lots of lentil. They cooked it, [then] diced lots of onions and fried them in oil, and they *tashshû* (sizzled) the fried onions [onto the lentil]. They kept on drinking, drinking, and drinking that lentil [soup]; they didn't even use any bread. Before morning time came, their stomach[s] became that high [narrator laughs, and places the palm of her hand in front of her stomach to indicate how high]—as if [their pregnancy was in its] ninth month.

The man took his three daughters and went to the sultan's son: "Here are my three daughters: pregnant and virgin!"

The sultan's son said, "No, they are not pregnant! How do we know that they are pregnant?"

The young[est] girl said, "Pregnant ones crave!"

So the sultan's son said to the eldest, "What do you crave?"

She [immediately and simple-mindedly] replied, "Apples!"

They got some apples for her; she sat down in total absorption in [devouring] them.

Then he asked the middle one, "What do you crave?"

She [immediately and simple-mindedly] answered, "Pears."

They got some for her; she sat down in total absorption in [devouring] them.

He said to the youngest, "And what about you, damned one—you who are the youngest!?"

She replied [emphatically], "I want a male radish planted in the heart of stone."

He [the sultan's son] asked his servants, and his guards—(his people, I mean)—to fetch for her what she has requested. They said to him, "We don't have her request[ed item]!" He said to her, "Ask for something else!" She replied [defiantly], "No! This is what I want!" He said to his soldiers and guards, "Find what she has asked for!" They answered him, "Impossible. How can a radish be planted in [solid] stone?!" So he turned to the girl and said to her, "What you have craved is impossible: there is no 'male radish planted in stone!'"

She immediately [in a taunting tone] retorted, "How could it be, then, that you want virgin girls to have become pregnant without a male!"

She said to her father and the other two [sisters], who were still immersed in their total absorption [with eating their apples and pears], "Let us go home!"

And she left the sultan's son sitting there—(of course she confounded him in front of everyone). He became more vexed with her.

So, what did he say [to himself]? He said, "I must marry her in order to break her spirit, and bring her nose [down] to the ground just like she brought my nose to the ground!" So he went to her father and said, "I wish to marry your [youngest] daughter." The man said, "No!" He, [the sultan's son], said to him, "Just consult with her and find out what she might say!" [When her father asked her,] she said, "Yes, father, I would marry him; I agree to marry. You tell him that you [also] agree."

Her father went to the sultan's son, and they agreed on the marriage. Meanwhile she had gone to the sweets man and said to him, "I want you to make me a [sugar] doll: in my size, looks like me, and with strings which when pulled would cause her [it] to move her head, eyelashes, arms, waist, … I mean move exactly like a [living] human being!

ASIDE

A child comments: "Like a 'Prophet's-Birthday doll'"….

[Narrator continues, repeating listener's comment:] Just like the doll of the Prophet's Birthday celebration, but very much bigger and with moving hands, head, and everything.

When the time came for the actual consummation of marriage (*dukhlah*), she went into the room of the bride and groom before anyone else was there. She set the doll on the bed, covered her [the doll] with the [lace] shawl, put out the lights, and hid inside the wardrobe; (and of course, she held the strings in her hands). The sultan's son entered the room: [he was] bent on getting even with her, for all what she had done to him. He held the sword in his hand and said to her [in a taunting tone], "Do you remember the time you [insulted me by] saying 'You, son of a clog!?' Do you remember, or have you forgotten!? And do you remember the time you did to me [such and such]!?, And do you remember ... ?!" He unreeled before her (*karr-e-lhâ*) all she had done to him.

Meanwhile, she pulled the strings and the doll kept on winking, fluttering her eyelashes (*titrammishsh*), and swaying her body coquettishly (*titqaṣṣaʿ*)—like this and like that. [Narrator, while sitting on a cushion on the floor, shows how it is done.] Every time he would say to her, "Do you remember the time you did such and such to me?" she would pull the strings, and the doll would keep on winking (*titghammiz*), fluttering her eyelashes, and swaying her waist. He became more and more vexed and said to her, "This is the end for you!" He struck her with his sword. The doll broke up into a thousand pieces and scattered everywhere. One piece flew into his mouth; he found it to be sweet. [Suddenly] he was saddened and said, [in a sorrowful voice], "Your beginning [in this affair] is bitterness (enmity), but your end is sweetness!"

That was it! She got out of the wardrobe, and said to him, "There need not be bitterness [between us]. I am your wife: legitimate for you."

And they repeated the wedding celebration [in a more joyful manner].

And they lived in stability and prosperity and begot boys and girls.

EL-SHAMY: How could they live together after all that has happened?

NARRATOR: That which happened between the two of them took evil and went away [with it]. When something bad (away from you) happens, this is what we would say. With marriage, they will have to get along.

Two years earlier, Nabawiyyah M.Y., the narrator of another variant of this tale, gave the following answer to the same question:

> Of course, now that she is a married woman, she will have to relax the tension [of her pride] somewhat; she will have to obey her man. Or, maybe he will not be so uptight: [because] "a pillow would not carry two [of a kind]." A man and his wife cannot be too much alike; for if both are handsome, proud, or moody, both will be demanding; neither will yield to the other and there will be no give and take.

42. Donald Braid, *Scottish Traveller Tales: Lives Shaped Through Stories* (2002)[1]

In introducing his study of contemporary storytelling among Scottish Travellers, Donald Braid notes that "most Travellers speak in a dialect that combines English, Scots, and Traveller cant (their own secret language—and cant is the term they call it by)." To render his printed versions of tales accessible and readable, Braid uses "predominantly English spellings" (Braid xi). The formatting of the text itself (most notably the line breaks and arrangement of chunks of text into something like stanzas) follows a scholarly tradition of experimentation with transcription and the creation of written records of oral performance, aimed at revealing "formal patterning of the stories while preserving a sense of the rhythms of performance" (Braid xi). The line breaks mark performer Duncan Williamson's pauses and also the repetition of syntactical structures.

The particular story included here, called "The Boy and the Blacksmith," is an example of what Scottish Travellers refer to as "dream stories" (see Braid 250–82). In the context of this anthology, this tale is interesting in many ways, including its blending of fairy tale and legend elements and its foregrounding of the ways in which seemingly serious and violent plot elements can be used for comic effect—something that can be lost on a reader who is not privy to the details of a specific performance, such as the one that Donald Braid has documented here.

THE BOY AND THE BLACKSMITH, PERFORMED BY DUNCAN WILLIAMSON, 1987

Now I'd like to tell you a story tonight, which I hope you'll enjoy.
It's called "The Boy and the Blacksmith."
A long time ago in the West Highlands of Scotland,
there lived an old blacksmith and his old wife.
And they had a small smithy up there in the Highlands.
And they were very poor, but they did little work.
Just the local farmers brought in their horses to get shod, you know?
Because it was mostly all horses in these days.
And the old woman she was a very (knacky?) old woman.
She was all getting onto her old husband John
  to get out to the smiddy,
    and do some work,
      and not sit around the house.
He never got much peace from her.

1 [Source: Donald Braid, *Scottish Traveller Tales: Lives Shaped Through Stories* (Jackson, MS: UP of Mississippi, 2002): 258–65.]

So.
He'd usually escape into the smiddy.
And there, he would kindle up his fire,
and sit there by himself,
just to get away from her nagging tongue, as we say.

But one particular morning,
she hunted him out of the house again,
saying, "John, get out to the blacksmith's shop and do something.
There must be something you can find to do for yourself in the blacksmith's shop."
He says, "Woman, there havna been a horse come near the blacksmith's shop for days."
"Well," she says, "do something.
Get out of my sight." [laughter]

So old John walks up to the blacksmith's shop,
 and he kindles up the blacksmith's fire,
  does little jobs around,
   tidies up round the smiddy.
And then a knock comes to the smiddy door,
because he'd closed the door with the wind.
And he goes to the door,
and there stands a young man
 dressed in green,
  with a young lady on his back.
He said, "Are you the blacksmith?"
And he said, "Yes, I am the blacksmith."
He said, "What can I do for you?"
"Well," he says, "look, blacksmith," he said.
"I'll pay you if you let me use your smiddy fire for a few moments."
And old John says, "Well, I'm not very busy," he said.
"Come on in."
And he brought the young woman in,
and he placed her on the anvil.

Now her head was back to front. [laughter]
And she was very still and quiet. [laughter]
She never moved, as if she was in some kind of a coma.

Now the young man says, "Look, blacksmith," he said.
"I'll tell you what I'm gonna do with you.
I'm gonna pay you."
"But," he says, "remember one thing.
Never you try and do what you see me or anyone else doing."
And the old smiddy man said,
"I hear you," he said.
"Well," he said, "just sit there quietly."
And he put his hand in his pocket,
and he gave the old blacksmith seven gold pieces.

And then the young boy blew up the smiddy fire til it was red hot.
He said to the old blacksmith,
"Can I borrow one of your knives you use for cutting the horses' hooves?"
The old blacksmith said, "There's plenty there and they are all sharp.
I've nothing else to do."

So the young man goes over and he cuts off the woman's head.
There was no blood from her neck or anything.
And then he puts her head in the fire.
And he puffs up
  and he blows
    and he blows
      and he blows,
'til he burned her head away until nothing but the bones was left.

And the old blacksmith,
  he's standing there,
    and he's watching this, [laughter]

And then he gathers the white, burnt bones, the young boy does,
  and he puts them on the anvil,
    and he beats them to a powder with a hammer.

And then he spits on them and he makes a paste,
  And he goes over to the girl who's lying there,
    And he puts it round her neck.

And then there is an amazing thing that happened.
All this blue smoke came up from the burning bones.

And ... when the smoke faded,
there stood the head of the most beautiful young woman you ever saw.
And her eyes opened,
and she smiled,
and she stood up,
and she put her arms round the young man.
And the young man turned to the blacksmith,
and he said, "Now, old man, remember, never try and do what you see me doing." And they walked away. [laughter]

The old blacksmith stood there in amazement, [loud laughter]
He had never seen anything like this in his life before, [laughter]

And then he heard a knock on the door.
And in comes his old, bended wife with a cup of tea.
She said, "Are you there, you lazy old bachel?
I've brought in your tea."
And *bachel* in Gaelic means *old man.*
He said, "Yes, I'm here."

And he thought to himself what a beautiful young woman had walked out the door.
And he takes a look at his old wife, [extended, loud laughter]
And he grabs her. [laughter]
She says, "Let me go, you old bachel."
But he held on to her.
He took her to the blacksmith's—, to the anvil,
and he cut off her head, [laughter]
And there her poor old body fell on the floor.
Blood all over the place.

He catched her head,
and he put it in the fire.
And he pumped up the fire,
and he burnt her head until it was white, nothing but the bone.
And then he done what the boy done:
gathered all the bones,
put them on the anvil,
tap, tap, til he made some dust.
And then he rubbed his hands in glee.

And he walked over to the old woman.
And he got all this dust,
and he spat on it and made a paste.
And he wrapped it round her neck.
But it fell off on the floor. [laughter]

He gathered it up again with some of the ashes from the floor,
and his fingers was shakin,
and he made another paste.
But still it fell off again.
There lay the old woman, no head.
"Oh, my God," he said.
"What have I done?"

So he quickly, he gathered the remains of the body of the old woman,
and he went to the bunker that held his coal.
And he buried her in the coal.
Covered her up,
  swept up the smiddy,
    locked the door,
      goes into his little house,
        takes a few possessions with him,
          locks the little house door,
            and off he goes.

He travels far and wide through the country.
His old wife, she's forgotten about.
And he travels for over a year doing little jobs around the country.
Til one day he was down and out and broke.
And he came to this large town.
And sitting by the roadside was an old man.

And he said to the old man,
"Have you a piece of tobacco you could spare me," said the old blacksmith,
"for my pipe?"
The old man said, "Yes," he said,
"I'll give you some tobacco for your pipe."
And he gave the old blacksmith a bit of tobacco.
And the old blacksmith [*sic*] said, "What do you do?"
He said, "I'm a blacksmith."

"Oh, well," he said, "you should find plenty of jobs in the town today
because there is a great fair and a great fete going on in town."
But he said, "sad, sad, it's oh, so sad," said the old man.
And the blacksmith said, "What's so sad about it?"
"Och," he said, "the poor girl.
The king's daughter," he said, "the princess,
she'll never make it this year.
Something terrible happened to her."
"And what happened to her?" said the old blacksmith.
"Oh, well," he said, "something queer."
He said, "She cannot walk.
And her head is back to front." [laughter]
"Oh, dear," said the old blacksmith, "that's terrible."
And in his mind,
he remembers back what happened with his own self.
"And," he said, "the king has offering a large reward
to anyone who can help her." [laughter]
Now the old blacksmith says to himself, he says,
"Maybe it didn't work the first time—
maybe the second time—." [words drowned in laughter]

So he makes his way into the town,
and he makes his way up to the palace.
He was soon stopped with the guards with their crossed spears, you see?
He said, "Where are you going?"
He said, "I want to see the king."
And he said, "What would an old man want to see the king for?"
He said, "What are you?
Are you a quack of some kind?
Or a magician who's come to help the king's daughter, the princess?"
"No," he said, "I'm better than that."
He said, "I'm a blacksmith.
And," he said, "I think I can help the king's daughter."

Soon word was passed and he was led before the king.
And the king said, to the old blacksmith, he said,
"You've come up to help my daughter.
Well," he said, "if you can help my daughter, I'll make it worthwhile for you.
You'll never need to be a blacksmith again.
But," he said, "if anything else happens," he said,

"you'll never live five minutes later."
He said to the king, he said, "Do you have a blacksmith's shop in the place."
The king said, "Yes, there is a blacksmith's shop," he says, "in the palace.
We need it," he said, "for shoeing the horses for the riders of the palace."
"Right," said the old blacksmith.
"Lead me to the blacksmith's shop."
"And," he says, "then bring down the princess."
See?

So.
The old blacksmith was led down to the beautiful blacksmith's shop,
and there was everything he needed.
He kindled up the blacksmith's fire as usual,
swept the anvil.
And then they came down carrying the princess.
Poor little princess lying still and quiet,
with her head back to front.
"Now," said the old blacksmith, he said,
"close the door and leave me in peace."
"How long will you need?" said the king.
"Oh," said the blacksmith, he said, "about ten, fifteen minutes.
Come back, and she'll be well."
This made the king very happy.

So they left the old blacksmith
with the princess lying there on the anvil.
He took off the princess's head with one of the knives, sharp knife,
and he put it in the fire as usual.
And he pumped it up.
And he blowed
    and he blowed
        and he blowed
until he burnt her head away to the white bone.
And then like what the boy done,
he put it on the anvil and he tapped, tap, tapped it again
and made some dust.
And then, he spat on the dust and made a paste.
And he went over to the princess' neck,
and he put it all round her neck,

and it fell off. [gentle laughter]
And he said, "I couldn't have done it right."
So he gathered it up from the floor again,
with some ashes mixed through it.
And he tried again.
It fell off.
Now the old blacksmith was in real trouble. [laughter]
The King was coming in another five minutes,
And he's really upset,
and he's shaking and he doesn't know what to do.
When slowly behind him, the door opened.
And then he got a skelp [loud slap noise] on the ear
that knocked him scattering across the blacksmith's shop.

And there stood the boy once more.
He said, "Didn't I tell you, old man, never to do what you saw me doing?
I WARNED you," he said.
"Now," he said, "SIT there and behave yourself.
"But," he says, "here, for the last time."
Seven gold pieces.

"Now," he said, "I'm going to save your life this time, but no more."
Quickly the boy gathered what was left of the remains of the dust.
And he just done that [holds hands out palm down] from the floor,
and it rose up to meet his hands.
And he put it on the anvil and he made a paste.
And he put it round the girl's neck.
And then the blue smoke began to come.
And then she took the form of a beautiful young woman.
The princess was as beautiful as ever before.
"Now, remember," said the boy.
"Never do what you see another person doing."

And they turned and walked through the door and was gone.
The old blacksmith sat there in a daze for a long, long time.
And then the door opened,
and he heard a voice saying, "Are you there, you old bachel?
I see a man coming down the road with a pair of horses,
and you've been sitting there asleep."

And the old blacksmith stood up.
And there was his old wife with a wee cup of tea.
She said, "John, here's tea for you."
And he was so happy,
he ran to her,
put his arms round her,
and kissed her for the first time in fifty years. [loud laughter]

She said, "Let me go, you old bachel," she said.
"You know I'm so weak I can hardly stand up for the want of food."
"And," she said, "there is not a penny in the house."
He said, "Not a penny in the house?"

She said, "Get the horses shod; we need some food.
We need some money."
And the old blacksmith put his hand in his pocket.
And he took out seven gold pieces.
And he gave them to the old woman.
He says, "Buy as much food as you like for that."
"And," he says, "I'll get you some more
when the man comes with the horses."
[laughter and applause]

PART II

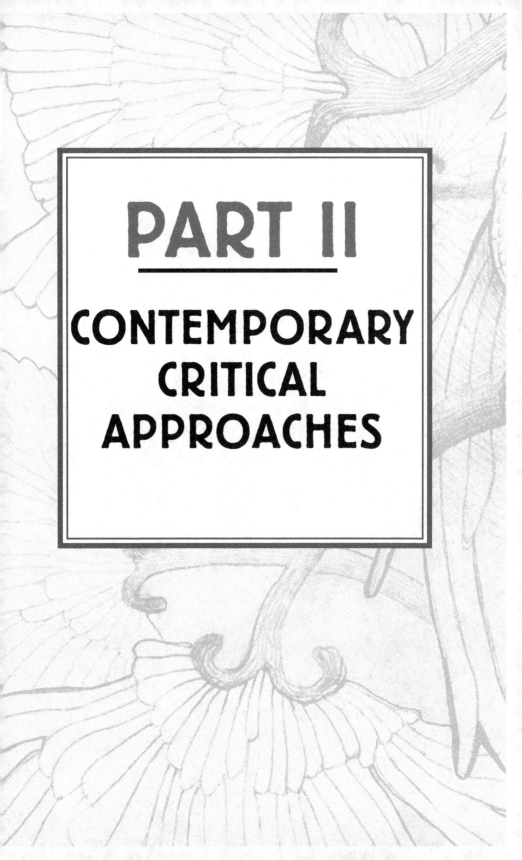

CONTEMPORARY CRITICAL APPROACHES

INTRODUCTION: HOW TO READ THE CRITICAL ESSAYS

Jennifer Schacker and Christine A. Jones

AN IMPORTANT GOAL OF THIS anthology as we articulated it in the Introduction to Part I is to make texts that feel familiar look strange to us. Fresh vision often promotes new insight and allows us to see things we may have missed before in our comfort. Similarly, this critical Introduction to Part II serves two purposes. The first follows convention: below we introduce the themes that guided the scholars in writing the essays and we summarize our vision of how each theme relates to fairy-tale studies. Second, and no less importantly, this introduction fills the pedagogical function of suggesting a way to approach critical essays as a savvy and concerned reader—the kind of interlocutor that the Grimms' Little Red Cap wishes she had been!

Why go the extra mile of discussing how to read criticism?

Part I and Part II have been paired together in this volume to illustrate the intimate relationship that stories and readers have developed through the mediation of scholarly study. The pioneers in the discipline have necessarily opened *and* delimited the fields of folk/fairy-tale studies. For example, sixteenth-, seventeenth-, and eighteenth-century print versions of stories appeared almost exclusively in anthologies or were inserted into novels, leaving modern researchers in the dark about which individual tales were most popular in their day. Often what makes a tale seem important today is not its early reception but how often it has been reproduced in nineteenth- and twentieth-century critical editions.

The genre of the critical essay has been no less important to the reception, transmission, and cultural vitality of tales than Disney. Bruno Bettelheim's mid-century psychoanalytic analysis of Little Red Riding Hood as a story of maturation and coming to sexuality is an excellent example of this influence. Insofar as we are taught to read by such theories, it becomes very difficult *not* to see these meanings in the color red. New theories bring new ways of seeing. With that in mind, we consider it just as important to disseminate current scholarship on the fairy tale as it is to make a wide range of stories available to readers.

In the essays that follow we have asked scholars from a range of fields, backgrounds, and disciplinary perspectives to address issues at the heart of debates in fairy-tale studies. As these scholars address issues of Genre, Ideology, Authorship, Reception, and Translation—key terms both in the field's past and its present—you will find that each addresses his or her topic from a unique perspective that is grounded in a discipline and also a personal intellectual vision. Our goal in providing multiple critical essays on each key issue is to offer our readers a sense not only of the diversity of perspectives characteristic of this field but also of the complexity of each of these ideas. As a result, no one essay stands as the definitive statement on the topic but rather as a contribution to dialogue—a dialogue that will ideally be perpetuated by the volume's readers.

Several schools of thought had a tremendous influence on the study of the fairy tale in the recent past; among them, psychology, feminism, and Marxist social history have had the greatest impact on popular ideas about the genre. Critics working in these areas brought new questions to bear on the fairy tale for the first time. Many current scholars are indebted to these movements and have developed fresh perspectives from that foundation. If we have not commissioned separate essays on the important issues of race, class, gender, and sexuality, it is because contemporary criticism is suffused with interest in all of these theoretical and thematic concerns. These schools of thought weave their way through each of the essays in this volume in new and often fascinating combination, and often scholars seek to move beyond them to imagine other paths of inquiry. In that sense, the shared intellectual history of our contributors provides and becomes evidence of a common thread among contemporary perspectives that are otherwise quite divergent.

The key terms that we present here are all thorny issues in fairy-tale studies—and more broadly in Folklore and literary studies. If scholars wrangle with them (and with each other over them), it is because they are at the core of how we understand our subject and our method of study. Below we explain some of the background that has made them particularly contentious and dynamic questions in fairy-tale studies.

Genre

Few types of writing feel as comfortable and obvious to us as what we call the "fairy tale." Perhaps because it appears so self-evident, the genre of fairy tale is the source of endless debate among scholars. When we teach a course on the subject, many of us will begin by debunking what we consider commonplace *mis*understandings of the genre. Students easily provide this list when asked what a fairy tale looks like: It is a story about fairies. It is a story with a universal moral. It is a story for children. One by one, we complicate these inherited notions in our classrooms. But if fairy tales are not what we think they are, what are they and how do we recognize them? That is the inexorable question that critics struggle to answer for themselves and for their fields.

This volume's essays reflect a relatively recent conception of the "fairy tale," one that is generally shared among scholars working today. Most of us think of the genre not as a blueprint for plot or a story that teaches common sense (and includes fairies!), but as a loose framework for the production and reception of inventive narratives across a variety of media, including oral performance, poems, and even theater scripts. If such a "definition" sounds dissatisfying, it may be because we have been lulled into believing that fairy tales are fantasies for children that were one day animated by Walt Disney. But when we concede—as the study of tale history across cultures strongly suggests we should—that "fairy tale" is a fluid, flexible, and changeable enterprise, the discussion gets a good bit fuzzier and, we think, more interesting.

It can be most productive, in fact, to think about the label "fairy tale" as an indicator of what people have considered "of a kind" rather than as an *a priori* category. An unusual and significant characteristic of tale history is that for hundreds of years the genre circulated without any set of fixed conventions: efforts to define it happened predominantly in the twentieth century. Even early discussions of genre, such as those that occurred in seventeenth-century France, indicate that authors played with audience expectations about narrative by being inventive with what we might call stylistic techniques. They did not, however, prescribe them as defining elements of the fairy tale. (It was instead their critics who began to make such prescriptions.) Indeed, instances of self-parody, metacommentary, grammatical flourish, and many other unexpected stylistics that we encounter in written and recorded tales upset modern notions of what a fairy tale was, is, and should be. Other strategies such as framing devices, claims to the truth value of a text, and other cues pointing to a writer's creativity (a moral written in poetic verse, a witty dedication to a patron or fellow writer) further highlight the narrative's constructedness. Authors often found opportunities for novelty, originality, and distinctiveness in precisely such maneuvers: while plots and motifs may recirculate and repeat, every telling configures them in a new way.

As you read the reflections on genre that follow, consider that the idea of fairy tale might be better understood as an open-ended, playful way of engaging social and political issues in a form that defies the constraints of realist fiction rather than as a *fixed* discursive form that corresponds to a set of narrative rules. If you do, you will see how complex and provocative the conversation can be.

Ideology

The common assumption that fairy tales are universal and timeless sends up red flags to anyone who is thinking critically about matters of "ideology." As the essays on this key word demonstrate, ideologies—understood as sets of values and beliefs that are generally taken for granted and assumed to be "natural" or commonsensical—get much of their power from their seeming invisibility. So what seems self-evident—including assumptions about what fairy tales are, what they do, where they come from, and what they mean—demands our attention as critical readers and should become the subject of inquiry and critique.

Recent critical work on the fairy tale has focused very productively on issues of ideology and has done so from several angles—including the study of ideologies conveyed or critiqued by specific texts, the ways in which ideology can shape reception (what we take from a tale and what we tend to overlook), and the ideological underpinnings of various chapters of the genre's history. For example, the study of the fairy tale in the nineteenth and early twentieth centuries, and in particular that of tales from oral traditions, was often carried out in ways that purported to be "scientific" and "objective"—in other words, ideologically neutral. Compilations done by the Brothers Grimm and those who sought to emulate and to amplify their field-based methods advocate documentation and preservation. In turn, work that drew on the immense archives of tales produced by these early folklorists tended to emphasize systematic classification and comparison. But behind all of those seemingly empirical practices are beliefs and values that had a shaping effect on every aspect of this work, the written records it produced, the theories it inspired, and so on.

We also have to account for the fact that the fairy tale flourishes in many distinct political contexts. For example, Antoine Galland introduced *Alf Layla wa Layla*—translated as *Les Mille et Une Nuits, Contes Arabes* (One Thousand and One Nights, Arabian Tales)—in the context of Louis XIV's absolutist monarchy, French trade and diplomatic missions in the Arab world, and the vogue for exoticism in courtly entertainment. Political ideologies are also vital to understanding the use of the fairy tale in Soviet Russia: tales from the nineteenth-century archive collected by

Aleksandr Afanas'ev and his followers were renounced in the 1930s, and a new set of tales was generated to create a new tradition for a society in the process of being remade and a history being refashioned.

In short, reading critically requires being attentive to *layers* of ideology, from marks of official state apparatus to an author's idiosyncratic biases, and also to our own presuppositions. Ideology can never be eradicated—there is no such thing as an ideologically neutral reading—but the essays on this key word help us to become aware of how ideology shapes texts and interpretations.

Authorship

The common presumption that fairy tales began as anonymously transmitted oral performances, the natural product of a collective (a culture), is misleading in its causality and simplistic in its view of the art of telling as a social practice. The anonymity of oral narrators is not a cultural reality—in fact, skilled storytellers often hold a kind of celebrity status in their communities—but is instead a by-product of cultural conditions in which a particular conception of "the author" (both as original and individual genius and as writer) was distinguished sharply from the masses or the folk. This distinction is used strategically by literary writers in the early history of the tale (Charles Perrault and Marie-Jeanne LHéritier, for example). With the publication of print texts that claimed to be representations of oral traditions, initiated by the Brothers Grimm in the early nineteenth century, the conception of orally told tales as collective and "anonymous" became a foundational paradigm of tale history, and this conception continues to shape many current assumptions about the genre. It has had the effect of downplaying (or even erasing) the creativity and individuality of oral narrators, thereby limiting our sense of "author" to figures who control print media.

This foundational paradigm can also have the effect of obscuring the usually complex history that brought a given "folk tale" into print form: by framing a text as anonymous, oral, or folk, readers are often *encouraged* to suspend their curiosity about the book's provenance (what exactly does this text represent, how did it come to be, whose interests does it serve?). Finally, the very tradition that rendered the folk "anonymous" also, somewhat paradoxically, can grant a tremendous amount of agency to the individual named person to whom a given collection or volume is attributed—whether as writer (Charles Perrault, for example) or as collector (such as Jacob and Wilhelm Grimm). Analogously, we are lulled by the big name author into forgetting about how a story finds its way into a printed book that then finds its way into our hands. (Some of these issues will come up in the essays on translation.)

Every text you encounter in this volume (indeed every text you encounter in print), whether it has come down to us as "collected" or "invented" or both, has been shaped by a set of hands that perform a function we associate with an "author"; that is, they borrow and invent ideas that they then shape into something that can be "published" as public performance or print matter. An "author" as we understand it here would more accurately be described as a network of players—from tellers, writers, and editors to publishers, critics, and even readers—who together create what we understand a tale to be. Each of the three essays in this section engages with some part of this complex legacy, addressing or challenging the ways in which we think about this figure.

Reception

Folklore and literary studies often focus on acts of production—making, telling, writing, publishing—but acts of reception can be just as complex and interesting to our understanding of tale history. In fact, reception in relation to the fairy tale might be said to incorporate ideas about all the other key words included here: genre, ideology, authorship, and translation.

One of the challenges for the study of reception has been the lack of readily available documentation or obvious evidence. How do we ascertain, or even make educated guesses, about the ways in which tales were and are understood by various audiences? In contemporary folklore study the focus has shifted away from decontextualized "texts" and artifacts towards the study of performance and process. This performance-oriented perspective has brought study of the dynamic relation between performer and audience to the fore, but while this has radically shifted the critical analysis of contemporary living traditions, how might one apply a performance studies approach to the past or to written traditions, when such matters were not documented in any kind of systematic way (if at all)?

For scholars working on specific print traditions, forms of paratextual material—including prefaces, editorial introductions, advertisements, and so on—are valuable sources of information about the social, economic, and ideological positioning of an implied readership. Research in this area can also focus on tales' material histories: the various forms in which they circulated in print and other media; the price, size, and format of a book; numbers of editions; the histories of distribution, translation, and pirating; and so on. On the other hand, and as the essays in this section will show, another approach to this conundrum is to focus on the ways in which all texts that have come down to us through history *imply* an audience.

When working with tale texts on their own in a volume such as this one, you can actually use your skills of textual analysis to think about reception, focusing on a given text's structure, logic, style, intertextual allusions, and so on. For instance, one might ask, what kind of reader is implied by references to culturally or historically specific details? What might one need to know to understand a text's humor? While this kind of analysis cannot generate conclusive evidence about how the text *was* read and who actually read it (some tales may have missed the mark, may be misconstrued, or may be understood differently than we assume), it nevertheless enables us to see that no fairy tale is produced or circulates in a void but always anticipates an audience.

Whether you are reading criticism or a fairy tale, reader-response theory (first developed in the 1960s) encourages you to be attentive to the fact that texts offer you particular subject positions from which to receive them: they invite you to share certain assumptions, beliefs, interests, and so on. When you accept that invitation, you have stepped into the readerly role implied by the text—but you always have the option of resistance. Either way, you have entered into a dynamic relationship with a text—and it is through this transaction that you make meaning.

Translation

Translation is ultimately about rewriting. On the one hand, every teller or writer engaging with this genre is acting (in some sense) as translator, drawing on and then reworking or extending prior texts or performances. On the other hand, every act of translation (in the more conventional sense) is also a creative act. A translator's words are the lens through which we see a foreign tale, which gives translators an extraordinarily prominent role in the transmission and reception of stories across the world. Recent scholarship in the discipline of Comparative Literature has brought the ethics of linguistic translation to the fore by exploring it as a form of cultural comparison and encounter. Translators indeed forge connections across the seemingly unbridgeable impasse of language barrier. Some critics have argued that to understand these connections, we must understand better the crucial position of the translator, who stands between one language and another. And they understand this practitioner not as a vehicle for meaning or as a master imitator but instead as a writer reaching back to one culture's experience of language and towards another, a writer who faces all the conflict, trauma, and euphoria of discovery in each direction. From this perspective, the act of translation includes both loss and (re)creation: as the translator works, one version of the story begins to disappear, but the other does not yet exist. This suggests that the translator does not carry a story to us in any kind of straightforward way; he or she necessarily stands in the way of our relationship to that "original" story. Nevertheless, translators are often invisible players in the histories of the fairy tale.

This novel way of viewing the translator's agency implies a set of questions for critical study. One way of incorporating this vision when you read the stories in this volume is to put aside concerns about how "good" or "bad" or "accurate" the translation is (a highly subjective and contentious activity) and focus on it as a multicultural production: a tree with foreign roots that are not visible, except insofar as they inform the limbs and leaves you can see. Your job as readers discovering the tale in translation is not to worry about digging up the roots to see how they feed the tree branches (although some critics will work on that question) but rather to accept the story "Cinderella" by Charles Perrault with help from Christine Jones, for example, as a hybrid literary creation with a logic and a vocabulary of its own.

The essays on translation all address matters of linguistic translation, but they also situate their case studies in relation to translation theory and broader histories of the fairy tale as a border-crossing genre. To think critically about translation and/of the fairy tale, we need to expand our vision to include the translation—sometimes subtle, sometimes radical, but always substantive at the level of meaning—from one rendition to another, one cultural context to another, one historical context to another, one ideological framework to another.

By presenting three original critical essays on each of five key issues, we aim to offer an opportunity for dialogue and debate both on the page and, we hope, in the classrooms that use this text. The essays are deliberately very short—far more concise than traditional scholarly articles. Our intention was to raise many issues within the constraints of an anthology. Each author makes a clear but complex and ideally provocative statement to encourage response. We invite our readers to be provoked and to think about the various perspectives, methodologies, preoccupations, and materials that each author draws upon to make his or her argument. What questions are raised by each piece? What evidence is offered? What is set aside? In other words, what concerns does this critic hope to encourage in us as readers of the fairy tale? We invite you further to discover the other work that each author has published to have a better sense of the voice behind the essay.

Alphabetical order serves as a neutral way to present these essays on each key word, but we hope that it will not determine the way a particular reader chooses to encounter them. Skip around, move back and forth among them, and especially reread the first ones once you have read others, as new ideas will surely emerge.

GENRE

ON FAIRY TALES AND THEIR ANTHOLOGIES

Christine A. Jones and Jennifer Schacker

THE QUESTION OF GENRE, CENTRAL to this volume, is a complicated matter indeed. Each person who picks up a volume of fairy tales does so with some preconceived ideas about what a "fairy tale" is. In our everyday lives, generic expectations, which generally remain unspoken, shape the ways in which we communicate: whether texting a good friend, looking at the phone bill, greeting a casual acquaintance on the street, hearing about a political scandal on the news, or reading a thing called a fairy tale. Each of these communicative forms, which we might call "genres," is associated with a certain set of interpretive conventions; for instance, one doesn't expect metaphors and symbols to be part of the phone bill, nor does one expect a full, verifiable, and accurate account of current world events in response to a casual salutation ("Hi.").

In fact, we are often only made aware of generic expectations when they are violated, when something occurs that feels out of place, unexpected, even bizarre. Some of the tales in this volume may strike you as odd or as (somehow) *not* fairy tales, given your inherited or learned sense of how a story called by that name should look. But they all are or were at one time considered part of an unruly herd of things collectively known in English as "fairy tales." The fact that they all look so different offers some indication of the remarkable malleability of this term—which comes from the French *contes de fées*, coined by Marie-Catherine d'Aulnoy in 1697—throughout its 300-year history.

One thing we can say about the word is that it now conjures the expectation of relatively brief self-contained stories, which we tend to approach as though they speak for themselves. This was not always the case, due at least in part to how fairy tales were published for centuries before editors took the habit (discussed below) of printing them individually or in small groupings with little or no introduction. Today this common editorial practice influences the way many of us first encounter fairy tales. And it has led to commonplace assumptions, such as the notions that they are timeless, universal, and carry a single meaning that can be summarized in a pithy sentence. One example of this phenomenon is the platitude that Perrault's Sleeping Beauty is "waiting for Mr. Right." Yet, while this tale of a slumbering princess appears to reinforce and even promote the idea that woman's role is to be passive, especially in courtship, reading Perrault's "Sleeping Beauty" for its complexity reveals that Perrault acknowledges but does not condemn the women of his day who *won't* wait endlessly for men to marry them (unless enchanted by a magical spell). The reader who approaches tales with a single-minded stereotype in mind is doomed to find just what she seeks—and to overlook the linguistic and thematic virtuosity in each version of the tale, that is, the particular transformational and marvelous dimensions of each text. Critical reading and attention to a story's complexity can actually *reverse* our conventional understanding of how morality is being portrayed in fairy tales.

The current volume emphasizes a radical reorientation of conventional approaches to the genre of the fairy tale and it can do that partially because it presents pedagogical devices that suggest a way for you to receive the stories. You're reading one of those devices right now, and as a critical reader it is good to have an awareness of the book's agenda and the techniques it uses to influence your reading practice. In fact, all "anthologies" or collections of tales engage in the practice of de- and re-contextualization, that is, reshaping the form, function, and meaning (the immediate reading context) of each tale found between its covers. And since anthologizing accounts for much of the tale's print history across cultures, we want to take a moment to discuss how print collections have shaped current preconceptions about "genre."

Until the eighteenth century, the "anthology," whose Greek roots refer to gathering flowers, was reserved for poetry (the flowers of the mind). When gathering together prose narrative, authors in antiquity cultivated a practice of "intercalating," or weaving tales into longer narratives whose characters then served as narrators of the tales. Apuleius's *The Golden Ass* is structured in this way—as a long continuous narrative that intercalates stories throughout (see "The Old Woman's Tale," p. 50). By the seventeenth century, Italian writers such as Straparola and Basile had reversed the balance of Apuleius's model and developed a technique called a "frame story." Frame stories present a logical premise for the tales they group together by inscribing multiple tellers as characters in a loose fictive storyline that begins, punctuates, and concludes the text. In this kind of volume, the tales "told" by characters from the frame story truly take center stage. Frame tales are narratives unto themselves but they also serve the important function of offering a pretext for their characters to *tell* stories. This technique followed from the narrative tradition of Boccaccio's *Decameron* (the title refers to a time span of ten days) and Marguerite de Navarre's *Heptameron* (seven days), both of whose frames are narratives of natural disaster that leave a group of people stranded somewhere they did not expect to be. In one the Black Death keeps people indoors, and in the other a flood blocks the path of pilgrims on their way to a holy site. In both cases, telling helps the victims of fate pass the time enjoyably.

The reliance on externally imposed logic tells us something about how the tale fits into predominant definitions of written literature before the eighteenth century. The presence of a pretext may suggest that tales could not stand alone in written form. The dominance of this model from antiquity onward further suggests that tales were perceived as narrative resources that could be adapted readily for particular social situations, were always in potential dialogue with other stories and experiences, and lent themselves to virtuosic flourishes. In other words, tales did not occur in isolation, but in the context of a shared experience and often in a performance mode where someone presented, others listened, and the storytelling event inspired conversation. Their print form reflects that cultural expectation.

At a key point in tales' European history, another way of presenting them emerged that became an equally compelling way of sharing such stories in print. French writers of the late seventeenth century began publishing their narratives—now known as "fairy tales"—without a fictive frame story tying them together. Henceforth, fairy tales could be published in bound volumes whose logic resided in an authorial persona (a different kind of interpretative strategy), not a frame story. The titles of these volumes highlight the multiplicity of stories between their covers: *Stories or Tales of Past Times* (Perrault, 1697), *Tales of the Fairies* (D'Aulnoy, 1698), *Ingenious Diversions* (Lhéritier, 1697). Several inferences can be drawn from the insistence on multiplicity and entertainment in these titles. On the one hand, if earlier tales found their way into print only by being subsumed into a larger rationale, from this period forward they could also appear on their own as individual pieces of short fiction.

On the other hand, simplification, both in the length of the narratives and in their entertainment value, is a literary strategy. Taken out of epic frames, fairy tales appear, in the words of the French writers, to be "trifles," nothing to get excited about—or be censured for!—because each one is just a little entertaining story. Identifying their literary production as "insignificant" strategically masks the fact that these writers were establishing very short prose as a legitimate literary form at a time when tragic drama and long romantic novels were the norm. Partially because French writers of the 1690s individualize tales in these crucial ways, they are sometimes known as the "inventors" of the modern literary fairy tale even though many, many stories were published before that time.

Partially in consequence of the "new" genre's popularity in Europe, the collection of self-contained, short fairy tales became the dominant format for publishing tales in France and beyond. Since we have inherited the expectation of this form as readers, we have to become aware of our preconceptions and cast them aside when working closely with texts that were once embedded in longer complicated narrative frames, since these frames impart shades of meaning to tales that are easily overlooked if they are read out of context. For example, the medieval *Alf Layla wa Layla* (*1001 Nights*) begins with the image of Shahrazad poised to tell each of the tales in the volume in an effort to save her life, and the lives of other women, and to dampen the misogynistic rage of a king (her new husband, Shahrayar). She works with her sister to achieve this goal, just as Shahrayar's murderous plan emerged through experiences shared with his brother. The themes of the frame story resonate in the tales that Shahrazad "tells": to read those tales in relation to the frame highlights their preoccupation with homosocial bonds, desire and sexual betrayal, revenge, suffering, and the transformational potential of storytelling.

While recovering the frame of *1001 Nights* can shift our perception of tales from that text, it is also a reminder that every tale collection offers a series of "frames" through which we experience the stories in them. Critical reading demands that we transfer the lesson of the *1001 Nights* frame even to volumes that look very different, such as authored collections and contemporary classroom anthologies. Perrault's *Stories or Tales of Times Past*, for example, contained a dedication/preface that illuminates his stories in interesting ways but is rarely reprinted in modern editions. Similarly, classroom anthologies such as the present one supply subtle frames that are powerful at shaping our perceptions of literary history. Let us look at one example of how this works: in the twentieth century, both fairy-tale scholarship and anthologies were dominated by the tales of seventeenth-century France and nineteenth-century Germany. We could argue that these anthologies, or more accurately their editors/publishers, *created* the academic fields of folk- and fairy-tale studies as we know them. The repertoire of fairy tales known by the general public and read in the typical university classroom is consequently quite narrow.[1] Although Disney films are often blamed for this narrowness, we might wonder what effect our anthologizing practices have always had on cultural media. Disney, too, drew on a limited

1 There are myriad issues surrounding what texts are anthologized, not the least of which are 1) marketability, 2) availability in translation, and 3) affordable copyright.

repertoire based on what writers and filmmakers of the early century had access to and what they knew.

Underpinning every collection of fairy tales—indeed, every expression of fairy-tale plot, whether it be an anthology or a Disney film—is a conception of the genre; although it is not always made explicit, an understanding of genre shapes the choice and organization of tale material presented. Attention to how anthologizing practices have drawn the maps of folk- and fairy-tale studies helps us recognize and take a modest stab at redrawing those borders. Based on our own research, study, and teaching, we have come to see the fairy tale as a messy genre that resists clear or facile definition (just as it does clear or facile interpretation). Our choices in this volume reflect that messiness, being eclectic and different from those of extant anthologies. Tested across a wide range of cultural production, theories of a development in the fairy tale over time from simple and formulaic to complex and satirical, for example, do not hold up. The strategies and characteristics associated with contemporary writers—those deemed modern or postmodern—can in fact be found throughout fairy-tale history, both in print and performance. Analogously, by consciously looking beyond Europe, we encounter traditions such as Mexican folklore in contemporary New Mexico and Japanese manga that reinvent the tradition in fascinating and sometimes surprising ways.

The fairy tale genre *for centuries* has been malleable and dynamic; it has provided an outlet for coded social commentary that is highly self-aware and even parodic. Narrators and storytellers have played strategically with style and have not shied away from the "darker" dimensions of human nature and experience. Anthologies are the primary vehicles through which stories find readers and until the tales of other times and cultures are anthologized, they simply won't enjoy the same level of attention as "Little Red Riding Hood" or "Snow White." New interpretive and editorial practices that rethink this history for the twenty-first century will help us rediscover the many facets of this marvelous genre.

Works Cited

Apuleius, Lucius. *The Golden Ass*. Ed. and trans. Jack Lindsay. Bloomington, IN: Indiana UP, 1960. [See "The Old Woman's Tale," included in this volume.]

Basile, Giambattista. *The Tale of Tales, or Entertainment for Little Ones*. Ed. and trans. Nancy Canepa. Detroit, MI: Wayne State UP, 2007. [See "The Cinderella Cat," "The Old Woman Who Was Skinned," "Cagliuso," and "Sun, Moon, and Talia," included in this volume.]

Boccaccio, Giovanni. *The Decameron*. 2nd ed. Ed. and trans. G.H. McWilliam. London: Penguin, 2003.

D'Aulnoy, Marie-Catherine. "The Fairies' Tales" [from *Les Contes des Fées*]. Trans. Christine A. Jones. In *Marvelous Transformations: An Anthology of Fairy Tales and Contemporary Critical Perspectives*, eds. Christine A. Jones and Jennifer Schacker, Peterborough, ON: Broadview P, 2012. [Included in this volume.]

Lhéritier de Villandon, Marie-Jeanne. "The Discreet Princess; or the Adventures of Finetta. A Novel" [from *Oeuvres meslées*]. In *Histories or Tales of Past Times*, trans. Robert Samber. London: J. Pote and R. Montagu, 1729: 137–214. [Included in this volume.]

Navarre, Marguerite de. *The Heptameron*. Ed. and trans. P.A. Chilton. London: Penguin, 2004.

Perrault, Charles. Select tales from *Histoires ou Contes du temps passé*. Trans. Christine A. Jones. In *Marvelous Transformations: An Anthology of Fairy Tales and Contemporary Critical Perspectives*, eds. Christine A. Jones and Jennifer Schacker, Peterborough, ON: Broadview P, 2012. [See "Blue Beard," "Cinderella, or the Little Glass Slipper," "The Little Red Riding Hood," and "Sleeping Beauty," included in this volume.]

Straparola, Giovan Francesco. Select tales from *Le Piacevoli notti*. Trans. Nancy Canepa. In *Marvelous Transformations: An Anthology of Fairy Tales and Contemporary Critical Perspectives*, eds. Christine A. Jones and Jennifer Schacker, Peterborough, ON: Broadview P, 2012. [See "Crazy Pietro," "Constantino Fortunato," and "King Pig," included in this volume.]

INTERTEXTUALITY

Gina M. Miele

INTERTEXTUALITY—THE LINK, EITHER DIRECT OR indirect, among texts—is inextricably linked to the notion of genre. The assignment of a given text to a genre connects it to other texts with similar form, content, or technique. When we read the generic framing device "once upon a time," we expect a specific narrative form and content common to fairy tales. In other words, strategic devices such as the English opening line remind us that fairy tales are in constant dialogue with other fairy tales. What may be less obvious to the modern reader is how much they also dialogue with other genres, even those as far afield as epic poetry. This case study takes up the stories of Italian author Luigi Capuana to show how much his vision of the fairy tale as a genre depends upon "intertextuality," that is, how it conceives itself in dialogue with many forms of story that precede and inform it.

Let us begin with a brief word about intertextuality. Coined by Julia Kristeva in 1966, the idea of "intertextuality" has its roots in twentieth-century linguistics, specifically in Swiss linguist Ferdinand de Saussure's semiotics and Russian literary theorist M.M. Bakhtin's dialogism, or the way language and literature are in continual dialogue with other texts. French theorist Roland Barthes later employed an intertextual theory to problematize the role the author plays in constructing meaning. According to Barthes, because each reader recognizes and interprets unique intertextual relations in a given literary work, and therefore creates a unique meaning for it based on his/her experience, its author does not exist as the absolute authority over the work. Instead, the author's "only power is to mix writings, to counter the ones with the others, in such a way as never to rest on any one of them" (Barthes 146).

If we approach intertextuality in this way, then we can see in oral folktales and literary fairy tales a most intertextual of fictional forms. The critic Jonathan Culler explains how the classic formulaic fairy-tale opening implies an intertextual context: "It relates the story to a series of other stories, identifies it with the conventions of a genre, asks us to take certain attitudes towards it.... The presuppositionless sentence is a powerful intertextual operator" (Culler 1392). Culler draws our attention to the fact that when we enter the realm of fairy tales, a set of readerly expectations is activated: we expect the requisite characters and plot elements that currently seem germane to the genre—talking animals, people with supernatural powers, magic, journeys to far-off lands, and battles between the forces of good and evil. In this sense, reading a single text catalyzes a network of experiences and influences drawn from both other fairy tales and examples of other genres.

The Italian author Luigi Capuana (1839–1915) drew on just such an intertextual network when composing his five collections of literary fairy tales (see "The Talking Tree" [p. 343] from Capuana's *C'era una volta ... fiabe* in this volume). Capuana frequently referenced the folk narratives published by fellow Sicilian Giuseppe Pitré (1841–1916), but he also drew on literary inscriptions of popular culture, ones that were granted a higher literary value in Italian culture than were print collections of oral narrative. Dante Alighieri, who found images for his epic poem *The Divine Comedy* in popular culture, thus became an important source for Capuana. For example, there are echoes of Dante in Capuana's "The Talking Tree," the story of a king who believes he has gathered at his palace all of the most precious things in the world. Learning from a stranger that he lacks the "talking tree," the king embarks on a successful journey to find it. The talking tree explains that she is the daughter of the King of Spain, now cursed by a malevolent witch to live as a tree. When the king reverses the witch's spell with a charm, the tree is transformed into a damsel so beautiful that the king can scarcely look at her. Although this could be read simply in terms of the common fairy-tale preoccupation with beauty, the scene is distinctly reminiscent of Dante's first vision of Beatrice in Paradise: she is so beautiful and full of heavenly light that he is nearly blinded. This intertextual resonance places Capuana's story into a productive tension with Dante's epic poem, one that he exploits throughout the tale.

An example of this extended allusion can be found in Capuana's use of the talking tree itself, which explicitly recalls in dialogue and description Dante's configuration of Hell in Canto XIII of "Inferno." The second sub-circle of the seventh circle is a dark knotted woods, an infernal forest whose trees are the souls of suicide victims imprisoned for eternity. Upon hearing one of the trees lament, Dante treats it with kindness, but his guide Virgil goes so far as to request the tree-soul's earthly name in the hope that Dante can redeem the sinner among the living (45, 52–55). The tone and action of the episode strongly evoke Christian spirituality. Drawing also from the use of this motif in popular tales (see Thompson's *Motif Index*, E631.04), Capuana secularizes "The Talking Tree," effacing the spiritual undertones from Dante's *Comedy*. Capuana's talking tree resides in "a valley where there was no living soul," where "a voice that seemed to cry" echoes through the barren space (see above, p. 343). And unlike the suicide victims in Dante's underworld who pay eternally for their sins against God, Capuana's imprisoned princess is punished for a ridiculous interdiction against a witch. While the tone of Capuana's tale is generally secular, upon hearing a voice emanate from a tree, the surprised king invokes the Lord and demands to know the soul's Christian name: "Who are you? If you are a baptized soul, respond, in the name of God!" (see above, p. 344).

In order to maintain the immediacy of language within dialogue characteristic of folk and fairy tales, Capuana tends to simplify the glorious rhetoric of the *Comedy* but often retains the wording of Dante's illustrious poem. When the king pulls two leaves off a branch, the talking tree cries out with the nearly identical words of the imprisoned suicide victim in "Inferno": "Ahhh! Why do you tear me?" (see above, p. 344). And in the passage cited above on the barren valley "where there was no living soul," but "a voice that seemed to cry" (see above, p. 343), both phrases pick up language from Dante. Early in Canto XIII, he describes the unusual aural character of the sub-circle: "From every side I heard the sound of cries, / but I could not see any source for them, / so that, in my bewilderment, I stopped. / I think that he was thinking that I thought / so many voices moaned among those trunks / from people who had been concealed from us" (22–27).

Beyond tropes and language, there are also plot elements in Capuana that appear to echo the *Comedy*. After meeting the evil witch, the king in Capuana's narrative gets lost in a great wood, where he encounters a blood-hungry ogre and his mastiffs (see above, p. 344). This could be an oblique reference to Dante, whose pilgrim finds himself in the dark of night, lost within a shadowed forest whose exit is blocked by three beasts: a leopard, a lion, and a she-wolf. Yet, a theme as broad as being lost in the forest occurs frequently in literature and popular culture alike (think Hansel and Gretel); as Culler's principle of intertextuality suggests, this should give us pause when attempting too strictly to find one-to-one correspondence between writers in traditions as supple as the fairy tale. More than likely, both Dante and Capuana borrowed from the fund of motifs and images common to both oral and written narratives.

As a final example of how freely traditions that we call "literature" and "popular culture" mingle through intertextual allusion, I will end on a tradition that may be more familiar to the reader: Charlotte Brontë's nineteenth-century novel *Jane Eyre*. At its core, *Jane Eyre* is a story of domestic enslavement and resistance. A young Jane is fascinated with fairy tales but also defies and revises typical fairy-tale plots. She resists the role of servitude found in Cinderella and the model of sacrifice in Beauty and the Beast. When she flees an unlawful marriage later in the novel, she disguises her identity and emerges triumphant, much like the fairy-tale heroine in Donkeyskin. The novel also contains an explicit reference to the Bluebeard tale when Jane, who is exploring the dark hall of Thornfield's third floor, states, "I lingered in the long passage to which this led ... with only one little window at the far end, and looking, with its two rows of small black doors all shut, like a corridor in some Bluebeard's castle" (Brontë 111). Brontë utilizes intertextuality here to create immediate suspense and mystery. Readers who recall Bluebeard's forbidden chamber populated by his murdered wives are intrigued by the suggestion that Rochester too has a dark secret. Indeed, as readers soon discover, Rochester's first wife, Bertha, is locked away from society in a hidden room on the third floor of Thornfield.

In the late twentieth and early twenty-first centuries, fairy tales continue to enjoy tremendous popularity in written and cinematic form. Feminist retellings of classic fairy tales such as Angela Carter's "The Bloody Chamber," a reworking of Perrault's "Bluebeard," were often meant to challenge or displace the patriarchal versions already in circulation. The popular film *Shrek* and its sequels *Shrek 2*, *Shrek the Third*, and *Shrek Forever After* all employ the fairy tale as an intertext. As Culler reminds us, these stories may achieve success precisely because many of us who grew up in North America were raised on a steady diet of classic tales. Fairy-tale intertext then elicits ready identification in us as readers and viewers—and invites us to interpret through our extensive network of references.

As you continue your voyage through the fairy-tale corpus and scholarship in this volume, you will join in the game of intertextuality, mining your knowledge to identify moments of overlap among fairy tales and between fairy tales and other genres. What this essay has endeavored to show, in fact, is that the fairy tale is not and never has been a single and bounded genre. Consider revisiting in this light such modern classics as L. Frank Baum's novel *The Wonderful Wizard of Oz* (1900), Walt Disney's film *Sleeping Beauty* (1959), or Roald Dahl's *Revolting Rhymes* (1987). All of them assume the reader's familiarity with, rescript, and cleverly build upon codes and discourses from print fairy tales—themselves a labyrinth of intertextual relations that presume other labyrinths—and so on and so on.

Works Cited

Alighieri, Dante. *The Divine Comedy*. Trans. Allen Mandelbaum. 3 vols. New York, NY: Bantam, 1982.

Barthes, Roland. *Image-Music-Text*. Trans. Stephen Heath. New York, NY: Hill and Wang, 1977.

Brontë, Charlotte. *Jane Eyre*. New York, NY: Carleton, 1864.

Capuana, Luigi. *Tutte le fiabe*. Ed. Maurizio Vitta. 2 vols. Milano: Mondadori, 1983.

Culler, Jonathan. "Presupposition and Intertextuality." *Modern Language Notes* 91.6 (1976): 1380–96.

FAIRY TALES AS METACOMMENTARY IN MANGA AND ANIME

Bill Ellis

When studying European fairy tales, Westerners are often limited by familiarity with the ways institutions have chosen to adapt and use them. So, one presumes that they are about females who are victimized by sly beasts or wicked stepmothers, and how they escape and find a handsome, high-status husband. Vladimir Propp's structural study of Russian fairy tales, in fact, presumes that a wedding and a throne are the logical goals of all such stories. In addition, it's taken for granted that such tales are intended for children, showing them how to find a heterosexual mate that will give them status and wealth. However, Jack Zipes notes that such assumptions are based on generations of institutional interference, in which the fairy tale's fluid and dynamic elements have been replaced by seemingly static texts that support the values of the cultural elite. In addition, tales that originally were told to adults as well as to children have become sanitized to the point that the advice they give is increasingly irrelevant for young people once they enter adolescence.

It is instructive to see how non-Western cultures have understood these same tales. In Japan, the flourishing narrative tradition of manga/anime[1] has become a major cultural phenomenon, appealing especially to adolescents and young adults. This new genre, as Dani Cavallaro observes, has a strong affinity with the fairy tale. Both genres, she proposes, are ways of opening the participants' minds to the unknown, to asking questions about the way things are, and to tolerating the absence of conclusive answers (21–22). In addition, Western fairy tales often play an explicit part in these narratives in a form that is less influenced by Western cultural norms. For this reason, elements that are intrinsic to the genre of the fairy tale become more visible when we see how Japanese authors read and reinterpret these narratives, not as all-too-familiar stories but as exotic and novel ways of reimagining universal human dilemmas.

Western fairy tales have been a familiar part of Japanese popular culture at least since 1960 when the Disney Studio mounted a huge promotional campaign to promote a Japanese-language version of the classic film *Sleeping Beauty*.[2] As Fredrik Schodt has

1 The two are quite different media: manga comprises graphic novels published in weekly magazines and collected in volumes of their own, while anime is a distinctive form of animated entertainment that may be broadcast on television, released as movies for theatrical screening, or published directly in DVD form. However, the two media are tightly interrelated in Japan, so that it is normal for a popular manga to be adapted at once in anime form and vice versa. In addition, many manga artists are also important artists in anime studios. For this reason I have discussed the two as one popular culture tradition in this short essay.

2 See Solomon. Walt Disney loaned a large amount of original animation art from *Sleeping Beauty* and other films, which was exhibited during the original run of the Japanese-dubbed version in major shopping centers and department stores. Disney then attempted to donate the art to the Japan Museum of Modern Art,

shown, the Disney animation style proved to be an important influence on the development of manga and anime, two important forms of Japanese popular culture that are increasingly popular in the rest of the world as well. Manga, a form of graphic novel, is based on a long tradition of using pictures and text to tell stories; in fact, the important Japanese folklorist Kunio Yanagita initiated a fieldwork project on traditional tales after finding in a used bookstore the Asian equivalent of a chapbook (an early form of cheap paperback) that presented ten folktales in graphic form (Mayer xx). Similarly, the first animated feature made for a Japanese audience was *Three Tales*, an anthology of children's stories broadcast on the Japanese NHK TV channel in January 1960. The manga and anime industries are now major media forces that have substantial audiences both among Japanese and North American children and youth.

These popular forms retain their roots in the traditional fairy tale, however, and it is common to find references to specific storylines and characters, as well as the use of motifs associated with familiar fantasy characters. More importantly, familiar Western fairy tales such as "Sleeping Beauty," "Cinderella," and "Little Red Riding Hood" are embedded in manga and anime plots self-reflexively, highlighting the ways in which these genres interpenetrate. In short, these uses of the fairy tale often function as a metacommentary on the larger plots in which they have been recast.

Western tales make appearances in manga and anime in a variety of ways. Sometimes these are relatively simple, as in a scene in which a mother reads a storybook to a child at bedtime (as in the anime *Sailor Moon*). In other cases, the entire plot of the narrative parallels that of a fairy tale, as in the feature animated film *A Tree of Palme* (2001), which (as the director admitted) was intended to suggest the story of *Pinocchio* in a dark dystopian alternative world. But more often the fairy tale is "quoted" inside the larger narrative, usually in the form of a "school play" that the protagonists are staging. This technique provides opportunities for complex metacommentary, in which the familiar but exotic story of the fairy tale provides ways of seeing the larger plot of the series in which it's embedded.

The foundation of the now vast Japanese anime industry was developed in the 1970s through adaptations of Western children's classics such as *The Tales of Hans Christian Andersen* (Mushi Productions, 1971) and the very successful *Heidi, Girl of the Alps* (Zuiyo Enterprises, 1974). The second of these was successfully marketed to a wide international audience and rendered into many European languages, making a surprisingly large profit. This success led to development of a long-running *World Masterpiece Theatre* project, in which anime series were created from a wide variety

---

which decided that the material was not relevant to its mission. Passed on to a technical school with a program in graphic design, the art languished in a janitor's closet until being rediscovered in 2004 and returned to Disney's Animation Research Library for safekeeping.

of Western children's books, including *Anne of Green Gables* (1979), *Tom Sawyer* (1980), and *Maeterlinck's Blue Bird* (1980).[1]

As part of this project, Nippon Animation produced a series of 41 adaptations of European fairy tales titled *Grimm Masterpiece Theater* (1987–88).[2] The series included fresh versions of three tales already familiar from the Disney movies—"Snow White," "Cinderella," and "Sleeping Beauty"—along with many others including "Little Red Riding Hood," "Rapunzel," and "Allerleirauh." This anime made many Western fairy-tale plots familiar to young Japanese audiences. But these adaptations were not simple imitations of the Disney approach: they were creatively interpreted with a middle- and high-school audience in mind. They are often darker and retain more of the sexual tensions of early print and many oral tales (such as the father's incestuous longing for his daughter in "Allerleirauh") than do contemporary Western adaptations intended for younger audiences. Susan Napier has proposed that one important function of anime is to find symbolic ways for children and young adults to understand the disorienting process through which their minds and bodies are transformed into sexual beings. Several Western commentators, notably Bruno Bettelheim, have insisted the same about the fairy-tale genre more generally,[3] despite popular assumption about the genre's inherent "innocence." The ability of fairy tales to embody such psychosexual tensions makes it useful in both anime and manga to provide metacommentary, focusing the reader's attention on issues raised in the context of complex story lines that deal directly with sexual awakening.

An important form of metacommentary is *mirroring* the fairy-tale situation. When they stage a fairy-tale play, characters in the larger plot are given roles in the performance that reflect situations in the broader trajectory of the manga/anime. For instance, in *Cardcaptor Sakura*,[4] the school decides to put on a play based on "Sleeping Beauty." In the larger plot, the female and male protagonists are playing out a courtship of their own; it seems logical that they are cast respectively as the

1 These proved hugely popular in French and Italian adaptations and have also been distributed in Spanish versions for European and Latin American audiences. Relatively few of these, surprisingly, were marketed in the United Kingdom or North America, though English versions were produced for audiences in India and the Philippines.

2 Rights to this series were acquired by Saban International, who produced an English-language version that was on the North American cable channel Nickelodeon during the late 1980s and early 1990s as *Grimm's Fairy Tale Classics*.

3 For an overview of the psychoanalytic approach to fairy tales, see Dundes and Jorgensen.

4 *Cardcaptor Sakura* was first published as a manga (1996–2000) and then adapted to anime form (1998–2001). As Nanase Ohkawa supervised the scripts for both versions, the "Sleeping Beauty" episode is very similar in both versions. In the manga it appears in Volume 5 (48–137), while in the anime it occupies Episodes 41–42. There are differences in details, but the discussion here deals only with the story line that is identical in both.

Princess who falls into the magical sleep and the Prince who awakens her. In the anime *Kamikaze Kaitou Jeanne*,[1] it is the choice of fairy-tale plot that is important. This is a magical girl series in which the high-school heroine Maron is secretly the master thief Jeanne who steals valuable objects that expose their owners to demonic possession. The plot is filled with elaborate disguises and ruses, so it is not surprising that the puppet show that the characters choose to perform in their school is "Little Red Riding Hood"—a story that centers on masquerade and impersonation.

On another level, metacommentary is used to subvert generic expectations through role switching. While the general situation of the fairy tale is quite similar to the new context in the manga/anime, the characters rarely remain within the gender and social roles in which they seem to have been cast. Hence the "Sleeping Beauty" performance in *Cardcaptor Sakura* becomes more complex when the male protagonist has to play the Princess and his female counterpart becomes the Prince who comes to administer the awakening kiss. In *Kamikaze Kaitou Jeanne*, the production of "Little Red Riding Hood" is highjacked by Maron's rival for the affections of the handsome new boy who has transferred to the school. She insists on playing the part of Red Riding Hood, relegating Maron to the bit part of the Grandmother who gets eaten, while the hunk is cast as the play-director-star's savior.

Another twist in the use of the fairy tale comes when the plot is rescripted, often by the participants in a performance. As a narrator reads a standard version of "Sleeping Beauty" in *Cardcaptor Sakura*, and the characters perform the actions on stage, the male protagonist—now playing the princess—is anxious to show that he is by no means effeminate and delivers every line in a forceful "manly" way. His part concludes when he portrays the princess accidentally pricking her finger on the spindle, but he does so deliberately, actually wounding himself on stage to show that he has no fear of pain. It is the puppet master (Maron's rival) in *Kamikaze Kaitou Jeanne* who radically changes the plot. Casting herself as Red Riding Hood, she rescripts the story to have the title character fall into a deep sleep from which she must be awakened with a kiss from the hunter who saves her (played by the boy she desires). These adolescent characters clearly possess a repertoire of fairy-tale plots and generic expectations. Objecting to this reworking of Red Riding Hood, the jealous protagonist Maron/Jeanne exclaims: "You stole that from 'Snow White'!"[2]

---

1 *Kamikaze Kaitou Jeanne* means roughly, "Jeanne, the Phantom Thief," though "kamikaze" also implies "lightning quick" and "sent by Heaven" as well. It was first published as a manga (1998–2000) and produced at nearly the same time in anime form (1999–2000). As the manga artist, Arina Tanemura, and the script supervisor for the anime, Sukehiro Tomita, were producing episodes simultaneously, the two stories parallel each other but differ considerably in detail. This adventure appears only in the anime (Episode 16: "A First Kiss Illuminated by Moonlight"), though it incorporates details from a similar situation in the manga (Vol. 1, Ch. 4, 166–67), which does not include the fairy tale.

2 Kissing in public is considered more transgressive in Japanese culture, particularly in the presence of young children. So it is significant that in the anime versions of three famous Western fairy tales in which the "kiss

Finally, the tale performance never goes quite as planned but is always interrupted, sometimes more than once. This moment of frame-breaking represents the ultimate metacommentary in which actions that occur "onstage" (that is, within the fairy-tale frame) become, for a time, identical with the events in the larger frame of the main plot. Like fairy tales, the main plots of each of these manga and anime examples combine magical elements with the mundane. In fact, the turning point for a protagonist's development is sometimes located in frame-breaking moments in a fairy-tale performance that have consequences in the larger plot. In the middle of the "Sleeping Beauty" performance in *Cardcaptor Sakura*, for instance, the protagonist has to confront and overcome a frightening magical entity called "The Dark," and the words she speaks at the crucial moment become a magical mantra that she repeats at each successive crisis in the manga plot.

In *Kamikaze Kaitou Jeanne*, an undisciplined child interrupts the puppet show and the longed-for magical kiss from the hunter is left undelivered in the play and will be redirected towards the end of the anime episode. This mishap in Little Red Riding Hood alerts our heroine Maron/Jeanne to a demon that has taken over the child's mother (much as the evil wolf impersonates the kindly grandmother). That night Maron (like Red Riding Hood) visits the possessed mother and carelessly falls into a trap. A rival masked thief (actually the hunk in disguise) saves her and helps her fulfill her mission. Not wishing to remain in her rival's debt, Jeanne asks his price which he exacts with a kiss. The moment is a turning point in the larger narrative arc, awakening Jeanne's sleeping sexual nature.

Hence the fairy tale functions in larger manga/anime plots as a concentrated expression of social and sexual tensions, which serves to advance the plot of the larger narrative trajectory in especially interesting ways. They are not simply markers of how successful Disney and other popularizers have been in exporting Western cultural material. Rather, they are opportunities for artists well aware of their psychosexual content to use them to symbolize and focus intense social issues present in the larger narrative arcs of their own works. In the way that they help manga and anime artists advance their stories, they can show, in a new context, many of the ways in which these stories are successful, not in giving pat social lessons, but in capturing the dilemmas of young people in the immediate post-puberty period. And in the implied metacommentary that narrative strategies such as mirroring, role-switching, rescripting, and frame-breaking provide, they can help us understand that fairy tales—which are sometimes assumed to have singular stable meanings—can be reread, rescripted, and rethought in unexpected ways.

---

of true love" saves the day—"Snow White," "Sleeping Beauty," and "The Frog Prince"—some accident occurs just before the kiss is performed, and the happy ending takes place through some other means.

Works Cited

Bettelheim, Bruno. *The Uses of Enchantment: The Meaning and Importance of Fairy Tales.* New York, NY: Alfred A. Knopf, 1976.

Cavallaro, Dani. *The Fairy Tale and Anime: Traditional Themes, Images and Symbols at Play on Screen.* Jefferson, NC: McFarland, 2011.

Dundes, Alan. "The Psychoanalytic Study of the Grimms' Tales: 'The Maiden Without Hands' (AT 706)." In *Folklore Matters,* ed. Alan Dundes. Knoxville, TN: U of Tennessee P, 1993. 112–50.

Ellis, Bill. "Sleeping Beauty Awakens Herself: Folklore and Gender Inversion in *Cardcaptor Sakura.*" In *The Japanification of Children's Popular Culture: From Godzilla to Spirited Away,* ed. Mark I. West. Lanham, MD: Scarecrow P, 2008. 249–66.

Jorgensen, Jeana. "Psychological Approaches." In *The Greenwood Encyclopedia of Folktales and Fairy Tales,* ed. Donald Haase. Westport, CT: Greenwood P, 2008. 778–82.

Mayer, Fanny Hagin, trans. and ed. *The Yanagita Kunio Guide to the Japanese Folk Tale.* Bloomington, IN: Indiana UP, 1986.

Napier, Susan J. *Anime from Akira to Howl's Moving Castle: Experiencing Contemporary Japanese Animation.* New York, NY: Palgrave, 2000.

Propp, Vladimir. *Morphology of the Folktale.* [1928] Trans. Laurence Scott. Ed. Louis Wagner and Alan Dundes. 2nd rev. ed. Austin, TX: U of Texas P, 1968.

Schodt, Fredrik L. *Dreamland Japan: Writings on Modern Manga.* Berkeley, CA: Stone Bridge P, 1996.

Solomon, Charles. "Animated Repatriation: Disney Art Returns." *The New York Times,* 18 March 2008. Available at http://www.nytimes.com/2008/03/18/arts/design/18anim.html, accessed 22 July 2011.

Zipes, Jack. "The Evolution and Dissemination of the Classical Fairy Tale." In his *Why Fairy Tales Stick: The Evolution and Relevance of a Genre.* New York, NY: Routledge, 2006. 41–89.

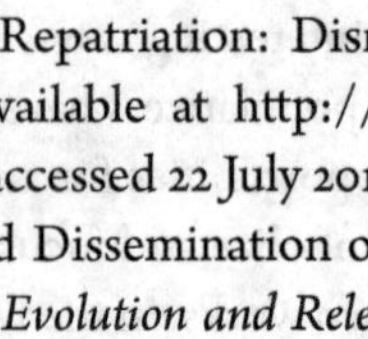

IDEOLOGY

FAIRY TALES AND THE IDEOLOGY OF GENDER

Cristina Bacchilega

ARE FAIRY TALES SEXIST? NORTH-AMERICAN feminists in the 1970s fought over this question, some saying yes, they perpetuate the gendered stereotype of the passive, helpless, and desirable young woman of the Sleeping Beauty or Snow White type; others, no, they represent active, resourceful, and brave heroines, such as Molly Whuppie or Kate Crackernuts, who save the day. This debate was primarily concerned with the role of fairy tales in the education of children, the subject formation of girls in particular. Whether blaming or praising the tales' powers of acculturation, scholars on both sides of the debate focused on representation—what do female characters do, say, and look like in fairy tales? The common assumption was that the most popular fairy-tale images had succeeded in their interpellation of "girls" as "princesses." But the power of ideology is hardly that straightforward or absolute. What girls and women *do* with fairy tales far exceeds consuming them passively, or being consumed by them (see Haase, *Fairy Tales*; Hearne; Rowe; Stone; Warner). And, while fairy tales are marketed more for girls than boys, their ideological impact is far more pervasive and complex, for, as writer Neil Gaiman reminds us, "the road between dreams and reality is one that must be negotiated, not walked" (61). In thinking about gender, ideology, and genre, scholars of fairy-tale studies in the late twentieth and early twenty-first centuries have thus tended to resist the yes or no alternatives of the 1970s debate and taken a multi-perspectival approach.

"Fairy tales are ideologically variable desire machines," I wrote a few years ago (Bacchilega 7); and I stand by this statement. The more we know about cross-cultural and localized histories of the fairy tale, the more we become aware of how over the centuries fairy tales have circulated in multiple versions and media, have functioned to varying performative effects in different contexts, and continue to exercise their powers, with emphasis on the plural. Enlisting these powers, storytellers and institutions alike are constantly adapting fairy tales to different situations and purposes, so that in fairy-tale production and reception there is no one "text" or "message." In Jeanne-Marie Leprince de Beaumont's classic eighteenth-century version of "Beauty and the Beast," the reassuring transformation of Beast was one of several, varied fairy-tale responses to the challenges of arranged marriages. In Angela Carter's 1979 adaptation, "The Tiger's Bride" (in *The Bloody Chamber*), the heroine's protest to being traded as a commodity brings about *her* metamorphosis into a different species. In "The Tale of the Rose" by Emma Donoghue (included in her 1997 collection *Kissing the Witch*), amorous Beauty discovers a woman behind the Beast's mask. And the 2001 animated film *Shrek* comments humorously on the value of "inner beauty" when both the ogre Shrek and his ogre princess reject any cosmetic transformation. Each retelling—including orally transmitted tales, literary narratives shaped by an author-narrator, and literary as well as popular culture adaptations across media—twists the fairy-tale metaphor and plot in ways that stage *located* possibilities for imaginatively negotiating with social scripts, desire, and otherness.

But which scripts and desires, both social and narrative, are most commonly associated with the fairy tale? Recognizing a genre's ideological variability does not exonerate us from reflecting on its hegemonic uses, such as today's image of the fairy tale and its gendered scripts in the culture industry. No doubt, in contemporary popular perception, the signature mark of the fairy-tale genre is the "happily ever after" ending. Getting there, to the HEA as we tag it in my classes, involves magic; and ritually marking the HEA are the wedding and the beautiful bride. This fairy-tale alliance of fantasy and romance "sells." It is no accident that the trope of fairy-tale magic is often utilized in advertising (Dégh; Jorgensen), or that the Disney Company has made a thriving business of "fairy-tale weddings." Fairy-tale magic sells as wish fulfillment, the regulated pathways of which are made to appear natural.

What is at work to sustain such magic? While for some the fairy tale functions as a form of escape from reality, others see it as a form of enchantment that epitomizes, to borrow from Slavoj Žižek, some of the fantasies that are at work in producing our shared sense of reality. Fairy tales are fictional narratives whose storyworlds unabashedly lack realism; and yet the most popular, endlessly reinforced view of the fairy tale is that it grounds itself in things as they ought to be or "truly" are, representing a world in which what the hero or heroine attains in the end is not only possible but good and natural. It is no accident that in Walt Disney's 1937 film, Snow White received "magic" help from birds and bunnies even to accomplish her domestic tasks. To suspend disbelief is to accept that it is "natural" for the queen to persecute Snow White, just as it is for everyone else she encounters in the forest to help her because, like the magic mirror, they conflate her outer beauty with her pure nature and natural purity. It's as if the fairy tale were holding a magic mirror to the world.

This magic, then, as Stuart Hall points out of ideology more generally, is the product of rhetorical and symbolic coding. From talking mirrors and impersonal or voice-over narration to the externalization of characters' inner traits and their reflection in nature, the symbols and rhetoric of reflection or mimesis sustain the artful magic and romance of fairy tales. Also playing a crucial role in the production of fairy-tale magic is framing, as both enclosure and exclusion. For instance, the pop-up fairy-tale books and voice-over narration that consistently open Disney movies from *Snow White and the Seven Dwarves* to *Enchanted* (2007) do the work of enlisting the authority of older technologies to enhance the screen's magic (Haase, "Hypertextual"); this connection also frames these earlier fairy-tale traditions as having one voice, that of print fairy tales for children only. To denaturalize hegemonic uses of fairy-tale magic involves questioning the work of the magic mirror, interrogating the mirror not for what it reveals, but what it frames, reproduces, enshrines, glamorizes, vilifies, obfuscates, and leaves out.

In scholarship, a powerfully anti-hegemonic strategy has been to expose how narrowly, in popular and mass media, fairy-tale traditions are framed when they are labeled as narratives for children that we associate with Disney's magic screen and with authors or "author-narrators" such as Charles Perrault, the Brothers Grimm, perhaps Andrew Lang and Hans Christian Andersen (Zipes). It is on *these* tales in print that the hegemonic image of fairy tales I sketched above was built; and even within the Perrault and Grimm collections, only a few tales were selected and endlessly serialized and adapted to support that image. These tales' "compact" form (Harries) has become exemplary of the genre to the exclusion or marginalization—until fairly recently even in the scholarly arena—of "complex" fairy-tale narratives by French aristocratic women in the late seventeenth to early eighteenth centuries, as well as of fairy-tale cycles such as the *Arabian Nights* or Basile's *Lo cunto de li cunti*. Embedded in a larger fiction or linked together as in a chain, these tales are explicitly framed within storytelling situations, where narrators have fictive bodies, histories, motives, philosophies—and are in conversation with one another or with their listeners. This kind of narrative framing encourages us to read the tales not as universal truths, but as performances; as "instructions" that, as Gaiman's homonymous poem (see "Instructions" in this text, p. 405) tells us, are of variable use but kindle a sense of opportunity; and as a mapping out of varied possibilities, arguments, and perspectives. These textual representations of fairy tales in action are a reminder of how the social life of stories involves so much more struggle and wonder than HEA magic would lead us to believe.

Even when one version or understanding of the fairy tale prevails in people's consciousness, in order to make their magic "work" in practice, tellers, writers, and producers of fairy tales necessarily engage in intertextual conversation and/or struggle with one another. This conversation has been especially self-conscious in so-called postmodern literature, where writers such as Angela Carter in *The Bloody Chamber* (1979) and Robert Coover from *Pricksongs & Descants* (1969) to *Stepmother* (2004) have engaged fairy tales metanarratively, playing with their topoi (symbols, plots, stock characters) and taking readers on complex journeys of re-orientation for individual stories and the genre itself. If sex and violence—in their sanctioned and unsanctioned scripts—are at the core of fairy tales (Tatar), Carter's and Coover's fictions for adults confront us with what the HEA-sanitized fairy tale for children leaves out as well as with what it habituated us to. In different ways and from different perspectives, Coover and Carter both provide devastating critiques of the "innocent persecuted heroine" plot *and* reactivate desires that mainstream fairy tales had witchified.

Commenting critically on a related violence, the regulatory power of hetero-normativity in fairy tales (Orme), Emma Donoghue has written fairy tales for young adults where sex is, just as in "classic" fairy tales, powerfully only a matter of indirection. There is no magic mirror in Emma Donoghue's adaptation of "Snow White"; rather, when two young women—the king's daughter and her new stepmother—look at each other in "The Story of the Apple," one of them notices that their "eyes were like mirrors set opposite each other, making a corridor of reflections, infinitely hollow" (47). In these mirrors, their faces are neither comparable nor the outer image of their nature. There is no poisoned apple, only the first-person narrator's story of her *misrecognition* of the apple and of her relationship with her stepmother. Her learning to decode the script that her own story enacts turns her refusal to compete with the other woman into the beginning of a different story, the sketching of a different storyworld. Here we come to the other side of Žižek's proposition of how fantasy is at work in the production of reality, in Judith Butler's claim that the critical promise of fantasy "is to challenge the contingent limits of what will/will not be called reality" (29).

But parodic self-consciousness of fairy tales is hardly limited to experimental literature these days, when twists on the fairy tale animate a wide range of cultural practices in various media, from DreamWork's *Shrek* films and Guillermo del Toro's *Pan's Labyrinth* to YouTube music videos and electronic hypertexts. The electronic accessibility of a wide range of fairy tales, the impact of feminist and other social critiques on children's literature and education, and the greater possibilities for any reader to generate new media adaptations—together these contemporary dynamics mean that the canonized Perrault-Grimms-Disney triad is no longer *the* central pre-text for the fairy tale. Like Donoghue's 13 first-person women narrators, many today are learning to read the Grimms and other fairy tales in ideologically transgressive ways so as to tell their own stories, whether they are published or not.

If, in today's fairy-tale web, the interests of the entertainment industry and the dynamics of globalization in a "post-feminist" climate are put in competition with more multivocal and unpredictable uses of the genre, new questions concerning genre ideology and the ideologies informing our approaches confront scholars of fairy tales. Among them, how does making the fairy-tale genre or a specific fairy tale "do new things" relate to renewing its powers as fantasy? What is the ideological valence of parody? With which other popular genres and storyworlds are storytellers, in different media and with unequal resources, allying the fairy tale? Could film be "assuming the mantle of storyteller, inheritor of fairy tale" (Tiffin 212)? What justifies privileging literature in fairy-tale studies? Questions of gender representation or poetics have not been superseded, but go hand in hand with considerations of multiple power dynamics in our globalized consumer society and the role of agency in storytelling reception and production.

Works Cited

Bacchilega, Cristina. *Postmodern Fairy Tales: Gender and Narrative Strategies.* Philadelphia, PA: U of Pennsylvania P, 1997.

Butler, Judith. *Undoing Gender.* New York, NY: Routledge, 2004.

Carter, Angela. *The Bloody Chamber and Other Stories* [1979]. New York, NY: Penguin Books, 1993.

Coover, Robert. *Pricksongs & Descants: Fictions* [1969]. New York, NY: Grove P, 2000.

____. *Stepmother.* San Francisco, CA: McSweeney's Books, 2004.

Dégh, Linda. *American Folklore and the Mass Media.* Bloomington, IN: Indiana UP, 1994.

Donoghue, Emma. "The Tale of the Rose." In *Kissing the Witch: Old Tales in New Skins.* New York, NY: Harper Collins, 1997. 27–42.

Gaiman, Neil. "Four Poems." In *Brothers & Beasts: An Anthology of Men on Fairy Tales*, ed. Kate Bernheimer. Detroit, MI: Wayne State UP, 2007. 61–71.

Haase, Donald. "Hypertextual Gutenberg: The Textual and Hypertextual Life of Folktales and Fairy Tales in English-Language Popular Print Editions." *Fabula* 47.3–4 (2006): 222–30.

____, ed. *Fairy Tales and Feminism: New Approaches.* Detroit, MI: Wayne State UP, 2004.

Hall, Stuart. "The Rediscovery of 'Ideology': Return of the Repressed in Media

Studies." In *Culture, Society, and the Media*, ed. Michael Gurevitch, Tony Bennett, James Curran, and Janet Woollacott. London and New York, NY: Methuen, 1982. 56–90.

Harries, Elizabeth. *Twice Upon a Time: Women Writers and the History of the Fairy Tale*. Princeton, NJ: Princeton UP, 2001.

Hearne, Betsy. "Disney Revisited, Or, Jiminy Cricket, It's Musty Down There." [1997] Reprinted in *Folk & Fairy Tales*, ed. Martin Hallett and Barbara Karasek. 4th ed. Peterborough, ON: Broadview P, 2009. 386–93.

Jorgensen, Jeana. "A Wave of the Magic Wand: Fairy Godmothers in Contemporary American Media." *Marvels & Tales* 21.2 (2007): 216–27.

Orme, Jennifer. "Mouth to Mouth: Queer Desires in Emma Donoghue's *Kissing the Witch*." *Marvels & Tales* 24.1 (2010): 116–30.

Rowe, Karen E. "To Spin a Yarn: The Female Voice in Folklore and Fairy Tale." In *Fairy Tales and Society: Illusion, Allusion, and Paradigm*, ed. Ruth B. Bottigheimer. New Haven, CT: Yale UP, 1986. 53–74.

Stone, Kay. *Some Day Your Witch Will Come*. Detroit, MI: Wayne State UP, 2008.

Tatar, Maria. "Sex and Violence: The Hard Core of Fairy Tales." [1987] In *Classic Fairy Tales*, ed. Maria Tatar. New York, NY: Norton, 1999. 364–73.

Tiffin, Jessica. *Marvelous Geometry: Narrative and Metafiction in Modern Fairy Tale*. Detroit, MI: Wayne State UP, 2009.

Warner, Marina. *From the Beast to the Blonde: On Fairy Tales and Their Tellers*. London: Chatto & Windus, 1994.

Zipes, Jack. *Fairy Tales and the Art of Subversion*. New York, NY: Routledge, 2006.

Žižek, Slavoj. *The Sublime Object of Ideology*. New York, NY and London: Verso, 1989.

IDEOLOGY, STATECRAFT, AND SUBVERSION

Marina Balina

STORIES WRITTEN UNDER POWERFUL STATE regimes offer fascinating examples of the link between ideology and the fairy tale. Among the most vivid cases of states using fairy tales to political ends are fairy tales of the Soviet period in Russia and those written under the Nazi regime in Germany. In both cases, classical tales were transformed to incorporate politically expedient messages: Soviet tales painted utopian visions of the communist future, while Nazi writers carefully recast traditional German folktales to support an Aryan vision of national character and ethnicity. These notorious cases are related through direct influence, but they also model an explicitly ideological use of the fairy tale that others would follow—sometimes with very surprising results. To take one example of this trajectory, Weimar period writer Hermynia Zur Mühlen's *Fairy Tales for Workers' Children* (1921) provided equally important influence on new literature for children in Russia of the 1920s and 1930s and, once translated, served as inspiration for similar works by American leftist writers. Traditional fairy-tale features became widely employed in reaching out to various audiences to deliver political messages of various kinds.

Julia Mickenberg observes that because of their protean nature, "fairy tales [...] provided a model for how the content and meanings attached to familiar literary forms could be transformed to radical ends" (61). The preferred *modus operandi* of ideologically charged tales was the transfiguration of classical fairy-tale plots by which authors infused them with contemporary references and new, politically expedient meanings. Stories abound in the early part of the twentieth century, for example, in which Socialism provides the happy ending to the worker's narrative of struggle. In the fairy-tale novel *Hans Urian, The Story of a Trip Around the World* (1931) by German writer Lisa Tetzner, the traditional fairy-tale motif of the protagonist who leaves home in order to grow up and mature is converted into proof of hardship and exploitation of all working people all over the world to serve a Soviet cause. Reading about the adventures of the main protagonist in Germany, the United States, China, and Mongolia and comparing those countries with the happy paradise in Communist Russia, readers are reassured of the necessity of a worldwide revolution that will defeat injustice.

Although this example uses specific geographical locations, straying a bit from the "classical" formula, we can observe other cases where the storytellers forsake the coordinates of the world map to make their ideological point allegorically. In his "Adventures of the Little Onion" (1951) the Italian writer Gianni Rodari, whose story "Nino and Nina" appears in this volume (see p. 381), created a vision of a world full of injustice and oppression by placing it in the vegetable garden; his young readers follow the adventures of a little onion named Cipollino, a traditional fairy-tale simpleton and truth-seeker who hits the road to look for justice and liberation for his wrongly accused father. A successful revolt against exploitation by Senior Tomato and Prince Lemon, the "nobility" of the vegetable garden, concludes the fairy tale and brings to all oppressed characters their utopian dream of universal happiness.

The conventional transformation of a fairy-tale protagonist from "rags to riches" has likewise been given new ideological twists. In Lazar Lagin's 1938 fairy tale "The Old Genie Khottabych: A Story of Make-Believe," Khottabych—an old genie liberated from centuries of imprisonment in a bottle by a simple schoolboy named Vol'ka—has to learn that his ability as a magic helper (creating palaces and providing riches) are not needed in the new Soviet society, since the new socialist reality is much better than any fairy-tale utopia. Every magic trick the genie performs gets him and his master in trouble: his knowledge of past history is polluted by "imperialist" statements so Vol'ka fails his school test; Khottabych's lack of understanding of the rules of the soccer game leads to the defeat of his master's favorite team. The "happily-ever-after" status of the main protagonist is achieved only when he stops using magic and completely converts to the Soviet cause.

But the potential for fairy tales to take on various ideological guises does not only serve state regimes and was not new in the twentieth century. On the contrary, its protean nature has always allowed the fairy tale to become an outlet for narratives that have been *critical* of dominant ideologies or state order. In his study of subversion in fairy tales, Jack Zipes attests to this potential in the genre: "Such nineteenth-century writers as Charles Dickens, George MacDonald, John Ruskin, George Sand, Oscar Wilde, Andrew Lang, L. Frank Baum, and others, designated now as 'classical,' opposed the authoritarian tendencies of the civilization process and expanded horizons of the fairy-tale discourse for children. They prepared the way for utopian and subversive experiments, which altered the fairy-tale discourse at the beginning of the twentieth century" (171).

Mark Lipovetsky adds to this broad statement about the fairy tale's potential for subversion, noting that in the twentieth century a form of satirical fairy tale developed, "as perhaps the most consistent exploration of the questions illuminating the people's responsibility for totalitarian terror and moral corruption" (236). The anti-totalitarian fairy tales of the Soviet period provided harsh critique of the socialist order and serve as excellent illustrations of this use of the genre. The "liberating potential of the fantastic" (Zipes 178) was employed in the works of such diverse writers of the Soviet period as Yevgeny Zamyatin (*Fairy Tales for Grown-Up Children*, 1922), Evgeny Shvartz (*The Dragon*, 1943), and Grigory Gorin (*That Very Munchausen*, 1976). By playing with the generic structural devices and plot developments associated with the genre, these fairy tales reveal the dark secrets of the Soviet utopia. But written in conventional fairy-tale "coding," they survived the vigilance of Soviet censorship precisely. By carefully avoiding any temporal or local references to the Soviet regime, writers were protected by the magical worlds of their stories.

The transformative power of the fairy tale has always and will continue to create an outlet from oppression—though it be illusory and perhaps short-lived—for writers and readers alike.

Works Cited

Balina, Marina, "Sowjetische Magie: die subversive Macht des Maerchens." In *Filme der Kindheit/Kindheit im Film: Beispiele aus Skandinavien, Mittel- und Osteuropa*, ed. Christine Goelz, Karin Hoff, and Anja Tippner. Kulturwissenschaftliche Beitraege, Band 66. Frankfurt/Main: Peter Lang, 2010.

Gorin, Grigory. *That Very Munchausen* [1976]. Trans. Christopher Hunter and Larissa Rudova. In *Politicizing Magic: An Anthology of Russian and Soviet Fairy Tales*, eds. Marina Balina, Helena Goscilo, and Mark Lipovetsky. Evanston, IL: Northwestern UP, 2005. 381–416.

Lagin, Lazar. *The Old Genie Khottabych* [1938]. Adapted from a translation by Faina Solasko. In *Politicizing Magic: An Anthology of Russian and Soviet Fairy Tales*, eds. Marina Balina, Helena Goscilo, and Mark Lipovetsky. Evanston, IL: Northwestern UP, 2005.

Lipovetsky, Mark, "Fairy Tales in Critique of Soviet Culture." In *Politicizing Magic: An Anthology of Russian and Soviet Fairy Tales*, ed. Marina Balina, Helena Goscilo, and Mark Lipovetsky. Evanston, IL: Northwestern UP, 2005.

Mickenberg, Julia. *Learning from the Left: Children's Literature, the Cold War, and the Radical Politics in the United States*. New York, NY: Oxford UP, 2006.

Rodari, Gianni. *Il Romanzo di Cipollino*. Rome: Ed. di Cultura Sociale, 1951.

Shvartz, Evgeny. *The Dragon* [1943]. Trans. Elizabeth Reynolds Hapgood. New York, NY: Theatre Arts Books, 1963.

Tetzner, Lisa. *Hans Urian. Die Geschichte einer Weltreise*. Hannover, GE: 1931.

Zamyatin, Yevgeny. *Fairy Tales for Grown-Up Children* [1922]. Trans. Seth Graham. In *Politicizing Magic: An Anthology of Russian and Soviet Fairy Tales*, eds. Marina Balina, Helena Goscilo, and Mark Lipovetsky. Evanston, IL: Northwestern UP, 2005. 251–66.

Zipes, Jack. *Fairy Tales and the Art of Subversion: The Classical Genre for Children and the Process of Civilization*. New York, NY: Methuen, 1988.

Zur Mühlen, Hermynia. *Fairy Tales for Workers' Children* [1921]. Trans. Ida Dailes and Lydia Gibson. Chicago, IL: Daily Worker Pub. Co., 1925.

IDEOLOGY AND THE IMPORTANCE OF SOCIO-POLITICAL AND GENDER CONTEXTS

Anne E. Duggan

It is important to take into account the relationship between ideology and the fairy tale for several related reasons. First, the genre has been deemed innocent and childlike, universal and timeless, which effaces any notion that the genre has a history and can be used to communicate motivated notions of class, gender, and race. Second, precisely because the fairy tale is viewed as innocent and unmotivated, it has become, since the mid-eighteenth century, a genre believed perfectly suited for children, even in the case of tales expressly written for adults. Given the ubiquity of the fairy tale within the world of children's literature and film, and more generally within popular culture, it is essential that we look seriously into what we are feeding our children's as well as our own minds. Third, some of the early works that defined approaches to the folk and fairy tale, such as Vladimir Propp's *The Morphology of the Folktale* (1928) and the AT classification system established by Antti Aarne and Stith Thompson, first developed in 1910, also universalize the genre, "abstracting it from its context and positioning it within a scientifically inspired taxonomy" (Haase 27). Such abstract, allegedly ideologically neutral methodologies attempting to scientifically classify folk and fairy tales persist today, as Donald Haase has eloquently shown in his critique of Jonathan Gottschall's evolutionary approach to the genre, which views even tales translated by colonial powers as unmediated and unmotivated stories (see Haase).

Before examining the relation between the fairy tale and ideology, a few words need to be said about the term "ideology." For Louis Althusser, ideology has the function of reproducing the conditions of production that uphold a particular sociopolitical order (127). The reproduction of such conditions involves not only education (reproduction of skills necessary for production) and wages (financial support for the reproduction of labor) but also the reproduction of the class relations that underpin a particular sociopolitical order. Such relations are supported by ideological discourses and representations that serve to naturalize this order. Ideology, then, operates to shape individuals into subjects of a particular sociopolitical order, differentiating them in such a way as to reproduce that order in terms of its class structure. Teresa de Lauretis draws from Althusser's formulation of ideology to insist that gender is "an instance of ideology" (7) insofar as it maintains or contests roles between the sexes that uphold a particular sociopolitical order. Such a definition can be expanded to think about ideology with respect to race, ethnicity, and sexual orientation.

For his part, Fredric Jameson focuses on the aesthetic act as ideological, by which he means that it functions in such a way as to invent "imaginary or formal 'solutions' to unresolvable social contradictions" (79). He considers both the perspective of a ruling class ideology, which strives for the "*legitimation* of its own power position" through representations, and that of an oppositional ideology, which "seek[s] to contest and to undermine the dominant 'value system'" (84). Insisting on the importance of questions of power as they relate to ideology, Terry Eagleton also views ideology in terms of conflict, remarking, "To say that the statement is ideological is then to claim that it is powered by an ulterior motive bound up with the legitimation of certain interests in a power struggle" (16).

Keeping in mind these different notions of ideology, approaching a fairy tale from an ideological perspective means examining the ways in which a tale perpetuates or contests normative values constitutive of subjectivity and that uphold a specific sociopolitical and cultural order from the perspective of class, gender, race, ethnicity, and/or sexual orientation. It means looking at the ways in which a tale engages in and resolves power struggles among different groups, which often entails situating a tale within broader discourses about class, gender, race, etc. In short, it means looking at fairy tales as motivated, historically specific texts produced from a particular sociopolitical and cultural order.

For instance, fairy tales emphasizing female domesticity, such as those penned by Charles Perrault or the Brothers Grimm, tend to reassert women's domestic roles and submission to male authority to maintain a particular type of patriarchal order. The implicit or explicit engagement these writers take with respect to gender can be foregrounded by situating their texts in relation to contemporaneous treatises and other publications about women. Strong, independent, and cunning heroines provide quite another model of female subjectivity. In her study of Marie-Catherine d'Aulnoy's tale "Belle-Belle," Adrienne Zuerner focuses not only on d'Aulnoy's representation of a woman who saves a kingdom but also on how the *conteuse* constructs "an oppositional discourse" (207), contesting the court society of Louis XIV. With respect to the imaginary resolution of class conflict, Ruth B. Bottigheimer points to the emergence of rags-to-riches tales in Renaissance Venice, in which "magic mediates an escape from class-defined poverty by means of marriage to royalty" (286). Such tales could be read as contestatory, for they appear to challenge the class status quo by elevating the lower-class hero. However, they can also be read in terms of reinforcing the current sociopolitical order by allowing lower classes to imagine their fantastic social elevation, without putting into question the oppressive order that originally had them in rags.

Perhaps no scholar has done more to bring ideology to bear on the genre of the folk and fairy tale than Jack Zipes. Zipes's work focuses on how fairy tales ideologically shape subjectivity, and how they function as "social symbolical acts" that provide an imaginary resolution to sociopolitical conflict (*Breaking* 6). Together his studies trace the broad ideological shifts that occur within the history of the genre. Seventeenth- and eighteenth-century tales by French writers such as d'Aulnoy, Henriette-Julie de Murat, and Gabrielle-Suzanne Barbot de Villeneuve supported an aristocratic agenda, with tales, as Lewis Seifert has shown, that sought to recuperate a threatened aristocratic identity in the imaginary realm of fiction (see, for instance, Seifert 84–85). In the nineteenth century, Jacob and Wilhelm Grimm remolded "oral folk tales explicitly for a bourgeois socialization process," continued in the work of Hans Christian Andersen (Zipes, *Subversion* 81). Zipes has also looked at the ways in which, in the twentieth century, socialists and communists tried to formulate their own brand of fairy tales for children, while the Nazis, appropriating classic bourgeois tales in the tradition of the Grimms, carried out "a cleansing policy to recover the pure Aryan tradition of the folktale" (*Subversion* 142).

Whereas Zipes examines the ideology of fairy tales by focusing on the sociopolitical context in which they were produced, other scholars have challenged traditional approaches that ignore ideological aspects of tale, or present themselves as being ideologically neutral but in fact reveal themselves to be ideologically motivated. David Pace criticizes Propp's morphology, which looks at tales as if they were "Platonic forms" (249), "isolated from the society in which they are told" (250). Pace then proposes the work of Claude Lévi-Strauss, which provides scholars with a more dynamic model for analyzing tales, and demonstrates how Lévi-Strauss's theories "can be used to relate a story back to its social and ideological context" (251). To this end, Pace examines "Cinderella" as a tale about what constitutes low and high status, which works through the conflictual relations between the female characters in such a way that the external signs of virtue and status end up corresponding to the internal signs: by the end of the tale, Cinderella is assigned her "proper" place within the social hierarchy.

Taking on Aarne and Thompson, Torborg Lundell demonstrates how the AT classification system promotes a sex-biased image of the folk and fairy-tale heroine. Lundell looks at how, through selective labeling, misleading plot summaries, and a focus on the male character instead of the heroine, the AT system downplays female agency even in tales in which female characters play strong leading roles. Thus, the very typology used to categorize tales proves ideologically motivated in the conscious or unconscious ways its authors classify differently, according to gender, characters who carry out similar tasks. Wittingly or unwittingly, they legitimate a sociopolitical order that privileges men as active agents, despite messages valorizing female agency present in many of the tales from which they draw.

When considering the question of ideology and the fairy tale, we must not only consider published tales, their material contexts, and the methods we use to analyze them. We must also take into account issues arising from the ways in which ideology shapes how a tale gets edited, translated, and canonized, which is also related to the ideological concerns of the field of folk and fairy-tale studies at a particular historical moment. As Maria Tatar has compellingly shown, the Grimms "actively and deliberately altered the folkloristic material they claimed to have tried so hard to preserve in its pristine state" (30). Some of the changes made served to enhance the "Germanness" of the tales of their collection, which was both "a scholarly venture and a patriotic project" (11). While the Brothers Grimm framed folk and fairy tales to suit German nationalism, in France during the same period, folklore studies were regionalist in nature. Nineteenth-century French folklorists sought to legitimate the unique culture and identity of the inhabitants of provinces such as Brittany, Lorraine, and Provence against the increasing threats of Parisian cultural and economic hegemony (see, for instance, Hopkin on Lorraine). Published collections of regional folklores thus served as oppositional discourses.

Translation can also frame tales in specific ways. With respect to Sir Richard Burton's translation of *The Arabian Nights*, Edward Said firmly situates it within the history of Orientalism, which itself could be considered, like gender, an instance of ideology. Published during the heyday of British imperialism, Burton's translation reproduces Western racist, sexist, and imperialist prejudices throughout the main text and in annotations. Antoine Galland, on the other hand, wrote within the context of Louis XIV's court society, and his own ideological concerns regarding French decorum and aristocratic culture informed his translation of the *Nights*.

Finally, the texts that make up a folk or fairy-tale canon at a specific moment in time are shaped by ideological concerns. Within the domain of French studies, for instance, scholars privileged the tales of Charles Perrault until the 1980s, when the tales penned by women writers such as d'Aulnoy, Murat, Marie-Jeanne Lhéritier de Villandon, and Catherine Bernard gained scholarly attention. Tales by these women authors were regularly published well into the nineteenth century, falling into decline when the aristocratic public from which they emerged, and which they legitimated, also began to wane. Perrault's tales, however, were perfectly suited to bourgeois audiences whose ideology found justification in his Mother Goose tales. With the rise of feminism within academia, however, fairy tales by the seventeenth-century *conteuses* could validate the counter-discourse of feminism, which resulted in the reframing of the classical canon of fairy tales that we know today.

Works Cited

Aarne, Antti and Stith Thompson. *The Types of the Folktale: A Classification and Bibliography*. Helsinki: Academia Scientiarum Fennica, 1987.

Althusser, Louis. *Lenin and Philosophy and Other Essays*. New York, NY: Monthly Review P, 1971.

Bottigheimer, Ruth B. "Straparola's *Piacevoli Notti*: Rags-to-Riches. Fairy Tales as Urban Creations." *Merveilles et Contes* 8.2 (December 1994): 281–96.

De Lauretis, Teresa. *Technologies of Gender*. Bloomington, IN: Indiana UP, 1987.

Eagleton, Terry. *Ideology: An Introduction*. New York, NY: Verso, 1991.

Haase, Donald. "Decolonizing Fairy-Tale Studies." *Marvels & Tales* 24.1 (2010): 17–38.

Hopkin, David. "Identity in a Divided Province: The Folklorists of Lorraine, 1860–1960." *French Historical Studies* 23.4 (2000): 639–82.

Jameson, Fredric. *The Political Unconscious*. Ithaca, NY: Cornell UP, 1981.

Lundell, Torborg. "Gender Related Biases in the Type and Motif Indexes of Aarne and Thompson." In *Fairy Tales and Society: Illusion, Allusion, and Paradigm*, ed. Ruth B. Bottigheimer. New Haven, CT: Yale UP, 1986. 146–63.

Pace, David. "Beyond Morphology: Lévi-Strauss and the Analysis of Folktales." In *Cinderella: A Casebook*, ed. Alan Dundes. Madison, WI: U of Wisconsin P, 1988. 245–58.

Propp, Vladimir. *Morphology of the Folktale*. [1928] Trans. Laurence Scott. Ed. Louis Wagner and Alan Dundes. 2nd rev. ed. Austin, TX: U of Texas P, 2009.

Said, Edward. *Orientalism*. New York, NY: Vintage, 1979.

Seifert, Lewis. *Fairy Tales, Sexuality, and Gender in France 1690–1715*. Cambridge: Cambridge UP, 2000.

Tatar, Maria. *The Hard Facts of the Grimms' Fairy Tales*. Princeton, NJ: Princeton UP, 1987.

Zipes, Jack. *Fairy Tales and the Art of Subversion*. [1983] New York, NY: Routledge, 2006.

____. *Breaking the Magic Spell: Radical Theories of Folk and Fairy Tales*. [1979] Lexington, KY: UP of Kentucky, 2002.

Zuerner, Adrienne E. "Reflections on Monarchy in d'Aulnoy's *Belle-Belle ou le chevalier Fortuné*." In *Out of the Woods: The Origins of the Literary Fairy Tale in Italy and France*, ed. Nancy L. Canepa. Detroit, MI: Wayne State UP, 1997. 194–217.

AUTHORSHIP

AUTHORSHIP IN ORAL NARRATIVE

Henry Glassie

IF THERE IS A TEXT before us, there is an author behind it. Someone put it into the world. One complication is collaborative creation—some texts have many authors. Actors combine their voices in a play, while a story is normally created in performance by a lone speaker. The more interesting complication is that all plays and stories are built out of other plays and stories, and acts of creation range from replication, the fastidious reproduction of old models, to radical innovations that plunder the past for novelty—from singing, once again, the old folksong "Finnegan's Wake" to writing the bewildering book *Finnegans Wake*. The range is wide, but, always new, always old, every text is a fresh configuration of dormant possibilities.

The narrative's author is the one who put this text before us, writing it for the eye or speaking it for the ear. Through copyright, the writer claims authorship and it is granted, but in the case of oral narrative, though the speaker is logically the author, I have found during half a century of fieldwork among storytellers in many locations that claims and attributions of authorship vary by genre.

Genres of oral narrative divide, just as the books on your newspaper's list of bestsellers divide, into two great classes: fiction and nonfiction.[1] Within the class

1 The division of oral narrative into fiction and nonfiction in many cultures was patiently documented by William Bascom, first in a paper, "The Forms of Folklore: Prose Narratives," then in an update; both can be found in Bascom, *Contributions to Folkloristics* (95–123, 217–19).

of the true, two main genres share in compositional dynamic: the myth and the historical legend.[1] Myths feature supernatural characters acting amid unsettled conditions. They abound in the context of polymorphous religions, in ancient Greece and Rome, and today, in my experience, among Hindus in South Asia and followers of the old faith in the Yorubaland of Nigeria. Historical legends feature people from the past acting amid familiar conditions. They abound in contexts of anger and aspiration, among people inadequately served by written history. With eight centuries of bitter colonial experience, Ireland is—I know at first hand—rich in historical legends. Myths and historical legends blend easily—in tales of the saints, for example—and their styles of textual construction and presentation are the same. Truth is what matters. Exactly as academic historians do, their narrators gather information from every available source, weigh it carefully, and compose the truest tale possible. The stress is on information, on the completeness and accuracy of the facts absorbed into sequential tellings. The tellers are acknowledged as experts; their authorship is but a byproduct of their roles as priests or historians.

There is a clear exception to this rule, the rule that tellers do not claim, and are not granted, rights of authorship over religious and historical tales of truth (in which plots follow the course of actual events). It comes when a storyteller recasts a narrative in verse, as Hesiod and Homer did. In the village of Kagajipara in Bangladesh, Amulya Chandra Pal created a *pala,* a long narrative poem, out of an ancient Hindu myth. In the community of Ballymenone on the Irish border, Hugh McGiveney composed a ballad out of a legend about a battle that raged in his place in 1594. Both thought of themselves as authors and were considered authors by their neighbors. Poetic form brought attention to the artistry and personal creativity implicit in every narrative.[2]

When the nonfictional tale turns personal, the narrative suffuses with the subjectivity of authorship. Amusing or moving autobiographical tales are peculiarly common at this moment in the United States, whether they are oral personal narratives or written memoirs.[3] But generally in the world, personal tales witness to mystery. If I tell of my encounter with the supernatural, the tale is mine, I am the author, but to support my claim to real experience and provide evidence for others to consider,

1 Skeptical and secular scholars might use the words legend and myth to signal unreliability and falsehood, but historical legends in performance meet every requirement of history—they are true to the best of the author's ability—and the myth, to the believer, is an explanatory narrative that carries theological truth.

2 Amulya Chandra Pal's *pala* can be found in Glassie, *Art and Life in Bangladesh* (103–15). The myth Amulya recast as a poem was analyzed by David Shulman in *The Hungry God* (18–47). For Hugh McGiveney and the Battle of the Ford of Biscuits, see Glassie, *The Stars of Ballymenone* 69–70, 77–99, 441–42.

3 American pioneers in the study of the oral personal story include William Labov—see his *Language in the Inner City,* chapter 9—and Sandra Dolby in her paper "The Personal Narrative as Folklore" and her book *Literary Folkloristics and the Personal Narrative.*

I must, while telling my story, deny the role of artful author, securing my status as an innocent observer. And if I relay the experiences of others, I will cite them, assuring you that they were not inventive storytellers but bland, objective reporters of truth, as I am.[1] That is how I found it to be among Irish country people, most of whom had not seen a ghost, heard the banshee, or met a fairy, but who spoke of such things to keep the mind from narrowing down around a materialistic worldview that precluded the need for faith.[2]

But when the personal shifts across the generic divide into fiction, when the story is a fabrication of the self—an instance of the genre that Americans call "tall tales," that my Irish friends call "pants" and describe as lies no one would believe—then the narrator claims and gains the rights of an author. The story is his—the genre is generally for males—his alone to tell, and when others tell it they ascribe it honorably to him. "Composer" was the word the Irish storyteller Hugh Nolan used; "author" was his word for writers, but Mr. Nolan argued that composers of oral stories and authors of books are one in gift: both gather scattered ideas into original, artful, communicative tales.[3]

Parallel to the myth and historical legend in the realm of fictional oral literature is the genre at question in this book, the one that the Grimms called *Märchen*, but that Irish narrators cannot call fairy tales, for those are accounts of encounters with tricky fairies, so they call them "fireside tales," a synonym for the wonder tales or fairy tales of the scholar. In Ireland, and in the Appalachian region of the United States, where I also heard these old stories told by old people, the tales, like the saints' legends of medieval Europe, combined mythical and historical qualities. Enchanted and miraculous happenings were firmly grounded in a recent, realistically described, premodern past, a time when farmers plowed with oxen, women drew water from springs, and fires provided warmth and light.

In Ireland and the uplands of Virginia and North Carolina, fairy tales were not assembled from multiple versions; they were said to be accurate renderings of particular

1 That is, in this essay I am saying only what I have experienced and believe to be true.

2 Carl von Sydow named personal narratives of the supernatural "memorates" in his *Selected Papers on Folklore* (73–74, 87). In Ballymenone they were called "experiences," a rigorous generic term; see Glassie, *The Stars of Ballymenone*, 289–334. The great Irish collection of such stories is Lady Gregory's *Visions and Beliefs in the West of Ireland*.

3 Though many kinds of story drift into anonymity to become attributed only to tradition itself, or to nameless elders and friends of friends, the American tall tale attaches to named individuals, as Richard Dorson noted (5–8, 226–29), and as American collections attest, from Hardin Taliaferro's early *Fisher's River (North Carolina) Scenes and Characters* to studies by professional folklorists, such as William Hugh Jansen's *Abraham "Oregon" Smith: Pioneer, Folk Hero and Tale-Teller* and Richard Lunt's "Jones Tracy: Tall-Tale Hero from Mount Desert Island." It is true in Ireland too: extravagant fictions of the self are composed by, and attributed to, famed individual narrators; see Glassie, *Stars of Ballymenone*, 85–113, 345–80, 445–47.

tales heard in the past. The tales had titles, which most oral narratives do not, and they were credited to specific sources. One was print. Other kinds of story were generally learned, as Hugh Nolan said, by listening while the old people talked, but fairytales were sometimes learned from books and newspapers. Most, though, were learned from an elder, usually a parent. Though it is often written that traditions pass from mother to daughter, father to son, I have found that when an oral tradition is robust, youngsters intent on becoming storytellers might begin at home, but they range through the community, seeking the best narrators and learning their craft from the masters. The Irish storyteller Michael Boyle learned first from his uncle at home, then built his style and repertory during study with Hugh McGiveney, John Brodison, and James Quigley, men to whom he was not related. But fairy tales, as their Irish name implies, were told to children and learned by children at the familial fireside.

Taken from authority, a book or parent, fairy tales demand an accuracy of reproduction that preserves form as well as content over time, and when learned from a parent, they carry a mood of nostalgia, of love, loss, and filial devotion. The story is told, in part, commemoratively, and a retentive memory is essential to the teller's right to perform. The teller of fairy tales credits a source; the audience credits the teller. In the minds of the audience the teller comes to possess the tale by memory and through two performative moves: voicing and elaboration.

In the high blue mountains of Madison County, North Carolina, the neighbors gathered in the home of Lee Wallin, farmer, banjo-picker, and riflesmith, to hear his famous tale, "Little Nippy." Number 328 in Aarne and Thompson's *Types of the Folktale*, the story is usually known as "Jack and the Beanstalk," though in Mr. Wallin's telling there is neither a Jack nor a beanstalk. He sat, his eyes closed, his hands on his knees, and told the tale smoothly to his neighbors and my tape recorder, laughing at the finish with the triumph of repetition. He was an old man, but his memory was sharp: he kept the intricate episodes in perfect order, right to the end. That would have been easy had he merely reported the story, outlining its plot, but he performed it with panache, pitching his voice high like a ballad singer, adopting the steady rhythms of the preacher or auctioneer, ornamenting his telling with repetitions that cracked the narrative into the long, sweeping lines of a poem. Set away from common speech by tone, made poetic in cadence, richly voiced, the tale became—in committed performance—Lee Wallin's creation.[1]

1 I transcribed "Little Nippy" from tape in Glassie, "Three Southern Mountain Jack Tales." The transcript would have been better if I had understood the poetic nature of oral narrative, which Dell Hymes would articulate in his mighty book *"In Vain I Tried to Tell You": Essays in Native American Ethnopoetics* (see chapter 9), but I was still an undergraduate when I recorded the story and wrote the paper; I did not yet know that oral narratives are not prose, but speech, and in performance they are apt to break into lines by breaths and repetitions, so they need to be scored in a technique that borrows from the conventions of both prose and verse.

On the low green hills of County Fermanagh in Northern Ireland, young people told me I should record the story "Huddon and Duddon and Donald O'Leary," which was told to them in childhood by their community's leading historian, the farmer and saintly old bachelor Hugh Nolan. The story, number 1535 in Aarne and Thompson, Mr. Nolan learned from a special Christmas number of *The Fermanagh Herald*, the local paper in which it had been reprinted from *Fairy and Folk Tales of the Irish Peasantry*, edited by W.B. Yeats. Published in 1888, it was the great poet's first book, and Yeats took the story from a chapbook, *Royal Hibernian Tales*, published in 1825. Here is a rare chance to compare a text from the field with its source. Hugh Nolan localized the story in diction and detail, expanded on the personalities of the characters, enriched the episodes, enlivened the texture with repetitions, and his telling was three times longer than Yeats's. The story Mr. Nolan read was little more than a clear sketch of the plot; the story he performed was an entertaining narration, designed, he said, to teach children the virtue of endurance through adversity. The story became his by dint of artful, personal elaboration.[1]

To conclude. If the author is the one who first contrived the outline of the plot, then most folktales and many literary masterpieces—*Hamlet* and *King Lear*, for example—will lack known authors. But logically the author is the one who fills the plot into the compelling presence of a story, whether it is an old woman at the hearth who speaks it to her grandchildren or a young man at the desk who writes it down and sends it through the press to unknown readers. There is no author of "Cinderella"; there are thousands of authors of thousands of "Cinderellas." The issue of authorship, though, needs more than the logic of theory; it deserves empirical inquiry—historical research and patient work among the world's living narrators. From work in the field, I would generalize that all narratives are simultaneously informational and artful, and that the more the artful prevails over the informational, the more likely are narrators to think of themselves as authors and to be taken as authors by others.[2] And since fairy tales lie toward the artful end of the narrative spectrum, they invite the critic's attention and should drive the critic's quest to discover who those authors, these artists of the verbal, were and are.

---

1 Hugh Nolan's source is found in W.B. Yeats, *Fairy and Folk Tales of the Irish Peasantry*, 299–303. I present and analyze Mr. Nolan's text in Glassie, *The Stars of Ballymenone*, 234–49.

2 The great informational tales—myths and historical legends—are in the hands of knowledgeable experts, personal nonfiction seems open to everyone, but the patently artful narratives are performed by the rarely talented or peculiarly inclined. In Ballymenone, the composers of personal fictions were known as "artists" and called "stars" (Glassie, *The Stars of Ballymenone*, chapter 6), and in the book that is, by my lights, the best on the topic, *Interpretation of Fairy Tales: Danish Folklore in a European Perspective*, Bengt Holbek reports that among Evald Tang Kristensen's informants in Denmark only one in 50 told fairy tales (86, 140). Students of fairy tales, like students of literary masterworks, deal with rare but important creations.

Works Cited

Aarne, Antti and Stith Thompson. *The Types of the Folktale: A Classification and Bibliography*. Helsinki: Academia Scientiarum Fennica, 1987.

Bascom, William. *Contributions to Folkloristics*. Meerut: Archana Publications, 1981.

____. "The Forms of Folklore: Prose Narratives." *Journal of American Folklore* 78.307 (1965): 3–20.

Dolby, Sandra. *Literary Folkloristics and the Personal Narrative*. Bloomington, IN: Indiana UP, 1989.

____. "The Personal Narrative as Folklore." *Journal of the Folklore Institute* 14.1–2 (1977): 9–30.

Dorson, Richard. *Jonathan Draws the Longbow*. Cambridge: Harvard UP, 1946.

Glassie, Henry. *Art and Life in Bangladesh*. Bloomington, IN: Indiana UP, 1997.

____. *The Stars of Ballymenone*. Bloomington, IN: Indiana UP, 2006.

____. "Three Southern Mountain Jack Tales." *Tennessee Folklore Society Bulletin* 30.3 (1964): 88–102.

Holbek, Bengt. *Interpretation of Fairy Tales: Danish Folklore in a European Perspective*. FFC 239. Helsinki: Suomalainen Tiedeakatemia, 1987.

Hymes, Dell. *"In Vain I Tried to Tell You": Essays in Native American Ethnopoetics*. Philadelphia, PA: U of Pennsylvania P, 1981.

Jansen, William Hugh. *Abraham "Oregon" Smith: Pioneer, Folk Hero and Tale-Teller*. New York, NY: Arno P, 1977.

Labov, William. *Language in the Inner City: Studies in the Black English Vernacular*. Philadelphia, PA: U of Pennsylvania P, 1972.

Lady Gregory. *Visions and Beliefs in the West of Ireland*. 2 vols. New York, NY: G.P. Putnam's Sons, 1920.

Lunt, Richard. "Jones Tracy: Tall-Tale Hero from Mount Desert Island." *Northeast Folklore* 10 (1968): 5–75.

Shulman, David. *The Hungry God: Hindu Tales of Filicide and Devotion*. Chicago, IL: U of Chicago P, 1993.

Taliaferro, Hardin. *Fisher's River (North Carolina) Scenes and Characters*. New York, NY: Harper and Brothers, 1859.

von Sydow, Carl. *Selected Papers on Folklore*. Copenhagen: Rosenkilde and Bagger, 1948.

Yeats, William Butler. *Fairy and Folk Tales of the Irish Peasantry*. London: Walter Scott, 1888.

THE CASE OF THE DISAPPEARING AUTHOR

Elizabeth Wanning Harries

Sometimes literary critics focus intensely on the relationship between authors and what they write. They find sources for fiction or poetry in the writer's biography and reading. They try to study the writer's intention in writing the work, using drafts, notes, letters, or offhand comments to friends. Sometimes, on the other hand, critics try to play down this relationship, arguing that the writer's stated intention is not a good guide to the words of a poem (Wimsatt) or that the writer is simply a conduit for or a nexus of contemporary ideas and concerns, his text "a tissue of quotations drawn from innumerable centers of culture" (Barthes 6).

Sometimes critics also look back nostalgically to cultures where, they imagined, there were no identifiable authors, as Virginia Woolf does in her very late essay "Anon." As she says, "Anonymity was a great possession ... It allowed us to know nothing of the writer: and so to concentrate on his song" (397). She talks about such writers' work as close to bird song, arising naturally and un-self-consciously in their response to their environment. She links "Anon" to the transmission of tales and rituals: "It was Anon who gave voice to the old stories, who incited the peasants ... to put off their working clothes and deck themselves in green leaves. He it was who found words for them to sing ..." (383). Woolf has invented a romantic version of the distant past where a nameless poet could inspire folk-song and folk dance.

Many people still tend to believe that fairy tales are a product of this kind of culture, passed on orally from generation to generation. Tales are often thought to be the relics or traces of a long national and linguistic tradition, evidence of an earlier and purer way of life, handed down by word of mouth. The Grimm brothers, for example, insisted in the prefaces that the tales they included in their collections were evidence of a long German tradition: in their 1814 preface they wrote that "these folktales have kept intact German myths that were thought to be lost" (trans. and qtd. in Tatar 213). Yet recent scholarship has shown that many of the tales we think of as anonymous have identifiable authors, often in fact a series of authors who added their own touches and spins of plot to an existing version (or removed things they thought improper, as the Grimms themselves did). Though the writers and editors who shaped the tales sometimes claimed that they were simply reproducing a traditional tale they had heard from a nursemaid or governess, they usually had created their own versions of written tales, mixing tradition and invention. These authors usually had learned the tales they passed on not through word of mouth but through intercultural reading, often through translations of works from other European cultures. In this process they also concealed their own names and identities, part of a literary strategy designed to highlight the "ageless" appeal of their tales.

Let me give an example. In 1694 a small pamphlet appeared in Paris called "Peau d'asne: Conte" (Donkey Skin: A Tale). Though the title page includes a dedication to a marquise, the name of the author does not appear. At the end of the tale, written in quite elaborate rhyming verse, we hear

Ils ne sont pas aisez à croire;
Mais tant que dans le monde on verra des enfants,
    Des Meres & des Meres-grands
    On en gardera la mémoire.

[These stories are not easy to believe, but as long as there are children, mothers, and grandmothers in the world, they will be remembered.]

Lines like these link written stories to an ongoing tradition of oral storytelling and also mark them as transmitted by women to children. We now know that the prominent writer and Academician Charles Perrault wrote and published this verse tale; it was an open secret in his lifetime. But, rather than affix his name to it, he hid behind a cloak of invisibility, a pretense that his elegant verses derived from oral tradition and women's stories. Interestingly enough, his niece Marie-Jeanne Lhéritier echoed the same lines in the dedication to one of her own tales, "Les Enchantements de l'éloquence" (1696). Both uncle and niece shied away from claiming authorship, preferring to attribute their tales to the well-known writer "Anon." and to the tradition of women's oral storytelling.[1]

Now it is certainly true that the outline of the story of "Donkey Skin" had a long history. Scholars have traced it back to medieval French romances like *Perceforêt* and *La Belle Helaine de Constantinople*, as well as to Straparola's "Doralice" in his *Piacevole Notte* (I,4) and many other early modern tales that turn on a daughter's disguising herself, usually in an animal skin, to escape her father's incestuous desires. But, though there may have been a history of oral retellings, we now have only the history of a sequence of written texts. Perrault almost certainly drew on some of these written sources.

Why then does Perrault obscure both his written sources and his name as author? And why does he locate the tale's origin in a line of oral transmission by women? Why do his niece Marie-Jeanne Lhéritier and many of the other women who wrote and published tales in the 1690s sometimes follow his lead? These are complex

1 For further discussion of this question, see Harries, *Twice upon a Time* (3–6, 10–12).

questions, with several answers. Though fairy tales apparently had been part of upper-class *salon* entertainments for decades, they still retained powerful cultural links to women's oral story-telling. Perrault may have felt that it was somewhat beneath his dignity as a well-known writer and Academician to produce such tales. (In 1697 he attributed his famous small volume of nine prose tales, *Histoires ou Contes du Temps Passé* [Stories or Tales of Times Past], to his young son Pierre Darmancour.) But he may also have wanted to use "the privileges of anonymity" that Joan DeJean has granted his female contemporaries to create controversy and discussion in the complex literary marketplace of his day.[1] The stance of anonymity had become, paradoxically, a way of generating public notice.

Whatever his motives, Perrault's authorial tactics became part of the dominant ideology of the fairy tale. Though earlier collections often had the writer's name on the title page (Straparola's in 1561, for example), Perrault's contemporaries and many later writers tended to remain anonymous or to pose as the editor of tales they themselves had composed. The women who wrote fairy tales in France in the late seventeenth century, Perrault's exact contemporaries, often identified themselves only by title and initials on the title page and in their forewords, omitting their full names. Later the Grimms often suggested that they had transcribed their tales directly from oral versions, though we now know that they usually used written sources and rewrote the tales quite drastically from edition to edition. Their editorial practices, particularly the ways they played up the supposed orality of their tales and downplayed writing, have influenced the ways many people still think about fairy tales.

In other words, the tales most North Americans know best are by and large not products of an oral culture or of that mythical world that Woolf evokes in her essay "Anon." Rather, they are products of a culture of writing, of a history of texts, rewritings, translations, and words on the page. Most of them have a series of identifiable authors, and fairy-tale scholars are still discovering new ones. Though we may not want to emphasize their intentions, as Wimsatt, Barthes, and Foucault warn us not to do, we need to acknowledge that most European fairy tales come down to us through a print tradition—not directly from the "illiterate folk" (an appealing concept for many early writers and collectors), but from a series of highly literate authors who engineered their own disappearance.

---

1 See DeJean's article, "Lafayette's Ellipses: The Privileges of Anonymity."

Works Cited

Barthes, Roland, "The Death of the Author." In *The Death and Resurrection of the Author?*, ed. William Irwin. Contributions in Philosophy, 83. Westport, CT: Greenwood P, 2002. 3–8.

DeJean, Joan. "Lafayette's Ellipses: The Privileges of Anonymity." *PMLA* 99 (October, 1984): 884–902.

Foucault, Michel. "What Is an Author?" In *The Death and Resurrection of the Author?*, ed. William Irwin. Contributions in Philosophy, 83. Westport, CT: Greenwood P, 2002. 9–22.

Harries, Elizabeth Wanning. *Twice upon a Time: Women Writers and the History of the Fairy Tale.* Princeton, NJ: Princeton UP, 2001.

Tatar, Maria. *The Hard Facts of the Grimms' Fairy Tales.* Princeton, NJ: Princeton UP, 1987.

Wimsatt, W.K. "The Intentional Fallacy." In his *The Verbal Icon: Studies in the Meaning of Poetry.* [1954] Lexington, KY: U of Kentucky P, 1967.

Woolf, Virginia. "'Anon' and 'The Reader': Virginia Woolf's Last Essays." Ed. Brenda Silver. *Twentieth-Century Literature* 25 (1979): 356–441.

ORAL VERSUS LITERARY TALES: A NEW APPROACH TO ISSUES OF AUTHORSHIP

Armando Maggi

THE AGE-OLD DISCUSSION OF THE relationship between oral and written folk literature needs to be rethought and updated. Within literary studies, which privileges the print tradition, the terms "oral" and "written" have not been treated equally—and commonly held notions of "authorship" reflect this imbalance. In Heather Maring's words, "expectations associated with the literary arts do not adequately take into consideration how oral traditions work and may even obscure their aesthetic vitality" (712). One problem is that literary critics have generally neglected the "aesthetic vitality" of oral tales—or, more specifically, orally told tales that have been collected and rendered in print.

Examining the crucial importance in the West of "the author's name," Michel Foucault writes that it "performs a certain role with regard to narrative discourse." That is, it grants the text a "certain status" (107). That status has often been denied to texts that document oral traditions, which for the past two centuries have been assumed to be anonymous, the property of the folk rather than the products of individual creativity. Such assumptions are themselves ideological and downplay the roles of individual tellers and performances. The author-function is, however, often attached to collectors of tales—for example, the Brothers Grimm are widely known, while Dorothea Viehmann (their primary informant) remains obscure.

Granting oral and written literature the same "status," as Foucault says, brings about mutually beneficial effects because the relationship between these two poles of artistic expression (the oral and the written) is porous and dynamic. As mythic narratives existed through infinite (oral and written) variations that mirrored and enlightened each other, as Roberto Calasso's *The Marriage of Cadmus and Harmony* (*Le nozze di Cadmo e Armonia*, 1988) has masterfully shown, so do fairy tales live through their multiple forms and infinite contaminations, which cannot and should not be separated or discriminated according to their alleged value. The notorious dilemma about the origins of a fairy tale (does the oral version precede the written one, or is it the other way around?) will never be solved because "in the beginning" fairy tales are adulterated products. My essay aims at bringing back that "spell" that so many scholars have successfully broken in recent times. By spell I mean what Max Lüthi defines as the "miracle" of the oral tale, which often results from what is left unsaid, what is apparently useless, what is mentioned and then forgotten, the so-called "blind or blunted motifs" (*Fairy Tale* 67). What is challenging today is not to determine how to break the oppressive moralistic spell of fairy tales, but rather how to restore its basic sense of magic, that is, how to learn to appreciate these hybrid artifacts as independent artistic manifestations that inform and are informed by other (written and oral) texts.[1] Oral and literary traditions are not easily untangled, but scholars have operated as though they are. The "spell" of this genre results from this *marvelous* contamination.

The hybrid nature of Western European fairy tales is already detectable in Giambattista Basile's *The Tale of Tales* (*Lo cunto de li cunti*, 1634–36), the father of the European fairy tale.[2] Basile's book is not only the first collection of fairy tales of the modern Western tradition, it is also the source of innumerable written and oral variations. Basile's seminal volume offers the first versions of tales such as Sleeping Beauty and Cinderella and the first early modern rewriting of the myth of Cupid and Psyche. Adaptations of his marvelous tales are also present in French late seventeenth-century literature and in collections of oral tales in early twentieth-century Spain.[3] Basile's volume had a lasting impact on both oral and written European traditions of fairy tales.

Writing in a highly literary version of Neapolitan dialect, which is an essentially oral idiom, Basile composed his tales as forms of entertainment for the local courts. What is essential to understand, therefore, is that Basile's book has a deeply ambiguous structure. It is a written text that invokes orality both in its style and content, being structured around fictive moments of tale-telling and positioning the reader as a (hypothetical) audience.[4] *Lo cunto de li cunti* is a written work that draws powerfully on notions of and representations of orality.[5] There is a sense in which Basile may be seen both as a kind of collector of oral tales, nearly 200 years before the systematic gathering of oral traditions began *and* as the learned exploiter of ancient and modern literature (recasting moments from Ovid's *Metamorphoses*, Apuleius's *The Golden Ass*, or Boccaccio's *Decameron*).

German writers of the early nineteenth century were attentive to the dynamic interaction of the oral and the written in Basile's book, which they considered a seminal work. Nevertheless, the Brothers Grimm and Clemens Brentano read *Lo cunto de li cunti* in two distinct ways. Whereas the Brothers Grimm wished to uncover the timeless wisdom of the German people through their oral tales, Brentano used images and motifs from the fairy-tale tradition to give form to his personal poetics.

1 Lüthi's work is a seminal point of reference for this kind of academic research. See, for instance, his analysis of "blunted" motifs (*European Folktale* 61). Lüthi's analysis has an essentially abstract character and presupposes the existence of an "ideal type" of oral fairy tale that all narrators keep in mind. For the limits of Lüthi's approach, see Bausinger (161–69).

2 For a recent translation of Basile's book, see Canepa.

3 Caumont de la Force borrows from Basile's version of Cupid and Psyche in her tale "More Beautiful than A Fairy" ("Plus belle que Fée" 1–95). In Espinosa's *Cuentos populares españoles*, we find a version of Basile's famous tale "The Three Citrons" ("Las tres naranjas" 238–39).

4 For the theatrical nature of *Lo cunto de li cunti*, see Rak (8–9, 13).

5 For discussion of "simulated orality" as a literary strategy, see Harries.

For the Grimms, *Lo cunto de li cunti* was not only the first collection of European fairy tales and an essential model for subsequent works in this genre, it was also, and more importantly, "the best and the richest" collection ever written in any European culture (*Kinder- und Hausmärchen* 277). They saw it as a trove of images, motifs, and plots that, with substantial variations, were also present in the German tales they were collecting during the first decade of the nineteenth century.

In the appendix to the second edition of *Kinder- und Hausmärchen*, the Grimms offered a detailed summary of the 50 tales of *Lo cunto de li cunti* and argued that Basile essentially agreed with their own view of fairy tales as expressions of national wisdom, or the voice of the "folk." For the Brothers Grimm, however, Basile's tales presented moral and narrative problems when they sounded too vulgar or inappropriate for the contemporary German sense of "decency."[1] The Grimms' most relevant editorial interventions, however, concerned the complexity or ambiguities of the Italian tales. Their summaries greatly simplify the plots of Basile's stories in order to make them similar to their clear and uncomplicated fairy tales. In some cases, their summaries also include mistranslated words or expressions to make them sound more poetic and "magical." For instance, "The Padlock," the most literal translation of one of Basile's tale titles, becomes "The Small Magic Box" in the Grimms' summaries (Grimm 1822, 314–15).

Clemens Brentano, on the other hand, emphasized Basile's literary skillfulness and explicitly criticized the Grimms' reading of Basile as a model for their own nationalist project of collecting oral traditional tales. In his *Italian Fairy Tales* (*Italianische Märchen*, 1810–20), Brentano sought to establish a "correct" view of Basile by rewriting ten of the Neapolitan stories in a very ornate and literarily sophisticated style. Despite differences in interpretation, both the Brothers Grimm and Brentano turned Basile into an authoritative proto-romantic author-figure, as if instead of living during the Italian Baroque, he had been a direct precursor of German Romanticism. The Basile case shows the central relevance of a critical approach to the issue of authorship in the study of oral and written fairy tales alike.

The significance of *Lo cunto de li cunti* was a major point of contention among German intellectuals and also served as the source of some subsequent oral tales, collected in Sicily and then translated and published in Germany by Laura Gonzenbach as *Sicilianische Märchen* (1870).[2] Born to German-Swiss parents in Messina,

---

1 In the preface to Felix Liebrecht's first German translation of *Lo cunto de li cunti* in 1846, Jacob Grimm notes that certain of Basile's images or words would be considered unsuitable to a German audience (Grimm 1846, vi).

2 For a succinct introduction to this author, see Lee 417. For Gonzenbach's book, see Rubini's first complete Italian version. Jack Zipes published the first English translation in two books, gave it a different title, and modified the original order of the tales. The two-part translation came out in one volume in 2005.

Sicily, Gonzenbach is credited with having interviewed very humble women (peasants, maids), and her published versions of those tales betray a distinctly literary origin. Consider, for instance, "The Maiden with the Seven Veils" ("Die Schöne mit den sieben Schleiern"), the thirteenth tale of Gonzenbach's book. This story recalls two of the most famous narratives from Basile's *Lo cunto*: the frame tale and "The Three Citrons," the last tale of Basile's text. Like the frame tale of *Lo cunto*, the Sicilian story opens with the image of a beautiful fountain of oil. In Basile, a melancholic princess laughs when a boy throws a stone at an old woman's pitcher filled with oil and breaks it. The old woman curses the princess, "May you never pluck a blossom of a husband unless you take the prince of Round Field" (Basile 37).

In Gonzenbach's version, an arrogant prince becomes melancholic when an old woman curses him because he has thrown a stone at her pitcher and shattered it. The woman says, "May you never marry until you find the maiden with the seven veils." Both the Neapolitan princess and the Sicilian prince embark on a journey that will change their lives. The second half of the Sicilian "The Maiden with the Seven Veils" is based on "The Three Citrons," the final tale of Basile's *Lo cunto*. In both the Sicilian and the Neapolitan tales a tiny woman pops out of a small object (a citron in Basile; a little box in Gonzenbach) and cries out, "Give me some water!" In both tales, a malicious dark-skinned slave pricks a beautiful lady with a sharp pin, marries the prince in her stead, and is eventually executed in a cruel manner. Not only does the relationship between the seventeenth-century Neapolitan book (*Lo cunto de li cunti*) and the nineteenth-century Sicilian tale collection (*Sicilianische Märchen*) remain necessarily obscure, but Basile's tales did not metamorphose on their own. Whether this literary phenomenon was integrated to an oral tradition by Sicilian storytellers or by Gonzenbach herself cannot be determined with any certainty. The single steps of this transmission are impossible to determine: collectors and editors such as Gonzenbach have the power of manipulating the printed text—including various forms of erasure and addition.

A close examination of the intimate dialogue among oral and written tales, among texts written by credited authors or transmitted by individuals whose identities have been erased not only compels us to question our notion of authorship (who owns a tale if innumerable writers and tellers tell it with seemingly minimal variations?). It also leads us to recognize the intrinsic aliveness (the "spell") of narratives that otherwise may appear to be static and immutable fossils.

Works Cited

Basile, Giambattista. *The Tale of Tales.* Trans. Nancy Canepa. Detroit, MI: Wayne State UP, 2007.

Bausinger, Hermann. *Formen der Volkspoesie.* Berlin: Schmidt, 1968.

Brentano, Clemens. *Briefe.* Ed. Friedrich Seebass. Vol. 2. Nürnberg: Carl, 1951.

Calasso, Roberto. *Le nozze di Cadmo e Armonia.* Milan: Adelphi, 1988.

Espinosa, Aurelio M., ed. *Cuentos populares españoles.* New York, NY: AMS P, 1967.

Foucault, Michel. "What Is an Author?" In *The Michel Foucault Reader,* ed. Paul Rabinow. New York, NY: Pantheon Books, 1984. 101–20.

Gonzenbach, Laura. *Beautiful Angiola.* Trans. Jack Zipes. New York, NY: Routledge, 2005.

____. *Fiabe siciliane.* Ed. Luisa Rubini. Rome: Donzelli, 1999.

____. *Sicilianische Märchen.* Leipzig: Engelmann, 1870.

Grimm, Jacob. "Vorrede." *Der Pentamerone oder: Das Märchen aller Märchen von Giambattista Basile.* Trans. Felix Liebrecht. 2 vols. Breslau: Verlag bei Josef Mar und Komp, 1846.

Grimm, Wilhelm and Jacob Grimm. *Kinder- und Hausmärchen.* Vol. 3. Berlin: Reimer, 1822.

Harries, Elizabeth Wanning. "Simulating Oralities: French Fairy Tales of the 1690s." *College Literature* 23.2 (June 1996): 100–11.

La Force, Charlotte-Rose de Caumont de. *Les contes des contes.* Paris: Simon Benard, 1698.

Lee, Linda J. "Gonzenbach, Laura." In *The Greenwood Encyclopedia of Folktales and Fairy Tales,* ed. Donald Haase. Vol. 2. Westport, CT: Greenwood P, 2008. 417.

Lüthi, Max. *The European Folktale: Form and Nature.* Trans. John D. Niles. Bloomington, IN: Indiana UP, 1982.

____. *The Fairy Tale as Art Form and Portrait of a Man.* Trans. Jon Erickson. Bloomington, IN: Indiana UP, 1987.

Maring, Heather. "Oral Theory." In *The Greenwood Encyclopedia of Folktales and Fairy Tales,* ed. Donald Haase. Vol. 2. Westport, CT: Greenwood P, 2008. 708–17.

Rak, Michele. *Logica della fiaba.* Milan: Bruno Mondadori, 2005.

RECEPTION

DEAR READER

Donald Haase

THE EDITORS OF THIS TEXTBOOK have asked me to write about the topic of fairy-tale reception. When I agreed to do that, I automatically envisioned writing for them an *essay*, which is the scholarly genre that both teachers and students would expect to find in a textbook of this sort. However, as I began to think about what I would write and for whom I would be writing it—you—it occurred to me that whatever I had to say about reception should really take the form of a letter.

Perhaps more clearly than any other written genre, the letter—from its opening salutation to its closing—owns up to the fact that it is written by someone for someone else. The letter does not disguise that it is an act of communication that involves (in the language of reception studies) a *sender* who is writing in the first person from a personal perspective (in this case, me) and a *receiver or recipient* (in this case, you). A letter perfectly illustrates that communication is a transaction requiring a sender, a message, and a receiver/recipient. That's true, of course, of any written document, including all the other parts of this textbook—from the title, preface, and introduction to the other scholars' essays and even the fairy tales themselves. However, in these other cases the personal role of the sender or the receiver may not be so obvious. The text or message may seem to transcend history, to offer itself as a timeless, universal statement whose meaning is fixed and forever the same. And once the text is viewed as timeless or unchanging, the role of recipient—your role—may also be underestimated or obscured. So it's easy, especially when reading published fairy tales, to forget that every tale was produced by a certain author at a certain time for a certain audience (just like this letter). And it's easy to overlook the fact that fairy tales published for some other audience in a different place and time now depend on us as readers to give them meaning.

Folktales and fairy tales in particular are notorious for appearing to have an aura of timelessness and universality. Tales that have been published in edited collections are often not attributed to any specific author or storyteller—no sender—and appear to us to be anonymous. Or we may get the impression that the sender—the storyteller or author—is unimportant. When early folklorists were collecting and publishing tales in the nineteenth century, they were operating on the premise that folktales expressed the worldview of a specific culture or nation. Introductions to collections of folktales claimed that the stories spoke in the collective voice of the "people" or the "folk." Accordingly, these collectors and editors were less interested in the idea of individual authorship and therefore gave less attention to the identity of individuals who actually told, transmitted, or wrote down tales for them. This is the case, for example, in Jacob and Wilhelm Grimm's *Kinder- und Hausmärchen* (Children's and Household Tales), an influential nineteenth-century collection of German tales that served as a model for other collectors and significantly influenced our notion of the collective voice that speaks in fairy tales.

The tendency to minimize or obscure the role of the actual tale-teller is paralleled by the tendency to construct a stereotypical storyteller. Behind the idea of the anonymous fairy tale produced by a collective voice, there is often the image of an ideal storyteller. In the preface to their folktale collection, for example, the Brothers Grimm described one of their informants—Dorothea Viehmann—whom they considered to be an ideal storyteller. No doubt she was a stellar storyteller, but the Grimms' description of this woman, who was also depicted in the now-famous frontispiece to the second edition of their collection, helped to establish the popular image of the traditional storyteller as a peasant woman. Similar stereotypical images, descriptions, and attributions can be found in many other collections. Scholarly and popular understanding of the folktale and fairy tale has been profoundly shaped by this stereotype, which not only carries an unearned aura of authenticity but also obscures the role of the actual sender.

So when it comes to fairy tales, one function of reception studies has been to reexamine the role and identity of the sender. Focusing on the sender makes a whole range of important questions possible: Who is the actual author or teller of a given tale? Is it possible to determine the sender's identity in the case of a tale that is presented anonymously? Does what we know about an actual author or storyteller give us any insight into the tale or affect the way we respond to it? What is the nature of the *implied sender* in any folktale or fairy tale—that is, what does the text imply about the narrator, what can we deduce about the narrator from the story itself? Note that the implied sender is distinct from the actual human being who has told or written the tale. For example, Wilhelm Grimm rewrote many of the folktales in his and his brother's collection so that that they seem to be the products of the stereotypical folk storyteller highlighted in their preface. The creation of a seemingly timeless once-upon-a-time atmosphere can also imply a storyteller who speaks from within that timelessness.

You should understand that reception studies inquire not only about the role of the storyteller or author but also about the role of collectors, editors, and translators. On one hand, they are the recipients of the texts produced by storytellers and authors, but on the other they are also senders because they act as transmitters of those texts. Take, once again, the Grimms. They not only tried to shape our understanding of their tales by constructing for us an image of the ideal storyteller. Through their editing they also significantly changed and rewrote many of the tales they had collected so that they better reflected the social and cultural values that they wanted to promote. So editors and collectors have a shaping, authorial role in the construction of the texts they are transmitting. This is also true of translators, who transmit and spread tales by recasting them in other languages.

The insight that those who assemble folktale collections try—whether consciously or unconsciously—to influence your response to the tales raises still more questions: What kind of storyteller has the collector or editor of a folktale collection constructed? What devices do collectors, editors, and translators use to frame the stories they are making available to you? How do their prefaces, introductions, notes, and other paratexts try to shape your understanding and response to folktales and fairy tales? In this context, you might ask yourself about the editors who have assembled this very textbook, which is itself a collection of tales. What motivates the editors' selection of tales? How have they arranged, presented, and contextualized the tales? How do they want you to understand the individual tales, the fairy tale as a genre, and the history of fairy tales? What is their purpose or agenda in doing this?

If you think about these questions, you'll realize that they prompt you to think not only about the role of the sender who is responsible for putting the text into the form in which it appears before you, but also about the reader/recipient with whom the sender is communicating. Although reception theory has developed various terms for the different kinds of readers that have been conceptualized, I want to mention just two of these, which I think are especially important for fairy-tale studies: *intended reader* (used by Erwin Wolff) and *real reader* (used by Wolfgang Iser).

The questions I posed for you above suggest that authors, editors, collectors, and translators not only have specific expectations about how their readers should receive their publications but also expectations about who those readers will be. (For example, I imagine that your Facebook postings and tweets would tell me a lot about who your intended readers are, just as this letter tells you a lot about mine.) So when you study fairy-tale reception, you will want to think about the target audience—the intended reader—for which a specific tale or collection of tales has been produced. The historical audience being targeted by the sender may be defined by categories such as class, gender, age, or nationality and can reveal a great deal about the history of the fairy tale and the many agendas it has been asked to serve. Fairy-tale studies have devoted a lot of attention to the deceptively simple question "Who are fairy tales for?" Like most question about "*the* fairy tale," this one has no universal answer and can only be addressed by doing a nuanced, case-by-case historical investigation of the intended reader.

Reception studies may also consider the actual recipients—the real readers—who encounter a text at any given time in history. With this kind of recipient in mind, you would document the reception history of a folktale collection or a specific fairy tale by investigating how a real reader or readers have responded to it. Studying reception history in this way requires that you document what actual historical readers have said or written about their experience and understanding of the fairy tale. Your focus in this case would not be on the text of the tale itself but on the response of consumers and readers as made evident in documents and utterances about the text. In shifting the focus from the text to the experience of the recipient, this kind of study also resists the idea that any text has a fixed meaning (whether historical or timeless) and that the reader's personal or subjective reading of the text has its own validity and is worthy of investigation. Traditionally, scholars have used the resources in archives and libraries to find what individuals have written about fairy tales in essays, interviews, reviews, memoirs, autobiographies, diaries, letters, and the like. Now you can also google and otherwise search the Internet to study the response of real readers to fairy tales, from classical versions to the latest film adaptations (in which case we're talking about real *viewers* or *spectators* and not, literally, readers).

Studying the responses of real readers can show fairy tales in a surprising new light. Once, in my own undergraduate course on the fairy tale, my students and I were discussing Grimms' "The Stubborn Child," which Wilhelm Grimm called "a simple moral tale for children." In my opinion, based on my historical understanding of the tale, it's a troubling didactic story that tells of a child who falls ill and dies, and is even beaten into submission in the grave, because of his stubborn disobedience. So I was all the more taken aback when, after class, a student came up to me and said the story meant a great deal to her because it evoked very fond childhood memories of her late father, who had read it to her. Clearly, no amount of historical interpretation or textual analysis—no matter how legitimate, necessary, and appropriate—would explain or invalidate my student's subjective response to Grimms' otherwise disturbing story.

I felt compelled, in closing my letter, to tell you that story about a story to demonstrate that there will always be tensions between the historical interpretation of texts and the study of their reception. Don't misunderstand me. I don't mean "anything goes." I believe that as students of the fairy tale, you and I have a responsibility to understand it historically and culturally. But even as we study and write about the fairy tale, you and I are its mortal recipients—real readers—whose identity as scholars still does not allow us to transcend time, place, or culture.

Having said that, I'm prompted to ask what the benefit of fairy-tale studies might really be, and what it is that we can know absolutely about fairy tales? These are important questions, but I'm afraid I have to bring this letter to a close. Maybe you can give them some thought and, when you have a chance, let me know what you think.

Best wishes,
Donald Haase

PS. If you're interested in reading more about reception and the related topics I mentioned, I can recommend a few selections:

Classic Works on Reception and Reader Response

Iser, Wolfgang. *The Act of Reading: A Theory of Aesthetic Response*. Baltimore, MD: The Johns Hopkins UP, 1978.

_____. *The Implied Reader: Patterns of Communication in Prose Fiction from Bunyan to Beckett*. Baltimore, MD: The Johns Hopkins UP, 1974.

Tompkins, Jane P., ed. *Reader Response Criticism: From Formalism to Post-Structuralism*. Baltimore, MD: Johns Hopkins UP, 1980.

The Authorial Role of Fairy-Tale Editors

Schacker, Jennifer. *National Dreams: The Remaking of Fairy Tales in Nineteenth-Century England*. Philadelphia, PA: U of Pennsylvania P, 2003.

Tatar, Maria. *The Hard Facts of the Grimms' Fairy Tales*. 2nd ed. Princeton, NJ: Princeton UP, 2003.

Paratexts and the Framing of Fairy Tales

Genette, Gérard. *Paratexts: Thresholds of Interpretation*. Trans. Jane E. Lewin. Cambridge: Cambridge UP, 1997.

Haase, Donald. "Framing the Brothers Grimm: Paratexts and Intercultural Transmission: English-Language Editions of the *Kinder- und Hausmärchen*." *Fabula* 44 (2003): 55–69.

Fairy-Tale Translation

Bacchilega, Cristina. "Translation." In *The Greenwood Encyclopedia of Folktales and Fairy Tales*, ed. Donald Haase. Vol. 3. Westport, CT: Greenwood, 2008. 988–90.

Fairy Tales and Translation, special issue of *Marvels & Tales* 23.1 (2009): 1–213.

Personal Responses to Fairy Tales

Bernheimer, Kate, ed. *Brothers and Beasts: An Anthology of Men on Fairy Tales*. Detroit, MI: Wayne State UP, 2007.

_____. *Mirror, Mirror: Women Writers Explore Their Favorite Fairy Tales*. New York, NY: Anchor, 2002.

Haase, Donald. "Response and Responsibility in Reading Grimms' Fairy Tales." In *The Reception of Grimms' Fairy Tales: Responses, Reactions, Revisions*, ed. Donald Haase. Detroit, MI: Wayne State UP, 1993. 230–49.

THE FAIRY TALE IN VICTORIAN ENGLAND

Molly Clark Hillard

EARLY IN THE NINETEENTH CENTURY, Sir Walter Scott urged a study "on the origin of popular fiction, and the transmission of popular tales from age to age," which he hoped would explain why "such fictions, however wild and childish," continue to "possess such charms for the populace" (188). His words characterize the particularly British nineteenth-century reception of the fairy tale. In one way, the Victorian reception of the tale can be measured by its very proliferation, and its rising consumption for family entertainment.[1] However, these print media only partially account for the veritable fairy tale industry that flourished in nineteenth-century England. An equally important form of reception, though one much less critically accounted for, was the tale's subtle "intercalation" into other English literary genres: poetry, fiction, and drama.[2] The fairy tale—its plots, motifs, and characters—inhabited popular, mainstream, and elite literatures, from the Victorian theater, to the novels of Charles Dickens, the Brontës, and George Eliot, to the poetry of Alfred Lord Tennyson, Robert Browning, and Christina Rossetti.

When re-minted as Victorian coin, tales encoded discourse about social issues. As this anthology shows, the fairy tale is a capacious form. It can serve multiple agendas, conservative and liberal, male and female, popular and elite. A single

1 Though fairy tales took passage to England in many ways, it is through print history of the eighteenth and nineteenth centuries that we can most easily trace the reception of the tale. The most abiding, oft read, and oft repeated of tale cycles came from Arabic, Italian, French, and German traditions, as well as from Britain itself. *Alf Layla wa Layla* (literally, 1001 Nights or "The Arabian Nights," as it is best known in English) is a tale tradition spanning six centuries of manuscript forms in Arabic. Antoine Galland's *Les Mille et Une Nuits: Contes Arabes* (1704–17) began the tales' European circulation, and English translations began as early as 1706. From the Italian tradition came the tales of Giovan Francesco Straparola, *Le Piacevoli Notti* (1550), and those of Giambattista Basile, *Il Pentamerone* (1634–36). Basile's work was translated into English in 1848 and Straparola's in 1894. The seventeenth-century French *salon* culture introduced the French fairy tale to England. Madame d'Aulnoy, the grande dame of the *conteuses*, produced *Contes de Fées* in 1697. The tales of Charles Perrault, *Histoires ou Contes du Temps Passé* (1697), was first translated into English by Robert Samber as *Histories, or Tales of Past Times: With Morals* (1729). A few decades later, the work of the Brothers Grimm, *Kinder- und Hausmärchen* (1812) and *Deutsche Sagen* (1815), brought the German tale into prominence. It was first translated into English by Edgar Taylor in 1823, and throughout the century remained a staple of English reading. During the nineteenth century, these works enjoyed multiple reprintings and retellings, both in their entirety and as selections of tales.

2 Robert Patten argues that we should not use the word "interpolation" when referring to tales, legends, and other fantastic material imbedded in the Victorian novel. The term wrongly explains away the fantastic intertext as idiosyncratic. I would also point out that "interpolation" carries the pejorative associations of adulteration, or inserting spurious matter into a genuine work. Instead, if tales are "intercalated," it means that they are interstratified, organically a *part* of Victorian literature ("Pickwick Redivivus").

fairy-tale plot will illustrate the diversity of Victorian reception. When we think of Sleeping Beauty, we might recall the princess's 100-year slumber, the sleeping palace surrounding her, and the prince who breaks the briar hedge and awakens her with a kiss. While the plot of Sleeping Beauty can be traced through a complex print history (including precursors from the fourteenth century; see Basile's "Sun, Moon and Talia" in this volume, p. 135), the now familiar elements of the narrative (title included) are features of seventeenth- and eighteenth-century stories, ones that emphasized the princess's 100-year sleep and the prince's revivifying kiss. The conventions of the tale inherited by the Victorians cast sleep as something specifically feminine and blamable, a somnolence that radiates outward from the princess to infect the kingdom around her.

This essay suggests that "Sleeping Beauty" in Victorian literary adaptations enacted a subtle debate over gender relations in political and social life. In *Past and Present*, for instance, Thomas Carlyle distinguishes between "a virtual Industrial Aristocracy, as yet only half alive—spell-bound amid money-bags and ledgers; and an actual idle aristocracy seemingly near dead in somnolent delusions" (1117). He implores his "Princes of Industry" to wake: "It is you who are already half-alive, whom I will welcome into life; whom I conjure in God's name to shake off your enchanted sleep and live wholly!" (1118). In casting himself as author-prince, giving the kiss of life to the capitalists, Carlyle refers overtly to the narrative of Sleeping Beauty, a fairy tale that, I argue, not only inhabited, but also *shaped* diverse Victorian socio-political discourses.

Alfred Tennyson's 1842 poem "The Day Dream" constructs a frame narrative in which the Victorian speaker uses the Sleeping Beauty thematic to instruct and woo the drowsy, self-involved Lady Flora. In Tennyson's hands, the story also becomes an allegory of nation, where England is figured as recumbent, feminine, and in need of masculine leadership. The prince's arrival is described as a messianic rebirth:

When will the hundred summers die,
And thought and time be born again,
And newer knowledge, drawing nigh,
Bring truth that sways the souls of men?
Here all things in their place remain,
As all were order'd, ages since.
Come Care and Pleasure, Hope and Pain,
And bring the fated Fairy Prince. (*Sleeping Palace* 49–56)[1]

1 "The Day Dream" is divided into nine sections. Each section is titled (i.e., *Prologue, The Sleeping Palace, The Arrival, The Sleeping Beauty, The Revival, The Departure, The Moral, L'Envoi, Epilogue*).

The world is righted and "thought and time" are "born again" only when this questing prince, with priapic hyperbole, awakens the princess and the castle: "the charm was snap't / There rose a noise of striking clocks ... And sixty feet the fountain leapt" (*L'Envoi* 1–2, 8). In Tennyson's version, Sleeping Beauty fades into the background in subordination to the prince. Her self-absorbed—indeed, all-absorbing—sleep ends in her absorption in another: "Beyond the night, across the day, / Thro' all the world she follow'd him" (31–32). Thoughtless, timeless, and radiating lassitude, the princess occasions a pregnant pause in a world that cannot deliver itself of the enchantment. The prince who penetrates this feminine languor brings "care" and "pain" with him, but these are productive labor pains, corollary to "knowledge," "truth," and "hope." And the speaker urges Lady Flora to follow suit, she who

> all too dearly self-involved,
> Yet sleeps a dreamless sleep to me;
> A sleep by kisses undissolved,
> That lets thee neither hear nor see:
> But break it. In the name of wife,
> And in the rights that name may give,
> Are clasp'd the moral of thy life,
> And that for which I care to live. (*L'Envoi* 49–56)

For men, the "moral" of "The Day Dream" is soul-swaying "truth," but for women it is "the name of wife."

In his massive 1853 novel *Bleak House*, Charles Dickens juxtaposes two worlds: the fashionable sphere of the aristocracy and the monolithic Court of Chancery. In describing the grand, but torpid, traditions of both kinds of "courts," he compares these worlds as two "sleeping beauties whom the knight will wake one day, when all the stopped spits in the kitchen shall begin to turn prodigiously!" (20). This Sleeping Beauty reference becomes a repeated and extended plot device in the novel. The principal aristocratic family in the novel are aptly named "Dedlock," and their ancestral home, Chesney Wold, is figured as Sleeping Beauty's castle:

> The house, with gable and chimney, and tower, and turret, and dark doorway, and broad terrace-walk, twining among the balustrades of which, and lying heaped upon the vases, there was one great flush of roses, seemed scarcely real in its light solidity and in the serene and peaceful hush that rested on all around it ... On everything, house, garden, terrace, green slopes, water, old oaks, fern, moss, woods again, and far away across the openings in the prospect to the distance lying wide before us with a purple bloom upon it, there seemed to be such undisturbed repose. (287)

The mistress of Chesney Wold, Lady Dedlock, is depicted as an "exhausted deity," who is figuratively and eventually literally "bored to death" (196). For Dickens, the "Sleeping Beauty" story and its heroine symbolize a lack of healthy occupation. His aristocratic characters are countered by the vigorous endeavor of middle-class characters. For instance, *Bleak House*'s narrator Esther Summerson is the "summer's sun" of the novel; discovered to be the illegitimate daughter of Lady Dedlock, her role is to "sweep the cobwebs" (121) from the stagnant institutions in the novel, both revealing them for what they are and repairing them with an abundance of cheerful domestic employment. Then, too, the son of the Dedlock's housekeeper, Mr. Rouncewell, becomes the successful owner of an iron foundry. He returns to Chesney Wold to claim the Dedlock's maid, Rosa, whom he will educate and marry to his youngest son. In a neat reworking of the tale, Dickens suggests that Mr. Rouncewell's earned wealth and social position makes him a fit "prince" of industry to rescue this Briar Ros(a) from the sleeping castle. In both poetic and novelistic examples, the tale is made into an allegory not only for sexual politics but also national policy; it is no coincidence that both Tennyson's and Dickens's Victorian "sleepers" are landed gentry. They reflect an England ruled by an aristocracy that authors increasingly characterized as an effeminate threat to progress. The middle classes are charged with heroically arousing the nation.

Not all nineteenth-century revisions of the tale champion the masculine hero and the domestic angel. Victorian men and women received and reflected on Sleeping Beauty very differently. When re-envisioned by certain female authors, the tale reflects upon the dullness of propriety, and the toxicity of a passive, useless existence. In Christina Rossetti's "The Prince's Progress" (1866), the prince makes a belated and slothful journey toward the enchanted princess, stopping to carouse with milkmaids and otherwise satisfy his own desires. He arrives at the tower to find the princess dead—killed, evidently, by sheer boredom. Her handmaidens recall:

We never saw her with a smile
Or with a frown;
Her bed seemed never soft to her,
Though tossed of down;
She little heeded what she wore,
Kirtle, or wreath, or gown ...
We never heard her speak in haste;
Her tones were sweet,
And modulated just so much
As it was meet:
Her heart sat silent through the noise

And concourse of the street.
There was no hurry in her hands,
No hurry in her feet. (511–28)

It is her "modulation," the absence of "hurry," a lack of "concourse," indeed, the dearth of any purpose other than waiting for a prince that proves deadly to her. Long before her actual death, Rossetti shows, the princess is moribund—heedless, affectless, and silent. Rossetti appears to battle not only with the diminishing of women to marital objects, but on a larger scale with the entire national patriarchal model championed by Tennyson before her.

In her 1875 collection of short stories, *Five Old Friends,* Anne Thackeray Ritchie writes five Victorian drawing room comedies into which she weaves five fairy tales. "The Sleeping Beauty in the Wood" features Cecilia Lulworth, a pathologically bored young woman, whose waking life, which is "unutterably dull, commonplace, respectable, stinted, ugly, and useless" (11) is likened to an enchanted sleep. Her days are punctuated only by walks around the grounds of Lulworth Hall ("up and down, down and up, up and down," 12), and by sewing: "she worked a great deal, embroidering interminable quilts and braided toilet covers and fish napkins" (16). This "spell" continues for 25 years, until her perfectly nice cousin Frank, a lawyer, comes to call and gives her a playful kiss. Cecilia is so startled at anything resembling normal human contact that, "blushing and blinking ... she at last gave three little sobs" (27). Ritchie makes overt her parody of the fairy tale: "the princess had awakened, but in tears ... the prince still stood by ... feeling horribly guilty, and yet scarcely able to help laughing" (29). Though with very different results, Rossetti and Ritchie employ Sleeping Beauty to chafe against the social expectations that women be passive homebodies, those who wait, not those who do. The "cult of true womanhood" is at best stultifying, and at worst, deadly.

In conclusion, I would suggest that reception is a form of interpretation and adaptation. These collected passages read social progress through the spells and slumbers of "Sleeping Beauty." In these brief examples of literary "intercalations" of a single tale we can see the glimmers of a Victorian socio-political conversation. Further research and extrapolation on your own can reveal the fairy tale's ability in other cultural contexts to serve as a catalyst for more extended debates on the relationship between the sexes, methods of raising and training girls, and models of political governance.

Works Cited

Carlyle, Thomas. *Past and Present*. In *The Norton Anthology of English Literature*, ed. M.H. Abrams, et al. Vol. 2, 7th ed. New York: Norton, 2000. 1110–19.

Dickens, Charles. *Bleak House*. London: Penguin, 2000.

Patten, Robert. "Pickwick Redivivus." University of California Dickens Project. Santa Cruz, CA, August, 2007. Lecture.

Ritchie, Anne Thackeray. "The Sleeping Beauty in the Wood." In *Five Old Friends*. Leipzig: Bernhard Tauchnitz, 1875. 9–31.

Rossetti, Christina. "The Prince's Progress." In *Christina Rossetti: The Complete Poems*, ed. R.W. Crump and Betty S. Flowers. London: Penguin, 2001. 89–104.

Scott, Walter. *The Lady of the Lake*, ed. William J. Rolfe. Boston, MA: J.R. Osgood, 1883.

Tennyson, Alfred. "The Day Dream." *The Poems of Tennyson in Three Volumes*. Vol. II, ed. Christopher Ricks. Essex: Longman, 1987. 48–59.

Zipes, Jack, ed. *Oxford Companion to Fairy Tales*. Oxford: Oxford UP, 2000.

SEXUALITY AND THE WOMEN FAIRY-TALE WRITERS OF THE 1690s

Sophie Raynard

WHEN WE APPROACH THE READING of a fairy tale, we do so with certain preconceived expectations and ideas. Critics such as Jack Zipes and Maria Tatar have suggested that most readers today understand fairy tales in the terms set out by the Brothers Grimm in the early nineteenth century. The Romantic transformation that the Grimms brought to bear on pre-existing tales has had a significant impact on how modern readers view fairy tales: largely as child-like and moral narratives. We also tend to impute transcendent meaning to fairy tales based on the belief that they incorporate universal meaning. It becomes then a real challenge to question such strongly held preconceived notions and to begin to accept the results of innovative scholarship that proposes readings of fairy tales based on re-contextualizations stemming from their socio-historical markings. In seventeenth-century France, literary tales or *contes de fées* were often prefaced, illustrated, dedicated, or embedded in larger and less fictional narratives. The entire paratextual apparatus stood ready to be used as an interpretative tool.

Such complex settings were favored by the early *conteuses*, those aristocratic women writers who literally took over the nascent literary genre of the *conte de fées* (alongside their now more famous male counterpart Charles Perrault). Mme d'Aulnoy was the leader of that group with the most prolific production of fairy tales and the first historically dated literary fairy tale of the era (1690) embedded in a novel. With this corpus in mind, as Jennifer Schacker explained, we can understand *contes de fées*, as "earlier French experiments," setting a "tradition of self-aware, self-reflexive, and frequently satirical engagement of narrators and performers with readers and audiences" (384). They were thus clearly a product of the literary salons frequented by these writers and not of the nursery, as Perrault implied and the Grimms claimed, writing more than a century later. Lewis Seifert suggests that women's *contes de fées*, with their sometimes unhappy endings, propose a rethinking of sexual desire and gender, a subversive recuperation of the traditional format of fairy tales. Christine Jones has pointed out that the moral function sometimes assumed to be inherently attached to fairy tales is called into question with the conteuses' open vindication of frivolity and triviality. The fact that *contes de fées* were extremely popular (as attested by the large number of re-editions and translations in the eighteenth and nineteenth centuries) proves that readers happily aligned themselves with those subversive narrators. There is undeniably a great deal of pleasure to be found in the discovery of unexpected cases of subversion in such texts, even though fairy tales and scandalous sexuality may not appear to be an easy pairing.

My case study here will compare three types of documentation—the *conteuses*' own memoirs versus historical biographies, and their representation of *eros* in fairy tales. For some of the early *conteuses*, sexual scandal was a first-hand experience. This was the case for Mme d'Aulnoy,[1] Mme de Murat,[2] and Mlle de La Force,[3] whose fiction was permeated by similar scandals. By invoking their memoirs, which often resemble fictional creations rather than autobiography, I propose here to show the link between the *conteuses'* biographies and their works—links that have the potential to help us rethink the reception of their tales. While their memoirs celebrated sexual transgression, their fairy tales explored many of the same themes but in coded ways. If we take seriously these memoirs and their connections to the *contes de fées*, then we can recognize the more transgressive elements in the fantasies.

Mme d'Aulnoy's *Mémoires des Avantures singulières de la Cour de France* (1692) and Mme de Murat's *Mémoires de Madame la Comtesse de M**** (1697) are modeled on pseudo-autobiographical memoirs[4] that were popular at the time and that glorified immorality (Démoris). What is striking about them is that their authors inscribed specifically female "crimes," such as adultery, as normal behavior even though these had previously been treated only as tragedy or comedy. Another important feature of these texts is that their authors do not hide behind a veil of innocence but admit those acts with complete candor. Murat invokes influential factors, such as the neglected education that women like her received in convents, and even points at the danger of reading love novels for girls.

The vision that Murat offers of herself in her memoirs is in fact more idealized and novelistic than the often cynical and pessimistic reality depicted in her own *contes de fées*. It may be because memoirs tend to be "contaminated by novelistic exaltation and by an excessive desire of exculpation" (Hipp 317, my translation). This may be because readers do not expect fairy tales to reveal something intimate about their tellers or writers. The *conteuses* exploited those readerly expectations to avoid autobiographical connection between their heroines and themselves.

Moreover, it seems that the fairy tale of the seventeenth century was received as a potentially subversive genre in many respects. It was "qualified as monstrous, frivolous, or at the very least marginal" (Vallois 119, my translation), and the implausibility of the plots bore much responsibility for their outsider status (Miller). It is

1 Marie-Catherine Le Jumel de Barneville, Baroness d'Aulnoy (1650/51–1705) was accused of treason against her own husband. Her mother appears to have been the instigator of the plot, but Marie-Catherine is indirectly responsible for the hanging of her mother's two accomplices. Later estranged from her husband, she gave birth to two daughters of unknown paternity.

2 Henriette-Julie de Castelnau, Comtesse de Murat (1670–1716), although married, was accused of lesbianism and related sexual "misconduct." Despite her prominent social status, she was exiled by order of Louis XIV because of the perceived gravity of the charges.

3 Charlotte-Rose Caumont de La Force (1654–1724), also born to a high-ranking noble family, was associated with several public scandals: numerous love affairs, a misalliance that ended in an annulment, and finally the composition of impious verses directed against the royal family. She too was exiled by Louis XIV.

4 The famous memoirs by Mme de Villedieu and Hortense Mancini are two prime examples.

certainly true that the Abbé de Villiers, the most famous critic of the fairy tale during its late seventeenth-century heyday, was the first to accuse fairy tales of being implausible, even impossible, and therefore outside the bounds of acceptable writing. At the same time, he criticized their lack of naïveté and their affected style, but he seems to have misunderstood that *conteuses* like Mme d'Aulnoy, Mme de Murat, Mlle de La Force, and Mlle Bernard were exploiting the playfulness of the marvelous, including its erotic potential for adult readers.

This kind of exploitation of erotic potential can be found in Mme d'Aulnoy's "Serpentin vert," a tale inspired by Apuleius's story of sexual awakening, "Cupid and Psyche." D'Aulnoy describes her heroine Laideronnette as reading the classic text, a case of intertextuality that Catherine Marin interprets "as a subversive use of literature" because "the reading of 'Cupid and Psyche' did not enable Laideronnette to follow the path of wisdom and to avoid repeating the faults committed by the heroine of the Latin tale" (Marin 126, my translation). On the contrary, it was Laideronnette's reading of the classic tale that prompted her to follow her ill-considered impulses.

Mlle de La Force also challenges the institution of marriage in both her life and her tales, leading Jacques Barchilon to qualify "L'Enchanteur" (The Enchanter) as "an apology for adultery" (Barchilon 73, my translation), because of its ambiguous concluding morality: "Through different routes one can reach happiness, / Vice can lead us there as well as honor" (La Force 354, my translation). Her "Persinette" similarly seems to challenge official morality by using polite language and tone to describe sexual union that produces illegitimate children.

It might be tempting, based on these examples of subversion, to assume that fairy tales advocated female rebellion against the social order. But the *conteuses* were exceptionally skillful writers: in all of their work, compositional style plays a role as significant as content, and sexual transgression in their tales operates symbolically. The genre allows for metamorphoses that are sexual in nature without being subject to censure. The *conteuses* may frequently display in their tales—just as they did in their lives—sexual behaviors that were at odds with the dominant morals of their times, and they do so indirectly through innuendo and metaphor. Rehabilitating the power of these strategies of indirection in marvelous fairy tales can help to retrieve the freedom of interpretation that once lay at their core. This accounts for the unexpected modernity of seventeenth-century women's *contes de fées* and their appeal to modern readers.

Works Cited

Aulnoy, Marie-Catherine Le Jumel de Barneville, Baroness d'. *Mémoires des Avantures Singulières de la Cour de France.* 2nd ed. La Haye: J. Alberts, 1692.

Barchilon, Jacques. *Le conte merveilleux français de 1690 à 1790. Cent ans de féerie et de poésie ignorées de l'histoire littéraire*. Paris: Honoré Champion, 1975.

Bernard, Catherine. "Inès de Cordoue, nouvelle espagnole." [1696] In *Contes: Mademoiselle Lhéritier, Mademoiselle Bernard, Mademoiselle de La Force, Madame Durand, Madame d'Auneuil*, ed. Raymonde Robert. Paris: Champion, 2005.

Démoris, René. *Le roman à la première personne. Du classicisme aux Lumières*. Paris: A. Colin, 1975.

Hipp, Marie-Thérèse. *Enquête sur le roman et les mémoires (1660–1700)*. Paris: Klincksieck, 1976.

Jones, Christine. "The Poetics of Enchantment (1690–1715)." *Marvels & Tales* 17.1 (2003): 55–74.

La Force, Charlotte-Rose Caumont de. "Les contes des contes, par mademoiselle de ***." [1698] In *Contes: Mademoiselle Lhéritier, Mademoiselle Bernard, Mademoiselle de La Force, Madame Durand, Madame d'Auneuil*, ed. Raymonde Robert. Paris: Champion, 2005.

Mancini, Hortense. *Mémoires D.M.L.D.M. à M.* ***. Cologne: Pierre Marteau, 1675.

Marin, Catherine. "Les Contes de fées de la fin du dix-septième siècle et la problématique de la morale." *Romance Language Annual* 6 (1994): 125–29.

Miller, Nancy K. "Plots and Plausibility in Women's Fiction." *PMLA* 96.1 (January 1981): 36–48.

Murat, Henriette-Julie de Castelnau, comtesse de. *Mémoires de Madame la Comtesse de M****. Paris: C. Barbin, 1697.

Schacker, Jennifer. "Unruly Tales: Ideology, Anxiety, and the Regulation of Genre." *Journal of American Folklore* 120.478 (Fall 2007): 381–400.

Seifert, Lewis C. *Fairy Tales, Sexuality, and Gender in France, 1690–1715*. Cambridge: Cambridge UP, 1996.

Tatar, Maria. *The Hard Facts of the Grimms' Fairy Tales*. Princeton, NJ: Princeton UP, 1987.

Vallois, Marie-Claire. "Des *Contes de ma Mère L'Oye* ou des caquets de Madame d'Aulnoy: nouvelle querelle chez les Modernes ?" In *La littérature, le XVIIe siècle et nous: dialogue transatlantique*, ed. Hélène Merlin-Kajman. Paris: Presses Sorbonne Nouvelle, 2008. 119–33.

Villedieu, Marie Catherine Hortense Desjardins, dame de. *Mémoires de la vie de Henriette Sylvie de Molière*. Paris: Claude Barbin, 1671–74.

Villiers, Pierre de. *Entretiens sur les contes de fées et sur quelques autres ouvrages du temps pour servir de préservatif contre le bon goût. Dédiés à Messieurs de l'Académie française*. Paris: Jacques Collombat, 1699.

Zipes, Jack. "The Struggle for the Grimms' Throne: The Legacy of the Grimms' Tales in the FRG and GDR since 1945." In *The Reception of Grimms' Fairy Tales: Responses, Reactions, Revisions*, ed. Donald Haase. Detroit, MI: Wayne State UP, 1993. 167–206.

TRANSLATION

GEOGRAPHICAL TRANSLOCATIONS AND CULTURAL TRANSFORMATIONS

Ruth B. Bottigheimer

In literary studies translation looms large as an area of research. In this word-based discipline, it is easy to forget that the root meaning of "translation" is physical movement, a transfer from one place to another, such as from one bishopric to another, from one government department to another, or even from earth to heaven without dying, as in the Old Testament translation of Enoch. These exemplify the Webster definition of translation as "to bear, remove, or change from one place or condition to another."

Physical "translation" is relevant to many aspects of the history of fairy tales. Modern translations of early fairy tales carried forward most of the tales' content (as it was written by their sixteenth-, seventeenth-, and early eighteenth-century authors) to another place through later editions of those same tales. That same editing process also involved the *non*-translation, or carrying forward, of those parts of fairy-tale plots that later editors found offensive or irrelevant.

The fairy tales in Giovan Francesco Straparola's The Pleasant Nights (*Piacevoli Notte*, 1551, 1553) offer telling examples of what later fairy-tale authors and editors left out. We could choose any of his fairy tales about poor boys or girls who rise to royal station or princes or princesses who are restored to the throne, but I'm particularly fond of "Costantino Fortunato." The first tale of the eleventh night of Straparola's storytelling, it has been known for over two centuries as "Puss in Boots" in versions that communicate a range of visions of a poor boy, his magic cat, their respective characteristics, and their individual actions. Straparola's poor hero in "Costantino Fortunato" is engagingly sweet, repellently filthy, and undeniably dim-witted; his fairy cat is canny and capable. But readers rarely see Straparola's introductory summary of the tale or its first paragraph. For that they would have to return to William George Waters's *Facetious Nights of Straparola* published in 1898 or to new translations by Donald Beecher or Suzanne Magnanini. There they would find the kind of plot summary that routinely prefaced a tale in late medieval and early modern tale collections, that is, from the fourteenth to the eighteenth centuries. Such a summary was brief and to the point, and often reappeared in the book's table of contents. In the case of "Costantino Fortunato," the brief Italian summary preceding the story reads as follows in Waters's nineteenth-century translation:

> Soriana viene a morte e lascia tre figliuoli, Dusolino, Tesifone e Costantino Fortunato, il quale per virtú d'una gatta acquista un potente regno. (2:668)
>
> Soriana dies and leaves three sons, Dusolino, Tesifone, and Costantino. The last-named, by the aid of his cat, gains the lordship of a powerful kingdom. (trans. Waters 4:6)

It is possible that Straparola himself did not write these words; his publisher or one of the printshop employees could just as well have summarized the tale.

The first paragraph of "Costantino Fortunato," however, is an integral part of the story. Here is the opening paragraph in the original Italian, followed once again by Waters's English translation:

> Molte volte, amorevoli donne, vedesi un gran ricco in gran povertà cadere, e quello che è in estreme miseria ad alto stato salite. Il che intervene ad uno poverello, il quale essendo mendico, pervenne al stato regale. (2:668)
>
> It is no rare event, beloved ladies, to see a rich man brought to extreme poverty, or to find one who from absolute penury has mounted to high estate. And this last-named fortune befell a poor wight of whom I have heard tell, who from being little better than a beggar attained the full dignity of a king. (trans. Waters 4:6)

The opening sentences position the tale within human experience and thus implicitly assess the tale as worthy of being told, because it corresponds to things that have actually happened in the real world. "Costantino Fortunato," however, mixes implausible magic into its characters' plausible cunning, and that may be why, when the tales appeared without the framing narrative, the opening paragraph was routinely omitted.

Another component of early fairy tales that was rarely carried over into later translations comprised early authors' own internal commentary on their work. Sometimes such comments were put into the mouths of characters from the framing tale, as when Marie-Jeanne Lhéritier de Villandon herself as author directed chatty commentary about "The Enchantments of Eloquence" (Les enchantements de l'éloquence, 1696) to the Duchess of Epernon, its dedicatee. Shorn of commentary, plots alone survived in later editions, without their original authorial explanations and comments.

The discussion so far has treated evidence of decisions to exclude parts of a tale that had once been an integral part of it. The next section will treat translation in its conventional sense, namely, the ways in which literary translations of a fairy tale do or do not communicate the overall sense and style of the original text. As one example, Straparola can tell outrageous events in a straightforward manner. Take for instance, Princess Bellisandra's brazen murder of her husband:

> La damigella non molto lenta ad ubidire il comandamento del soldano, prese l'acuto coltello che del giovenil sangue era bagnato ancora, e postali la mano sinistra sopra il cavezzzo e quello forte tenendo, nel petto un mortal colpo li diede; ... (1:106)

> Then the princess, who tarried not a moment to obey this command of the sultan, took up the sharp knife which was still wet with Livoretto's blood, and having seized him by the throat with her left hand, held him fast while she dealt him a mortal blow in the breast. (trans. Waters 1:298)

Waters's translation above captures Straparola's spare narrative style exactly.

When translators perform minor departures from original grammatical constructions they can produce subtle but important changes to a text. Examples abound in tale history. For instance, to communicate urgency and inevitability in her description of a prince who has caught sight of Persinette in her tower, seventeenth-century French writer Charlotte-Rose Caumont de La Force uses a series of simple subject-verb clauses within a single sentence (highlighted in bold):

> **Il fit** vingt fois le tour de cette fatale tour, et n'y voyant point d'entrée, **il pensa** mourir de douleur, **il avait** de l'amour, **il avait** de l'audace, **il eût voulu** pouvoir escalader la tour. (333)

In the following translation of "Persinette," La Force's distinctive sentence construction is remade as two complex sentences with dependent clauses and conjunctions (highlighted in bold) that suggest prior cause and resulting effect:

> He went around that fatal tower twenty times, **and when** he could not find an entrance, he thought he would die of agony; **for** he had fallen in love. **But since** he was daring, he kept looking for a way to scale the tower. (trans. Zipes 481)

These translation choices alter the tale's meaning at this point by replacing a pressing emotional simultaneity with a rationally accounted for cause and effect.

Nineteenth-century German collectors Jacob and Wilhelm Grimm stressed authenticity in their volume, introducing several dialect tales as evidence of popular voicing. But the language of the Grimms' dialect tales has proven so difficult to translate that it was not until 1978 that Brian Alderson "gave a regional English colouring to a few of the tales which the Grimms printed in Low German dialect" (Luke 43), which David Luke then continued in 1982 with additional translations of other Grimm tales into socially corresponding dialects of the British Isles.

Translation has carried individual tales such as sixteenth-century Straparola's "Pietro Pazzo" (Peter the Fool), seventeenth-century Perrault's "Cendrillon" (Cinderella), and the nineteenth-century Grimms' "Rotkäppchen" (Little Red Cap) throughout the world. Their widespread distribution led some nineteenth-century theorists to posit polygenesis: such fairy tales—they believed—had sprung into life under varying cultural conditions in locations far distant from one another, because—so they believed—similar human needs had brought forth the same story.

Increasingly, however, research indicates that books themselves, translated into new languages and transplanted into new cultures, have transformed European fairy tales into shapes that fit the local expectations of cultures around the world. The Reverend Lal Day introduced the feline "Puss in Boots" to India as a jackal (Bottigheimer 2010); the Grimms' version of "Red Riding Hood" reached Japan in the 1860s, and the mutually legible characters of the written languages carried it to China in the early years of the twentieth century (Farquhar 127). The tale tradition of click-speaking peoples in Namibia, a former German colony, contains among its local stories tales that are recognizably Grimmian (Schmidt). Research on the spread of fairy tales suggests that physical translations, that is, transfers of books, from Europe to distant parts of the world carried fairy tales from one country to another (Bottigheimer 1993). Translators adapt fairy tales in simple ways by changing characters' names (the Italian "Pietro" to the French "Pierre"). They also acknowledge profound cultural differences when they change heroes' and heroines' emotions to fit into the target language and culture (Bottigheimer 1987, 1993). Because of translation changes like these, new translations are often new tellings of an old tale.

Works Cited

Bottigheimer, Ruth B. "*Fairy Godfather*, Fairy-Tale History, and Fairy-Tale Scholarship: A Response to Dan Ben-Amos, Jan Ziolklowski, and Francisco Vaz da Silva." *Journal of American Folklore* 123 (Fall 2010): 447–96.

____. *Fairy Godfather: Straparola, Venice, and the Fairy Tale Tradition*. Philadelphia, PA: U of Pennsylvania P, 2002.

____. *Grimms' Bad Girls and Bold Boys. The Moral and Social Vision of the Tales*. New Haven, CT: Yale UP, 1987.

____. "Luckless, Witless, and Filthy-Footed: A Socio-Cultural Study and Publishing History Analysis of 'The Lazy Boy' (AT 675)." *Journal of American Folklore* 106 (Summer 1993): 259-84.

Farquhar, Mary Ann. *Children's Literature in China: From Lu Xun to Mao Zedong*. Armonk, NY: M.E. Sharpe, 1999.

La Force, Charlotte-Rose Caumont de. "Persinette." [1697] In *Contes: Mademoiselle Lhéritier, Mademoiselle Bernard, Mademoiselle de La Force, Madame Durand, Madame d'Auneuil*, ed. Raymonde Robert. Paris: Honoré Champion, 2005.

Lhéritier de Villandon, Marie-Jeanne. "Les Enchantements de l'éloquence." [1696] In *Contes: Mademoiselle Lhéritier, Mademoiselle Bernard, Mademoiselle de La Force, Madame Durand, Madame d'Auneuil*, ed. Raymonde Robert. Paris: Honoré Champion, 2005.

Luke, David. *Jacob and Wilhelm Grimm. Selected Tales*. Harmondsworth, UK: Penguin, 1982.

Schmidt, Sigrid. *Märchen aus Namibia*. Cologne: Diederichs, 1980.

Straparola, Giovan Francesco. *The Entertaining Nights*. Ed. and trans., Suzanne Magnanini. Toronto, ON: Center for Renaissance and Reformation Studies P, forthcoming 2013.

____. *The Facetious Nights of Straparola*. Ed. and trans., W.G. Waters. 4 vols. London: Society of Bibliophiles, 1898.

____. *Le Piacevoli Notti*. 2 vols. Ed. Donato Pirovano. Rome: Salerno Editrice, 2000.

____. *The Pleasant Nights: Giovan Francesco Straparola*. 2 vols. Ed. and trans., Donald Beecher. Toronto, ON: U of Toronto P, 2012.

Zipes, Jack. *The Great Fairy Tale Tradition: From Straparola and Basile to the Brothers Grimm*. New York, NY: W.W. Norton, 2001.

THE TRANSLATION OF ENCHANTMENT

Nancy L. Canepa

THE FAIRY TALE IS ONE of the most universally familiar of narrative forms. Even those incapable of recognizing Odysseus or Medea, Don Quixote or Desdemona will invariably be acquainted in some way with the adventures of Little Red Riding Hood and Snow White. And few other narrative forms have been and continue to be so consistently refashioned as the fairy tale, which over time has simultaneously preserved its distinctiveness as a genre and reconceptualized its forms and functions to engage with new realities. Within the European literary tradition alone, fairy tales have been written for sophisticated court and salon entertainment, social criticism, and metaphysical parable, but also as moralizing children's tales and, more recently, as a forum for experimenting with postmodern narratives and ideologies. Among the many adaptations and revisions of fairy tales also number translations, those other "invisible" retellings in which the history of the genre abounds.[1] Any discussion of fairy tales—and translation—necessarily includes, then, a broader reflection on the authorship, dissemination, and reception of cultural material.

I'd like to focus my comments on my own translation of a fairy-tale collection, Giambattista Basile's *The Tale of Tales, or Entertainment for Little Ones* (*Lo cunto de li cunti, overo Lo trattennemiento de' peccerille*, 1634–36), also known as the *Pentamerone*. Basile, a courtier and feudal administrator who used Tuscan, or literary Italian, in his "official" output, adopted Neapolitan dialect in *The Tale of Tales* and several shorter works, elevating what had until then been a predominantly non-literary vernacular to literary status. Fairy tales had previously appeared in European novella collections, most notably, in Giovan Francesco Straparola's *The Pleasant Nights* (*Le piacevoli notti*, 1550–53), but Basile was the first European author to conceive of an entire framed cycle of fairy-tale narratives, and his innovative narrative model—the authored, literary fairy tale—would reach extraordinary levels of popularity throughout the following centuries.

To translate: according to the *Oxford English Dictionary*, "to turn from one language into another," but also "to transfer, transport," and "to change in form, appearance, or substance; to transmute, to transform." What exactly does Basile himself transport, and how does he change its form? The stories that make up *The Tale of Tales*, of the sort that "old women usually tell for the entertainment of little ones," derive from folk and popular traditions. Although in Italy the interest in the "popular" and the cross-fertilization between high and low cultures was evident from at least

1 Here I use the polemical epithet adopted by Venuti, *Translator's Invisibility*.

the fourteenth century onward, the exploration of the New World and the increasingly anthropological attention to the discoveries therein substantiated "the myth of the primitive" (Cocchiara 5) and the fascination with "unknown human societies with strange languages, religions, and customs" (Ben-Amos xviii). This in turn helped to inspire, locally, an interest in Europe's own "exotic" folk traditions and the cataloguing and literary re-elaboration of its materials, especially in the sixteenth and seventeenth centuries.

Both the language and narrative form that Basile adopts reflect in a very concrete way this general interest. What is "translated"—transported, but also transformed into sophisticated artful narratives for a literate courtly public—involves, however, much more than popular tales of magic. Basile borrows materials and discursive modes from sources as disparate as myths and legends, animal tales, epic, chapbooks, novellas, travel accounts, theater, and the love lyric, as well as translating the "wonders" of everyday life in the Naples and Italy of his time into the many descriptions of contemporary people, places, customs, and practices that pepper the text. Basile was not alone in his role of transporter and transformer, balancing on the threshold of multiple cultures. His work appeared during a period—the early seventeenth century, the "Baroque"—of epistemic discontinuity and reflection on "the arbitrariness of inherited forms of knowledge, social values, and structures" (Castillo 100). In this context, translating meaning, in the widest sense of the term, can be seen as an emblematic activity, reflecting the impulse to experiment with new ways of perceiving, comprehending, and representing a rapidly changing world.

Translating this uniquely polyphonic and unruly work—one that has virtually no precedents or epigones in Italian literature—involved engaging with a full spectrum of the complexities of the process of translation itself. Once I had confronted the substantial semantic hurdles, I still had every translator's most difficult question in front of me: how to render Basile's distinctive voice? How to translate a work that flaunts such spectacular and innovative hybridization, a major work of "minor literature" that exposes "the contradictory conditions of ... the literary canon [and] the dominant culture"? (Venuti, *Scandals* 10).[1] Should the translator attempt to reproduce the idiosyncrasies of a work that is "strange" or "foreign" even in Italy, possibly to the detriment of fluidity? Or, instead, to bow to the temptation to domesticate and render more fluid and transparent a text that, for all of its delights, is none of these? Ultimately, I aimed to craft a productively foreignizing translation, attempting to avoid the simplification, abridgment, or "scandalous decorum" to which even Basile's most illustrious translators have succumbed.[2]

1 This use of the term "minor literature" was coined in Deleuze and Guattari (100 ff).

2 I borrow the term from Borges (37).

But what difference does it really make? How are different degrees of "domestication" or "foreignization" in translation linked to the larger question of what it means to transport cultural material? In order to begin to formulate an answer, let us consider several passages from Basile's tales in two representative English translations of the nineteenth and twentieth centuries, both by eminent British folklorists, Sir Richard Burton (1893) and Norman Penzer (1932). At the start of Tale 1.10, "The Old Woman Who Was Skinned," a king's attentions are occupied by his mysterious downstairs neighbors, two ancient sisters, until, in Burton's translation (who tones the tale's title down to "The Old Woman Discovered"):

> he could not even belch but that these two would talk and observe his doings; sometimes saying, that a jasmine had fallen upon their heads, and had given them an head-ache; another time, that a letter had fallen upon their shoulders and disturbed them; and at another, that the dust had suffocated them.

Penzer's version reads:

> he was not even able to sneeze without upsetting these old hags, for they grumbled and complained about everything. First they said that a sprig of jessamine had fallen from the window and bruised their heads, then that a torn letter had hurt their shoulders, and then that some powder had crushed their hips.

Finally, my translation:

> he couldn't even fart without causing those old pains in the neck to wrinkle their noses, for they grumbled and threw themselves about like squid over the smallest thing. First they said that a jasmine flower fallen from above had given one of them a lump on her head, then that a torn-up letter had dislocated one of their shoulders, and then that a pinch of dust had bruised one of their thighs.

Whereas some part of the earlier translators' choices may be attributed to the opacity of the Neapolitan (Penzer relied more heavily on Benedetto Croce's Italian translation than on the original, and Neapolitan was perhaps not at the top of the list of the close to 30 languages in which Burton was reputably versed), their general tendency to both clean up and flatten Basile's language and imagery is quite evident. The king's bodily eruption is rendered as a belch by Burton and an even more innocuous sneeze by Penzer, whereas in Neapolitan the term—*pideto*—explicitly refers to a function of the less decorous lower-body stratum. The graphic, theatrical nature of the sisters' displeasure is likewise elided into a bland generality of terms. The overall effect of such qualitative and quantitative impoverishment[1] is to downplay the women's physicality, in the process compromising the potency of this prologue to a tale whose theme centers on, precisely, physical appearance. But it also, and no less potently, both dilutes Basile's formidable, and comic, descriptive abilities and erases allusions to local culture and customs (e.g., the squid).

Translations from Tale 5.1, "The Goose," offer another example of the reductive treatment of "difficult" passages. At the start of the tale two penniless sisters spend their last resources to buy a goose. When they arrive home with it they are awarded a surprise. Burton's translation:

> But sweep today and look tomorrow, the good day came, and the goose began to drop golden crowns, in such a manner that one by one they filled a large chest, and the dropping was such that the sisters began to lift their heads, and to look well fed and happy.

And Penzer's:

> But dawn comes and it turns out a fine day: the worthy goose began to make golden ducats, so that, little by little, they filled a great chest with them; and, such was that excrement, that they began to carry their heads high with shining countenances.

In both translations all derivatives of the verb *cacare* (to shit), which obsessively punctuates the original, are expunged (as they are in Croce's Italian translation), resulting in a staid and lifeless rendition. What is lost, once again, is the peculiarly exuberant flavor of Basile's text, which can careen from the most Petrarchan of metaphors to ... a chest of shit. *Dalle stelle alle stalle*—from the stars to the stables—as an Italian saying goes. And, in passing, also lost is the reader's awareness of the commonality of Basile's hybridizing "bad writing" with other early modern masters such as Rabelais or Cervantes.[2] My translation reads:

> And when morning breaks it's a nice day, for the good goose began to shit hard cash, until, shitload upon shitload, they had filled up a whole chest. There was

1 These are two of the 12 "deforming tendencies" outlined in Berman.

2 Berman comments on "the loss of control, [...] the proliferation, the welling of the text" in such works of literary prose, which "collects, reassembles, and intermingles the polylingual space of a community. It mobilizes and activates the totality of 'languages' that coexist in any language" (297).

so much shit, in fact, that the two sisters began to raise their heads and see their fur shine ...

Increasing the familiarity of texts from the early history of the fairy tale and treating them more philologically in translation certainly offers new insights into the early modern culture in which these works were written. But it also sheds a new light on the history of the literary fairy tale and on the relevance and relation of these early narrative modes to other literary forms. For example, as in recent decades scholars of fairy tales have denaturalized and historicized their readings of the dominant "classic" versions of tales, focusing on the cultural and ideological specificity of the tales and the dynamics of canon formation, the accessibility to the often darker and racier Italian tales has been crucial.[1]

Equally intriguing, though relatively little attended to, is the "translation" of the narrative model of the early fairy tale into later forms. The itineraries of subject formation that the fairy tale recounts, in however formulaic or pared-down fashion; the "comic familiarization of the image of man" that we find in its characters; the busy subtexts of daily life in all of its aspects, from the highest to, especially, the lowest; and the refusal of the "absolutism of a single or unitary language" foreshadow the more complex paths that the novel will take in the following centuries (Bakhtin 35, 366). And in our own centuries the fairy tale has even more explicitly permeated other literary forms, as both model and material, in authors as diverse as Italo Calvino, Angela Carter, Margaret Atwood, Robert Coover, and Salman Rushdie.

Informed translations thus beget deep thinking of the processes involved in the transference of cultural material over time and across space, a sort of thinking that, as we have seen, was not foreign to the early fabulists themselves. One of the things that most astounds my students of fairy tales is that much of what we read is so different from what they consider the "real" (usually, Disney or Disneyfied) versions. This can be disorienting at first—What do you mean, Cinderella is an assassin?—but it is ultimately eye-opening, for these same students come to understand that these remote, curious old tales can still speak to them. And, in the process, they experience their own initiations into new fictional—and nonfictional—worlds and into a new awareness of the profoundly vital nature of narrative. It constitutes a wonderful irony that we, citizens of an increasingly rootless world, continue to look for guidance

1 Two of the best-known examples are Basile's version of "Sleeping Beauty" ("Sun, Moon and Talia," 5.5), in which the "prince charming" character, actually a married king, rapes his Sleeping Beauty, Talia, *while* she is asleep, then abandons her to return to his wife, and later nearly eats, unaware, the twins born to Talia; and Basile's "The Cinderella Cat" (1.6), whose heroine is a conniving murderess who shapes her own destiny with cold determination.

in tales of quests for belonging, but also that for so long we have been drawn to translate, transport, and transform these tales of the marvelous in order to better decipher our own past and present *and* to venture into worlds far from our own.

Works Cited

Bakhtin, Mikhail. *The Dialogic Imagination*. Ed. Michael Holquist. Trans. Caryl Emerson and Michael Holquist. Austin, TX: U of Texas P, 1982.

Basile, Giambattista. *Il Pentamerone, or The Tale of Tales by Giovanni Batiste Basile*. Trans. Sir Richard Burton. [1893] Honolulu, HI: UP of the Pacific, 2003.

____. The *Pentamerone of Giambattista Basile*. Trans. and ed. Norman M. Penzer. London: John Lane the Bodley Head, 1932.

____. *The Tale of Tales, or Entertainment for Little Ones*. Trans., ed. and notes Nancy L. Canepa. Detroit, MI: Wayne State UP, 2007.

Ben-Amos, Dan. "Foreword" to Giuseppe Cocchiara, *The History of Folklore in Europe*. Philadelphia, PA: Institute for the Study of Human Issues, 1981. xvii-xix.

Berman, Antoine "Translation and the Trials of the Foreign." In *The Translation Studies Reader*, ed. Lawrence Venuti. London and New York: Routledge, 2000. 284–97.

Borges, Jorge Luis. "The Translators of The Thousand and One Nights." In *The Translation Studies Reader*, ed. Lawrence Venuti. London and New York, NY: Routledge, 2000. 34–48.

Castillo, David. "Horror (Vacui): The Baroque Condition." In *Hispanic Baroques: Reading Culture in Context*, ed. Nicholas Spadaccini and Luis Martin-Estudillo. Nashville, TN: Vanderbilt UP, 2005. 87–104.

Cocchiara, Giuseppe. *Popolo e letteratura in Italia*. Turin: Einaudi, 1959.

Deleuze, Gilles and Félix Guattari. *A Thousand Plateaus: Capitalism and Schizophrenia*. Minneapolis, MN: U of Minnesota P, 1987.

Venuti, Lawrence. *The Translator's Invisibility: A History of Translation*. London and New York, NY: Routledge, 1995.

____. *The Scandals of Translation: Towards an Ethics of Difference*. London and New York, NY: Routledge, 1998.

THE WONDER OF THE *ARABIAN NIGHTS* IN ENGLISH

Muhsin al-Musawi

In a neat conclusion to her 1908 reading of *The Oriental Tale in England in the Eighteenth Century*, Martha Pike Conant baptizes the *Arabian Nights* (or *The Thousand and One Nights*) as the "fairy godmother of the English novel" (243). The *Nights* functions that way in more than one sense. Its appearance in Antoine Galland's French translation, 1704–11, and simultaneously in English, made it the most surprising literary phenomenon. It swept journals, dailies, and weeklies, and it elicited comments from almost every writer or scholar of renown. Its appeal and impact, influx, and dynamic acceleration of a literary scene and culture industry, were stupendous and multidimensional. But was it only the fantastical elements of the text that captured the imagination of Europe? There are many fairy tales that could have provided Europeans with something to which, in comparison, Shakespeare's fairies pale. Indeed, many a scholar and critic in the eighteenth century belittled Shakespeare's fairies and medieval fairy lore when they came upon Scheherazade's legacy of the wonderful and the fantastic. It was a particular use of wonder that gave the *Nights* its inimitable charm, but, importantly, this dimension of the text was handled and interpreted in strikingly varied ways by eighteenth- and nineteenth-century Europeans. The story of the *Arabian Nights* and its fate in English print history is nothing less than the story of the power of translation to shape a narrative's history.

In the *Nights*, the tales of wonder are many, and they certainly make up a significant portion in the frame tale cycle of merchants and demons: "The Porter and the Three Ladies of Baghdad," the story of "Nur al-Din Ali Masri," and also the story of "Jullanar of the Sea," along with the tales of the three mendicants. These narratives abound with magic, demons, jinns, and ifrits. But in these tales the wonderful or the fantastic does not arise by itself or in isolation from human agency. Jinns or demons appear in response to a human situation, out of curiosity or in internal competitions and strife that center on a human situation. In other words, the wonderful and the representational or realistic blend together. There lies the power of this dimension of the stories: these tales of wonder titillate the mind without necessarily upsetting its empirical reasoning in an age that was known for its rationality.

By and large, eighteenth-century European translators and redactors, appropriators, imitators, and editors did not feel alienated by this blend of the real and the fantastical. Nevertheless, this amalgam did arouse curiosity and surprise among some critics. The case of Bishop Atterbury in England is well-documented: presented with a volume by Alexander Pope, Atterbury was appalled and responded with alarm and great unease. Horace Walpole did not spare the bishop in his sarcastic remarks on rigidity in the age of reason, and the bishop's responses to the *Nights* and other popular texts became the object of sarcastic commentary throughout the century. Writers in the vein of Joseph Addison and Richard Steele used some of these tales for a moral or satirical purpose, with an eye to social commentary. In other words, fairy tales or stories of wonder could be appropriated in translation to fit or to mock a rising middle-class morality. As I argued in *Scheherazade in England*, the collection passed through some trimming or tailoring here and there to fit into readers' expectations, and on the whole its many translations or redactions serve as an index of taste, alternately mirroring and critiquing the expectations of the rising bourgeoisie.

Galland's French edition (1704–11) served as the basis for all English versions of the *Nights* in the eighteenth century, and it offered itself easily to adaptors, theater directors, journalists, and novelists who could pick and choose whatever suited their own dispositions and those of their audiences. In these early adaptations of the *Nights*, the fairy component did not sound as jarring as it would to many later audiences whose pragmatic mindset attracted them to tales that conclude with some material achievement (as do Sindbad's adventures). Victorians would once again reshape the *Nights*' fantastical landscape to their own ends.

This process began with one of the more attentive readers of the *Nights*' cultural dimension: Edward William Lane. Lane's early Victorian edition of the *Nights* (1838–41) maintained the fantastical elements of the text but also included elaborate footnotes that translate the fantastical into something practical: a guide or manual on foreign manners and customs. In this way, he believed, a seemingly absurd element of the narrative could be made palatable and relevant to British readers. Lane's footnotes were so detailed that his nephew was able to publish them under separate cover, 40 years later, as an historical and ethnographic guide, entitled *Arabian Society in the Middle Ages* (1883). In Lane's footnotes, comments on the world of magic are many, and situate the fantastical within a system of faith and belief. Lane addresses the abundance of the supernatural and erotic elements in oral storytelling and in the *Nights* in terms of social and religious elements of a society that he prided himself on knowing intimately from his sojourn in Egypt. The erotic is not explained as part of the conviviality and joyfulness that comes with storytelling as a street profession but as an anthropological detail that was noticed by the undisputed authoritative Orientalist himself. The supernatural element led Lane to argue the case as a Quranic premise: the natural and the supernatural were not as separate as they might have become later and especially not as Europeans imagined them to be. By acknowledging and demonstrating in his footnotes that rewriting a text for a different cultural environment meant altering its value system as well as its language, Lane exposed the ideological implications of translation.

The Quranic formula that opens Muslim literature appears in the *Arabian Nights*: "call on Me and I respond," which attests to the availability of God to human needs and requests. The universe as such harbors a combination of the human and the spirit world in the form of emissaries: fairies and spirits make an ordinary appearance in the everyday. In many tales they are there to strike arrangements, abide by pledges and oaths, and form pacts. In the *Arabian Nights* as in the Quran there are both good and bad jinns. Scheherazade's tales are a celebration of the relationship between the human and the spirit world, expressed in a fairy element that expands imaginatively beyond apprehensible restrictions and bindings.

What Lane perceived in the *Arabian Nights* is that for a long time these tales circulated among audiences in the Islamic regions without causing many qualms or raising many questions. Fairies worked with humans and had at times the same appreciation of beauty. The story of "Nur al-Din and Budur," for example, shows how love and beauty can be brought together in an arrangement that defies time and space. Love is triumphant as a transcending power. But you need some spirits, jinns, to make this possible or at least feasible in narrative terms. The two jinn, Danhash and Maimuna, are available to make this union possible.

In the case of the *Nights*, the role of wonder in the everyday underwent particularly dramatic transformation in its nineteenth-century European translation. By the end of the nineteenth century, Richard Burton's translation of the *Nights* included an even more expansive anthropological apparatus, preoccupied with erotic Orientalism and standing as a challenge to British middle-class values. He translated the fairy dimension of the text in terms of the erotic, a subconscious urge to go beyond limits. Like Lane before him, he recognized how important the fantastical dimension was to the story and "translated" it according to his own values and interests.

This combination of the material and the spiritual, the factual and the imaginary, has sustained the *Nights* even through periods in which the "fantastical" was largely out of favor. In this defiance of our intellectual limits lies the power that led Samuel Taylor Coleridge to appreciate the tales of the merchant and the demon, in which the demon comes out of the blue in a seemingly abandoned wilderness. For Coleridge this appearance or apparition stands for the power of imagination itself: bold and surprising or even terrifying, bringing together the familiar and the wonderful into a poetic tradition that requires only "the willing suspension of disbelief for the moment, that constitutes poetic faith" (174). Today, we may return to reading this supernatural presence as a narrative strategy that allows the story to fulfill the premise that love and beauty can make their case despite obstacles and boundaries.

Works Cited

al-Musawi, Muhsin [Muhsin Jassim Ali]. *Scheherazade in England.* Washington, DC: Three Continents P, 1981.

Coleridge, Samuel Taylor. *Biographia Literaria.* Book XIV. [1817] New York, NY: Leavitt, Lord and Co., 1834.

Conant, Martha Pike. *The Oriental Tale in England in the Eighteenth Century.* New York, NY: Columbia UP, 1908.

Lane-Poole, Stanley. *Arabian Society in the Middle Ages.* London: Chatto & Windus, 1883.

NOTES ON CONTRIBUTORS

Muhsin al-Musawi is Professor of Arabic and Comparative Studies at Columbia University. He is the editor of the *Journal of Arabic Literature* and the author of many books in English and Arabic, including *Scheherazade in England* (1982), *The Islamic Context of the Thousand and One Nights* (2009), the *Postcolonial Arabic Novel* (2003), *Arabic Poetry: Trajectories of Modernity and Tradition* (2006), *Reading Iraq: Culture and Power in Conflict* (2006), and *Islam on the Street: Religion in Modern Arabic Literature* (2009). He is the editor of the Barnes and Noble *Arabian Nights*.

Cristina Bacchilega is Professor of English at the University of Hawai'i at Mānoa, where she teaches folklore and literature, fairy tales and their adaptations, and cultural studies. She has published *Legendary Hawai'i and the Politics of Place: Tradition, Translation, and Tourism* (2007) and *Postmodern Fairy Tales: Gender and Narrative Strategies* (1997), and she is the review editor of *Marvels & Tales: Journal of Fairy-Tale Studies*. Recent essays include "Generic Complexity in Early 21st-Century Fairy-Tale Film" with John Rieder (2010) and work on nineteenth-century translations of *The Arabian Nights* into Hawaiian with historian Noelani Arista and translator Sahoa Fukushima (2007). With Donatella Izzo and Bryan Kamaoli Kuwada, Bacchilega co-edited "Sustaining Hawaiian Sovereignty," a special issue of *Anglistica*, an online journal of international interdisciplinary studies (2011). Her current book project focuses on the poetics and politics of twenty-first-century fairy-tale adaptations.

Marina Balina is Isaac Funk Professor of Russian Studies at Illinois Wesleyan University. Her published research has focused on contemporary Russian life writing—autobiography, memoir, and travelogue—as well as Soviet children's literature and culture. She has co-edited *Endquote: Sots-Art Literature and Soviet Empire Style* (with Nancy Condee and Evgeny Dobrenko, 2000), *Sovetskoe Bogatstvo: Stat'i o literature, kul'ture i kino* (with Evgeny Dobrenko and Yuri Murashov, 2002), *Dictionary of Literary Biography: Russian Writers since 1980* (with Mark Lipovetsky, 2003), an anthology of Russian and Soviet fairy tales, *Politicizing Magic* (with Helena Goscilo and Mark Lipovetsky, 2005), *Russian Children's Literature and Culture* (with Larissa Rudova, 2008), *Petrified Utopia: Happiness Soviet Style* (with Evgeny Dobrenko, 2009), and most recently *The Cambridge Companion to Twentieth-Century Russian Literature* (with Evgeny Dobrenko, 2011).

Ruth B. Bottigheimer, Research Professor in the Department of Comparative Literary and Cultural Studies at Stony Brook University, teaches and does research on fairy tales and children's literature. She is editor of *Fairy Tales and Society: Illusion, Allusion, and Paradigm* (1986) and *Gender and Story in South India* (with Leela Prasad and Lalita Handoo, 2006), and author of *Grimms' Bad Girls and Bold Boys: The Moral and Social Vision of the Tales* (1987), *The Bible for Children from the Age of Gutenberg to the Present* (1996), *Fairy Godfather: Straparola, Venice, and the Fairy Tale Tradition* (2002), and *Fairy Tales: A New History* (2009). She has published on the history and theory of fairy tales in *Marvels & Tales: Journal of Fairy-Tale Studies* and *Journal of American Folklore.* She has most recently edited a volume of translations of early edition prefaces, titled *Fairy Tales Framed: Early Forewords, Afterwords, and Critical Words* (2012).

Nancy L. Canepa is Associate Professor of Italian at Dartmouth College. Her teaching and research interests include seventeenth-century Italian literature and culture, fairy tales, Italian dialect literature, and translation studies. In the area of fairy tales, she has published *Out of the Woods: The Origins of the Literary Fairy Tale in Italy and France* (1997), *From Court to Forest: Giambattista Basile's "Lo cunto de li cunti" and the Birth of the Literary Fairy Tale* (1999), and translations of Carlo Collodi's *The Adventures of Pinocchio* (2002) and Giambattista Basile's *The Tale of Tales* (2007). She is currently working on an anthology of Italian fairy tales in translation, titled *The Enchanted Boot*, as well as an edited volume of essays on teaching the fairy tale.

Anne E. Duggan is Associate Professor of French Literature at Wayne State University and Associate Editor of *Marvels & Tales: Journal of Fairy-Tale Studies.* She is author of *Salonnières, Furies, and Fairies: The Politics of Gender and Cultural Change in*

Absolutist France (2005) and *Enchanting Subversions: The Fairy-Tale Cinema of Jacques Demy* (manuscript under consideration). Along with her work on fairy tales, she has published on early modern women writers as well as on the genre of the tragic story.

Bill Ellis is Professor Emeritus of English and American Studies at Penn State University. He has served as President of the American Folklore Society's Children's Folklore Section, as well as of the AFS's Folk Narrative Section. The author of several books and numerous articles on storytelling and on contemporary legend, he recently published a fuller study of the use of the fairy tale "Sleeping Beauty" in the manga/anime *Cardcaptor Sakura*, published in *The Japanification of Children's Popular Culture*, edited by Mark I. West (2008). He resides in Berlin, Maryland.

Donald Haase is Professor of German and Associate Dean of the College of Liberal Arts and Sciences at Wayne State University. He has edited *The Reception of Grimms' Fairy Tales: Responses, Reactions, Revisions* (1993), an edition of Joseph Jacobs's *English Fairy Tales and More English Fairy Tales* (2002), *Fairy Tales and Feminism: New Approaches* (2004), and the three-volume *Greenwood Encyclopedia of Folktales and Fairy Tales* (2007). He also edits the international journal *Marvels & Tales: Journal of Fairy-Tale Studies* and the Series in Fairy-Tale Studies for Wayne State University Press.

Henry Glassie is College Professor Emeritus at Indiana University and author of many books on folklore, folk art, and vernacular architecture. Recently he was given the award for a lifetime of scholarly achievement from the American Folklore Society and the Charles Homer Haskins Prize of the American Council of Learned Societies for a distinguished career of humanistic scholarship.

Elizabeth Wanning Harries is Helen and Laura Shedd Professor Emerita of Modern Languages at Smith College. Her work on literary fairy tales includes *Twice upon a Time: Women Writers and the History of the Fairy Tale* (2001) and several recent essays including "The Violence of the Lambs," "'Ancient Forms': Myth, Fairy Tale, and Narrative in A.S. Byatt's Fiction," "Old Men and Comatose Virgins: Nobel Prize Winners Re-Write 'Sleeping Beauty,'" and "Water Music: Dvořák's *Rusalka* and the Tale of Melusine." She also writes about eighteenth- and nineteenth-century fragments and novels, particularly Sterne's *Tristram Shandy*.

Molly Clark Hillard is an Assistant Professor at Seattle University, where she specializes in nineteenth-century literature. She is the author of *Spellbound: The Fairy Tale and the Victorians* (forthcoming). Her essays appear in *Dickens Studies Annual*,

Partial Answers, *Narrative*, and *SEL*. She is currently at work on her next book project, about the networking of Victorian and postmodern literatures, with the working title of *Re-reading the Victorians*.

Christine A. Jones is Associate Professor of French and Comparative Literary and Cultural Studies in the Department of Languages and Literature at the University of Utah. Her scholarship explores the literary and material arts that emerged during the reign of Louis XIV and the cultural relevance of trades in the eighteenth century. Her first monograph, *Shapely Bodies: The Image of Porcelain in Eighteenth-Century France* (forthcoming), is on material culture and national identity. Current projects include a study on the representation of trades and luxury consumerism in the *Encyclopédie* and new translations of Charles Perrault's *Histoires ou contes du temps passé*.

Armando Maggi is Professor of Romance Languages and Literatures at the University of Chicago, where he also serves on the Committee on History of Culture. He has published several books on early modern philosophy and spirituality. He is currently completing a volume titled *Preserving the Spell: Basile, The Brothers Grimm, and the Future of Storytelling*.

Gina M. Miele is Assistant Professor of Italian and former Director of the Coccia Institute for the Italian Experience in America at Montclair State University. While she specializes in nineteenth- and twentieth-century Italian folktales, particularly those of Luigi Capuana and Italo Calvino, she teaches courses on various periods, authors, and genres of the Italian literary tradition. She has published in *Italica*, *Marvels & Tales: Journal of Fairy-Tale Studies*, *Fabula*, *Italian Quarterly*, the *Greenwood Encyclopedia of Folktales and Fairy Tales*, the *Harvard College Journal of Italian American History and Culture*, the *Italian American Review*, *Altreitalie*, the *Paterson Literary Review*, and *Primo Magazine*. She is currently working on an annotated translation of Luigi Capuana's fairy tales.

Sophie Raynard is Associate Professor of French in the Department of European Languages, Literatures, and Cultures at the State University of New York at Stony Brook. She specializes in women's seventeenth-century French literature. She is the author of the book *La Seconde préciosité. Floraison des conteuses de 1690 à 1756* (2002), as well as several articles on the poetics of early *contes de fées* and the various connections between the *conteuses*, preciosity, and libertinism. She also served as the guest editor for a special issue on fairy tales in the *Romanic Review*, edited *The Teller's Tale: Lives of the Classic Fairy-Tale Writers* (forthcoming), and is co-editing a volume on fairy-tale paratexts. She is completing a monograph on the poetics of early *contes de fées*.

Jennifer Schacker is an Associate Professor in the School of English and Theatre Studies at the University of Guelph. She is the author of *National Dreams: The Remaking of Fairy Tales in Nineteenth-Century England* (2003), which received the Mythopoeic Scholarship Award in 2006. She has contributed to *The Encyclopedia of Folklore and Literature* and *The Greenwood Encyclopedia of Folktales and Fairy Tales*, and has published articles on the histories of folklore, the fairy tale, and Christmas pantomime in *Journal of American Folklore*, *Folklore Historian*, and *Marvels & Tales: Journal of Fairy-Tale Studies*. She is currently completing a manuscript titled *Cross-Dressed Tales: English Pantomime and Fairy-Tale History*, which was supported by a three-year grant from the Social Sciences and Humanities Research Council of Canada.

SOURCES

Marius Barbeau and Michael Hornyansky. "Princess Tomboso," from *The Golden Phoenix and Other Fairy Tales from Quebec*. Collected by Marius Barbeau; retold by Michael Hornyansky. Copyright © Oxford University Press Canada, 1980. Reprinted by permission of the publisher.

Donald Braid. "The Boy and the Blacksmith," from *Scottish Traveller Tales: Lives Shaped Through Stories*. Copyright © 2002, University Press of Mississippi. Reprinted with the permission of University Press of Mississippi.

Nancy L. Canepa (Translator). "Cinderella Cat, Sixth Entertainment of the First Day," "Old Woman Who Was Skinned, Tenth Entertainment of the First Day," "Cagliuso, Fourth Entertainment of the Second Day," "Sun, Moon, and Talia, Fifth Entertainment of the Fifth Day," from Giambattista Basile's *The Tale of Tales, or Entertainment for Little Ones*, translated by Nancy Canepa; illustrated by Carmelo Lettere. Copyright © 2007, Wayne State University Press. Reprinted with the permission of Wayne State University Press.

Robert Coover. Excerpt from *Briar Rose*, copyright © 1996 by Robert Coover. New York: Grove Press, 1996. Used by permission of Grove/Atlantic, Inc., and Penguin Books Ltd.

Hasan M. El-Shamy (Editor). "The Daughters of the Bean Vendor," from *Tales Arab Women Tell, and the Behavioral Patterns They Portray*. Copyright © 1999, Indiana University Press. Reprinted with the permission of Indiana University Press.

Neil Gaiman. "Instructions," from *A Wolf at the Door and Other Retold Fairy Tales*, edited by Ellen Datlow and Terri Windling. New York: Simon and Schuster Books for Young Readers, 2000. Reprinted with the permission of Writers House LLC.

George Gibian (Translator). "A Children's Story" by Daniil Kharms, from *Russia's Lost Literature of the Absurd*, edited and translated by George Gibian. Ithaca: Cornell University Press, 1971. Reprinted with the permission of the Estate of George Gibian and Literary Agency Galina Dursthoff.

Helena Goscilo (Translator). "The Frog Princess," "Baba Yaga," "The Maiden Tsar," "Danilo the Luckless," "Tale of the Military Secret, Malchish-Kibalchish and His Solemn Word," from *Politicizing Magic: An Anthology of Russian and Soviet Fairy Tales*, edited by Marina Balina, Helena Goscilo, and Mark Lipovetsky. Evanston: Northwestern University Press, 2005. Reprinted with the permission of Northwestern University Press.

Husain Haddawy (Translator). "Prologue: The Story of King Shahrayar and Shahrazad, His Vizier's Daughter," from *The Arabian Nights: The Thousand and One Nights*. Copyright © 1990 by W.W. Norton and Company, Inc. Used by permission of W.W. Norton and Company, Inc.

Joe Hayes (Translator). "The Enchanted Frog," from *Cuentos de Cuanto Hay/Tales from Spanish New Mexico*. University of New Mexico Press, 1998. Reprinted with the permission of University of New Mexico Press.

Nalo Hopkinson. "The Glass Bottle Trick," from *Skin Folk*. New York: Aspect/Warner Books, 2001. First published in *Whispers from the Cotton Tree Root: Caribbean Fabulist Fiction*, edited by Nalo Hopkinson. Invisible Cities Press, 2000. Reprinted with the permission of the author.

Vera Kalm (Translator). "The Serpent Prince," from *Hungarian Folktales: The Art of Zsuzanna Palkó*, edited by Linda Dégh and Vera Kalm. New York: Garland, 1995. Reprinted with permission of Taylor & Francis Group LLC; permission conveyed through Copyright Clearance Center, Inc.

Jack Lindsay (Translator). Excerpt from "The Old Woman's Tale," from *The Golden Ass* by Lucius Apuleius. Copyright © 1960, Indiana University Press. Reprinted with permission of Indiana University Press.

Kelly Link. "Swans," from *A Wolf at the Door and Other Retold Fairy Tales*, edited by Ellen Datlow and Terri Windling. New York: Simon and Schuster Books for Young Readers, 2000. Copyright © 2000 by Kelly Link. Reprinted with the permission of the author.

William Bernard McCarthy (Translator). "Juan Bobo and the Riddling Princess," from *Marvels & Tales: Journal of Fairy-Tale Studies*, Vol. 19, No. 2. Copyright © 2009 Wayne State University Press. Reprinted with the permission of Wayne State University Press.

Tiina Nunnally (Translator); Jackie Wullschlager (Editor). "The Tinderbox," "The Princess and the Pea," "The Red Shoes," from *Fairy Tales* by Hans Christian Andersen. Translation copyright © 2004 by Tiina Nunnally. Used by permission of Viking Penguin, a division of Penguin Group (USA) Inc., and Penguin Books Ltd.

A.K. Ramanujan (Translator). "Hanchi," from *Folktales from India: A Selection of Oral Tales from Twenty-Two Languages*, edited by A.K. Ramanujan. New York: The Pantheon Fairy Tale and Folklore Library, Pantheon Books/Random House, 1991.

Judith P. Shoaf (Translator). "Le Fresne," by Marie de France. Translation copyright © 1996 by Judith P. Shoaf. http://www.clas.ufl.edu/users/jshoaf/Marie/fresne.pdf. Reprinted with the permission of Judith P. Shoaf.

Marina Warner. "The Difference in the Dose: A Story after Rapunzel," from *Marvels & Tales: Journal of Fairy-Tale Studies*, Vol. 24, No. 2. Copyright © 2009 Wayne State University Press. Reprinted with the permission of Wayne State University Press.

Sylvia Townsend Warner. "Bluebeard's Daughter," from *The Cat's Cradle-Book*. New York: Viking Press, 1940. Reprinted with the permission of the Estate of Sylvia Townsend Warner.

Edward F. Wente, Jr. (Translator). "The Tale of the Two Brothers," from *The Literature of Ancient Egypt*, 3rd edition, edited by William Kelley Simpson. Copyright © Yale University Press, 2003. Reprinted with the permission of Yale University Press.

from the publisher

A name never says it all, but the word "broadview" expresses a good deal of the philosophy behind our company. We are open to a broad range of academic approaches and political viewpoints. We pay attention to the broad impact book publishing and book printing has in the wider world; we began using recycled stock more than a decade ago, and for some years now we have used 100% recycled paper for most titles. As a Canadian-based company we naturally publish a number of titles with a Canadian emphasis, but our publishing program overall is internationally oriented and broad-ranging. Our individual titles often appeal to a broad readership too; many are of interest as much to general readers as to academics and students.

Founded in 1985, Broadview remains a fully independent company owned by its shareholders—not an imprint or subsidiary of a larger multinational.

If you would like to find out more about Broadview and about the books we publish, please visit us at **www.broadviewpress.com**. And if you'd like to place an order through the site, we'd like to show our appreciation by extending a special discount to you: by entering the code below you will receive a 20% discount on purchases made through the Broadview website.

Discount code: **broadview20%**

Thank you for choosing Broadview.

MIX
Paper from responsible sources
FSC www.fsc.org
FSC® C004071

Please note: this offer applies only to sales of bound books within the United States or Canada.